THE ANNOTATED POE

THE ANNOTATED

POE

EDITED BY KEVIN J. HAYES

WITH A FOREWORD BY WILLIAM GIRALDI

THE BELKNAP PRESS OF
HARVARD UNIVERSITY PRESS
Cambridge, Massachusetts
London, England
2015

FIRST PRINTING

Frontispiece: Harry Clarke, "She Now Stands Without the Door!" Illustration for
"The Fall of the House of Usher," *Tales of Mystery and Imagination*
(London: George G. Harrap, 1919).

BOOK DESIGN BY TIM JONES & ANNAMARIE MCMAHON WHY

Library of Congress Cataloging-in-Publication Data

Poe, Edgar Allan, 1809–1849.
[Works. Selections. 2015]
The Annotated Poe / Edgar Allan Poe ;
edited by Kevin J. Hayes ; with a foreword by William Giraldi.
pages cm
Includes bibliographical references.
ISBN 978-0-674-05529-2 (alk. paper)
1. Horror tales, American.   2. Fantasy poetry, American.   3. Detective and
mystery stories, American.   I. Hayes, Kevin J., editor.   II. Title.
PS2603 2015
818'.309—dc23
2015019303

For Myung-Sook

◄◄-►►

Contents

Note on the Text

Thomas Ollive Mabbott's *Collected Works of Edgar Allan Poe* remains the standard scholarly edition of Poe's work and forms the basis for the poems and most of the tales contained in the present edition. Ever hoping to publish a collected edition of his short stories, Edgar Allan Poe tinkered with his texts throughout his career. Mabbott's edition incorporates the final revisions Poe made before his death in 1849. But last isn't always best. There is no magic formula that can be applied indiscriminately to every literary text. The principles of modern textual editing demand that when a work exists in different versions, the editor must evaluate each version individually, taking into account all surviving evidence, internal and external, anything and everything that bears on the history of a work's composition and publication. Then, and only then, can the editor decide which version to use as copy text. Poe usually improved his work in revision, but sometimes his first impulses were his best ones. In a few instances, Poe marred earlier texts by engaging in a process of self-censorship. For the present edition, the texts of three works—"Metzengerstein," "Berenice," and "The Philosophy of Furniture"—are based on their first published versions.

Throughout I have drawn on Mabbott's research and notes, as have all Poe scholars who follow him. But Mabbott's edition is now decades old and "full text search" was unavailable to Mabbott. Poe was very sneaky in his use of sources, often taking his quotations at third or fourth hand but pretending to have examined primary sources. In many instances, I have been able to uncover for the first time Poe's sources and reveal his deliberate obfuscations. The extensive new information contained within my annotations helps to reveal the extraordinary complexity of Poe's work.

In selecting the tales and poems for this one-volume annotated edition I have tried to give a sense of the great range and diversity of Poe's achievement. "Were all my tales now before me in a large volume and as the composition of another," Poe once wrote, "the merit which would principally arrest my attention would be the wide *diversity and* variety." On the other hand, this is a one-volume selection of Poe's tales and poems, not a collected works; in deference to the reader I have included many of Poe's "greatest hits." Again with the reader in mind, I have devoted more space to the tales than to the poetry. Speaking of Poe's significant verse, William Carlos Williams, Poe's great American champion, once said that "there are but five poems, possibly three."

Foreword

William Giraldi

It's the most recognizably anguished face in American letters, impossible to be mistaken for any other—the face of the writer we think we know—a doughy face, lopsided in letdown, harrowed and blanched by loss. With Whitman you get the searing soulfulness, with Melville the fixed intransigence, with Thoreau the contented sedition, and Dickinson is that milky, marble-eyed beauty from beyond. But in S. W. Hartshorn's famous 1848 daguerreotype of Poe, so much of his work is somehow perfectly there, myriad threads from the poems and tales. In this pallid photo, Poe's face speaks the dread truth of his depth.

The forehead is glaringly wide, both temples slightly dented, the hairline in retreat, the hair itself styled by a storm—all that messiness atop an endless intellection, a daimonic imagination, the introduction of chaos into the reliable obedience of order. There's a pinch between his brows, another pensive strain—even now, even here in front of Hartshorn's camera, Poe can't stay the wonder, the probing of possibilities, and the confusion he feels is the confusion of his hard life, yes, but also the confusion of eons. Under thatched brows the eyes are averted to his left, not because the lens would thieve his soul, and not in the fashion of the time, but because Poe is forever looking past what stands before us—our essence lies behind what we typically see, above the tangible, in the mysterious folds of some other domain.

Those devastating crescents sag beneath his eyes in exhaustion, in evidence of too much time looking into the dark, questing for whatever hints of us are to be found in the nooks and corners most are too afraid to step into. The mustache is unevenly shaven, longer on the right side, perhaps in an attempt to balance his skewed face, the left jawbone fuller, that cheek droopier than its twin; and it occurs to you how much of his work is an effort in equipoise, at augmenting appearances, the balancing of a nature split against itself, insisting that the night have its say against the common revelations of day, that dreams be allowed their fruitful intrusion into our waking selves—Poe was intent on "dreaming dreams no mortals ever dared to dream be-

fore." There's the faintest trace of disgust in his visage—the tight mouth, the rueful
stare—as if the quotidian crush of our lives, of which photographs are a part, vex
and irk a poet, leaving him eager for the shadows, where he can croon a truth in hiding. Not a beautiful man, Poe spent his art in pursuit of higher beauty, and this photo
is what the agonized beauty of genius looks like.

The heartwreck you glimpse in the photo is lifelong and inherited. A debtor and
drunk, flustered and ineffectual, Poe's father abandoned the family and disappeared.
Poe was almost three years old when he watched his loving twenty-four-year-old
mother die of consumption. A pretty, tiny woman, an able actress and singer, she'd
suffered horrendous losses most of her life. Poe and his two siblings were separated after her death, adopted by families who would never be real families. Imagine that child, just shy of his third birthday, at his cherished mother's bedside as
she dies; imagine the sunder inside him, the searing, the cosmic aloneness and fear—
"the dawn/ Of a most stormy life." How does such a sensitive boy, a boy born
with darkness in his strands ("Darkness there, and nothing more"), ever recover
from a blow such as that? He doesn't. How is he ever whole again? He isn't. "From
childhood's hour I have not been/ As others were—I have not seen/ As others
saw."

All through his childhood and adolescence he was smitten with young maternal
figures who were ill and guaranteed to die on him. It will happen again in a major
way, again when the woman was twenty-four: his cousin-wife, Virginia Clemm, a
miniscule beauty like his mother, her middle name the same as his mother's first
name, "Eliza"—she was thirteen years old when she married Poe and was dead of
consumption eleven years later. Poe was inconsolable; he slept at her grave. ("And
so, all the night-tide, I lie down by the side/ Of my darling—my darling—my life
and my bride.") His imagination was fired by remembrance of these frail ingénues,
wisps of women filched from him by some foul wind—"the wind came out of the
cloud, chilling/ And killing my Annabel Lee." In his essay "The Philosophy of
Composition," Poe writes that "the death . . . of a beautiful woman is unquestionably the most poetical topic in the world." Even if you find "unquestionably" a tad
questionable, you take Poe's point if you understand his life. Alluring as death was
for him, a beautiful woman made it all the more alluring, which goes to show how his
interest in women was meta-sensual, unerotic, ethereal.

Biographers differ on whether Poe ever consummated his marriage to his cousin.
W. H. Auden rather uncharitably said that Poe was "an unmanly sort of man whose
love-life seems to have been largely confined to crying in laps and playing house."[1]
And Richard Wilbur floated a similar notion: "What he sought from all these
women, with the frantic anxiety of a lost child, was the equivalent of adoption."[2]
Notorious as a cutthroat critic when the writer was a talented male, Poe was also notorious as a fawn when the writer was a talentless female—it was as if he believed a

poetess would devote herself to him, nurse him to health with her love, *become his mother,* if only he praised her promiscuously in print.

Poe's dead girls remained for him as alive in death as they were in life—he imbued the dead with life and at every turn in life spied death. Catalog his losses and it all makes sense, the warmed flesh of the dead and the corpselike cold that brushed across the living. In his essay "The Poetic Principle," he speaks of "the glories beyond the grave," and those aren't Christian glories, to be sure, but glories that are both pagan and uniquely Poesque—he wants it both ways: "determined to depart, yet live—to leave the world, yet continue to exist," as he puts it in "Hans Phaall" (a tale about a moon mission that beat by thirty years Jules Verne's popular novel *From the Earth to the Moon*).

Everywhere in Poe's work "Death looks gigantically down"—such a masterful mobilizing of an adverb in that line—and everywhere you are confronted with a cocktail of youth and demise, of the female and the Ideal, of death and beauty: "I could not love except where Death/ Was mingling his with Beauty's breath." His narrators and poetic personas—in "Berenice," in "Morella," in "Ligeia," in "Lenore," in "Annabel Lee"—are helpless to keep from losing their fairy queens, and helpless to keep from pining after them once they're gone, from attempting to reach them in that misty realm of the dead, a realm that begins to look and feel a lot like our own. The "other side," it's often called, but for Poe the deceased inhabit the selfsame side as the living. In his poems and tales the dead don't really ever die because they heave still in the heart, breathe still in dreams. They prowl the daytime cloaked as ghosts and at nightfall disrobe to reveal themselves in flesh.

Poe's limited conception of flesh stays prelibidinal, and his asexuality, his erotic lacuna, is one of the factors that endears him to adults who feed him to schoolchildren. Curious how Poe has often been considered suitable for young readers—"The Raven," especially: at the apex of Poe's fame children would accost him on the sidewalk with chants of "Nevermore!"—because the truth is that he's not altogether easy to understand. T. S. Eliot was never more wrongheaded than when he accused Poe of having a "pre-adolescent mentality," and although I'm loath ever to disagree with Henry James, his snipe about Poe, "enthusiasm for Poe is the mark of a decidedly primitive stage of reflection," misses the mark in a most un-Jamesian way.[3] The sing-song lilt of Poe's poems might appeal to the ears of youth—Emerson, bothered by Poe's lack of gravity, dubbed him "the Jingle Man"—but break from the lulling of his meter, look at the individual words and, with scant exceptions, his syntax and diction need much unknotting.[4] Add to that Poe's ceaseless courtship with death, his "mournful and terrible *engine* of horror and of crime," as he describes the gallows in "The Black Cat," and you must have some mightily perplexed, upset children.

It's something of a platitude to say that Poe can't shake his death obsession. What major writer does not unleash his talents upon the problem of our mortality? All of literature has only two motors, love and death, and everything else—envy, hatred, sin, devotion, whatever else you can name—is a variation, a capillary off those two throbbing arterioles. That rule holds in tragedy and comedy both. Poe's reclusive sleuth, Auguste Dupin—the character who would help inspire the creation of Sherlock Holmes—is "enamored of the Night for her own sake," but that doesn't quite describe Poe himself. His gothic grasping after the occult, after the mysteries of death, was no affectation, no mere wish to join the alphas at the altar of literature. If you could take Schopenhauer, Nietzsche, and Freud and distill them, shave their work to the bone, extract their dark marrow, you'd have someone who looks a lot like Poe. It's fruitless, because obvious, to apply Freud to Poe, but apply Poe to Freud and you'll be on to something.

This affliction in his art was not his choice. I submit that an imaginative writer doesn't choose his tenor, his topics, his taste, any more than you chose your parents. The death impulse in Poe's work seems intelligible enough: it derives from his perennial mourning, his fanged grief over the loss of so many beloveds. At about the time Poe knew for certain that he'd become a writer, and just as he'd reestablished contact with him, his older brother, Henry, from whom Poe was estranged most of his life, drank himself into the grave at the age of—guess—*twenty-four*. Tidy as it is to spot the nexus between Poe's losses and his literary expression of those losses, something much more complex is going on in his gruesome vision.

The horror of so many of his tales happens through claustrophobia, yes—in Poe's best known work ("The Black Cat," "The Tell-Tale Heart," "The Pit and the Pendulum"), he favors the cramped indoors, as if in reminder that the grave is never far away—but also by virtue of unfolding during "the raven-winged hours," because Poe also favors the dark. We take it for granted that horror happens after nightfall, that the dark is the proper place for a vampire such as Poe (that was D. H. Lawrence's typically colorful assertion, that Poe didn't write about vampires as much as he was himself a vampire). There are evolutionary reasons for our fear of the dark: bedded down in a sable thickness on the African savanna, our ancestors were vulnerable to nocturnal predators, to those monsters that came to devour us, and our double helix has never forgotten that fright. Like every horror artist, Poe exploits our fear of the dark—even when he doesn't have to, when he isn't in horror mode, as with Auguste Dupin's preference for drawn shutters—but that exploitation is only half the point. Poe favors the dark because only in the dark do we stand naked; only in the dark is the truth open for detection. If you want someone to tell you the truth, said Wilde, give him a mask. The dark is Poe's mask, and his mission is Truth with a hollering upper-case.

In "The Fall of the House of Usher," as Roderick Usher slumps further into a madness from which he will not recover, the narrator perceives "the futility of all attempt at cheering a mind from which darkness, as if an inherent positive quality, poured forth upon all objects of the moral and physical universe in one unceasing radiation of gloom." That begins to get at an important part of Poe's reaching for Truth: the "inherent positive quality" of darkness. Harold Bloom once suggested that "Poe's genius was for negativity and opposition," and that's accurate in a certain sense—and certainly in Poe's novella, *The Narrative of Arthur Gordon Pym*—but not when it comes to key tales in which our essence is illuminated by darkness.[5] In Poe's worldview, the illuminating darkness is a positive quality because truth always trumps falsehood: better to be true in the dark than false in the light.

The tale "Manuscript Found in a Bottle," about a ghost ship swallowed by an abyss, makes reference to "the severe precincts of truth." Again, in his essay "The Poetic Principle," Poe writes that "the demands of Truth are severe," and in the same paragraph, he contends that "in enforcing a truth, we need severity." He might have been writing there about the technical methods and applications of poetry, but you see how the truth/severity duet sings inside his own themes. Look at the opening of "The Premature Burial," when the narrator admits that "certain themes . . . are with propriety handled only when the severity and majesty of Truth sanctify and sustain them." You see what he means: hard to think of a fate more horrible than being buried alive, and our presumption is that only the morbidly misfit would choose to tell or hear such a story. Many over the decades have accused Poe of just that: R. L. Stevenson said Poe was so morbidly misfit that he had "ceased to be a human being," and, worse, that "one is glad to think of him as dead."[6] But the "severity and majesty of Truth" demands that the severest tales be told and heard, because they unveil something intrinsic to the human makeup, and that unveiling, contra Stevenson, doesn't make Poe less human—it makes him more.

In Poe's cruelest tale, "The Black Cat"—about a man who cuts out the eye of his cat before lynching it, and then axes his wife's skull before entombing her in the basement—the narrator is certain that "perverseness is one of the primitive impulses of the human heart." You rightly think him a madman, until you run it by your own heart, a heart that has known, if you are honest, the pitch of the perverse. This is what Bloom means when he says that Poe depicts "the universalism of a common nightmare."[7] We all of us have a darkness thrumming within; the difference between most individuals and the narrator of "The Black Cat" is that he can no longer discern the distinction between a nightmare and a common night.

For the sheer horror of a diseased psyche, Edmund Wilson, for one, preferred Poe to Kafka (and that pairing, so stylistically inapposite at first glance, becomes outright tantalizing the more you look at it). Every diseased psyche has its own idiopathic rationale, and in Poe's psyche, his mother and his cousin-bride are perfect pictures of beauty. If they live still in death, if their beauty abides still in the murky glow of dreams, and if beauty is indeed the Keatsian assurance of Truth, as Poe believed it was, then death itself becomes a revealer of Truth—not just the physical truth of the fate of every living thing, but a Platonic Ideal wherein the world spins in equilibrium and souls are once again fused ("Morella" begins with an epigraph from Plato: "Itself, by itself, solely, ONE everlasting, and single"). This is, above all, what the Dupin stories show, especially "The Murders in the Rue Morgue" and "The Mystery of Marie Roget": the gruesomeness of death is occasion for the uncovering of Truth. Dupin feels his way to a truth that becomes Truth—he's all hubris and intuition; whatever logic he asserts is unimportant because he has already ascertained the truth by poetical guessing—just as Poe was convinced that the poeticizing of death, through the bringing forth of deathly dreams, would itself become its own Truth.

Poe's life was downright miserable, "a Sahara of dreariness, pain, and drudgery," in Richard Wilbur's unimprovable wording.[8] The first two lines of "Berenice" are: "Misery is manifold. The wretchedness of the earth is multiform," and although it's normally the uninspired reader-as-voyeur who wants to spy an author in every crevice of his work, Poe's well-advertised anguish invites such searching. His is a heart "whose woes are legion"—the exaggerator of much, he didn't exaggerate about that. It's no shock he took some consolation in imagining death, in death as a work of art, death augmented by fillips of beauty ("the delight of its horror," as he puts it in "The Imp of the Perverse"). Let's also give him credit for his fearlessness in staring down the Reaper—"The Masque of the Red Death" hammers home the pitiful futility of denying death's grip—and let's not look upon him as a reality dodger who dreamt away his talents.

In its manufacture of dreams, sleep is a kind of portal to death: "By sleep and its world alone is *Death* imagined," he writes in "The Colloquy of Monos and Una," and by "imagined" he intends "experienced." His preference for dreams over reality won't be a mystery to fellow depressives because they know how hard it is to be alive, and they know that dreams, after all, happen in sleep. And sleep—a cavernous sleep that presses comfortingly upon you, a sleep with heft that hovers just above your body—is about the only place a depressive finds relief. Poe would have chosen a round-the-clock dream state if he had been able. In the tale "Eleonora," he writes: "They who dream by day are cognizant of many things which escape those who dream only by night."

It occurs to you that Poe's tales aren't actually happening to his characters, but are instead unfurling inside Poe's sleep, deep inside his dreamland. These aren't stories as we normally understand stories, not those Gogolian models of perfection, not even fables or black fairy tales, but fever dreams we've been allowed access to, fever dreams whose logic is loyal only to Poe's personal syntax of seeing. (In "Ligeia," the narrator describes the vision of his beloved as "the radiance of an opium-dream.") "The typical Poe story," Richard Wilbur writes, "is, in its action, an allegory of dream experience" that happens "within the mind of a poet; the characters are not distinct personalities, but principles or faculties of the poet's divided nature."[9] In other words: the characters aren't really characters at all, but ciphers in two meanings of the term: nonentities, and messages in code. They are embodiments of psychic states.

The realist conception of character that has come to reign over so much of American literature, a conception codified in the mid-to-late nineteenth century after Poe's death, would have struck him as somewhat beside the point. Who needs another representation of played-out reality, another simulacrum of the actual? Look around you—there it is. Instead, Poe's tales strive to impart a different reality altogether, a reality that awakens while consciousness slumbers. In "The Assignation," the narrator remarks, "There are surely other worlds than this—other thoughts than the thoughts of the multitude—other speculations than the speculations of the sophist." In this sense Poe was a true Romantic despite his struggles to ditch the Romantic blueprint: literature should not reflect the world but transform it, imbue it with a new and fiercer fire, and in his creative capacities, in his forging of worlds, the poet achieves his own apotheosis.

There are problems that arise when a writer's characters are not bone and blood human beings but stand-ins for the rips and rasps of a psyche—"the disintegration-processes of his own psyche," as D. H. Lawrence put it.[10] One of those problems was noticed by Edmund Wilson, who claimed that there's no love in Poe's world, and it's true: love is usually the first casualty of the insistently allegorical.[11] Write about Love and love takes a hit. Another of those problems is one that Leslie Fiedler pointed out: Poe's tales are bereft of sin, of the pitched awareness of sin, and so have no moral weight. Across the decades a quiver of critics has been eager to conflate the lack of moral reckoning in Poe's work with the absence of morality in Poe himself, a folly any way you cut it. Poe had great surfeits of love in him, and felt great responsibility to care for his young wife and mother-in-law.

Moral reckoning—morality transferred and fertilized, imagined and asserted in style—might be the highest aim of some writers, but it is also, somewhat paradoxically, the quotidian concern of churchgoers, and Poe was having none of that. His essay "The Heresy of the Didactic" blasts the "happy idea" that literature "should inculcate a moral." Poe's concerns were of an entirely different order, *beyond good and evil* in the Nietzschean sense of dismissing the dichotomy.

In *Love and Death in the American Novel* (1960), Fiedler makes a vital observation about Poe's understanding of the soul or spirit. Poe doesn't mean what we typically mean by those terms—the Christian soul, the spirit redeemed through sacrifice—but rather, says Fiedler, he means something more akin to "sensibility."[12] The problem with sensibility in a work of fiction—sensibility only, unaided by the strafings and strainings of the soul—is that it has no consequence, no inevitable way to be enacted, no necessary manifestation and so no urgency. This is the reason, by the way, it won't quite do to speak of Poe's tales as investigations of evil, as some insist on doing: true evil is no metaphysical mystery, no obscurantist's plaything, but rather the real result of real human beings doing the worst that can be imagined.

Evil has heavy consequences for the soul, so when your idea of soul is "sensibility," then those consequences are neutered. "Poe lacks as a writer *a sense of sin,*" writes Fiedler, "and therefore cannot raise his characters to the Faustian level which alone dignifies gothic fiction."[13] That "alone" might be contestable, but nothing else in Fiedler's idea is. "Poe fails finally to transform the gothic into the tragic," says Fiedler, because of his "immunity to Calvinism," by which he means the pervasive sense of original sin that permitted Melville his soaring to heights both tragic and sublime.[14] When Ahab bleeds, you check yourself for bleeding too. When Poe's people bleed, the blood is movie blood, colored corn syrup.

But as Wilbur suggests, we must not confer on Poe's people "a credibility of character, motive, and feeling which they do not possess. . . . Poe's characters escape our everyday understanding, and are meant to."[15] That's precisely what we love about Poe: his eschewing of typical comprehension. Say what you will about him, he's always compelling, and he's never afraid. More important, there's William Carlos Williams's assertion, in his essay-length airing of frisson from *In the American Grain* (1925): "Poe gives the sense for the first time in America that literature is *serious,* not a matter of courtesy but of truth."[16]

Poe seems to me to hold a rather shaky status as a particularly American mind. Whereas Whitman's exuberant American-ness is barely containable (without Whitman, American selfhood is an impotent affair), and Hawthorne's and Melville's aesthetic is a kind of religious roar augmented by American individualism, Poe's relationship to our national identity presents a bit of a problem. There's his penchant for setting his tales outside America, in Paris or Italy, in the Netherlands or the Arctic, or in some hallucinatory locale he considered more exotic than Baltimore or Richmond or Philadelphia, even though he knew those cities best. His chosen settings are necessary for his storytelling mission of disassociation, of course, but there's something else going on there. Although, in his *Marginalia,* Poe foresaw such a gripe as mine: "That an American should confine himself to American themes, or even prefer them, is rather a political than a literary idea—and at best is a questionable point."

Still, reading Poe you can see quite clearly that he doesn't feel much like crooning homage to America, and it's no wonder when you look at how he suffered in this supposed land of plenty—in his unstinting poverty and daily drudgery, hyperaware of his own genius and ability, repeatedly passed over for literary awards and jobs that were beneath him, always unable to start the magazine he'd intensely dreamed of, Poe must have felt that America had let him down, that the notion of American promise did not apply to him. He despised the national worship of money; in his essay "The Philosophy of Furniture," he laments that Americans yearn for a large "purse" while not giving a damn about the size of their "soul." He tended to see his fellow countrymen as not very bright, as easily, eagerly bamboozled, willing to lionize writers who didn't deserve it, such as Longfellow, about whom Poe penned an annihilating critique. Unlike the darling Longfellow, Poe was orphaned in more ways than one, the quintessential outcast, at home nowhere—and every outcast feels resentment at last.

In *Waiting for the End* (1964), Leslie Fiedler wrote of Poe: "He is at once too banal and too unique, too decadent and too revolutionary, too vulgar and too subtle, all of which is to say, too American, for us to bear," and there, I think, Fiedler goes one adjective too many.[17] In *Love and Death in the American Novel*, Fiedler sees Poe's *Arthur Gordon Pym* as "the archetypal American story" that would have formidable effects on both *Moby-Dick* and *Huckleberry Finn*.[18] But Fiedler calls *Arthur Gordon Pym* "the private world of his own tortured psyche," and therein lies the trouble with seeing it as archetypally American: *private* and *tortured* are not American qualities.[19]

Luminous others disagree. H. L. Mencken referred to Poe as "this most potent and original of Americans."[20] Van Wyck Brooks was convinced that Poe had birthed an entirely new American literature, wholly apart from Washington Irving's efforts. (Indeed, it's difficult to take *The Legend of Sleepy Hollow* seriously after being jolted and convulsed by the demonic energies of Poe.) About Poe's status as an American, William Carlos Williams wrote: "He was the astounding, inconceivable growth of his locality. Gape at him they did, and he at them in amazement. Afterward with mutual hatred; he in disgust, they in mistrust. It is only that which is under your nose which seems inexplicable"—and yet earlier in the essay Williams can't help admitting that Poe's "doctrine" was essentially "anti-American" in its ferocious pessimism.[21]

Like "Kafkaesque," the term "existential" is bandied about willy-nilly to describe everything from warfare to a rained-on picnic, but Poe is more deserving than most of the tag because his anomic vision results from an outsider's status, from his denied ambitions, from his faithlessness in cultural structures, and from America's rescinded promise of happiness. Put another way: the awful plight of Poe's life and art is partly social, and in that regard he's as American as Dreiser. In some of the most refulgent lines ever set down about Poe, Williams said this:

> He is American, understandable by a simple exercise of reason; a light in the morass—which *must* appear eerie, even to himself, by force of terrific contrast, an isolation that would naturally lead to drunkenness and death, logically and simply—by despair, as the very final evidence of a too fine seriousness and devotion.[22]

Leslie Fiedler is not alone in seeing Poe the myth as Poe's best creation, but he perhaps overestimates the agency Poe exerted in his own literary immortality.

Choosing an enemy for a biographer (a vitriolic hack with a taste for sensation whose name, Rufus Griswold, perfectly captures the creep he was), concocting stories about himself that aspired to Byronic gallantry and excitation, melodramatizing his own situation (Poe's letters to his family members, in the 1830s especially, are freshets of self-pity about perishing of illness, poverty, or heartache), even drinking in part because he suspected readers wanted their writers outcast and unstrung— all this overlooks how unstrung and outcast Poe actually was. Not to say that he gave no thought to posterity, only that someone continually crushed in the molars of melancholy, someone so persistently pestled by circumstance, doesn't have the gumption to manipulate the levers of fame-making. He's mostly trying just to survive the day.

It's certainly fitting that a writer who made death his muse would himself suffer a death that would help make him a myth. Ask death to be your Muse and she responds by becoming your Siren. We still have trouble saying for sure how Poe died. In October 1849, at only forty years of age, he was found whiskey-soaked and insensate in a Baltimore tavern dressed horrendously in clothes that were not his. The fullest account of Poe's baffling end is given in *Midnight Dreary* (1998) by John Evangelist Walsh: a model of research, it eventually morphs into a circus of extrapolation (in short, Walsh thinks Poe was murdered by his wealthy fiancée's three brothers). Poe would have ascended into his posthumous literary glow without this unclear and sickening fate, but as he understood better than most, all the world loves an enigma. In American history, only JFK's assassination has more competing, and nuttier, theories than the demise of Poe.

Whitman felt the "indescribable magnetism" of Poe's myth (and Whitman was the only major presence at the ceremony to give Poe's grave a headstone, an unforgivable twenty-six years after his death—America has a shameful track record of treating its writers poorly, but nowhere is that track record more shameful than in the neglect of Edgar Poe).[23] The true magnetism of Poe, naturally, is generated by the work, a wand which transforms the quotidian into the wondrous, the mundane into the macabre, or as Poe himself once expressed it: "the ludicrous heightened into the grotesque; the fearful colored into the horrible; the witty exaggerated into the burlesque; the singular wrought out into the strange and mystical."

He eventually resented being known as the cartoonish author of "The Raven," and for good reason: in its gimmickry and plumed metaphors, the poem lives several zip codes over from his best work. There have been vociferous claims made for his originality—by Mencken, by Wilson, by Williams—and yet Poe was, to be a gentleman about it, a great borrower of others' ideas. He also borrowed tropes from the German and British Gothic traditions in making a challenge to all that was knowable and trusted in the world, and in showing that our lives will not be denuded of the strange just because science has explained away the supernatural. His poem "Sonnet—to Science" follows Keats in damning the imagination-killing materialism of the scientific worldview.

To one extent or another, all writers are robbers, and so what's indisputable about him is this: without an understanding of Poe—his methods, his meanings, his dazzling magic—there is simply no complete understanding of American literature. Williams maintained that "in him American literature is anchored, in him alone, on solid ground," and Edmund Wilson spoke of "the masterpieces excreted like precious stones by the subterranean chemistry of his mind" —there's no quarrelling with that, with either the quality of the chemistry or with the torque of the mind.[24]

Edgar Poe was the saddest writer who ever lived. That enormous sadness is, ultimately and unforgettably, what you see in S. W. Hartshorn's 1848 daguerreotype. We can't wish that it had been any other way unless we're willing to admit that we can go without his genius. He transformed the tremors of his beaten soul, the storm and stress of his psyche, into an exuberant literature of the night, a disturbed chronicle of those innermost journeys that both tempt and repel us. Doyen of diabolism, he understood that "the world of our sad Humanity may assume the semblance of a Hell." About the "demon in my view" and his question "what demon has tempted me here?" Those are our demons, too, our own devilish temptations. In his conjuring of the irrationalism that would blitz the twentieth century, Poe was our first truly modern sage, our seer of the absurd. For that reason we remain in need of him—we require his darkling truths and the witness he gave to those ancient, unspoken urges in us.

NOTES

1. W. H. Auden, *Prose: Volume III, 1949–1955*, ed. Edward Mendleson (Princeton: Princeton University Press, 2008), 222.

2. Richard Wilbur, *Responses: Prose Pieces, 1953–1976* (New York: Harcourt Brace Jovanovich, 1976), 44.

3. T. S. Eliot, *To Criticize the Critic and Other Writings* (Lincoln: University of Nebraska Press, 1965), 35. Henry James, "Comments," in Eric W. Carlson, ed., *The Recongnition of Edgar Allan Poe: Selected Criticism Since 1829* (Ann Arbor: University of Michigan Press, 1966), 66.

4. William Dean Howells, *Literary Friends and Acquaintance: A Personal Retrospect of American Authorship*, ed. David F. Hiatt and Edwin H. Cady (Bloomington: Indiana University Press, 1968), 58.

5. Harold Bloom, ed., *The Tales of Poe* (New York: Chelsea House, 1987), 12.

6. Robert Louis Stevenson, "Literature," *Academy*, January 2, 1875, 1.

7. Bloom, ed., *Tales of Poe*, 8.

8. Wilbur, *Responses*, 43.

9. Wilbur, *Responses*, 58.

10. D. H. Lawrence, "Edgar Allan Poe," in Carlson, ed., *Recognition*, 110.

11. Edmund Wilson, *Classics and Commercials: A Literary Chronicle of the Forties* (New York: Farrar, Straus and Giroux, 1950), 391.

12. Leslie Fiedler, *Love and Death in the American Novel*, rev. ed. (New York: Stein and Day, 1966), 428.

13. Fiedler, *Love and Death*, 428.

14. Fiedler, *Love and Death*, 430.

15. Wilbur, *Responses,* 50-51.

16. William Carlos Williams, *In the American Grain* (1956; reprinted, New York: New Directions, 2009), 216.

17. Leslie Fiedler, *Waiting for the End* (New York: Stein and Day, 1964), 199.

18. Fiedler, *Love and Death,* 393.

19. Fiedler, *Love and Death,* 393.

20. H. L. Mencken, *A Mencken Chrestomathy* (1949; reprinted, New York: Vintage, 1982), 481.

21. Williams, *In the American Grain,* 226.

22. Williams, *In the American Grain,* 222.

23. Walt Whitman, "Edgar Poe's Significance," in Carlson, ed., *Recognition,* 74.

24. Williams, *In the American Grain,* 226; Wilson, *Classics and Commercials,* 113.

THE ANNOTATED POE

Introduction

The Path of a Poet

Though best known as the author of weird and terrifying stories such as "Ligeia," "The Fall of the House of Usher," "The Pit and the Pendulum," and "The Masque of the Red Death," Edgar Allan Poe (1809-1849) never wished to be so narrowly cast. By his teen years, he had already decided to devote his life to literature, but, first and foremost, he wanted to be a poet. As a schoolboy in Richmond, he longed to publish a collection of his own verse. Pursuing this ambition, he urged his foster father, John Allan, to consult his teacher Joseph Clarke on the matter. Clarke, however, convinced Allan that it would not be in the boy's best interest to let him publish a book of poetry, which would give his headstrong ward an overinflated sense of his own literary abilities. Disappointed but undaunted, Poe kept compiling poems with an eye toward publishing a book-length collection.

After receiving a good classical education in Richmond, he continued his studies at the University of Virginia, matriculating in February 1826, just one year after Thomas Jefferson had opened his "academical village." Poe excelled at Latin and French but also ran up enormous gambling debts, which he maintained were accumulated as an unfortunate consequence of Allan's failure to provide sufficient money for his expenses. Poe may have dined with Jefferson, who frequently invited students from the university to Monticello for dinner. Later that year, Poe attended Jefferson's funeral. Poe took advantage of the university's outstanding facilities, especially its library collection, which Jefferson had developed for the purpose of encouraging students to read beyond the curriculum. The many arcane literary allusions in Poe's early writings suggest that he took full advantage of the library's holdings at the University of Virginia.[1]

Jefferson had planned the undergraduate curriculum as a two-year program, but Allan, outraged by Poe's gambling debts, pulled him from school at the end of his first academic year and put him to work in the counting house of Ellis and Allan, the

The Rotunda at the University of Virginia. Thomas Jefferson designed the Rotunda, modeled on the Pantheon in Rome, as the university's library. The books were moved there in 1826, during Poe's first and only year at the university.

mercantile firm he owned and operated with his partner, Charles Ellis. For someone who dreamed of becoming a great poet, Allan's dollars-and-cents world was intolerable. Just months after his return to Richmond, Poe quarreled viciously with his foster father—over his unpaid debts and other issues—and stormed out of the Allan household. Writing to Allan the next day, he declared his determination "to find some place in this wide world, where I will be treated—not as *you* have treated me."[2] Poe set out for Boston—his birthplace—taking with him his most precious possession: a manuscript volume of his verse, which he published anonymously as *Tamerlane and Other Poems* (1827). On the title page of the forty-page booklet, the eighteen-year-old Southerner from Richmond identified himself only as a "Bostonian."

Two additional collections of verse soon followed. On May 27, 1827, Poe, in need of money, enlisted in the U.S. army under the name "Edgar A. Perry." Then on February 28, 1828, Poe's foster mother, Frances Allan, died, bringing a temporary reconciliation between Poe and Allan. With Allan's permission and assistance, Poe was

William James Bennett, *Baltimore from Federal Hill*, 1831.

discharged from the army and successfully applied to the U.S. Military Academy at West Point. Not feeling entirely welcome at home, Poe sought out his father's relatives in Baltimore, where he stayed with them in what he described in a letter to Allan as "a most uncomfortable situation."[3] Orphaned before the age of three and brought up in the Allan household, Poe hardly knew his blood relatives. Residing together were his sickly grandmother (Mrs. David Poe), his widowed Aunt Maria Clemm, her daughter (Virginia), her son (Henry Clemm), and Poe's own elder brother, Henry. It was during this time in Baltimore that Poe published *Al Aaraaf, Tamerlane, and Minor Poems* (1829).

When Poe matriculated to West Point in 1830, he was older than most of the other cadets, who looked up to him. He endeared himself to them by writing satirical verses lampooning their instructors. When Poe arranged to publish a new collection of poetry by subscription toward the end of his time at West Point, fellow cadets eagerly subscribed, assuming it would include more of the same. The volume, titled

Poems: Second Edition (1831) and dedicated "To the U.S. Corps of Cadets," did not appear until after Poe had been court-martialed and dismissed from the academy for a series of infractions deliberately incurred by Poe, again in debt, to spite his foster father. When the cadets received their subscription copies, they were sorely disappointed. Poe understood something about poetry they did not: nonce poems that circulate in manuscript do not necessarily deserve the permanence of print.[4]

The 1831-1834 period is a black hole in Poe's biography. Poe returned to Baltimore to take refuge once again with his Aunt Maria Clemm, but we know little about his personal life and activities at this time, nor much about his apprentice work as a fiction writer. Few letters survive from these years. It was during this undocumented period of his life that the young poet made the decision to turn to fiction writing. In response to a contest advertised in the Philadelphia *Saturday Courier* in June 1831, offering a premium of one hundred dollars for "the best American Tale," Poe supplied five stories. None of them won, but the submissions made an impression. The *Courier* would publish all five. On January 14, 1832, Poe's debut tale, the gothically inflected "Metzengerstein," made its appearance in the *Courier,* followed in the same year by four lesser tales that spoof contemporary genres or authors.

These parodies and satires, and Poe's willingness to adapt genre to his own aesthetic aims, show that he was reading widely during this period. Along with the good, he was consuming a lot of bad writing—but he found ways to learn from whatever he read. Poe divided books into two basic types: those that allow readers to immerse themselves in the author's thought; and those that encourage readers to develop their own thought. The second category, which he labeled "suggestive books," Poe subdivided into the positively and the negatively suggestive. The first type suggests by what it says, the second by what it could have or should have said. Whether positively or negatively suggestive, a book could fulfill its essential purpose: to provoke the reader's (or writer's) thought.[5]

The motivation for the switch from verse to fiction was financial: Poe believed he could make more money writing fiction. Contests such as the one sponsored by the *Saturday Courier,* or the one advertised in the June 15, 1833, issue of the *Baltimore Saturday Visiter* that earned Poe a $50 prize for "Manuscript Found in a Bottle," illustrate an appetite for short fiction in antebellum America. With the growth of periodical literature, short stories now commanded greater prize money than poetry.[6] And Poe remained in dire need of money. There would be no further assistance coming from John Allan. Soon after Poe had made good on his threat to get himself kicked out of West Point, Allan severed the relationship. Allan's remarriage in 1830 had further complicated matters. When John Allan died on March 17, 1834, Poe may have held out some slender hope that he would be remembered in his will, but if so that hope was soon crushed. With an irony no doubt not lost on Poe, Allan—whose

Stefanie Rocknak, *Poe Returning to Boston*, 2014, bronze. This sculpture, located at Edgar Allan Poe Square, a triangular brick plaza at the intersection of Charles and Boylston streets across from Boston Common, represents the city's attempt to bring Poe back to his birthplace and reclaim him as a native son.

great wealth was inherited from a wealthy childless uncle—made no mention of his ward in his will.

In "Metzengerstein," Poe created a young protagonist in possession of vast riches, indulging a fantasy he would return to time and again in his fiction. A periodical press growing by fits and starts, new cost-lowering technologies, and the emergence of a mass-market readership created exciting new opportunities for writers, but these were difficult times—made yet more difficult by the Panic of 1837. Many new magazines were short-lived. Poe's repeated and humiliating pleas for assistance in his letters make for depressing reading. In his correspondence and periodical writings, Poe

William James Bennett,
Richmond, from the Hill above the
Waterworks, 1834.
This print depicts the city as it
looked around the time Poe
moved to Richmond and started
working for the *Southern Literary*
Messenger.

complains bitterly about the lack of international copyright law, which permitted American publishers to freely reprint books published in Britain instead of supporting American authors.[7] In "Some Secrets from the Magazine Prison-House"(1845), he grouses that the absence of international copyright drove authors into writing for magazines and reviews. In fact, Poe would never be able to live by the efforts of his pen alone, supplementing his writing income with editorial jobs at various periodicals, including the *Southern Literary Messenger* in Richmond, *Burton's Gentleman's Magazine* and *Graham's Magazine* in Philadelphia, and the *Broadway Journal* in New York City. Throughout his adult life Poe would continue to struggle financially, often living at or below the poverty level.

Poe would never stop writing verse even if it was no longer the focus of his creative energies. The best of the poems composed between 1831 and 1845 he incorporated into his short fiction. "To One in Paradise," for example, was first published as part of "The Visionary" (1834), a short story set in Venice and based on an episode from the life of Lord Byron. He nestled "The Conqueror Worm" within a revised version of "Ligeia" (1845), and put "The Haunted Palace" within "The Fall of the House of Usher" (1839), after both poems had appeared separately elsewhere. In the preface to *Poems,* Poe explains why he had embedded "The Lake," an early lyric poem, in a revised version of the much longer narrative poem "Tamerlane": he hoped to give the shorter poem "some chance of being seen by posterity."[8] The same logic applies to his inclusion of poetry in the tales, whether or not, as many commentators suppose, the poems comment on the enveloping tales, or vice versa. Embedding poetry within his fiction, Poe tacitly acknowledged that fiction has more staying power than verse.

The tale—the term Poe preferred for his short fiction—was a new development, closely connected to the growth of periodical literature, and an outgrowth of the early nineteenth-century magazine sketch.[9] (Not until the 1880s did the term "short story" come to have the meaning it has today. Originally, it referred to children's tales.) With the possible exception of Nathaniel Hawthorne, no previous writer in American literature had approached short fiction with the seriousness and level of artistry Poe now brought to it. Samuel Taylor Coleridge once said that every word counted. He was speaking about poetry. Not only does every word count, Poe believed, so does the position of every word. It was a principle Poe applied equally to his poetry and his tales.

There could be no truly original subjects and themes, Poe believed. He once declared that "the truest and surest test of *originality* is the manner of handling a hackneyed subject. The more hackneyed the theme, indeed, the better chance the display of originality in its conduct."[10] In his criticism, Poe often employed the figure of the griffin to illustrate his approach to creative writing. A mythical beast with the body of a lion, the head and wings of an eagle, and a serpentlike tail, the griffin vividly embodies a central tenet of Poe's aesthetic: his theory of novel combinations.

Reviewing the work of the popular British poet Thomas Moore, Poe explained how the creative process works—or does not work, as the case may be. He called Moore a poet of fancy, not imagination, borrowing critical terms from Coleridge, who defined and distinguished both concepts. Whereas the fancy combines, the imagination creates. Poe repeated Coleridge's distinction mainly to challenge it. Essentially, Poe saw no difference between these two creative abilities: "The fancy as nearly creates as the imagination; and neither creates in any respect. All novel conceptions are merely unusual combinations. The mind of man can *imagine* nothing which has not really existed."[11] It is impossible to create anything totally original, Poe believed. Originality, properly understood, is the creation of new combinations of pre-existing elements—genres, motifs, styles, themes. The griffin symbolizes how various elements that exist in nature can be combined to create something that does not exist in nature: an original image. The best authors combine different pre-existing aspects of literature to create something completely original.

Poe continued to develop his theory of novel combinations, subsequently explaining in detail how an author or, for that matter, any artist could put the theory into practice:

> Imagination, Fancy, Fantasy and Humor have in common the elements Combination and Novelty. The Imagination is the artist of the four. From novel arrangements of old forms which present themselves to it, it selects only such as are harmonious; the result, of course, is *beauty* itself—using the term in its most extended sense, and as inclusive of the sublime. The pure Imagination chooses, *from either beauty or deformity,* only the most combinable things hitherto uncombined.[12]

The emphasized phrase reveals a crucial aspect of Poe's aesthetic. The creation of beauty did not necessarily involve the combination of beautiful images or motifs or language: it could also incorporate "deformity." Poe thus built the grotesque into his critical theory. Beauty and deformity could be combined in original ways to create art.

Though Poe would not fully articulate his theory of novel combinations until later in his career, his short stories exemplify novelty from the beginning of his fiction career. Poe was a shameless magpie, borrowing and appropriating freely. In "Morella" (1835), for example, one of the tales that appeared in the *Southern Literary Messenger,* he combines aspects of sentimental fiction, supernatural tales, German metaphysics, and folk legends to create a challenging and original tale about death, resurrection, and the power of the will. It was Poe's friend, a Baltimore man of letters named John Pendleton Kennedy, who paved the way for Poe's contributions to the *Messenger* by putting him in contact with the magazine's editor and proprietor, Thomas W. White. Writing to White from Baltimore, Poe dispensed advice, perhaps angling for a job. He urged White to publish the kinds of sensational stories readers desired, for their impact "will be estimated better by the circulation of the Magazine than by any comments upon its contents."[13] After a few of his stories appeared in the magazine, Poe left Baltimore for Richmond hoping to obtain a more permanent position either at the *Messenger* or perhaps elsewhere. In any case, shortly after Poe's arrival in Richmond, White put him to work in the *Messenger* offices, where he handled a variety of editorial duties: editing copy and checking proof, reviewing submissions, and writing fiction, poetry, reviews, and whatever else was needed. Having secured full-time employment, Poe now brought Aunt Maria and his thirteen-year-old cousin Virginia to Richmond, where he and Virginia were married on May 16, 1836.

Over the next two years Poe published a number of new tales and poems in the *Messenger* and reprinted several earlier works. It was the critical writings that ap-

H. B. Hall, portrait of John Pendleton Kennedy, engraved frontispiece to Henry T. Tuckerman, *Life of John Pendleton Kennedy*, 1871. Based on a daguerreotype, this portrait depicts Kennedy as he looked around 1850.

peared in the *Messenger*, however, that established his literary reputation. White gave him considerable latitude when it came to reviewing books, and Poe took full advantage of it. During his time with the *Messenger* Poe developed his singular critical voice—trenchant, acerbic, not above ridicule and withering satire. If Poe's brand of hard-hitting criticism did not significantly increase the magazine's circulation, as he liked to claim, it did bring the *Southern Literary Messenger* to national attention.[14] It also made Poe famous, or perhaps infamous, depending on one's point of view. His uncompromising standards irked some readers, especially authors, who expected reviews to be at least respectful. Poe's reputation as a literary "savage" was already circulating in 1836, when the *Cincinnati Mirror* called attention to Poe's "savage skill" in wielding his pen like a "tomahawk and scalping knife" and the *New Yorker* reported that Poe had "tomahawked and scalped" Morris Mattson's novel *Paul Ulric* "after the manner of a Winnebago." Both notices were reprinted by Poe in the *Messenger*.[15] It is worth noting that the *Cincinnati Mirror* nonetheless expressed respect for Poe's temerity. Other readers were less inhibited in their praise. One contempo-

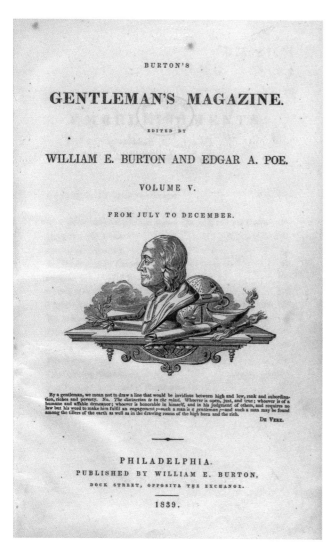

By a gentleman, we mean not to draw a line that would be invidious between high and low, rank and subordina-
tion, riches and poverty. No. *The distinction is in the mind.* Whoever is open, just, and true; whoever is of a
humane and affable demeanor; whoever is honorable in himself, and in his judgment of others, and requires no
law but his word to make him fulfil an engagement;—such a man is *a gentleman;*—and such a man may be found
among the tillers of the earth as well as in the drawing rooms of the high born and the rich.
                                                                                         DE VERE.

PHILADELPHIA.
PUBLISHED BY WILLIAM E. BURTON,
DOCK STREET, OPPOSITE THE EXCHANGE.
1839.

Title page for the fifth volume of *Burton's Gentleman's Magazine and American Monthly Review.* This volume, which contains the last six monthly issues of 1839, includes "The Man That Was Used Up" (August), "The Fall of the House of Usher" (September), and "William Wilson" (October).

rary newspaperman called Poe "the best critic among us and withal the most independent."[16]

Hoping to obtain a more prestigious editorial position in New York, Poe left Richmond with Virginia and her mother in early 1837. His hopes went for naught. After months of poverty and frustration, he moved the family again, this time to Philadelphia, where he secured a position as assistant editor with *Burton's Gentleman's Magazine,* owned and edited by William Burton, a former stage comedian. Determined to rein in his editor, Burton did not grant Poe the same leeway he had enjoyed in the review pages of the *Messenger.* Poe resented the restraints, but Burton knew what he was doing. Unable to write lengthy reviews, Poe devoted more of his energy to fiction, and consequently some of his finest tales would appear in *Burton's:* "The Business Man," "The Fall of the House of Usher," "The Man of the Crowd," "The Man That Was Used Up," and "William Wilson." Poe's stint at *Burton's* lasted barely a year. After a quarrel precipitated by Burton's decision to sell the magazine without consulting his editor, Poe was dismissed from the magazine in June 1840. The relationship ended acrimoniously, with personal accusations on both sides. Fortunately, Poe was able to obtain a similar position at the Philadelphia-based *Graham's Magazine,* created from the recent merger of the *Casket* and *Burton's* after Burton sold his interest in the magazine. A sociable and enterprising publisher, George R. Graham encouraged Poe to write the kind of reviews he thought were needed and paid him a generous salary of $800 per year, with additional compensation for his own literary contributions. Graham's policy meant that Poe could develop his fiction and his criticism simultaneously.

The April 1841 issue of *Graham's* carried a short notice by "the Proprietor" announcing Poe's association with the magazine, "commencing with the present number." As a critic, the notice continues, Poe "is surpassed by no man in the country; and as in this Magazine his critical abilities shall have free scope, the rod will be very generously, and at the same time, justly administered."[17] The same issue of *Graham's* included two substantial contributions by Poe: "The Murders in the Rue Morgue," the first of his tales of ratiocination, which established the key features of the modern detective story, and his review of Edward Bulwer-Lytton's novel *Night and Morning.*

Along with his well-known review of Hawthorne's *Twice-Told Tales* (which appeared in *Graham's* the following year), the analysis of *Night and Morning* contains some of Poe's most important statements on the art of fiction. Poe has plenty to say about Bulwer-Lytton's novel, but the real object of the review is to demonstrate the shortcomings of the novel form and the superiority of the brief tale. "We could never bring ourselves to attach any idea of merit to mere *length*," he says. "The ordinary talk about 'continuous and sustained effort' is pure twaddle and nothing more."[18] The need to maintain suspense and keep a story going over hundreds of pages forces the novelist to supply much additional exposition and incidental detail, which do not necessarily enhance a story's effectiveness. These inherent shortcomings of the form are only magnified by the "absurd fashion" of serial publication of novels, a point emphasized by Poe slightly later in his review of Dickens's *Barnaby Rudge*.[19]

The brevity of the prose tale, on the other hand, Poe argues, allows the author to control plot, action, and character, to achieve that which is "alone worth the attention of the critic—the unity or totality of *effect*."[20] In his review of Hawthorne's *Twice-Told Tales*, Poe stresses his theory of totality, which he also calls the "single

Paolo Fumagalli, *A Market Square, Philadelphia, Pennsylvania, ca.* 1830. Although Poe's five years in Philadelphia were widely considered his most prolific, he often had trouble making ends meet. The charming depiction of the city in this color lithograph belies the hand-to-mouth-existence that characterized Poe's time there.

effect." Working from the premise that "immense force" may be gained from totality, he argues that a tale composed according to a "pre-established design" —toward whose end every word must contribute—and brief enough to be read in a single sitting, affords, with the single exception of the rhymed poem, "the fairest field for the exercise of loftiest talent."[21]

Unlike the novel, the short story allows an author to grab hold of the reader's attention and not let go for "a half-hour to one or two hours." Poe's single-sitting requirement applies equally to verse and fiction. "During the hour of perusal," he maintains, "the soul of the reader is at the writer's control."[22] If the reader's attention is broken, then so too is the spell cast by the writer: "Worldly interests intervening during the pauses of perusal, modify, annul, or counteract, in a greater or less degree, the impressions of the book. But simple cessation in reading, would, of itself, be sufficient to destroy the true unity."[23]

Much as today's new technologies have become the focus of intense cultural, political, and economic debate, the popular magazine in Poe's day elicited fascination, worries, and considerable hyperbole. Critics were quick to blame the magazine for America's cultural and moral degeneration. Not Poe. Though he complained bitterly and frequently about being stuck in "the magazine prison-house" and the paying practices of periodicals, he believed the magazine, for good or bad, merely reflected the pace of modern life. "The whole tendency of the age," he recognized, "is Magazine-ward."[24] People traveled faster, moved more often, thought more rapidly, and made decisions more quickly than ever before. In his "Marginalia," published in *Godey's Lady's Book* in September 1845, he makes the point plainly:

> The increase, within a few years, of the magazine literature, is by no means to be regarded as indicating what some critics would suppose it to indicate— a downward tendency in American taste or in American letters. It is but a sign of the times, an indication of an era in which men are forced upon the curt, the condensed, the well-digested, in place of the voluminous . . . I will not be sure that men at present think more profoundly than half a century ago, but beyond question they think with more rapidity, with more skill, with more tact, with more of method and less of excrescence in the thought. Besides all this, they have a vast increase in the thinking material; they have more facts, more to think about. For this reason, they are disposed to put the greatest amount of thought in the smallest compass.[25]

This remarkably modern view adds another dimension to Poe's emphasis on brevity, which we now see was not solely motivated by aesthetics. Poe advances a larger cultural agenda about changing reading habits and the direction and pace of modern society. Whatever its "merits and demerits," magazine literature suited "the *rush* of

Evert Augustus Duyckinck, ca. 1860–1878. Duyckinck (1816-1878), one of the most influential figures on the antebellum literary scene, was the editor of Wiley and Putnam's Library of American Books. Duyckinck recruited some of the finest American authors, including Poe, who contributed a volume of tales and a volume of poems to the prestigious series.

the age."[26] What such times demanded was "the curt, the condensed, the pointed, the readily diffused—in place of the verbose, the detailed, the voluminous, the inaccessible."[27]

Poe's own experiments in novel writing were limited to the commercially unsuccessful book *The Narrative of Arthur Gordon Pym* (1838) and the never-finished western narrative *The Journal of Julius Rodman* (1840). Perhaps these forays into the novel were motivated by Poe's frustrations in trying to find a book publisher for his proposed "Tales of the Folio Club" and his belief, in the mid-to-late 1830s, that if he were going to publish a book of fiction, it would have to be a novel-length narrative.[28] Book publishers have never much liked story collections. In any case, the failure of *Pym* may only have hardened him in his views about the novel.

In 1840, the Philadelphia publishing firm of Lea and Blanchard finally took the chance on a collection of twenty-five of Poe's stories, *Tales of the Grotesque and Arabesque.* It sold poorly enough that a year later the publisher declined Poe's proposal for a revised edition. In 1842, Poe planned a new collection he now hoped to call "Phantasy-Pieces," referring to the German musical term *Fantasiestück,* a short composition in which the composer's imagination drives both the form and the progress of the movement. Speaking before the Harvard Musical Association the same year Poe planned this collection, William Wetmore Story defined the phantasy piece as a work "full of wild changes, flights and freaks—full of coquetry, brilliancy and bravura."[29] These words might just as easily describe Poe's short fiction.

"Phantasy-Pieces" never saw print, but Poe's growing renown as a fiction writer prompted editor Evert A. Duyckinck to approach him about publishing a selection of his tales in the Library of American Books, a prestigious series he was editing for Wiley and Putnam. Poe's *Tales* (1845) appeared as the second volume in the series. Though Poe wasn't entirely happy with Duyckinck's selection (which he felt emphasized the tales of ratiocination at the expense of variety), he did what he could to help promote it. In an anonymous self-review of *Tales*, Poe pointedly summarizes his achievement: "The evident and most prominent aim of Mr. Poe is originality, either of idea, or the combination of ideas. . . . Thus it is that he has produced works of the most notable character, and elevated the mere 'tale,' in this country, over the larger 'novel'—conventionally so termed."[30]

Since the mid-1830s Poe had dreamed of one day publishing a literary magazine of his own. Such a magazine might usher in a national republic of letters, in which diverse and independent criticism would prevail. Then, too, his experiences had taught him that he could never really be content working under someone else's direction. As he told a correspondent in 1841, "So far I have not only labored solely for the benefit of others (receiving for myself a miserable pittance) but have been forced to model my thoughts at the will of men whose imbecility was evident to all but themselves."[31] Immediately after his dismissal from *Burton's*, Poe embarked on an ambitious plan to realize his dream. In a paid advertisement in the June 6, 1840, issue of the Philadelphia *Saturday Evening Post*, he printed a 750-word announcement: "Prospectus of the Penn Magazine, a Monthly Literary Journal, to Be Edited and Published in the City of Philadelphia, by Edgar A. Poe." Critical notices in the "Penn," he promised, would offer "the calmest and sternest sense of literary justice," while contributions, from "the loftiest regions of literature," would exhibit "versatility, originality and pungency." From the summer through the winter months, Poe attempted to raise money for the magazine and build a list of subscribers, but a new bank panic in February 1841 temporarily put an end to his plans— "scotched, not killed," Poe wrote to his friend Joseph Snodgrass—and forced him to accept the position at *Graham's*.[32]

Both Poe and *Graham's* benefited from his association with the magazine, its subscription base increasing sevenfold over the initial 5,500 subscribers as Poe's growing reputation as an author of fiction started to rival the fame of his tomahawk.[33] Besides "The Murders in the Rue Morgue," several other important works appeared in *Graham's*, including "A Descent into the Maelström," "The Oval Portrait," and "The Masque of the Red Death." Things had gone well at *Graham's*—or well

Rufus W. Griswold, undated engraving. During their professional literary careers, Poe and Griswold developed a public animosity, part genuine and part contrived. Both men realized that controversy could sell books, so they exaggerated their critical disputes in the press. After Poe's death, Griswold savaged him in an obituary notice but also undertook the task of editing a collected edition of Poe's works.

enough that Poe tried to enlist George Graham's backing for the "Penn," in an equal partnership that would have put the publication under Poe's design and control. After expressing interest in the proposition, Graham either changed his mind or understood all along that he would be working against the interests of the magazine that carried his name. In May 1842, one year after Graham had hired him, Poe remained on good terms with his employer, but again chaffing under someone else's editorial direction, growing disgusted with his situation, and still hoping to start his own magazine, he left the security of his job at *Graham's* for an uncertain future. Poe's replacement at *Graham's* was an ambitious young anthologist named Rufus Griswold. Hearing that Griswold had replaced Poe at the magazine, newspaperman Jesse Dow editorialized: "We would give more for Edgar A. Poe's toe nail, than we would for Rueful Grizzle's soul, unless we wanted a milk-strainer. Them's our sentiments."[34]

Poe kept trying to raise capital for his magazine that would reshape American letters (now called "The Stylus"), but prospects remained poor. Worse, his wife, Virginia, was showing the unmistakable signs of consumption (tuberculosis), a death sentence in the nineteenth century. Her illness, the inability to raise money for his magazine, and worsening money problems led to periodic escape in binge drinking, followed by inevitable self-recriminations and promises to stop. Poe nevertheless continued to publish tales, poems, and reviews in magazines and newspapers. In January 1843, "The Tell-Tale Heart" appeared in his friend James Russell Lowell's short-lived Boston literary magazine, *The Pioneer*. Then in June 1843, Poe won $100 in a contest sponsored by Philadelphia's *Dollar Newspaper* for "The Gold-Bug," his tale of ratiocination that brilliantly capitalized on renewed interest in cryptology following the discovery of the Rosetta Stone, and on the perennial fascination with buried pirate treasure. Later that year, "The Black Cat" appeared in the *United States Saturday Post*.

In April 1844, Poe moved his family from Philadelphia to New York, where he temporarily joined the staff of the daily *Evening Mirror*. The position was undemanding. It mostly involved writing editorial squibs to fill white spaces. It was the kind of editorial work Poe hated, but at least it left time and energy for more important work. The publication of his hoax about a trans-Atlantic balloon crossing in the April 13 issue of the New York *Sun* created a sensation in an era when readers were hungry for stories about progress. In 1844 he also produced a few comic tales as well as "The Oblong Box," "A Tale of the Ragged Mountains," "The Premature Burial," "Mesmeric Revelation," and the last of his Dupin tales, "The Purloined Letter." In January 1845, Poe's pointless attacks on Henry Wadsworth Longfellow in the *Mirror*, in which he accused Longfellow of plagiarism, initiated a protracted print war between Poe and Longfellow's defenders that eclipsed Poe's earlier, more even-handed reviews of Longfellow and—whether calculated or not—brought new notoriety.

While employed by the *Evening Mirror*, Poe had begun to contribute to the weekly *Broadway Journal*. In February 1845 he signed a contract with its proprietor to co-edit the magazine. During his time with the *Broadway Journal*, Poe went from co-editor to editor to co-owner to sole proprietor, borrowing heavily to acquire the magazine. As a weekly, the *Broadway Journal* was not the ideal magazine he had dreamed of publishing, but it was the first over which he exercised full control. Predictably, editorial responsibilities sapped his energy and prevented him from writing many new stories.

Before the troubled *Broadway Journal* ceased operations in January 1846, Poe, however, did manage to reprint about forty of his tales. Reprinting was a common practice in Poe's antebellum literary world, when printed material became widely and cheaply available. Some of the tales Poe reprinted in the *Broadway Journal* had already appeared multiple times elsewhere. As a storyteller, Poe prided himself on his versatility but realized that the diversity of his achievement in short fiction had gone unrecognized because his stories had been published too diffusely. Unable to publish the comprehensive edition of tales he wanted, he accepted the *Broadway*

Journal as the next best thing. Separate issues of the magazine could be bound together in one or two volumes to attract investors and subscribers to the ideal magazine Poe envisioned. He always saw the *Broadway Journal* as a stepping-stone to "The Stylus."[35]

These late New York years also brought the kind of fame Poe had always dreamed of achieving, with the publication of "The Raven" in the January 29, 1845, issue of the *Evening Mirror*. Recognizing a hit when he saw one, N. P. Willis, the paper's editor, printed the poem ahead of its scheduled appearance in the February issue of the *American Review*. In his headnote, Willis praises the poem as "unsurpassed in English poetry for subtle conception, masterly ingenuity of versification, and consistent, sustaining of imaginative lift and 'pokerishness' [eeriness]." He accurately predicted that it would "stick to the memory of everybody who reads it."[36] The poem's vivid imagery, its insistent meter, its rhyme and interior rhyme scheme of very particular complexity, and of course the catchy refrain, quickly established it as part of American vernacular culture. "The Raven" was reprinted in numerous magazines and newspapers across the nation, memorized by countless readers, and parodied by many wits, wags, and poetasters. Poe, whose first three collections of poems had attracted little notice, now found himself more famous for his poem than for his other work. "The Raven" remains his single most famous and quotable work, and elements from it, especially the image of the raven perched atop the bust of Pallas, have become part of Poe iconography.

To capitalize on the popularity of "The Raven," Poe's former employer George Graham invited him to contribute an article about it to his magazine. The request sounded simple enough: Graham wanted him to describe the process of writing the poem. The result was "The Philosophy of Composition" (1846). Poe's mock-serious essay on the composition of "The Raven" has intrigued readers ever since it appeared in *Graham's*. Creative writing handbooks, premised on the notion that creativity can be taught, have often cited Poe's essay to illustrate the power of craftsmanship over inspiration. Poe promises his readers an unprecedented and indeed forbidden "peep behind the scenes" at the tricks of the trade: "at the wheels and pinions—the tackle for scene-shifting—the step-ladders and demon-traps—the cock's feathers, the red paint and the black

"Edgar A. Poe," a trading card in the "Great Americans" series issued in packs of Duke cigarettes around the turn of the century. Other distinguished figures featured on the cards include Benjamin Franklin, Patrick Henry, Thomas Jefferson, and Captain John Smith.

patches, which in ninety-nine cases out of a hundred, constitute the properties of the literary *histrio*."[37] T. S. Eliot, whose attitude toward Poe was ambivalent at best, acknowledged the importance of "The Philosophy of Composition." Eliot understood that the essay embodies a vital question all poets must ask themselves: "What am I doing when I write a poem?"[38]

What Poe did when he wrote "The Raven" or, at least, what he said he did, was to reject widely accepted Romantic notions regarding poetic inspiration. By and large, Romantics believed that poets reacted to external stimuli, letting what their senses perceive inspire them to write great poetry. The aeolian harp was one of their favorite metaphors. An oblong box with strings stretched across its top, the aeolian harp would be placed on the casement of an open window. As the wind wafted across the strings, it would resonate, creating what Coleridge called "a soft floating witchery of sound."[39] According to this Romantic view, poets functioned similarly. What they saw and heard and felt from nature inspired them to create their own kind of music.

In "The Philosophy of Composition," Poe downplays or dismisses intuition as important in the creative process. Most writers, especially poets, avoid telling others how they write, because, he says, they prefer to keep things a mystery, hoping readers would think they "compose by a species of fine frenzy—an ecstatic intuition."[40] Elsewhere in his writings, however, Poe emphasizes the crucial role intuition and chance play in the creative process. Even Poe's supersleuth Dupin relies on intuition. In any case, whether satire or braggadocio, "The Philosophy of Composition" reiterates the key principles of single effect, originality, and novel combinations.

In May 1846, Poe moved his family out of New York City, first to Turtle Bay then to a cottage in the rural village of Fordham. It was there that Virginia, now twenty-four, died of consumption on January 30, 1847. The years following Virginia's death were marked by Poe's own illness and depression, more binge drinking, and continuing economic hardship. He became briefly engaged to the poet Sarah Helen Whitman, but the engagement was called off after Poe broke his promise to Whitman to abstain from drink. In the summer of 1848, he published *Eureka*, his prose poem on the origin and destination of the universe. And he continued to try to find backing for "The Stylus." In a letter of August 9, 1846, Poe calls "The Stylus" "the one great purpose of my literary life. Undoubtedly (unless I die) I will accomplish it . . . I wish to establish a journal in which the men of genius may fight their battles; upon some terms of equality, with those dunces the men of talent. But, apart from this, I have *magnificent* objects in view—may I but live to accomplish them!"[41]

In the summer of 1849, Poe embarked on a lecture tour in another effort to raise money for "The Stylus." The tour brought him to Richmond, where after a brief courtship he became engaged to his childhood sweetheart, the widowed Elmira Royster Shelton. The last two weeks of Poe's life, the circumstances surrounding his death, and the causes of his death, must remain mysterious in the absence of contemporary documentation. On September 27, 1849, he sailed from Richmond to Baltimore, on his way to New York, possibly intending to bring his Aunt Maria back to Richmond. On October 3, he was found in need of medical assistance inside or perhaps just outside a tavern, 4th Ward Polls, also known as Gunner's Hall, where Joseph W. Walker happened upon him. Walker sent the following note to Poe's acquaintance Dr. Joseph E. Snodgrass: "DEAR SIR,—There is a gentleman, rather the worse for wear, at Ryan's 4th ward polls, who goes under the cognomen of Edgar A. Poe, and who appears in great distress, and he says he is acquainted with you, and I assure you, he is in need of immediate assistance. Yours, in haste, Jos. W. Walker."[42] Snodgrass and Henry Herring, Poe's uncle, arranged for a carriage to convey Poe, whom they assumed to be drunk, to the Washington Hospital, where he died four days later, on October 7, 1849.

A Posthumous Footnote

"EDGAR ALLAN POE is dead," began an obituary by "Ludwig" in the October 9, 1849, issue of the *New York Tribune*. "He died in Baltimore the day before yesterday. This announcement will startle many, but few will be grieved by it." The pseudonymous Ludwig was none other than Poe's old professional rival Rufus Griswold. He went on to depict Poe as a "brilliant but erratic" writer, a friendless loner who "walked the streets, in madness or melancholy, with lips moving in indistinct curses."[43] Perhaps by misrepresenting his interests and his relationship with Poe, Griswold became Poe's literary executor, after Maria Clemm transferred power of attorney to him. In any case, in a third volume of Poe's works that he edited, Griswold enlarged his scandalous portrait of Poe in his "Memoir of the Author."

Numerous explanations have been advanced for Griswold's posthumous attacks on Poe. But always at the heart of Griswold's resentment seems to be his inability to forgive Poe for his review of Griswold's anthology *The Poets and Poetry of America* (1842)—a positive but not uncritical review that Griswold had paid Poe to write (privately Poe thought the collection "outrageous humbug").[44] Friends and supporters defended Poe's reputation as best they could, but Griswold's portrait circulated widely and was largely responsible for shaping the myth of Edgar Allan Poe that persists today. Committed to the notion that literature should perform a moral function, Anglo-American readers were quick to question the value of Poe's work even as—or precisely because—they found it so compelling. In France and Europe it was a different story. Griswold's portrait may have enhanced his literary reputation: Poe's great French champion Baudelaire embraced Poe as a *poète maudit*, an accursed seer, spewing his "scorn and disgust for democracy, progress and *civiliza-tion*." If there was a fault it lay within America, "a nation more infatuated with itself than any other," not within the breast of Edgar Allan Poe.[45]

The Notes in the Margin

The publication of an annotated selection of the tales and poems of Edgar Allan Poe seems appropriate, given his penchant for parodies, satires, and hoaxes, and his belief that true originality expresses itself in new combinations of old forms and ideas. Inevitably, some of the objects of his satire have fallen from view, just as the ingenuity of some of his inventions is not entirely obvious for the reason that Poe has influenced so many writers who have come after him. His works are fiendishly dense with allusions, quotations (both real and made-up), and near quotations. He was fond of ciphers, puns, neologisms (tintinnabulation, deskism, scoriac, Neufchatel-ish), and word play of all kind. For all of these reasons readers may want to consult the margins of the book for guidance.

An annotated edition of selected tales and poems is fitting in another way, since in his "Marginalia" Poe himself offers the rationale for such an undertaking. In the first of his "Marginalia," published in installments between 1844 and 1849 in the *Democratic Review, Godey's Lady's Book, Graham's,* and the *Messenger,* he meditates on his design: "In getting my books, I have been always solicitous of an ample margin; this not so much through any love of the thing in itself, however agreeable, as for the facility it affords me of pencilling suggested thoughts, agreements and differences of opinion, or brief critical comments in general."[46]

The conceit here is that Poe's published marginalia are transcriptions of the pencil markings in his own books. Poe presents himself to his readers as the seemingly well-to-do owner of a personal library, "sufficiently miscellaneous" and "not a little *recherché,*" consulted in his apparently abundant leisure hours to escape boredom. In truth, Poe never had more than a modest collection of books, about as many as could be accommodated on the hanging bookshelf that was among the spare furnishings in the Fordham cottage. He was never able to afford a good library. As a book review editor, of course, he received many books for free, but always in need of extra income, he sold his review copies almost as soon as he read them. Would he have marked them up when he needed to sell them? It seems unlikely. But it doesn't matter. Poe's rationale for recording his thoughts in the margins of his books makes good sense. The margins of a book—literal or figurative—are that place where author and reader meet.

Marginal notes in the best sense are thoughts provoked by the text, which is why, Poe says, the "mind of the reader" feels it must "unburthen itself of a *thought;* —however flippant—however silly—however trivial."[47] In the margins, too, because we speak to ourselves, we feel free to "talk freshly—boldly—originally— with *abandonnement*—without conceit."[48] As a medium of expression, the margin offers other distinct advantages. However ample a book's margins, it's still a relatively small space. Confined to the margins, readers must therefore articulate their thoughts as clearly and succinctly as possible. "The circumscription of space," Poe says in the headnote to "Marginalia," "compels us (whatever diffuseness of idea we may clandestinely entertain), into Montesquieu-ism."[49] Finally, a book's margins accommodate "multitudinous opinion," meaning both our own disparate thoughts as well as the views of other readers (Poe was keenly aware that in publishing his marginal notes he had turned an essentially private dialogue between author and reader into a public forum).

In my own margins I supply in addition to literary contexts a range of other helpful contexts (biographical, historical, political, philosophical), and gloss allusions and sources, topical references, obscure words and phrases, and words whose connotations may not be clear to modern readers. While offering my own penciled thoughts on the tales and poems selected for this volume, I admit into the margins the "multitudinous opinion" of biographers, critics, theorists, literary historians, editors, poets, and fiction writers, from Poe's circle of acquaintances and the larger antebellum literary world to present-day scholars. In preparing this edition, I have tried to remain mindful of the fact that the margins must accommodate new views, including those of the readers of *The Annotated Poe*: Poe's tales and poems admit many interpretations, and there is no final way of reading any of his works.

From his early European admirers Charles Baudelaire and Fyodor Dostoyevsky to Cormac McCarthy, Poe has inspired generations of writers. As a pioneer in the short story, he influenced all practitioners of the form who came after him. More particularly, he shaped the development of the horror story and science fiction, and established the modern detective genre with his Dupin tales. My notes draw liberally on creative writers to take measure of his influence. But Poe's influence on the arts extends well beyond the realm of literature, and his presence in popular culture is pervasive. The history of modern book illustration can be told through the artists who have illustrated his works, while his influence in the history of cinema has been profound. He has since the early days of motion pictures provided filmmakers with subjects, while influencing the development of cinematic theory and technique. Here too in the margins I trace the story of Poe's influence.

NOTES

1. Kevin J. Hayes, *The Road to Monticello: The Life and Mind of Thomas Jefferson* (New York: Oxford University Press, 2008), 639–640; James A. Bear, Jr., "The Last Few Days in the Life of Thomas Jefferson," *Magazine of Albemarle County History* 32 (1974), 63-80; Kevin J. Hayes, *Edgar Allan Poe* (London: Reaktion, 2009), 41-42.

2. Edgar Allan Poe to John Allan, March 19, 1827, *Collected Letters of Edgar Allan Poe*, ed. John Ward Ostrom, Burton R. Pollin, and Jeffrey A. Savoye, 2 vols. (New York: Gordian Press, 2008), I, 10.

3. Poe to John Allan, August 10, 1829, *Collected Letters*, I, 43.

4. Kevin J. Hayes, *Poe and the Printed Word* (New York: Cambridge University Press, 2000), 27.

5. Edgar Allan Poe, *The Complete Works of Edgar Allan Poe*, ed. James A. Harrison, 17 vols. (New York: T. Y. Crowell, 1902), XVI, 36–37.

6. Hayes, *Edgar Allan Poe*, 18.

7. Meredith L. McGill, *American Literature and the Culture of Reprinting, 1834-1853* (Philadelphia: University of Pennsylvania Press, 2003), 76-108.

8. Edgar Allan Poe, *Private Perry and Mister Poe: The West Point Poems, 1831*, ed. William F. Heckler (Baton Rouge: Louisiana State University Press, 2005), 14.

9. Kevin J. Hayes, *A Journey through American Literature* (New York: Oxford University Press, 2012), 70-75.

10. Edgar Allan Poe, *Collected Works of Edgar Allan Poe*, ed. Thomas Ollive Mabbott, 3 vols. (Cambridge, MA: The Belknap Press of Harvard University Press, 1969-1978), III, 802.

11. Poe, *Complete Works*, X, 61-62.

12. Poe, *Complete Works*, VII, 38.

13. Poe to Thomas W. White, April 30, 1835, *Collected Letters*, I, 85.

14. Terence Whalen, *Edgar Allan Poe and the Masses: The Political Economy of Literature in Antebellum America* (Princeton: Princeton University Press, 1999), 65-71.

15. Dwight Thomas and David K. Jackson, *The Poe Log: A Documentary Life of Edgar Allan Poe, 1809-1849* (Boston: G. K. Hall, 1987), 201, 204.

16. "We Understand," *Brooklyn Eagle*, January 3, 1846.

17. Thomas and Jackson, *Poe Log*, 320.

18. Poe, *Complete Works*, X, 122.

19. Poe, *Complete Works*, XI, 54.

20. Poe, *Complete Works*, X, 122.

21. Poe, *Complete Works*, X, 106.

22. Poe, *Complete Works*, VIII, 153.

23. Poe, *Complete Works*, X, 108.

24. Poe, *Complete Works*, XVI, 117.

25. Poe, *Complete Works*, XVI, 82.

26. Poe, *Complete Works*, XVI, 117-118.

27. Poe, *Complete Works*, XVI, 117-118.

28. J. Gerald Kennedy, "America's Europe: Irving, Poe, and the Foreign Subject," in *The American Novel to 1870*, ed. J. Gerald Kennedy and Leland S. Person (New York: Oxford University Press, 2014), 159-176.

29. William W. Story, *Address Delivered before the Harvard Musical Association in the Chapel of the University at Cambridge, August 24, 1842* (Boston: S. N. Dickinson, 1842), 20.

30. Edgar Allan Poe, *Essays and Reviews*, ed. G. R. Thompson (New York: Library of America, 1984), 873.

31. Poe to Robert T. Conrad, January 22, 1841, *Collected Letters*, I, 260.

32. Poe to Joseph E. Snodgrass, April 1, 1841, *Collected Letters*, I, 264.

33. Kenneth Silverman, *Edgar A. Poe: Mournful and Never-Ending Remembrance* (New York: HarperCollins, 1991), 174-175.

34. Thomas and Jackson, *Poe Log*, 370.

35. Hayes, *Edgar Allan Poe*, 141.

36. Nathaniel Parker Willis, "Introductory Note in the New York *Evening Mirror*," in *Edgar Allan Poe: The Critical Heritage*, ed. I. M. Walker (New York: Routledge and Kegan Paul, 1986), 140.

37. Poe, *Complete Works*, XIV, 195.

38. T. S. Eliot, "From Poe to Valéry," in Eric W. Carlson, ed., *The Recognition of Edgar Allan Poe: Selected Criticism since 1829* (Ann Arbor: University of Michigan Press, 1966), 218.

39. Samuel Taylor Coleridge, *The Poetical Works of Samuel Taylor Coleridge, Including Poems and*

Harry Clarke, portrait of Edgar Allan Poe from *Tales of Mystery and Imagination* (London: George G. Harrap, 1919). Clarke (1881–1931), an Irish artist renowned for his stained-glass creations, produced twenty-four eerie and exotic illustrations and several vignettes for this first edition of *Tales*. His work for Poe's collection secured his reputation as a book illustrator.

Versions of Poems Now Published for the First Time, ed. Ernest Hartley Coleridge (London: Henry Frowde, 1912), 101.

40. Poe, *Complete Works*, XIV, 194.
41. Poe to Philip P. Cooke, August 9, 1846, *Collected Letters*, I, 597.
42. Poe, *Complete Works*, I, 328.
43. Rufus Wilmot Griswold, "The 'Ludwig' Article," in Carlson, ed., *Recognition*, 32-33.
44. Poe to Joseph E. Snodgress, June 4, 1842, *Collected Letters*, I, 341.
45. Charles Baudelaire, "New Notes on Edgar Poe," in Carlson, ed., *Recognition*, 45-46.
46. Poe, *Complete Works*, XVI, 1.
47. Poe, *Complete Works*, XVI, 2.
48. Poe, *Complete Works*, XVI, 2.
49. Poe, *Complete Works*, XVI, 2.

Metzengerstein

Pestis eram vivus, moriens tua mors ero.

Martin Luther[1]

Horror and fatality have been stalking abroad in all ages. Why then give a date to the story I have to tell? I will not. Besides I have other reasons for concealment.[2] Let it suffice to say that, at the period of which I speak, there existed, in the interior of Hungary,[3] a settled although hidden belief in the doctrines of the Metempsychosis.[4] Of the doctrines themselves—that is, of their falsity, or probability—I say nothing. I assert, however, that much of our incredulity (as La Bruyère observes of all our unhappiness,) *vient de ne pouvoir etre seuls.*[5]

But there were some points in the Hungarian superstition (the Roman term was religio,)[6] which were fast verging to absurdity. They, the Hungarians, differed essentially from the Eastern authorities. For example—"The soul," said the former, (I give the words of an acute, and intelligent Parisian,) *"ne demeure, quun seul fois, dans un corps sensible—au reste—ce quon croit d'etre un cheval —un chien—un homme—n'est que le resemblance peu tangible de ces animaux."*[7]

The families of Berlifitzing, and Metzengerstein had been at variance for centuries. Never, before, were two houses so illustrious mutually embittered by hostility so deadly. Indeed, at the era of this history, it was remarked by an old crone of haggard, and sinister appearance, that fire and water might sooner mingle, than a Berlifitzing clasp the hand of a Metzengerstein. The origin of this enmity seems to be found in the words of an ancient prophecy. "A lofty name shall have a fearful fall, when, like the rider over his horse, the mortality of Metzengerstein shall triumph over the immortality of Berlifitzing."[8]

Poe's remarkable debut tale, "Metzengerstein," appeared in the Philadelphia Saturday Courier *on January 14, 1832, one of five tales Poe had submitted to a contest sponsored by the magazine (none of Poe's stories won). He was just shy of his twenty-third birthday. After taking a job with the* Southern Literary Messenger, *where Poe was the magazine's editor in every sense but perhaps in name, he republished several of his early stories in its pages, including "Metzengerstein," which appeared in the January 1836 issue. He also reprinted the work in* Tales of the Grotesque and Arabesque *(1840). Poe later revised the text of "Metzengerstein," cancelling several significant passages. In his 1850 edition of Poe's collected works, Rufus W. Griswold published a version incorporating its author's latest revisions. Subsequent editors have typically followed Griswold's text. For its significance as Poe's first published story and its greater complexity, the 1832 version forms the basis of the present text of "Metzengerstein."*

The Messenger *reprint appeared under the title "Metzengerstein: A Tale in Imitation of the German." Poe added the subtitle to forestall complaints about his gothicism or, as the gothic style was also known, "Germanism." In his preface to* Tales of the Grotesque and Arabesque, *Poe offers a defense of his Germanism. "If in many of my productions terror has been the thesis," he observes, "I maintain that terror is not of Germany, but of the soul" (I, 6). Several gothic elements are present in "Metzengerstein"—death, decay, madness, a menacing chateau, a murder plot, supernatural transformations— but in Poe's hands they are used not only to thrill and frighten but also to extend the limits of narrative point of view, portray the perverse, and explore the world of the imagination and the role of the artist.*

1 "I was a plague to thee, O Pope, whilst living, and will be thy death when I die." Martin Luther (1483–1546) addressed these words to Pope Clement VII (1478–1534).

2 Though Poe's story is told in the first person, his narrator does not inhabit its fictional world. Even so, the occasionally intrusive narrator possesses a distinct personality and is a character in his own right. The narrator asserts himself to defend various aesthetic decisions but hesitates to reveal much about himself. Poe had second thoughts about this narrative strategy. Without changing the first person to third, he did minimize the first-person voice, omitting this sentence, the previous one, and others in a late revision.

3 Eastern European settings are characteristic of much gothic fiction. Some of Poe's contemporaries believed American authors should set their stories in America.

From Niagara Falls to the Rockies, the West offered great literary potential. Poe disagreed. He felt American authors should strive for originality. They must be free to use whatever settings they wish. From his perspective, imaginary landscapes have greater literary potential than actual ones. It is his quest for originality, not his use of native materials, that makes Poe an American literary pioneer. William Carlos Williams turns the tables on Poe's jingoistic critics, equating his originality with the American journey west and comparing Poe to Daniel Boone: "His greatness is in that he turned his back and faced inland, to originality, with the identical gesture of a Boone" (Eric W. Carlson, ed., *The Recognition of Edgar Allan Poe: Selected Criticism since 1829* [Ann Arbor: University of Michigan Press, 1966], 136).

4   Metempsychosis is the belief in the transmigration of souls, or the passing of the soul at death into another body. Poe would continue to make creative use of this concept. American authors from Benjamin Franklin to Ambrose Bierce to Philip K. Dick have played with the notion that a person's identity could take another form after death.

5   This quote from Jean de La Bruyère (1645–1696), the French essayist and moralist, may be translated "comes from being unable to be alone."

6   "Superstition" is one possible translation of the word "religio" (William Young, *Latin-English Dictionary* [London: A. Wilson, 1810], 311).

7   "The soul . . . dwells but once in a material body—for the rest—a horse, a dog, even a human being—it is only an intangible phantom of those creatures." Poe coined this quotation himself.

8   The ancient prophecy is confusing because it is paradoxical. Essentially, it says that only when Metzengerstein triumphs over the immortal Berlifitzing will the name of Metzengerstein fall: a temporary triumph will lead to a permanent fall.

9   Poe draws an analogy between the feudal castle and the modern apartment building, from which one neighbor could gaze into the windows of another with jealousy and curiosity.

10   A poetical phrase popularized by "The Squire and the Cur," one of John Gay's *Fables* (1727), lines 37–38:

> Antiochus, with hardy pace,
> Provok'd the dangers of the chase.

To be sure, the words themselves had little or no meaning—but more trivial causes have given rise (and that no long while ago,) to consequences equally eventful. Besides, the estates, which were contiguous, had long exercised a rival influence, in the affairs of a busy government. Moreover, near neighbours are seldom friends, and the inmates of the Castle Berlifitzing might look, from their lofty buttresses, into the very windows of the Chateau Metzengerstein;[9] and least of all was the more than feudal magnificence thus discovered, calculated to allay the irritable feelings of the less ancient, and less wealthy Berlifitzings. What wonder then, that the words, however silly, of that prediction, should have succeeded in setting, and keeping at variance, two families, already predisposed to quarrel, by every instigation of hereditary jealousy? The words of the prophecy implied, if they implied any thing, a final triumph on the part of the already more powerful house, and were, of course, remembered, with the more bitter animosity, on the side of the weaker, and less influential.

Wilhelm, Count Berlifitzing, although honourably, and loftily descended, was, at the epoch of this narrative, an infirm, and doting old man, remarkable for nothing but an inordinate, and inveterate personal antipathy to the family of his rival, and so passionate a love of horses, and of hunting, that neither bodily decrepitude, great age, nor mental incapacity, prevented his daily participation in the dangers of the chace.[10]

Frederick, Baron Metzengerstein, was, on the other hand not yet of age. His father, the Minister G———, died young. His mother, the Lady Mary, followed quickly after. Frederick was, at that time, in his fifteenth year. In a city fifteen years are no long period—a child may be still a child in his third lustrum.[11] But in a wilderness—in so magnificent a wilderness as that old principality, fifteen years have a far deeper meaning.

The beautiful Lady Mary!—how could she die?—and of consumption! But it is a path I have prayed to follow. I would wish all I love to perish of that gentle disease. How glorious! to depart in the hey-day of the young blood—the heart all passion—the imagination all fire—amid the remembrances of happier days—in the fall of the year, and so be buried up forever in the gorgeous, autumnal leaves. Thus died the Lady Mary. The young Baron Frederick stood, without a living relative, by the coffin of his dead mother. He laid his hand upon her placid forehead. No shudder came over his delicate frame—no sigh from his gentle bosom—no curl upon his kingly lip. Heartless, self-willed, and impetuous from his childhood, he had arrived at the age of which I speak, through a career of unfeeling, wanton, and reckless dissipation, and a barrier had long since arisen in the channel of all holy thoughts, and gentle recollections.[12]

From some peculiar circumstances attending the administration of his father, the young Baron, at the decease of the former, entered immediately upon his vast possessions. Such estates were, never before, held by a nobleman of Hungary.[13] His castles were without number—of these, the chief, in point of splendour and extent, was the Chateau Metzengerstein. The boundary line of his dominions was never clearly defined, but his principal park embraced a circuit of one hundred and fifty miles.

Upon the succession of a proprietor so young, with a character so well known, to a fortune so unparalleled, little speculation was afloat in regard to his probable course of conduct. And, indeed, for the space of three days, the behaviour of the heir, out-heroded Herod,[14] and fairly surpassed the expectations of his most enthusiastic admirers. Shameful debaucheries—flagrant treacheries—unheard-of atrocities, gave his trembling vassals quickly to understand, that no servile submission on their part—no punctilios of conscience on his own were, thenceforward, to prove any protection against the bloodthirsty and remorseless fangs of a petty Caligula.[15] On the night of the fourth day, the stables of the Castle Berlifitzing were discovered to be on fire—and the neighbourhood unanimously added the crime of the incendiary, to the already frightful list of the Baron's misdemeanors and enormities.[16] But, during the tumult occasioned by this occurrence, the young nobleman himself, sat, apparently buried in meditation, in a vast, and desolate upper apartment of his family palace of Metzengerstein. The rich, although faded tapestry hangings which swung gloomily upon the walls, represented the majestic, and shadowy forms of a thousand illustrious ancestors.[17] Here rich-ermined priests, and pontifical dignitaries, familiarly seated with the autocrat, and the sovereign, put a veto on the wishes of some temporal king, or restrained, with the fiat of papal supremacy, the rebellious sceptre of the Arch-Enemy.[18] Here the dark, tall statures of the

11 A period of five years.

12 Tuberculosis, or consumption, was an endemic disease of the urban poor in the nineteenth and early twentieth centuries. Highly romanticized and often associated with artistic temperaments, it was considered a disease of "passion" or "inward burning," an affliction that consumed the life force. The narrator, who possesses a strong death wish, considers tuberculosis a good way to die. Poe had second thoughts about the disease. He would strike this paragraph after his wife, Virginia, had contracted tuberculosis, which had already claimed the lives of both his mother and his brother Henry.

13 Poe's protagonists often inherit vast riches. "Metzengerstein" appeared two years before his wealthy foster father, John Allan, died. At this point in his troubled, volatile relationship with Allan, Poe had abandoned hope of inheriting Allan's fortune but still expected some sort of bequest. When Allan left him nothing, Poe could only fantasize about inherited wealth.

14 Herod the Great (*ca.* 74–4 BCE) was a king of Judea known for his murderous cruelty. The phrase "it out-Herods Herod" comes from Shakespeare's *Hamlet*, III. ii.14, but it had become proverbial. Though Poe would reuse the phrase in "William Wilson" and "The Masque of the Red Death," he often avoided proverbs in his writing. Unlike Herman Melville, who recorded sailor proverbs for posterity, Poe would use proverbs and proverbial phrases for either rhetorical or humorous effect: to emphasize a point or spoof a character.

15 Caligula (12–41 CE) was a Roman emperor known for his pride, selfishness, and wanton behavior. Speaking of Caligula in *Bibliotheca Classica*, fourth edition, John Lemprière says: "Wild beasts were constantly fed in his palace with human victims, and a favorite horse was made high priest and consul, and kept in marble apartments, and adorned with the most valuable trappings and pearls the Roman empire could furnish."

16 Since Metzengerstein is at home when Berlifitzing's stables catch fire, he has presumably dispatched a servant as an arsonist, but this carefully worded sentence never definitively makes Metzengerstein responsible for the fire. It is more concerned with perceived than real guilt. Once Metzengerstein earns a reputation for debauchery, his neighbors easily attribute other crimes to him.

17 Delusional and detached from the world around him, Metzengerstein exhibits psychotic behavior as he ponders a work of art while his neighbor perishes in the fire. David H. Hirsch observes: "This kind of 'psychotic' detachment, this eerie disjunction between stimulus and response, is common among Poe's heroes. But the detachment here, as elsewhere in Poe, is not gratuitous, testifying, as it does, to a growing rift taking place within Metzengerstein's psyche between the world of spirit and the world of matter." Whatever one thinks of Metzengerstein's odd behavior, the scene demonstrates Poe's already sophisticated narrative technique this early in his career. "Metzengerstein" shows how narrative can present multiple perspectives by varying the focalization, that is, the "lens" through which the story is seen. In a fairly short space, Poe shifts from the perspective of his narrator to external, observable events to those mediated through the mind of Metzengerstein and then back again (David H. Hirsch, "Poe's 'Metzengerstein' as a Tale of the Subconscious," *University of Mississippi Studies in English* 3 [1982], 41; Luc Herman and Bart Vervaeck, *Handbook of Narrative Analysis* [Lincoln: University of Nebraska Press, 2005], 71–72).

18 Satan. Compare John Milton, *Paradise Lost*, book I, lines 81–83:

> To whom th' Arch-Enemy,
> And thence in Heaven call'd Satan, with bold words
> Breaking the horrid silence thus began.

19 Nero Claudius Caesar Augustus Germanicus (37–68 CE) was a Roman emperor infamous for his cruelty, insensitivity, and self-absorption. The saying "Nero fiddled while Rome burned" was already current in Poe's day.

20 The term "Saracen," which can mean Arab or Muslim, was often used in reference to the Crusades. Since Berlifitzing is a descendent of Saracens, the feud between Metzengerstein and his neighbor takes on the dimensions of the clash of civilizations, a battle between Muslim and Christian, East and West.

21 In subsequent works, especially "The Pit and the Pendulum," Poe would continue to ponder the overlap between consciousness and unconsciousness. Can we know precisely when consciousness ends and sleep begins?

22 A master of chiaroscuro for dramatic effect, Poe uses light and shadow here to create a visual contrast that also makes his imagery more dynamic. The flash of light sup-

Princes Metzengerstein—their muscular war coursers plunging over the carcass of a fallen foe—startled the firmest nerves with their vigorous expression—and here, the voluptuous, and swan-like figures of the dames of days gone by, floated away, in the mazes of an unreal dance, to the strains of imaginary melody.

But as the Baron listened, or affected to listen, to the rapidly increasing uproar in the stables of the Castle Berlifitzing, or perhaps pondered, like Nero,[19] upon some more decided audacity, his eyes were unwittingly rivetted to the figure of an enormous and unnaturally coloured horse, represented, in the tapestry, as belonging to a Saracen ancestor of the family of his rival.[20] The horse, itself, in the foreground of the design, stood motionless, and statue-like; while, farther back, its discomfited rider perished by the dagger of a Metzengerstein. There was a fiendish expression on the lip of the young Frederick, as he became aware of the direction which his glance had, thus, without his consciousness, assumed. But he did not remove it. On the contrary, the longer he gazed, the more impossible did it appear that he might ever withdraw his vision from the fascination of that tapestry. It was with difficulty that he could reconcile his dreamy and incoherent feelings, with the certainty of being awake.[21] He could, by no means, account for the singular, intense, and overwhelming anxiety which appeared falling, like a shroud, upon his senses. But the tumult without, becoming, suddenly, more violent, with a kind of compulsory, and desperate exertion, he diverted his attention to the glare of ruddy light thrown full by the flaming stables upon the windows of the apartment. The action was but momentary; his gaze returned mechanically to the wall. To his extreme horror and surprise, the head of the gigantic steed had, in the meantime, altered its position. The neck of the animal, before arched, as if in compassion, over the prostrate body of its lord, was now extended at full length, in the direction of the Baron. The eyes, before invisible, now wore an energetic, and human expression; while they gleamed with a fiery, and unusual red, and the distended lips of the apparently enraged horse left in full view his sepulchral and disgusting teeth.

Stupified with terror, the young nobleman tottered to the door. As he threw it open, a flash of red light, streaming far into the chamber, flung his shadow, with a clear, decided outline, against the quivering tapestry:[22] and he shuddered to perceive that shadow,

Angelo Biasioli,
*The Stables of
Caligula's Horse,
Incitata, ca.* 1800–1818.

as he staggered, for a moment, upon the threshold, assuming the exact position, and precisely filling up the contour of the relentless, and triumphant murderer of the Saracen Berlifitzing.

With the view of lightening the oppression of his spirits, the Baron hurried into the open air. At the principal gate of the Chateau he encountered three equerries.[23] With much difficulty, and, at the imminent peril of their lives, they were restraining the unnatural, and convulsive plunges of a gigantic, and fiery-coloured horse.

"Whose horse is that? Where did you get him?" demanded the youth, in a querulous, and husky tone of voice, as he became instantly aware that the mysterious steed, in the tapestried chamber, was the very counterpart of the furious animal before his eyes.[24]

"He is your own property, Sire," replied one of the equerries— "at least, he is claimed by no other owner. We caught him, just

plies movement, which the shadow, outlined against the tapestry, freezes. Red light has special significance for Poe. Sometimes he uses it to convey insanity; other times he uses it, as he does here, to intensify the mood.

23   An obsolete term for a groom.

24   That the horse jumps from the tapestry into the action of the story is a supernatural detail readers must accept as part of the fictional world of "Metzengerstein." Yet the behavior of this tapestry horse has broader ramifications at the symbolic level. Poe implies that works of art from the past are available for artists of the present to appropriate. The movement of the horse from tapestry to tale parallels Poe's habit of borrowing quotations from previous works of literature. Exploiting the tapestry's artistic potential, Poe presents one of several details in "Metzengerstein" that form comments on the creative process.

25   An estray is "any *beast* not being wild, found wandering within some lordship or manor, without authority"
(John Scriven, *A Treatise on Copyholds*, 2 vols. [London:
for Henry Butterworth, 1823], II, 766).

26   Folklore offers numerous instances of men transformed into horses and stories of the devil appearing as a
horse.

now, flying all smoking, and foaming with rage, from the burning
stables of the Castle Berlifitzing. Supposing him to have belonged
to the old Count's stud of foreign horses, we led him back as an
estray.[25] But the grooms there disclaim any title to the creature,
which is singular, since he bears evident marks of a narrow escape
from the flames"—

"The letters W. V. B. are, moreover, branded very distinctly
upon his forehead," interrupted a second equerry. "We, at first,
supposed them to be the initials of Wilhelm Von Berlifitzing."

"Extremely singular!" said the young Baron, with a musing air,
apparently unconscious of the meaning of his words. "He is, as
you say, a remarkable horse—a prodigious horse! Although, as
you very justly observe, of a suspicious and untractable character.
Let him be mine, however," added he, after a pause, "perhaps a
rider, like Frederick of Metzengerstein, may tame even the devil,
from the stables of Berlifitzing."[26]

"You appear to be mistaken, my lord, the horse (as I think we
mentioned) is *not* from the stables of the Count. If such were the
case, we know our duty better than to bring him in the presence of
a noble of your name."

"True!" observed the Baron, dryly, and, at that instant, a page
of the bed-chamber came from the Chateau with a heightened colour, and a precipitate step. He whispered into his master's ear, an
account of the miraculous, and sudden disappearance of a small
portion of the tapestry in an apartment which he designated—entering, at the same time, into particulars of a minute, and circumstantial character, but, from the low tone of voice in which these
latter were communicated, nothing escaped to gratify the excited
curiosity of the equerries.

The young Frederick, however, during the conference, seemed
agitated by a variety of emotions. He soon, however, recovered
his composure, and an expression of determined malignancy settled upon his countenance, as he gave peremptory orders that a
certain chamber should be immediately locked up, and the key
placed, forthwith, in his own possession.

"Have you heard of the unhappy death of the hunter Berlifitzing?"
said one of his vassals to the Baron, as, after the affair of the page,
the huge and mysterious steed, which that nobleman had adopted

as his own, plunged, and curvetted with redoubled, and supernatural fury down the long avenue which extended from the Chateau to the stables of Metzengerstein.

"No!" said the Baron, turning abruptly toward the speaker, "dead! say you?"

"It is true, my lord, and is no unwelcome intelligence, I imagine, to a noble of your family?"

A rapid smile, of a peculiar and unintelligible meaning, shot over the beautiful countenance of the listener—"How died he?"

"In his great exertions to rescue a favourite portion of his hunting-stud, he has, himself, perished miserably in the flames."

"I-n-d-e-e-d!" ejaculated the Baron, as if slowly, and deliberately impressed with the truth of some exciting idea.

"Indeed," repeated the vassal.

"Shocking!" said the youth, calmly, and returned into the Chateau.

From this date, a marked alteration took place in the outward demeanour of the dissolute young Baron, Frederick, of Metzengerstein. Indeed, the behaviour of the heir disappointed every expectation, and proved little in accordance with the views of many a manoeuvring mamma,[27] while his habits and manners, still less than formerly, offered any thing congenial with those of the neighbouring aristocracy. He was seldom to be seen at all; never beyond the limits of his own domain. There are few, in this social world, who are utterly companionless, yet so seemed he; unless, indeed, that unnatural, impetuous, and fiery-coloured horse which he thenceforward continually bestrode, had any mysterious right to the title of his friend. Numerous invitations on the part of the neighbourhood for a long time, however, continually flocked in. "Will the Baron attend our excursions? Will the Baron honour our festivals with his presence?"—"Baron Frederick does not hunt—Baron Frederick will not attend," were the haughty, and laconic answers. These repeated insults were not to be endured by an imperious nobility. Such invitations became less cordial—less frequent. In time they ceased altogether. The widow of the unfortunate Count Berlifitzing, was even heard to express a hope "that the Baron might be at home, when he did not choose to be at home, since he disdained the company of his equals—and ride when he did not wish to ride, since he preferred the society of a horse."[28] This, to be sure, was a very silly explosion of hereditary pique,

27 A proverbial phrase. Compare the following sentence by the contemporary British novelist Samuel Beazley: "A young man of high birth and expectations, has been inveigled into a match by some manoeuvring mamma" (*The Oxonians: A Glance at Society*, 2 vols. [New York: Harpers, 1830], II, 133).

28 Metzengerstein's behavior is reminiscent of that of Jonathan Swift's famous hero at the end of *Gulliver's Travels* (1726). After returning home from the land of the Houyhnhnms, a race of talking, intelligent horses, Lemuel Gulliver prefers his horses' company to that of his countrymen.

29   This phrase is often attributed to Samuel Johnson, who explains: "My reigning sin, to which perhaps many others are appendant, is waste of time, and general sluggishness, to which I was always inclined, and, in part of my life, have been almost compelled by morbid melancholy and disturbance of mind" (*Prayers and Meditations*, ed. George Strahan [London: T. Cadell, 1785], 154).

30   The phrase "in sickness or in health" comes from the marriage ceremony in *The Book of Common Prayer*, of course. Elsewhere Poe makes rhetorical use of the language of the marriage ceremony. In a letter of May 1829 to Philadelphia publisher Isaac Lea, he expresses his commitment to being a poet "for better or worse" (*Collected Letters of Edgar Allan Poe*, ed. John Ward Ostrom, Burton R. Pollin, and Jeffrey A. Savoye, 2 vols. [New York: Gordian Press, 2008], I, 26). For Poe, the relationship between the poet, or artist, and his work is a sacred union that cannot be broken. His reuse of language from the marriage ceremony in "Metzengerstein" suggests a compelling allegorical reading of the story. If Metzengerstein, who has lost himself in reverie in the world of the tapestry, represents the artist, then the demonic horse, which leaps from the tapestry, represents art. The relationship between horse and master is analogous to the artist's intense, all-or-nothing relationship with his art: he sticks to it, though it dooms him.

31   Poe echoes Milton, *Paradise Lost*, book I, lines 174–177:

> the Thunder,
> Wing'd with red Lightning and impetuous rage,
> Perhaps hath spent his shafts, and ceases now
> To bellow through the vast and boundless Deep.

32   At one point, Poe considered changing the title of his story to "The Horse-Shade." By "Shade," in this context, Poe means a ghost, that is, a dead person's visible yet impalpable form. That none of the grooms remember placing their hands on the horse's body reinforces its ghostly, or perhaps unreal, status. The oral tradition provides legends about suicides and murder victims who return in the shape of ghostly horses foreboding evil (Grace P. Smith, "Poe's 'Metzengerstein,'" *Modern Language Notes* 48 [1933], 356–359).

33   If Metzengerstein is an artist figure, then this dwarfish, peevish observer represents the critic, a small-minded person who cannot fathom the creative mind.

and merely proved how singularly unmeaning our sayings are apt to become, when we desire to be unusually energetic.

The charitable, nevertheless, attributed the alteration in the conduct of the young nobleman, to the natural sorrow of a son for the untimely loss of his parents; forgetting, however, his atrocious, and reckless behaviour, during the short period immediately succeeding that bereavement. Some there were, indeed, who suggested a too haughty idea of self-consequence and dignity. Others again, among whom may be mentioned the family physician, did not hesitate in speaking of morbid melancholy,[29] and hereditary ill health; while dark hints of a more equivocal nature, were current among the multitude.

Indeed the Baron's perverse attachment to his lately acquired charger, an attachment which seemed to attain new strength from every fresh example of the brute's ferocious, and demon-like propensities; at length became, in the eyes of all reasonable men, a hideous, and unnatural fervour. In the glare of noon, at the dead hour of night, in sickness or in health,[30] in calm or in tempest, in moonlight or in shadow, the young Metzengerstein seemed rivetted to the saddle of that colossal horse, whose untractable audacities so well accorded with the spirit of his own. There were circumstances, moreover, which coupled with late events, gave an unearthly, and portentous character to the mania of the rider, and the capabilities of the steed. The space passed over in a single leap, had been accurately measured, and was found to exceed, by an incalculable distance, the wildest expectations of the most imaginative; while the red lightning, itself, was declared to have been outridden in many a long-continued, and impetuous career.[31] The Baron, besides had no particular name for the animal, although all the rest of his extensive collection, were distinguished by characteristic appellations. Its stable was appointed at a distance from the others, and with regard to grooming, and other necessary offices, none but the owner, in person, had ever ventured to officiate, or even to enter the enclosure of that particular stall. It was also to be observed, that although the three grooms who had caught the horse, as he fled from the conflagration at Berlifitzing, had succeeded in arresting his course, by means of a chain-bridle and noose, yet no one of the three could, with any certainty affirm, that he had, during that dangerous struggle, or at any period thereafter, actually placed his hand upon the body of the beast.[32]

Hermann Wögel, engraving depicting the Baron charging, with "superhuman exertion," into the burning Chateau Metzengerstein, from *The Tales and Poems of Edgar Allan Poe* (Philadelphia: George Barrie, 1895).

Among all the retinue of the Baron, however, none were found to doubt the ardour of that extraordinary affection which existed, on the part of the young nobleman, for the fiery qualities of his horse; at least, none but an insignificant, and misshapen little page, whose deformities were in every body's way, and whose opinions were of the least possible importance.[33] He, if his ideas are worth mentioning at all, had the effrontery to assert, that his master never vaulted into the saddle without an unaccountable, and almost imperceptible shudder, and that upon his return from every habitual ride, during which his panting and bleeding brute was never known to pause in his impetuosity, although he, himself, evinced no appearance of exhaustion, yet an expression of triumphant malignity distorted every muscle in his countenance.

34 A poetical phrase popularized by Henry Kirke White's "Lines, Supposed to Be Spoken by a Lover, at the Grave of His Mistress," lines 17–22:

> And oh! thy voice it rose so musical,
> Betwixt the hollow pauses of the storm,
> That at the sound the winds forgot to rave,
> And the stern demon of the tempest, charmed
> Sunk on his rocking throne, to still repose,
> Lock'd in the arms of silence.

35 References to Azrael, the Angel of Death in Judaism, Sikhism, and Islam, occur frequently in the works of the British Romantic poets. See, for example, Lord Byron's "The Bride of Abydos," canto I, lines 323–326:

> Even Azrael, from his deadly quiver
>   When flies that shaft, and fly it must,
> That parts all else, shall doom for ever
>   Our hearts to undivided dust!

36 The cinema has much to offer when it comes to understanding Poe, partly because his work has contributed so much to its development. The great Soviet filmmaker Sergei Eisenstein found that Poe's writings anticipated visual techniques that would not be fully utilized until the invention of motion pictures. This paragraph provides a good example. Poe depicts Metzengerstein in close-up (the "agony of his countenance"), pulls back to show him from a distance ("the convulsive struggling of his frame"), and then supplies an extreme close-up ("his lacerated lips, which were bitten through and through"). The rapid shifting of images quickens the narrative pace, which the ensuing cacaphony of sound—the shriek of Metzengerstein, the clatter of hoofs, the roar of the flames, and the shriek of the wind—further intensifies, thus providing a narrative running start for the horse's final bound up the staircase.

37 If Metzengerstein represents the artist, then this final image reveals the artist on his chosen path, even as it leads to his destruction. It's a heavy price the artist must pay for his art.

These ominous circumstances portended in the opinion of all people, some awful, and impending calamity. Accordingly one tempestuous night, the Baron descended, like a maniac, from his bed-chamber, and, mounting in great haste, bounded away into the mazes of the forest.

An occurrence so common attracted no particular attention, but his return was looked for with intense anxiety on the part of his domestics, when, after some hours absence, the stupendous, and magnificent battlements of the Chateau Metzengerstein were discovered crackling, and rocking to their very foundation, under the influence of a dense, and livid mass of ungovernable fire. As the flames, when first seen, had already made so terrible a progress, that all efforts to save any portion of the building were evidently futile, the astonished neighbourhood stood idly around in silent, and apathetic wonder. But a new, and fearful object soon rivetted the attention of the multitude, and proved the vast superiority of excitement which the sight of human agony excercises in the feelings of a crowd, above the most appalling spectacles of inanimate matter.

Up the long avenue of aged oaks, which led from the forest to the main entrance of the Chateau Metzengerstein, a steed bearing an unbonneted and disordered rider, was seen leaping with an impetuosity which outstripped the very demon of the tempest,[34] and called forth from every beholder an ejaculation of "Azrael!"[35]

The career of the horseman was, indisputably, on his own part, uncontrollable. The agony of his countenance, the convulsive struggling of his frame gave evidence of superhuman exertion; but no sound, save a solitary shriek, escaped from his lacerated lips, which were bitten through and through, in the intensity of terror.[36] One instant, and the clattering of hoofs resounded sharply, and shrilly, above the roaring of the flames and the shrieking of the winds—another, and clearing, at a single plunge, the gateway, and the moat, the animal bounded, with its rider, far up the tottering staircase of the palace, and was lost in the whirlwind of hissing, and chaotic fire.[37]

The fury of the storm immediately died away, and a dead calm suddenly succeeded. A white flame still enveloped the building, like a shroud, and streaming far away into the quiet atmosphere, shot forth a glare of preternatural light, while a cloud of wreathing

Byam Shaw, "A Cloud of Smoke Settled Heavily over the Battlements in the Distinct Colossal Figure of—*A Horse*." George Liston Byam Shaw (1872–1919), an Indian-born British painter, printmaker, illustrator, and theater designer, illustrated Poe's *Selected Tales of Mystery* (London: Sidgwick and Jackson, 1909).

smoke settled heavily over the battlements, and slowly, but distinctly assumed the appearance of a motionless and colossal horse.

Frederick, Baron Metzengerstein, was the last of a long line of princes. His family name is no longer to be found among the Hungarian aristocracy.

Manuscript Found in a Bottle

Qui n'a plus qu'un moment à vivre
N'a plus rien à dissimuler.

Quinault, *Atys*[1]

O f my country and of my family I have little to say. Ill usage and length of years have driven me from the one, and estranged me from the other. Hereditary wealth afforded me an education of no common order, and a contemplative turn of mind enabled me to methodise the stores which early study very diligently garnered up. Beyond all things, the works of the German moralists[2] gave me great delight; not from any ill-advised admiration of their eloquent madness, but from the ease with which my habits of rigid thought enabled me to detect their falsities. I have often been reproached with the aridity of my genius; a deficiency of imagination has been imputed to me as a crime; and the Pyrrhonism[3] of my opinions has at all times rendered me notorious. Indeed, a strong relish for physical philosophy has, I fear, tinctured my mind with a very common error of this age—I mean the habit of referring occurrences, even the least susceptible of such reference, to the principles of that science.[4] Upon the whole, no person could be less liable than myself to be led away from the severe precincts of truth by the *ignes fatui* of superstition.[5] I have thought proper to premise thus much, lest the incredible tale I have to tell should be considered rather the raving of a crude imagination, than the positive experience of a mind to which the reveries of fancy have been a dead letter and a nullity.

After many years spent in foreign travel, I sailed in the year 18—,[6] from the port of Batavia, in the rich and populous island of Java, on a voyage to the Archipelago of the Sunda islands.[7] I went as passenger—having no other inducement than a kind of nervous restlessness which haunted me as a fiend.[8]

A suspenseful tale of shipwreck and supernatural adventure, "Manuscript Found in a Bottle" marks Poe's first major success in the realm of fiction. He submitted the story—along with several others and a poem—to a fiction and poetry contest sponsored by the Baltimore Saturday Visiter. "Manuscript Found in a Bottle" was unanimously selected by the judges as the best tale. An announcement of the award appeared in the pages of the Visiter on October 12, 1833. The magazine gave him a choice of prizes: a silver cup or fifty dollars. Poe took the cash. After the story appeared in the next issue of the Visiter (along with the winning poem "Song of the Wind" by "Henry Wilton"), it would be reprinted several times in Poe's lifetime. Some printings abbreviate the title as "MS. Found in a Bottle," but Poe preferred to write out the first word, as the handwritten table of contents for his planned collection, Phantasy Pieces, indicates. Since its initial publication, "Manuscript Found in a Bottle" has earned the praise of many different readers. The judges of the Visiter competition praised "Manuscript Found in a Bottle," along with Poe's other submissions, for "singular force and beauty," "wild, vigorous and poetical imagination," "rich style," "fertile invention, and a varied and curious learning." Biographer Kenneth Silverman calls it "a sustained crescendo of ever-building dread in the face of ever-stranger and ever-more-imminent catastrophe." And in a letter to John Livingston Lowes, November 29, 1921, Joseph Conrad called the tale "a very fine piece of work—about as fine as anything of that kind can be—and so authentic in detail that it might have been told by a sailor of a sombre and poetical genius in the invention of the phantastic."

1 "Whoever has but a moment to live has nothing left to hide." Philippe Quinault (1635–1688) was a French dramatist, librettist, and poet.

2 Poe uses this phrase to mean authors concerned with a variety of philosophical topics. He may not have had any specific kind of writing in mind. Elsewhere he mentions "the mass of that German morality which is indeed purely wild, purely vague, and at times purely fantastical" (Thomas Ollive Mabbott, ed., *Collected Works of Edgar Allan Poe*, 3 vols. [Cambridge, MA: The Belknap Press of Harvard University Press, 1969-1978], II, 225).

3 A type of extreme skepticism named after Pyrrho, an ancient Greek philosopher who doubted everything, never passed judgment on anything, and avoided making conclusions altogether.

4 The antagonistic relationship between science and poetic truths finds pointed expression in other of Poe's works.

Our vessel was a beautiful ship of about four hundred tons, copper-fastened, and built at Bombay of Malabar teak.[9] She was freighted with cotton-wool and oil, from the Lachadive islands. We had also on board coir, jaggeree, ghee, cocoa-nuts, and a few cases of opium.[10] The stowage was clumsily done, and the vessel consequently crank.[11]

We got under way with a mere breath of wind, and for many days stood along the eastern coast of Java, without any other incident to beguile the monotony of our course than the occasional meeting with some of the small grabs[12] of the Archipelago to which we were bound.

One evening, leaning over the taffrail,[13] I observed a very singular, isolated cloud, to the N. W. It was remarkable, as well for its color, as from its being the first we had seen since our departure from Batavia. I watched it attentively until sunset, when it spread all at once to the eastward and westward, girting in the horizon with a narrow strip of vapor, and looking like a long line of low beach. My notice was soon afterwards attracted by the dusky-red appearance of the moon, and the peculiar character of the sea. The latter was undergoing a rapid change, and the water seemed more than usually transparent. Although I could distinctly see the bottom, yet, heaving the lead,[14] I found the ship in fifteen fathoms. The air now became intolerably hot, and was loaded with spiral exhalations similar to those arising from heated iron. As night came on, every breath of wind died away, and a more entire calm it is impossible to conceive. The flame of a candle burned upon the poop without the least perceptible motion, and a long hair, held between the finger and thumb, hung without the possibility of detecting a vibration. However, as the captain said he could perceive no indication of danger, and as we were drifting in bodily in to shore, he ordered the sails to be furled, and the anchor let go. No watch was set, and the crew, consisting principally of Malays,[15] stretched themselves deliberately upon deck. I went below—not without a full presentiment of evil. Indeed, every appearance warranted me in apprehending a Simoom.[16] I told the captain my fears; but he paid no attention to what I said, and left me without deigning to give a reply. My uneasiness, however, prevented me from sleeping, and about midnight I went upon deck. As I placed my foot upon the upper step of the companion-ladder, I was startled by a loud, humming noise,[17] like that occasioned by the

In his early poem "Sonnet—To Science" (1829), he argues that science does harm by diminishing our capacity to perceive beauty and truth through art:

> Science! true daughter of Old Time thou art!
> Who alterest all things with thy peering eyes.
> Why preyest thou thus upon the poet's heart,
> Vulture, whose wings are dull realities?
> How should he love thee? or how deem thee wise?
> Who wouldst not leave him in his wandering
> To seek for treasure in the jewelled skies,
> Albeit he soared with an undaunted wing?
> Hast thou not dragged Diana from her car?
> And driven the Hamadryad from the wood
> To seek a shelter in some happier star?
> Hast thou not torn the Naiad from her flood,
> The Elfin from the green grass, and from me
> The summer dream beneath the tamarind tree?

Firmly establishing his narrator as a man who has "a strong relish for physical philosophy," Poe puts in motion a dynamic between the narrator's love of scientific explanation and the supernatural events of the story.

5 *Ignis fatuus*—also called will-o'-the-wisp, jack-o'-lantern, and corpse candle—means the phosphorescent light sometimes seen at night flitting through a marshy area. According to folklore, the will-o'-the-wisp is a mischievous sprite or spirit of the dead leading lone travelers astray. Used figuratively, the term refers to delusive aims, hopes, or principles.

6 Poe often uses blanks to avoid providing specific dates, family names, and place names. A conventional device, the blank enhances mystery, giving a narrative the aura of a true story whose details have been deliberately withheld to protect those involved.

7 Contemporary geographical handbooks divided Oceania into three parts, the Western Archipelago, Australasia, and the Eastern Archipelago. Java was one of the Sunda Islands, which formed part of the Western Archipelago.

8 The narrator's nervous restlessness anticipates Ishmael's inducements for going to sea in *Moby-Dick* (1851): "Whenever I find myself growing grim about the mouth; whenever it is a damp, drizzly November in my soul; whenever I find myself involuntarily pausing before coffin warehouses, and bringing up the rear of every funeral I meet; and especially whenever my hypos get such an upper hand of me, that it requires a strong moral principle to pre-

vent me from deliberately stepping into the street, and me-thodically knocking people's hats off—then, I account it high time to get to sea as soon as I can." Some readers see Poe's story as a source for *Moby-Dick*.

9   These details reinforce the importance the narrator places on physical reality, on objects that can be quantified. And as Daniel Hoffman observes, they also help to es-tablish the narrator's reliability: "Poe has learned well the need, in a fantastic adventure tale, of a credible witness—learned well from *Gulliver's Travels* and *Robinson Crusoe* the indispensability, to the fabulist, of a downright, com-monsensical narrator (*Poe Poe Poe Poe Poe Poe Poe* [Gar-den City, NY: Doubleday, 1972], 140).

10   Coir is fiber prepared from coconut husks and used to make rope and mats; jaggeree is a coarse brown sugar made from the sap of palm trees; ghee is clarified butter made from buffalo's milk. Poe appropriated details from Edward John Trelawny's novel *Adventures of a Younger Son* (1831): "She proved to be a country trader from Bom-bay, bound to China. Having heard that a French cruiser was off the Cochin-China coast, she had, with extreme precaution, kept along the opposite one of Borneo, and thus fell into our hands. She was a beautiful copper-fastened brig, built of Malabar teak by the Parsees of Bom-bay, freighted with cotton-wool, a few cases of opium, guns, pearls from Arabia, sharks' fins, birds' nests, and oil from the Lackadive islands, with four or five sacks of ru-pees" (*Adventures of a Younger Son* [1831; Paris: Galignani, 1835], 437).

11   "Crank" vessels are liable to lean over or capsize, be-ing too narrow or containing insufficient ballast.

12   Large, two-masted vessels common to the coastal re-gions of India.

13   The aftmost railing around the stern of a ship.

14   To heave the lead means to throw a lead weight into the sea for the purpose of sounding the depth.

15   Malays, that is, people from Malaysia, had a reputation for warlike ferocity. In *Adventures of a Younger Son*, Tre-lawny sardonically observes that the Malays "of all eastern nations, and all human beings except kings, hold human life in least respect."

16   In English, the term "simoom" means a "hot, dry, suf-

rapid revolution of a mill-wheel, and before I could ascertain its meaning, I found the ship quivering to its centre. In the next in-stant, a wilderness of foam hurled us upon our beam-ends, and, rushing over us fore and aft, swept the entire decks from stem to stern.

The extreme fury of the blast proved, in a great measure, the salvation of the ship. Although completely water-logged, yet, as her masts had gone by the board,[18] she rose, after a minute, heavily from the sea, and, staggering awhile beneath the immense pressure of the tempest, finally righted.

By what miracle I escaped destruction, it is impossible to say. Stunned by the shock of the water, I found myself, upon recovery, jammed in between the stern-post and rudder. With great diffi-culty I gained my feet, and looking dizzily around, was at first struck with the idea of our being among breakers; so terrific, be-yond the wildest imagination, was the whirlpool of mountainous and foaming ocean within which we were ingulfed. After a while, I heard the voice of an old Swede,[19] who had shipped with us at the moment of our leaving port. I hallooed to him with all my strength, and presently he came reeling aft. We soon discovered that we were the sole survivors of the accident. All on deck, with the exception of ourselves, had been swept overboard; the captain and mates must have perished as they slept, for the cabins were deluged with water. Without assistance, we could expect to do lit-tle for the security of the ship, and our exertions were at first para-lyzed by the momentary expectation of going down. Our cable had, of course, parted like pack-thread, at the first breath of the hurricane, or we should have been instantaneously overwhelmed. We scudded with frightful velocity before the sea, and the water made clear breaches over us. The frame-work of our stern was shattered excessively, and, in almost every respect, we had re-ceived considerable injury; but to our extreme joy we found the pumps unchoked, and that we had made no great shifting of our ballast. The main fury of the blast had already blown over, and we apprehended little danger from the violence of the wind; but we looked forward to its total cessation with dismay; well believing, that in our shattered condition, we should inevitably perish in the tremendous swell which would ensue. But this very just apprehen-sion seemed by no means likely to be soon verified. For five entire

Louis Haghe after David Roberts, *Approach of the Simoom—Desert of Gizeh*, color lithograph from *Egypt and Nubia* (London: F. G. Moon, 1849).

focating sand-wind which sweeps across the African and Asiatic deserts at intervals during the spring and summer" *(Oxford English Dictionary;* hereafter *OED)*. In Arabic, "simoom" means the wind of hell. Poe's reference to a simoom here creates a sense of foreboding. The term was so widely used in the early nineteenth century that it became part of a proverbial comparison—"like the simoom"—which could describe anything that moved quickly and destructively. Poe would use this figurative comparison in "Berenice."

17   Poe often uses humming or buzzing sounds as auditory symbols that suggest a transition to a dreamlike state (Richard Wilbur, "Edgar Allan Poe," *Major Writers of America*, ed. Perry Miller [New York: Harcourt, Brace, 1962], 399).

18   Nautical etymologist W. H. Smyth defines "by the board" as "over the ship's side. When a mast is carried away near the deck it is said to go by the board" (*The Sailor's Word-Book: An Alphabetical Digest of Nautical Terms* [London: Blackie and Son, 1867], 149).

19   According to tradition, old sailors from northern Europe or the outlying regions of Great Britain had the second sight, a supernatural gift for interpreting signs, making prophecies, and looking into the future. Recall the Manxman in *Moby-Dick* or the Old Dansker in *Billy Budd*. The Swede's intuition contrasts with the narrator's rationality.

20   Sudden gusts.

21   Australia.

22   Poe had several precedents for the motif of perpetual darkness in both folklore and literature.

23   Poe draws upon a commonly held superstition that weather conditions nearer the Pole lessened in severity.

24   Here the narrator means at a height beyond which the albatross, a large seabird that ranges widely in the Southern Ocean, is accustomed to flying. His reference recalls Coleridge's "Rime of the Antient Mariner" (1798; 1817), in which the Mariner must endure a fate worse than death for his thoughtless act ("with my cross-bow / I shot the albatross"). Coleridge's poem influenced many elements of Poe's tale: both involve a ship driven off course by a storm, the death of everyone on board except the narrator, and the encounter of a ghostly vessel. In "Letter to B," Poe says: "Of Coleridge I cannot speak but with reverence. His towering intellect! his gigantic power! . . . In reading his poetry I tremble—like one who stands upon a volcano, conscious, from the very darkness bursting from the crater, of the fire and the light that are weltering below" (*Essays and Reviews*, ed. G. R. Thompson [New York: Library of America, 1984], 10-11).

25   Traditional stories about the legendary sea creature known as the kraken, supposedly the largest creature in the seven seas, circulated orally in Poe's day.

days and nights—during which our only subsistence was a small quantity of jaggeree, procured with great difficulty from the forecastle—the hulk flew at a rate defying computation, before rapidly succeeding flaws of wind,[20] which, without equalling the first violence of the Simoom, were still more terrific than any tempest I had before encountered. Our course for the first four days was, with trifling variations, S. E. and by S.; and we must have run down the coast of New Holland.[21] On the fifth day the cold became extreme, although the wind had hauled round a point more to the northward. The sun arose with a sickly yellow lustre, and clambered a very few degrees above the horizon—emitting no decisive light. There were no clouds apparent, yet the wind was upon the increase, and blew with a fitful and unsteady fury. About noon, as nearly as we could guess, our attention was again arrested by the appearance of the sun. It gave out no light, properly so called, but a dull and sullen glow without reflection, as if all its rays were polarized. Just before sinking within the turgid sea, its central fires suddenly went out, as if hurriedly extinguished by some unaccountable power.[22] It was a dim, sliver-like rim, alone, as it rushed down the unfathomable ocean.

We waited in vain for the arrival of the sixth day—that day to me has not arrived—to the Swede, never did arrive. Thenceforward we were enshrouded in pitchy darkness, so that we could not have seen an object at twenty paces from the ship. Eternal night continued to envelop us, all unrelieved by the phosphoric sea-brilliancy to which we had been accustomed in the tropics. We observed too, that, although the tempest continued to rage with unabated violence, there was no longer to be discovered the usual appearance of surf, or foam, which had hitherto attended us. All around were horror, and thick gloom, and a black sweltering desert of ebony. Superstitious terror crept by degrees into the spirit of the old Swede, and my own soul was wrapped up in silent wonder. We neglected all care of the ship, as worse than useless, and securing ourselves, as well as possible, to the stump of the mizen-mast, looked out bitterly into the world of ocean. We had no means of calculating time, nor could we form any guess of our situation. We were, however, well aware of having made farther to the southward than any previous navigators, and felt great amazement at not meeting with the usual impediments of ice.[23] In the meantime every moment threatened to be our last—every mountainous bil-

Thomas Phillips, *Samuel Taylor Coleridge,*
ca. 1818–1821.

low hurried to overwhelm us. The swell surpassed anything I had
imagined possible, and that we were not instantly buried is a miracle. My companion spoke of the lightness of our cargo, and reminded me of the excellent qualities of our ship; but I could not
help feeling the utter hopelessness of hope itself, and prepared
myself gloomily for that death which I thought nothing could de-
fer beyond an hour, as, with every knot of way the ship made, the
swelling of the black stupendous seas became more dismally appalling. At times we gasped for breath at an elevation beyond the
albatross[24]—at times became dizzy with the velocity of our descent into some watery hell, where the air grew stagnant, and no
sound disturbed the slumbers of the kraken.[25]

We were at the bottom of one of these abysses, when a quick
scream from my companion broke fearfully upon the night. "See!

26   A ship of the line is a ship large enough to take a place among a fleet of ships arranged for battle. An East Indiaman is a vessel employed in the East India trade.

27   Poe introduces a favorite theme: how does the surface of something reflect what lies beneath? Without external detail—"customary carvings"—this ship bears no legible signs, nothing for the narrator to read and interpret. It is an unreadable text.

28   Poe's contrast between static and dynamic imagery intensifies the horror of the fantastic spectacle. Typically, battle lanterns illuminate the deck during a nighttime engagement. We are told the lantern light "dashed" from the polished surfaces of the (idle) canons. Dash means to strike with violence and break into fragments. In the midst of impossible hurricane-like conditions, the gigantic ship bears up "under a press of sail," meaning its sails have not been furled to ride out the storm.

29   To heave in stays means to bring a ship's head into the wind in tacking.

see!" cried he, shrieking in my ears, "Almighty God! see! see!" As he spoke, I became aware of a dull, sullen glare of red light which streamed down the sides of the vast chasm where we lay, and threw a fitful brilliancy upon our deck. Casting my eyes upwards, I beheld a spectacle which froze the current of my blood. At a terrific height directly above us, and upon the very verge of the precipitous descent, hovered a gigantic ship, of perhaps four thousand tons. Although upreared upon the summit of a wave more than a hundred times her own altitude, her apparent size still exceeded that of any ship of the line or East Indiaman in existence.[26] Her huge hull was of a deep dingy black, unrelieved by any of the customary carvings of a ship.[27] A single row of brass cannon protruded from her open ports, and dashed from their polished surfaces the fires of innumerable battle-lanterns, which swung to and fro about her rigging. But what mainly inspired us with horror and astonishment, was that she bore up under a press of sail in the very teeth of that supernatural sea, and of that ungovernable hurricane. When we first discovered her, her bows were alone to be seen, as she rose slowly from the dim and horrible gulf beyond her. For a moment of intense terror she paused upon the giddy pinnacle, as if in contemplation of her own sublimity, then trembled and tottered, and—came down.[28]

At this instant, I know not what sudden self-possession came over my spirit. Staggering as far aft as I could, I awaited fearlessly the ruin that was to overwhelm. Our own vessel was at length ceasing from her struggles, and sinking with her head to the sea. The shock of the descending mass struck her, consequently, in that portion of her frame which was already under water, and the inevitable result was to hurl me, with irresistible violence, upon the rigging of the stranger.

As I fell, the ship hove in stays,[29] and went about; and to the confusion ensuing I attributed my escape from the notice of the crew. With little difficulty I made my way, unperceived, to the main hatchway, which was partially open, and soon found an opportunity of secreting myself in the hold. Why I did so I can hardly tell. An indefinite sense of awe, which at first sight of the navigators of the ship had taken hold of my mind, was perhaps the principle of my concealment. I was unwilling to trust myself with a race of people who had offered, to the cursory glance I had taken, so many points of vague novelty, doubt, and apprehension. I therefore thought proper to contrive a hiding-place in the hold. This I did by removing a small portion of the shifting-boards, in such a manner as to afford me a convenient retreat between the huge timbers of the ship.

I had scarcely completed my work, when a footstep in the hold forced me to make use of it. A man passed by my place of concealment with a feeble and unsteady gait. I could not see his face, but had an opportunity of observing his general appearance. There was about it an evidence of great age and infirmity. His knees tottered beneath a load of years, and his entire frame quivered under the burthen. He muttered to himself, in a low broken tone, some words of a language which I could not understand, and grouped in a corner among a pile of singular-looking instruments, and decayed charts of navigation. His manner was a wild mixture of the peevishness of second childhood and the solemn dignity of a God. He at length went on deck, and I saw him no more.

A feeling, for which I have no name, has taken possession of my soul[30]—a sensation which will admit of no analysis, to which the lessons of by-gone time are inadequate, and for which I fear futurity itself will offer me no key.[31] To a mind constituted like my own, the latter consideration is an evil. I shall never—I know that I shall never—be satisfied with regard to the nature of my conceptions. Yet it is not wonderful that these conceptions are indefinite, since they have their origin in sources so utterly novel. A new sense—a new entity is added to my soul.

It is long since I first trod the deck of this terrible ship, and the rays of my destiny are, I think, gathering to a focus. Incomprehensible men! Wrapped up in meditations of a kind which I cannot divine, they pass me by unnoticed. Concealment is utter folly on my part, for the people *will not* see. It was but just now that I passed directly before the eyes of the mate; it was no long while ago that I ventured into the captain's own private cabin, and took thence the materials with which I write, and have written. I shall from time to time continue this journal. It is true that I may not find an oppor-

30 Note the shift from past to present tense that occurs here and continues for the next several paragraphs. Poe anticipates the technique of a cinematic montage, in which brief shots are joined together to form a sequence that compresses space, time, and information. Through similar compression, Poe accelerates the action of the story, propelling readers toward its climax.

31 Futurity may or may not offer insights into the feeling that has taken hold of the narrator, but the prolific British novelist Margaret Oliphant would coin the expression "the thrill of the unknown" in her novel *The Ladies Lindores* (1883).

32 Though Poe could speak contemptuously about allegory, he seems to invite an allegorical reading here. If we are meant to equate the narrator's predicament with the vocation of the writer, then the writer transmits his message to the world with little hope that it will be read.

33 "Ratlin stuff" means the thin ropes used on sailing ships to climb the rigging. A yawl is a ship's small boat, usually with four or six oars.

34 The narrator's aimless tar-brush markings on the edges of the folded canvas have created—visible once the sails are unfurled—a legible text, indeed, a text that celebrates its own discovery. The idea that chance plays an integral part in the creative process is one that aligns Poe with modernists such as André Breton (automatic writing), William Burroughs (cut-up method), and Jack Kerouac (spontaneous prose).

tunity of transmitting it to the world, but I will not fail to make the endeavor. At the last moment I will enclose the manuscript in a bottle, and cast it within the sea.[32]

An incident has occurred which has given me new room for meditation. Are such things the operation of ungoverned chance? I had ventured upon deck and thrown myself down, without attracting any notice, among a pile of ratlin-stuff and old sails, in the bottom of the yawl.[33] While musing upon the singularity of my fate, I unwittingly daubed with a tar-brush the edges of a neatly-folded studding-sail which lay near me on a barrel. The studding-sail is now bent upon the ship, and the thoughtless touches of the brush are spread out into the word DISCOVERY.[34]

I have made many observations lately upon the structure of the vessel. Although well armed, she is not, I think, a ship of war. Her rigging, build, and general equipment, all negative a supposition of this kind. What she *is not*, I can easily perceive; what she *is*, I fear it is impossible to say. I know not how it is, but in scrutinizing her strange model and singular cast of spars, her huge size and overgrown suits of canvass, her severely simple bow and antiquated stern, there will occasionally flash across my mind a sensation of familiar things, and there is always mixed up with such indistinct shadows of recollection, an unaccountable memory of old foreign chronicles and ages long ago.

I have been looking at the timbers of the ship. She is built of a material to which I am a stranger. There is a peculiar character about the wood which strikes me as rendering it unfit for the purpose to which it has been applied. I mean its extreme *porousness,* considered independently of the worm-eaten condition which is a consequence of navigation in these seas, and apart from the rottenness attendant upon age. It will appear perhaps an observation somewhat over-curious, but this wood would have every characteristic of Spanish oak, if Spanish oak were distended by any unnatural means.

In reading the above sentence, a curious apothegm of an old

weather-beaten Dutch navigator comes full upon my recollection. "It is as sure," he was wont to say, when any doubt was entertained of his veracity, "as sure as there is a sea where the ship itself will grow in bulk like the living body of the seaman."[35]

About an hour ago, I made bold to thrust myself among a group of the crew. They paid me no manner of attention, and, although I stood in the very midst of them all, seemed utterly unconscious of my presence.[36] Like the one I had at first seen in the hold, they all bore about them the marks of a hoary old age. Their knees trembled with infirmity; their shoulders were bent double with decrepitude; their shrivelled skins rattled in the wind; their voices were low, tremulous, and broken; their eyes glistened with the rheum of years; and their gray hairs streamed terribly in the tempest. Around them, on every part of the deck, lay scattered mathematical instruments of the most quaint and obsolete construction.[37]

I mentioned, some time ago, the bending of a studding-sail. From that period, the ship, being thrown dead off the wind, has continued her terrific course due south, with every rag of canvass packed upon her, from her trucks to her lower studding-sail booms, and rolling every moment her top-gallant yard-arms into the most appalling hell of water which it can enter into the mind of man to imagine. I have just left the deck, where I find it impossible to maintain a footing, although the crew seem to experience little inconvenience. It appears to me a miracle of miracles that our enormous bulk is not swallowed up at once and for ever. We are surely doomed to hover continually upon the brink of eternity, without taking a final plunge into the abyss. From billows a thousand times more stupendous than any I have ever seen, we glide away with the facility of the arrowy sea-gull; and the colossal waters rear their heads above us like demons of the deep,[38] but like demons confined to simple threats, and forbidden to destroy. I am led to attribute these frequent escapes to the only natural cause which can account for such effect. I must suppose the ship to be within the influence of some strong current, or impetuous under-tow.

35 This quotation is apparently Poe's invention.

36 In his letter to Lowes, Joseph Conrad compares the attitude of these mysterious sailors—"secular ghosts," he calls them—to the "indifference of the animated corpses to the living people" in Coleridge's "Rime of the Ancient Mariner."

37 Poe's story draws upon the legend of the Flying Dutchman, which originated in seventeenth-century maritime folklore. In one of the earliest written accounts of the legend, John Leyden in his *Scenes of Infancy* (1803) writes, "The crew of [the Flying Dutchman] are supposed to have been guilty of some dreadful crime, in the infancy of navigation; and to have been stricken with pestilence . . . and are ordained still to traverse the ocean on which they perished, till the period of their penance expire." Reviewing Frederick Marryat's novel *The Phantom Ship*, Poe refers to the story of the Flying Dutchman as "a legend, by the bye, possessing all the rich *materiel* which a vigorous imagination could desire (*Gentleman's Magazine* 4 [1839], 359). Joseph Conrad characterized "Manuscript Found in a Bottle" as an "impressive version of the Flying Dutchman."

38 Compare Barry Cornwall, "The Flood of Thessaly" (1823):

> Below, the Ocean rose boiling and black,
> And flung its monstrous billows far and wide
> Crumbling the mountain joints and summit hills;
> Then its dark throat it bared and rocky tusks,
> Where, with enormous waves on their broad backs,
> The demons of the deep were raging loud

39 Making narrator and captain the same height (5'8"), Poe draws the reader's attention to a deeper resemblance between the two men. Both are men of science—both guilty "of a very common error of [their] age," that is, of relying too heavily upon science to explain everything (note in this same paragraph the captain's "mouldering instruments of science, and obsolete long-forgotten charts," navigational tools not likely to be of much help on this particular journey). Poe's own height was 5'8", a biographical fact that projects the writer into the story in an amusing and ironical way.

40 Poe echoes Byron's "The Dream," lines 12–13:

> They pass like spirits of the past,—they speak
> Like sybils of the future

Gray eyes—the color of Poe's eyes—are traditionally associated with keen perceptive powers.

41 Vellum tends to curl at the corners, so vellum books were typically bound with clasps to keep the pages flat. Poe's description not only suggests the books' extreme age but also gives them magic associations. A volume bound with iron clasps, like other forms of iron (think horseshoe), supposedly had supernatural powers.

42 Balbec and Tadmor (also known as Palmyra) are cities in ancient Syria known for their magnificent ruins. Persepolis, a city in ancient Persia, is also marked by the ruins of a once-great civilization. In "Al Aaraaf" (1829), part II, lines 36–38, Poe mentions:

> Friezes from Tadmor and Persepolis—
> From Balbec, and the stilly, clear abyss
> Of beautiful Gomorrah!

Glossing this passage, Richard Wilbur observes, "The thirst for ruins is the thirst to recapture the primal state of self and world" (*Poe* [New York: Dell, 1959], 138).

43 A proverbial phrase.

44 In Western culture, the two most prominent narratives of forbidden knowledge are the story of Adam and Eve and the Faust legend. Elsewhere Poe would make use of the Book of Genesis; the Faust legend seems more pertinent here. Poe implies that some knowledge should remain beyond human comprehension; any mortal who dares to seek the knowledge of the gods deserves to be struck down.

I have seen the captain face to face, and in his own cabin—but, as I expected, he paid me no attention. Although in his appearance there is, to a casual observer, nothing which might bespeak him more or less than man, still, a feeling of irrepressible reverence and awe mingled with the sensation of wonder with which I regarded him. In stature, he is nearly my own height; that is, about five feet eight inches.[39] He is of a well-knit and compact frame of body, neither robust nor remarkable otherwise. But it is the singularity of the expression which reigns upon the face—it is the intense, the wonderful, the thrilling evidence of old age, so utter, so extreme, which excites within my spirit a sense—a sentiment ineffable. His forehead, although little wrinkled, seems to bear upon it the stamp of a myriad of years. His gray hairs are records of the past, and his grayer eyes are sybils of the future.[40] The cabin floor was thickly strewn with strange, iron-clasped folios,[41] and mouldering instruments of science, and obsolete long-forgotten charts. His head was bowed down upon his hands, and he pored, with a fiery, unquiet eye, over a paper which I took to be a commission, and which, at all events, bore the signature of a monarch. He muttered to himself—as did the first seaman whom I saw in the hold—some low peevish syllables of a foreign tongue; and although the speaker was close at my elbow, his voice seemed to reach my ears from the distance of a mile.

The ship and all in it are imbued with the spirit of Eld. The crew glide to and fro like the ghosts of buried centuries; their eyes have an eager and uneasy meaning; and when their figures fall athwart my path in the wild glare of the battle-lanterns, I feel as I have never felt before, although I have been all my life a dealer in antiquities, and have imbibed the shadows of fallen columns at Balbec, and Tadmor, and Persepolis, until my very soul has become a ruin.[42]

When I look around me, I feel ashamed of my former apprehensions. If I trembled at the blast which has hitherto attended us, shall I not stand aghast at a warring of wind and ocean, to convey

any idea of which, the words tornado and simoom are trivial and ineffective? All in the immediate vicinity of the ship is the blackness of eternal night,[43] and a chaos of foamless water; but, about a league on either side of us, may be seen, indistinctly and at intervals, stupendous ramparts of ice, towering away into the desolate sky, and looking like the walls of the universe.

As I imagined, the ship proves to be in a current—if that appellation can properly be given to a tide which, howling and shrieking by the white ice, thunders on to the southward with a velocity like the headlong lashing of a cataract.

To conceive the horror of my sensations is, I presume, utterly impossible; yet a curiosity to penetrate the mysteries of these awful regions, predominates even over my despair, and will reconcile me to the most hideous aspect of death. It is evident that we are hurrying onwards to some exciting knowledge—some never-to-be-imparted secret, whose attainment is destruction.[44] Perhaps this current leads us to the southern pole itself.[45] It must be confessed

Balbec (undated print), site of one of the great engineering mysteries of ancient times. The ruins of this town in modern-day Lebanon contain a temple with enormous stones weighing more than 800 tons each. The question of how the ancients moved these stones remains unanswered. According to the *Encyclopaedia Britannica; or A Dictionary of Arts, Sciences, and Miscellaneous Literature* (1823), "The inhabitants of Balbec have a very commodious manner of explaining it, by supposing these edifices to have been constructed by *Djenoun*, or genii, who obeyed the orders of King Solomon; adding, that the motive of such immense works was to conceal in subtereanneous caverns vast treasures, which still remain there" (Edinburgh: Archibald Constable and Co., 1823), vol. 3, 347.

45 John Cleves Symmes theorized that the earth was hollow, making it possible to enter its interior at a hole in the South Pole and travel all the way through to the North

Pole. A contemporary reader joked that Poe's aim "seems to be to give the credulous well *bottled* proof of Capt. Symmes' theory of polar apertures and concentric circles" (*The Floridian*, November 21, 1835).

46   The "eagerness of hope" and the "apathy of despair" are clichéd proverbial phrases. The narrator's growing reliance on stock phrases suggests that he is lost for words as he approaches the unknown. Having been afloat for countless centuries, the mariners seem relieved to be approaching their final doom, which will release them from their life-in-death existence.

47   Poe adumbrates Kurtz's final words in Joseph Conrad's *Heart of Darkness* (1899): "The horror! The horror!"

48   Drawing parallels with two of Poe's poems, "To Helen" (1831) and "The Coliseum" (1833), Wilbur observes: "When the narrator descends at the close into a 'gigantic amphitheatre' or Coliseum of ice and whirling water, we are to understand that he has reclaimed, among other things, 'the grandeur that was Rome'" (*Poe* [New York: Dell, 1959], 138).

49   "The 'Manuscript Found in a Bottle,' was originally published in 1831 [1833]; and it was not until many years afterwards that I became acquainted with the maps of Mercator, in which the ocean is represented as rushing, by four mouths, into the (northern) Polar Gulf, to be absorbed into the bowels of the earth; the Pole itself being represented by a black rock, towering to a prodigious height [Poe's note]." Poe refers to Gerardus Mercator (1512–1594), the Dutch cartographer and geographer who introduced his famous projection in his 1569 map of the world.

that a supposition apparently so wild has every probability in its favor.

The crew pace the deck with unquiet and tremulous step; but there is upon their countenances an expression more of the eagerness of hope than of the apathy of despair.[46]

In the meantime the wind is still in our poop, and, as we carry a crowd of canvass, the ship is at times lifted bodily from out the sea! Oh, horror upon horror![47]—the ice opens suddenly to the right, and to the left, and we are whirling dizzily, in immense concentric circles, round and round the borders of a gigantic amphitheatre, the summit of whose walls is lost in the darkness and the distance.[48] But little time will be left me to ponder upon my destiny! The circles rapidly grow small—we are plunging madly within the grasp of the whirlpool—and amid a roaring, and bellowing, and thundering of ocean and of tempest, the ship is quivering—oh God! and—going down![49]

Berenice: A Tale

When this gruesome tale of suspense originally appeared in the March 1835 issue of the Southern Literary Messenger, *some readers wrote proprietor Thomas W. White to complain. White passed the complaints on to Poe. Hoping to forge a lasting relationship with the* Messenger's *editor, Poe defended his story, emphasizing its utility in increasing the magazine's reputation and circulation. "The history of all magazines," he argued, "shows plainly that those which have attained celebrity were indebted for it to articles similar in nature—to Berenice . . . I say similar in nature. You ask me in what does this nature consist? In the ludicrous heightened into the grotesque: the fearful coloured into the horrible: the witty exaggerated into the burlesque: the singular wrought out into the strange and mystical. You may say all this is bad taste. . . . But whether the articles of which I speak are, or are not in bad taste is little to the purpose. To be appreciated you must be read, and these things are invariably sought after with avidity" (*Collected Letters of Edgar Allan Poe, ed. John Ward Ostrom, Burton R. Pollin, and Jeffrey A. Savoye, 2 vols. [New York: Gordian Press, 2008], I, 84-85).*

Then living in Baltimore with his Aunt Maria Clemm and her adolescent daughter Virginia, Poe continued his correspondence with White, in which the two men further discussed the magazine's business. Their mutual friend John Pendleton Kennedy encouraged White to hire Poe. Shortly after Poe moved to Richmond, White offered him a full-time editorial position. Poe would be both the magazine's editor as well as a frequent contributor to its pages (his hard-hitting book reviews in particular helped to increase the Messenger's *readership). Poe's time with the magazine, from August 1835 to January 1837, established his own reputation as an editor and fueled his dreams of owning and editing a magazine himself one day.*

Poe made a few changes to "Berenice" when he included the story in Tales of the Grotesque and Arabesque, *but when he revised it in 1845 for the* Broadway Journal *he softened the tale considerably. Poe scholars tend to assume that every time Poe revised a story he did so for aesthetic reasons. With "Berenice," his reasons were pragmatic. Using the* Broadway Journal *as a showcase to attract financial supporters for the ideal magazine he was planning, he was leery about offending potential backers and therefore toned down its most graphic content—to the story's detriment. The first published text is followed here.*

Misery is manifold. The wretchedness of earth is multiform. Overreaching the wide horizon like the rainbow, its hues are as various as the hues of that arch, as distinct too, yet as intimately blended. Overreaching the wide horizon like the rainbow! How is it that from Beauty I have derived a type of unloveliness?—from the covenant of Peace a simile of sorrow?[1] But thus is it. And as, in ethics, Evil is a consequence of Good, so, in fact, out of Joy is sorrow born.[2] Either the memory of past bliss is the anguish of today, or the agonies which *are*, have their origin in the ecstasies which *might have been*. I have a tale to tell in its own essence rife with horror—I would suppress it were it not a record more of feelings than of facts.

My baptismal name is Egaeus[3]—that of my family I will not mention. Yet there are no towers in the land more time-honored than my gloomy, grey, hereditary halls.[4] Our line has been called a race of visionaries:[5] and in many striking particulars—in the character of the family mansion—in the frescos of the chief saloon—in the tapestries of the dormitories—in the chiseling of some buttresses in the armory—but more especially in the gallery of antique paintings—in the fashion of the library chamber—and, lastly, in the very peculiar nature of the library's contents, there is more than sufficient evidence to warrant the belief.

The recollections of my earliest years are connected with that chamber, and with its volumes—of which latter I will say no more. Here died my mother. Herein was I born.[6] But it is mere idleness to say that I had not lived before—that the soul has no previous existence. You deny it. Let us not argue the matter. Convinced

---

1   The rainbow is a Christian symbol of God's covenant with the earth. Breaking through the clouds of human guilt and divine wrath, it represents God's mercy. Poe's narrator, commenting on his own use of figurative language, rebukes himself—not very harshly—for transforming this symbol of God's love into a simile for misery and wretchedness.

2   The narrator's association between beauty and sorrow indicates how closely the two were associated in Poe's aesthetic. In "The Philosophy of Composition" (1846), Poe famously said, "The death . . . of a beautiful woman is, unquestionably, the most poetical topic in the world—and equally is it beyond doubt that the lips best suited for such topic are those of a bereaved lover" (*Essays and Reviews*, ed. G. R. Thompson [New York: Library of America, 1984], 19).

3   In Greek mythology, Aegeus is a king of Athens. In Shakespeare's *Midsummer Night's Dream*, Egeus is the name of Hermia's father.

4   Like Metzengerstein, Egaeus is an aristocrat from a time-honored family who lives in a gloomy, sprawling ancestral mansion—a basic ingredient of gothic fiction. Unlike "Metzengerstein," which is set in Hungary, "Berenice" has no specific geographical setting. Poe's deliberate vagueness reflects an advance in his technique. A specific setting could compete with, and detract from, the imaginary landscapes he wished to create.

5   From Poe's perspective, visionaries typically indulge in fantastic, impractical ideas or schemes. In his story "The Visionary" (1834), Poe makes clear with whom his sympathies lie: "There are surely other worlds than this—other thoughts than the thoughts of the multitude—other speculations than the speculations of the sophist. Who then shall call thy conduct into question? who blame thee for thy visionary hours, or denounce those occupations as a wasting away of life, which were but the overflowing of thine everlasting energies?" (Thomas Ollive Mabbott, ed., *Collected Works of Edgar Allan Poe*, 3 vols. [Cambridge, MA: The Belknap Press of Harvard University Press, 1969–1978], II, 151).

6   Compare Coleridge, "Christabel," line 197: "She died the hour that I was born." In *Sexual Personae* (1990), Camille Paglia briefly compares "Berenice" and "Christabel." Though she does not mention this verbal echo, it reinforces her theory that "Berenice" redramatizes "Christabel," with Poe's title character representing the vampiric Geraldine. Much as Geraldine's sexuality disturbs Christabel, Berenice's sexuality unsettles Egaeus, causing him to react in ways he does not comprehend.

7   By "aerial" Poe means ethereal, insubstantial, immaterial, but also unreal, imaginary, fanciful, otherworldly.

myself I seek not to convince. There is, however, a remembrance of aerial forms[7]—of spiritual and meaning eyes—of sounds musical yet sad—a remembrance which will not be excluded: a memory like a shadow, vague, variable, indefinite, unsteady—and like a shadow too, in the impossibility of my getting rid of it, while the sunlight of my reason shall exist.

In that chamber was I born. Thus awaking, as it were, from the long night of what seemed, but was not, nonentity at once into the very regions of fairy land—into a palace of imagination—into the wild dominions of monastic thought and erudition—it is not singular that I gazed around me with a startled and ardent eye—that I loitered away my boyhood in books, and dissipated my youth in reverie—but it *is* singular that as years rolled away, and the noon of manhood found me still in the mansion of my fathers[8]—it is wonderful what stagnation there fell upon the springs of my life— wonderful how total an inversion took place in the character of my common thoughts. The realities of the world affected me as visions, and as visions only, while the wild ideas of the land of dreams became, in turn,—not the material of my every-day existence—but in very deed that existence utterly and solely in itself.

Berenice[9] and I were cousins, and we grew up together in my paternal halls—Yet differently we grew. I ill of health and buried in gloom—she agile, graceful, and overflowing with energy. Hers the ramble on the hill side—mine the studies of the cloister. I living within my own heart, and addicted body and soul to the most intense and painful meditation—she roaming carelessly through life with no thought of the shadows in her path, or the silent flight of the raven-winged hours.[10] Berenice!—I call upon her name— Berenice!—and from the grey ruins of memory a thousand tumultuous recollections are startled at the sound! Ah! vividly is her image before me now, as in the early days of her light-heartedness and joy! Oh! gorgeous yet fantastic beauty! Oh! Sylph amid the shrubberies of Arnheim![11]—Oh! Naiad among her fountains![12]— and then—then all is mystery and terror, and a tale which should not be told. Disease—a fatal disease—fell like the Simoom[13] upon her frame, and, even while I gazed upon her, the spirit of change swept over her, pervading her mind, her habits, and her character, and, in a manner the most subtle and terrible, disturbing even the

Sidney Hall, *Bootes Canes Venatici, Coma Berenices, and Quadrans Muralis*, plate 10 in *Urania's Mirror*, a set of celestial cards accompanying *A Familiar Treatise on Astronomy* by Jehoshaphat Aspin (London: Samuel Leigh, 1825). This astronomical chart shows Bootes the Ploughman holding a spear, a sickle, and two dogs on a leash. Berenice's hair forms the constellations.

8   This nostalgic phrase derives from Charles de Moor's lament in Friedrich Schiller's tragedy *The Robbers*, first translated into English in 1793 and frequently excerpted in early nineteenth-century classroom readers: "There was a time when I could weep with ease.—O days of bliss!—Mansion of my fathers! O vales so green, so beautiful! scenes of my infant years, enjoy'd by fond enthusiasm! will you no more return? no more exhale your sweets to cool this burning bosom!—Oh never, never shall they return—no more refresh this bosom with the breath of peace. They are gone! gone for ever!"

9   The name Berenice was common to many queens and princesses in the Ptolemean family in Egypt. Catullus, Rome's greatest lyric poet, relates the story of the most famous Berenice from classical times in "Berenice's Hair." In this poem, Berenice, the daughter of Philadelphus and Arisinoe, marries her brother Evergetes. When he goes on a dangerous expedition, she pledges her long flowing locks of hair to Venus to ensure his safe return and places them in the temple of Venus, from which they quickly disappear. An astronomer reports that Jupiter took them to make a constellation. Coma Bernices is a galactic star cluster about 250,000 light years from the earth.

   Mabbott notes that in Poe's own day "Berenice was pronounced as four syllables, and [rhymed] with 'very spicey'" (*Collected Works*, II, 219).

10   A circumlocution for night.

11   A sylph is an imaginary spirit of the air. The word "Arnheim" refers to the fanciful setting of Sir Walter Scott's novel *Anne of Geirstein* (1829), which also inspired Poe's 1847 tale "The Domain of Arnheim."

12   In Greek mythology, naiads were female figures associated with fountains, lakes, rivers, and other bodies of water.

13   A proverbial comparison. Byron, for example, uses the phrase in "The Giaour" (1813), lines 282–285:

> He came, he went, like the simoom,
> That harbinger of fate and gloom,
> Beneath whose widely-wasting breath
> That very cypress droops to death

14   Early readers of Poe's "Berenice" appreciated it as a psychological case study. A contributor to the *Daily National Intelligencer* (May 15, 1835) expressed his admiration: "It delineates, with thrilling accuracy, a species of *monomania* of a striking and original character. The state of mind, made up of weakness and energy, which, in the absence of the capacity of exercising sane and useful thought, broods over trifling fancies and insignificant objects, until they become invested with terrific associations, is drawn in a striking manner, evincing great ability in the delineation of the more intricate workings of the human mind."

15   By his own admission, Egaeus is a drug addict. The claim that Poe was an opium addict dates back to his own lifetime, when his detractors were quick to confuse the author with his characters. No evidence survives to support the claim. Poe's one-time friend and adversary Dr. Thomas Dunn English wrote that "had Poe the opium habit when I knew him, I should, both as a physician and a man of observation, have discovered it in his frequent visits to my rooms, my visits to his house, and our meetings elsewhere" (*The Independent*, October 15, 1896). Poe does refer to opium elsewhere. The standard concordance to Poe's fiction lists eighteen instances of the word "opium" plus one usage each of the following compounds: "opium-dream," "opium-eater," and "opium-engendered."

16   In "How One Forces Inspiration" (1933), the German painter Max Ernst articulates automatic methods for painting reminiscent of Egaeus's obsession with physical objects. The artist's creativity is a kind of concentrated attendance at the birth of the work. Ernst explains the method: "This process rests on nothing other than the *intensification of the mind's powers of irritability,* and in view of its technical features I have dubbed it *frottage* (rubbing), and it has had in my own personal development an even larger share than *collage*, from which I do not believe it differs *fundamentally*" (*Beyond Painting*, ed. Robert Motherwell [New York: Wittenborn, Schultz, 1948], 6).

17   Revising "Tamerlane" for *Al Aaraaf, Tamerlane, and Minor Poems* (1829), Poe added a passage conveying this same idea:

> Thus I remember having dwelt
>   Some page of early lore upon,
> With loitering eye, till I have felt
>   The letters—with their meaning—melt
>   To fantasies—with none.
>
>   (lines 81–85)

very identity of her person! Alas! the destroyer came and went, and the victim—where was she? I knew her not—or knew her no longer as Berenice.

Among the numerous train of maladies, superinduced by that fatal and primary one which effected a revolution of so horrible a kind in the moral and physical being of my cousin, may be mentioned as the most distressing and obstinate in its nature, a species of epilepsy not unfrequently terminating in *trance* itself—trance very nearly resembling positive dissolution, and from which her manner of recovery was, in most instances, startlingly abrupt. In the meantime my own disease—for I have been told that I should call it by no other appelation—my own disease,[14] then, grew rapidly upon me, and, aggravated in its symptoms by the immoderate use of opium,[15] assumed finally a monomaniac character of a novel and extraordinary form—hourly and momentarily gaining vigor—and at length obtaining over me the most singular and incomprehensible ascendancy. This monomania—if I must so term it—consisted in a morbid irritability of the nerves[16] immediately affecting those properties of the mind, in metaphysical science termed the *attentive*. It is more than probable that I am not understood—but I fear that it is indeed in no manner possible to convey to the mind of the merely general reader, an adequate idea of that nervous *intensity of interest* with which, in my case, the powers of meditation (not to speak technically) busied, and, as it were, buried themselves in the contemplation of even the most common objects of the universe.

To muse for long unwearied hours with my attention rivetted to some frivolous device upon the margin, or in the typography of a book[17]—to become absorbed for the better part of a summer's day in a quaint shadow falling aslant upon the tapestry, or upon the floor—to lose myself for an entire night in watching the steady flame of a lamp, or the embers of a fire—to dream away whole days over the perfume of a flower—to repeat monotonously some common word, until the sound, by dint of frequent repetition, ceased to convey any idea whatever to the mind—to lose all sense of motion or physical existence in a state of absolute bodily quiescence long and obstinately persevered in—Such were a few of the most common and least pernicious vagaries induced by a condition of the mental faculties, not, indeed, altogether unparalleled, but certainly bidding defiance to any thing like analysis or explanation.[18]

Yet let me not be misapprehended. The undue, intense, and morbid attention thus excited by objects in their own nature frivolous, must not be confounded in character with that ruminating propensity common to all mankind, and more especially indulged in by persons of ardent imagination. By no means. It was not even, as might be at first supposed, an extreme condition, or exaggeration of such propensity, but primarily and essentially distinct and different. In the one instance the dreamer, or enthusiast, being interested by an object usually *not* frivolous, imperceptibly loses sight of this object in a wilderness of deductions and suggestions issuing therefrom, until, at the conclusion of a day-dream *often replete with luxury,* he finds the *incitamentum* or first cause of his musings utterly vanished and forgotten. In my case the primary object was *invariably frivolous,* although assuming, through the medium of my distempered vision,[19] a refracted and unreal importance. Few deductions—if any—were made; and those few pertinaciously returning in, so to speak, upon the original object as a centre. The meditations were *never* pleasurable; and, at the termination of the reverie, the first cause, so far from being out of sight, had attained that supernaturally exaggerated interest which was the prevailing feature of the disease. In a word, the powers of mind more particularly exercised were, with me, as I have said before, the *attentive,* and are, with the day-dreamer, the *speculative.*

My books, at this epoch, if they did not actually serve to irritate the disorder, partook, it will be perceived, largely, in their imaginative, and inconsequential nature, of the characteristic qualities of the disorder itself. I well remember, among others, the treatise of the noble Italian Coelius Secundus Curio *de amplitudine beati regni Dei*[20]—St. Austin's great work the *City of God*[21]—and Tertullian *de Carne Christi*, in which the unintelligible sentence *"Mortuus est Dei filius; credible est quia ineptum est: et sepultus resurrexit; certum est quia impossibile est"*[22] occupied my undivided time, for many weeks of laborious and fruitless investigation.

Thus it will appear that, shaken from its balance only by trivial things, my reason bore resemblance to that ocean-crag spoken of by Ptolemy Hephestion, which steadily resisting the attacks of human violence, and the fiercer fury of the waters and the winds,

18 Egaeus suffers from what is now called obsessive-compulsive disorder (OCD). *Campbell's Psychiatric Dictionary,* ninth edition, supplies a useful definition: "Considered a form of anxiety disorder, its characteristics are recurrent, disturbing, unwanted, anxiety-provoking obsessions (insistent thoughts or ruminations that at least initially are experienced as intrusive or absurd) or compulsions (repetitive ritualistic behaviors, or mental actions such as praying or counting, and purposeful actions that are intentional, even though they may be reluctantly performed because they are considered abnormal, undesirable, or distasteful to the subject). The compulsion may consist of ritualistic, stereotyped behavior or it may be a response to an obsession or to rules that the person feels obliged to follow. The obsession often involves the thought of harming others or ideas that the subject feels are gory, sexually perverse, profane, or horrifying."

19 "Distempered" in this instance means diseased or disordered. Gothic and sentimental novelists often attribute "distempered vision" to their characters. Anna Maria Porter, for one, writes: "The late events had thrown an unusual degree of gloom over Rupert's soul. For the first time in his life, he saw with distempered vision, and believed every thing dark and lowering. Whichever way he turned, whether reverting back, or looking forward, a black and dismal waste, haunted by the spectre forms of objects lost, and hopes foully murdered, seemed stretching before him" (*The Village of Mariendorpt*, 4 vols. [London: Longman, Hurst, Rees, Orme, and Brown, 1821], IV, 26).

20 Coelius Secundus Curio (1503–1569), a Protestant Italian professor of eloquence, wrote *De Amplitudine Beati Regni Dei* (1550) to prove "that *Heaven* has more inhabitants than *Hell*, or in his own phrase that the *elect* are more numerous than the *reprobate*" (Isaac Disraeli, *Curiosities of Literature*, new ed., 3 vols. [London: John Murray, 1824], I, 360).

21 St. Augustine (354–430) wrote *De Civitate Dei* (413–425), or *The City of God*, to answer hostile attacks on Christianity. His ideal republic demonstrates the relationship between Christianity and secular government, church and state, and the realms of man and God.

22 "The Son of God has died, it is to be believed because it is incredible; and, buried, He is risen, it is sure because it is impossible." Tertullian (*ca.* 160–*ca.* 240), the most important church father after St. Augustine, was known for his use of paradox. The sentence Poe quotes from *De Carne Christi* is one of Tertullian's most famous paradoxes.

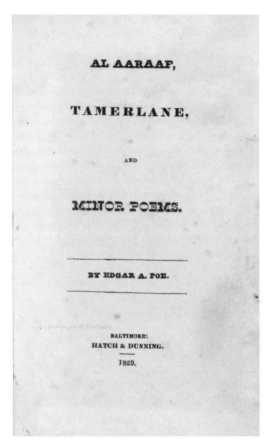

Title page of *Al Aaraaf, Tamerlane, and Minor Poems*, published by Hatch and Dunning in 1829. Little is known about the publication of Poe's second collection of verse, but Hatch and Dunning specialized in medical books, so the imprint provides a tantalizing clue, suggesting that Poe had befriended Baltimore's leading literati, many of whom were physicians, and they helped him secure publication.

23 The entry for "Stones" in *Encyclopaedia Britannica*, sixth edition, explains: "Ptolemy Hephistion mentions a gygonian stone near the ocean, which was agitated when struck by the stalk of an asphodel, but could not be removed by a great exertion of force."

24 Compare 1 Corinthians 15:47: "The first man is of the earth, earthy: the second man is the Lord from heaven."

trembled only to the touch of the flower called Asphodel.[23] And although, to a careless thinker, it might appear a matter beyond doubt, that the fearful alteration produced by her unhappy malady, in the *moral* condition of Berenice, would afford me many objects for the exercise of that intense and morbid meditation whose nature I have been at some trouble in explaining, yet such was not by any means the case. In the lucid intervals of my infirmity, her calamity indeed gave me pain, and, taking deeply to heart that total wreck of her fair and gentle life, I did not fail to ponder frequently and bitterly upon the wonder-working means by which so strange a revolution had been so suddenly brought to pass. But these reflections partook not of the idiosyncrasy of my disease, and were such as would have occurred, under similar circumstances, to the ordinary mass of mankind. True to its own character, my disorder revelled in the less important but more startling changes wrought in the *physical* frame of Berenice, and in the singular and most appalling distortion of her personal identity.

During the brightest days of her unparalleled beauty, most surely I had never loved her. In the strange anomaly of my existence, feelings, with me, *had never been* of the heart, and my passions *always were* of the mind. Through the grey of the early morning—among the trellissed shadows of the forest at noonday—and in the silence of my library at night, she had flitted by my eyes, and I had seen her—not as the living and breathing Berenice, but as the Berenice of a dream—not as a being of the earth—earthly[24]—but as the abstraction of such a being—not as a thing to admire, but to analyze—not as an object of love, but as the theme of the most abstruse although desultory speculation. And *now*—now I shuddered in her presence, and grew pale at her approach; yet, bitterly lamenting her fallen and desolate condition, I knew that she had loved me long, and, in an evil moment,[25] I spoke to her of marriage.

And at length the period of our nuptials was approaching, when, upon an afternoon in the winter of the year, one of those unseasonably warm, calm, and misty days which are the nurse of the beautiful Halcyon,[26] I sat, and sat, as I thought alone, in the inner apartment of the library. But uplifting my eyes Berenice stood before me.

Was it my own excited imagination—or the misty influence of the atmosphere—or the uncertain twilight of the chamber—or the grey draperies which fell around her figure—that caused it to loom up in so unnatural a degree? I could not tell. Perhaps she had grown taller since her malady. She spoke, however, no word, and I—not for worlds could I have uttered a syllable. An icy chill ran through my frame; a sense of insufferable anxiety oppressed me; a consuming curiosity pervaded my soul; and, sinking back upon the chair, I remained for some time breathless, and motionless, and with my eyes rivetted upon her person. Alas! its emaciation was excessive, and not one vestige of the former being lurked in any single line of the contour. My burning glances at length fell upon her face.

The forehead was high, and very pale, and singularly placid; and the once golden hair fell partially over it, and overshadowed the hollow temples with ringlets now black as the raven's wing,[27] and jarring discordantly, in their fantastic character, with the reigning melancholy of the countenance. The eyes were lifeless, and lustreless, and I shrunk involuntarily from their glassy stare to the contemplation of the thin and shrunken lips. They parted: and, in a smile of peculiar meaning, the teeth of the changed Berenice disclosed themselves slowly to my view. Would to God that I had never beheld them, or that, having done so, I had died!

The shutting of a door disturbed me, and, looking up, I found my cousin had departed from the chamber. But from the disordered chamber of my brain, had not, alas! departed, and would not be driven away, the white and ghastly *spectrum* of the teeth. Not a speck upon their surface—not a shade on their enamel—not a line in their configuration—not an indenture in their edges—but what that brief period of her smile had sufficed to brand in upon my memory. I saw them *now* even more unequivocally than I beheld them *then*. The teeth!—the teeth!—they were here, and there, and every where, and visibly, and palpably before me, long, narrow, and excessively white, with the pale lips writhing about them, as in the very moment of their first terrible development.[28] Then came the full fury of my *monomania*, and I struggled in vain against its strange and irresistible influence. In the multiplied objects of the external world I had no thoughts but for the teeth. All other matters and all different interests became absorbed in their single contemplation. They—they alone were present to the mental eye, and

25 This idea, that someone might not only feel but also act upon a momentary evil impulse, intrigued Poe. He would return to it often, refining the concept and, in 1845, giving it a name: the imp of the perverse. This phrase marks a clarification over "evil moment": it refrains from attributing a moral dimension to the idea. The murderous narrator of "The Imp of the Perverse" explains: "There is no intelligible principle: and we might, indeed, deem this perverseness a direct instigation of the arch-fiend, were it not occasionally known to operate in furtherance of good" (Mabbott, ed., *Collected Works*, III, 1223). Though the effects of acting on a perverse impulse can be positive, they usually are not. We spend months in careful planning only to surrender to the imp of the perverse, sabotaging ourselves, others, and all our plans on a momentary whim.

Poe is not the only major writer intrigued with this self-destructive impulse. Dostoevsky was fascinated with our capacity for sabotaging ourselves. This impulse also forms a leitmotif of much hard-boiled crime fiction of the twentieth century. The concept and Poe's name for it have entered the legal, philosophical, and psychological literature, as well.

26 "For as Jove, during the winter season, gives twice seven days of warmth, men have called this clement and temperate time the nurse of the beautiful Halcyon.—*Simonides* [Poe's note]." Beyond a handful of elegies and epigrams, few works of Simonides (*ca.* 556–468 BCE), a celebrated Greek poet, survive.

27 Revising this sentence when he republished "Berenice" in 1845, Poe omitted the phrase "black as the raven's wing." Having published "The Raven" earlier that year, he perhaps worried that readers would see the simile as an allusion to the poem and an attempt to capitalize on its author's newfound fame. In revision, Berenice's hair is "jetty" initially; it turns to a "vivid yellow" once she falls sick.

28 Berenice's teeth present several possible interpretations. Seen with her pale, sunken face, the teeth give her the appearance of a skeleton. Her face thus serves as a traditional image in Western iconography: a *memento mori*, or a reminder of mortality. Berenice's teeth also represent the stereotype of the devouring female. It was this interpretation that appealed to Max Ernst, whose painting *Berenice* (1935) borrows its inspiration and central theme from Poe's story. Depicting two long-armed, long-legged figures, the painting invokes a favorite misogynistic image of the Surrealists—the praying mantis—an insect species whose female sex devours the male following intercourse.

Alternatively, the teeth may symbolize Berenice's sexual desire. Karen Weekes observes: "Showing one's teeth in a smile can indicate sexual interest, and if the 'peculiar meaning' of Berenice's grin is of carnal desire, the cerebral narrator would be doubly overcome" (Robert Belton, "Edgar Allan Poe and the Surrealists' Image of Women," *Woman's Art Journal* 8 [1987], 12; Karen Weekes, "Poe's Feminine Ideal," *The Cambridge Companion to Edgar Allan Poe*, ed. Kevin J. Hayes [New York: Cambridge University Press, 2002], 156).

29   "Her every step was a sentiment": such was said about Marie Sallé (1707–1756), a French dancer with a graceful and expressive style. Poe's adaptation of these words to describe Berenice means that "all her teeth were ideas."

30   When Poe revised "Berenice" for the *Broadway Journal*, he omitted the next four paragraphs.

they, in their sole individuality, became the essence of my mental life. I held them in every light—I turned them in every attitude. I surveyed their characteristics—I dwelt upon their peculiarities—I pondered upon their conformation—I mused upon the alteration in their nature—and shuddered as I assigned to them in imagination a sensitive and sentient power, and even when unassisted by the lips, a capability of moral expression. Of Mad'selle Sallé it has been said, *"que tous ses pas etoient des sentiments,"* and of Berenice I more seriously believed *que touts ses dents etoient des ideés.*[29]

And the evening closed in upon me thus—and then the darkness came, and tarried, and went—and the day again dawned—and the mists of a second night were now gathering around—and still I sat motionless in that solitary room, and still I sat buried in meditation, and still the *phantasma* of the teeth maintained its terrible ascendancy as, with the most vivid and hideous distinctness, it floated about amid the changing lights and shadows of the chamber. At length there broke forcibly in upon my dreams a wild cry as of horror and dismay; and thereunto, after a pause, succeeded the sound of troubled voices intermingled with many low moanings of sorrow, or of pain. I arose hurriedly from my seat, and, throwing open one of the doors of the library, there stood out in the antechamber a servant maiden, all in tears, and she told me that Berenice was—no more. Seized with an epileptic fit she had fallen dead in the early morning, and now, at the closing in of the night, the grave was ready for its tenant, and all the preparations for the burial were completed.[30]

With a heart full of grief, yet reluctantly, and oppressed with awe, I made my way to the bed-chamber of the departed. The room was large, and very dark, and at every step within its gloomy precincts I encountered the paraphernalia of the grave. The coffin, so a menial told me, lay surrounded by the curtains of yonder bed, and in that coffin, he whisperingly assured me, was all that remained of Berenice. Who was it asked me would I not look upon the corpse? I had seen the lips of no one move, yet the question had been demanded, and the echo of the syllables still lingered in the room. It was impossible to refuse; and with a sense of suffocation I dragged myself to the side of the bed. Gently I uplifted the sable draperies of the curtains.

As I let them fall they descended upon my shoulders, and shut-

ting me thus out from the living, enclosed me in the strictest communion with the deceased.

The very atmosphere was redolent of death. The peculiar smell
of the coffin sickened me; and I fancied a deleterious odor was already exhaling from the body. I would have given worlds to escape—to fly from the pernicious influence of mortality—to
breathe once again the pure air of the eternal heavens. But I had no
longer the power to move—my knees tottered beneath me—and I
remained rooted to the spot, and gazing upon the frightful length
of the rigid body as it lay outstretched in the dark coffin without a
lid.

God of heaven!—is it possible? Is it my brain that reels—or
was it indeed the finger of the enshrouded dead that stirred in the
white cerement that bound it? Frozen with unutterable awe I
slowly raised my eyes to the countenance of the corpse. There had
been a band around the jaws, but, I know not how, it was broken
asunder. The livid lips were wreathed into a species of smile, and,
through the enveloping gloom, once again there glared upon me
in too palpable reality, the white and glistening, and ghastly teeth
of Berenice. I sprang convulsively from the bed, and, uttering no
word, rushed forth a maniac from that apartment of triple horror,
and mystery, and death.

I found myself again sitting in the library, and again sitting there
alone. It seemed that I had newly awakened from a confused and
exciting dream. I knew that it was now midnight, and I was well
aware that since the setting of the sun Berenice had been interred.
But of that dreary period which had intervened I had no positive,
at least no definite comprehension. Yet its memory was rife with
horror—horror more horrible from being vague, and terror more
terrible from ambiguity. It was a fearful page in the record of my
existence, written all over with dim, and hideous, and unintelligible recollections. I strived to decypher them, but in vain—while
ever and anon, like the spirit of a departed sound, the shrill and
piercing shriek of a female voice seemed to be ringing in my ears. I
had done a deed—what was it? And the echoes of the chamber
answered me—"what was it?"

On the table beside me burned a lamp, and near it lay a little box

31 "My companions told me I might find some little alleviation of my misery, in visiting the grave of my beloved
[Poe's note, written from Egaeus's perspective]." Written
by the ninth-century Arab poet Muhammad Ibn Abd al-
Malik al-Zayyat, these words appear in George Moir's essay "Early Narrative and Lyrical Poetry of Spain," which
includes a brief appreciation of Arabic verse (*Edinburgh
Review* 39 [1824], 422).

32 Poe would frequently return to the theme of premature burial. His contemporaries also found the subject fascinating. Accounts of premature burial appeared often in
the contemporary press. Coffins were sometimes constructed with built-in lifesaving devices—bells, breathing
tubes, and the like—just in case a person should find himself or herself buried alive.

33 Stories of the dead returning to punish the theft of
their teeth occur in the oral tradition. Anna K. Stimson
identifies "Berenice" as a type of startle story centered on
the "resurrection bone," that is, a small bone in the body
upon which the body's resurrection depends. Stimson explains: "A woman dies and is buried. Her husband broods
and finally robs the grave of the interesting anatomic detail. He is awakened in the night by a faroff voice wailing,
'Who took my resurrection bone?' The voice comes nearer
and is more and more ominous; it comes into the house, up
the stairs, and at last the door slowly swings open and a figure is on the threshold. 'Who took my resurrection
bone?—*You did!*'" ("Cries of Defiance and Derision, and
Rhythmic Chants of West Side New York City, 1893–
1903," *Journal of American Folklore* 58 [1945], 126).

of ebony. It was a box of no remarkable character, and I had seen it
frequently before, it being the property of the family physician;
but how came it *there* upon my table, and why did I shudder in regarding it? These things were in no manner to be accounted for,
and my eyes at length dropped to the open pages of a book, and to
a sentence underscored therein. The words were the singular, but
simple words of the poet Ebn Zaiat. *"Dicebant mihi sodales si sepul-
chrum amicae visit arem curas meas aliquantulum fore levatas."*[31]
Why then, as I perused them, did the hairs of my head erect themselves on end, and the blood of my body congeal within my veins?

There came a light tap at the library door, and, pale as the tenant of a tomb, a menial entered upon tiptoe. His looks were wild
with terror, and he spoke to me in a voice tremulous, husky, and
very low. What said he?—some broken sentences I heard. He told
of a wild cry heard in the silence of the night—of the gathering
together of the household—of a search in the direction of the
sound—and then his tones grew thrillingly distinct as he whispered me of a violated grave—of a disfigured body discovered
upon its margin—a body enshrouded, yet still breathing, still pal-
pitating, still alive![32]

He pointed to my garments—they were muddy and clotted
with gore. I spoke not, and he took me gently by the hand—but it
was indented with the impress of human nails. He directed my attention to some object against the wall—I looked at it for some
minutes—it was a spade. With a shriek I bounded to the table, and
grasped the ebony box that lay upon it. But I could not force it
open, and in my tremor it slipped from out my hands, and fell
heavily, and burst into pieces, and from it, with a rattling sound,
there rolled out some instruments of dental surgery, intermingled
with many white and glistening substances that were scattered to
and fro about the floor.[33]

Morella

Αυτο καθ' αυτο μεθ' αυτου, μονο ειδες αιει ον.
Itself, by itself solely, ONE everlasting, and single.

Plato, Sympos[1]

With a feeling of deep yet most singular affection I regarded my friend Morella.[2] Thrown by accident into her society many years ago, my soul, from our first meeting, burned with fires it had never before known; but the fires were not of Eros,[3] and bitter and tormenting to my spirit was the gradual conviction that I could in no manner define their unusual meaning, or regulate their vague intensity. Yet we met; and fate bound us together at the altar; and I never spoke of passion, nor thought of love. She, however, shunned society, and, attaching herself to me alone, rendered me happy. It is a happiness to wonder;—it is a happiness to dream.

Morella's erudition was profound. As I hope to live, her talents were of no common order—her powers of mind were gigantic. I felt this, and, in many matters, became her pupil.[4] I soon, however, found that, perhaps on account of her Presburg education,[5] she placed before me a number of those mystical writings which are usually considered the mere dross of the early German literature.[6] These, for what reason I could not imagine, were her favorite and constant study—and that, in process of time they became my own, should be attributed to the simple but effectual influence of habit and example.

In all this, if I err not, my reason had little to do. My convictions, or I forget myself, were in no manner acted upon by the ideal, nor was any tincture of the mysticism which I read, to be discovered, unless I am greatly mistaken, either in my deeds or in my thoughts. Persuaded of this, I abandoned myself implicitly to the guidance of my wife, and entered with an unflinching heart into the intricacies of her studies. And then—then, when, poring

When Elizabeth Arnold Poe died of tuberculosis in Richmond, Virginia, on December 8, 1811, her son Edgar, one month shy of his third birthday, witnessed her death. This fact has influenced critical interpretations of "Morella." According to Marie Bonaparte's psychoanalytical interpretation, Morella represents Poe's mother, and her daughter symbolizes Virginia Clemm, Poe's thirteen-year-old cousin, whom Poe would marry shortly after "Morella" debuted. The tale manifests a process Freud defines as mother transference. As Poe supposedly transferred the love for his mother to Virginia Clemm, the narrator transfers his feelings for Morella to their daughter.

Attempts to correlate facts in Poe's life with "Morella" and other of his writings have been largely misguided. In The Limits of Interpretation (1990), Umberto Eco provides a necessary corrective: "When Bonaparte says that Poe was dominated by the impression he felt as a child when he saw his mother, dead of consumption, lying on the catafalque, when she says that in his adult life and in his work he was so morbidly attracted by women with funereal features, when she reads his stories populated by living corpses in order to explain his personal necrophilia—then she is using, not interpreting texts." Freed from reductive biographical moorings, "Morella" offers expansive opportunities for critical interpretation. When he published the tale in the April 1835 issue of the Southern Literary Messenger, Poe thought it was the best story he had ever written (Collected Letters of Edgar Allan Poe, ed. John Ward Ostrom, Burton R. Pollin, and Jeffrey A. Savoye. 2 vols. [New York: Gordian Press, 2008], I, 115). He included it in Tales of the Grotesque and Arabesque (1840), reprinting "Morella" in the November 1839 issue of Burton's as a prepublication extract to promote the forthcoming book.

1   This quotation from Plato's *Symposium* is from H. N. Coleridge's *Introductions to the Study of the Greek Classic Poets* (1830).

2   The name "Morella" may have been inspired by a real-life woman of formidable intellect and learning, Donna Juliana Morella, a native of Barcelona, whom Poe could have read about in an article entitled "Women Celebrated in Spain for Their Extraordinary Powers of Mind" in the September 1834 issue of *The Lady's Book*. Alternatively, Poe may have taken the name from the title character of an Eliza Haywood novel: *The Agreeable Caledonian, or, Memoirs of Signior di Morella* (1728). Haywood's Morella was also highly learned.

3   The god of love in Greek mythology.

4   Most marriages in the nineteenth century were lopsided

affairs—but here it is the better-educated wife who plays the role of mentor to a somewhat childlike partner. In "Ligeia," we see the same reversal of the power relationship between the sexes: "I saw not then what I now clearly perceive, that the acquisitions of Ligeia were gigantic, were astounding; yet I was sufficiently aware of her infinite supremacy to resign myself, with a child-like confidence, to her guidance through the chaotic world of metaphysical investigation at which I was most busily occupied during the earlier years of our marriage."

In *A Vindication of the Rights of Woman* (1792), Mary Wollstonecraft had argued that women were not innately inferior to men but only appeared so owing to a lack of education. Radical social reform was still in its early days when Poe wrote "Morella." In the United States, Margaret Fuller's *Woman in the Nineteenth Century* (1845) would not appear for another decade.

In what "many matters" does Morella instruct the narrator? He doesn't say. The sentence suggests the possibility that Morella is the narrator's teacher in the bedroom as well as in the classroom. There is no indication in the story how soon after the marriage Morella becomes pregnant with child.

5 Presburg (Bratislava), a German-speaking city for many centuries, was often associated with the supernatural.

6 Mystical writings attempt to illuminate hidden meanings about spiritual matters that otherwise evade human understanding. Poe may have in mind the works of Jakob Böhme (1575–1624), whose most ambitious mystical work, *De signatura rerum*, sought to understand the meaning of all things in creation.

7 Likely "forbidden pages" refers to German mystical writings. The "forbidden spirit" the narrator feels enkindled within, however, may have found a more material explanation in his close physical proximity to his instructor. In Genesis, God forbids Adam to eat from the tree of knowledge, under penalty of death. Traditionally, the forbidden fruit has been associated with carnal knowledge. Jules Zanger sees Morella as the incarnation of "the principle of forbidden female sexuality originally embodied in the Garden myth" ("Poe and the Theme of Forbidden Knowledge," *American Literature* 49, IV [1978], 536).

8 The biblical valley of the son of Hinnom is also known as Gehenna. It became associated with an idolatrous ancient rite that involved burning children alive in a slow fire.

over forbidden pages, I felt a forbidden spirit enkindling within me[7]—would Morella place her cold hand upon my own, and rake up from the ashes of a dead philosophy some low, singular words, whose strange meaning burned themselves in upon my memory. And then, hour after hour, would I linger by her side, and dwell upon the music of her voice—until, at length, its melody was tainted with terror,—and there fell a shadow upon my soul—and I grew pale, and shuddered inwardly at those too unearthly tones. And thus, joy suddenly faded into horror, and the most beautiful became the most hideous, as Hinnom became Ge-Henna.[8]

It is unnecessary to state the exact character of those disquisitions which, growing out of the volumes I have mentioned, formed, for so long a time, almost the sole conversation of Morella and myself. By the learned in what might be termed theological morality they will be readily conceived, and by the unlearned they would, at all events, be little understood. The wild Pantheism of Fichte; the modified Παλιγγενϵσια of the Pythagoreans; and, above all, the doctrines of *Identity* as urged by Schelling, were generally the points of discussion presenting the most of beauty to the imaginative Morella.[9] That identity which is termed personal, Mr. Locke, I think, truly defines to consist in the sameness of a rational being. And since by person we understand an intelligent essence having reason, and since there is a consciousness which always accompanies thinking, it is this which makes us all to be that which we call *ourselves*—thereby distinguishing us from other beings that think, and giving us our personal identity. But the *principium individuationis,* the notion of that identity *which at death is or is not lost forever,* was to me, at all times, a consideration of intense interest; not more from the perplexing and exciting nature of its consequences, than from the marked and agitated manner in which Morella mentioned them.[10]

But, indeed, the time had now arrived when the mystery of my wife's manner oppressed me as a spell. I could no longer bear the touch of her wan fingers, nor the low tone of her musical language, nor the lustre of her melancholy eyes. And she knew all this, but did not upbraid; she seemed conscious of my weakness or my folly, and, smiling, called it Fate. She seemed, also, conscious of a cause, to me unknown, for the gradual alienation of my regard; but she gave me no hint or token of its nature.[11] Yet was she woman, and pined away daily. In time, the crimson spot settled steadily upon the cheek, and the blue veins upon the pale forehead became prominent;[12] and one instant, my nature melted into pity, but, in the next, I met the glance of her meaning eyes, and then my soul sickened and became giddy with the giddiness of one who gazes downward into some dreary and unfathomable abyss.[13]

Shall I then say that I longed with an earnest and consuming desire for the moment of Morella's decease? I did; but the fragile spirit clung to its tenement of clay[14] for many days—for many weeks and irksome months—until my tortured nerves obtained the mastery over my mind, and I grew furious through delay, and, with the heart of a fiend, cursed the days, and the hours, and the bitter moments, which seemed to lengthen and lengthen as her gentle life declined—like shadows in the dying of the day.

But one autumnal evening, when the winds lay still in heaven, Morella called me to her bed-side.[15] There was a dim mist over all the earth, and a warm glow upon the waters, and, amid the rich October leaves of the forest, a rainbow from the firmament had surely fallen.

"It is a day of days," she said, as I approached; "a day of all days either to live or die. It is a fair day for the sons of earth and life—ah, more fair for the daughters of heaven and death!"[16]

I kissed her forehead, and she continued:

"I am dying, yet shall I live."[17]

"Morella!"

"The days have never been when thou couldst love me—but her whom in life thou didst abhor, in death thou shalt adore."[18]

"Morella!"

"I repeat that I am dying. But within me is a pledge of that affection—ah, how little!—which thou didst feel for me, Morella. And when my spirit departs shall the child live—thy child and mine, Morella's. But thy days shall be days of sorrow—that sorrow which is the most lasting of impressions, as the cypress is the most enduring of trees.[19] For the hours of thy happiness are over;[20] and joy is not gathered twice in a life, as the roses of Paestum[21] twice in a year. Thou shalt no longer, then, play the Teian[22] with time, but, being ignorant of the myrtle and the vine,[23] thou shalt bear about with thee thy shroud on earth, as do the Moslemin at Mecca."[24]

"Morella!" I cried, "Morella! how knowest thou this?"—but she turned away her face upon the pillow, and, a slight tremor

To be burnt with the fire of Gehenna thus became a proverbial expression for undergoing any sort of dreadful torment.

9 Παλιγγενσια, or palingenesia, means "birth again," or metempsychosis. Poe conflates the thought of Johann Gottlieb Fichte (1762–1814) and Friedrich Wilhelm Joseph von Schelling (1775–1854). Schelling is more typically associated with pantheism. Both thinkers devoted considerable attention to the theme of personal identity.

10 The narrator paraphrases John Locke in his *Essay Concerning Human Understanding* where he maintains that personal identity is a matter of neither the soul nor the body but of consciousness ("the sameness of a rational being"): "In this alone consists personal identity, i.e. the sameness of a rational being: and as far as this consciousness can be extended backwards to any past action or thought, so far reaches the identity of that person" (*Essay Concerning Human Understanding*, 2 vols. [1690; reprinted, Glasgow: D. M'Vean, 1819], I, 338). According to Locke, consciousness may be transferred from one soul to another, or from one body to another. The parsing of Locke's doctrine of identity, however, is of less interest to the narrator than the question of whether or not we survive death.

11 Like many of Poe's narrators, this one possesses a dim understanding of his own feelings and motivations. Morella anyway seems to understand the cause of her husband's growing resentment and ill will.

12 These tell-tale physical symptoms would have suggested to nineteenth-century readers that Morella suffers from consumption (tuberculosis).

13 Though the phrase "the fascination of the abyss" would not be coined until the late nineteenth century, the idea itself was prevalent in gothic and Romantic literature. It involves the lure of danger and an attraction to the unknown. When we are fascinated by the abyss, we are frozen at its edge, unable to move. In "Morella," the narrator speaks figuratively: it is a moral abyss he peers into that causes terror—he desires the destruction of his wife.

14 John Dryden, *Absalom and Achitophel* (1681), lines 156–158:

> A fiery Soul, which working out its way,
> Fretted the Pigmy-Body to decay;
> And o'er inform'd the Tenement of Clay.

coming over her limbs, she thus died, and I heard her voice no more.

Yet, as she had foretold, her child—to which in dying she had given birth, and which breathed not until the mother breathed no more—her child, a daughter, lived.[25] And she grew strangely in stature and intellect, and was the perfect resemblance of her who had departed, and I loved her with a love more fervent than I had believed it possible to feel for any denizen of earth.

But, ere long, the heaven of this pure affection became darkened, and gloom, and horror, and grief, swept over it in clouds. I said the child grew strangely in stature and intelligence.—Strange indeed was her rapid increase in bodily size—but terrible, oh! terrible were the tumultuous thoughts which crowded upon me while watching the development of her mental being. Could it be otherwise, when I daily discovered in the conceptions of the child the adult powers and faculties of the woman?—when the lessons of experience fell from the lips of infancy? and when the wisdom or the passions of maturity I found hourly gleaming from its full and

15   Here, Poe inverts perhaps the greatest cliché of sentimental fiction: the tear-filled deathbed scene. Neither Morella on her deathbed nor her nameless husband for that matter shows much emotion. Instead, Morella asserts her intellect, maintains her decorum, and acknowledges that her husband does not love her.

16   Unlike the sentimental deathbed scenes in Victorian and nineteenth-century American literature, Poe's doesn't attempt to evoke the sympathies or finer feelings of his characters—or of the reader. Morella's death, as she gives birth to her daughter, seems the opportunity for one final lesson: you can't escape me.

17   Compare John 11:25: "Jesus said unto her, I am the resurrection, and the life: he that believeth in me, though he were dead, yet shall he live."

18   Poe echoes Milton, *Paradise Lost*, book V, lines 119–121:

>   Which gives me hope
> That what in sleep thou didst abhor to dream,
> Waking thou never wilt consent to do.

19   A traditional symbol of mourning.

20   What hours of happiness might these possibly be, the reader may wonder, since the narrator's wife has become a terror to him.

21   An ancient Greek city in Lucania, Paestum was celebrated for its rich soil, which produced highly fragrant roses that blossomed twice a year.

22   By the "Teian," Morella refers to Anacreon (b. *ca.* 570 BCE), the renowned Greek lyric poet who was born at Teos in Ionia. Poe borrowed this phrase from Edward Bulwer-Lytton's *Conversations with an Ambitious Student in Ill Health* (1832): "Let us play the Teian with life, think only of the Rose and Vine, and since our most earnest endeavours can effect so little to others, let us not extend our hopes and our enjoyments beyond the small and safe circle of Self!"

23   The myrtle and the vine symbolize idyllic luxury.

24   Travel writer John Lewis Burckhardt explains: "Many hadjys purchase at Mekka the shroud in which they wish to be buried, and wash it themselves at the well of Zemzem, supposing that, if the corpse be wrapped in linen which has been wetted with this holy water, the peace of the soul after death will be more effectually secured" (*Travels in Arabia: Comprehending an Account of Those Territories in Hedjaz which the Mohammedans Regard as Sacred*, 2 vols. [London: Henry Colburn, 1829], I, 276–277).

25   Immersed as he is in mystical writings, the narrator implies that Morella's soul had transmigrated to her daughter.

speculative eye? When, I say, all this became evident to my appalled senses—when I could no longer hide it from my soul, nor throw it off from those perceptions which trembled to receive it— is it to be wondered at that suspicions, of a nature fearful and exciting, crept in upon my spirit, or that my thoughts fell back aghast upon the wild tales and thrilling theories of the entombed Morella? I snatched from the scrutiny of the world a being whom destiny compelled me to adore, and in the rigorous seclusion of my home, watched with an agonizing anxiety over all which concerned the beloved.

And, as years rolled away, and I gazed, day after day, upon her holy, and mild, and eloquent face, and pored over her maturing form, day after day did I discover new points of resemblance in the child to her mother, the melancholy and the dead. And, hourly, grew darker these shadows of similitude, and more full, and more definite, and more perplexing, and more hideously terrible in their aspect.[26] For that her smile was like her mother's I could bear; but then I shuddered at its too perfect *identity*—that her eyes were like Morella's I could endure; but then they too often looked down into the depths of my soul with Morella's own intense and bewildering meaning. And in the contour of the high forehead, and in the ringlets of the silken hair, and in the wan fingers which buried themselves therein, and in the sad musical tones of her speech, and above all—oh, above all—in the phrases and expressions of the dead on the lips of the loved and the living, I found food for consuming thought and horror—for a worm that *would* not die.[27]

Thus passed away two lustra of her life, and, as yet, my daughter remained nameless upon the earth.[28] "My child," and "my love," were the designations usually prompted by a father's affection, and the rigid seclusion of her days precluded all other intercourse. Morella's name died with her at her death. Of the mother I had never spoken to the daughter;—it was impossible to speak.[29] Indeed, during the brief period of her existence the latter had received no impressions from the outward world save such as might have been afforded by the narrow limits of her privacy. But at length the ceremony of baptism presented to my mind, in its unnerved and agitated condition, a present deliverance from the terrors of my destiny.[30] And at the baptismal font I hesitated for a name. And many titles of the wise and beautiful, of old and modern times, of my own and foreign lands,[31] came thronging to my

26 As the daughter grows more and more to resemble her mother, the narrator comes to feel the same growing resentment toward her as he did toward her mother. In looking at his daughter he can see her mother's face, her eyes, and her smile and hear the manner and cadence of her speech.

27 Compare Mark 9:43–44: "And if thy hand offend thee, cut it off: it is better for thee to enter into life maimed, than having two hands to go into hell, into the fire that never shall be quenched: Where their worm dieth not, and the fire is not quenched."

28 Since a lustrum is five years, the daughter is now ten years old. Never has she been baptized or even named. Because the narrator has so far kept her hidden away in "rigid seclusion," there has been little need to name her: she has no other human contact. The narrator addresses her as "my child" or "my love," and she him, presumably, as "Father"—and, unthinkably, perhaps as "my love."

29 The daughter has never been told the name of her mother. The narrator's name (never given) seems to have died as well, not with his wife's death, but perhaps much earlier, with his marriage to Morella.

30 The doctrinal purpose of the ceremony of baptism, of course, is to make it possible for the baptized person to enter the kingdom of God, not to deliver a parent from his own terrors.

31 As in "Berenice," Poe never says where his story is set, preferring to leave the location vague.

32   According to superstition, a person's name, when uttered aloud, can function as a magic spell. Names of the deceased are especially potent. Ghosts can be summoned by name, and calling the name of a dead person requires them to answer. Apparently, the narrator refrains from uttering his dead wife's name to prevent her from haunting him or afflicting their daughter. He is so paranoid and so cautious that he manages to avoid saying her name for ten years. But when he eventually decides to baptize his daughter, he inexplicably christens her "Morella." What compelled him to utter his dead wife's name at this crucial moment, especially after he had been so careful for so many years? A demon? A fiend? These are the terms he uses in conjecture, but his behavior is compelled by the same internal creature that motivates Egaeus in "Berenice," indeed, that motivates so many of Poe's protagonists: the imp of the perverse. As soon as he utters the name, a bond is established between the dead mother and the living daughter. By pronouncing the name, he creates a portal between the world of the living and that of the dead through which his wife can escape the underworld and reanimate herself in the body of her daughter.

33   Multiple interpretations of this conclusion are possible. Since every story observes its own logic, readers may choose to accept the supernatural as part of the fictional world of "Morella" and take for granted that the spirit of the first Morella has left the grave to inhabit the body of her daughter. Some critics see the lady Morella as the incarnation of the human desire (or Poe's desire) to transcend the limitations of human knowledge and mortality. Others see the narrator as a delusional madman. Harry Levin glosses the story this way: "The junior Morella so completely takes her mother's place that, if we do not believe in reincarnation, we must perforce suspect incest. The crucial scene enacts a ceremonial, as the narrator carries his dead daughter from her baptismal font to her mother's empty tomb" (*The Power of Blackness: Hawthorne, Poe, Melville* [New York: Knopf, 1958], 157).

lips, with many, many fair titles of the gentle, and the happy, and the good. What prompted me, then, to disturb the memory of the buried dead? What demon urged me to breathe that sound, which, in its very recollection was wont to make ebb the purple blood in torrents from the temples to the heart? What fiend spoke from the recesses of my soul, when, amid those dim aisles, and in the silence of the night, I whispered within the ears of the holy man the syllables—Morella? What more than fiend convulsed the features of my child, and overspread them with hues of death, as starting at that scarcely audible sound, she turned her glassy eyes from the earth to heaven, and, falling prostrate on the black slabs of our ancestral vault, responded—"I am here!"[32]

Distinct, coldly, calmly distinct, fell those few simple sounds within my ear, and thence, like molten lead rolled hissingly into my brain. Years—years may pass away, but the memory of that epoch—never! Nor was I indeed ignorant of the flowers and the vine—but the hemlock and the cypress overshadowed me night and day. And I kept no reckoning of time or place, and the stars of my fate faded from heaven, and therefore the earth grew dark, and its figures passed by me, like flitting shadows, and among them all I beheld only—Morella. The winds of the firmament breathed but one sound within my ears, and the ripples upon the sea murmured evermore—Morella. But she died; and with my own hands I bore her to the tomb; and I laughed with a long and bitter laugh as I found no traces of the first, in the charnel where I laid the second—Morella.[33]

Ligeia

And the will therein lieth, which dieth not. Who knoweth the mysteries of the will, with its vigor? For God is but a great will pervading all things by nature of its intentness. Man doth not yield himself to the angels, nor unto death utterly, save only through the weakness of his feeble will.

Joseph Glanvill[1]

I cannot, for my soul, remember how, when, or even precisely where, I first became acquainted with the lady Ligeia.[2] Long years have since elapsed, and my memory is feeble through much suffering. Or, perhaps, I cannot *now* bring these points to mind, because, in truth, the character of my beloved, her rare learning, her singular yet placid cast of beauty, and the thrilling and enthralling eloquence of her low musical language, made their way into my heart by paces so steadily and stealthily progressive that they have been unnoticed and unknown.[3] Yet I believe that I met her first and most frequently in some large, old, decaying city near the Rhine.[4] Of her family—I have surely heard her speak. That it is of a remotely ancient date cannot be doubted. Ligeia! Ligeia! Buried in studies of a nature more than all else adapted to deaden impressions of the outward world, it is by that sweet word alone—by Ligeia—that I bring before mine eyes in fancy the image of her who is no more. And now, while I write, a recollection flashes upon me that I have *never known* the paternal name of her who was my friend and my betrothed,[5] and who became the partner of my studies, and finally the wife of my bosom. Was it a playful charge on the part of my Ligeia? or was it a test of my strength of affection, that I should institute no inquiries upon this point? or was it rather a caprice of my own—a wildly romantic offering on the shrine of the most passionate devotion? I but indistinctly recall the fact itself—what wonder that I have utterly forgotten the circumstances which originated or attended it? And, indeed, if ever that spirit which is entitled *Romance*—if ever she, the wan and the misty-winged *Ashtophet*[6] of idolatrous Egypt, presided, as they

"Ligeia," which debuted in the September 1838 issue of American Museum, *was the first new short story Poe had written in three years, that is, since he had published "Morella" in the* Southern Literary Messenger. *After he joined the* Messenger *staff, his demanding editorial responsibilities prevented him from completing any new tales. "Hans Phaall," an elaborate story of a balloon voyage to the moon, appeared after "Morella," but he had written that work earlier. While he was with the magazine, Poe also drafted his only novel,* The Narrative of Arthur Gordon Pym *(1838).*

In February 1837, with his wife, Virginia, and his mother-in-law, Maria Clemm, Poe moved to New York, where he unsuccessfully sought an editorial position with one of the city's magazines. He published only one story while living in New York that year, "Von Jung, The Mystific," but that too he had written before "Morella." The financial depression that struck the United States in 1837 forced publishers and editors to tighten belts. With many magazine contributors willing to write for nothing, Poe found few outlets for his work and, therefore, had little motivation to keep writing. In early 1838, he moved his family again, to Philadelphia, then a significant publishing center, where he spent months in search of editorial work. Late that summer, Nathan C. Brooks invited him to contribute to the inaugural issue of the American Museum. *Given this opportunity, Poe resumed his short fiction career, picking up where he had left off three years earlier. Many readers have noted the similarities between "Morella" and "Ligeia." Both are concerned with death, resurrection, and communication beyond the grave; and both are narrated by husbands whose educated, intellectually powerful wives look and think alike. But there are key differences between the stories: the more complex, richly ambiguous "Ligeia" is in some senses a rewriting of the earlier story.*

In a letter of December 1, 1835, to his friend Nathaniel Beverly Tucker, Poe wrote: "Generally, people praise extravagantly those [tales] of which I am ashamed, and pass in silence what I fancy to be praise worthy. The last tale I wrote was Morella *and it was my best. When I write again I will write something better than Morella." In Poe's own estimation he accomplished that goal with "Ligeia." Eight years after its publication, he still considered it "undoubtedly the best story I have written." Others agree. George Bernard Shaw remarked: "The story of the Lady Ligeia is not merely one of the wonders of literature: it is unparalleled and unapproached. There is really nothing to be said about it: we others simply take off our hats and let Mr. Poe go first"* (Collected Letters of Edgar Allan Poe, ed. *John Ward Ostrom, Burton R. Pollin, and Jeffrey A. Savoye, 2 vols. [New York: Gordian Press, 2008], I, 115, 550; Eric W. Carlson, ed.,* The Recognition of Edgar Allan Poe: Selected Criticism since 1829 *[Ann Arbor: University of Michigan Press, 1966], 99).*

Currier and Ives,
View on the Rhine,
undated.

1   Joseph Glanvill (1636–1680), an Anglican clergyman, attacked Nonconformism and scholastic philosophy yet defended the pre-existence of souls and the belief in witchcraft. This particular quotation does not appear in Glanvill's published writings: most likely Poe invented it. D. H. Lawrence considers the epigraph the clue to understanding Poe. "It is a profound saying," Lawrence writes, "and a deadly one. Because if God is a great will, then the universe is but an instrument." According to Lawrence, Poe resolved to set his own will "against the whole of the limitations of nature"(Carlson, ed., *Recognition*, 113). Lawrence enjoyed the epigraph to "Ligeia" so much that he appropriated it for *Lady Chatterley's Lover* (1928).

2   Poe took his heroine's name from one of the Sirens of Greek mythology, creatures half bird and half woman that lure sailors to their death with song. In Milton's *Comus*, lines 878–882, Ligeia appears as a luxuriant-haired and alluring siren seated upon diamond rocks. Discussing the significance of the Sirens's names, English essayist and poet Leigh Hunt suggests that Ligeia means "shrill and high-sounding; expressive of the triumphant nature of the female voice,—which rises above all others, in a very peculiar and consummate manner" ("The Sirens and Mermaids of the Poets," *New Monthly Magazine* 47 [1836], 276).

3   These mellifluous word pairs—"thrilling and enthralling," "steadily and stealthily," "unnoticed and unknown"—reveal a narra-

tor deliberately shaping personal experience into ornate literary prose. Dorothea E. von Mücke argues that the deceased Lady Ligeia functions as a muse: "We see in [the] plot not merely the telling of some past event but also the narrator's presence as a writer who attempts to conjure up the presence of his lost beloved in the act of writing" (*The Seduction of the Occult and the Rise of the Fantastic Tale* [Stanford: Stanford University Press, 2003], 181).

4   The Rhine, one of Europe's longest rivers, flows from the Swiss Alps north and west to the North Sea. It passes through or borders several countries, including Liechtenstein, Austria, Germany, France, and the Netherlands. The castles that line its banks testify to its importance as a waterway. If the narrator cannot remember where he met Ligeia, he may not know either where their courtship began. Poe scholars generally place the narrator's home in Germany.

5   Ligeia may not have had a paternal name. Until mandated by law in the eighteenth and nineteenth centuries, Eastern European Jews rarely used surnames. The narrator never directly identifies Ligeia as Jewish, but he does compare her profile to faces depicted on Hebrew medallions. With the words "my friend," Poe repeats a phrase from "Morella," but he changes the way the narrator and his betrothed feel toward each other, replacing an intense hatred with an equally intense, all-consuming love.

tell, over marriages ill-omened, then most surely she presided over mine.

There is one dear topic, however, on which my memory fails me not. It is the *person* of Ligeia. In stature she was tall, somewhat slender, and, in her latter days, even emaciated. I would in vain attempt to portray the majesty, the quiet ease, of her demeanor, or the incomprehensible lightness and elasticity of her footfall. She came and departed as a shadow. I was never made aware of her entrance into my closed study save by the dear music of her low sweet voice, as she placed her marble hand upon my shoulder.[7] In beauty of face no maiden ever equalled her. It was the radiance of an opium dream—an airy and spirit-lifting vision more wildly divine than the phantasies which hovered about the slumbering souls of the daughters of Delos.[8] Yet her features were not of that regular mould which we have been falsely taught to worship in the classical labors of the heathen. "There is no exquisite beauty," says Bacon, Lord Verulam, speaking truly of all the forms and *genera* of beauty, "without some *strangeness* in the proportion."[9] Yet, although I saw that the features of Ligeia were not of a classic regularity—although I perceived that her loveliness was indeed "exquisite," and felt that there was much of "strangeness" pervading it, yet I have tried in vain to detect the irregularity and to trace home my own perception of "the strange." I examined the contour of the lofty and pale forehead—it was faultless—how cold indeed that word when applied to a majesty so divine!—the skin rivalling the purest ivory, the commanding extent and repose, the gentle prominence of the regions above the temples; and then the raven-black, the glossy, the luxuriant and naturally-curling tresses, setting forth the full force of the Homeric epithet, "hyacinthine!"[10] I looked at the delicate outlines of the nose—and nowhere but in the graceful medallions of the Hebrews had I beheld a similar perfection. There were the same luxurious smoothness of surface, the same scarcely perceptible tendency to the aquiline, the same harmoniously curved nostrils speaking the free spirit. I regarded the sweet mouth. Here was indeed the triumph of all things heavenly—the magnificent turn of the short upper lip—the soft, voluptuous slumber of the under—the dimples which sported, and the color which spoke—the teeth glancing back, with a brilliancy almost startling, every ray of the holy light which fell upon them in her serene and placid, yet most exultingly radiant of all smiles. I

6   Poe apparently had in mind Ashtoreth, also known as Astarte, one of the three great Canaanite goddesses, the one primarily associated with fertility and love.

7   D. H. Lawrence objects to Poe's diction and Ligeia's relationship with the narrator: "'Her marble hand' and 'the elasticity of her footfall' seem more like chair-springs and mantel-pieces than a human creature. She never was quite a human creature to him. She was an instrument from which he got his extremes of sensation. His *machine à plaisir,* as somebody says" (Carlson, ed., *Recognition,* 114).

8   The island of Delos, located in the Aegean Sea, is the legendary birthplace of Apollo, god of music and poetry.

9   In his essay "Of Beauty," Sir Francis Bacon observes, "There is no excellent beauty, that hath not some strangeness in the proportion." Poe gave this idea considerable currency in the nineteenth century, and it had a significant impact on French literature and painting. Describing Des Esseintes, the hero of Joris-Karl Huysmans's decadent novel *Against Nature* (1884), the narrator observes, "He realized first of all that to attract him a book had to have that quality of strangeness that Edgar Allan Poe called for." Eugène Delacroix copied out Poe's sentence about the strangeness of beauty, and Paul Gauguin, discussing one of the first paintings he did in Tahiti—*Woman with a Flower* (1891)—wrote: "And her forehead . . . with the majesty of upsweeping lines, reminded me of that saying of Poe's, 'There is no perfect beauty without a certain singularity in the proportions'" (quoted in Kevin J. Hayes, "One-Man Modernist," *The Cambridge Companion to Edgar Allan Poe* [New York: Cambridge University Press, 2002], 232).

10   It is in Alexander Pope's famous English translation of Homer's *Odyssey* (1725-1726), book 6, lines 271-274, that the epithet "hyacinthine locks" appears. Hyacinthine means having tight curls, like the petals of the hyacinth.

11 Poe refers to the Venus de Medici, a life-size Hellenis-
tic marble sculpture of the Greek goddess of love, Aphro-
dite, which carries on its base the inscription: "Cleomenes
Son of Apollodorus of Athens." By Poe's day, this inscription was recognized as a modern forgery intended to increase the sculpture's market value. Poe chose to ignore
recent scholarly findings to draw upon the traditional story
that the image of Venus had been revealed to Cleomenes in
a dream, which chimes with his own belief in the importance of dreams to the creative process.

12 The Greeks and Romans created remarkably lifelike
figures in stone and bronze, but the eyes presented a particular challenge. Most statues were painted in antiquity,
and eyes were often inlaid with glass, jewels, or bone.

13 Poe refers to Frances Sheridan's Oriental romance
The History of Nourjahad (1767). Sheridan makes no mention of "gazelle eyes," but this phrase is common to Oriental tales and other Romantic fiction. A French traveler observes: "When the Arabs wish to describe the beauty of a
woman, they say, that she has the eyes of a Gazelle. All
their songs, in which they celebrate their mistresses, speak
of nothing but Gazelle eyes, and they need only compare
them to this animal, to describe, in one word, a perfect
beauty" (quoted in Samuel Burder, *Oriental Literature*, 2
vols. [London: Longman, Rees, Orme, and Brown, 1822],
II, 60).

14 The word "houris" derives from the classical Arabic
word for eyes. A houri is a voluptuous young woman, especially one of the virginal maidens who await devout
Muslim men in Paradise. *Encyclopaedia Americana* (1831)
offers the following account of the Houris of Mohammed's
Paradise: "According to the description of the Koran, they
surpass, in their dazzling beauty, both pearls and rubies;
they are subject to no impurity, and reserve the languishing
glances of their dark black eyes for individual admirers.
They dwell in green gardens, beautiful beyond description,
where they are to be found in bowers lying upon green
cushions, and the most beautiful tapestry, and flourishing
in perpetual youth."

15 Poe's description may be partly indebted to Byron's
"The Giaour" (1813), lines 739–742:

> But him the maids of Paradise
>   Impatient to their halls invite,
> And the dark Heaven of Houri's eyes
>   On him shall glance for ever bright

Byron's description of Margaret Parker, the young woman
who supposedly inspired him, also anticipates Poe's de-

scrutinized the formation of the chin—and here, too, I found the
gentleness of breadth, the softness and the majesty, the fullness
and the spirituality, of the Greek—the contour which the God
Apollo revealed but in a dream, to Cleomenes, the son of the Athenian.[11] And then I peered into the large eyes of Ligeia.

For eyes we have no models in the remotely antique.[12] It might
have been, too, that in these eyes of my beloved lay the secret to
which Lord Verulam alludes. They were, I must believe, far larger
than the ordinary eyes of our own race. They were even fuller
than the fullest of the gazelle eyes of the tribe of the valley of
Nourjahad.[13] Yet it was only at intervals—in moments of intense
excitement—that this peculiarity became more than slightly noticeable in Ligeia. And at such moments was her beauty—in my
heated fancy thus it appeared perhaps—the beauty of beings either above or apart from the earth—the beauty of the fabulous
Houri of the Turk.[14] The hue of the orbs was the most brilliant
of black, and, far over them, hung jetty lashes of great length.[15]
The brows, slightly irregular in outline, had the same tint. The
"strangeness," however, which I found in the eyes, was of a nature
distinct from the formation, or the color, or the brilliancy of the
features, and must, after all, be referred to the *expression*. Ah, word
of no meaning! behind whose vast latitude of mere sound we in-
trench our ignorance of so much of the spiritual. The expression
of the eyes of Ligeia! How for long hours have I pondered upon it!
How have I, through the whole of a midsummer night, struggled
to fathom it! What *was* it—that something more profound than
the well of Democritus[16]—which lay far within the pupils of my
beloved? What *was* it? I was possessed with a passion to discover.[17]
Those eyes! those large, those shining, those divine orbs! they became to me twin stars of Leda,[18] and I to them devoutest of as-
trologers.

There is no point, among the many incomprehensible anomalies of the science of mind, more thrillingly exciting than the
fact—never, I believe, noticed in the schools—that, in our endeavors to recall to memory something long forgotten, we often
find ourselves *upon the very verge* of remembrance, without being
able, in the end, to remember. And thus how frequently, in my intense scrutiny of Ligeia's eyes, have I felt approaching the full
knowledge of their expression—felt it approaching—yet not
quite be mine—and so at length entirely depart! And (strange, oh

Paul Gauguin (1848–1903), *Vahine No Te Tiare* [Woman with a Flower], 1891. Gauguin's continued fascination with Poe is evident in his painting *Nevermore* (1897), completed more than fifty years after *The Raven* was first published.

strangest mystery of all!) I found, in the commonest objects of the universe, a circle of analogies to that expression. I mean to say that, subsequently to the period when Ligeia's beauty passed into my spirit, there dwelling as in a shrine, I derived, from many existences in the material world, a sentiment such as I felt always

scription of Ligeia: "It would be difficult for me to forget her—her dark eyes—her long eyelashes—her completely Greek cast of face and figure!" D. H. Lawrence thought Poe overdid the length of Ligeia's eyelashes. To Lawrence they sounded like the lashes of a whip (Carlson, ed., *Recognition*, 115).

16   The Greek philosopher Democritus (*ca.* 460–*ca.* 370 BCE) offered one of the first materialist accounts of the natural world, which must be credited with laying the foundations of modern atomic theory. When Poe speaks of "something more profound than the well of Democritus," he means to suggest, in a figurative way, something beyond, or deeper, than the furthest reaches of human knowledge. See the motto to "A Descent into the Maelström," which Poe took from Joseph Glanvill: "The ways of God in Nature, as in Providence, are not as *our* ways; nor are the models that we frame any way commensurate to the vastness, profundity, and unsearchableness of His works *which have a depth in them greater than the well of Democritus.*"

17   D. H. Lawrence glosses this and the previous few sentences: "Beware, oh woman, of the man who wants to *find out what you are.* . . . It is the temptation of a vampire fiend, is this knowledge. . . . But Poe wanted to know—wanted to know what was the strangeness in the eyes of Ligeia. She might have told him it was horror at his probing, horror at being vamped by his consciousness. . . . But she wanted to be vamped. She wanted to be probed by his consciousness, to be KNOWN. She paid for wanting it too." For Lawrence "Ligeia" is ultimately a love story—a great battle of wills between two lovers: "But Ligeia, true to the great tradition and mode of womanly love, by her will kept herself submissive, recipient. She is the passive body who is explored and analyzed to death. And yet, at times, her great female will must have revolted" (Carlson, ed., *Recognition*, 115–16, 117).

18   The twin stars are Castor and Pollux, brightest in the constellation Gemini. In Greek mythology, Castor and Pollux are the sons of Leda, wife of King Tyndareus of Sparta, who was seduced or raped by Zeus. The figurative comparison of the eyes of the beloved to the twin stars recurs frequently in early nineteenth-century literature. A character in Sir Walter Scott's *Peveril of the Peak* (1823) similarly compares a woman's eyes to "the twin stars of Leda." Scott calls his character "a great admirer of lofty language." The narrator's figurative comparison in "Ligeia" suggests that he, too, is a great admirer of lofty language—another indication that he is a writer deliberately shaping his personal experience into a tale.

19   Visible in the northern hemisphere from spring through autumn, Lyra (the Harp) is a small constellation. Its principal star, Vega, is one of the largest and brightest in the sky. The changeable star to which Poe refers is Epsilon Lyrae, also known as the Double Double, a multiple star system of variable brightness.

20   Unable to state clearly what it is he sees in Ligeia's eyes, the narrator produces instead a catalog of "the commonest objects of the universe" that evoke the same sentiment aroused by her "large and luminous orbs." He tells us that these objects form not a series but "a circle of analogies" to Ligeia's eyes. This puzzling and humorous inventory includes "a rapidly-growing vine," "a moth," "a butterfly," "a chrysalis," "a stream of running water," "the ocean," a falling meteor, "the glances of unusually old people," "one or two stars in heaven (especially, a star of the sixth magnitude, double and changeable, to be found near the large star in Lyra)," "certain sounds from stringed instruments," and "passages from books." What do we make of this list—or rather *circle*—of things, which completes itself by returning us to the text ("passages in books")? Some of the items suggest transformation—more obviously the moth, butterfly, chrysalis, or the flowing stream (Heraclitus claimed no one can step twice into the same stream). Others perhaps suggest death (a falling meteor, the glances of unusually old people, who are presumably closer to death than the young). Matthew A. Taylor argues that "the association of these disparate things and Ligeia registers a trace of their shared material and spiritual origin . . . clues to the aforementioned 'something long forgotten,' or to *Eureka*'s 'spiritual shadows' and '*Memories* of a Destiny more vast.' Perhaps these things, in other words, are the forensic evidence of what *Eureka* describes as God's past self-dispersal and eventual reconstitution, reminders of our origin and fate" (*Universes without Us: Posthuman Cosmologies in American Literature* [Minneapolis: University of Minnesota Press, 2013], 54–55).

aroused within me by her large and luminous orbs. Yet not the more could I define that sentiment, or analyze, or even steadily view it. I recognized it, let me repeat, sometimes in the survey of a rapidly-growing vine—in the contemplation of a moth, a butterfly, a chrysalis, a stream of running water. I have felt it in the ocean; in the falling of a meteor. I have felt it in the glances of unusually aged people. And there are one or two stars in heaven—(one especially, a star of the sixth magnitude, double and changeable, to be found near the large star in Lyra)[19] in a telescopic scrutiny of which I have been made aware of the feeling. I have been filled with it by certain sounds from stringed instruments, and not unfrequently by passages from books.[20] Among innumerable other instances, I well remember something in a volume of Joseph Glanvill, which (perhaps merely from its quaintness—who shall say?) never failed to inspire me with the sentiment;—"And the will therein lieth, which dieth not. Who knoweth the mysteries of the will, with its vigor? For God is but a great will pervading all things by nature of its intentness. Man doth not yield him to the angels, nor unto death utterly, save only through the weakness of his feeble will."

Length of years, and subsequent reflection, have enabled me to trace, indeed, some remote connection between this passage in the English moralist and a portion of the character of Ligeia. An *intensity* in thought, action, or speech, was possibly, in her, a result, or at least an index, of that gigantic volition which, during our long intercourse, failed to give other and more immediate evidence of its existence. Of all the women whom I have ever known, she, the outwardly calm, the ever-placid Ligeia, was the most violently a prey to the tumultuous vultures of stern passion. And of such passion I could form no estimate, save by the miraculous expansion of those eyes which at once so delighted and appalled me—by the almost magical melody, modulation, distinctness and placidity of her very low voice—and by the fierce energy (rendered doubly effective by contrast with her manner of utterance) of the wild words which she habitually uttered.

I have spoken of the learning of Ligeia: it was immense—such as I have never known in woman. In the classical tongues was she deeply proficient, and as far as my own acquaintance extended in regard to the modern dialects of Europe, I have never known her at fault. Indeed upon any theme of the most admired, because sim-

Harry Clarke, illustration for "Ligeia," from *Tales of Mystery and Imagination* (London: George G. Harrap, 1819).

ply the most abstruse of the boasted erudition of the academy, have I *ever* found Ligeia at fault? How singularly—how thrillingly, this one point in the nature of my wife has forced itself, at this late period only, upon my attention! I said her knowledge was such as I have never known in woman—but where breathes the man who has traversed, and successfully, *all* the wide areas of moral, physical, and mathematical science? I saw not then what I now clearly perceive, that the acquisitions of Ligeia were gigantic, were astounding; yet I was sufficiently aware of her infinite supremacy to resign myself, with a child-like confidence, to her guidance through the chaotic world of metaphysical investigation at which I was most busily occupied during the earlier years of our marriage. With how vast a triumph—with how vivid a delight—with how much of all that is ethereal in hope—did I *feel*, as she

21 While the narrator may never before have encountered a woman of such prodigious learning, the reader who
comes to this story after "Morella" certainly has. The Lady
Ligeia would have met her match in Morella, in a world
of melding fictions. Morella's favorite reading is the German mystics, but she also knows the Pythagoreans, Fichte,
Schelling, and Locke. Mabbott surmises that Ligeia may be
an alchemist.

22 Compare Proverbs 23:5: "Wilt thou set thine eyes
upon that which is not? for riches certainly make themselves wings; they fly away as an eagle toward heaven."

23 By the end of the 1830s the term "transcendentalism"
would come to mean New England Transcendentalism, the
movement associated with the thought, writings, and activities of Ralph Waldo Emerson, William Ellery Chan-
ning, Margaret Fuller, George Ripley, Theodore Parker,
Frederic Henry Hedge, Bronson Alcott, Orestes Brown-
son, Henry David Thoreau, and others. Describing the
origins of the intellectual ferment of his day, Ralph Waldo
Emerson said in his 1841 lecture "The Transcendentalist":
"It is well known to most of my audience, that the Ideal-
ism of the present day acquired the name of Transcendental, from the use of that term by Immanuel Kant, of Ko-
nigsberg, who replied to the skeptical philosophy of Locke,
which insisted that there was nothing in the intellect which
was not previously in the experience of the senses, by
showing that there was a very important class of ideas, or
imperative forms, which did not come by experience, but
through which experience was acquired; that these were
intuitions of the mind itself; and he denominated them
Transcendental forms" (*Emerson: Essays and Lectures* [New
York: The Library of America, 1983], 198). Poe uses the
term here in this more general sense, meaning any transcendental thought that placed an emphasis on intuition.

Beginning in 1840, however, Poe would engage in a series of personal attacks against the New England Transcendentalists. He was contemptuous of Transcendentalism's faith in social progress, and he chaffed under the
cultural authority of its most prominent members. He
would characterize Emerson, for example, as a writer interested "in mysticism for mysticism's sake," while often
derisively referring to the Transcendentalists as "Frogpon-
dians." His satirical tale "Never Bet the Devil Your Head"
(1841) is an attack on Transcendentalism. But Poe's relationship to the Transcendentalists, however vexed, was
multidimensional and complex. See Heidi Silcox, "Transcendentalism," *Edgar Allan Poe in Context*, ed. Kevin J.
Hayes (New York: Cambridge University Press, 2013),
269–278.

bent over me in studies but little sought—but less known—that
delicious vista by slow degrees expanding before me, down whose
long, gorgeous, and all untrodden path, I might at length pass onward to the goal of a wisdom too divinely precious not to be forbidden![21]

How poignant, then, must have been the grief with which, after
some years, I beheld my well-grounded expectations take wings to
themselves and fly away![22] Without Ligeia I was but as a child
groping benighted. Her presence, her readings alone, rendered
vividly luminous the many mysteries of the transcendentalism in
which we were immersed.[23] Wanting the radiant lustre of her eyes,
letters, lambent and golden, grew duller than Saturnian lead.[24] And
now those eyes shone less and less frequently upon the pages over
which I pored. Ligeia grew ill. The wild eyes blazed with a too—
too glorious effulgence; the pale fingers became of the transparent
waxen hue of the grave, and the blue veins upon the lofty forehead
swelled and sank impetuously with the tides of the most gentle
emotion. I saw that she must die—and I struggled desperately in
spirit with the grim Azrael.[25] And the struggles of the passionate
wife were, to my astonishment, even more energetic than my own.
There had been much in her stern nature to impress me with the
belief that, to her, death would have come without its terrors;—
but not so. Words are impotent to convey any just idea of the
fierceness of resistance with which she wrestled with the Shadow.
I groaned in anguish at the pitiable spectacle. I would have
soothed—I would have reasoned; but, in the intensity of her wild
desire for life,—for life—*but* for life—solace and reason were
alike the uttermost of folly. Yet not until the last instance, amid the
most convulsive writhings of her fierce spirit, was shaken the external placidity of her demeanor. Her voice grew more gentle—
grew more low—yet I would not wish to dwell upon the wild
meaning of the quietly uttered words. My brain reeled as I hearkened, entranced, to a melody more than mortal—to assumptions
and aspirations which mortality had never before known.

That she loved me I should not have doubted; and I might have
been easily aware that, in a bosom such as hers, love would have
reigned no ordinary passion. But in death only, was I fully impressed with the strength of her affection. For long hours, detain-
ing my hand, would she pour out before me the overflowing of a
heart whose more than passionate devotion amounted to idolatry.

How had I deserved to be so blessed by such confessions?—how had I deserved to be so cursed with the removal of my beloved in the hour of her making them? But upon this subject I cannot bear to dilate. Let me say only, that in Ligeia's more than womanly abandonment to a love, alas! all unmerited, all unworthily bestowed, I at length recognized the principle of her longing with so wildly earnest a desire for the life which was now fleeing so rapidly away. It is this wild longing—it is this eager vehemence of desire for life—*but* for life—that I have no power to portray—no utterance capable of expressing.

At high noon of the night in which she departed, beckoning me, peremptorily, to her side, she bade me repeat certain verses composed by herself not many days before.[26] I obeyed her.—They were these:

> Lo! 'tis a gala night
>   Within the lonesome latter years!
> An angel throng, bewinged, bedight
>   In veils, and drowned in tears,
> Sit in a theatre,[27] to see
>   A play of hopes and fears,
> While the orchestra breathes fitfully
>   The music of the spheres.[28]
>
> Mimes, in the form of God on high,
>   Mutter and mumble low,
> And hither and thither fly—
>   Mere puppets they, who come and go
> At bidding of vast formless things
>   That shift the scenery to and fro,
> Flapping from out their Condor wings
>   Invisible Wo!
>
> That motley drama!—oh, be sure
>   It shall not be forgot!
> With its Phantom chased forevermore,
>   By a crowd that seize it not,
> Through a circle that ever returneth in
>   To the self-same spot,
> And much of Madness and more of Sin,
>   And Horror the soul of the plot.

24 Here "Saturnian" alludes to both the Golden Age of verse and a duller, leaden one that follows. Glossing the phrase "a new Saturnian age of lead" in *The Dunciad*, book I, line 28, Alexander Pope notes: "The ancient Golden Age is by Poets styled *Saturnian*, as being under the reign of Saturn . . . but in the Chemical language *Saturn* is Lead."

25 Pairing Azrael, the Angel of Death in Judaisim, Sikhism, and Islam, with the adjective "grim," Poe offers a highfalutin take on the proverbial comparison "like grim death." The usage of the word "grim" survives today with "The Grim Reaper," but that phrase was not current in Poe's day.

26 When "Ligeia" first appeared in the September 1838 issue of *American Museum*, it did not contain Poe's poem "The Conqueror Worm" (yet to be written). Poe later incorporated it into "Ligeia" when he revised the story for republication in 1845. "The Conquerer Worm" first appeared as an independent poem in the January 1843 issue of *Graham's Magazine*. Here, however, within the context of the story, we are asked to believe that the poem is the invention of the Lady Ligeia. The title of Ligeia's poem is not given in Poe's story. Mabbott believes that the "insertion of the poem with its accompanying paragraphs is the indication that Ligeia's struggle [to overcome death by force of will] cannot succeed" (Thomas Ollive Mabbott, ed., *Collected Works of Edgar Allan Poe*, 3 vols. [Cambridge, MA: The Belknap Press of Harvard University Press, 1969-1978], II, 333).

27 Klaus Lubbers reminds us that the idea that the world is a theater has a long and distinguished literary tradition. More particularly, in the Elizabethan and Jacobean imagination it became "a convenient device to voice the struggle of life within the framework of a theocentric world picture. . . . The world was viewed as a theatre, the earth as a stage, life as a play from womb to tomb, birth as the first act or prologue, death as the exit or epilogue, the grave as drawn curtains" ("Poe's 'The Conqueror Worm,'" *American Literature* 39 [1967], 377). Here, however, the eschatology is entirely Poe's: if life is a grotesque pantomime, death is equally meaningless. The poem describes the tragedy "Man," performed by "mimes, in the form of God on high" for an audience of weeping angels, on its opening night. At the bidding of supernatural forces, the mimes run about in meaningless circles, chasing a Phantom they can never apprehend. In the final act, a "blood-red thing," a monstrous worm, comes writhing onto the stage and devours the mimes. Then, with "the rush of a storm," the curtain, "a funeral pall," comes clanging down. The

poem's final line—the real kicker—reveals that the Conqueror Worm is the hero of this tragedy. God has withdrawn his attention from the play. The angels sob for the mimes but cannot intercede on their behalf.

Going further than Klaus Lubbers, Jerome McGann argues that Poe has staged for his readers a play within a play: the poem invites "its mortal audience—ourselves—to watch [the ancient and familiar tragedy *Man*] in a larger theatrical setting: the play called *The Conqueror Worm* in which *Man* is a theatrical interlude, or play within a play. Stage, backstage, orchestra, and auditorium provide the setting for this enveloping play's virtually cosmic action" (*The Poet Edgar Allan Poe: Alien Angel* [Cambridge: Harvard University Press, 2014], 137). For McGann *The Conqueror Worm* is a seriocomical restaging of the kind of amateurish, clumsy productions that typified American theater in Poe's day—the kind of productions in which Poe's own parents were actors.

28   Attributed to Pythagoras (*ca.* 570–*ca.* 495 BCE), "the music of the spheres" is the ancient philosophical and religious concept that the movements of the planets are modulated according to musical proportions or ratios, each celestial body producing its own tone, according to its size, velocity, and distance from the center, but together producing beautiful music and demonstrating the supreme perfection of the universe. In Ligeia's poem, however, the celestial orchestra plays "fitfully."

29   From Shakespeare to writers of the present day, the worm figures prominently as a symbol of death and decay. See, for example, what Hamlet says of Polonius: "Not where he eats, but where he is eaten: a certain convocation of politic worms are e'en at him. Your worm is your only emperor for diet: we fat all creatures else to fat us, and we fat ourselves for maggots: your fat king and your lean beggar is but variable service,—two dishes, but to one table: that's the end" (*Hamlet*, IV.iii.20–25).

But see, amid the mimic rout,
    A crawling shape intrude!
A blood-red thing that writhes from out
    The scenic solitude!
It writhes!—it writhes!—with mortal pangs
    The mimes become its food,
And the seraphs sob at vermin fangs
    In human gore imbued.

Out—out are the lights—out all!
    And over each quivering form,
The curtain, a funeral pall,
    Comes down with the rush of a storm,
And the angels, all pallid and wan,
    Uprising, unveiling, affirm
That the play is the tragedy, "Man,"
    And its hero the Conqueror Worm.[29]

"O God!" half shrieked Ligeia, leaping to her feet and extending her arms aloft with a spasmodic movement, as I made an end of these lines—"O God! O Divine Father!—shall these things be undeviatingly so?—shall this Conqueror be not once conquered? Are we not part and parcel in Thee? Who—who knoweth the mysteries of the will with its vigor? Man doth not yield him to the angels, *nor unto death utterly,* save only through the weakness of his feeble will."

And now, as if exhausted with emotion, she suffered her white arms to fall, and returned solemnly to her bed of Death. And as she breathed her last sighs, there came mingled with them a low murmur from her lips. I bent to them my ear and distinguished, again, the concluding words of the passage in Glanvill—"*Man doth not yield him to the angels, nor unto death utterly, save only through the weakness of his feeble will.*"

She died;—and I, crushed into the very dust with sorrow, could no longer endure the lonely desolation of my dwelling in the dim and decaying city by the Rhine. I had no lack of what the world calls wealth. Ligeia had brought me far more, very far more than ordinarily falls to the lot of mortals. After a few months, therefore, of weary and aimless wandering, I purchased, and put in some repair, an abbey, which I shall not name, in one of the wildest and least frequented portions of fair England.[30] The gloomy and dreary grandeur of the building, the almost savage aspect of the domain, the many melancholy and time-honored memories connected with both, had much in unison with the feelings of utter abandonment which had driven me into that remote and unsocial region of the country. Yet although the external abbey, with its verdant decay hanging about it, suffered but little alteration, I gave way, with a child-like perversity, and perchance with a faint hope of alleviating my sorrows, to a display of more than regal magnificence within.—For such follies, even in childhood, I had imbibed a taste, and now they came back to me as if in the dotage of grief. Alas, I feel how much even of incipient madness might have been discovered in the gorgeous and fantastic draperies, in the solemn carvings of Egypt, in the wild cornices and furniture, in the Bedlam patterns of the carpets of tufted gold! I had become a bounden slave in the trammels of opium, and my labors and my orders had taken a coloring from my dreams.[31] But these absurdities I must not pause to detail. Let me speak only of that one chamber, ever accursed, whither in a moment of mental alienation,[32] I led from the altar as my bride—as the successor of the unforgotten Ligeia—the fair-haired and blue-eyed Lady Rowena Trevanion, of Tremaine.[33]

There is no individual portion of the architecture and decoration of that bridal chamber which is not now visibly before me. Where were the souls of the haughty family of the bride, when, through thirst of gold, they permitted to pass the threshold of an apartment *so* bedecked, a maiden and a daughter so beloved? I have said that I minutely remember the details of the chamber—yet I am sadly forgetful on topics of deep moment—and here there was no system, no keeping, in the fantastic display, to take hold upon the memory. The room lay in a high turret of the castellated abbey, was pentagonal in shape, and of capacious size.[34] Occupying the whole southern face of the pentagon was the sole window—an immense sheet of unbroken glass from Venice—a single pane, and tinted of a leaden hue, so that the rays of either the sun or moon, passing through it, fell with a ghastly lustre on the objects within. Over the upper portion of this huge window, extended the trellice-work of an aged vine, which clambered up the massy walls of the turret. The ceiling, of gloomy-looking oak, was excessively lofty, vaulted, and elaborately fretted with the wildest

30 With the dissolution of the monasteries in England under Henry VIII, the numerous abbeys that dotted the countryside fell into disrepair. Some were refurbished as private residences, but most became ruins. By the mid-eighteenth century they would become tourist destinations and function as Romantic symbols of the ultimate decay of all earthly things.

31 Earlier, the narrator had spoken of "the radiance of an opium dream": it seems he was not speaking figuratively.

32 The use of the word "moment" may be redundant. Mental alienation, a synonym for insanity, was generally assumed to be a temporary affliction. According to contemporary medical theory, poets and artists, that is, those who indulged their imagination more than others, were highly susceptible to mental alienation.

33 D. H. Lawrence calls Lady Rowena Trevanion of Tremaine "a sort of Saxon-Cornish blue-blood." Her literary pedigree is somewhat less aristocratic: she is a fictional composite of elements in several popular nineteenth-century novels. R. Plumer Ward's *Tremaine; or, The Man of Refinement* (1825) gave Poe the source for Lady Rowena's ancestral home. Miss Trevanion, the heroine of Anna Maria Porter's novel *The Barony* (1830), provides Rowena's family name plus another curious parallel: "She was like one of those torpid creatures who lie through the winter in deathly insensibility, but wake to life and motion by the first breath of spring." Poe's character owes her Christian name, her fair hair, and her blue eyes to Scott's heroine Rowena in *Ivanhoe* (1819). Clive Bloom goes so far as to call "Ligeia" a "partial pastiche of *Ivanhoe*" (*Gothic Histories: The Taste for Terror, 1764 to the Present* [New York: Continuum, 2010], 14).

34 In folklore and literature, the pentagon, which forms the inner part of the pentagram, possesses great magic powers.

35 Druids serve as magicians, soothsayers, and sorcerers in ancient Celtic legend. Though they existed in fact, little is known about their actual practices. In his *Commentarii* on the Gallic War, Julius Caesar states that the chief tenet of Druidical thought was belief in the indestructibility of the human soul, which upon death passes from one body to the next.

36 A Saracenic pattern is characterized by abstract geometric designs.

37 A city in Upper Egypt on the east bank of the Nile and the site of the ancient city of Thebes.

38 With its single window of leaden hue and heavy arabesque draperies, its vaulted ceiling and censer, the ebony bed and pall-like canopy, and the two large black granite sarcophagi, the apartment seems to have been designed by the narrator not as a bridal chamber but as a tomb—which perhaps explains why he envisions how it would appear to a visitor as he enters and then moves through the space. Describing the bridal chamber as "a torture chamber," J. Gerald Kennedy sees the narrator's interior decorating efforts as part of a "deadly plot" to frighten Rowena to death ("Poe, 'Ligeia,' and the Problem of Dying Women," in *New Essays on Poe's Major Tales*, ed. Kenneth Silverman [New York: Cambridge University Press, 1993], 113–127).

39 Poe means to conjure in the reader's mind the grotesque shapes and forms of Norman transformation legends. One of the most renowned figures of Norman legend is *Loup-garou*, a man who changes into a wolf. Another ghastly figure from Norman legend is the *Rongeur d'Os*, a phantom in the shape of a great dog. Stories of one woman transforming into the likeness of another also occur in the oral tradition.

40 Widely popular in Europe and America in the early nineteenth century, the phantasmagoria show was a form of theatrical entertainment intended to give audiences the willies. Central to the phantasmagoria show was a magic lantern, or projector, that cast ghoulish images such as ghosts, skeletons, and demons onto a screen. Currents of air fluttered the surrounding drapery to create a sense of movement. Eerie musical noises accompanied the visual imagery. A characteristic aspect of the phantasmagoria show was the "transmutation," during which a projected human image, often a beautiful woman, would change into a skeleton. Poe's allusion to phantasmagoria at this point in "Ligeia" foreshadows the eerie transformation that con-

and most grotesque specimens of a semi-Gothic, semi-Druidical device.[35] From out the most central recess of this melancholy vaulting, depended, by a single chain of gold with long links, a huge censer of the same metal, Saracenic[36] in pattern, and with many perforations so contrived that there writhed in and out of them, as if endued with a serpent vitality, a continual succession of parti-colored fires.

Some few ottomans and golden candelabra, of Eastern figure, were in various stations about—and there was the couch, too—the bridal couch—of an Indian model, and low, and sculptured of solid ebony, with a pall-like canopy above. In each of the angles of the chamber stood on end a gigantic sarcophagus of black granite, from the tombs of the kings over against Luxor,[37] with their aged lids full of immemorial sculpture. But in the draping of the apartment lay, alas! the chief phantasy of all. The lofty walls, gigantic in height—even unproportionably so—were hung from summit to foot, in vast folds, with a heavy and massive-looking tapestry—tapestry of a material which was found alike as a carpet on the floor, as a covering for the ottomans and the ebony bed, as a canopy for the bed, and as the gorgeous volutes of the curtains which partially shaded the window. The material was the richest cloth of gold. It was spotted all over, at irregular intervals, with arabesque figures, about a foot in diameter, and wrought upon the cloth in patterns of the most jetty black. But these figures partook of the true character of the arabesque only when regarded from a single point of view. By a contrivance now common, and indeed traceable to a very remote period of antiquity, they were made changeable in aspect. To one entering the room, they bore the appearance of simple monstrosities; but upon a farther advance, this appearance gradually departed; and step by step, as the visiter[38] moved his station in the chamber, he saw himself surrounded by an endless succession of the ghastly forms which belong to the superstition of the Norman,[39] or arise in the guilty slumbers of the monk. The phantasmagoric effect was vastly heightened by the artificial introduction of a strong continual current of wind behind the draperies—giving a hideous and uneasy animation to the whole.[40]

In halls such as these—in a bridal chamber such as this—I passed, with the Lady of Tremaine, the unhallowed hours of the first month of our marriage—passed them with but little disquietude. That my wife dreaded the fierce moodiness of my temper—

that she shunned me and loved me but little—I could not help perceiving; but it gave me rather pleasure than otherwise. I loathed her with a hatred belonging more to demon than to man. My memory flew back, (oh, with what intensity of regret!) to Ligeia, the beloved, the august, the beautiful, the entombed.[41] I revelled in recollections of her purity, of her wisdom, of her lofty, her ethereal nature, of her passionate, her idolatrous love. Now, then, did my spirit fully and freely burn with more than all the fires of her own. In the excitement of my opium dreams (for I was habitually fettered in the shackles of the drug) I would call aloud upon her name,[42] during the silence of the night, or among the sheltered recesses of the glens by day, as if, through the wild eagerness, the solemn passion, the consuming ardor of my longing for the departed, I could restore her to the pathway she had abandoned— ah, *could* it be forever?—upon the earth.

About the commencement of the second month of the marriage, the Lady Rowena was attacked with sudden illness, from which her recovery was slow. The fever which consumed her rendered her nights uneasy; and in her perturbed state of half-slumber, she spoke of sounds, and of motions, in and about the chamber of the turret, which I concluded had no origin save in the distemper of her fancy, or perhaps in the phantasmagoric influences of the chamber itself. She became at length convalescent— finally well. Yet but a brief period elapsed, ere a second more violent disorder again threw her upon a bed of suffering; and from this attack her frame, at all times feeble, never altogether recovered. Her illnesses were, after this epoch, of alarming character, and of more alarming recurrence, defying alike the knowledge and the great exertions of her physicians. With the increase of the chronic disease which had thus, apparently, taken too sure hold upon her constitution to be eradicated by human means, I could not fail to observe a similar increase in the nervous irritation of her temperament, and in her excitability by trivial causes of fear. She spoke again, and now more frequently and pertinaciously, of the sounds—of the slight sounds—and of the unusual motions among the tapestries, to which she had formerly alluded.

One night, near the closing in of September, she pressed this distressing subject with more than usual emphasis upon my attention. She had just awakened from an unquiet slumber, and I had been watching, with feelings half of anxiety, half of a vague terror,

cludes the tale (Terry Castle, "Phantasmagoria: Spectral Technology and the Metaphorics of Modern Reverie," *Critical Inquiry* 15 [1988], 26–61).

41   The psychological complexity of "Ligeia," according to Kenneth Silverman, comes from the narrator's wish to memorialize Ligeia and his simultaneous and almost equally strong desire to forget his first wife, upon whom he was so dependent when she was living. Though he marries Rowena to forget Ligeia, his intrusive memories of Ligeia prevent him from loving Rowena. "In furnishing the bridal chamber," Silverman observes, "he selects among other funeral pieces, a 'gigantic sarcophagus of black granite,' revealing that his effort to forget conceals a stronger need to remember. Ligeia's ultimate rebirth only dramatizes more horrifyingly how those most deeply beloved live on within oneself, never dead and ever ready to return" (*Edgar A. Poe: Mournful and Never-Ending Remembrance* [New York: HarperCollins, 1991], 140).

42   As he does in "Morella," Poe makes use of the superstition that calling out a dead person's name requires them to answer. Poe's words also echo Psalms 99:6: "Moses and Aaron among his priests, and Samuel among them that call upon his name; they called upon the Lord, and he answered them."

43   Laudanum or tincture of opium was ruby colored. In an older but still influential interpretation of the story, Roy P. Basler suggests that the narrator—unhinged but nevertheless cunning in his madness—poisons Rowena in a maniacal effort to bring his dead wife back to life: "This is to say that Poe's psychological effect in 'Ligeia' is similar to that of later delvers in psychological complexity like Henry James, whose stories told by a narrator move on two planes. There is the story which the narrator means to tell, and there is the story which he tells without meaning to, as he unconsciously reveals himself" ("The Interpretation of 'Ligeia,'" *College English* 5 [1944], 367). In Basler's reading, it is not Ligeia's but the megalomaniacal narrator's will to conquer death that finds expression in the story.

the workings of her emaciated countenance. I sat by the side of her ebony bed, upon one of the ottomans of India. She partly arose, and spoke, in an earnest low whisper, of sounds which she *then* heard, but which I could not hear—of motions which she *then* saw, but which I could not perceive. The wind was rushing hurriedly behind the tapestries, and I wished to show her (what, let me confess it, I could not *all* believe) that those almost inarticulate breathings, and those very gentle variations of the figures upon the wall, were but the natural effects of that customary rushing of the wind. But a deadly pallor, over-spreading her face, had proved to me that my exertions to reassure her would be fruitless. She appeared to be fainting, and no attendants were within call. I remembered where was deposited a decanter of light wine which had been ordered by her physicians, and hastened across the chamber to procure it. But, as I stepped beneath the light of the censer, two circumstances of a startling nature attracted my attention. I had felt that some palpable although invisible object had passed lightly by my person; and I saw that there lay upon the golden carpet, in the very middle of the rich lustre thrown from the censer, a shadow— a faint, indefinite shadow of angelic aspect—such as might be fancied for the shadow of a shade. But I was wild with the excitement of an immoderate dose of opium, and heeded these things but little, nor spoke of them to Rowena. Having found the wine, I recrossed the chamber, and poured out a goblet-ful, which I held to the lips of the fainting lady. She had now partially recovered, however, and took the vessel herself, while I sank upon an ottoman near me, with my eyes fastened upon her person. It was then that I became distinctly aware of a gentle foot-fall upon the carpet, and near the couch; and in a second thereafter, as Rowena was in the act of raising the wine to her lips, I saw, or may have dreamed that I saw, fall within the goblet, as if from some invisible spring in the atmosphere of the room, three or four large drops of a brilliant and ruby colored fluid.[43] If this I saw—not so Rowena. She swallowed the wine unhesitatingly, and I forbore to speak to her of a circumstance which must, after all, I considered, have been but the suggestion of a vivid imagination, rendered morbidly active by the terror of the lady, by the opium, and by the hour.

Yet I cannot conceal it from my own perception that, immediately subsequent to the fall of the ruby-drops, a rapid change for the worse took place in the disorder of my wife; so that, on the third subsequent night, the hands of her menials prepared her for the tomb, and on the fourth, I sat alone, with her shrouded body, in that fantastic chamber which had received her as my bride.— Wild visions, opium-engendered, flitted, shadow-like, before me. I gazed with unquiet eye upon the sarcophagi in the angles of the room, upon the varying figures of the drapery, and upon the writhing of the parti-colored fires in the censer overhead. My eyes then fell, as I called to mind the circumstances of a former night, to the spot beneath the glare of the censer where I had seen the faint traces of the shadow. It was there, however, no longer; and breathing with greater freedom, I turned my glances to the pallid and rigid figure upon the bed. Then rushed upon me a thousand memories of Ligeia—and then came back upon my heart, with the turbulent violence of a flood, the whole of that unutterable wo with which I had regarded *her* thus enshrouded. The night waned; and still, with a bosom full of bitter thoughts of the one only and supremely beloved, I remained gazing upon the body of Rowena.

It might have been midnight, or perhaps earlier, or later, for I had taken no note of time, when a sob, low, gentle, but very distinct, startled me from my revery.—I *felt* that it came from the bed of ebony—the bed of death. I listened in an agony of superstitious terror—but there was no repetition of the sound. I strained my vision to detect any motion in the corpse—but there was not the slightest perceptible. Yet I could not have been deceived. I *had* heard the noise, however faint, and my soul was awakened within me. I resolutely and perseveringly kept my attention riveted upon the body. Many minutes elapsed before any circumstance occurred tending to throw light upon the mystery. At length it became evident that a slight, a very feeble, and barely noticeable tinge of color had flushed up within the cheeks, and along the sunken small veins of the eyelids. Through a species of unutterable horror and awe, for which the language of mortality has no sufficiently energetic expression, I felt my heart cease to beat, my limbs grow rigid where I sat. Yet a sense of duty finally operated to restore my self-possession. I could no longer doubt that we had been precipitate in our preparations—that Rowena still lived. It was necessary that some immediate exertion be made; yet the turret was altogether apart from the portion of the abbey tenanted by the servants— there were none within call—I had no means of summoning them to my aid without leaving the room for many minutes—and this I could not venture to do. I therefore struggled alone in my endeavors to call back the spirit still hovering. In a short period it was certain, however, that a relapse had taken place; the color disappeared from both eyelid and cheek, leaving a wanness even more than that of marble; the lips became doubly shrivelled and pinched up in the ghastly expression of death; a repulsive clamminess and coldness overspread rapidly the surface of the body; and all the usual rigorous stiffness immediately supervened. I fell back with a shudder upon the couch from which I had been so startlingly aroused, and again gave myself up to passionate waking visions of Ligeia.

An hour thus elapsed when (could it be possible?) I was a second time aware of some vague sound issuing from the region of the bed. I listened—in extremity of horror. The sound came again—it was a sigh. Rushing to the corpse, I saw—distinctly saw—a tremor upon the lips. In a minute afterward they relaxed, disclosing a bright line of the pearly teeth. Amazement now struggled in my bosom with the profound awe which had hitherto reigned there alone. I felt that my vision grew dim, that my reason wandered; and it was only by a violent effort that I at length succeeded in nerving myself to the task which duty thus once more had pointed out. There was now a partial glow upon the forehead and upon the cheek and throat; a perceptible warmth pervaded the whole frame; there was even a slight pulsation at the heart. The lady *lived;* and with redoubled ardor I betook myself to the task of restoration. I chafed and bathed the temples and the hands, and used every exertion which experience, and no little medical reading, could suggest. But in vain. Suddenly, the color fled, the pulsation ceased, the lips resumed the expression of the dead, and, in an instant afterward, the whole body took upon itself the icy chilliness, the livid hue, the intense rigidity, the sunken outline, and all the loathsome peculiarities of that which has been, for many days, a tenant of the tomb.

And again I sunk into visions of Ligeia—and again, (what marvel that I shudder while I write?) *again* there reached my ears a low sob from the region of the ebony bed. But why shall I minutely detail the unspeakable horrors of that night? Why shall I pause to relate how, time after time, until near the period of the gray dawn, this hideous drama of revivification was repeated; how each terrific relapse was only into a sterner and apparently more irredeemable death; how each agony wore the aspect of a struggle with some invisible foe; and how each struggle was succeeded by I know not what of wild change in the personal appearance of the corpse? Let me hurry to a conclusion.

The greater part of the fearful night had worn away, and she who had been dead, once again stirred—and now more vigorously than hitherto, although arousing from a dissolution more appalling in its utter hopelessness than any. I had long ceased to struggle or to move, and remained sitting rigidly upon the ottoman, a helpless prey to a whirl of violent emotions, of which extreme awe was perhaps the least terrible, the least consuming. The corpse, I repeat, stirred, and now more vigorously than before. The hues of life flushed up with unwonted energy into the countenance—the limbs relaxed—and, save that the eyelids were yet pressed heavily together, and that the bandages and draperies of the grave still imparted their charnel character to the figure, I might have dreamed that Rowena had indeed shaken off, utterly, the fetters of Death. But if this idea was not, even then, altogether adopted, I could at least doubt no longer, when, arising from the bed, tottering, with feeble steps, with closed eyes, and with the manner of one bewildered in a dream, the thing that was enshrouded advanced bodily and palpably into the middle of the apartment.

I trembled not—I stirred not—for a crowd of unutterable fancies connected with the air, the stature, the demeanor of the figure, rushing hurriedly through my brain, had paralyzed—had chilled me into stone. I stirred not—but gazed upon the apparition. There was a mad disorder in my thoughts—a tumult unappeasable. Could it, indeed, be the *living* Rowena who confronted me? Could it indeed be Rowena *at all*—the fair-haired, the blue-eyed Lady Rowena Trevanion of Tremaine? Why, *why* should I doubt it? The bandage lay heavily about the mouth—but then might it not be the mouth of the breathing Lady of Tremaine? And the cheeks—there were the roses as in her noon of life—yes, these might indeed be the fair cheeks of the living Lady of Tremaine. And the chin, with its dimples, as in health, might it not be hers?— but *had she then grown taller since her malady?* What inexpressible madness seized me with that thought? One bound, and I had reached her feet! Shrinking from my touch, she let fall from her head the ghastly cerements which had confined it, and there

44   Earlier versions had read "the raven wings." When Poe revised the story in 1848, readers strongly identified him with "The Raven" (1845), which had been widely reprinted and frequently parodied. He revised his text to avoid the distraction.

45   The ending leaves many questions unanswered. The reappearance of Ligeia can be interpreted as a phantasmagoric illusion, an opium-induced hallucination, a psychological fantasy, a modern recurrence of a traditional transformation legend, or an actual event. If we are to believe that Ligeia really did return in the body of Rowena, then what has happened since then? According to the narrator in the opening paragraph, "long years" have passed since the events of the story took place. Did the narrator and Ligeia resume their forbidden studies, picking up where they left off? Do they live happily ever after? It's amusing to think so.

When his friend Philip Pendleton Cooke questioned the tale's ending, Poe responded by suggesting how he might have improved it. In a September 21, 1839, letter to Cooke, Poe explained: "One point I have not fully carried out—I should have intimated that the *will* did not perfect its intention—there should have been a relapse—a final one—and Ligeia (who had only succeeded in so much as to convey an idea of the truth to the narrator) should be at length entombed as Rowena—the bodily alterations having gradually faded away" (*Collected Letters*, I, 193).

streamed forth, into the rushing atmosphere of the chamber, huge masses of long and dishevelled hair; it *was blacker than the wings*[44] *of the midnight!* And now slowly opened *the eyes* of the figure which stood before me. "Here then, at least," I shrieked aloud, "can I never—can I never be mistaken—these are the full, and the black, and the wild eyes—of my lost love—of the lady—of the LADY LIGEIA!"[45]

The Man That Was Used Up: A Tale of the Late Bugaboo and Kickapoo Campaign

Pleurez, pleurez, mes yeux, et fondez vous en eau!
La moitié de ma vie a mis l'autre au tombeau.

Corneille[1]

I cannot just now remember when or where I first made the acquaintance of that truly fine-looking fellow, Brevet Brigadier General John A. B. C. Smith.[2] Some one *did* introduce me to the gentleman, I am sure—at some public meeting, I know very well—held about something of great importance, no doubt at some place or other, I feel convinced,—whose name I have unaccountably forgotten. The truth is—that the introduction was attended, upon my part, with a degree of anxious embarrassment which operated to prevent any definite impressions of either time or place. I am constitutionally nervous—this, with me, is a family failing, and I can't help it. In especial, the slightest appearance of mystery—of any point I cannot exactly comprehend—puts me at once into a pitiable state of agitation.

There was something, as it were, remarkable—yes, *remarkable*, although this is but a feeble term to express my full meaning—about the entire individuality of the personage in question. He was, perhaps, six feet in height, and of a presence singularly commanding.[3] There was an *air distingué* pervading the whole man, which spoke of high breeding, and hinted at high birth. Upon this topic—the topic of Smith's personal appearance—I have a kind of melancholy satisfaction in being minute. His head of hair would have done honor to a Brutus;—nothing could be more richly flowing, or possess a brighter gloss.[4] It was of a jetty black;—which was also the color, or more properly the no color, of his unimaginable whiskers. You perceive I cannot speak of these latter without

When William Burton hired Poe to help edit Burton's Gentleman's Magazine *in June 1839, Poe had not worked since leaving the* Southern Literary Messenger *in 1837. After moving to Philadelphia, he, Virginia, and her mother had been living a hand-to-mouth existence. One friend found them subsisting solely on bread and molasses. As the assistant editor of* Burton's, *Poe chose submissions, prepared manuscripts, proofread copy, supervised production, and wrote book reviews. Burton paid him extra for contributing original tales to the magazine's pages, so Poe made the most of the opportunity, experimenting with different types of fiction. In the August 1839 issue, he published this remarkable but often overlooked satire about the bloody anti-Indian campaigns of the Jacksonian era and the ways in which we honor and talk about war veterans. In the face of the growing number of wounded veterans now returning home from the service fitted with prosthetic devices, "The Man That Was Used Up" finds disturbing resonances today. David Haven Blake observes: "What we find in 'The Man That Was Used Up' is that the publicity surrounding the hero's experience is ultimately more significant than a narration of his suffering" ("'The Man That Was Used Up': Edgar Allan Poe and the Ends of Captivity," Nineteenth-Century Literature 57 [2002], 324). Also unacknowledged, of course, is the terrible suffering of many Native Americans.*

1 "Weep, eyes; melt into tears these cheeks to lave: / One half myself lays the other in the grave." This quotation comes from *Le Cid*, III.iii.7–8, by Pierre Corneille (1606–1684). That a motto from Corneille, the founder of classical French tragedy, serves as an epigraph to a darkly humorous tale is only the first of many ironies in the story.

2 Some readers see General Winfield Scott (1786–1866), the seasoned veteran known as "Old Fuss and Feathers" and the "Grand Old Man of the Army," as the inspiration for General Smith. Scott was injured in the Seminole and Creek Indian removal campaigns.

3 The word "perhaps" casts doubt on Smith's actual height. Six feet is the height of the archetypal hero. Poe's physical description of Smith looks forward to the opening sentence of Joseph Conrad's *Lord Jim* (1900), which also makes ironic use of the conventional height of a hero: "He was an inch, perhaps two, under six feet, powerfully built, and he advanced straight at you with a slight stoop of the shoulders, head forward, and a fixed from-under stare which made you think of a charging bull."

4 After the Revolutionary era, fashion-conscious men on both sides of the Atlantic discarded their powdered wigs in

favor of the more natural, classically inspired "Brutus" head-dress—closely cropped hair that was brushed forward onto the forehead. There is nothing at all natural about Smith's hair, as the reader will discover.

5 The peak of perfection. This is the first of several Latin or French phrases the pretentious narrator interjects.

6 The femur, or thigh bone.

7 A humorous typename for an Italian sculptor. In "Lionizing" (1835), Poe had used a similar name for a character who prides himself on his knowledge of painting: Signor Tintontintino.

8 A proverbial comparison that goes back to Shakespeare, *1 Henry IV*, II.iv.239–240, in which Falstaff says: "If reasons were as plentiful as blackberries, I would give no man a reason upon compulsion."

9 Etymologist N. Wanostrocht observes: "*Je ne sais quoi* is only said of things, and signifies an object which cannot precisely be named or defined" (*Grammar of the French Language with Practical Exercises* [Boston: Richardson, Lord, and Holbrook, 1831], 142).

10 Noticing a stiffness and rectangular precision in Smith's movements, the narrator attributes them to his military deportment, but there may be other reasons to explain the general's mechanical actions.

11 A person who takes pleasure in a fight, especially a firefight.

enthusiasm; it is not too much to say that they were the handsomest pair of whiskers under the sun. At all events, they encircled, and at times partially overshadowed, a mouth utterly unequalled. Here were the most entirely even, and the most brilliantly white of all conceivable teeth. From between them, upon every proper occasion, issued a voice of surpassing clearness, melody, and strength. In the matter of eyes, my acquaintance was preeminently endowed. Either one of such a pair was worth a couple of the ordinary ocular organs. They were of a deep hazel, exceedingly large and lustrous: and there was perceptible about them, ever and anon, just that amount of interesting obliquity which gives pregnancy to expression.

The bust of the General was unquestionably the finest bust I ever saw. For your life you could not have found a fault with its wonderful proportion. This rare peculiarity set off to great advantage a pair of shoulders which would have called up a blush of conscious inferiority into the countenance of the marble Apollo. I have a passion for fine shoulders, and may say that I never beheld them in perfection before. The arms altogether were admirably modelled. Nor were the lower limbs less superb. These were, indeed, the *ne plus ultra*[5] of good legs. Every connoisseur in such matters admitted the legs to be good. There was neither too much flesh, nor too little,—neither rudeness nor fragility. I could not imagine a more graceful curve than that of the *os femoris*,[6] and there was just that due gentle prominence in the rear of the *fibula* which goes to the conformation of a properly proportioned calf. I wish to God my young and talented friend Chiponchipino,[7] the sculptor, had but seen the legs of Brevet Brigadier General John A. B. C. Smith.

But although men so absolutely fine-looking are neither as plenty as reasons or blackberries,[8] still I could not bring myself to believe that *the remarkable* something to which I alluded just now—that the odd air of *je ne sais quoi*[9] which hung about my new acquaintance,—lay altogether, or indeed at all, in the supreme excellence of his bodily endowments. Perhaps it might be traced to the *manner;* yet here again I could not pretend to be positive. There *was* a primness, not to say stiffness, in his carriage—a degree of measured, and, if I may so express it, of rectangular precision,[10] attending his every movement, which, observed in a more diminutive figure, would have had the least little savor in the world

Gray and James, *Attack of the Seminoles on the Block House*, 1837. This hand-colored lithograph shows an attack by the Seminole Indians, possibly on a fort on the Withlacoochee River in December 1835.

of affectation, pomposity or constraint, but which noticed in a gentleman of his undoubted dimensions, was readily placed to the account of reserve, *hauteur,* of a commendable sense, in short, of what is due to the dignity of colossal proportion.

The kind friend who presented me to General Smith whispered in my ear some few words of comment upon the man. He was a *remarkable* man—a *very* remarkable man—indeed one of the *most* remarkable men of the age. He was an especial favorite, too, with the ladies—chiefly on account of his high reputation for courage.

"In *that* point he is unrivalled—indeed he is a perfect desperado—a downright fire-eater,[II] and no mistake," said my friend, here dropping his voice excessively low, and thrilling me with the mystery of his tone.

"A downright fire-eater, and no mistake. Showed *that*, I should say, to some purpose, in the late tremendous swamp-fight away

12   Poe refers to the ongoing Second Seminole War (1835–1842), fought between the U.S. Army and the Seminole Indians of Florida, following the refusal of many Seminoles to relocate west under the Indian Removal Act. The Second Seminole War was the longest and costliest of U.S.-Indian wars. Retreating to the Everglades and employing guerrilla tactics, the Seminoles protracted the war and inflicted heavy casualties on American soldiers and volunteers. The U.S. Army employed the Kickapoo as scouts during the conflict. Presumably Poe chose the word "bugaboo" because of its resemblance to the word "Kickapoo." A bugaboo or bugbear is an object of terror more imagined than real.

13   This and other, similar phrases—the age of mechanical invention, wonderful age for invention—are euphemisms for maiming, loss of limbs, and prosthetics. They are not dissimilar to current euphemisms—assets, clean bombing, collateral damage, friendly fire—phrases that obscure rather than illuminate meaning.

14   Man-traps and spring-guns are cruel and dangerous mechanical devices used to snare trespassers and poachers.

15   Constructed by English balloonist Charles Green (1785–1870), the Great Nassau balloon made numerous ascents, including its historic flight on November 7, 1836, from Vauxhall Gardens in London to Nassau, Germany, covering almost five hundred miles in eighteen hours: a record unsurpassed until 1907. One of the two men accompanying Green on the continental flight was balloonist Monck Mason, perhaps now as famous for a trip he never made as for any of his real exploits, thanks to Poe. On April 13, 1844, the New York *Sun* ran the story of Monck Mason's trip across the Atlantic in three days in a gas balloon. The story was a hoax perpetrated on the *Sun*'s readers by Poe. Timbuctoo or Timbuktu (a West African city in present-day Mali) symbolizes a place at the end of the earth: "from here to Timbuctoo." The "age of invention," Smith asserts, has obliterated the constraints of time and space, making it possible to travel anywhere in the world.

16   Developments in electromagnetism, the branch of physics that deals with the relationship between electricity and magnetism, would lead to the invention of the telegraph in Poe's day.

17   These are both proverbial comparisons. The phrase "springing up like mushrooms," commonplace in Poe's day, can still be heard today. The comparison with grasshoppers was more unusual. The traveler John Madox, for

down South, with the Bugaboo and Kickapoo Indians.[12] (Here my friend opened his eyes to some extent.) "Bless my soul!—blood and thunder, and all that!—*prodigies* of valor!—heard of him, of course?—you know he's the man—"

"Man alive, how *do* you do? why how *are* ye? *very* glad to see ye, indeed!" here interrupted the General himself, seizing my companion by the hand as he drew near, and bowing stiffly but profoundly, as I was presented. I then thought, (and I think so still,) that I never heard a clearer nor a stronger voice nor beheld a finer set of teeth: but I *must* say that I was sorry for the interruption just at that moment, as, owing to the whispers and insinuations aforesaid, my interest had been greatly excited in the hero of the Bugaboo and Kickapoo campaign.

However, the delightfully luminous conversation of Brevet Brigadier General John A. B. C. Smith soon completely dissipated this chagrin. My friend leaving us immediately, we had quite a long *tête-à-tête*, and I was not only pleased but *really*—instructed. I never heard a more fluent talker, or a man of greater general information. With becoming modesty, he forbore, nevertheless, to touch upon the theme I had just then most at heart—I mean the mysterious circumstances attending the Bugaboo war—and, on my own part, what I conceive to be a proper sense of delicacy forbade me to broach the subject; although, in truth, I was exceedingly tempted to do so. I perceived, too, that the gallant soldier preferred topics of philosophical interest, and that he delighted, especially, in commenting upon the rapid march of mechanical invention.[13] Indeed, lead him where I would, this was a point to which he invariably came back.

"There is nothing at all like it," he would say; "we are a wonderful people, and live in a wonderful age. Parachutes and railroads—man-traps and spring-guns![14] Our steam-boats are upon every sea, and the Nassau balloon packet is about to run regular trips (fare either way only twenty pounds sterling) between London and Timbuctoo.[15] And who shall calculate the immense influence upon social life—upon arts—upon commerce—upon literature—which will be the immediate result of the great principles of electro magnetics![16] Nor, is this all, let me assure you! There is really no end to the march of invention. The most wonderful—the most ingenious—and let me add, Mr.—Mr.—Thompson, I believe, is your name—let me add, I say, the most *useful*—the

This broadside print of 1838 advertises Charles Green's forthcoming ride in the balloon *Nassau*. It reads: "Royal Gardens, Vauxhall. Grand Day and Evening Fete, Next Tuesday, August 7, 1838. Ascent of the Nassau Balloon, Combined with the Evening Entertainments."

most truly *useful* mechanical contrivances, are daily springing up like mushrooms, if I may so express myself, or, more figuratively, like—ah—grasshoppers[17]—like grasshoppers, Mr. Thompson—about us and ah—ah—ah—around us!"

Thompson, to be sure, is not my name; but it is needless to say that I left General Smith with a heightened interest in the man, with an exalted opinion of his conversational powers, and a deep sense of the valuable privileges we enjoy in living in this age of mechanical invention. My curiosity, however, had not been altogether satisfied, and I resolved to prosecute immediate inquiry among my acquaintances touching the Brevet Brigadier General himself,[18] and particularly respecting the tremendous events *quorum pars magna fuit*,[19] during the Bugaboo and Kickapoo campaign.

The first opportunity which presented itself, and which *(horresco referens)*[20] I did not in the least scruple to seize, occurred at the

one, uses it: "In the land of the Philistines, I had seen the Arabs spring up like grasshoppers, where, at first, only two or three seemed visible, and I felt very sensibly that our situation was now dangerous" (*Excursions in the Holy Land, Egypt, Nubia, Syria, &c.*, 2 vols. [London: Richard Bentley, 1834], II, 364).

18 In his quest to learn more about Smith, the narrator calls to mind the reporter in *Citizen Kane* (1941) who approaches Charles Foster Kane's friends to learn more about the great man, only to be frustrated at every turn. Orson Welles was an admirer of Poe's writing.

19 "Of which things he was a great part." This quotation, which comes from the *Aeneid*, book II, line 6, occurs frequently in the contemporary literature. In *Essays of Elia* (1823), Charles Lamb, for example, refers to "some lucky dog of a reporter, who . . . sits down and reports what he had heard and seen, *(quorum pars magna fuit,)* for the *Morning Post* or the *Courier*."

20   "I shudder recalling it." This phrase also comes from the *Aeneid*, book II, line 204.

21   Poe's use of the word "drum" is a double entendre, suggesting "drummer," that is, a salesman who goes about drumming up customers, and "to drum," that is, to shape another's opinion through persistent repetition or admonition.

22   An inside joke: "The Psyche Zenobia" (1838), an earlier Poe tale, contains a backbiting, rumor-mongering character named Tabitha Turnip.

23   Job 14:1–2: "Man that is born of a woman is of few days, and full of trouble. He cometh forth like a flower, and is cut down: he fleeth also as a shadow, and continueth not."

24   The word "rantipole" can be a noun or an adjective. As an adjective, it means boisterous, crazy, disorderly, rakish, or wildly irrational or eccentric. Situating a performance of *Othello* in the Rantipole Theatre, Poe alludes to an episode in *Salmagundi* (1807–1808), the periodical written by Washington Irving in collaboration with Irving's brother William, and James Kirke Paulding: "As the house was crowded, we were complimented with seats in Box No. 2, a sad little rantipole place, which is the stronghold of a set of rare wags, and where the poor actors undergo the most merciless tortures of verbal criticism. The play was *Othello*, and, to speak my mind freely, I think I have seen it performed much worse in my time."

25   The word "cognoscenti" means people who are connoisseurs of the arts, but it can more generally mean everyone "in the know."

Church of the Reverend Doctor Drummummupp,[21] where I found myself established, one Sunday, just at sermon time, not only in the pew, but by the side, of that worthy and communicative little friend of mine, Miss Tabitha T.[22] Thus seated, I congratulated myself, and with much reason, upon the very flattering state of affairs. If any person knew anything about Brevet Brigadier General John A. B. C. Smith, that person, it was clear to me, was Miss Tabitha T. We telegraphed a few signals, and then commenced, *sotto voce*, a brisk *tête-à-tête*.

"Smith!" said she, in reply to my very earnest inquiry; "Smith!—why, not General John A. B. C.? Bless me, I thought you *knew* all about *him!* This is a wonderfully inventive age! Horrid affair that!—a bloody set of wretches, those Kickapoos!—fought like a hero—prodigies of valor—immortal renown. Smith!—Brevet Brigadier General John A. B. C.!—why, you know he's the man—"

"Man," here broke in Doctor Drummummupp, at the top of his voice, and with a thump that came near knocking the pulpit about our ears; "man that is born of a woman hath but a short time to live; he cometh up and is cut down like a flower!"[23] I started to the extremity of the pew, and perceived by the animated looks of the divine, that the wrath which had nearly proved fatal to the pulpit had been excited by the whispers of the lady and myself. There was no help for it; so I submitted with a good grace, and listened, in all the martyrdom of dignified silence, to the balance of that very capital discourse.

Next evening found me a somewhat late visitor at the Rantipole theatre,[24] where I felt sure of satisfying my curiosity at once, by merely stepping into the box of those exquisite specimens of affability and omniscience, the Misses Arabella and Miranda Cognoscenti.[25] That fine tragedian, Climax was doing Iago to a very crowded house, and I experienced some little difficulty in making my wishes understood; especially, as our box was next the slips, and completely overlooked the stage.

"Smith?" said Miss Arabella, as she at length comprehended the purport of my query; "Smith?—why, not General John A. B. C.?"

"Smith?" inquired Miranda, musingly. "God bless me, did you ever behold a finer figure?"

"Never, madam; but *do* tell me—"

"Or so inimitable grace?"

"Never, upon my word!—but pray inform me—"

"Or so just an appreciation of stage effect?"

"Madam!"

"Or a more delicate sense of the true beauties of Shakespeare? Be so good as to look at that leg!"

"The devil!" and I turned again to her sister.

"Smith?" said she, "why, not General John A. B. C.? Horrid affair that, wasn't it?—great wretches, those Bugaboos—savage and so on—but we live in a wonderfully inventive age!—Smith!—O yes! great man!—perfect desperado—immortal renown—prodigies of valor! *Never heard!* (This was given in a scream.) Bless my soul!—why, he's the man—"

> "———mandragora
> Nor all the drowsy syrups of the world
> Shall ever medicine thee to that sweet sleep
> Which thou ow'dst yesterday!"[26]

here roared out Climax just in my ear, and shaking his fist in my face all the time, in a way that I *couldn't* stand, and I *wouldn't*. I left the Misses Cognoscenti immediately, went behind the scenes forthwith, and gave the beggarly scoundrel such a thrashing as I trust he will remember to the day of his death.

At the *soirée* of the lovely widow, Mrs. Kathleen O'Trump,[27] I was confident that I should meet with no similar disappointment. Accordingly, I was no sooner seated at the card-table, with my pretty hostess for a *vis-à-vis*, than I propounded those questions the solution of which had become a matter so essential to my peace.

"Smith?" said my partner, "why, not General John A. B. C.? Horrid affair that, wasn't it?—diamonds, did you say?—terrible wretches, those Kickapoos!—we are playing *whist,* if you please, Mr. Tattle—however, this is the age of invention, most certainly—*the* age, one may say—*the* age *par excellence*—speak French?—oh, quite a hero—perfect desperado!—*no hearts,* Mr. Tattle? I don't believe it—immortal renown and all that—prodigies of valor! *Never heard!!*—why, bless me, he's the man———"

"Mann?—*Captain* Mann?"[28] here screamed some little feminine interloper from the farthest corner of the room. "Are you talking about Captain Mann and the duel?—oh, I *must* hear—do

26 *Othello,* III.iii.330–333.

27 The loquacious Kathleen O'Trump would make a poor whist player. According to Hoyle, "Whist is a well-known game at cards, which requires great attention and silence: hence the name" (*Hoyle's Improved Edition of the Rules for Playing Fashionable Games* [Philadelphia: Thomas Cowperthwait, 1838], 5).

28 Poe refers to Captain Daniel Mann, who was party to a fraud led by Thomas W. Dyott. Mann's trial began in March 1839 and continued through August, the month Poe published "The Man That Was Used Up." Throughout the period, the *Philadelphia Public Ledger* referred to the trial almost every day (Cornelia Varner, "Notes on Poe's Use of Contemporary Materials in Certain of His Stories," *Journal of English and German Philology* 32 [1933], 77).

29   A fashionable yet difficult dance step. Compare Poe's use of the phrase with another facetious reference to it in the song "Run, Neighbours, Run, All London Is Quadrilling It": "Dandies, turning *figurantes*, conceive they've made a clever hit; / And widows, weighing thirty stone, attempt to *pas de Zephyr* it" (*Universal Songster*, 3 vols. [London: Jones, 1834], I, 192).

30   Bas-Bleu, or "bluestocking," refers to a learned woman with literary interests or ambitions. In mid-eighteenth century England, the Blue Stocking Society evolved as a social movement and a women's literary discussion group. Gradually, the terms "bluestockings," "Blues," and "Bas-Bleus" gathered negative connotations. In *Don Juan*, canto XI, stanza L, Byron offers this unflattering portrait:

> The Blues, that tender tribe, who sigh o'er sonnets,
>   And with the pages of the last Review
> Line the interior of their heads or bonnets,
>   Advanced in all their azure's highest hue:
> They talked bad French or Spanish and upon its
>   Late authors ask'd him for a hint or two.
> And which was softest, Russian or Castilian?
> And whether in his travels he saw Ilion?

31   First performed in London in 1834, *Man-Fred: A Burlesque Ballet Opera in One Act* is Gilbert Abbott À Beckett's popular spoof of Byron's poetic drama *Manfred* (1817). In À Beckett's burlesque, Byron's heroic, yet tortured Count Manfred is transformed into a melancholy chimney sweep named "Man-Fred." Miss Bas-Bleu's friends may be thinking of À Beckett's play. The similarity between "Man-Fred" and "Man-Friday" introduces further confusion. Man Friday, of course, is the name of the native servant in *Robinson Crusoe*.

32   A British extrapolation of an African-American dialect, "sinivate" means insinuate. In *Jim Crow*, Tom Taylor's one-act burlesque, the title character resents the derogatory racial epithet Sambo has used to characterize him and questions, "Wot oo dare to sinivate?" (*Jim Crow: or, The Creole Ball* [1836; reprinted, London: J. Pattie, 1839], 15).

tell—go on, Mrs. O'Trump!—do now go on!" And go on Mrs. O'Trump did—all about a certain Captain Mann, who was either shot or hung, or should have been both shot and hung. Yes! Mrs. O'Trump, she went on, and I—I went off. There was no chance of hearing anything farther that evening in regard to Brevet Brigadier General John A. B. C. Smith.

Still I consoled myself with the reflection that the tide of ill luck would not run against me for ever, and so determined to make a bold push for information at the rout of that bewitching little angel, the graceful Mrs. Pirouette.

"Smith?" said Mrs. P., as we twirled about together in a *pas de zéphyr*,[29] "Smith?—why not General John A. B. C.? Dreadful business that of the Bugaboos, wasn't it?—terrible creatures, those Indians!—*do* turn out your toes! I really am ashamed of you—man of great courage, poor fellow!—but this is a wonderful age for invention—O dear me, I'm out of breath—quite a desperado—prodigies of valor—*never heard!!*—can't believe it—I shall have to sit down and enlighten you—Smith! why he's the man——"

"Man-*Fred*, I tell you!" here bawled out Miss Bas-Bleu,[30] as I led Mrs. Pirouette to a seat. "Did ever anybody hear the like? It's Man-*Fred*, I say, and not at all by any means Man-*Friday*."[31] Here Miss Bas-Bleu beckoned to me in a very peremptory manner; and I was obliged, will I nill I, to leave Mrs. P. for the purpose of deciding a dispute touching the title of a certain poetical drama of Lord Byron's. Although I pronounced, with great promptness, that the true title was Man-*Friday*, and not by any means Man-*Fred*, yet when I returned to seek Mrs. Pirouette she was not to be discovered, and I made my retreat from the house in a very bitter spirit of animosity against the whole race of the Bas-Bleus.

Matters had now assumed a really serious aspect, and I resolved to call at once upon my particular friend, Mr. Theodore Sinivate;[32] for I knew that here at least I should get something like definite information.

"Smith?" said he, in his well-known peculiar way of drawling out his syllables; "Smith?—why, not General John A. B. C.? Savage affair that with the Kickapo-o-o-os, was'nt it? Say! don't you think so?—perfect despera-a-ado—great pity, 'pon my honor!—wonderfully inventive age!—pro-o-odigies of valor! By the by, did you ever hear about Captain Ma-a-a-n?"

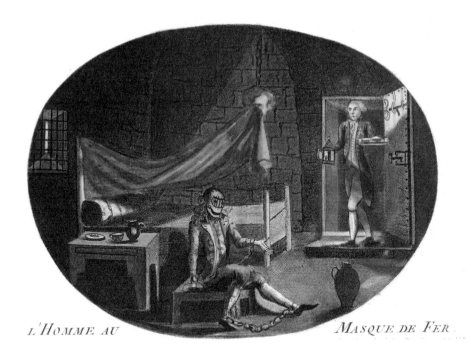

L'Homme au masque de fer
[The Man in the Iron Mask],
1789. This etching demon-
strates the relevance of Poe's
comparison of the French prisoner with General John
A. B. C. Smith. Whereas technology literally imprisons the
Man in the Iron Mask, it figuratively imprisons Smith, allowing him to function, but effectively dehumanizing him.
Technology thus shapes the
identity of both characters.

"Captain Mann be d——d!" said I, "please to go on with your story."

"Hem!—oh well!—quite *la même cho-o-ose*,[33] as we say in France. Smith, eh? Brigadier General John A—B—C.? I say—(here Mr. S. thought proper to put his finger to the side of his nose)—"I say, you don't mean to insinuate now, really and truly, and conscientiously, that you don't know all about that affair of Smith's, as well as I do, eh? Smith? John A—B—C.? Why, bless me, he's the ma-a-an——"

"*Mr.* Sinivate," said I, imploringly, "*is* he the man in the mask?"[34]

"No-o-o!" said he, looking wise, "nor the man in the mo-o-on."

This reply I considered a pointed and positive insult, and so left the house at once in high dudgeon,[35] with a firm resolve to call my friend, Mr. Sinivate, to a speedy account for his ungentlemanly conduct and ill-breeding.

In the meantime, however, I had no notion of being thwarted touching the information I desired. There was one resource left me yet. I would go to the fountain-head. I would call forthwith upon the General himself, and demand, in explicit terms, a solution of this abominable piece of mystery. Here, at least, there

33   The same thing.

34   Many contemporary storybooks perpetuated the story of the French prisoner known as the Man in the Iron Mask, who was held captive for thirty-four years during the reign of Louis XIV (1643–1715). It would receive its most famous treatment by Alexandre Dumas in 1847.

35   A strong feeling of anger or resentment.

36   A proverbial comparison. Byron, for one, had used it: "Milan has very handsome streets, a corso, and four or five thousand columns of granite; the people are a paradox; as concise as Tacitus in conversation; and, in writing, as they aim at using the finest Tuscan periods, as prolix as Cicero" (*The Life, Writings, Opinions, and Times of the Right Hon. George Gordon Noel Byron, Lord Byron*, 3 vols. [London: Matthew Iley, 1825], II, 385).

37   In Sir Walter Scott's novel *The Bride of Lammermoor* (1819), Captain Dalgetty descends a dark, narrow staircase, at the bottom of which he stumbles over "a bundle of something soft, which stirred and uttered a groan." Speaking in a "hollow and broken voice," the bundle calls itself "a wretched trunk, from which the boughs have one by one been lopped away." In the English translation of Victor Hugo's *Hunchback of Notre-Dame* (1834), a priest stumbles over "a bundle of something lying across the doorway," which turns out to be Quasimodo. Whatever Poe's literary sources, there appears to be so little left of Brevet Brigadier General John A. B. C. Smith that he has been reduced to a mere object, a *thing*.

38   Did Smith give his servant, Pompey, his name? In any case, Pompey is named after Gnaeus Pompeius Magnus (106–48 B.C), a Roman military officer. Pompey forged a political alliance with Julius Caesar, married his daughter, and later fought against him in a civil war for control of the Roman state.

39   A prosthetic cork-leg is "made of light wood usually *willow*," explains folk etymologist B. W. Green, "but never of *cork*" (*Word-Book of Virginia Folk-Speech* [Richmond: William Ellis Jones's Sons, 1912], 127).

40   Several of the tradesmen mentioned were real people working in Philadelphia during the years Poe lived there. Much as modern consumers buy designer clothing, expensive watches, and other personal accessories as status symbols, General Smith "accessorizes" with brand-name prosthetics, which make the man.

41   In Alain René Le Sage's *Le Diable Boiteaux* (1707), the Devil reveals to Cleofas what goes on behind closed doors. In one home, he spies two people retiring for the night, a superannuated coquette going to bed after removing her hair, eyebrows, and teeth and an amorous dotard who has removed a glass eye, false whiskers, and a peruke, or wig, and awaits a servant to remove his wooden arm and leg.

should be no chance for equivocation. I would be plain, positive, peremptory—as short as pie-crust—as concise as Tacitus or Montesquieu.[36]

It was early when I called, and the General was dressing; but I pleaded urgent business, and was shown at once into his bed-room by an old negro valet, who remained in attendance during my visit. As I entered the chamber, I looked about, of course, for the occupant, but did not immediately perceive him. There was a large and exceedingly odd-looking bundle of something which lay close by my feet on the floor, and, as I was not in the best humor in the world, I gave it a kick out of the way.[37]

"Hem! ahem! rather civil that, I should say!" said the bundle, in one of the smallest, and altogether the funniest little voices, between a squeak and a whistle, that I ever heard in all the days of my existence.

"Ahem! rather civil that, I should observe."

I fairly shouted with terror, and made off, at a tangent, into the farthest extremity of the room.

"God bless me! my dear fellow," here again whistled the bundle, "what—what—what—why, what *is* the matter? I really believe you don't know me at all."

What *could* I say to all this—what *could* I? I staggered into an arm-chair, and, with staring eyes and open mouth, awaited the solution of the wonder.

"Strange you shouldn't know me though, isn't it?" presently re-squeaked the nondescript, which I now perceived was performing, upon the floor, some inexplicable evolution, very analogous to the drawing on of a stocking. There was only a single leg, however, apparent.

"Strange you shouldn't know me, though, isn't it? Pompey,[38] bring me that leg!" Here Pompey handed the bundle a very capital cork leg,[39] ready dressed, which it screwed on in a trice; and then it stood up before my eyes.

"And a bloody action it *was*," continued the thing, as if in a soliloquy; "but then one musn't fight with the Bugaboos and Kickapoos, and think of coming off with a mere scratch. Pompey, I'll thank you now for that arm. Thomas" (turning to me) "is decidedly the best hand at a cork leg; but if you should ever want an arm, my dear fellow, you must really let me recommend you to Bishop."[40] Here Pompey screwed on an arm.[41]

"We had rather hot work of it, that you may say. Now, you dog, slip on my shoulders and bosom! Pettitt makes the best shoulders, but for a bosom you will have to go to Ducrow."[42]

"Bosom!" said I.

"Pompey, will you *never* be ready with that wig? Scalping is a rough process after all; but then you can procure such a capital scratch at De L'Orme's."

"Scratch!"

"Now, you nigger, my teeth! For a *good* set of these you had better go to Parmly's at once; high prices, but excellent work. I swallowed some very capital articles, though, when the big Bugaboo rammed me down with the butt end of his rifle."

"Butt end! ram down!! my eye!!"

"O yes, by-the-by, my eye—here, Pompey, you scamp, screw it in! Those Kickapoos are not so very slow at a gouge; but he's a belied man, that Dr. Williams, after all; you can't imagine how well I see with the eyes of his make."[43]

I now began very clearly to perceive that the object before me was nothing more nor less than my new acquaintance, Brevet Brigadier General John A. B. C. Smith. The manipulations of Pompey had made, I must confess, a very striking difference in the appearance of the personal man. The voice, however, still puzzled me no little; but even this apparent mystery was speedily cleared up.

"Pompey, you black rascal," squeaked the General, "I really do believe you would let me go out without my palate."

Hereupon the negro, grumbling out an apology, went up to his master, opened his mouth with the knowing air of a horse-jockey, and adjusted therein a somewhat singular-looking machine, in a very dexterous manner, that I could not altogether comprehend. The alteration, however, in the entire expression of the General's countenance was instantaneous and surprising. When he again spoke, his voice had resumed all that rich melody and strength which I had noticed upon our original introduction.

"D——n the vagabonds!" said he, in so clear a tone that I positively started at the change, "D——n the vagabonds! they not only knocked in the roof of my mouth, but took the trouble to cut off at least seven-eighths of my tongue. There isn't Bonfanti's[44] equal, however, in America, for really good articles of this description. I can recommend you to him with confidence, (here the General

42 Andrew Ducrow (1793–1842) was a famous equestrian performer.

43 Oculist Dr. John Williams was subjected to much contemporary ridicule. His dubious cures helped to make his fortune. In "Enigmatical and Conundrumical," a collection of conundrums written for *Alexander's Weekly Messenger* (December 18, 1839), Poe referred to Williams: "Why is Dr. Williams' cash, the oculist, like a divorced wife's pension? Because it's all eye-money.—*alimony.*"

44 Joseph Bonfanti, a New York retailer, sold talking dolls, among many other knick-knacks and gew-gaws.

Peter Weller as the title character of the original *Robocop* movie (1987). Weller, a police officer brutally murdered by gang members in a futuristic Detroit, returns as a crime-fighting cyborg. He is a postmodern example of a man who has been used up.

45   The phrase "used up" means "killed," according to *Grose's Classical Dictionary of the Vulgar Tongue* (1823), which traces the derivation to General John Guise. On the expedition to Cartagena, Guise asked for "some more grenadiers, for those he had were all *used up*." General Smith prefigures fictional characters of more recent vintage: "The General was 'used up' in his campaigns, like the postmodern Robocop or Six Million Dollar Man, consumed by the state, and technologically recuperated" (Tim Armstrong, *Modernism, Technology, and the Body: A Cultural Study* [New York: Cambridge University Press, 1998], 92).

bowed,) and assure you that I have the greatest pleasure in so doing."

I acknowledged his kindness in my best manner, and took leave of him at once, with a perfect understanding of the true state of affairs—with a full comprehension of the mystery which had troubled me so long. It was evident. It was a clear case. Brevet Brigadier General John A. B. C. Smith was the man——was *the man that was used up.*[45]

The Fall of the House of Usher

Son coeur est un luth suspendu;
Sitôt qu'on le touche il résonne.

De Béranger[1]

During the whole of a dull, dark, and soundless day in the autumn of the year, when the clouds hung oppressively low in the heavens, I had been passing alone, on horseback,[2] through a singularly dreary tract of country; and at length found myself, as the shades of the evening drew on, within view of the melancholy House of Usher.[3] I know not how it was—but, with the first glimpse of the building, a sense of insufferable gloom pervaded my spirit. I say insufferable; for the feeling was unrelieved by any of that half-pleasurable, because poetic, sentiment, with which the mind usually receives even the sternest natural images of the desolate or terrible. I looked upon the scene before me—upon the mere house, and the simple landscape features of the domain—upon the bleak walls—upon the vacant eye-like windows[4]—upon a few rank sedges[5]—and upon a few white trunks of decayed trees—with an utter depression of soul which I can compare to no earthly sensation more properly than to the after-dream of the reveller upon opium[6]—the bitter lapse into every-day life—the hideous dropping off of the veil. There was an iciness, a sinking, a sickening of the heart—an unredeemed dreariness of thought which no goading of the imagination could torture into aught of the sublime.[7] What was it—I paused to think—what was it that so unnerved me in the contemplation of the House of Usher? It was a mystery all insoluble;[8] nor could I grapple with the shadowy fancies that crowded upon me as I pondered. I was forced to fall back upon the unsatisfactory conclusion, that while, beyond doubt, there *are* combinations of very simple natural objects which have the power of thus affecting us, still the analysis of this power lies

One of Poe's most memorable tales of terror, "The Fall of the House of Usher" first appeared in the September 1839 issue of Burton's Gentleman's Magazine. "Usher" greatly impressed contemporary readers, even if it did unsettle them. Reading Poe's tale in the September issue of Burton's, the reviewer for the Washington Globe (September 16, 1839) admitted, "To one of weak nerves—writing, as I am, at midnight—his ghostly figures assume a bodily form and fashion, which incline me to pass on as rapidly as possible to some more pleasing contemplation." James Russell Lowell commented, "Had its author written nothing else it would alone have been enough to stamp him as a man of genius, and the master of a classic style" (I. M. Walker, Edgar Allan Poe: The Critical Heritage [New York: Routledge and Kegan Paul, 1986], 165). The gothic moment of the late eighteenth century that produced Horace Walpole's The Castle of Otranto (1764), Ann Radcliffe's The Mysteries of Udolpho (1794), and Matthew Lewis's The Monk (1796) had come and gone. Two decades before Poe wrote "Usher," Jane Austen had parodied already outworn conventions of gothic fiction in Northanger Abbey (1818). Poe was arriving even later to the party, but, unlike Austen, he saw new possibilities in the genre and sought to reinvent it. In "Usher," he took the gothic clichés—an ancestral mansion, a bleak landscape, a mysterious family background, subterranean passageways and supernatural occurrences, even a dark and stormy night—and combined them in new ways to create an original masterpiece.

What, exactly, Poe was doing with the gothic form has become an issue of considerable interest to scholars. Some critics believe that "Usher" is about the way its author uses gothic conventions to call into question the act of reading or interpretation. Others have recognized how Poe imbued aspects of the gothic world with psychological insight to explore the depths of the mind and the darkness of the soul. H. P. Lovecraft, Richard Wilbur, and Daniel Hoffman have seen the characters, motifs, and setting of "Usher" as external manifestations of internal impulses. From this viewpoint, the narrator represents the conscious mind and Roderick Usher, his sister Madeline, and the house itself symbolize the subconscious. Wilbur suggests that the narrator's visit to the House of Usher resembles a person entering a hypnagogic state, that transitional realm between wakefulness and sleep that leads to the world of dreams.

Poe deliberately refrains from providing a specific geographical setting for his story. Roger Corman set House of Usher (1960)—a low-budget feature film starring Vincent Price as Roderick—in New England, somewhere outside of Boston, but Poe is not so specific. Usher is an Anglo-Norman name, so the fen-filled regions of the Brontës' England form one possible setting, but Poe leaves it to his readers to imagine where the story occurs. Does it much matter? The story's true setting, most would agree, is the shadowy landscape of the mind.

1   "His heart is a hanging lute; / As soon as it is touched, it responds." When Poe revised the story for *Tales* (1845), he added this motto from French poet and songwriter Pierre-Jean de Béranger (1780–1857), slightly modifying the original text.

2   This opening image of the lone figure on horseback echoes a recurrent motif in the fiction of prolific British novelist G. P. R. James (1799–1860), who wrote numerous biographies, histories, and novels, including *Richelieu* (1829) and *Life of Edward, The Black Prince* (1836). He used the motif so often in his fiction that he became known as "Solitary Horseman" James.

3   The name "Usher" has a biographical antecedent. The accomplished husband-and-wife acting team of Noble Luke Usher and Harriet L'Estrange Usher were friends and fellow members of the same acting company as Poe's parents. As Mabbott notes, it is impossible to say to what extent Poe modeled his characters on the Ushers (likely, not much).

4   The anthropomorphic House of Usher is a forerunner of other big, scary gothic mansions in American literature that might also qualify as characters in their own right, from the ancestral Pyncheon house in Nathaniel Hawthorne's *The House of the Seven Gables* (1851) to Hill House in Shirley Jackson's *The Haunting of Hill House* (1959) and the Overlook Hotel in Stephen King's *The Shining* (1977). American directors have created a whole subgenre of horror films that feature malevolent houses, including memorable adaptations of all of the above.

5   When used to describe plant matter, the adjective "rank" usually has negative connotations, meaning to grow too rampantly. The term "sedge" refers to various coarse, rushlike plants that thrive in wet places.

6   Though there is no evidence that Poe was ever an opium user, his portrayal of the deep depression that follows an ecstatic high suggests that he understood the way the drug worked. He did know all too well the painful hangovers that come after drinking binges, hangovers filled with regret, remorse, and profound self-loathing.

7   Edmund Burke in his *Philosophical Enquiry into the Origin of Our Ideas of the Sublime and Beautiful* (1757) defines the sublime as "a sort of delightful horror" that sets in "when without danger we are conversant with terrible objects." In other words, it is a kind of literary or aesthetic pleasure: spine-tingling awe filled with dread and terror. The sublime was understood in contrast to two rival modes, the beautiful and the picturesque. What Poe's narrator, clearly a literary man, says here is that the aspect of the House of Usher is far too grim to be pleasurable or sublime.

8   Commonplace in his day, the phrase "insoluble mystery" had special resonance for Poe: he prided himself in his ability to solve mysteries that others considered insoluble. The year after the appearance of "Usher," he challenged readers of *Alexander's* to submit cryptograms for him to solve. Though the narrator characterizes the disturbing impression of the Usher mansion as an insoluble mystery, he still tries to solve it.

9   A tarn is a small mountain lake with no significant tributaries. Compare Sir Walter Scott, *The Bridal of Triermain* (1813), canto I, stanza 10, lines 10–13:

> Though never sun-beam could discern
> The surface of that sable tarn,
> In whose black mirror you may spy
> The stars, while noon-tide lights the sky.

10   The reflection of the house within the tarn is the first of many instances of mirroring that occur in the story: Usher's face resembles the façade of the House, which is mirrored in the tarn; Usher's song, "The Haunted Palace," describes a house that symbolizes Usher's head; and Madeline Usher and her brother seem remarkably similar. Note, for example, the pains Poe takes to connect Roderick's face and the "aspect" of the house—its unhealthy complexion, "vacant, eyelike windows," and "the fine tangled webwork" of fungi that hangs from its eaves. See Renata R. Mautner Wasserman, "The Self, the Mirror, the Other: 'The Fall of the House of Usher,'" *Poe Studies* 10 (1977), 33–35.

11   In Poe's only novel, *The Narrative of Arthur Gordon Pym* (1838), Pym describes the close relationship that he and his friend Augustus share: "I used frequently to go home with him, and remain all day, and sometimes all night. We occupied the same bed, and he would be sure to keep me awake until almost light, telling me stories of the natives of the Island of Tinian, and other places he had visited in his travels."

12   In the first published version of this tale, Poe used the phrase "pitiable mental idiosyncrasy" in place of "mental disorder." His later revision eliminates the awkward repetition of the *l*-sound at the end of the first two words of the original phrase. But the earlier version provides insight into the nature of Roderick Usher's malady. In the early nineteenth century, "mental idiosyncrasy" was a medico-scientific diagnosis often applied to poets. A contemporary medical writer comments: "The maladies of the body in patients so spiritual and intellectual as Goethe and Byron, are always more or less different, or are at least modified, from their ordinary features; for they seem to receive, so to speak, a colouring or hue from the character of the being in whom they occur. There is what may be called a 'mental

among considerations beyond our depth. It was possible, I re-flected, that a mere different arrangement of the particulars of the scene, of the details of the picture, would be sufficient to modify, or perhaps to annihilate its capacity for sorrowful impression; and, acting upon this idea, I reined my horse to the precipitous brink of a black and lurid tarn[9] that lay in unruffled lustre by the dwelling, and gazed down—but with a shudder even more thrilling than be-fore—upon the remodelled and inverted images of the gray sedge, and the ghastly tree-stems, and the vacant and eye-like windows.[10]

Nevertheless, in this mansion of gloom I now proposed to my-self a sojourn of some weeks. Its proprietor, Roderick Usher, had been one of my boon companions in boyhood; but many years had elapsed since our last meeting.[11] A letter, however, had lately reached me in a distant part of the country—a letter from him—which, in its wildly importunate nature, had admitted of no other than a personal reply. The manuscript gave evidence of nervous agitation. The writer spoke of acute bodily illness—of a mental disorder[12] which oppressed him—and of an earnest desire to see me, as his best, and indeed his only personal friend, with a view of attempting, by the cheerfulness of my society, some alleviation of his malady. It was the manner in which all this, and much more, was said—it was the apparent *heart* that went with his request—which allowed me no room for hesitation; and I accordingly obeyed forthwith what I still considered a very singular summons.

Although, as boys, we had been even intimate associates, yet I really knew little of my friend. His reserve had been always exces-sive and habitual. I was aware, however, that his very ancient fam-ily had been noted, time out of mind, for a peculiar sensibility of temperament, displaying itself, through long ages, in many works of exalted art, and manifested, of late, in repeated deeds of munifi-cent yet unobtrusive charity, as well as in a passionate devotion to the intricacies, perhaps even more than to the orthodox and eas-ily recognisable beauties, of musical science. I had learned, too, the very remarkable fact, that the stem of the Usher race, all time-honored as it was, had put forth, at no period, any enduring branch; in other words, that the entire family lay in the direct line of descent, and had always, with very trifling and very temporary variation, so lain. It was this deficiency, I considered, while run-ning over in thought the perfect keeping of the character of the premises with the accredited character of the people, and while

temperament' or 'mental idiosyncrasy,' just as there is a sanguineous temperament, or a lymphatic temperament, and so forth" ("History of the Last Illness of Goethe," *Medico-Chirurgical Review* 20 [1834], 499).

13 The house and family merge in the appellation the "House of Usher" not only in the minds of the peasantry but also in the reader's mind. The story's title *plays* on this ambiguity between family and mansion, since both "fall" together. Hawthorne's *The House of the Seven Gables* provides an interesting parallel: Hepzibah, a descendent of Colonel Pyncheon, has lived in the house so long and is so bewildered with its chimney-corner traditions that "her very brain was impregnated with the dry-rot of its timbers."

14 Poe formulates a psychological problem: getting in touch with one's feelings is not always a great thing. In other words, being conscious of anxiety, paranoia, or fear can increase these feelings.

15 With the dead trees and dark tarn surrounding it, the house exudes an evil and ominous atmosphere. Planning his cinematic adaptation of "Usher," Roger Corman pitched the project as a horror film. Doubtful whether the story suited the horror genre, his producer asked him where the monster was. Corman exclaimed, "The house is the monster!"

16 Discussing the fungi-covered house, Angela Carter observed, "It must look as if it had been born in a caul." Her comparison reinforces the story's supernatural associations: according to tradition, babies born in a caul have the power of second sight. To more literal-minded readers, the fungi still seem scary. Identifying the types of fungi that afflict the House of Usher, Nicholas P. Money confirms the damage they could do to wood: "*Meruliporia* and *Serpula* can turn the interior of a plank into dust before anything more than bubbling of paintwork is visible. Once the cellulose is extracted by the fungus, a screwdriver can be pushed through a 2x4 without any resistance" (Angela Carter, *Shaking a Leg: Collected Writings* [New York: Penguin, 1998], 484; Nicholas P. Money, *Carpet Monsters and Killer Spores: A Natural History of Toxic Mold* [New York: Oxford University Press, 2004], 141).

speculating upon the possible influence which the one, in the long lapse of centuries, might have exercised upon the other—it was this deficiency, perhaps, of collateral issue, and the consequent undeviating transmission, from sire to son, of the patrimony with the name, which had, at length, so identified the two as to merge the original title of the estate in the quaint and equivocal appellation of the "House of Usher"—an appellation which seemed to include, in the minds of the peasantry who used it, both the family and the family mansion.[13]

I have said that the sole effect of my somewhat childish experiment—that of looking down within the tarn—had been to deepen the first singular impression. There can be no doubt that the consciousness of the rapid increase of my superstition—for why should I not so term it?—served mainly to accelerate the increase itself. Such, I have long known, is the paradoxical law of all sentiments having terror as a basis.[14] And it might have been for this reason only, that, when I again uplifted my eyes to the house itself, from its image in the pool, there grew in my mind a strange fancy—a fancy so ridiculous, indeed, that I but mention it to show the vivid force of the sensations which oppressed me. I had so worked upon my imagination as really to believe that about the whole mansion and domain there hung an atmosphere peculiar to themselves and their immediate vicinity—an atmosphere which had no affinity with the air of heaven, but which had reeked up from the decayed trees, and the gray wall, and the silent tarn—a pestilent and mystic vapor, dull, sluggish, faintly discernible, and leaden-hued.[15]

Shaking off from my spirit what *must* have been a dream, I scanned more narrowly the real aspect of the building. Its principal feature seemed to be that of an excessive antiquity. The discoloration of ages had been great. Minute fungi overspread the whole exterior, hanging in a fine tangled web-work from the eaves.[16] Yet all this was apart from any extraordinary dilapidation. No portion of the masonry had fallen; and there appeared to be a wild inconsistency between its still perfect adaptation of parts, and the crumbling condition of the individual stones. In this there was much that reminded me of the specious totality of old wood-work which has rotted for long years in some neglected vault, with no disturbance from the breath of the external air. Beyond this indication of extensive decay, however, the fabric gave little token of instability.

Perhaps the eye of a scrutinizing observer might have discovered a barely perceptible fissure, which, extending from the roof of the building in front, made its way down the wall in a zigzag direction, until it became lost in the sullen waters of the tarn.[17]

Noticing these things, I rode over a short causeway to the house.[18] A servant in waiting took my horse, and I entered the Gothic archway of the hall. A valet, of stealthy step, thence conducted me, in silence, through many dark and intricate passages in my progress to the *studio* of his master. Much that I encountered on the way contributed, I know not how, to heighten the vague sentiments of which I have already spoken. While the objects around me—while the carvings of the ceilings, the sombre tapestries of the walls, the ebon blackness of the floors, and the phantasmagoric armorial trophies which rattled as I strode, were but matters to which, or to such as which, I had been accustomed from my infancy[19]—while I hesitated not to acknowledge how familiar was all this—I still wondered to find how unfamiliar were the fancies which ordinary images were stirring up. On one of the staircases, I met the physician of the family. His countenance, I thought, wore a mingled expression of low cunning and perplexity. He accosted me with trepidation and passed on. The valet now threw open a door and ushered me into the presence of his master.[20]

The room in which I found myself was very large and lofty. The windows were long, narrow, and pointed, and at so vast a distance from the black oaken floor as to be altogether inaccessible from within. Feeble gleams of encrimsoned light made their way through the trellissed panes, and served to render sufficiently distinct the more prominent objects around; the eye, however, struggled in vain to reach the remoter angles of the chamber, or the recesses of the vaulted and fretted ceiling. Dark draperies hung upon the walls. The general furniture was profuse, comfortless, antique, and tattered. Many books and musical instruments lay scattered about, but failed to give any vitality to the scene. I felt that I breathed an atmosphere of sorrow. An air of stern, deep, and irredeemable gloom hung over and pervaded all.

Upon my entrance, Usher arose from a sofa on which he had been lying at full length, and greeted me with a vivacious warmth which had much in it, I at first thought, of an overdone cordiality—of the constrained effort of the *ennuyé* man of the world.[21] A

17 Many readers note the corollary between this barely perceptible but nonetheless worrisome fissure and Roderick's broken, increasingly unstable mind. They are a source of considerable tension in the story.

18 The causeway spanning the mysterious tarn emphasizes the tale's mythological or fablelike dimensions and suggests the traditional passage to the underworld. Many belief systems in the East contend that the souls of the dead must pass over a perilous causeway before they reach their final resting place.

19 The narrator's longstanding familiarity with such trappings suggests that he, too, is an aristocrat.

20 With every step taken inside the House of Usher, the reader is reminded that it is a haunted House of Fiction whose architect is Edgar Allan Poe: "Even as we're getting 'lost' in the House of *Usher*, the self-referential devices—elaborate sentence structures, texts within the text, relentless use of doubling and reflection—keep pushing us back outside the story, reminding us that *Poe* is the real master of the house" (Scott Peeples, "Poe's 'Constructiveness' and 'The Fall of the House of Usher,'" *The Cambridge Companion to Edgar Allan Poe*, ed. Kevin J. Hayes [New York: Cambridge University Press, 2002], 186).

21 The *ennuyé* is someone troubled by *ennui* or boredom. Elsewhere, Poe commented, "The ennuyé who travels in the hope of dissipating his ennui by the perpetual succession of novelties, will invariably be disappointed in the end. He receives the impression of novelty so continuously that it is at length no novelty to receive it" ("Anastatic Printing," *Broadway Journal* 1 [April 12, 1845], 230).

22 In Poe's day, self-proclaimed phrenologists traveled the nation, charging fees for phrenological diagnoses, which involved feeling the contours of the skull to provide a "scientific" picture of the client's innate character. Franz-Joseph Gall and Johann Gaspar Spurzheim, the leading founders of phrenology, mapped the skull, dividing it into different regions or organs, each representing a personal characteristic. Creativity and aesthetic appreciation, for example, were represented by the organ of ideality, located on the upper forehead. The term "ideality" entered Poe's critical vocabulary through the medium of phrenology, and the concept influenced his aesthetic theory. In the phrenological sense, a true idealist was, in Poe's words, "sensitively alive to beauty in every development" (*Essays and Reviews*, ed. G. R. Thompson [New York: Library of America, 1984], 1208). According to phrenology, great poets, being attuned to the beautiful, should naturally have giant foreheads. Like Roderick Usher, Poe himself possessed a large forehead. When he sat for daguerreotypes, Poe deliberately posed in such a way as to emphasize his prominent forehead (Kevin J. Hayes, "Poe, the Daguerreotype, and the Autobiographical Act," *Biography* 25 [2002], 477–492).

23 The term "Arabesque" and its bedfellow "grotesque" referred to styles of decorative art, much discussed and debated in journals and encyclopedias in Poe's day. The title Poe coined for his first published collection of short fiction, *Tales of the Grotesque and Arabesque*, draws upon the currency of these terms. Here, however, Poe uses "Arabesque" to mean simply "strangely mixed, fantastic" (*OED*).

glance, however, at his countenance, convinced me of his perfect sincerity. We sat down; and for some moments, while he spoke not, I gazed upon him with a feeling half of pity, half of awe. Surely, man had never before so terribly altered, in so brief a period, as had Roderick Usher! It was with difficulty that I could bring myself to admit the identity of the wan being before me with the companion of my early boyhood. Yet the character of his face had been at all times remarkable. A cadaverousness of complexion; an eye large, liquid, and luminous beyond comparison; lips somewhat thin and very pallid, but of a surpassingly beautiful curve; a nose of a delicate Hebrew model, but with a breadth of nostril unusual in similar formations; a finely moulded chin, speaking, in its want of prominence, of a want of moral energy; hair of a more than web-like softness and tenuity; these features, with an inordinate expansion above the regions of the temple, made up altogether a countenance not easily to be forgotten.[22] And now in the mere exaggeration of the prevailing character of these features, and of the expression they were wont to convey, lay so much of change that I doubted to whom I spoke. The now ghastly pallor of the skin, and the now miraculous lustre of the eye, above all things startled and even awed me. The silken hair, too, had been suffered to grow all unheeded, and as, in its wild gossamer texture, it floated rather than fell about the face, I could not, even with effort, connect its Arabesque expression[23] with any idea of simple humanity.

In the manner of my friend I was at once struck with an incoherence—an inconsistency; and I soon found this to arise from a series of feeble and futile struggles to overcome an habitual trepidancy—an excessive nervous agitation. For something of this nature I had indeed been prepared, no less by his letter, than by reminiscences of certain boyish traits, and by conclusions deduced from his peculiar physical conformation and temperament. His action was alternately vivacious and sullen. His voice varied rapidly from a tremulous indecision (when the animal spirits seemed utterly in abeyance) to that species of energetic concision—that abrupt, weighty, unhurried, and hollow-sounding enunciation—that leaden, self-balanced and perfectly modulated guttural utterance, which may be observed in the lost drunkard, or the irreclaimable eater of opium, during the periods of his most intense excitement.

It was thus that he spoke of the object of my visit, of his ear-

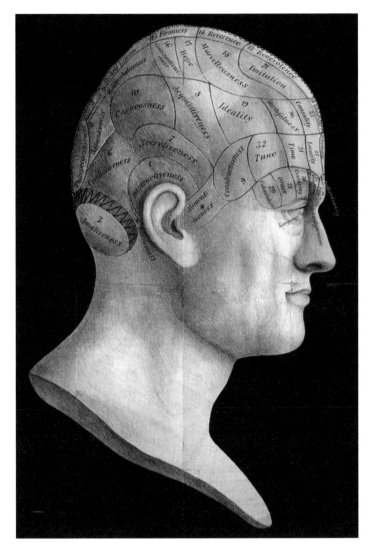

William S. Pendleton, *Dr. Spurzheim: Divisions of the Organs of Phrenology Marked Externally*, 1834.

nest desire to see me, and of the solace he expected me to afford him. He entered, at some length, into what he conceived to be the nature of his malady. It was, he said, a constitutional and a family evil, and one for which he despaired to find a remedy—a mere nervous affection, he immediately added, which would un-doubtedly soon pass. It displayed itself in a host of unnatural sen-sations. Some of these, as he detailed them, interested and be-wildered me; although, perhaps, the terms, and the general manner of the narration had their weight. He suffered much from a mor-bid acuteness of the senses; the most insipid food was alone endur-

24 Whereas Usher's alternating moods of vivacity and sullenness may suggest that he suffers from what is now called bipolar disorder, his other symptoms—sensitivity to light, smell, sound, taste, and texture, in addition to his sleeping disorder, crippling anxiety, and minimal social interaction—meet today's diagnostic criteria for the developmental disorder known as autism.

25 At this point in the first published version of "Usher," Poe clarified the reason for the narrator's astonishment and dread: "Her figure, her air, her features—all, in their very minutest development were those—were identically (I can use no other sufficient term) were identically those of the Roderick Usher who sat beside me" (Thomas Ollive Mabbott, ed., *Collected Works of Edgar Allan Poe*, 3 vols. [Cambridge, MA: The Belknap Press of Harvard University Press, 1969-1978], II, 404).

The omission of this sentence delays the narrator's recognition of the physical similarities between Roderick and Madeline until much later, thus increasing his (and our) shock.

able; he could wear only garments of certain texture; the odors of all flowers were oppressive; his eyes were tortured by even a faint light; and there were but peculiar sounds, and these from stringed instruments, which did not inspire him with horror.[24]

To an anomalous species of terror I found him a bounden slave. "I shall perish," said he, "I *must* perish in this deplorable folly. Thus, thus, and not otherwise, shall I be lost. I dread the events of the future, not in themselves, but in their results. I shudder at the thought of any, even the most trivial, incident, which may operate upon this intolerable agitation of soul. I have, indeed, no abhorrence of danger, except in its absolute effect—in terror. In this unnerved—in this pitiable condition—I feel that the period will sooner or later arrive when I must abandon life and reason together, in some struggle with the grim phantasm, FEAR."

I learned, moreover, at intervals, and through broken and equivocal hints, another singular feature of his mental condition. He was enchained by certain superstitious impressions in regard to the dwelling which he tenanted, and whence, for many years, he had never ventured forth—in regard to an influence whose suppositious force was conveyed in terms too shadowy here to be restated—an influence which some peculiarities in the mere form and substance of his family mansion, had, by dint of long sufferance, he said, obtained over his spirit—an effect which the *physique* of the gray walls and turrets, and of the dim tarn into which they all looked down, had, at length, brought about upon the *morale* of his existence.

He admitted, however, although with hesitation, that much of the peculiar gloom which thus afflicted him could be traced to a more natural and far more palpable origin—to the severe and long-continued illness—indeed to the evidently approaching dissolution—of a tenderly beloved sister—his sole companion for long years—his last and only relative on earth. "Her decease," he said, with a bitterness which I can never forget, "would leave him (him the hopeless and the frail) the last of the ancient race of the Ushers." While he spoke, the lady Madeline (for so was she called) passed slowly through a remote portion of the apartment, and, without having noticed my presence, disappeared. I regarded her with an utter astonishment not unmingled with dread—and yet I found it impossible to account for such feelings.[25] A sensation of stupor oppressed me, as my eyes followed her retreating steps.

When a door, at length, closed upon her, my glance sought instinctively and eagerly the countenance of the brother—but he
had buried his face in his hands, and I could only perceive that a
far more than ordinary wanness had overspread the emaciated fingers through which trickled many passionate tears.

The disease of the lady Madeline had long baffled the skill of
her physicians. A settled apathy, a gradual wasting away of the
person, and frequent although transient affections of a partially
cataleptical character, were the unusual diagnosis.[26] Hitherto she
had steadily borne up against the pressure of her malady, and had
not betaken herself finally to bed; but, on the closing in of the evening of my arrival at the house, she succumbed (as her brother
told me at night with inexpressible agitation) to the prostrating
power of the destroyer; and I learned that the glimpse I had obtained of her person would thus probably be the last I should obtain—that the lady, at least while living, would be seen by me no
more.

For several days ensuing, her name was unmentioned by either
Usher or myself: and during this period I was busied in earnest endeavors to alleviate the melancholy of my friend. We painted and
read together; or I listened, as if in a dream, to the wild improvisations of his speaking guitar. And thus, as a closer and still closer
intimacy admitted me more unreservedly into the recesses of his
spirit, the more bitterly did I perceive the futility of all attempt at
cheering a mind from which darkness, as if an inherent positive
quality, poured forth upon all objects of the moral and physical
universe, in one unceasing radiation of gloom.

I shall ever bear about me a memory of the many solemn hours
I thus spent alone with the master of the House of Usher. Yet I
should fail in any attempt to convey an idea of the exact character
of the studies, or of the occupations, in which he involved me, or
led me the way. An excited and highly distempered ideality threw
a sulphureous lustre over all. His long improvised dirges will ring
forever in my ears. Among other things, I hold painfully in mind a
certain singular perversion and amplification of the wild air of the
last waltz of Von Weber.[27] From the paintings over which his elaborate fancy brooded, and which grew, touch by touch, into vague-
nesses at which I shuddered the more thrillingly, because I shuddered knowing not why;—from these paintings (vivid as their
images now are before me) I would in vain endeavor to educe[28]

26 Catalepsy, according to *Encyclopaedia Americana* (1830), is "a universal spasmodic disease of the organs of locomotion. The body remains in the position in which it may have been when attacked with the fit, and the limbs preserve any situation in which they may be placed. The senses are obliterated, and the mind totally inactive, noth-ing being able to rouse the patient. . . . This disease is an obstinate one, and is very liable to recur, even when the patient seems in the least respect liable to a recur-rence." Madeline Usher's catalepsy is severe yet transient. Poe would find catalepsy a convenient plot device again in "The Premature Burial," in which the story's narrator re-covers from the condition—but only after he awakens in the dark, confined quarters of his berth, believing his worst fears have been realized.

27 The *Last Waltz* of Karl Maria, Baron von Weber (1786–1826) was actually composed by his friend Karl Gottlieb Reissiger (1798–1859). The reference to Weber may indicate an aesthetic debt. Poe's friend and champion Evert Duyckinck (1816–1878) saw similarities between the opening of "Usher" and the introduction to Weber's most famous opera, *Der Freischütz* (1821). Poe's story, in turn, has appealed to subsequent composers, having inspired op-eratic versions by Claude Debussy and Philip Glass.

28 To elicit a conclusion from a set of data.

I. P. Simon after
Henry Fuseli,
"Midsummer
Nights Dream Act
IV Scene I," 1796.

29   Henry Fuseli (1741–1825), born in Zurich, established a reputation as a leading history painter while working in England. He illustrated many literary works, including the plays of Shakespeare. Fuseli was renowned for his bizarre, psychologically complex subjects. Poe's phrase—"concrete reveries"—conveys a sense of Fuseli's highly detailed, nightmarish paintings. Describing his art in *The Botanic Garden* (1789), canto III, line 58, Erasmus Darwin says that Fuseli "gave to the airy phantom form and place."

30   "Phantasmagoria" refers to a popular theatrical entertainment that employed magic lanterns to project ghoulish images such as ghosts, skeletons, and demons. The word stayed in the language after the phantasmagoria craze waned in the early nineteenth century to describe hallucinatory mental images. Poe's writings capture this shift from external to internal imagery, amusement to psychology (Terry Castle, "Phantasmagoria: Spectral Technology and the Metaphorics of Modern Reverie," *Critical Inquiry* 15 [1988], 26–61).

more than a small portion which should lie within the compass of merely written words. By the utter simplicity, by the nakedness of his designs, he arrested and overawed attention. If ever mortal painted an idea, that mortal was Roderick Usher. For me at least—in the circumstances then surrounding me—there arose out of the pure abstractions which the hypochondriac contrived to throw upon his canvass, an intensity of intolerable awe, no shadow of which felt I ever yet in the contemplation of the certainly glowing yet too concrete reveries of Fuseli.[29]

One of the phantasmagoric conceptions[30] of my friend, partaking not so rigidly of the spirit of abstraction, may be shadowed forth, although feebly, in words. A small picture presented the interior of an immensely long and rectangular vault or tunnel, with low walls, smooth, white, and without interruption or device. Certain accessory points of the design served well to convey the idea that this excavation lay at an exceeding depth below the surface of the earth. No outlet was observed in any portion of its vast extent, and no torch, or other artificial source of light was discernible; yet a flood of intense rays rolled throughout, and bathed the whole in a ghastly and inappropriate splendor.[31]

I have just spoken of that morbid condition of the auditory nerve which rendered all music intolerable to the sufferer, with the exception of certain effects of stringed instruments. It was, perhaps, the narrow limits to which he thus confined himself upon the guitar, which gave birth, in great measure, to the fantastic character of his performances. But the fervid *facility* of his *impromptus* could not be so accounted for. They must have been, and were, in the notes, as well as in the words of his wild fantasias[32] (for he not unfrequently accompanied himself with rhymed verbal improvisations), the result of that intense mental collectedness and concentration to which I have previously alluded as observable only in particular moments of the highest artificial excitement.[33] The words of one of these rhapsodies I have easily remembered. I was, perhaps, the more forcibly impressed with it, as he gave it, because, in the under or mystic current of its meaning, I fancied that I perceived, and for the first time, a full consciousness on the part of Usher, of the tottering of his lofty reason upon her throne. The verses, which were entitled "The Haunted Palace,"[34] ran very nearly, if not accurately, thus:

I.

In the greenest of our valleys,
By good angels tenanted,
  Once a fair and stately palace[35]—
Radiant palace—reared its head.
  In the monarch Thought's dominion—
It stood there!
  Never seraph spread a pinion
Over fabric half so fair.[36]

II.

Banners yellow, glorious, golden,
On its roof did float and flow;
  (This—all this—was in the olden
Time long ago)
  And every gentle air that dallied,
In that sweet day,
  Along the ramparts plumed and pallid,
A winged odor went away.

31   Roderick's weird, creepy painting of an underground vault, illuminated by a sourceless light, offers a glimpse into the terrible, frightening terminus—madness or despair—into which the artist has fallen. Oliver Evans suggests: "The intense underground light proceeds from hell, not from heaven, and in the painting Usher has projected his own personality, whose brilliance has a satanic rather than a divine source" ("Infernal Illumination in Poe," *Modern Language Notes* 75 [1960], 297).

32   The phrase "wild fantasias" is redundant: fantasias are instrumental compositions with no preset form. They are limited solely by the imagination and ingenuity of their composer. Their formal and stylistic qualities can thus vary considerably.

33   In "The Philosophy of Composition," Poe describes how he composed his most famous poem, "The Raven": "The work proceeded, step by step, to its completion with the precision and rigid consequence of a mathematical problem" (*Essays*, 15). Elsewhere he celebrates the role that accident plays in the creative process. As André Breton says about Poe, "It would be hard to imagine this lover of Chance not allowing for chance expressions" (*Anthology of Black Humor*, trans. Mark Polizzotti [San Francisco: City Lights, 1997], 83). Improvisation is the defining feature of Usher's own bizarre musical compositions.

34   This poem by Poe first appeared as "The Haunted Palace" in the April 1839 issue of the *American Museum*. Writing to Rufus Wilmot Griswold on May 29, 1841, he explained the title: "By the Haunted Palace I mean to imply a mind haunted by phantoms—a disordered brain" (*Collected Letters of Edgar Allan Poe*, ed. John Ward Ostrom, Burton R. Pollin, and Jeffrey A. Savoye. 2 vols. [New York: Gordian Press, 2008], I, 272).

35   Poe echoes a passage in Edward Bulwer-Lytton's novel *Rienzi, The Last of the Tribunes* (1835): "After proceeding thus somewhat less than half an hour they turned up a green lane remote from the road, and came suddenly upon the porticoes of a fair and stately palace."

36   The word "fabric" was sometimes used to mean edifice, usually in a figurative sense. The universe—a God-made edifice—could be called a "fabric" as well.

37 *Oxford English Dictionary*, which defines "porphyro-gene" as born into royalty, identifies it as Poe's coinage. Poe derived the word from porphyry, a hard purplish rock polished and used for ornamentation. The color purple is traditionally associated with royalty.

38 Litten means "lighted," usually used in combination, as it is here.

39 "Watson, Dr. [Thomas] Percival, [Lazzaro] Spallan-zani, and especially the Bishop of Landaff.—See *Chemical Essays*, vol. V [Poe's note]." Poe's reference to Watson *and* the Bishop of Llandaff is redundant: After serving as professor of chemistry at Cambridge, Richard Watson (1737–1816) became the Bishop of Llandaff. His newfound clerical responsibilities did not stop his scientific research. He continued to study the sentience of plants.

40 Absence of organization or an unorganized condition.

41 In William Faulkner's *Absalom, Absalom!* (1936), family patriarch Thomas Sutpen shares a similar view about the sentience of the Sutpen mansion: "His presence alone compelled that house to accept and retain human life; as though houses actually possess a sentience, a personality and character acquired not from the people who breathe or have breathed in them so much as rather inherent in the wood and brick or begotten upon the wood and brick by the man or men who conceived and built them."

42 Poe conflates two separate works by Jean-Baptiste-Louis Gresset (1709–1777): *Ver-Vert* (1734) and *La Char-treuse* (1735).

43 The eponymous demon in Machiavelli's *Belfagor* travels from hell to earth on a mission to discover why so many ruined men in hell attribute their ruin to their wives. As per his instructions, Belfagor marries an earth woman, experiences no end of trouble, and ultimately flees from her.

44 Emanuel Swedenborg (1688–1772), the Swedish mystic, philosopher, and visionary, published *A Treatise Concerning Heaven and Hell* in 1758.

III.

Wanderers in that happy valley
Through two luminous windows saw
      Spirits moving musically
To a lute's well-tunéd law,
      Round about a throne, where sitting
(Porphyrogene!)[37]
      In state his glory well befitting,
The ruler of the realm was seen.

IV.

      And all with pearl and ruby glowing
Was the fair palace door,
      Through which came flowing, flowing, flowing,
And sparkling evermore,
      A troop of Echoes whose sweet duty
Was but to sing,
      In voices of surpassing beauty,
The wit and wisdom of their king.

V.

      But evil things, in robes of sorrow,
Assailed the monarch's high estate;
      (Ah, let us mourn, for never morrow
Shall dawn upon him, desolate!)
      And, round about his home, the glory
That blushed and bloomed
      Is but a dim-remembered story
Of the old time entombed.

VI.

      And travellers now within that valley,
Through the red-litten[38] windows, see
      Vast forms that move fantastically
To a discordant melody;
      While, like a rapid ghastly river,
Through the pale door,
      A hideous throng rush out forever,
And laugh—but smile no more.

I well remember that suggestions arising from this ballad led us into a train of thought wherein there became manifest an opinion of Usher's which I mention not so much on account of its novelty, (for other men[39] have thought thus,) as on account of the pertinacity with which he maintained it. This opinion, in its general form, was that of the sentience of all vegetable things. But, in his disordered fancy, the idea had assumed a more daring character, and trespassed, under certain conditions, upon the kingdom of inorganization.[40] I lack words to express the full extent, or the earnest *abandon* of his persuasion. The belief, however, was connected (as I have previously hinted) with the gray stones of the home of his forefathers.[41] The conditions of the sentience had been here, he imagined, fulfilled in the method of collocation of these stones—in the order of their arrangement, as well as in that of the many *fungi* which overspread them, and of the decayed trees which stood around—above all, in the long undisturbed endurance of this arrangement, and in its reduplication in the still waters of the tarn. Its evidence—the evidence of the sentience—was to be seen, he said, (and I here started as he spoke,) in the gradual yet certain condensation of an atmosphere of their own about the waters and the walls. The result was discoverable, he added, in that silent, yet importunate and terrible influence which for centuries had moulded the destinies of his family, and which made *him* what I now saw him—what he was. Such opinions need no comment, and I will make none.

Our books—the books which, for years, had formed no small portion of the mental existence of the invalid—were, as might be supposed, in strict keeping with this character of phantasm. We pored together over such works as the *Ververt et Chartreuse* of Gresset;[42] the *Belphegor* of Machiavelli;[43] the Heaven and Hell of Swedenborg;[44] the *Subterranean Voyage of Nicholas Klimm* by Holberg;[45] the *Chiromancy* of Robert Flud, of Jean D'Indaginé, and of De la Chambre;[46] the *Journey into the Blue Distance* of Tieck;[47] and the *City of the Sun* of Campanella.[48] One favorite volume was a small octavo edition of the *Directorium Inquisitorium*, by the Dominican Eymeric de Gironne;[49] and there were passages in Pomponius Mela, about the old African Satyrs and Aegipans, over which Usher would sit dreaming for hours.[50] His chief delight, however, was found in the perusal of an exceedingly rare and curious book in quarto Gothic—the manual of a forgotten church—the *Vigiliae Mortuorum secundum Chorum Ecclesiae Maguntinae.*

I could not help thinking of the wild ritual of this work, and of its probable influence upon the hypochondriac, when, one eve-

45 In *Iter Subterraneum* (1741), the Danish writer Baron Ludvig Holberg (1684–1754) takes his fictional narrator, Nicholas Klimm, on a fantastic underground voyage.

46 These three occult writers—Robert Fludd (1574–1637), Johannes ab Indagine (d. 1537), and Martin Cureau de La Chambre (1594–1669)—all wrote works on the practice of chiromancy or, as this fortune-telling technique is better known, palmistry.

47 "A Journey into the Blue Distance" by Johann Ludwig Tieck (1773–1854) is a satirical narrative embedded within a larger story. Thomas Wentworth Higginson offers a personal anecdote relating how his passion for Poe's writings encouraged him to try to read the books Poe had read: "I remember the chagrin with which I looked through Tieck, in my student-days, to find the 'Journey into the Blue Distance' to which Poe refers in the 'House of Usher'; and how one of the poet's intimates laughed me to scorn for being deceived by any of Poe's citations, saying that he hardly knew a word of German" (Eric W. Carlson, ed., *The Recognition of Edgar Allan Poe: Selected Criticism since 1829* [Ann Arbor: University of Michigan Press, 1966], 70).

48 In *City of the Sun* (1623), Tommaso Campanella (1568–1639) describes a utopian society inspired by Plato's vision of the universe, positing that the health of the individual family reflects the health of the political state in which they live.

49 Nicolau Eimeric (1320–1399) wrote *Directorium Inquisitorum* as a guidebook for fellow inquisitors. Poe took his description of this book from "The Bibliophilist," a short story that British *bon vivant* Thomas Raikes published in the June 1838 issue of *Bentley's*. Raikes is also the source for Poe's reference to *Vigiliae Mortuorum Secundum Chorum Ecclesiae Maguntinae* at the end of this paragraph (Kevin J. Hayes, "Another Source for 'The Fall of the House of Usher,'" *Notes and Queries* 57 (2010), 214–216).

50 Poe refers to Pomponius Mela's *De situ orbis*, the earliest surviving Latin work in geography. Aegipans are mythological deities of the mountains and woods with the horns and feet of a goat.

51 Angela Carter wryly comments: "Poe never tells us where the coffin has come from, anyway. The Ushers probably had a stock of empty coffins laid in, anyway, in case of sudden emergency. They probably felt about coffins like other people feel about spare beds."

52 A "donjon keep" is "the strongest part of a feudal castle; a high square tower, with walls of tremendous thickness, situated in the centre of the other buildings, from which, however, it was usually detached. Here, in case of the outward defences being gained, the garrison retreated to make their last stand. The donjon contained the great hall, and principal rooms of state for solemn occasions, and also the prison of the fortress; from which last circumstance we derive the modern and restricted use of the word *dungeon*" (Sir Walter Scott, *Marmion* [Edinburgh: Robert Cadell, 1835], 261–262).

53 Numerous articles about case studies demonstrating the sympathy between twins appeared in the early nineteenth-century press and caught the attention of the Romantic poets. In "A Fragment," Shelley describes "two cousins, almost like to twins," who

> grew together, like two flowers
> Upon one stem, which the same beams and
>   showers
> Lull or awaken in their purple prime,
> Which the same hand will gather—the same clime
> Shake with decay.
>
>   (lines 11, 15–19)

ning, having informed me abruptly that the lady Madeline was no more, he stated his intention of preserving her corpse for a fortnight, (previously to its final interment,) in one of the numerous vaults within the main walls of the building. The worldly reason, however, assigned for this singular proceeding, was one which I did not feel at liberty to dispute. The brother had been led to his resolution (so he told me) by consideration of the unusual character of the malady of the deceased, of certain obtrusive and eager inquiries on the part of her medical men, and of the remote and exposed situation of the burial-ground of the family. I will not deny that when I called to mind the sinister countenance of the person whom I met upon the staircase, on the day of my arrival at the house, I had no desire to oppose what I regarded as at best but a harmless, and by no means an unnatural, precaution.

At the request of Usher, I personally aided him in the arrangements for the temporary entombment. The body having been encoffined, we two alone bore it to its rest.[51] The vault in which we placed it (and which had been so long unopened that our torches, half smothered in its oppressive atmosphere, gave us little opportunity for investigation) was small, damp, and entirely without means of admission for light; lying, at great depth, immediately beneath that portion of the building in which was my own sleeping apartment. It had been used, apparently, in remote feudal times, for the worst purposes of a donjon-keep,[52] and, in later days, as a place of deposit for powder, or some other highly combustible substance, as a portion of its floor, and the whole interior of a long archway through which we reached it, were carefully sheathed with copper. The door, of massive iron, had been, also, similarly protected. Its immense weight caused an unusually sharp grating sound, as it moved upon its hinges.

Having deposited our mournful burden upon tressels within this region of horror, we partially turned aside the yet unscrewed lid of the coffin, and looked upon the face of the tenant. A striking similitude between the brother and sister now first arrested my attention; and Usher, divining, perhaps, my thoughts, murmured out some few words from which I learned that the deceased and himself had been twins,[53] and that sympathies of a scarcely intelligible nature had always existed between them. Our glances, however, rested not long upon the dead—for we could not regard her unawed. The disease which had thus entombed the lady in the ma-

turity of youth, had left, as usual in all maladies of a strictly cataleptical character, the mockery of a faint blush upon the bosom
and the face, and that suspiciously lingering smile upon the lip
which is so terrible in death. We replaced and screwed down the
lid, and, having secured the door of iron, made our way, with toil,
into the scarcely less gloomy apartments of the upper portion of
the house.

And now, some days of bitter grief having elapsed, an observable change came over the features of the mental disorder of my
friend. His ordinary manner had vanished. His ordinary occupations were neglected or forgotten. He roamed from chamber to
chamber with hurried, unequal, and objectless step. The pallor of
his countenance had assumed, if possible, a more ghastly hue—
but the luminousness of his eye had utterly gone out. The once
occasional huskiness of his tone was heard no more; and a tremulous quaver, as if of extreme terror, habitually characterized his
utterance. There were times, indeed, when I thought his unceasingly agitated mind was laboring with some oppressive secret, to
divulge which he struggled for the necessary courage. At times,
again, I was obliged to resolve all into the mere inexplicable vagaries of madness, for I beheld him gazing upon vacancy for long
hours, in an attitude of the profoundest attention, as if listening to
some imaginary sound. It was no wonder that his condition terrified—that it infected me. I felt creeping upon me, by slow yet certain degrees, the wild influences of his own fantastic yet impressive superstitions.

It was, especially, upon retiring to bed late in the night of the
seventh or eighth day after the placing of the lady Madeline within
the donjon, that I experienced the full power of such feelings.
Sleep came not near my couch—while the hours waned and waned
away. I struggled to reason off the nervousness which had dominion over me. I endeavored to believe that much, if not all of what I
felt, was due to the bewildering influence of the gloomy furniture
of the room—of the dark and tattered draperies, which, tortured
into motion by the breath of a rising tempest, swayed fitfully to
and fro upon the walls, and rustled uneasily about the decorations
of the bed. But my efforts were fruitless. An irrepressible tremor
gradually pervaded my frame; and, at length, there sat upon my
very heart an incubus of utterly causeless alarm.[54] Shaking this off
with a gasp and a struggle, I uplifted myself upon the pillows, and,

54 An incubus, from the Latin *incubare* or "to lie upon,"
is an evil spirit of the male sex that descends upon women
in their sleep to have carnal intercourse. A succubus refers
to a demon that takes the form of the female sex. Tradition says that intercourse with a demon may bring about
sickness and, if occurring with frequency, death. Poe's description of an incubus sitting on the narrator's heart may
allude to Henry Fuseli's famous painting *The Nightmare*
(1781). Engraved and frequently reprinted in Poe's day,
The Nightmare depicts a gruesome incubus seated atop a
sleeping woman. Though it does seem odd that a male-
form demon would perch atop the narrator, the figurative
meaning of "incubus" had largely lost its gender-specific
connotations and come to mean any oppressive burden.
Describing *The Knickerbocker*, the magazine edited by
Lewis Gaylord Clark, Poe wrote, "Some incomprehensible *incubus* has seemed always to sit heavily upon it, and it
has never succeeded in attaining *position* among intelligent
or educated readers" (*Essays*, 1205).

55   This ghastly illumination is yet another insoluble mystery. The narrator of "The Premature Burial" has a vision of "the graves of all mankind": "From each issued the faint phosphoric radiance of decay; so that I could see into the innermost recesses, and there view the shrouded bodies in their sad and solemn slumbers with the worm." Richard Wilbur sees the light in the vault beneath the House of Usher as an allusion to *Romeo and Juliet*, V.iii.84–86: "A grave? O no, a lanthorn, slaught'red youth; / For here lies Juliet, and her beauty makes / This vault a feasting presence full of light" ("Edgar Allan Poe," *Major Writers of America*, ed. Perry Miller [New York: Harcourt, Brace, 1962], 414).

56   The *Mad Trist* and its author, Sir Launcelot Canning, are fictional contrivances by Poe. However imprecisely the *Mad Trist* reflects or anticipates events in "Usher," it creates almost intolerable suspense for both Roderick and the reader.

peering earnestly within the intense darkness of the chamber, harkened—I know not why, except that an instinctive spirit prompted me—to certain low and indefinite sounds which came, through the pauses of the storm, at long intervals, I knew not whence. Overpowered by an intense sentiment of horror, unaccountable yet unendurable, I threw on my clothes with haste (for I felt that I should sleep no more during the night), and endeavored to arouse myself from the pitiable condition into which I had fallen, by pacing rapidly to and fro through the apartment.

I had taken but few turns in this manner, when a light step on an adjoining staircase arrested my attention. I presently recognised it as that of Usher. In an instant afterward he rapped, with a gentle touch, at my door, and entered, bearing a lamp. His countenance was, as usual, cadaverously wan—but, moreover, there was a species of mad hilarity in his eyes—an evidently restrained *hysteria* in his whole demeanor. His air appalled me—but anything was preferable to the solitude which I had so long endured, and I even welcomed his presence as a relief.

"And you have not seen it?" he said abruptly, after having stared about him for some moments in silence—"you have not then seen it?—but, stay! you shall." Thus speaking, and having carefully shaded his lamp, he hurried to one of the casements, and threw it freely open to the storm.

The impetuous fury of the entering gust nearly lifted us from our feet. It was, indeed, a tempestuous yet sternly beautiful night, and one wildly singular in its terror and its beauty. A whirlwind had apparently collected its force in our vicinity; for there were frequent and violent alterations in the direction of the wind; and the exceeding density of the clouds (which hung so low as to press upon the turrets of the house) did not prevent our perceiving the life-like velocity with which they flew careering from all points against each other, without passing away into the distance. I say that even their exceeding density did not prevent our perceiving this—yet we had no glimpse of the moon or stars—nor was there any flashing forth of the lightning. But the under surfaces of the huge masses of agitated vapor, as well as all terrestrial objects immediately around us, were glowing in the unnatural light of a faintly luminous and distinctly visible gaseous exhalation which hung about and enshrouded the mansion.[55]

"You must not—you shall not behold this!" said I, shudder-

ingly, to Usher, as I led him, with a gentle violence, from the window to a seat. "These appearances, which bewilder you, are merely electrical phenomena not uncommon—or it may be that they have their ghastly origin in the rank miasma of the tarn. Let us close this casement;—the air is chilling and dangerous to your frame. Here is one of your favorite romances. I will read, and you shall listen;—and so we will pass away this terrible night together."

The antique volume which I had taken up was the *Mad Trist* of Sir Launcelot Canning;[56] but I had called it a favorite of Usher's more in sad jest than in earnest; for, in truth, there is little in its

Henry Fuseli, *The Nightmare*, 1781. Perhaps Fuseli's best-known painting, *The Nightmare* captures the thin boundary between sex and fear. It was wildly controversial when first shown at the annual Royal Academy exhibition in 1782.

57 This sentence provides a good example of how Poe used sound imagery to create tension. After the noise in the passage from the *Mad Trist*, the narrator pauses to describe what is happening in the House of Usher. Anticipating a commensurate noise, the reader must nevertheless endure most of this eighty-two-word sentence before hearing it.

uncouth and unimaginative prolixity which could have had interest for the lofty and spiritual ideality of my friend. It was, however, the only book immediately at hand; and I indulged a vague hope that the excitement which now agitated the hypochondriac, might find relief (for the history of mental disorder is full of similar anomalies) even in the extremeness of the folly which I should read. Could I have judged, indeed, by the wild overstrained air of vivacity with which he harkened, or apparently harkened, to the words of the tale, I might well have congratulated myself upon the success of my design.

I had arrived at that well-known portion of the story where Ethelred, the hero of the *Trist*, having sought in vain for peaceable admission into the dwelling of the hermit, proceeds to make good an entrance by force. Here, it will be remembered, the words of the narrative run thus:

"And Ethelred, who was by nature of a doughty heart, and who was now mighty withal, on account of the powerfulness of the wine which he had drunken, waited no longer to hold parley with the hermit, who, in sooth, was of an obstinate and maliceful turn, but, feeling the rain upon his shoulders, and fearing the rising of the tempest, uplifted his mace outright, and, with blows, made quickly room in the plankings of the door for his gauntleted hand; and now pulling therewith sturdily, he so cracked, and ripped, and tore all asunder, that the noise of the dry and hollow-sounding wood alarummed and reverberated throughout the forest."

At the termination of this sentence I started, and for a moment, paused; for it appeared to me (although I at once concluded that my excited fancy had deceived me)—it appeared to me that, from some very remote portion of the mansion, there came, indistinctly, to my ears, what might have been, in its exact similarity of character, the echo (but a stifled and dull one certainly) of the very cracking and ripping sound which Sir Launcelot had so particularly described.[57] It was, beyond doubt, the coincidence alone which had arrested my attention; for, amid the rattling of the sashes of the casements, and the ordinary commingled noises of the still increasing storm, the sound, in itself, had nothing, surely, which should have interested or disturbed me. I continued the story:

"But the good champion Ethelred, now entering within the door, was sore enraged and amazed to perceive no signal of the maliceful hermit; but, in the stead thereof, a dragon of a scaly and prodigious demeanor, and of a fiery tongue, which sate in guard before a palace of gold, with a floor of silver; and upon the wall there hung a shield of shining brass with this legend enwritten—

> Who entereth herein, a conqueror hath bin;
> Who slayeth the dragon, the shield he shall win;

And Ethelred uplifted his mace, and struck upon the head of the dragon, which fell before him, and gave up his pesty breath, with a shriek so horrid and harsh, and withal so piercing, that Ethelred had fain to close his ears with his hands against the dreadful noise of it, the like whereof was never before heard."

Here again I paused abruptly, and now with a feeling of wild amazement—for there could be no doubt whatever that, in this instance, I did actually hear (although from what direction it proceeded I found it impossible to say) a low and apparently distant, but harsh, protracted, and most unusual screaming or grating sound—the exact counterpart of what my fancy had already conjured up for the dragon's unnatural shriek as described by the romancer.

Oppressed, as I certainly was, upon the occurrence of this second and most extraordinary coincidence, by a thousand conflicting sensations, in which wonder and extreme terror were predominant, I still retained sufficient presence of mind to avoid exciting, by any observation, the sensitive nervousness of my companion. I was by no means certain that he had noticed the sounds in question; although, assuredly, a strange alteration had, during the last few minutes, taken place in his demeanor. From a position fronting my own, he had gradually brought round his chair, so as to sit with his face to the door of the chamber; and thus I could but partially perceive his features, although I saw that his lips trembled as if he were murmuring inaudibly. His head had dropped upon his breast—yet I knew that he was not asleep, from the wide and rigid opening of the eye as I caught a glance of it in profile. The motion of his body, too, was at variance with this idea—for he rocked from side to side with a gentle yet constant and uniform sway. Having rapidly taken notice of all this, I resumed the narrative of Sir Launcelot, which thus proceeded:

"And now, the champion, having escaped from the terrible fury of the dragon, bethinking himself of the brazen shield, and of the

58   Compare Psalms 139:7: "Whither shall I go from thy spirit? or whither shall I flee from thy presence?"

59   An anonymous review of Poe's *Tales* in the October 1845 issue of the *Aristidean* describes "Usher," commenting, "The thesis of this tale, is the revulsion of feeling consequent upon discovering that for a long period of time we have been mistaking sounds of agony, for those of mirth or indifference." The authorship of this review has been subject to debate. Thomas Dunn English initialed it in the *Aristidean* index, but it is likely that Poe, then still friends with English, was largely responsible for the contents of the review (Walker, *Edgar Allan Poe*, 195, 192). The thesis the reviewer articulates provides no answers to the reader's questions. Did Roderick intentionally bury his sister *alive?* And if he really believed she was dead when he placed her in the vault, why, having recognized his error some days prior, when he first became aware of her "feeble movements in the hollow coffin," has he made no effort to rescue her?

breaking up of the enchantment which was upon it, removed the carcass from out of the way before him, and approached valorously over the silver pavement of the castle to where the shield was upon the wall; which in sooth tarried not for his full coming, but fell down at his feet upon the silver floor, with a mighty great and terrible ringing sound."

No sooner had these syllables passed my lips, than—as if a shield of brass had indeed, at the moment, fallen heavily upon a floor of silver—I became aware of a distinct, hollow, metallic, and clangorous, yet apparently muffled reverberation. Completely unnerved, I leaped to my feet; but the measured rocking movement of Usher was undisturbed. I rushed to the chair in which he sat. His eyes were bent fixedly before him, and throughout his whole countenance there reigned a stony rigidity. But, as I placed my hand upon his shoulder, there came a strong shudder over his whole person; a sickly smile quivered about his lips; and I saw that he spoke in a low, hurried, and gibbering murmur, as if unconscious of my presence. Bending closely over him, I at length drank in the hideous import of his words.

"Not hear it?—yes, I hear it, and *have* heard it. Long—long—long—many minutes, many hours, many days, have I heard it—yet I dared not—oh, pity me, miserable wretch that I am!—I dared not—I *dared* not speak! *We have put her living in the tomb!* Said I not that my senses were acute? I now tell you that I heard her first feeble movements in the hollow coffin. I heard them—many, many days ago—yet I dared not—I *dared not speak!* And now—to-night—Ethelred—ha! ha!—the breaking of the hermit's door, and the death-cry of the dragon, and the clangor of the shield!—say, rather, the rending of her coffin, and the grating of the iron hinges of her prison, and her struggles within the coppered archway of the vault! Oh whither shall I fly?[58] Will she not be here anon? Is she not hurrying to upbraid me for my haste? Have I not heard her footstep on the stair? Do I not distinguish that heavy and horrible beating of her heart? Madman!"—here he sprang furiously to his feet, and shrieked out his syllables, as if in the effort he were giving up his soul—*"Madman! I tell you that she now stands without the door!"*[59]

As if in the superhuman energy of his utterance there had been found the potency of a spell—the huge antique pannels to which the speaker pointed, threw slowly back, upon the instant, their

Thomas Dunn English.

ponderous and ebony jaws. It was the work of the rushing gust—but then without those doors there *did* stand the lofty and en-shrouded figure of the lady Madeline of Usher. There was blood upon her white robes, and the evidence of some bitter struggle upon every portion of her emaciated frame. For a moment she re-mained trembling and reeling to and fro upon the threshold—then, with a low moaning cry, fell heavily inward upon the person of her brother, and in her violent and now final death-agonies, bore him to the floor a corpse, and a victim to the terrors he had anticipated.

From that chamber, and from that mansion, I fled aghast. The storm was still abroad in all its wrath as I found myself cross-ing the old causeway. Suddenly there shot along the path a wild

Harry Clarke, "She Now Stands Without the Door!" from *Tales of Mystery and Imagination* (London: George G. Harrap, 1919).

60   Compare Ezekiel 43:2: "And, behold, the glory of the God of Israel came from the way of the east: and his voice was like a noise of many waters: and the earth shined with his glory"; and Revelation 1:15: "And his feet like unto fine brass, as if they burned in a furnace; and his voice as the sound of many waters."

61   "Usher" is one of those stories that seems to inspire as many interpretations as it does readers—and there can perhaps be no consensus about the story or its dramatic ending: "In the end, the House of Usher, as a building, emblem, or signifier, proves to be more powerful than any of the readings attached to it, and despite its collapse and dissolution into the tarn, it keeps coming back to life, exemplifying 'the imperative to repetition' and originating further interpretations of the tale" (Marita Nadal, "'The Fall of the House of Usher': A Master Text for [Poe's] American Gothic," *Journal of English Studies* 7 [2009], 59).

light, and I turned to see whence a gleam so unusual could have issued; for the vast house and its shadows were alone behind me. The radiance was that of the full, setting, and blood-red moon, which now shone vividly through that once barely-discernible fissure, of which I have before spoken as extending from the roof of the building, in a zigzag direction, to the base. While I gazed, this fissure rapidly widened—there came a fierce breath of the whirlwind—the entire orb of the satellite burst at once upon my sight—my brain reeled as I saw the mighty walls rushing asunder—there was a long tumultuous shouting sound like the voice of a thousand waters[60]—and the deep and dank tarn at my feet closed sullenly and silently over the fragments of the *"House of Usher."*[61]

William Wilson

What say of it? what say of CONSCIENCE grim,
That spectre in my path?

Chamberlayne's Pharonnida[1]

Let me call myself, for the present, William Wilson.[2] The fair page now lying before me need not be sullied with my real appellation. This has been already too much an object for the scorn—for the horror—for the detestation of my race. To the uttermost regions of the globe have not the indignant winds bruited its unparalleled infamy? Oh, outcast of all outcasts most abandoned!—to the earth art thou not forever dead? to its honors, to its flowers, to its golden aspirations?—and a cloud, dense, dismal, and limitless, does it not hang eternally between thy hopes and heaven?

I would not, if I could, here or to-day, embody a record of my later years of unspeakable misery, and unpardonable crime. This epoch—these later years—took unto themselves a sudden elevation in turpitude, whose origin alone it is my present purpose to assign. Men usually grow base by degrees. From me, in an instant, all virtue dropped bodily as a mantle. From comparatively trivial wickedness I passed, with the stride of a giant, into more than the enormities of an Elah-Gabalus.[3] What chance—what one event brought this evil thing to pass, bear with me while I relate. Death approaches; and the shadow which foreruns him has thrown a softening influence over my spirit. I long, in passing through the dim valley, for the sympathy—I had nearly said for the pity—of my fellow men. I would fain have them believe that I have been, in some measure, the slave of circumstances beyond human control. I would wish them to seek out for me, in the details I am about to give, some little oasis of *fatality* amid a wilderness of error. I would have them allow—what they cannot refrain from allowing—that, although temptation may have ere-while existed as

"William Wilson," the story of a doppelganger (in German, literally a "double goer"), has influenced numerous literary and cinematic works: Fyodor Dostoevsky's The Double *(1846), Robert Louis Stevenson's* The Strange Case of Dr. Jekyll and Mr. Hyde *(1886), Oscar Wilde's* The Picture of Dorian Gray *(1891), Joseph Conrad's* The Secret Sharer *(1912), and, to take just one example from the cinema, Joseph Losey's* Mr. Klein *(1976), which stars Alain Delon in the title role. Discussing Dostoevsky's novel, Thomas Mann comments, "Certainly he by no means improved on Edgar Allan Poe's 'William Wilson,' a tale that deals with the same old romantic motive in a way far more profound on the moral side and more successfully resolving the clinical in the poetic." Edmund Wilson preferred Poe's story to Stevenson's: "It is the lifelong 'agony' of his moral experience that gives to Poe's 'William Wilson' its superior sincerity and intensity over Stevenson's* Doctor Jekyll and Mr. Hyde" *(*The Thomas Mann Reader, ed. Joseph Warner Angell [New York: Knopf, 1950], 446; Eric W. Carlson, ed.,* The Recognition of Edgar Allan Poe: Selected Criticism since 1829 *[Ann Arbor: University of Michigan Press, 1966], 147).*

*Poe did not invent the double motif, of course. As biographer George Woodberry observes: "The conception of a double dogging one's steps and thwarting one's evil designs, is an old fancy of men that has taken many shapes since Zoroaster saw his phantom in the garden" (*Edgar Allan Poe *[Boston: Houghton Mifflin, 1885], 122–123). Poe himself took his inspiration from "An Unwritten Drama of Lord Byron," an article Washington Irving wrote for* The Gift: A Christmas and New Year's Present for 1836. *Irving relates the plot of a tragedy Byron had conceived yet never written. A mysterious stranger persistently follows an impetuous young Spanish nobleman named Alfonso, who becomes so perturbed by his shadow that he fatally stabs the stranger—only to discover his own face on the victim. Irving suggested that this plot could provide "a rich theme to a poet or dramatist of the Byron school." Never one to turn away from a challenge, Poe soon set to work on "William Wilson." The story, however, went through a long gestation period. Poe did not finish it until 1839—four years after he first encountered Irving's sketch. Appropriately, he published the tale in* The Gift: A Christmas and New Year's Present for 1840.

1 *Pharonnida* (1659), a heroic romance by the British poet and playwright William Chamberlayne (ca. 1619–1689), contains no such lines. Nor do Chamberlayne's other works. Most likely Poe invented this quotation. He may have been inspired by James Montgomery's hugely popular abolitionist poem *The West Indies* (1809), which portrays conscience as a spectre "shrieking through the

gloom." Given Poe's general contempt for Montgomery, it makes sense that he would attribute the motto to the well-respected seventeenth-century poet Chamberlayne instead.

2 Biographer Kenneth Silverman observes that Poe's psychological thriller owes something to the irritation we all experience upon learning that someone else—a colleague or acquaintance—shares our name, a wound to the feeling of uniqueness. Poe complicates the matter further by having his narrator assign himself a name only to admit that it is not his real one. The name "William Wilson" was quite common in Poe's day. *McElroy's Philadelphia Directory for 1839* lists thirteen William Wilsons, one William B. Wilson, three William H. Wilsons, one William R. Wilson, and a grocer, "William Wilson and Co."

3 Poe alludes to the notorious Roman emperor Elagabalus, sometimes erroneously called Heliogabalus. Born Varius Avitus Bassianus, he took his name from the sun-god of Emesa, Elah-Gabal. Elagabalus served as emperor of Rome (218–222 CE) and established a reputation for depravity during his rule.

4 Many readers have noted the confessional nature of "William Wilson." In Louis Malle's penetrating film adaptation of the same title, the narrator relates his story to a priest in a confessional.

5 Poe fictionalizes a school he attended while living in England during his adolescence, the Manor House School in Stoke Newington, then a suburb of London. On the evidence of information Poe supplied to him, Henry B. Hirst called "William Wilson" a "faithful description of this school and its principal" ("An Early Biography of Poe [1843]: The *Philadelphia Saturday Museum* Sketch," *Masques, Mysteries, and Mastodons: A Poe Miscellany*, ed. Benjamin Franklin Fisher [Baltimore: Edgar Allan Poe Society of Baltimore, 2006], 156).

6 By Wilson's description, the place seems more like a prison than a school. These walls, topped with broken glass set in mortar, not only keep out intruders but also prevent the students from escaping.

William Wilson (Alain Delon) tells his story to a priest in a confessional in Louis Malle's "William Wilson," the second segment of the film *Histoires extraordinaires* (1968).

great, man was never *thus*, at least, tempted before—certainly, never *thus* fell. And is it therefore that he has never thus suffered? Have I not indeed been living in a dream? And am I not now dying a victim to the horror and the mystery of the wildest of all sublunary visions?[4]

I am the descendant of a race whose imaginative and easily excitable temperament has at all times rendered them remarkable; and, in my earliest infancy, I gave evidence of having fully inherited the family character. As I advanced in years it was more strongly developed; becoming, for many reasons, a cause of serious disquietude to my friends, and of positive injury to myself. I grew self-willed, addicted to the wildest caprices, and a prey to the most ungovernable passions. Weak-minded, and beset with constitutional infirmities akin to my own, my parents could do but little to check the evil propensities which distinguished me. Some feeble and ill-directed efforts resulted in complete failure on their part, and, of course, in total triumph on mine. Thenceforward my voice was a household law; and at an age when few children have abandoned their leading-strings, I was left to the guidance of my own will, and became, in all but name, the master of my own actions.

My earliest recollections of a school-life, are connected with a large, rambling, Elizabethan house, in a misty-looking village of England, where were a vast number of gigantic and gnarled trees, and where all the houses were excessively ancient.[5] In truth, it was

"Rev. Dr. Bransby's Establishment at Stoke-Newington." Poe attended this school in London from 1818 to 1820.

a dream-like and spirit-soothing place, that venerable old town. At this moment, in fancy, I feel the refreshing chilliness of its deeply-shadowed avenues, inhale the fragrance of its thousand shrubberies, and thrill anew with undefinable delight, at the deep hollow note of the church-bell, breaking, each hour, with sullen and sudden roar, upon the stillness of the dusky atmosphere in which the fretted Gothic steeple lay imbedded and asleep.

It gives me, perhaps, as much of pleasure as I can now in any manner experience, to dwell upon minute recollections of the school and its concerns. Steeped in misery as I am—misery, alas! only too real—I shall be pardoned for seeking relief, however slight and temporary, in the weakness of a few rambling details. These, moreover, utterly trivial, and even ridiculous in themselves, assume, to my fancy, adventitious importance, as connected with a period and a locality when and where I recognise the first ambiguous monitions of the destiny which afterwards so fully overshadowed me. Let me then remember.

The house, I have said, was old and irregular. The grounds were extensive, and a high and solid brick wall, topped with a bed of mortar and broken glass, encompassed the whole.[6] This prison-like rampart formed the limit of our domain; beyond it we saw but thrice a week—once every Saturday afternoon, when, attended by two ushers, we were permitted to take brief walks in a body through some of the neighboring fields—and twice during Sun-

7   Draco, an Athenian lawmaker, created a legendary code of laws that rigorously imposed the death penalty for even the smallest infractions. Draco's legal code was supposedly so severe that his name became an adjective to describe any harsh set of laws.

8   A level space in a garden containing ornamentally arranged flower beds, the parterre in this story presents an ironic contrast to the barren quality of the rest of the landscaping. The parterre may be realistic: Poe's schoolmaster had an interest in botany and botanical experimentation. In Poe's day, the term "parterre" was sometimes used figuratively to refer to collections of flowery, sentimental literature designed for female readers.

day, when we were paraded in the same formal manner to the morning and evening service in the one church of the village. Of this church the principal of our school was pastor. With how deep a spirit of wonder and perplexity was I wont to regard him from our remote pew in the gallery, as, with step solemn and slow, he ascended the pulpit! This reverend man, with countenance so demurely benign, with robes so glossy and so clerically flowing, with wig so minutely powdered, so rigid and so vast,—could this be he who, of late, with sour visage, and in snuffy habiliments, administered, ferule in hand, the Draconian Laws[7] of the academy? Oh, gigantic paradox, too utterly monstrous for solution!

At an angle of the ponderous wall frowned a more ponderous gate. It was riveted and studded with iron bolts, and surmounted with jagged iron spikes. What impressions of deep awe did it inspire! It was never opened save for the three periodical egressions and ingressions already mentioned; then, in every creak of its mighty hinges, we found a plenitude of mystery—a world of matter for solemn remark, or for more solemn meditation.

The extensive enclosure was irregular in form, having many capacious recesses. Of these, three or four of the largest constituted the play-ground. It was level, and covered with fine hard gravel. I well remember it had no trees, nor benches, nor anything similar within it. Of course it was in the rear of the house. In front lay a small parterre,[8] planted with box and other shrubs; but through this sacred division we passed only upon rare occasions indeed—such as a first advent to school or final departure thence, or perhaps, when a parent or friend having called for us, we joyfully took our way home for the Christmas or Midsummer holydays.

But the house!—how quaint an old building was this!—to me how veritably a palace of enchantment! There was really no end to its windings—to its incomprehensible subdivisions. It was difficult, at any given time, to say with certainty upon which of its two stories one happened to be. From each room to every other there were sure to be found three or four steps either in ascent or descent. Then the lateral branches were innumerable—inconceivable—and so returning in upon themselves, that our most exact ideas in regard to the whole mansion were not very far different from those with which we pondered upon infinity. During the five years of my residence here, I was never able to ascertain with pre-

"The Rev. Dr. Bransby," 1877.

cision, in what remote locality lay the little sleeping apartment assigned to myself and some eighteen or twenty other scholars.

The school-room was the largest in the house—I could not
help thinking, in the world. It was very long, narrow, and dismally
low, with pointed Gothic windows and a ceiling of oak.[9] In a remote and terror-inspiring angle was a square enclosure of eight or
ten feet, comprising the *sanctum*, "during hours," of our principal,
the Reverend Dr. Bransby.[10] It was a solid structure, with massy
door,[11] sooner than open which in the absence of the "Dominie,"
we would all have willingly perished by the *peine forte et dure*.[12] In
other angles were two other similar boxes, far less reverenced, indeed, but still greatly matters of awe. One of these was the pulpit
of the "classical" usher, one of the "English and mathematical."[13]
Interspersed about the room, crossing and recrossing in endless
irregularity, were innumerable benches and desks, black, ancient,
and time-worn, piled desperately with much-bethumbed books,
and so beseamed with initial letters, names at full length, grotesque figures, and other multiplied efforts of the knife, as to have

9   The "pointed Gothic windows" are at odds with the
narrator's earlier characterization of the architecture as
Elizabethan.

10   Poe named William Wilson's schoolmaster after his
own teacher in Stoke Newington. Though the real John
Bransby did not have the Doctor of Divinity Poe gives
him, he was well educated and did have wide-ranging
scholarly interests. According to one obituary: "The Rev.
John Bransby, M.A., was educated at St. John's College,
Cambridge, where he took his Bachelor's degree in 1805,
and that of Master of Arts in 1808. For many years he was
curate of the parish of Stoke Newington, and in 1845 he became rector of Testerton, in the county of Norfolk. In 1814
he was elected a Fellow of the Linnean Society; and he was
also a Fellow of the Society of Antiquaries, of the Geological Society, and of the Cambridge Philosophical Society.
He died at King's Lynn, after a short illness, on the 5th of
March of the present year [1857], at the age of 74" (*Journal
of the Proceedings of the Linnean Society* 2 [1858], xxii).

11   A massy door is a heavy and imposing one, difficult to
open.

12   "Dominie" was another name for schoolmaster. *Peine
forte et dure* was a form of torture involving the placement
of a succession of heavy weights on a prisoner's body until
submission or death.

13   An usher was an assistant to a schoolmaster. Recall
Herman Melville's portrayal of an usher in *Moby-Dick*
(1851): "The pale Usher—threadbare in coat, heart, body,
and brain; I see him now. He was ever dusting his old lexi-
cons and grammars, with a queer handkerchief, mockingly
embellished with all the gay flags of all the known nations
of the world. He loved to dust his old grammars; it somehow mildly reminded him of his mortality."

14   In other words, Wilson attends the academy between the ages of eleven and fifteen.

15   Something unusual or unorthodox, beyond the bounds of propriety.

16   An exergue is a small space usually on the reverse of a coin or medal below the principal device and used for an inscription, date, engraver's initials, or other information. The term can also refer to the inscription itself. In *The Elements of Universal Erudition* (1771), a source Poe often used to add a veneer of learning to his fiction, Jacob Bielfeld describes Carthaginian medals as follows: "They are easily distinguished by their emblem, which is a crocodile resting against a palm tree; and was the arms of the republic of Carthage. There are some of them also that have a human figure on one side holding a spear in one hand, with this inscription Karthago; and on the other the head of a horse, in profile, and under, on the exergue is XLII." Poe reused the term "exergue" in a review of *The Critical and Miscellaneous Writings of Henry Lord Brougham:* "What impression Lord Brougham has stamped upon his age, cannot be accurately determined until Time has fixed and rendered definite the lines of the medal; and fifty years hence it will be difficult, perhaps, even to make out the deepest indentations of the *exergue*" (*Graham's* 20 [1843], 190).

17   Conning, a method of study involved scanning, scrutinizing, poring over a text.

18   Quarrels.

19   "Oh, what a good time it was, that era of iron!" This quotation from Voltaire's *Le Mondain* (1736) frequently occurs in early nineteenth-century French literature.

entirely lost what little of original form might have been their portion in days long departed. A huge bucket with water stood at one extremity of the room, and a clock of stupendous dimensions at the other.

Encompassed by the massy walls of this venerable academy, I passed, yet not in tedium or disgust, the years of the third lustrum of my life.[14] The teeming brain of childhood requires no external world of incident to occupy or amuse it; and the apparently dismal monotony of a school was replete with more intense excitement than my riper youth has derived from luxury, or my full manhood from crime. Yet I must believe that my first mental development had in it much of the uncommon—even much of the *outré*.[15] Upon mankind at large the events of very early existence rarely leave in mature age any definite impression. All is gray shadow—a weak and irregular remembrance—an indistinct regathering of feeble pleasures and phantasmagoric pains. With me this is not so. In childhood I must have felt with the energy of a man what I now find stamped upon memory in lines as vivid, as deep, and as durable as the *exergues* of the Carthaginian medals.[16]

Yet in fact—in the fact of the world's view—how little was there to remember! The morning's awakening, the nightly summons to bed; the connings,[17] the recitations; the periodical half-holidays, and perambulations; the play-ground, with its broils,[18] its pastimes, its intrigues;—these, by a mental sorcery long forgotten, were made to involve a wilderness of sensation, a world of rich incident, an universe of varied emotion, of excitement the most passionate and spirit-stirring. *"Oh, le bon temps, que ce siecle de fer!"*[19]

In truth, the ardor, the enthusiasm, and the imperiousness of my disposition, soon rendered me a marked character among my schoolmates, and by slow, but natural gradations, gave me an ascendancy over all not greatly older than myself;—over all with a single exception. This exception was found in the person of a scholar, who, although no relation, bore the same Christian and surname as myself;—a circumstance, in fact, little remarkable; for, notwithstanding a noble descent, mine was one of those everyday appellations which seem, by prescriptive right, to have been, time out of mind, the common property of the mob. In this narrative I have therefore designated myself as William Wilson,—a ficti-

tious title not very dissimilar to the real. My namesake alone, of
those who in school-phraseology constituted "our set," presumed
to compete with me in the studies of the class—in the sports and
broils of the play-ground—to refuse implicit belief in my assertions, and submission to my will—indeed, to interfere with my arbitrary dictation in any respect whatsoever. If there is on earth a
supreme and unqualified despotism, it is the despotism of a mastermind in boyhood over the less energetic spirits of its companions.

Wilson's rebellion was to me a source of the greatest embarrassment; the more so as, in spite of the bravado with which in
public I made a point of treating him and his pretensions, I secretly
felt that I feared him, and could not help thinking the equality
which he maintained so easily with myself, a proof of his true superiority; since not to be overcome cost me a perpetual struggle.
Yet this superiority—even this equality—was in truth acknowledged by no one but myself; our associates, by some unaccountable blindness, seemed not even to suspect it. Indeed, his competition, his resistance, and especially his impertinent and dogged
interference with my purposes, were not more pointed than private. He appeared to be destitute alike of the ambition which
urged, and of the passionate energy of mind which enabled me to
excel. In his rivalry he might have been supposed actuated solely
by a whimsical desire to thwart, astonish, or mortify myself; although there were times when I could not help observing, with a
feeling made up of wonder, abasement, and pique, that he mingled
with his injuries, his insults, or his contradictions, a certain most
inappropriate, and assuredly most unwelcome *affectionateness* of
manner. I could only conceive this singular behavior to arise from
a consummate self-conceit assuming the vulgar airs of patronage
and protection.

Perhaps it was this latter trait in Wilson's conduct, conjoined
with our identity of name, and the mere accident of our having
entered the school upon the same day, which set afloat the notion
that we were brothers, among the senior classes in the academy.
These do not usually inquire with much strictness into the affairs
of their juniors. I have before said, or should have said, that Wilson was not, in the most remote degree, connected with my family.
But assuredly if we *had* been brothers we must have been twins;
for, after leaving Dr. Bransby's, I casually learned that my name-

20   Poe himself was born on January 19, 1809. In giving his diabolical protagonist the same birthday as himself, as Daniel Hoffman explains, Poe made it much too easy for his literary executor and biographer Rufus W. Griswold to tarnish Poe's character.

21   Achilles, a hero of the Trojan War in Greek mythology, had a reputation for invulnerability. In his infancy, his mother dipped him into the River Styx, making his body invulnerable—except for the only part the water did not touch: the heel by which she held him. During the Trojan War, Paris shot Achilles in the heel with an arrow: a mortal blow.

22   The fauces is the cavity at the back of the mouth above the larynx. Glossing this sentence, Richard Wilbur explains that Poe alludes to the "still small voice" of I Kings 19:12, an expression that has become synonymous with "conscience" ("Edgar Allan Poe," *Major Writers of America*, ed. Perry Miller [New York: Harcourt, Brace, 1962], 422).

sake was born on the nineteenth of January, 1813—and this is a somewhat remarkable coincidence; for the day is precisely that of my own nativity.[20]

It may seem strange that in spite of the continual anxiety occasioned me by the rivalry of Wilson, and his intolerable spirit of contradiction, I could not bring myself to hate him altogether. We had, to be sure, nearly every day a quarrel in which, yielding me publicly the palm of victory, he, in some manner, contrived to make me feel that it was he who had deserved it; yet a sense of pride on my part, and a veritable dignity on his own, kept us always upon what are called "speaking terms," while there were many points of strong congeniality in our tempers, operating to awake in me a sentiment which our position alone, perhaps, prevented from ripening into friendship. It is difficult, indeed, to define, or even to describe, my real feelings towards him. They formed a motley and heterogeneous admixture;—some petulant animosity, which was not yet hatred, some esteem, more respect, much fear, with a world of uneasy curiosity. To the moralist it will be unnecessary to say, in addition, that Wilson and myself were the most inseparable of companions.

It was no doubt the anomalous state of affairs existing between us, which turned all my attacks upon him, (and they were many, either open or covert) into the channel of banter or practical joke (giving pain while assuming the aspect of mere fun) rather than into a more serious and determined hostility. But my endeavors on this head were by no means uniformly successful, even when my plans were the most wittily concocted; for my namesake had much about him, in character, of that unassuming and quiet austerity which, while enjoying the poignancy of its own jokes, has no heel of Achilles in itself,[21] and absolutely refuses to be laughed at. I could find, indeed, but one vulnerable point, and that, lying in a personal peculiarity, arising, perhaps, from constitutional disease, would have been spared by any antagonist less at his wit's end than myself;—my rival had a weakness in the faucial or guttural organs, which precluded him from raising his voice at any time *above a very low whisper.*[22] Of this defect I did not fail to take what poor advantage lay in my power.

Wilson's retaliations in kind were many; and there was one form of his practical wit that disturbed me beyond measure. How his sagacity first discovered at all that so petty a thing would vex me, is a question I never could solve; but, having discovered, he habitually practised the annoyance. I had always felt aversion to my uncourtly patronymic, and its very common, if not plebeian praenomen. The words were venom in my ears; and when, upon the day of my arrival, a second William Wilson came also to the academy, I felt angry with him for bearing the name, and doubly disgusted with the name because a stranger bore it, who would be the cause of its twofold repetition, who would be constantly in my presence, and whose concerns, in the ordinary routine of the school business, must inevitably, on account of the detestable coincidence, be often confounded with my own.

The feeling of vexation thus engendered grew stronger with every circumstance tending to show resemblance, moral or physical, between my rival and myself. I had not then discovered the remarkable fact that we were of the same age; but I saw that we were of the same height, and I perceived that we were even singularly alike in general contour of person and outline of feature. I was galled, too, by the rumor touching a relationship, which had grown current in the upper forms. In a word, nothing could more seriously disturb me, (although I scrupulously concealed such disturbance,) than any allusion to a similarity of mind, person, or condition existing between us. But, in truth, I had no reason to believe that (with the exception of the matter of relationship, and in the case of Wilson himself,) this similarity had ever been made a subject of comment, or even observed at all by our schoolfellows. That *he* observed it in all its bearings, and as fixedly as I, was apparent; but that he could discover in such circumstances so fruitful a field of annoyance, can only be attributed, as I said before, to his more than ordinary penetration.

His cue, which was to perfect an imitation of myself, lay both in words and in actions; and most admirably did he play his part. My dress it was an easy matter to copy; my gait and general manner were, without difficulty, appropriated; in spite of his constitutional defect, even my voice did not escape him. My louder tones were, of course, unattempted, but then the key, it was identical; and *his singular whisper, it grew the very echo of my own.*

How greatly this most exquisite portraiture harassed me, (for it could not justly be termed a caricature,) I will not now venture to describe. I had but one consolation—in the fact that the imitation, apparently, was noticed by myself alone, and that I had to en-

23   There is no evidence that the other schoolboys recognize the rivalry between the two Wilsons—or are even
aware of the namesake's existence. The namesake speaks
in a whisper, is invisibly well-behaved, and sleeps apart
from the other schoolboys in a closetlike space.

dure only the knowing and strangely sarcastic smiles of my namesake himself.[23] Satisfied with having produced in my bosom the
intended effect, he seemed to chuckle in secret over the sting he
had inflicted, and was characteristically disregardful of the public applause which the success of his witty endeavors might have
so easily elicited. That the school, indeed, did not feel his design,
perceive its accomplishment, and participate in his sneer, was, for
many anxious months, a riddle I could not resolve. Perhaps the
gradation of his copy rendered it not so readily perceptible; or,
more possibly, I owed my security to the masterly air of the copy-
ist, who, disdaining the letter, (which in a painting is all the obtuse
can see,) gave but the full spirit of his original for my individual
contemplation and chagrin.

I have already more than once spoken of the disgusting air of
patronage which he assumed toward me, and of his frequent offi-
cious interference with my will. This interference often took the
ungracious character of advice; advice not openly given, but
hinted or insinuated. I received it with a repugnance which gained
strength as I grew in years. Yet, at this distant day, let me do him
the simple justice to acknowledge that I can recall no occasion
when the suggestions of my rival were on the side of those errors
or follies so usual to his immature age and seeming inexperience;
that his moral sense, at least, if not his general talents and worldly
wisdom, was far keener than my own; and that I might, to-day,
have been a better, and thus a happier man, had I less frequently
rejected the counsels embodied in those meaning whispers which I
then but too cordially hated and too bitterly despised.

As it was, I at length grew restive in the extreme under his
distasteful supervision, and daily resented more and more openly
what I considered his intolerable arrogance. I have said that, in the
first years of our connexion as schoolmates, my feelings in regard
to him might have been easily ripened into friendship: but, in the
latter months of my residence at the academy, although the intrusion of his ordinary manner had, beyond doubt, in some measure,
abated, my sentiments, in nearly similar proportion, partook very
much of positive hatred. Upon one occasion he saw this, I think,
and afterwards avoided, or made a show of avoiding me.

It was about the same period, if I remember aright, that, in an
altercation of violence with him, in which he was more than usu-

ally thrown off his guard, and spoke and acted with an openness of demeanor rather foreign to his nature, I discovered, or fancied I discovered, in his accent, his air, and general appearance, a something which first startled, and then deeply interested me, by bringing to mind dim visions of my earliest infancy—wild, confused and thronging memories of a time when memory herself was yet unborn. I cannot better describe the sensation which oppressed me than by saying that I could with difficulty shake off the belief of my having been acquainted with the being who stood before me, at some epoch very long ago—some point of the past even infinitely remote. The delusion, however, faded rapidly as it came; and I mention it at all but to define the day of the last conversation I there held with my singular namesake.

The huge old house, with its countless subdivisions, had several large chambers communicating with each other, where slept the greater number of the students. There were, however, (as must necessarily happen in a building so awkwardly planned,) many little nooks or recesses, the odds and ends of the structure; and these the economic ingenuity of Dr. Bransby had also fitted up as dormitories; although, being the merest closets, they were capable of accommodating but a single individual. One of these small apartments was occupied by Wilson.

One night, about the close of my fifth year at the school, and immediately after the altercation just mentioned, finding every one wrapped in sleep, I arose from bed, and, lamp in hand, stole through a wilderness of narrow passages from my own bedroom to that of my rival. I had long been plotting one of those ill-natured pieces of practical wit at his expense in which I had hitherto been so uniformly unsuccessful. It was my intention, now, to put my scheme in operation, and I resolved to make him feel the whole extent of the malice with which I was imbued. Having reached his closet, I noiselessly entered, leaving the lamp, with a shade over it, on the outside. I advanced a step, and listened to the sound of his tranquil breathing. Assured of his being asleep, I returned, took the light, and with it again approached the bed. Close curtains were around it, which, in the prosecution of my plan, I slowly and quietly withdrew, when the bright rays fell vividly upon the sleeper, and my eyes, at the same moment, upon his countenance. I looked;—and a numbness, an iciness of feeling instantly pervaded

24   What the narrator saw when the lamp's rays fell on the sleeper's face he cannot bring himself to say, but presumably this incident constitutes the first time Wilson recognizes the namesake's countenance as his own.

25   The prestigious English boys' school near Windsor established in the fifteenth century and known for educating numerous British statesmen and writers, including Sir Robert Walpole, William Pitt the Elder, the first Duke of Wellington, William Ewart Gladstone, Henry Fielding, Thomas Gray, Horace Walpole, and Percy Bysshe Shelley.

my frame. My breast heaved, my knees tottered, my whole spirit became possessed with an objectless yet intolerable horror. Gasping for breath, I lowered the lamp in still nearer proximity to the face. Were these—*these* the lineaments of William Wilson? I saw, indeed, that they were his, but I shook as if with a fit of the ague in fancying they were not. What *was* there about them to confound me in this manner? I gazed;—while my brain reeled with a multitude of incoherent thoughts. Not thus he appeared—assuredly not *thus*—in the vivacity of his waking hours. The same name! the same contour of person! the same day of arrival at the academy! And then his dogged and meaningless imitation of my gait, my voice, my habits, and my manner! Was it, in truth, within the bounds of human possibility, that *what I now saw*[24] was the result, merely, of the habitual practice of this sarcastic imitation? Awe-stricken, and with a creeping shudder, I extinguished the lamp, passed silently from the chamber, and left, at once, the halls of that old academy, never to enter them again.

After a lapse of some months, spent at home in mere idleness, I found myself a student at Eton.[25] The brief interval had been sufficient to enfeeble my remembrance of the events at Dr. Bransby's, or at least to effect a material change in the nature of the feelings with which I remembered them. The truth—the tragedy—of the drama was no more. I could now find room to doubt the evidence of my senses; and seldom called up the subject at all but with wonder at the extent of human credulity, and a smile at the vivid force of the imagination which I hereditarily possessed. Neither was this species of skepticism likely to be diminished by the character of the life I led at Eton. The vortex of thoughtless folly into which I there so immediately and so recklessly plunged, washed away all but the froth of my past hours, ingulfed at once every solid or serious impression, and left to memory only the veriest levities of a former existence.

I do not wish, however, to trace the course of my miserable profligacy here—a profligacy which set at defiance the laws, while it eluded the vigilance of the institution. Three years of folly, passed without profit, had but given me rooted habits of vice, and added, in a somewhat unusual degree, to my bodily stature, when, after a week of soulless dissipation, I invited a small party of the most dissolute students to a secret carousal in my chambers. We met at a late hour of the night; for our debaucheries were to be faithfully protracted until morning. The wine flowed freely, and there were not wanting other and perhaps more dangerous seductions; so that the gray dawn had already faintly appeared in the east, while our delirious extravagance was at its height. Madly flushed with cards and intoxication, I was in the act of insisting upon a toast of more than wonted profanity, when my attention was suddenly diverted by the violent, although partial unclosing of the door of the apartment, and by the eager voice of a servant from without. He said that some person, apparently in great haste, demanded to speak with me in the hall.

Wildly excited with wine, the unexpected interruption rather delighted than surprised me. I staggered forward at once, and a few steps brought me to the vestibule of the building. In this low and small room there hung no lamp; and now no light at all was admitted, save that of the exceedingly feeble dawn which made its way through the semi-circular window. As I put my foot over the threshold, I became aware of the figure of a youth about my own height, and habited in a white kerseymere morning frock,[26] cut in the novel fashion of the one I myself wore at the moment. This the faint light enabled me to perceive; but the features of his face I could not distinguish. Upon my entering, he strode hurriedly up to me, and, seizing me by the arm with a gesture of petulant impatience, whispered the words "William Wilson!" in my ear.

I grew perfectly sober in an instant.

There was that in the manner of the stranger, and in the tremulous shake of his uplifted finger, as he held it between my eyes and the light, which filled me with unqualified amazement; but it was not this which had so violently moved me. It was the pregnancy of solemn admonition in the singular, low, hissing utterance; and, above all, it was the character, the tone, *the key*, of those few, simple, and familiar, yet *whispered* syllables, which came with a thousand thronging memories of by-gone days, and struck upon my soul with the shock of a galvanic battery.[27] Ere I could recover the use of my senses he was gone.

Although this event failed not of a vivid effect upon my disordered imagination, yet was it evanescent as vivid. For some weeks, indeed, I busied myself in earnest inquiry, or was wrapped in a cloud of morbid speculation. I did not pretend to disguise from my perception the identity of the singular individual who thus perseveringly interfered with my affairs, and harassed me with his

26 Kerseymere (or cassimere) was a lightweight, fine-quality twilled woollen cloth used for clothes favored by many well-to-do young men, including dandy Harvard undergraduates. One college reporter describes a Harvard commencement: "In one part of the procession, minced and tripped the college beau" wearing a "white Cassimere coat, laced waistcoat, green velvet breeches, silk stockings, and gold buckles" ("Commencement in Olden Time," *Harvard Register*, no. 10 [1827], 304).

27 Like Mary Shelley, Poe too was interested in contemporary debates over animal electricity and accounts of early electrochemistry. See, for example, "The Premature Burial," in which the narrator relates "a well known and very extraordinary case in point, where [a galvanic battery's] action proved the means of restoring to animation a young attorney of London, who had been interred for two days."

28 W. H. Auden describes this sentence: "In isolation, as a prose sentence, it is terrible, vague, verbose, the sense at the mercy of a conventional rhetorical rhythm. But dramatically, how right; how well it reveals the William Wilson who narrates the story in his real colors, as the fantastic self who hates and refuses contact with reality" (Carlson, ed., *Recognition*, 222).

29 Poe accumulated large gambling debts while a student at the University of Virginia. John Allan may not have provided his foster son with sufficient funds for textbooks and other living expenses, so Poe attempted to compensate for the shortfall by gambling. He incurred debts of about two thousand dollars, by contemporary estimates. Possessing a superior memory, an ability to imagine what others thought, and excellent math skills, Poe had the makings of a good gambler, but one crucial aspect of his personality prevented him from gambling success: he could not back down from a challenge. Allan refused to honor his debts and withdrew him from the university (Kevin J. Hayes, *Edgar Allan Poe* [London: Reaktion, 2009], 42–43).

insinuated counsel. But who and what was this Wilson?—and whence came he?—and what were his purposes? Upon neither of these points could I be satisfied—merely ascertaining, in regard to him, that a sudden accident in his family had caused his removal from Dr. Bransby's academy on the afternoon of the day in which I myself had eloped. But in a brief period I ceased to think upon the subject, my attention being all absorbed in a contemplated departure for Oxford. Thither I soon went, the uncalculating vanity of my parents furnishing me with an outfit and annual establishment, which would enable me to indulge at will in the luxury already so dear to my heart—to vie in profuseness of expenditure with the haughtiest heirs of the wealthiest earldoms in Great Britain.

Excited by such appliances to vice, my constitutional temperament broke forth with redoubled ardor, and I spurned even the common restraints of decency in the mad infatuation of my revels. But it were absurd to pause in the detail of my extravagance. Let it suffice, that among spendthrifts I out-Heroded Herod, and that, giving name to a multitude of novel follies, I added no brief appendix to the long catalogue of vices then usual in the most dissolute university of Europe.[28]

It could hardly be credited, however, that I had, even here, so utterly fallen from the gentlemanly estate, as to seek acquaintance with the vilest arts of the gambler by profession, and, having become an adept in his despicable science, to practise it habitually as a means of increasing my already enormous income at the expense of the weak-minded among my fellow-collegians.[29] Such, nevertheless, was the fact. And the very enormity of this offence against all manly and honorable sentiment proved, beyond doubt, the main if not the sole reason of the impunity with which it was committed. Who, indeed, among my most abandoned associates, would not rather have disputed the clearest evidence of his senses, than have suspected of such courses, the gay, the frank, the generous William Wilson—the noblest and most liberal commoner at Oxford—him whose follies (said his parasites) were but the follies of youth and unbridled fancy—whose errors but inimitable whim—whose darkest vice but a careless and dashing extravagance?

I had been now two years successfully busied in this way, when there came to the university a young *parvenu* nobleman, Glendinning[30]—rich, said report, as Herodes Atticus[31]—his riches, too, as easily acquired. I soon found him of weak intellect, and, of course, marked him as a fitting subject for my skill. I frequently engaged him in play, and contrived, with the gambler's usual art, to let him win considerable sums, the more effectually to entangle him in my snares. At length, my schemes being ripe, I met him (with the full intention that this meeting should be final and decisive) at the chambers of a fellow-commoner, (Mr. Preston,)[32] equally intimate with both, but who, to do him justice, entertained not even a remote suspicion of my design. To give to this a better coloring, I had contrived to have assembled a party of some eight or ten, and was solicitously careful that the introduction of cards should appear accidental, and originate in the proposal of my contemplated dupe himself. To be brief upon a vile topic, none of the low finesse was omitted, so customary upon similar occasions that it is a just matter for wonder how any are still found so besotted as to fall its victim.

We had protracted our sitting far into the night, and I had at length effected the manoeuvre of getting Glendinning as my sole antagonist. The game, too, was my favorite *écarté*.[33] The rest of the company, interested in the extent of our play, had abandoned their own cards, and were standing around us as spectators. The *parvenu*, who had been induced by my artifices in the early part of the evening, to drink deeply, now shuffled, dealt, or played, with a wild nervousness of manner for which his intoxication, I thought, might partially, but could not altogether account. In a very short period he had became my debtor to a large amount, when, having taken a long draught of port, he did precisely what I had been coolly anticipating—he proposed to double our already extravagant stakes. With a well-feigned show of reluctance, and not until after my repeated refusal had seduced him into some angry words which gave a color of pique to my compliance, did I finally comply. The result, of course, did but prove how entirely the prey was in my toils:[34] in less than an hour he had quadrupled his debt. For some time his countenance had been losing the florid tinge lent it by the wine; but now, to my astonishment, I perceived that it had grown to a pallor truly fearful. I say, to my astonishment, Glendinning had been represented to my eager inquiries as immeasurably wealthy; and the sums which he had as yet lost, although in themselves vast, could not, I supposed, very seriously annoy, much less

30 A parvenu is a person from a humble background who has rapidly gained wealth or social status. The term implies that the person lacks the manners or accomplishments necessary for the new social position. The name Glendinning comes from Sir Walter Scott's novel *The Monastery* (1820) and its sequel, *The Abbot* (1820). Herman Melville would reuse the name for the title character of his complex psychological novel *Pierre: or, The Ambiguities* (1852).

31 The proverbial comparison—"rich as Croesus"— was commonplace in Poe's day. Using Herodes Atticus, a wealthy Athenian citizen, instead, Poe makes his comparison original. The reference also reinforces Wilson's theatricality, his need to perform his evil deeds before an audience. Herodes Atticus was best known as a patron of the theater and went to great expense to erect or refurbish stadia and theaters in Athens.

32 A private joke. Poe refers to John Thomas Lewis Preston (1811–1890), an old school chum from Joseph H. Clarke's Richmond school. In 1839, Preston founded Virginia Military Institute (VMI), where he also served as professor of Latin.

33 Écarté, a two-handed card game, is played with a pack of thirty-two cards, omitting the two, three, four, five, and six of every suit. Success at écarté requires intense concentration.

34 The term "toil," usually used in the plural, refers to a net or nets designed to enclose a space into which hunters drive their quarry.

35 "William Wilson," as Ann Fabian reads it, illustrates "the pathological isolation of the professed gambler and the financial schemes that perpetuated isolation" (*Card Sharps and Bucket Shops: Gambling in Nineteenth-Century America* [New York: Routledge, 1999], 87).

so violently affect him. That he was overcome by the wine just swallowed, was the idea which most readily presented itself; and, rather with a view to the preservation of my own character in the eyes of my associates, than from any less interested motive, I was about to insist, peremptorily, upon a discontinuance of the play, when some expressions at my elbow from among the company, and an ejaculation evincing utter despair on the part of Glendinning, gave me to understand that I had effected his total ruin under circumstances which, rendering him an object for the pity of all, should have protected him from the ill offices even of a fiend.[35]

What now might have been my conduct it is difficult to say. The pitiable condition of my dupe had thrown an air of embarrassed gloom over all; and, for some moments, a profound silence was maintained, during which I could not help feeling my cheeks tingle with the many burning glances of scorn or reproach cast upon me by the less abandoned of the party. I will even own that an intolerable weight of anxiety was for a brief instant lifted from my bosom by the sudden and extraordinary interruption which ensued. The wide, heavy folding doors of the apartment were all at once thrown open, to their full extent, with a vigorous and rushing impetuosity that extinguished, as if by magic, every candle in the room. Their light, in dying, enabled us just to perceive that a stranger had entered, about my own height, and closely muffled in a cloak. The darkness, however, was now total; and we could only *feel* that he was standing in our midst. Before any one of us could recover from the extreme astonishment into which this rudeness had thrown all, we heard the voice of the intruder.

"Gentlemen," he said, in a low, distinct, and never-to-be-forgotten *whisper* which thrilled to the very marrow of my bones, "Gentlemen, I make no apology for this behavior, because in thus behaving, I am but fulfilling a duty. You are, beyond doubt, uninformed of the true character of the person who has to-night won at *écarté* a large sum of money from Lord Glendinning. I will therefore put you upon an expeditious and decisive plan of obtaining this very necessary information. Please to examine, at your leisure, the inner linings of the cuff of his left sleeve, and the several little packages which may be found in the somewhat capacious pockets of his embroidered morning wrapper."

While he spoke, so profound was the stillness that one might have heard a pin drop upon the floor. In ceasing, he departed at once, and as abruptly as he had entered. Can I—shall I describe my sensations? Must I say that I felt all the horrors of the damned? Most assuredly I had little time for reflection. Many hands roughly seized me upon the spot, and lights were immediately re-procured. A search ensued. In the lining of my sleeve were found all the court cards essential in *écarté*, and, in the pockets of my wrapper, a number of packs, facsimiles of those used at our sittings, with the single exception that mine were of the species called, technically, *arrondées;* the honors being slightly convex at the ends, the lower cards slightly convex at the sides. In this disposition, the dupe who cuts, as customary, at the length of the pack, will invariably find that he cuts his antagonist an honor; while the gambler, cutting at the breadth, will, as certainly, cut nothing for his victim which may count in the records of the game.[36]

Any burst of indignation upon this discovery would have affected me less than the silent contempt, or the sarcastic composure, with which it was received.

"Mr. Wilson," said our host, stooping to remove from beneath his feet an exceedingly luxurious cloak of rare furs, "Mr. Wilson, this is your property." (The weather was cold; and, upon quitting my own room, I had thrown a cloak over my dressing wrapper, putting it off upon reaching the scene of play.) "I presume it is supererogatory[37] to seek here (eyeing the folds of the garment with a bitter smile) for any farther evidence of your skill. Indeed, we have had enough. You will see the necessity, I hope, of quitting Oxford—at all events, of quitting instantly my chambers."

Abased, humbled to the dust as I then was, it is probable that I should have resented this galling language by immediate personal violence, had not my whole attention been at the moment arrested by a fact of the most startling character. The cloak which I had worn was of a rare description of fur; how rare, how extravagantly costly, I shall not venture to say. Its fashion, too, was of my own fantastic invention; for I was fastidious to an absurd degree of coxcombry,[38] in matters of this frivolous nature. When, therefore, Mr. Preston reached me that which he had picked up upon the floor, and near the folding-doors of the apartment, it was with an astonishment nearly bordering upon terror, that I perceived my own already hanging on my arm, (where I had no doubt unwittingly placed it,) and that the one presented me was but its exact counterpart in every, in even the minutest possible particular. The singular

36 Poe is talking about "brief cards," whose edges have either a concave or convex shape so that a sharper's opponent will cut the deck to the sharper's advantage.

37 Doing more than what is necessary.

38 Foppery.

39 Poe echoes "The Gamester," a sketch of a good brother and an evil one that forms part of William Wirt's *The Old Bachelor* (1814). Caught cheating at cards, the evil brother says, "I was kicked out of the room; and driven with scorn and contempt from the society of rogues." See Richard Beale Davis, "Poe and William Wirt," *American Literature* 16 (1944), 212–220.

40 This adverbial phrase, which means ineffectually or to no purpose, was common English usage, though its frequent occurrence in the Bible stresses the impossibility of escaping fate or the day of judgment.

41 The phrase "ends of the earth" comes from Deuteronomy 33:17: "His glory is like the firstling of his bullock, and his horns are like the horns of unicorns: with them he shall push the people together to the ends of the earth: and they are the ten thousands of Ephraim, and they are the thousands of Manasseh."

being who had so disastrously exposed me, had been muffled, I remembered, in a cloak; and none had been worn at all by any of the members of our party with the exception of myself. Retaining some presence of mind, I took the one offered me by Preston; placed it, unnoticed, over my own; left the apartment with a resolute scowl of defiance; and, next morning ere dawn of day, commenced a hurried journey from Oxford to the continent, in a perfect agony of horror and of shame.[39]

I fled in vain.[40] My evil destiny pursued me as if in exultation, and proved, indeed, that the exercise of its mysterious dominion had as yet only begun. Scarcely had I set foot in Paris ere I had fresh evidence of the detestable interest taken by this Wilson in my concerns. Years flew, while I experienced no relief. Villain!—at Rome, with how untimely, yet with how spectral an officiousness, stepped he in between me and my ambition! At Vienna, too—at Berlin—and at Moscow! Where, in truth, had I *not* bitter cause to curse him within my heart? From his inscrutable tyranny did I at length flee, panic-stricken, as from a pestilence; and to the very ends of the earth[41] *I fled in vain.*

And again, and again, in secret communion with my own spirit, would I demand the questions "Who is he?—whence came he?—and what are his objects?" But no answer was there found. And now I scrutinized, with a minute scrutiny, the forms, and the methods, and the leading traits of his impertinent supervision. But even here there was very little upon which to base a conjecture. It was noticeable, indeed, that, in no one of the multiplied instances in which he had of late crossed my path, had he so crossed it except to frustrate those schemes, or to disturb those actions, which, if fully carried out, might have resulted in bitter mischief. Poor justification this, in truth, for an authority so imperiously assumed! Poor indemnity for natural rights of self-agency so pertinaciously, so insultingly denied!

I had also been forced to notice that my tormentor, for a very long period of time, (while scrupulously and with miraculous dexterity maintaining his whim of an identity of apparel with myself,) had so contrived it, in the execution of his varied interference with my will, that I saw not, at any moment, the features of his face. Be Wilson what he might, *this,* at least, was but the veriest of affectation, or of folly. Could he, for an instant, have supposed that, in my admonisher at Eton—in the destroyer of my honor at Oxford,—in him who thwarted my ambition at Rome, my revenge at Paris, my passionate love at Naples, or what he falsely termed my avarice in Egypt,—that in this, my arch-enemy and evil genius, could fail to recognise the William Wilson of my school-boy days,—the namesake, the companion, the rival,—the hated and dreaded rival at Dr. Bransby's? Impossible!—But let me hasten to the last eventful scene of the drama.

Thus far I had succumbed supinely to this imperious domination. The sentiment of deep awe with which I habitually regarded the elevated character, the majestic wisdom, the apparent omnipresence and omnipotence of Wilson, added to a feeling of even terror, with which certain other traits in his nature and assumptions inspired me, had operated, hitherto, to impress me with an idea of my own utter weakness and helplessness, and to suggest an implicit, although bitterly reluctant submission to his arbitrary will. But, of late days, I had given myself up entirely to wine; and its maddening influence upon my hereditary temper rendered me more and more impatient of control. I began to murmur,—to hesitate,—to resist. And was it only fancy which induced me to believe that, with the increase of my own firmness, that of my tormentor underwent a proportional diminution? Be this as it may, I now began to feel the inspiration of a burning hope, and at length nurtured in my secret thoughts a stern and desperate resolution that I would submit no longer to be enslaved.

It was at Rome, during the Carnival of 18—,[42] that I attended a masquerade in the palazzo of the Neapolitan Duke Di Broglio. I had indulged more freely than usual in the excesses of the wine-table; and now the suffocating atmosphere of the crowded rooms irritated me beyond endurance. The difficulty, too, of forcing my way through the mazes of the company contributed not a little to the ruffling of my temper; for I was anxiously seeking, (let me not say with what unworthy motive) the young, the gay, the beautiful wife of the aged and doting Di Broglio. With a too unscrupulous confidence she had previously communicated to me the secret of the costume in which she would be habited, and now, having caught a glimpse of her person, I was hurrying to make my way into her presence. At this moment I felt a light hand placed upon my shoulder, and that ever-remembered, low, damnable *whisper* within my ear.

In an absolute frenzy of wrath, I turned at once upon him who

42 It makes sense that Wilson is attracted to the carnival, a time when social rules are suspended and people can freely engage in aberrant behavior. Given the fact that carnival precedes Lent, a time of penitence, it also makes sense that his better half should show up now to confront him.

Byam Shaw, "A Masquerade in the Palazzo of the Neopolitan Duke Di Broglio," the frontispiece to Edgar Allan Poe, *Selected Tales of Mystery* (London: Sidgwick & Jackson).

43   James Gargano observes: "It is not fortuitous that the resolution of 'William Wilson' takes place at a masquerade. With his passion for design in the smallest details of his fiction, Poe stages the masquerade at the palazzo of the Duke Di Broglio, whose suggestive Italian name means 'intrigue' or 'plot' . . . Wilson's last and decisive confrontation with the mysterious stranger at the masquerade encourages the inference that all of Wilson's flights and tergiversations should be interpreted as a masquerade of self-deception" (*The Masquerade Vision in Poe's Short Stories* [Baltimore: Edgar Allan Poe Society, 1977], 4).

had thus interrupted me, and seized him violently by the collar. He was attired, as I had expected, in a costume altogether similar to my own; wearing a Spanish cloak of blue velvet, begirt about the waist with a crimson belt sustaining a rapier.[43] A mask of black silk entirely covered his face.

"Scoundrel!" I said, in a voice husky with rage, while every syllable I uttered seemed as new fuel to my fury; "scoundrel! impostor! accursed villain! you shall not—you *shall not* dog me unto death! Follow me, or I stab you where you stand!"—and I broke my way from the ball-room into a small ante-chamber adjoining,—dragging him unresistingly with me as I went.

Upon entering, I thrust him furiously from me. He staggered against the wall, while I closed the door with an oath, and commanded him to draw. He hesitated but for an instant; then, with a slight sigh, drew in silence, and put himself upon his defence.

The contest was brief indeed. I was frantic with every species of wild excitement, and felt within my single arm the energy and power of a multitude. In a few seconds I forced him by sheer strength against the wainscoting, and thus, getting him at mercy, plunged my sword, with brute ferocity, repeatedly through and through his bosom.

At that instant some person tried the latch of the door. I hastened to prevent an intrusion, and then immediately returned to my dying antagonist. But what human language can adequately portray *that* astonishment, *that* horror which possessed me at the spectacle then presented to view? The brief moment in which I averted my eyes had been sufficient to produce, apparently, a material change in the arrangements at the upper or farther end of the room. A large mirror,—so at first it seemed to me in my confusion—now stood where none had been perceptible before; and, as I stepped up to it in extremity of terror, mine own image, but with features all pale and dabbled in blood, advanced to meet me with a feeble and tottering gait.[44]

Thus it appeared, I say, but was not. It was my antagonist—it was Wilson, who then stood before me in the agonies of his dissolution. His mask and cloak lay, where he had thrown them, upon the floor. Not a thread in all his raiment—not a line in all the marked and singular lineaments of his face which was not, even in the most absolute identity, *mine own!*

It was Wilson; but he spoke no longer in a whisper, and I could have fancied that I myself was speaking while he said:

"You have conquered, and I yield. Yet, henceforward art thou also dead—dead to the World, to Heaven and to Hope! In me didst thou exist—and, in my death, see by this image, which is thine own, how utterly thou hast murdered thyself."[45]

44 Momentarily perceiving a mirror in front of him, Wilson seems ready to look himself in the eye and own up to all the terrible things he has done, but he backs away from self-confrontation.

45 Though there is some ambiguity about the amount of time that passes between the final scene and the narrator's commitment of his story to paper, presumably he goes on to lead a long life of crime and debauchery, unburdening himself only on his deathbed. At the beginning of the story the narrator says: "I would not, if I could, here or to-day, embody a record of my later years of unspeakable misery, and unpardonable crime. This epoch—these later years—took unto themselves a sudden elevation in turpitude, whose origin alone it is my present purpose to assign. Men usually grow base by degrees. From me, in an instant, all virtue dropped bodily as a mantle." Daniel Hoffmann observes that in Stevenson's *Dr. Jekyll and Mr. Hyde*, the better of the two selves destroys its evil-doing double. Here we have the opposite. If the namesake is Wilson's double in conscience, then the narrator survives in a kind of death in life.

Though modern readers have ignored this story for the most part, Poe's contemporaries enjoyed it very much. Tales of the Grotesque and Arabesque *(1840) marks its first known appearance, but Poe may have published it earlier in a lost or unidentified newspaper or magazine. Once copies of* Tales of the Grotesque and Arabesque *reached Great Britain, William Harrison Ainsworth pirated the story and reprinted it as "The Irish Gentleman and the Little Frenchman" in the July 1840 issue of* Bentley's Miscellany, *thus making it the first of Poe's works to be reprinted overseas. Since Ainsworth published it anonymously, the reprint did nothing to advance Poe's British reputation. The title Ainsworth assigned the story provides a clearer indication of its principal characters—the two men who are rivals for a widow named Mrs. Treacle—but it ignores the comic playfulness of Poe's original title, which suggests a purely causal explanation, medical or physical, for a phenomenon, namely, the sling the Little Frenchmen wears. When William T. Porter, editor of* The Spirit of the Times, *a weekly New York sporting paper, came across the story in* Bentley's, *he liked it so well that he reprinted it in his paper without recognizing Poe's authorship or the tale's American origin. This reprint affirms the story's positive reception among readers in Poe's day: much of the best contemporary humor appeared in* The Spirit of the Times.

"Little Frenchman" represents a kind of light social satire not usually associated with Poe. It anticipates the short fiction of Ring Lardner, a twentieth-century American author who made light social satire his forté. As Lardner does in "Haircut" (1925), for example, Poe presents a story told by a narrator whose viewpoint is severely limited by his poor understanding, lack of sympathy and imagination, and paucity of language. Much as Lardner's obtuse barber-narrator relates the story of a murder without realizing it has occurred, Poe's narrator, Sir Patrick O'Grandison, relates the story of his rivalry with a neighboring Frenchman over the affections of the widow Mrs. Treacle without understanding how the widow feels toward him. Also as in Lardner's "Haircut," Poe's tale is related orally, and its telling forms a vital part of its context.

1   The name of Poe's narrator recalls the hero of Samuel Richardson's *History of Sir Charles Grandison* (1754). Since the appearance of Richardson's novel almost a full century earlier, its title character had become a masculine ideal among English and American readers. Only in the most ironic sense can Poe's O'Grandison be considered a masculine ideal. Poe uses the character to parody the concept. Sir Patrick's street address had biographical significance for Poe. With the intention of establishing a London branch of his firm, John Allan, along with his wife, Frances, and their foster son, Edgar, found lodgings in Bloomsbury at 47 Southampton Row, Russell Square near the British Museum. They later moved to 39 Southampton Row.

Why the Little Frenchman Wears His Hand in a Sling

It's on my wisiting cards sure enough (and it's them that's all o' pink satin paper) that inny gintleman that plases may behould the intheristhin words, "Sir Pathrick O'Grandison, Barronitt, 39 Southampton Row, Russell Square, Parrish o' Bloomsbury."[1] And shud ye be wantin to diskiver who is the pink of purliteness[2] quite, and the laider of the hot tun[3] in the houl city o' Lonon—why it's jist mesilf. And fait that same is no wonder at all at all, (so be plased to stop curlin your nose,)[4] for every inch o' the six wakes that I've been a gintleman, and left aff wid the bog-throthing[5] to take up wid the Barronissy, it's Pathrick that's been living like a houly imperor,[6] and gitting the iddication and the graces. Och! and would'nt it be a blessed thing for your sperrits if ye cud lay your two peepers jist, upon Sir Pathrick O'Grandison, Barronitt, when he is all riddy drissed for the hopperer, or stipping into the Brisky[7] for the drive into the Hyde Park.[8]—But it's the iligant big figgur that I ave, for the rason o' which all the ladies fall in love wid me. Isn't it my own swate silf now that'll missure the six fut, and the three inches more nor that, in me stockings, and that am excadingly will proportioned all over to match? And it is ralelly more than three fut and a bit that there is, inny how, of the little ould furrener Frinchman[9] that lives jist over the way, and that's a oggling and a goggling the houl day, (and bad luck to him,) at the purty widdy Misthress Tracle that's my own nixt door neighbor, (God bliss her) and a most particuller frind and acquaintance? You percave the little spalpeen[10] is summat down in the mouth, and wears his lift hand in a sling; and it's for that same thing, by yur lave, that I'm going to give you the good rason.[11]

The truth of the houl matter is jist simple enough; for the very first day that I com'd from Connaught,[12] and showd my swate little silf in the strait to the widdy, who was looking through the windy, it was a gone case althegither wid the heart o' the purty Misthress Tracle. I percaved it, ye see, all at once, and no mistake, and that's God's thruth. First of all it was up wid the windy in a jiffy, and thin she threw open her two peepers to the itmost, and thin it was a little gould spy-glass that she clapped tight to one o' them, and divil may burn me if it didn't spake to me as plain as a peeper

2   After mentioning the pinkish hue of his visiting cards, Sir Patrick attempts a clever play on words, identifying himself as being in the pink of politeness. Used in this manner, the word "pink" means "the most excellent example of something; the embodiment or model of a particular quality" *(OED)*. Having Sir Patrick use the word "pink" to describe both the color of his visiting cards and the essence of his personality, Poe reinforces the strong connection that existed in the nineteenth century between the visiting card and the person it identified. Sir Patrick's fascination with the color of his cards and the quality of their paper brings to mind Patrick Bateman's fascination with his handsomely printed business cards in Bret Easton Ellis's *American Psycho* (1991). In each instance, the elegant appearance of the card bears little resemblance to the person it identifies. In Sir Patrick's case, the falseness of the impression shows as soon as he opens his mouth. The spoken word exposes what the printed word masks (Kevin J. Hayes, "Understanding 'Why the Little Frenchman Wears His Hand in a Sling,'" in *Edgar Allan Poe: Beyond Gothicism*, ed. James M. Hutchisson [Newark: University of Delaware Press, 2011], 124).

3   Sir Patrick means "haut ton," which contemporary lexicographer Jon Bee defines as "the highest orders of society, who see life; they are so denominated by the *bon-ton* and *bon-genre*, and are all of high breeding and large fortune. Money alone does not confer the *haût-titre*, nor giving a ball in a fine house; nor commanding a play, nor driving four-in-hand, but these together may constitute *haût-ton* with very little trouble" (*Slang: A Dictionary of the Turf, the Ring, the Chase, the Pit, of Bon-Ton, and the Varieties of Life* [London: for T. Hughes, 1823], 94).

4   To express scorn or contempt, a person should curl the lip, not the nose. Sir Patrick's misuse of the phrase indicates his tenuous grasp of the English language, but the expression about curling the nose was not unprecedented. The pseudonymous author Peter Paragraph observes, "You must know, sir, that my nose has always had an inveterate tendency to curl its nostrils at presumption, vanity, self-importance, and folly" ("Another Hit at the Nose," *New-York Literary Gazette* 1 [December 24, 1825], 250).

5   "Bog-trotter" is derogatory slang for an Irishman.

6   The proverbial simile is "like an emperor." Poe's comparison to a holy emperor is original.

7   Once the German Britzschka was brought to England, it found favor among both coachmen and mechanics, who appreciated its lightness, a feature contributing to its anglicized name, Brisker or Brisky (William Bridges Adams, *English Pleasure Carriages: Their Origin, History, Varieties, Materials, Construction, Defects, Improvements, and Capabilities* [London: Charles Knight, 1837], 231).

8   Located in west London, Hyde Park, according to a contemporary guidebook, was "open every day in the year, to all ranks of society, from six in the morning till nine at night; and vehicles of every description are admitted, except hackney and stage carriages and loaded carts. The rides and walks in this park have long been noted for the assemblage of genteel and fashionable people for the benefit of the air. Saturday is a grand day for the select; but on Sundays, in particular, the broad footway, from Knightsbridge towards Kensington-gardens, and the spacious grounds around, are crowded with gay and fashionably-dressed persons, with equipages and horses of every description" (John H. Brady, *A New Pocket Guide to London and Its Environs* [London: John W. Parker, 1838], 73).

9   Poking fun at the Frenchman's diminutive stature, Sir Patrick implicitly denigrates his sexual prowess. Poe's use of a little Frenchman is typical of the times. In American culture, the little Frenchman had already become an object of humorous derision. Augustus Baldwin Longstreet, for example, includes "a gay, smerky little Frenchman" in *Georgia Scenes* (1835). The author who most strongly influenced Poe in this regard was George P. Morris, whose story "The Little Frenchman" was reprinted as part of "Biographical Sketch of George P. Morris," *Southern Literary Messenger* 4 (1838), 663–671.

10   A rascal.

11   Poe's use of dialect performs a significant rhetorical function, alerting readers to the possibility that the narrator is simply a fool. His violations of standard English thus prepare the way for his violations of behavioral standards. By the end of the opening paragraph, as

Wayne C. Booth observes, "everyone must feel very sure that all the ladies do *not* fall in love with the speaker and that, in fact, most of his claims about himself will prove false. In short, *that* the passage is ironic is unmistakably revealed through violations of stylistic norms that the reader shares with Poe" (*A Rhetoric of Irony* [Chicago: University of Chicago Press, 1974], 70).

12   Or Connacht, a province in western Ireland.

13   An Irish term for "my darling."

14   In another attempt at cleverness, Sir Patrick combines a proverbial phrase—"in the twinkling of an eye"—with the eye of a potato. In Irish-English slang, potatoes were called praties. Consider the following lines in praise of potatoes from "Dear Praties, We Can't Do Without Them":

> They make the boys stout, and they keep the girls slender,
> They soften the heart and they strengthen the mind;
> And the man from the bog, or the lord in high splendour,
> All live by praties, as all folks can find.

(*Universal Songster* [1834], I, 27–28)

15   Giving this dancing master a name that sounds like "Luchesi," Poe was making a private reference to Frederick Lucchesi, a Baltimore musician and music teacher.

16   Parlez-vous (Do you speak?), Voulez-vous (Would you like?).

cud spake, and says it, through the spy-glass, "Och! the tip o' the mornin to ye, Sir Pathrick O'Grandison, Barronitt, mavourneen;[13] and it's a nate gintleman that ye are, sure enough, and it's mesilf and me forten jist that'll be at yur sarvice, dear, inny time o' day at all at all for the asking." And it's not mesilf ye wud have to be bate in the purliteness; so I made her a bow that wud ha broken yur heart althegither to behould, and thin I pulled aff me hat with a flourish, and thin I winked at her hard wid both eyes, as much as to say, "Thrue for you, yer a swate little crature, Mrs. Tracle, me darlint, and I wish I may be drownthed dead in a bog, if it's not mesilf, Sir Pathrick O'Grandison, Barronitt, that'll make a houl bushel o' love to yur leddy-ship, in the twinkling o' the eye of a Londonderry purraty."[14]

And it was the nixt mornin, sure, jist as I was making up me mind whither it wouldn't be the purlite thing to sind a bit o' writin to the widdy by way of a love-litter, when up cum'd the delivery sarvant wid an illigant card, and he tould me that the name on it (for I niver cud rade the copper-plate printin on account of being lift handed) was all about Mounseer, the Count, A Goose, Look-aisy, Maiter-di-dauns,[15] and that the houl of the divilish lingo was the spalpeeny long name of the little ould furrener Frinchman as lived over the way.

And jist wid that in cum'd the little willian himself, and thin he made me a broth of a bow, and thin he said he had ounly taken the liberty of doing me the honor of the giving me a call, and thin he went on to palaver at a great rate, and divil the bit did I comprehind what he wud be afther the tilling me at all at all, excipting and saving that he said "pully wou, woolly wou,"[16] and tould me, among a bushel o' lies, bad luck to him, that he was mad for the love o' my widdy Misthress Tracle, and that my widdy Mrs. Tracle had a puncheon for *him*.

At the hearin of this, ye may swear, though, I was as mad as a grasshopper, but I remimbered that I was Sir Pathrick O'Grandison, Barronitt, and that it wasn't althegither gentaal to lit the anger git the upper hand o' the purliteness, so I made light o' the matter and kipt dark, and got quite sociable wid the little chap, and afther a while what did he do but ask me to go wid him to the widdy's, saying he wud give me the feshionable inthroduction to her leddyship.

"Is it there ye are?" said I thin to mesilf, "and it's thrue for you,

Pathrick, that ye're the fortunnittest mortal in life. We'll soon see now whither it's your swate silf, or whither it's little Mounseer Maiter-di-dauns, that Misthress Tracle is head and ears in the love wid."

Wid that we wint aff to the widdy's, next door, and ye may well say it was an illigant place; so it was. There was a carpet all over the floor, and in one corner there was a forty-pinny and a jews-harp[17] and the divil knows what ilse, and in another corner was a sofy, the beautifullest thing in all natur, and sitting on the sofy, sure enough, there was the swate little angel, Misthress Tracle.

"The tip o' the morning to ye," says I, "Mrs. Tracle," and thin I made sich an illigant obaysance that it wud ha quite althegither bewildered the brain o' ye.

"Wully woo, pully woo, plump in the mud,"[18] says the little furrenner Frinchman, "and sure Mrs. Tracle," says he, that he did, "isn't this gintleman here jist his reverence Sir Pathrick O'Grandison, Barronitt, and isn't he althegither and entirely the most particular frind and acquintance that I have in the houl world?"

And wid that the widdy, she gits up from the sofy, and makes the swatest curtchy nor iver was seen; and thin down she sits like an angel; and thin, by the powers, it was that little spalpeen Mounseer Maiter-di-dauns that plumped his silf right down by the right side of her. Och hon! I ixpicted the two eyes o' me wud ha cum'd out of my head on the spot, I was so dispirate mad! Howiver, "Bait who!" says I, after a while. "Is it there ye are, Mounseer Maiter-di-dauns?" and so down I plumped on the lift side of her leddyship, to be aven wid the willain. Botheration! it wud ha done your heart good to percave the illigant double wink that I gived her jist thin right in the face wid both eyes.

But the little ould Frinchman he niver beginned to suspict me at all at all, and disperate hard it was he made the love to her leddyship. "Woully wou," says he, "Pully wou," says he, "Plump in the mud," says he.

"That's all to no use, Mounseer Frog, mavourneen," thinks I; and I talked as hard and as fast as I could all the while, and throth it was mesilf jist that divarted her leddyship complately and intirely, by rason of the illigant conversation that I kipt up wid her all about the dear bogs of Connaught. And by and by she gived me such a swate smile, from one ind of her mouth to the ither, that it made

17 Sir Patrick apparently means a pianoforte and a harp, which he confuses with a jew's harp, a small, inexpensive instrument that fits in the mouth. Sir Patrick's confusion reveals his ignorance and also serves as a class marker.

18 Though the phrase "plump in the mud" does make fun of the way spoken French sounds, Poe's parody is unoriginal. He borrowed the phrase from Frederick Marryat's *Jacob Faithful* (1834), a novel that takes for its subject the life of a Thames waterman. Describing one of their dangerous escapes, Young Tom Beazley says to his father: "And if we had tumbled, father, we should have just died betwixt and between, not water enough to float us. It would have been *woolez wous parlez wous*, plump in the mud, as you say sometimes." See Kevin J. Hayes, "Poe's 'Little Frenchman' and Marryat's *Jacob Faithful*," *Notes and Queries* 59 (2012), 394–395.

19   According to a traditional folktale, two Kilkenny cats fought each other until there was nothing left but two tails and little fluff. The story was so well known that the Kilkenny cats became proverbial and frequently appeared in contemporary comparisons. In a letter to Frederick W. Thomas of September 12, 1842, Poe mentioned a literary battle between two contemporary litterateurs, Park Benjamin and Louis F. Tasistro: "Have you seen how Benjamin and Tasistro have been playing Kilkenny cats with each other?" (*Collected Letters of Edgar Allan Poe*, ed. John Ward Ostrom, Burton R. Pollin, and Jeffrey A. Savoye, 2 vols. [New York: Gordian Press, 2008], I, 359).

me as bould as a pig, and I jist took hould of the ind of her little finger in the most dillikittest manner in natur, looking at her all the while out o' the whites of my eyes.

And then ounly percave the cuteness of the swate angel, for no sooner did she obsarve that I was afther the squazing of her flipper, than she up wid it in a jiffy, and put it away behind her back, jist as much as to say, "Now thin, Sir Pathrick O'Grandison, there's a bitther chance for ye, mavourneen, for it's not altogether the gentaal thing to be afther the squazing of my flipper right full in the sight of that little furrenner Frinchman, Mounseer Maiter-di-dauns."

Wid that I giv'd her a big wink jist to say, "lit Sir Pathrick alone for the likes o' them thricks," and thin I wint aisy to work, and you'd have died wid the divarsion to behould how cliverly I slipped my right arm betwane the back o' the sofy, and the back of her leddyship, and there, sure enough, I found a swate little flipper all a waiting to say, "the tip o' the mornin to ye, Sir Pathrick O'Grandison, Barronitt." And wasn't it mesilf, sure, that jist giv'd it the laste little bit of a squaze in the world, all in the way of a commincement, and not to be too rough wid her leddyship? and och, botheration, wasn't it the gentaalest and dilikittest of all the little squazes that I got in return? "Blood and thunder, Sir Pathrick, mavourneen," thinks I to myself, "fait it's jist the mother's son of you, and nobody else at all at all, that's the handsomest and the fortunittest young bogthrotter that ever cum'd out of Connaught!" And wid that I giv'd the flipper a big squaze, and a big squaze it was, by the powers, that her leddyship giv'd to me back. But it would ha split the seven sides of you wid the laffin to behould, jist then all at once, the consated behavior of Mounseer Maiter-di-dauns. The likes o' sich a jabbering, and a smirking, and a parley-wouing as he begin'd wid her leddyship, niver was known before upon arth; and divil may burn me if it wasn't me own very two peepers that cotch'd him tipping her the wink out of one eye. Och, hon? if it wasn't mesilf thin that was mad as a Kilkenny cat[19] I shud like to be tould who it was!

"Let me infarm you, Mounseer Maiter-di-dauns," said I, as purlite as iver ye seed, "that it's not the gintaal thing at all at all, and not for the likes o' you inny how, to be afther the oggling and a goggling at her leddyship in that fashion," and jist wid that such another squaze as it was I giv'd her flipper, all as much as to say, "isn't it Sir Pathrick now, my jewel, that'll be able to the protecting o' you, my darlint?" and then there cum'd another squaze back, all by way of the answer. "Thrue for you, Sir Pathrick," it said as plain as iver a squaze said in the world, "Thrue for you, Sir Pathrick, mavourneen, and it's a proper nate gintleman ye are—that God's truth," and wid that she opened her two beautiful peepers till I belaved they wud ha com'd out of her hid althegither and intirely, and she looked first as mad as a cat at Mounseer Frog, and thin as smiling as all out o' doors at mesilf.

"Thin," says he, the willian, "Och hon! and a wolly-wou, pully-wou," and then wid that he shoved up his two shoulders till the divil the bit of his hid was to be diskivered, and then he let down the two corners of his purraty-trap,[20] and thin not a haporth more of the satisfaction could I git out o' the spalpeen.

Belave me, my jewel, it was Sir Pathrick that was unrasonable mad thin, and the more by token that the Frinchman kipt an wid his winking at the widdy; and the widdy she kipt an wid the squazing of my flipper, as much as to say, "At him again Sir Pathrick O'Grandison, mavourneen;" so I just ripped out wid a big oath, and says I,

"Ye little spalpeeny frog of a bog throtting son of a bloody-noun!"—and jist thin what d'ye think it was that her leddyship did? Troth she jumped up from the sofy as if she was bit, and made off through the door, while I turned my head round afther her, in a complete bewilderment and botheration, and followed her wid me two peepers. You percave I had a reason of my own for knowing that she could'nt git down the stares althegither and entirely; for I knew very well that I had hould of her hand, for the divil the bit had I iver lit it go. And says I,

"Isn't it the laste little bit of a mistake in the world that ye've been afther the making, yer leddyship? Come back now, that's a darlint, and I'll give ye yur flipper." But aff she wint down the stairs like a shot, and thin I turned round to the little Frinch furrenner. Och hon! if it wasn't his spalpeeny little paw that I had hould of in my own—why thin—thin it was'nt—that's all.

"And maybe it wasn't mesilf that jist died then outright wid the laffin, to behould the little chap when he found out that it wasn't the widdy at all at all that he had hould of all the time, but only Sir Pathrick O'Grandison. The ould divil himself niver behild sich a long face as he pet an! As for Sir Pathrick O'Grandison, Barronitt,

20 His mouth (potato trap).

it wasn't for the likes of his riverence to be afther the minding of a thrifle of a mistake. Ye may jist say, though (for it's God's thruth) that afore I lift hould of the flipper of the spalpeen, (which was not till afther her leddyship's futman had kicked us both down the stairs,) I gived it such a nate little broth of a squaze, as made it all up into raspberry jam.

"Wouly-wou," says he, "pully-wou," says he—"Cot tam!"

And that's jist the thruth of the rason why he wears his left hand in a sling.

The Business Man

Method is the soul of business.
                              Old Saying[1]

I am a business man.[2] I am a methodical man. Method is *the* thing, after all. But there are no people I more heartily despise, than your eccentric fools who prate about method without understanding it; attending strictly to its letter, and violating its spirit.[3] These fellows are always doing the most out-of-the-way things in what they call an orderly manner. Now here—I conceive is a positive paradox.[4] True method appertains to the ordinary and the obvious alone, and cannot be applied to the *outré*. What definite idea can a body attach to such expressions as "methodical Jack o' Dandy,"[5] or "a systematical Will o' the Wisp?"

My notions upon this head might not have been so clear as they are, but for a fortunate accident which happened to me when I was a very little boy. A good-hearted old Irish nurse (whom I shall not forget in my will) took me up one day by the heels, when I was making more noise than was necessary, and, swinging me round two or three times, d——d my eyes for "a shreeking little spalpeen,"[6] and then knocked my head into a cocked hat against the bed-post. This, I say, decided my fate, and made my fortune. A bump arose at once on my sinciput, and turned out to be as pretty an organ of *order* as one shall see on a summer's day.[7] Hence that positive appetite for system and regularity which has made me the distinguished man of business that I am.

If there is any thing on earth I hate, it is a genius.[8] Your geniuses are all arrant asses—the greater the genius the greater the ass—and to this rule there is no exception whatever. Especially, you cannot make a man of business out of a genius, any more than money out of a Jew,[9] or the best nutmegs out of pineknots. The

Poe could speak quite contemptuously of America's burgeoning democratic capitalist culture. Writing in the Southern Literary Messenger *in 1836, for example, he heaped scorn on a money-grubbing society that refused to support its writers: "When* shall *the artist assume his proper situation in society—in a society of thinking beings? How long shall he be enslaved? How long shall mind succumb to the grossest materiality? How long shall the veriest vermin of the Earth, who crawl around the altar of Mammon, be more esteemed of men than they, the gifted ministers to those exalted emotions which link us with the mysteries of Heaven? To our own query we may venture a reply. Not long. Not long will such rank injustice be committed or permitted. A spirit is already abroad at war with it. And in every billow of the unceasing sea of Change—and in every breath, however gentle, of the wide atmosphere of Revolution encircling us, is that spirit steadily yet irresistibly at work"* (Essays and Reviews, *ed. G. R. Thompson [New York: Library of America, 1984], 164). Four years later, still awaiting the cultural Revolution, Poe channeled his contempt into "The Business Man," which J. A. Leo Lemay has called "a splendid satirical epitome of that emerging cultural ideal of American middle-class society—the self-made wealthy businessman." This tale Lemay calls "one of the cruelest burlesques of antebellum American materialism" ("Poe's 'The Business Man': Its Contexts and Satire of Franklin's* Autobiography," *Poe Studies 15 [1982], 29–37).*

"Peter Pendulum, The Business Man," as Poe originally titled the story, debuted in the February 1840 issue of Burton's. *The tale is better known by its last version, "The Business Man," which Poe published in the August 2, 1845, issue of the* Broadway Journal. *Mabbott theorized that Poe published an interim version of "The Business Man," possibly in the* Philadelphia Saturday Museum, *many issues of which do not survive. John E. Reilly confirmed Mabbott's theory, locating two Rhode Island reprints from 1843. Reilly shows that when Poe republished the story that year, he revised its text significantly, turning his original subtitle into the main title, changing the name of his protagonist from "Peter Pendulum" to "Peter Proffit," adding six more paragraphs at the end, and revising the text elsewhere ("The 'Missing' Version of Edgar Allan Poe's 'The Business Man,'" American Periodicals 9 [1999], 1–14).*

1 Poe's motto has several precedents. In *The Compleat English Tradesman* (1727), for example, Daniel Defoe observes: "The Reason and End of the Tradesman is to get Money: 'Tis the Pole-Star and Guide, the Aim and Design of all his Motions; 'tis the Center and Point to which all his Actions tend; 'tis the Soul of Business, the Spur of Industry, the Wheel that turns within all the Wheels of his whole

Business, and gives Motion to all the rest." In *Letters to His Son* (1774), Lord Chesterfield advises: "Dispatch is the soul of business; and nothing contributes more to dispatch, than method. Lay down a method for every thing, and stick to it inviolably, as far as unexpected incidents may allow." Lemay suggests that the motto sounds like something from *Poor Richard's Almanac* and scathingly encapsulates Franklin's emphasis in the *Autobiography* on practical methods for self-improvement ("Poe's 'The Business Man,'" 29–31).

2   The first version of this story begins: "My name is Pendulum—Peter Pendulum. I am a business man." The revision gets to the heart of the matter: In a capitalist culture, we are defined by what we do for a living, not who we are.

3   Compare II Corinthians 3:6: "Who also hath made us able ministers of the new testament; not of the letter, but of the spirit: for the letter killeth, but the spirit giveth life." See also Romans 7:6: "But now we are delivered from the law, that being dead wherein we were held; that we should serve in newness of spirit, and not in the oldness of the letter."

4   This phrase repeats the name of a character in "Lionizing" (1835), one of Poe's early humorous tales: "There was Sir Positive Paradox. He said that all fools were philosophers, and all philosophers were fools."

5   Jack-o'-Dandy, according to slang etymologist Jon Bee, can mean anyone who affects dandy manners: "foolish, proud, and choleric as a turkey or *dindon* (the 'n' being mute) whence by easy transition to dandy.

> Handy, spandy, *Jack o' Dandy*,
> Lov'd plum-cake and sugar-candy;
> He bought some at a grocer's shop,
> And well pleas'd went off with a hop—hop, hop."

(*Slang: A Dictionary of the Turf, the Ring, the Chase, the Pit, of Bon-Ton, and the Varieties of Life* [London: for T. Hughes, 1823], 102)

6   A screeching little rascal.

7   The sinciput is the front part of the head or skull. The phrase "organ of order" reflects the vocabulary of phrenology. Those with prominent organs of order arrange the material objects around them with precision. This nasty

creatures are always going off at a tangent into some fantastic employment, or ridiculous speculation, entirely at variance with the "fitness of things,"[10] and having no business whatever to be considered as a business at all. Thus you may tell these characters immediately by the nature of their occupations. If you ever perceive a man setting up as a merchant or a manufacturer; or going into the cotton or tobacco trade, or any of those eccentric pursuits; or getting to be a dry-goods dealer, or soap-boiler,[11] or something of that kind; or pretending to be a lawyer, or a blacksmith, or a physician—anything out of the usual way—you may set him down at once as a genius, and then, according to the rule-of-three, he's an ass.[12]

Now I am not in any respect a genius, but a regular business man. My Day-book[13] and Ledger will evince this in a minute. They are well kept, though I say it myself; and, in my general habits of accuracy and punctuality, I am not to be beat by a clock. Moreover, my occupations have been always made to chime in with the ordinary habitudes of my fellow-men. Not that I feel the least indebted, upon this score, to my exceedingly weak-minded parents, who, beyond doubt, would have made an arrant genius of me at last, if my guardian angel had not come, in good time, to the rescue. In biography the truth is everything, and in auto-biography it is especially so—yet I scarcely hope to be believed when I state, however solemnly, that my poor father put me, when I was about fifteen years of age, into the counting-house of what he termed "a respectable hardware and commission merchant doing a capital bit of business!" A capital bit of fiddlestick![14] However, the consequence of this folly was, that in two or three days, I had to be sent home to my button-headed family in a high state of fever, and with a most violent and dangerous pain in the sinciput, all round about my organ of order. It was nearly a gone case with me then—just touch-and-go for six weeks—the physicians giving me up and all that sort of thing. But, although I suffered much, I was a thankful boy in the main. I was saved from being a "respectable hardware and commission merchant, doing a capital bit of business," and I felt grateful to the protuberance which had been the means of my salvation, as well as to the kind-hearted female who had originally put these means within my reach.

The most of boys run away from home at ten or twelve years of

Nathaniel Currier, *Benjamin Franklin: The Statesman and Philosopher*, 1847. This hand-colored Currier lithograph portrays Franklin in a dignified and respectful manner, reflecting the American public's high regard for him in the 1840s, an attitude "The Business-Man" parodies.

age, but I waited till I was sixteen. I don't know that I should have gone, even then, if I had not happened to hear my old mother talk about setting me up on my own hook in the grocery way. The *grocery* way!—only think of that! I resolved to be off forthwith, and try and establish myself in some *decent* occupation, without dancing attendance any longer upon the caprices of these eccentric old people, and running the risk of being made a genius of in the end. In this project I succeeded perfectly well at the first effort, and

knock on the head is a knock against both material greed and the tenets of phrenology. In Poe's day, many embraced phrenology as a valid scientific pursuit, as did Poe for a time anyway, but he would become increasingly skeptical of its claims.

8 Fairly or unfairly, Poe establishes an opposition between creative endeavor (genius) and the business of making money. Poe's businessman, however, is a mere swindler. If Proffit's success can be attributed to method, then it is method only and always in the service of making money, as the narrator's name suggests. He is clever, egotistic, opportunistic, unethical, and utterly ruthless.

Never far beneath the surface of "The Business Man" is Poe's anger at his own inability to make a living as a writer. In a letter of 1844 to Charles Anthon, Poe lamented the "sad poverty & the thousand consequent contumelies & other ills which the condition of the mere Magazinist entails upon him in America—where more than in any other region upon the face of the globe to be poor is to be despised" (*Collected Letters of Edgar Allan Poe*, ed. John Ward Ostrom, Burton R. Pollin, and Jeffrey A. Savoye, 2 vols. [New York: Gordian Press, 2008], I, 470).

In the wake of the Panic of 1837, Poe would come to understand painfully the ways in which literary production is tied to production more generally. The depression threw the publishing industry into chaos, increasing the demand for writing in the penny press but making it difficult for commercial writers to earn a living wage.

9 Poe finds a ready handle in the trope of the shrewd, tightfisted Jew: anti-Semitism was deeply ingrained in nineteenth-century American culture.

10 The phrase refers to the ethical theory of the English philosopher and clergyman Samuel Clarke (1675–1729), who believed that in relationship to human will moral conduct had a natural, objective fitness or suitableness, analogous to the laws that govern the physical universe. The "fitness of things" means human conduct that is naturally appropriate or suitable.

11 Poe alludes to the trade of Benjamin Franklin's father, who was a tallow chandler (maker of tallow candles) and soap boiler. Refusing his parents' occupational suggestions, Peter Proffit re-enacts Franklin's rejection of a series of trades his father chose for him. The close verbal parallels between "The Business Man" and Franklin's *Autobiography*, Lemay argues, demonstrate that Poe was consciously burlesquing Franklin ("Poe's 'The Business Man,'" 29–31).

12   The rule of three is a mathematical term referring to "a method of finding a fourth quantity, given three known quantities, which bears the same relation to the third as the second does to the first, or (equivalently) the same relation to the second as the third does to the first" *(OED)*.

13   A day-book is a ledger in which commercial transactions, both sales and purchases, are entered immediately in the order in which they occur.

14   The word "fiddlestick" means something insignificant or absurd.

15   Employed as an animated billboard, the sandwich-man—sandwiched between placards—was an increasingly prominent urban sight in Poe's day.

16   A maxim dating back to antiquity, and a cliché. Novelist Thomas Haynes Bayley, for instance, says: "He had heard from his father that money made the man, and while he could chink his purse in his pocket, he felt confident in being looked upon as a perfect gentleman" (*David Dumps; or, The Budget of Blunders* [Philadelphia: E. L. Carey and A. Hart, 1838], 13).

17   A proverbial phrase, "to cut and come again," means cutting a slice from, say, a roast and returning repeatedly to cut off more meat. It was used figuratively to denote an abundant, seemingly inexhaustible supply of something. In "The Mudfrog Papers," (1837–1838), Charles Dickens includes a character named Dr. Kutankumagen, a Russian physician who specializes in bleeding patients.

by the time I was fairly eighteen, found myself doing an extensive and profitable business in the Tailor's Walking-Advertisement line.[15]

I was enabled to discharge the onerous duties of this profession, only by that rigid adherence to system which formed the leading feature of my mind. A scrupulous *method* characterized my actions as well as my accounts. In my case, it was method—not money—which made the man:[16] at least all of him that was not made by the tailor whom I served. At nine, every morning, I called upon that individual for the clothes of the day. Ten o'clock found me in some fashionable promenade or other place of public amusement. The precise regularity with which I turned my handsome person about, so as to bring successively into view every portion of the suit upon my back, was the admiration of all the knowing men in the trade. Noon never passed without my bringing home a customer to the house of my employers, Messrs. Cut and Comeagain.[17] I say this proudly, but with tears in my eyes—for the firm proved themselves the basest of ingrates. The little account about which we quarrelled and finally parted, cannot, in any item, be thought overcharged, by gentlemen really conversant with the nature of the business. Upon this point, however, I feel a degree of proud satisfaction in permitting the reader to judge for himself. My bill ran thus:

Messrs. Cut and Comeagain, Merchant Tailors.
　　To Peter Proffit, *Walking Advertiser*,

		Drs.
July 10.	To promenade, as usual, and customer brought home,	$00 25
July 11.	To　　do　　do　　do	25
July 12.	To one lie, second class; damaged black cloth sold for invisible green,[18]	25
July 13.	To one lie, first class, extra quality and size; recommending milled sattinet[19] as broad-cloth,	75
July 20.	To purchasing bran new paper shirt collar or dickey, to set off gray Petersham,[20]	2
Aug. 15.	To wearing double-padded bobtail frock,[21] (thermometer 706 in the shade)	25

Aug. 16.	Standing on one leg three hours, to show off new-style strapped pants at 12½ cents per leg per hour,			37½
Aug. 17.	To promenade, as usual, and large customer brought home (fat man,)			50
Aug. 18.	To	do	do (medium size,)	25
Aug. 19.	To	do	do (small man and bad pay,)	6
				$2 96.½

The item chiefly disputed in this bill was the very moderate charge of two pennies for the dickey. Upon my word of honor, this *was not* an unreasonable price for that dickey. It was one of the cleanest and prettiest little dickeys I ever saw; and I have good reason to believe that it effected the sale of three Petershams. The elder partner of the firm, however, would allow me only one penny of the charge, and took it upon himself to show in what manner four of the same sized conveniences could be got out of a sheet of foolscap. But it is needless to say that I stood upon the *principle* of the thing. Business is business, and should be done in a business way. There was no *system* whatever in swindling me out of a penny—a clear fraud of fifty per cent.—no *method* in any respect. I left at once the employment of Messrs. Cut and Comeagain, and set up in the Eye-Sore line by myself—one of the most lucrative, respectable, and independent of the ordinary occupations.

My strict integrity, economy, and rigorous business habits, here again came into play. I found myself driving a flourishing trade, and soon became a marked man upon 'Change.[22] The truth is, I never dabbled in flashy matters, but jogged on in the good old sober routine of the calling—a calling in which I should, no doubt, have remained to the present hour, but for a little accident which happened to me in the prosecution of one of the usual business operations of the profession. Whenever a rich old hunks,[23] or prodigal heir, or bankrupt corporation, gets into the notion of putting up a palace, there is no such thing in the world as stopping either of them, and this every intelligent person knows. The fact in question is indeed the basis of the Eye-Sore trade. As soon, therefore, as a building project is fairly afoot by one of these parties, we merchants secure a nice corner of the lot in contemplation, or a

18 A dark shade of green, invisible green is difficult to distinguish from black. In other words, the scheming Peter Proffit palms off some old black cloth as new invisible green cloth.

19 An imitation satin made from cotton and wool or silk.

20 A style of heavy overcoat, originally with a short shoulder cape, named for Viscount Petersham. The word also puns on Peter Proffit's name and dubious occupation.

21 Though Peter Proffit considers the bobtail frock a fashionable, albeit stifling garment, the word "bobtail" had derogatory connotations. According to *Grose's Classical Dictionary of the Vulgar Tongue* (1823), a "bobtail" could mean "a lewd woman, or one that plays with her tail; also an impotent man, or an eunuch." The phrase "tag, rag, and bobtail," again according to *Grose's*, means a "mob of all sorts of low people." By wearing a bobtail frock, in other words, Peter Proffit either emasculates himself or associates with the rabble. Either way, it's another barb thrown at the American businessman.

22 In this context, the word "Change" refers to a place where merchants meet to transact business. In Poe's day it was chiefly used in the phrase "upon 'Change," meaning "at the Exchange" *(OED)*. The New York Stock Exchange began in 1792, when brokers and merchants gathered on Wall Street to sign the Buttonwood Agreement letting them trade securities on commission. In 1817, New York brokers established a formal organization, the New York Stock and Exchange Board (NYS & EB) at 40 Wall Street.

23 A surly, crusty old man.

24 In *Doings of Gotham*, a series of newspaper sketches he published in 1844, Poe describes similar architectural eyesores: "In point of *natural* beauty, as well as of convenience, the harbor of New York has scarcely its equal in the northern hemisphere; but, as in the case of Brooklyn, the Gothamites have most grievously disfigured it by display of landscape and architectural *taste*. More atrocious *pagodas*, or what not—for it is indeed difficult to find a name for them—were certainly never imagined than the greater portion of those which affront the eye, in every nook and corner of the bay, and, more particularly, in the vicinity of New Brighton. If these monstrosities appertain to taste, then it is to taste in its dying agonies."

25 A pigment consisting of almost pure carbon, lampblack was made by collecting the soot produced by burning oil. In Poe's day, lampblack was a key ingredient in the production of ink, a fact which opens up interesting interpretive possibilities for "The Business Man." To what extent should we understand the narrator as a writer who has merely adopted the persona of Peter Proffit?

26 A proverbial phrase. See Matthew 6:2: "Therefore when thou doest thine alms, do not sound a trumpet before thee, as the hypocrites do in the synagogues and in the streets, that they may have glory of men. Verily I say unto you, They have their reward."

27 In "The Spectacles" (1844), Poe observes that "the stern decrees of Fashion had, of late, imperatively prohibited the use of the opera-glass."

prime little situation just adjoining or right in front. This done, we wait until the palace is half-way up, and then we pay some tasty architect to run us up an ornamental mud hovel, right against it; or a Down-East or Dutch Pagoda,[24] or a pig-sty, or an ingenious little bit of fancy work, either Esquimau, Kickapoo, or Hottentot. Of course, we can't afford to take these structures down under a bonus of five hundred per cent. upon the prime cost of our lot and plaster. *Can* we? I ask the question. I ask it of business men. It would be irrational to suppose that we can. And yet there was a rascally corporation which asked me to do this very thing—this *very thing!* I did not reply to their absurd proposition, of course; but I felt it a duty to go that same night, and lamp-black[25] the whole of their palace. For this, the unreasonable villains clapped me into jail; and the gentlemen of the Eye-Sore trade could not well avoid cutting my connection when I came out.

The Assault and Battery business, into which I was now forced to adventure for a livelihood, was somewhat ill-adapted to the delicate nature of my constitution; but I went to work in it with a good heart, and found my account, here as heretofore, in those stern habits of methodical accuracy which had been thumped into me by that delightful old nurse—I would indeed be the basest of men not to remember her well in my will. By observing, as I say, the strictest system in all my dealings, and keeping a well-regulated set of books, I was enabled to get over many serious difficulties, and, in the end, to establish myself very decently in the profession. The truth is, that few individuals, in any line, did a snugger little business than I. I will just copy a page or so out of my Day-Book; and this will save me the necessity of blowing my own trumpet[26]— a contemptible practice, of which no high-minded man will be guilty. Now, the Day-Book is a thing that don't lie.

"Jan. 1.—New Year's Day. Met Snap in the street, groggy. Mem—he'll do. Met Gruff shortly afterwards, blind drunk. Mem—he'll answer too. Entered both gentlemen in my Ledger, and opened a running account with each.

"Jan. 2.—Saw Snap at the Exchange, and went up and trod on his toe. Doubled his fist and knocked me down. Good!—got up again. Some trifling difficulty with Bag, my attorney. I want the damages at a thousand, but he says that, for so simple a knockdown, we can't lay them at more than five hundred. Mem—must get rid of Bag—no *system* at all.

Laurent Deroy after
Augustus Köllner,
Wall Street, N.Y., 1847.
Poe decried such clusters
of commercial buildings,
or "monstrosities," which
he believed "grievously
disfigured" New York
harbor.

"Jan. 3.—Went to the theatre, to look for Gruff. Saw him sitting in a side box, in the second tier, between a fat lady and a lean one. Quizzed the whole party through an opera-glass,[27] till I saw the fat lady blush and whisper to G. Went round, then, into the box, and put my nose within reach of his hand. Wouldn't pull it—no go. Blew it, and tried again—no go. Sat down then, and winked at the lean lady, when I had the high satisfaction of finding him lift me up by the nape of the neck, and fling me over into the pit. Neck dislocated, and right leg capitally splintered. Went home in high glee, drank a bottle of champagne, and booked the young man for five thousand. Bag says it'll do.

"Feb. 15.—Compromised the case of Mr. Snap. Amount entered in Journal—fifty cents—which see.

"Feb. 16.—Cast by that villain, Gruff, who made me a present of five dollars. Costs of suit, four dollars and twenty-five cents. Nett profit—see Journal—seventy-five cents."

Now, here is a clear gain, in a very brief period, of no less than one dollar and twenty five cents—this is in the mere cases of Snap and Gruff; and I solemnly assure the reader that these extracts are taken at random from my Day-Book.

It's an old saying, and a true one, however, that money is noth-

28 A prig is a thief or, more generally, a disreputable person, an eyesore prig therefore some disreputable sort who has set himself up in the eyesore trade.

29 The idea of the "soulless corporation," which is pervasive in modern culture, was a fairly new concept in the early nineteenth century. The earliest known usage of the phrase "soulless corporation" occurs in 1827 in *Register of Debates in Congress, Comprising the Leading Debates and Incidents of the Second Session of the Nineteenth Congress.* Poe thought it appropriate to end his story here, with his indictment of corporations, in his first version of the story published in *Burton's* in 1840.

He added the next six paragraphs when he revised it in 1843.

ing in comparison with health. I found the exactions of the profession somewhat too much for my delicate state of body; and, discovering, at last, that I was knocked all out of shape, so that I didn't know very well what to make of the matter, and so that my friends, when they met me in the street, couldn't tell that I was Peter Proffit at all, it occurred to me that the best expedient I could adopt, was to alter my line of business. I turned my attention, therefore, to Mud-Dabbling, and continued it for some years.

The worst of this occupation is that too many people take a fancy to it, and the competition is in consequence excessive. Every ignoramus of a fellow who finds that he hasn't brains in sufficient quantity to make his way as a walking advertiser, or an eye-sore prig,[28] or a salt and batter man, thinks, of course, that he'll answer very well as a dabbler of mud. But there never was entertained a more erroneous idea than that it requires no brains to mud-dabble. Especially, there is nothing to be made in this way without *method*. I did only a retail business myself, but my old habits of *system* carried me swimmingly along. I selected my street-crossing, in the first place, with great deliberation, and I never put down a broom in any part of the town *but that*. I took care, too, to have a nice little puddle at hand, which I could get at in a minute. By these means I got to be well known as a man to be trusted; and this is one-half the battle, let me tell you, in trade. Nobody ever failed to pitch *me* a copper, and got over *my* crossing with a clean pair of pantaloons. And, as my business habits, in this respect, were sufficiently understood, I never met with any attempt at imposition. I wouldn't have put up with it, if I had. Never imposing upon any one myself, I suffered no one to play the possum with me. The frauds of the banks of course I couldn't help. Their suspension put me to ruinous inconvenience. These, however, are not individuals, but corporations; and corporations, it is very well known, have neither bodies to be kicked, nor souls to be damned.[29]

I was making money at this business, when, in an evil moment, I was induced to merge in the Cur-Spattering—a somewhat analogous, but, by no means, so respectable a profession. My location, to be sure, was an excellent one, being central, and I had capital blacking and brushes. My little dog, too, was quite fat and up to all varieties of snuff. He had been in the trade a long time, and, I may say, understood it. Our general routine was this;—Pompey, having rolled himself well in the mud, sat upon end at the shop door, until he observed a dandy approaching in bright boots. He then proceeded to meet him, and gave the Wellingtons[30] a rub or two with his wool. Then the dandy swore very much, and looked about for a boot-black. There I was, full in his view, with blacking and brushes. It was only a minute's work, and then came a sixpence. This did moderately well for a time;—in fact, I was not avaricious, but my dog was. I allowed him a third of the profit, but he was advised to insist upon half. This I couldn't stand—so we quarrelled and parted.

I next tried my hand at the Organ-grinding for a while, and may say that I made out pretty well. It is a plain, straight-forward business, and requires no particular abilities. You can get a music-mill for a mere song, and, to put it in order, you have but to open the works, and give them three or four smart raps with a hammer. It improves the tone of the thing, for business purposes, more than you can imagine. This done, you have only to stroll along, with the mill on your back, until you see tan-bark in the street, and a knocker wrapped up in buckskin.[31] Then you stop and grind; looking as if you meant to stop and grind till doomsday. Presently a window opens, and somebody pitches you a sixpence, with a request to "Hush up and go on," &c. I am aware that some grinders have actually afforded to "go on" for this sum; but for my part, I found the necessary outlay of capital too great, to permit of my "going on" under a shilling.

At this occupation I did a good deal; but, somehow, I was not quite satisfied, and so finally abandoned it. The truth is, I labored under the disadvantage of having no monkey—and American streets are *so* muddy, and a Democratic rabble is *so* obtrusive, and so full of demnition mischievous little boys.

I was now out of employment for some months, but at length succeeded, by dint of great interest, in procuring a situation in the Sham-Post. The duties, here, are simple, and not altogether unprofitable. For example:—very early in the morning I had to make up my packet of sham letters. Upon the inside of each of these I had to scrawl a few lines—on any subject which occurred to me as sufficiently mysterious—signing all the epistles Tom Dobson, or Bobby Tompkins, or anything in that way. Having folded and sealed all, and stamped them with sham postmarks— New Orleans, Bengal, Botany Bay, or any other place a great way off—I set out, forthwith, upon my daily route, as if in a very

30 "A high boot covering the knee in front and cut away behind," Wellingtons could also refer to "a somewhat shorter boot worn under the trousers" *(OED)*. The term was not used to mean rubberized waterproof boots, or "Wellies," until the early twentieth century.

31 Poe refers to a sick person's house. The door knocker is covered to quiet it, and the tanbark, or wood chips, in the street dampen the sound of passing traffic.

32   The Latin abbreviation "nem. con." means *nemine contradicente*, that is, without opposition.

33   Genesis 9:1: "And God blessed Noah and his sons, and said unto them, Be fruitful, and multiply, and replenish the earth."

34   This popular hair tonic gave British and American authors no end of fun. In *White-Jacket* (1850), Herman Melville explains its popularity among midshipmen: "Some of them are terrible little boys, cocking their caps at alarming angles, and looking fierce as young roosters. They are generally great consumers of Macassar oil and the Balm of Columbia; they thirst and rage after whiskers; and sometimes, applying their ointments, lay themselves out in the sun, to promote the fertility of their chins."

35   The long inventory of Proffit's business ventures ends, or seems to end, with his brilliant scheme of taking advantage of new legislation intended to cut down on the population of feral cats. Now that he is a "made man," he can contemplate running for, or illicitly buying, a political office. We can imagine what kind of politician he will be. But there is still a further, unstated joke here. Proffit may have since found another way of bilking the public: he has managed to pass himself off as an author.

great hurry. I always called at the big houses to deliver the letters, and receive the postage. Nobody hesitates at paying for a letter—especially for a double one—people are *such* fools—and it was no trouble to get round a corner before there was time to open the epistles. The worst of this profession was, that I had to walk so much and so fast; and so frequently to vary my route. Besides, I had serious scruples of conscience. I can't bear to hear innocent individuals abused—and the way the whole town took to cursing Tom Dobson and Bobby Tompkins, was really awful to hear. I washed my hands of the matter in disgust.

My eighth and last speculation has been in the Cat-Growing way. I have found that a most pleasant and lucrative business, and, really, no trouble at all. The country, it is well known, has become infested with cats—so much so of late, that a petition for relief, most numerously and respectably signed, was brought before the legislature at its late memorable session. The assembly, at this epoch, was unusually well-informed, and, having passed many other wise and wholesome enactments, it crowned all with the Cat-Act. In its original form, this law offered a premium for cat-*heads*, (fourpence a-piece) but the Senate succeeded in amending the main clause, so as to substitute the word *"tails"* for "heads." This amendment was so obviously proper, that the house concurred in it *nem. con.*[32]

As soon as the Governor had signed the bill, I invested my whole estate in the purchase of Toms and Tabbies. At first, I could only afford to feed them upon mice (which are cheap), but they fulfilled the Scriptural injunction[33] at so marvellous a rate, that I at length considered it my best policy to be liberal, and so indulged them in oysters and turtle. Their tails, at a legislative price, now bring me in a good income: for I have discovered a way, in which, by means of Macassar oil,[34] I can force three crops in a year. It delights me to find, too, that the animals soon get accustomed to the thing, and would rather have the appendages cut off than otherwise. I consider myself, therefore, a made man, and am bargaining for a country seat on the Hudson.[35]

The Philosophy of Furniture

An indictment of American taste and culture, "The Philosophy of Furniture" continues and extends Poe's critique of materialism undertaken in "The Business Man," bringing it now directly into the American parlor (the "well furnished apartment"). Lacking an "aristocracy of blood," Poe says, we have "therefore, as a natural, and, indeed, as an inevitable thing, fashioned for ourselves an aristocracy of dollars." Hence, our eagerness to confuse cost and size with beauty. Sometimes categorized as an essay, "The Philosophy of Furniture" has also been called a sketch. Mabbott and others have noted its fictional elements. It is less frequently recognized as an occasional piece. "The Philosophy of Furniture" was written for the occasion of New York City's annual Moving Day, that is, May 1, when the city's tenants customarily signed their leases. Motivated by a chronic housing shortage and high rents, nineteenth-century New Yorkers often took to the streets with their belongings on this day to improve their living situations. All trade ceased because Manhattan streets were chockablock with carts and carriages filled with tenants and their household goods. New Yorkers brought their interiors outside and effectively turned their lives inside out for all to see. When Poe was living in New York in 1837, he would have had the opportunity to witness the spectacle for himself. "The Philosophy of Furniture" was first published in the May issue of Burton's, *copies of which would have reached New York newsstands the last week of April. One contemporary reader said it "should be read by every housekeeper at least" (*Daily National Intelligencer, *May 8, 1840). When Poe published a revised and abridged version under the title "House Furniture" in 1845 in the* Broadway Journal, *he again timed its appearance to coincide with Moving Day. Conventionally, Poe's editors have coupled the later text with the earlier title. The present version follows the first printed text.*

Put side by side, Poe's original title and his later revision of it show he was not inattentive to the marketplace and was quite willing to adapt his own work to suit the moment: the original capitalizes on what was then a current fashion in middle-class American culture. In The Life and Adventures of Martin Chuzzlewit (1843–1844), *Charles Dickens satirizes the leisure-time activities of middle-class American women, among his targets such edifying lectures as "The Philosophy of Vegetables," "The Philosophy of Matter," and "The Philosophy of Crime." By the time Poe republished this work, however, "Philosophy of" titles had passed from vogue—partly through the cultural work of* Martin Chuzzlewit. *Poe apparently changed his title to avoid sounding passé.*

Philosophy," says Hegel, "is utterly useless and fruitless, and, *for this very reason*, is the sublimest of all pursuits, the most deserving of our attention, and the most worthy of our zeal"—a somewhat Coleridegy[1] assertion, with a rivulet of deep meaning in a meadow of words. It would be wasting time to disentangle the paradox—and the more so as no one will deny that Philosophy has its merits, and is applicable to an infinity of purposes. There is reason, it is said, in the roasting of eggs,[2] and there is philosophy even in furniture—a philosophy nevertheless which seems to be more imperfectly understood by Americans than by any civilized nation upon the face of the earth.[3]

In the internal decoration,[4] if not in the external architecture, of their residences, the English are supreme. The Italians have but little sentiment beyond marbles and colors. In France *meliora probant, deteriora sequuntur*[5]—the people are too much a race of gad-abouts to study and maintain those household proprieties, of which indeed they have a delicate appreciation, or at least the elements of a proper sense. The Chinese, and most of the Eastern races, have a warm but inappropriate fancy. The Scotch are *poor* decorists.[6] The Dutch have merely a vague idea that a curtain is not a cabbage. In Spain they are *all* curtains—a nation of *hang-men.* The Russians do not furnish. The Hottentots and Kickapoos are very well in their way—the Yankees alone are preposterous.

How this happens it is not difficult to see. We have no aristocracy of blood, and having, therefore, as a natural and, indeed, as an inevitable thing, fashioned for ourselves an aristocracy of dollars, the *display of wealth* has here to take the place, and perform

---

1 Poe coined the term "Coleridgey." The quotation from Georg Wilhelm Friedrich Hegel (1770–1831) comes word-for-word from a footnote to "Tieck's *Collected Tales*," *Foreign Quarterly Review* 32 (1839), 358.

2   This proverb circulated widely in Poe's day. Abraham Hayward observes: "When Boswell asked Burke's opinion of his definition of our species—'Man is a cooking animal,'—the great statesman answered—'Your definition is a good one; and I now see the force of the old proverb, "There is reason in the roasting of eggs"'" ("Cookery," *Quarterly Review* 52 [1834], 406).

3   Poe omitted this opening paragraph when he republished "The Philosophy of Furniture" as "House Furniture."

4   Many critics have noted Poe's preoccupation in his tales with interior spaces—most often taken as metaphors for some inner psychological state. Richard Wilbur, for example, argues that interior rooms in Poe's tales are carefully designed and furnished as "dream-chambers" (for example, Roderick Usher's studio or the bridal chamber in "Ligeia").

5   "Approve the better, follow the worse": a Latin proverb.

6   Poe coined the word "decorist." Reviewing Edward Bulwer-Lytton's *Night and Morning* (1841), Poe calls one of the novel's characters "a crafty man-of-the-world, whose only honesty consists in appearing honest—a scrupulous decorist" (*Essays and Reviews*, ed. G. R. Thompson [New York: Library of America, 1984], 146).

7   Michel Chevalier apparently introduced this phrase in 1839, when he said of the United States: "If there is a country in the world where it is preposterous to prate about the aristocracy of dollars, and about the filthy metals, it is this. For here, more than any where else, every body has some employment; whoever has capital is engaged in turning it to profit, and can neither increase nor even keep it without great activity and vigilance" (*Society, Manners and Politics in the United States: Being a Series of Letters on North America* [Boston: Weeks, Jordan, 1839], 78).

8   Poe anticipates the concept of "conspicuous consumption" that Thorstein Veblen would identify in *The Theory of the Leisure Class* (1899), that is, the spending of discretionary income on goods and services to reveal the spending power and social status of the consumer.

9   A contest of one-upmanship between two members of the *nouveau riche*.

the office, of the heraldic display in monarchical countries.[7] By a transition readily understood, and which might have been easily foreseen, we have been brought to merge in simple *show* our notions of taste itself.[8] To speak less abstractedly. In England, for example, no mere parade of costly appurtenances would be so likely as with us to create an impression of the beautiful in respect to the appurtenances themselves, or of taste as respects the proprietor—this for the reason, first, that wealth is not in England the loftiest object of ambition, as constituting a nobility; and, secondly, that there, the true nobility of blood rather avoids than affects costliness, in which a parvenu rivalry[9] may be successfully attempted, confining itself within the rigorous limits, and to the analytical investigation, of legitimate taste. The people naturally imitate the nobles, and the result is a thorough diffusion of a right feeling. But, in America, dollars being the supreme insignia of aristocracy, their display may be said, in general terms, to be the sole means of aristocratic distinction; and the populace, looking up for models, are insensibly led to confound the two entirely separate ideas of magnificence and beauty. In short, the cost of an article of furniture has, at length, come to be, with us, nearly the sole test of its merit in a decorative point of view. And this test, once established, has led the way to many analogous errors, readily traceable to the one primitive folly.

There could be scarcely any thing more directly offensive to the eye of an artist than the interior of what is termed, in the United States,[10] a well furnished apartment. Its most usual defect is a preposterous want of keeping. We speak of the keeping of a room as we would of the keeping of a picture; for both the picture and the room are amenable to those undeviating principles which regulate all varieties of art; and very nearly the same laws by which we decide upon the higher merits of a painting, suffice for a decision upon the adjustment of a chamber. A want of keeping is observable sometimes in the character of the several pieces of furniture, but generally in their colors, or modes of adaptation to use. Very often the eye is offended by their inartistical arrangement. Straight lines are too prevalent, too uninterruptedly continued, or clumsily interrupted at right angles. If curved lines occur, they are repeated into unpleasant uniformity. Undue precision spoils the appearance of many a room.

Curtains are rarely well disposed, or well chosen, in respect to the other decorations. With formal furniture curtains are out of place, and an excessive volume of drapery of any kind is, under any circumstances, irreconcilable with good taste; the proper quantum, as well as the proper adjustment, depends upon the character of the general effect.

Carpets are better understood of late than of ancient days, but we still very frequently err in their patterns and colors. A carpet is the soul of an apartment. From it are deduced not only the hues but the forms of all objects incumbent. A judge at common law *may* be an ordinary man; a good judge of a carpet *must* be a genius. Yet I have heard fellows discourse of carpets with the visage of a sheep in a reverie— *"d'un mouton qui rêve"*[11]—who should not and who could not be entrusted with the management of their own mustachios. Every one knows that a large floor should have a covering of large figures, and a small one of small; yet this is not all the knowledge in the world. As regards texture the Saxony is alone admissible. Brussels is the preter-pluperfect tense of fashion, and Turkey is taste in its dying agonies.[12] Touching pattern, a carpet should *not* be bedizened out like a Ricaree Indian—all red chalk, yellow ochre and cock's feathers.[13] In brief, distinct grounds and vivid circular figures, *of no meaning*, are here Median laws.[14] The abomination of flowers, or representations of well known objects of any kind should never be endured within the limits of Christendom. Indeed, whether on carpets, or curtains, or paper-hangings, or ottoman coverings, all upholstery of this nature should be rigidly Arabesque.[15] Those antique floor-cloths which are still seen occasionally in the dwellings of the rabble—cloths of huge, sprawling and radiating devices, stripe-interspersed, and glorious with all hues, among which no ground is intelligible—are but the wicked invention of a race of time servers and money lovers—children of Baal and worshippers of Mammon[16]—men[17] who, to save trouble of thought and exercise of fancy, first cruelly invented the Kaleidoscope, and then established a patent company to twirl it by steam.[18]

Glare is a leading error in the philosophy of American household decoration—an error easily recognized as deduced from the perversion of taste just specified. We are violently enamoured of gas and of glass. The former is totally inadmissible within doors. Its harsh and unsteady light is positively offensive. No man having both brains and eyes will use it. A mild, or what artists term a cool

10 For "House Furniture," Poe inserted the following phrase to modify "in the United States": "that is to say, in Appallachia." Washington Irving first suggested this alternate name in an article he contributed to the August 1839 issue of the *Knickerbocker*: "We have it in our power to furnish ourselves with such a national appellation, from one of the grand and eternal features of our country; from that noble chain of mountains which formed its back-bone, and ran through the 'old confederacy,' when it first declared our national independence. I allude to the Appalachian or Alleghany mountains. We might do this without any very inconvenient change in our present titles. We might still use the phrase, 'The United States,' substituting Appalachia, or Alleghania, (I should prefer the latter,) in place of America." The editor of the *Knickerbocker* found Poe's use of this new name to be the most notable aspect of "House Furniture": "We hold, with the *Broadway Journal*, that if a new name for our country can be adopted, Apalachia should be chosen" ("Editor's Table," *Knickerbocker* 25 [1845], 374).

11 A proverbial expression that literally means "of a sheep that dreams."

12 Brussels, Saxony, and Turkey are expensive and durable types of carpet, Brussels being used in the best apartments of the day.

13 In June 1821, General William H. Ashley led a trapping expedition to the Rocky Mountains, during which he agreed to trade with the Ricaree or Arickaree, who attacked his party, killing over a dozen men. Col. Henry Leavenworth, who commanded Fort Atkinson at Council Bluffs, subsequently led a punitive attack on the Ricaree. Poe took the name from American history, but his colorful description comes from British *belles lettres*. In an anonymous essay, George Croly observes: "The Americans rival even the metropolitan press in description, they paint nature as the American savage paints himself; all is red chalk, yellow ochre, and cock's feathers" ("The World We Live In," *Blackwood's* 42 [1837], 796–797).

14 Unchanging. See Daniel 6:8: "Now, O king, establish the decree, and sign the writing, that it be not changed, according to the law of the Medes and Persians, which altereth not."

15 A species of surface decoration composed in flowing lines of branches, leaves, and scrollwork fancifully intertwined.

16   Baal was a name for a false god. In the February 1839 issue of *Burton's*, William E. Burton had used the phrase "children of Baal." Mammon means a false god representing an inordinate desire for wealth but could be used as a synonym for money. Both phrases were commonplace; Poe's combination of the two is original.

17   In what may be the most inspired revision Poe made to his text for "House Furniture," he canceled the word "men" and substituted "Benthams," thus making the name of the utilitarian philosopher Jeremy Bentham (1748–1832) synonymous with any and all utilitarians.

18   Authors began using the word "kaleidoscope" figuratively soon after David Brewster made its invention public in 1819, finding in the kaleidoscope's brilliant display and changeable patterns an apt poetic metaphor. However, in Poe's writing, the kaleidoscope figures as a purely mechanical device, its varying patterns and colors controlled by neither the intellect nor the imagination. Steam-powered machines—such as those that produced the gaudy carpets Poe hates—might be labor-saving inventions, but there are no shortcuts when it comes to the creation of beauty, which can only be accomplished with the imagination (Kevin J. Hayes, "The Flaneur in the Parlor: Poe's 'Philosophy of Furniture,'" *Prospects* 27 [2002], 111).

19   Named for the Swiss physicist and chemist Aimé Argand (1750–1803), the Argand lamp was an oil-burning lamp with a glass chimney and tubular wick. It represented an improvement over the traditional oil lamp in several respects. Drawing air from the bottom of the lamp up through the chimney, it produced a brighter, steadier light. Its wick also required less trimming. Both Benjamin Franklin and Thomas Jefferson brought Argand lamps home with them when they returned from Europe.

20   Consider by way of contrast the ghastly, flickering illumination in the bridal chamber in "Ligeia": "From out the most central recess of [the ceiling], depended, by a single chain of gold with long links, a huge censer of the same metal, Saracenic in pattern, and with many perforations so contrived that there writhed in and out of them, as if endued with a serpent vitality, a continual succession of parti-colored fires."

21   In affluent antebellum homes, the use of mirrors was every bit as pervasive as Poe suggests. Some homeowners situated pier glass, floor-to-ceiling mirrors, in the narrow

light, with its consequent warm shadows, will do wonders for even an ill-furnished apartment. Never was a more lovely thought than that of the astral lamp. I mean, of course, the astral lamp proper, and do not wish to be misunderstood—the lamp of Argand[19] with its original plain ground-glass shade, and its tempered and uniform moonlight rays. The cut-glass shade is a weak invention of the enemy. The eagerness with which we have adopted it, partly on account of its *flashiness*, but principally on account of *its greater cost*, is a good commentary upon the proposition with which I began. It is not too much to say that the deliberate employer of a cut-glass shade is a person either radically deficient in taste, or blindly subservient to the caprices of fashion. The light proceeding from one of these gaudy abominations is unequal, broken, and painful. It alone is sufficient to mar a world of good effect in the furniture subjected to its influence. Female loveliness in especial is more than one half disenchanted beneath its evil eye.[20]

In the matter of glass, generally, we proceed upon false principles. Its leading feature is *glitter*—and in that one word how much of all that is detestable do we express! Flickering, unquiet lights, are *sometimes* pleasing—to children and idiots always so—but in the embellishment of a room they should be scrupulously avoided. In truth even strong *steady* lights are inadmissible. The huge and unmeaning glass chandeliers, prism-cut, gas-litten, and without shade, which dangle in our most fashionable drawing-rooms, may be cited as the quintessence of false taste, as so many concentrations of preposterous folly.

The rage for *glitter*—because its idea has become, as I before observed, confounded with that of magnificence in the abstract—has led us also to the exaggerated employment of mirrors.[21] We line our dwellings with great British plates, and then imagine we have done a fine thing. Now the slightest thought will be sufficient to convince any one who has an eye at all, of the ill effect of numerous looking-glasses, and especially of large ones. Regarded apart from its reflection the mirror presents a continuous, flat, colorless, unrelieved surface—a thing always unpleasant, and obviously so. Considered as a reflector it is potent in producing a monstrous and odious uniformity—and the evil is here aggravated in no direct proportion with the augmentation of its sources, but in a ratio constantly increasing. In fact a room with four or five mir-

A George III commode, eighteenth century, mahogany and ormolu.

rors arranged at random is, for all purposes of artistical show, a room of no shape at all. If we add to this, the attendant glitter upon glitter, we have a perfect farrago of discordant and displeasing effects. The veriest bumpkin, not addle-headed, upon entering an apartment so bedizened, would be instantly aware of something wrong, although he might be altogether unable to assign a cause for his dissatisfaction. But let the same individual be led into a room tastefully furnished, and he would be startled into an exclamation of surprise and of pleasure.

It is an evil growing out of our republican institutions, that here a man of large purse has usually a very little soul which he keeps in it. The corruption of taste is a portion and a pendant of the dollar-manufacture.[22] As we grow rich our ideas grow rusty.[23] It is therefore not among *our* aristocracy that we must look if at all, in the United States, for the spirituality of a British *boudoir*. But I have seen apartments in the tenure of Americans—men of exceedingly moderate means, yet *rarae aves*[24] of good taste—which, in negative merit at least, might vie with any of the or-moluled cabinets[25] of our friends across the water. Even now there is present to my

spaces between windows to reflect even more light, magnify a room's space, and further display the homeowner's wealth (Carolyn Brucken, "In the Public Eye: Women and the American Luxury Hotel" (*Winterthur Portfolio* 31 [1996], 219).

22 Using the word "pendant" in this sense, which antedates the earliest usage recorded in the *Oxford English Dictionary*, Poe applies a term meaning the counterpart or representation of something else.

23 Poe anticipates a comment Henry David Thoreau would make in "Resistance to Civil Government" (1849): "The more money, the less virtue."

24 The plural of *rara avis*, meaning a type of person rarely encountered.

25 The noun "ormolu" originally meant the process of applying an amalgam of powdered gold and mercury to ornament furniture and decorative objects. Later, gold-colored alloys were substituted. "Ormolu" may also refer to articles decorated with such materials. The use of the term as a past participial adjective is Poe's invention.

26 Poe catches the proprietor in the unconscious act of leaving his impression on the room as his body makes an indentation on the sofa. According to Walter Benjamin, this action suggests the tendency of the nineteenth-century urban middle-class to imprint themselves on their domestic environment (*The Arcades Project*, trans. Howard Eiland and Kevin McLaughlin, ed. Rolf Tiedemann [Cambridge, MA: The Belknap Press of Harvard University Press, 1999], 9).

27 The English painter Clarkson Stanfield (1793–1867) was best known as a marine artist. Poe also mentions Stanfield in his tale "The Landscape Garden," again referring to his fanciful imagery. The American John Gadsby Chapman (1808–1889) was a respected landscape painter and portraitist before earning success as an illustrator and history painter. When Poe republished this sketch as "House Furniture," he added a reference to another American painter, the portraitist Thomas Sully (1783–1872): "There are, nevertheless, three or four female heads, of an ethereal beauty—portraits in the manner of Sully."

28 Interestingly, when Poe later revised the sketch, he canceled this sentence, replacing it with the following: "But one mirror—and this not a very large one—is visible. In shape it is nearly circular—and it is hung so that a reflection of the person can be obtained from it in none of the ordinary sitting-places of the room." Borges took a similar attitude toward mirrors: "It is truly awful that there are mirrors; I have always been terrified by mirrors. I think that Poe felt it too. There is an essay of his, one of the least known, on the decoration of rooms. One of the conditions he insists on is that the mirrors be placed in such a way that a seated person is not reflected. This tells us his fear of seeing himself in the mirror" (*Seven Nights*, trans. Eliot Weinberger [New York: New Directions, 2009], 88).

mind's eye a small and not ostentatious chamber with whose decorations no fault can be found. The proprietor lies asleep upon a sofa[26]—the weather is cool—the time is near midnight—I will make a sketch of the room ere he awakes. It is oblong—some thirty feet in length and twenty-five in breadth—a shape affording the best opportunities for the adjustment of furniture. It has but one door, which is at one end of the parallelogram, and but two windows, which are at the other. These latter are large, reaching downwards to the floor, are situated in deep recesses and open upon an Italian *veranda*. Their panes are of a crimson-tinted glass, set in rose-wood framings, of a kind somewhat broader than usual. They are curtained, within the recess, by a thick silver tissue, adapted to the shape of the window and hanging loosely, but have no volumes. Without the recess are curtains of an exceedingly rich crimson silk, fringed with a deep network of gold, and lined with the silver tissue which forms the exterior blind. There are no cornices; but the folds of the whole fabric, (which are sharp rather than massive, and have an airy appearance) issue from beneath a broad entablature of rich gilt-work, which encircles the room at the junction of the ceiling and walls. The drapery is thrown open, also, or closed, by means of a thick rope of gold loosely enveloping it, and resolving itself readily into a knot—no pins or other such devices are apparent. The colors of the curtains and their fringe—the tints of crimson and gold—form the *character* of the room, and appear every where in profusion. The carpet, of Saxony material, is quite half an inch thick, and is of the same crimson ground, relieved simply by the *appearance* of a gold cord (like that festooning the curtains,) thrown upon it in such a manner as to form a close succession of short irregular curves, no one overlaying the other. This carpet has no border. The paper on the walls is of a glossy, silvery hue, intermingled with small Arabesque devices of a fainter tint of the prevalent crimson. Many paintings relieve the expanse of the paper. These are chiefly landscapes of an imaginative cast, such as the fairy grottoes of Stanfield, or the Lake of the Dismal Swamp of our own Chapman.[27] The tone of each is warm but dark—there are no brilliant effects. Not one of the pictures is of small size. Diminutive paintings give that *spotty* look to a room which is the blemish of so many a fine work of art overtouched. The frames are broad, *but not deep,* and richly carved, without being fillagreed. Their profuse gilding gives them

John Gadsby Chapman, *Lake of the Dismal Swamp*, 1825. Chapman (1908–1889), who at eighteen painted this scene of Lake Drummond, the swamp's principal feature, on a firescreen, was likely inspired by Thomas Moore's 1803 poem "A Ballad: The Lake of the Dismal Swamp." The swamp is located in southeastern Virginia and northeastern North Carolina.

the whole lustre of gold. They lie flat upon the walls, and do not hang off with cords. The designs themselves may, sometimes, be best seen in this latter position, but the general appearance of the chamber is injured. *No* mirror is visible[28]—nor chairs. Two large sofas, of rose-wood and crimson silk, form the only seats. There is a piano-forte—also of rose-wood, and without cover. Mahogany has been avoided. An octagonal table, formed entirely of the

29 Established in 1756 near the Marquise de Pompadour's chateau at Bellevue, between Paris and Versailles, the Sèvres Porcelain Factory produced some of the finest vases in the world.

30 In her "Reminiscences" of Poe, the radical social reformer Mary Gove Nichols (1810–1884) offers a glimpse of the interior of Poe's cottage in Fordham, where Poe spent the last years of his life: "The cottage had an air of taste and gentility that must have been lent to it by the presence of its inmates. So neat, so poor, so unfurnished, and yet so charming a dwelling I never saw. The floor of the kitchen was white as wheaten flour. A table, a chair, and a little stove that it contained, seemed to furnish it perfectly. The sitting-room floor was laid with check matting; four chairs, a light stand, and a hanging bookshelf completed its furniture. There were pretty presentation copies of books on the little shelves, and the Brownings had posts of honour on the stand" (*Reminiscences of Edgar Allan Poe* [New York: Union Square Book Shop, 1931], 9).

richest gold-threaded marble, is placed near one of the sofas— this table is also without cover—the drapery of the curtains has been thought sufficient. Four large and gorgeous Sevres vases,[29] in which grow a number of sweet and vivid flowers in full bloom, occupy the angles of the room. A tall and magnificent candelabrum, bearing a small antique lamp with strongly perfumed oil, is standing near the head of my sleeping friend. Some light and graceful hanging shelves, with golden edges and crimson silk cords with gold tassels, sustain two or three hundred magnificently-bound books.[30] Beyond these things there is no furniture, if we except an Argand lamp, with a plain crimson-tinted glass shade, which depends from the lofty ceiling by a single gold chain, and throws a subdued but magical radiance over all.

The Man of the Crowd

Ce grand malheur, de ne pouvoir être seul.

La Bruyère[1]

Lt was well said of a certain German book that *"er lasst sich nicht lesen"*—it does not permit itself to be read.[2] There are some secrets which do not permit themselves to be told.[3] Men die nightly in their beds, wringing the hands of ghostly confessors, and looking them piteously in the eyes—die with despair of heart and convulsion of throat, on account of the hideousness of mysteries which will not *suffer themselves* to be revealed. Now and then, alas, the conscience of man takes up a burthen so heavy in horror that it can be thrown down only into the grave. And thus the essence of all crime is undivulged.

Not long ago, about the closing in of an evening in autumn, I sat at the large bow window of the D——Coffee-House in London.[4] For some months I had been ill in health, but was now convalescent,[5] and, with returning strength, found myself in one of those happy moods which are so precisely the converse of *ennui*— moods of the keenest appetency, when the film from the mental vision departs—the αχλυς ος πριν επηεν[6]—and the intellect, electrified, surpasses as greatly its every-day condition, as does the vivid yet candid reason of Leibnitz,[7] the mad and flimsy rhetoric of Gorgias.[8] Merely to breathe was enjoyment; and I derived positive pleasure even from many of the legitimate sources of pain. I felt a calm but inquisitive interest in every thing. With a cigar in my mouth and a newspaper in my lap,[9] I had been amusing myself for the greater part of the afternoon, now in poring over advertisements, now in observing the promiscuous company in the room, and now in peering through the smoky panes into the street.[10]

This latter is one of the principal thoroughfares of the city,

Poe's enigmatic tale "The Man of the Crowd" recalls a singular day of crowd watching (one among presumably many other, if less remarkable, ones), in which its narrator observes a mysterious old man with an "idiosyncratic" expression. Intrigued, he leaves behind his newspaper and the coffeehouse where he has parked himself, plunges into the crowd, and pursues the old man through London's streets for the next twenty-four hours in a futile effort "to know more of him." The tale has attracted considerable scholarly attention. It has been seen as a proto-detective story that anticipates the Dupin tales, while other readings have emphasized its playfulness, indeterminacy, and self-reflexivity. But by far it has received the most sustained critical attention from a now long line of readers—beginning with Poe's great French champion and translator Charles Baudelaire and the German cultural theorist Walter Benjamin—who have drawn attention to the story's modern urban setting and new modes of visual perception to which the city gave birth in the nineteenth century, as urban dwellers tried to make sense of the crowds and a myriad of other stimuli.

In "The Painter of Modern Life" (1863), Charles Baudelaire holds up "The Man of the Crowd" as exemplary of the mind-set of the modern artist, who attempts to capture on canvas the fleeting, ephemeral experience of new urban life. To be successful, however, the artist must become like the flaneur, or urban idler—a new urban type, a man of leisure who strolls about the city observing the street and the people in it for his own pleasure. The flaneur immerses himself in the life of the modern city yet somehow remains apart from it. Benjamin speaks of the flaneur as a kind of "botanist on asphalt" who turns the Parisian boulevards into a drawing room in which he identifies and classifies the crowd. He interprets or "reads" the city and its inhabitants like a "text." In his essays and notes on Baudelaire, Benjamin revises Baudelaire's earlier reading of "The Man of the Crowd." For Benjamin, Poe's tale demonstrates the impossibility of the flaneur's cool detachment and his ultimate failure to read the city-as-text. "It is a magnificent touch in Poe's story," Benjamin writes, "that it includes along with the earliest description of the flaneur the figuration of his end."

"The Man of the Crowd" was originally published in the last issue of Burton's Gentlemen's Magazine *and revised and republished for Wiley and Putnam's* Tales *(1845). The text of the 1845 version is presented here.*

1 "That great evil, to be unable to be alone." This quotation also appears in "Metzengerstein." D. H. Lawrence interprets the phrase to mean that all men and women yearn for love, that our inherent impulses compel us to avoid loneliness and seek companionship (Eric W. Carlson, ed., *The Recognition of Edgar Allan Poe: Selected Criticism since 1829* [Ann Arbor: University of Michigan Press, 1966], 126).

Gustave Courbet,
Charles Baudelaire, 1847.

The phrase may be more complex than Lawrence realizes. The verb "pouvoir" is ambiguous. It signifies "to be able to," but it may also mean "to be allowed to."

2   Poe took this phrase from something Thomas De Quincey says: "Of a German book, otherwise entitled to respect, it was said—*er lässt sich nicht lesen*, it does not permit itself to be read: such and so repulsive was the style" ("Style," *Blackwood's* 48 [1840], 17).

3   The proverbial expression "to read someone like a book" meant in Poe's day what it does today: to know exactly what someone else is thinking or feeling without having to ask. Here, however, Poe draws an analogy between an unreadable book and secrets that "do not permit themselves to be told." In other words, neither people nor literary texts are so easily read as common wisdom would have us believe.

4   Commercial travelers from overseas frequented London coffeehouses, lodging at adjoining hotels and using the coffeehouse as their business address. After bringing his family to Great Britain to establish a London branch of his firm in 1815, Poe's foster father, John Allan, would have patronized the London coffeehouses regularly to learn the latest shipping news and establish business connections. The narrator's presence in the coffeehouse suggests that he, too, is an American in London (Kevin J. Hayes, "Visual Culture and the Word in Edgar Allan Poe's 'The Man of the Crowd,'" *Nineteenth-Century Literature* 56 [2002], 448–449).

5   In "The Painter of Modern Life" (1863), Baudelaire likens the modern artist to an "eternal convalescent" or "man-child" in his heightened perception and undiminished curiosity about all aspects of modern life: "The convalescent, like the child, is possessed in the highest degree of the faculty of keenly interesting himself in things, be they apparently of the most trivial. Let us go back, if we can, by a retrospective effort of the imagination, towards our most youthful, our earliest, impressions, and we will recognize that they had a strange kinship with those brightly coloured impressions which we were later to receive in the aftermath of a physical illness, always provided that that illness had left our spiritual capacities pure and unharmed" (*The Painter of Modern Life and Other Essays*, trans. and ed. Jonathan Mayne [1964; reprinted, London: Phaidon, 1995], 7–8).

6   "The mist that before was upon them": Pallas Athena speaks these words in Homer's *Iliad*, book V, line 127, telling Diomedes that she has taken the mist from his eyes so he can distinguish between god and man on the battlefield.

Rick Deckard (Harrison Ford) in the opening scene of Ridley Scott's *Blade Runner* (1982). Like the narrator in "The Man of the Crowd," Deckard is eventually compelled to wander among the teeming crowds in the city streets.

and had been very much crowded during the whole day. But, as the darkness came on, the throng momently increased; and, by the time the lamps were well lighted, two dense and continuous tides of population were rushing past the door. At this particular period of the evening I had never before been in a similar situation, and the tumultuous sea of human heads filled me, therefore, with a delicious novelty of emotion. I gave up, at length, all care of things within the hotel, and became absorbed in contemplation of the scene without.[11]

At first my observations took an abstract and generalizing turn. I looked at the passengers in masses, and thought of them in their aggregate relations. Soon, however, I descended to details, and regarded with minute interest the innumerable varieties of figure, dress, air, gait, visage, and expression of countenance.[12]

By far the greater number of those who went by had a satisfied business-like demeanor, and seemed to be thinking only of making their way through the press. Their brows were knit, and their eyes rolled quickly; when pushed against by fellow-wayfarers they evinced no symptom of impatience, but adjusted their clothes and hurried on. Others, still a numerous class, were restless in their movements, had flushed faces, and talked and gesticulated to themselves, as if feeling in solitude on account of the very denseness of the company around. When impeded in their progress, these people suddenly ceased muttering, but redoubled their gesticulations, and awaited, with an absent and overdone smile upon the lips, the course of the persons impeding them. If jostled, they

7   The 1840 text, which reads "the vivid, yet candid reason of Combe," pays homage to George Combe (1788–1858), one of the founders of phrenology. Omitting Combe in favor of philosopher and mathematician Gottfried Wilhelm Leibniz (1646–1716) when he revised the story, Poe substituted a reference of greater literary cachet. The revision does create a slight textual anomaly. The narrator's fascination with the "tumultuous sea of human heads" in the following paragraph makes more sense coming after his appreciation for a founder of phrenology than following a reference to the founder of differential calculus.

8   A native of Sicily, Gorgias (*ca.* 483–*ca.* 385 BCE) was a pre-Socratic philosopher and rhetorician. In a work that does not survive he emphasized the nonexistence, incomprehensibility, or incommunicability of all things.

9   Poe implicitly connects the activity of observing the urban landscape and reading a written text. In the early nineteenth century, as literacy became widespread in major cities, the relationship between the written word and visual culture was changing in the metropolis. Language was becoming more and more visible—in mass-market periodicals, on advertisements and shop signs, and on the placards carried up and down the street by sandwichmen. See Kevin J. Hayes, "Visual Culture and the Word in Edgar Allan Poe's 'The Man of the Crowd,'" *Nineteenth-Century Literature* 56 [2002], 448–449.

10   John D. Dorst is among those critics who prize "The Man of the Crowd" for its understanding of the modern urban experience. He notes parallels between Poe's tale and Ridley Scott's sublimely dystopian film *Blade Runner* (1982): "We first encounter Rick Deckard . . . as he sits reading the newspaper and waiting for service at a curbside 'noodle bar' in a nightmarish future Los Angeles. Like his mid-nineteenth century counterpart, he is confronted with a dense tide of motley humanity streaming by in front of him. And soon he too will find himself compelled to wander the night streets of a great metropolis in the effort to resolve ambiguities that go well beyond the immediate circumstances of the case assigned to him" ("Parsing the City," *American Quarterly* 50 [1998], 645).

11   Baudelaire observes: "The crowd is [the flaneur's] element, as the air is that of fishes. His passion and profession are to become one flesh with the crowd. For the perfect flaneur, for the passionate spectator, it is an immense joy to set up house in the heart of the multitude, amid the ebb and flow of movement, in the midst of the fugitive and the infinite (*The Painter of Modern Life and Other Essays*, 9).

12   Poe's description of life in urban London is characteristic of the "city sketch." Horace Greeley, one of the great newspaper editors of the day, recognized the affinity between Poe's tale and this subgenre, excerpting the next six paragraphs as "A London Thoroughfare" in the *New Yorker* (December 5, 1840), which the Washington *Daily National Intelligencer* reprinted (December 21, 1840).

13   Walter Benjamin observes: "These are less the movements of people going about their business than the movements of the machines they operate. With uncanny foresight, Poe seems to have modeled the gestures and reactions of the crowd on the rhythm of these machines" (*The Arcades Project*, ed. Rolf Tiedemann, trans. Howard Eiland and Kevin McLaughlin [Cambridge, MA: The Belknap Press of Harvard University Press, 1999], 337).

14   Unscrupulous stockbrokers.

15   The hereditary aristocracy of Athens or, more generally, a person of noble descent.

16   The *Oxford English Dictionary* defines the term "flash house" as either a resort of thieves or a brothel. Here, Poe twists the term to mean a newly established place of business, which he contrasts with "staunch firms" in the following paragraph.

17   Poe's coinage (not in the *OED*).

18   Polite or fashionable society.

19   Still played today in many cities around the world, the thimblerig or the shell game is a gambling game that in reality often involves sleight-of-hand. The operator or con-man places a pea under one of three thimbles or walnut shells and then, as he manipulates the shells on a flat surface, invites onlookers to place bets on where the pea will end up. Typically shell men set up shop on the busiest street corners to snare tourists and other unwary passers-by.

bowed profusely to the jostlers, and appeared overwhelmed with confusion.[13]—There was nothing very distinctive about these two large classes beyond what I have noted. Their habiliments belonged to that order which is pointedly termed the decent. They were undoubtedly noblemen, merchants, attorneys, tradesmen, stock-jobbers[14]—the Eupatrids[15] and the common-places of society—men of leisure and men actively engaged in affairs of their own—conducting business upon their own responsibility. They did not greatly excite my attention.

The tribe of clerks was an obvious one and here I discerned two remarkable divisions. There were the junior clerks of flash houses[16]—young gentlemen with tight coats, bright boots, well-oiled hair, and supercilious lips. Setting aside a certain dapperness of carriage, which may be termed *deskism*[17] for want of a better word, the manner of these persons seemed to me an exact facsimile of what had been the perfection of *bon ton*[18] about twelve or eighteen months before. They wore the cast-off graces of the gentry;—and this, I believe, involves the best definition of the class.

The division of the upper clerks of staunch firms, or of the "steady old fellows," it was not possible to mistake. These were known by their coats and pantaloons of black or brown, made to sit comfortably, with white cravats and waistcoats, broad solid-looking shoes, and thick hose or gaiters.—They had all slightly bald heads, from which the right ears, long used to pen-holding, had an odd habit of standing off on end. I observed that they always removed or settled their hats with both hands, and wore watches, with short gold chains of a substantial and ancient pattern. Theirs was the affectation of respectability;—if indeed there be an affectation so honorable.

There were many individuals of dashing appearance, whom I easily understood as belonging to the race of swell pick-pockets, with which all great cities are infested. I watched these gentry with much inquisitiveness, and found it difficult to imagine how they should ever be mistaken for gentlemen by gentlemen themselves. Their voluminousness of wristband, with an air of excessive frankness, should betray them at once.

The gamblers, of whom I descried not a few, were still more easily recognisable. They wore every variety of dress, from that of the desperate thimble-rig bully,[19] with velvet waistcoat, fancy neckerchief, gilt chains, and filagreed buttons, to that of the scrupulously inornate clergyman, than which nothing could be less liable to suspicion. Still all were distinguished by a certain sodden swarthiness of complexion, a filmy dimness of eye, and pallor and compression of lip. There were two other traits, moreover, by which I could always detect them;—a guarded lowness of tone in conversation, and a more than ordinary extension of the thumb in a direction at right angles with the fingers.—Very often, in company with these sharpers, I observed an order of men somewhat different in habits, but still birds of a kindred feather. They may be defined as the gentlemen who live by their wits. They seem to prey upon the public in two battalions—that of the dandies and that of the military men. Of the first grade the leading features are long locks and smiles; of the second frogged coats[20] and frowns.

Descending in the scale of what is termed gentility, I found darker and deeper themes for speculation. I saw Jew pedlars, with hawk eyes flashing from countenances whose every other feature wore only an expression of abject humility; sturdy professional street beggars scowling upon mendicants of a better stamp, whom despair alone had driven forth into the night for charity; feeble and ghastly invalids, upon whom death had placed a sure hand, and who sidled and tottered through the mob, looking every one beseechingly in the face, as if in search of some chance consolation, some lost hope; modest young girls returning from long and late labor to a cheerless home, and shrinking more tearfully than indignantly from the glances of ruffians, whose direct contact, even, could not be avoided; women of the town of all kinds and of all ages—the unequivocal beauty in the prime of her womanhood, putting one in mind of the statue in Lucian, with the surface of Parian marble, and the interior filled with filth[21]—the loathsome and utterly lost leper in rags—the wrinkled, bejewelled and paint-begrimed beldame, making a last effort at youth—the mere child of immature form, yet, from long association, an adept in the dreadful coquetries of her trade, and burning with a rabid ambition to be ranked the equal of her elders in vice;[22] drunkards innumerable and indescribable—some in shreds and patches, reeling, inarticulate, with bruised visage and lack-lustre eyes—some in whole although filthy garments, with a slightly unsteady swagger, thick sensual lips, and hearty-looking rubicund faces—others

20 A frogged coat is adorned with "frogs," ornamental fastenings made from spindle-shaped buttons, which pass through loops on the other breast of the garment.

21 This comparison refers to a passage found in "The Dream, or The Cock," by Lucian (*ca.* 120–after 180), an ancient Greek rhetorician and satirist. In the passage in question, the Cock (Pythagoras reincarnated) compares a monarch to "the great colossi that Phidias or Myron or Praxiteles made, each of which outwardly is a beautiful Poseidon or a Zeus, made of ivory and gold, with a thunderbolt or a flash of lightning or a trident in his right hand," the inside containing "bars and props and nails driven clear through, and beams and wedges and pitch and clay and a quantity of such ugly stuff housing within, not to mention numbers of mice and rats that keep their court in them sometimes. That is what monarchy is like" (*Lucian*, trans. A. M. Harmon, K. Kilburn, and M. D. Macleod, 8 vols. [Cambridge, MA: Harvard University Press, 1913–1967], II, 223).

22 In his edition, Mabbott notes Poe's indebtedness, here and elsewhere, to Charles Dickens. His description of the prostitutes owes much to Dickens in "The Pawnbroker's Shop" in his *Sketches by Boz* (Thomas Ollive Mabbott, ed., *Collected Works of Edgar Allan Poe*, 3 vols. [Cambridge, MA: The Belknap Press of Harvard University Press, 1969-1978], II, 516). More recently, Stephen Rachman has called attention to Poe's appropriation of Dickens: "While unabashedly relying on Dickens for the details of his London picture, and at times even for his turn of phrase, Poe transforms the socially intelligible world of Dickens into a diabolical parade of types, of urban hieroglyphs ostensibly significant to the narrator only in their potential decipherability" ("Reading Cities: Devotional Seeing in the Nineteenth Century," *American Literary History* 9 [1997], 659).

23 Coal gas was first used for street lighting along Pall Mall in London in 1807. The general illumination of London streets began within the next half dozen years.

24 Mabbott traces this comment about Tertullian (*ca.* 160–*ca.* 240), the early Christian theologian, to a quote by Jean-Louis Guez de Balzac (1594–1655) found in the second edition of Gilles Ménage's collection of anecdotes, *Menagiana* (1694). Poe, however, took the quotation from Edward Bulwer-Lytton's novel *Paul Clifford* (1830). In his dedicatory epistle, Bulwer-Lytton characterized the literary style of William Godwin by using "the simile applied somewhat too flatteringly to that of Tertullian,—that it is like ebony, at once dark and splendid."

25 The phrase "world of light" reads "world of life" in the earlier 1840 version of the story. Modest as it is, Poe's revision enhances the story considerably. It suggests that the narrator cannot really "read" the history of each passer-by, as he claims he can; rather, he takes in only the spectacle of the crowd—the light reflected from the surfaces of so many passing faces.

26 Middle-class consumers on both sides of the Atlantic eagerly purchased editions of literary works illustrated by German illustrator Friedrich August Moritz Retzsch (1799–1857), who made his early reputation with his etchings for Goethe's *Faust*. Retzsch worked in "outline," a style that combines rich symbolism with an austereness of line. In a review of Henry Wadsworth Longfellow's *Ballads and Other Poems*, Poe's observations about Retzsch's outline style invite reflection on his own methods: "It is curious to observe how very slight a degree of truth is sufficient to satisfy the mind, which acquiesces in the absence of numerous essentials in the thing depicted. An outline frequently stirs the spirit more pleasantly than the most elaborate picture. We need only refer to the compositions of . . . Retzsch. Here all details are omitted—nothing can be farther from truth. Without even color the most thrilling effects are produced" (*Essays and Reviews*, ed. G. R. Thompson [New York: Library of America, 1984], pp. 694–695). For a discussion of how Retzsch's style influenced Poe's aesthetics, see Kevin J. Hayes, "Retzsch's *Outlines* and Poe's 'The Man of the Crowd,'" *Gothic Studies* 12 [2010], 29–41.

27 Glossing this sentence, the poet Charles Simic observes: "On a busy street one quickly becomes a voyeur. An air of danger, eroticism, and crushing solitude play hide-and-seek in the crowd. The indeterminate, the unforeseeable, the ethereal, and the fleeting rule there. The city is the place where the most unlikely opposites come

clothed in materials which had once been good, and which even now were scrupulously well brushed—men who walked with a more than naturally firm and springy step, but whose countenances were fearfully pale, whose eyes hideously wild and red, and who clutched with quivering fingers, as they strode through the crowd, at every object which came within their reach; beside these, pie-men, porters, coal-heavers, sweeps; organ-grinders, monkey-exhibiters and ballad mongers, those who vended with those who sang; ragged artizans and exhausted laborers of every description, and all full of a noisy and inordinate vivacity which jarred discordantly upon the ear, and gave an aching sensation to the eye.

As the night deepened, so deepened to me the interest of the scene; for not only did the general character of the crowd materially alter (its gentler features retiring in the gradual withdrawal of the more orderly portion of the people, and its harsher ones coming out into bolder relief, as the late hour brought forth every species of infamy from its den,) but the rays of the gas-lamps, feeble at first in their struggle with the dying day, had now at length gained ascendancy, and threw over every thing a fitful and garish lustre.[23] All was dark yet splendid—as that ebony to which has been likened the style of Tertullian.[24]

The wild effects of the light enchained me to an examination of individual faces; and although the rapidity with which the world of light flitted before the window, prevented me from casting more than a glance upon each visage, still it seemed that, in my then peculiar mental state, I could frequently read, even in that brief interval of a glance, the history of long years.[25]

With my brow to the glass, I was thus occupied in scrutinizing the mob, when suddenly there came into view a countenance (that of a decrepid old man, some sixty-five or seventy years of age,)—a countenance which at once arrested and absorbed my whole attention, on account of the absolute idiosyncracy of its expression. Any thing even remotely resembling that expression I had never seen before. I well remember that my first thought, upon beholding it, was that Retzsch, had he viewed it, would have greatly preferred it to his own pictural incarnations of the fiend.[26] As I endeavored, during the brief minute of my original survey, to form some analysis of the meaning conveyed, there arose confusedly and paradoxically within my mind, the ideas of vast mental power, of caution, of penuriousness, of avarice, of coolness, of malice, of blood-thirstiness, of triumph, of merriment, of excessive terror, of intense—of supreme despair. I felt singularly aroused, startled, fascinated. "How wild a history," I said to myself, "is written within that bosom!"[27] Then came a craving desire to keep the man in view—to know more of him. Hurriedly putting on an overcoat, and seizing my hat and cane, I made my way into the street, and pushed through the crowd in the direction which I had seen him take; for he had already disappeared. With some little difficulty I at length came within sight of him, approached, and followed him closely, yet cautiously, so as not to attract his attention.[28]

I had now a good opportunity of examining his person. He was short in stature, very thin, and apparently very feeble. His clothes, generally, were filthy and ragged; but as he came, now and then, within the strong glare of a lamp, I perceived that his linen, although dirty, was of beautiful texture; and my vision deceived me, or, through a rent in a closely-buttoned and evidently second-handed *roquelaire*[29] which enveloped him, I caught a glimpse both of a diamond and of a dagger.[30] These observations heightened my

together, the place where our separate intuitions momentarily link up. The myth of Theseus, the Minotaur, Ariadne, and her thread continue here. The city is a labyrinth of analogies, the Symbolist forest of correspondences" (*Dime-Store Alchemy: The Art of Joseph Cornell* [Hopewell, NJ: Ecco Press, 1992], 10–11).

28 Walter Benjamin theorizes that the detective story has as its genesis the modern phenomenon of the big-city crowd. It is the criminal's frightening ability to hide in plain sight that gives birth to detective fiction. In "The Paris of the Second Empire in Baudelaire" (1938), he observes: "The masses appear as the asylum that shields an asocial person from his persecutors. Of all the menacing aspects of the masses, this one became apparent first. It lies at the origin of the detective story." Later, in the same essay, he famously calls "The Man of the Crowd" "something like an X-ray of a detective story. It does away with all the drapery that a crime represents. Only the armature remains: the pursuer, the crowd, and an unknown man who manages to walk through London in such a way that he always remains in the middle of the crowd" (*Selected Writings*, vol. 4, 1938–1940, ed. Howard Eiland and Michael W. Jennings, trans. Edmund Jephcott [Cambridge,

Friedrich August Moritz Retzsch, "Faust and Mephistopheles in the Witches' Cave," from *Illustrations of Goethe's Faust*, 1843. Poe was drawn to Retzsch's minimalist style.

MA: The Belknap Press of Harvard University Press, 2003], 21, 27). Poe had not yet invented the detective story with his Dupin tales, but Benjamin's observations initiated the critical debate about whether or not the tale serves as a prototype for the detective story. See Bran Nichol, "Reading and Not Reading 'The Man of the Crowd': Poe, the City, and the Gothic Text," *Philological Quarterly* 91 (2012), 465–493.

29   A roquelaure, as it was also spelled, was a knee-length cloak.

30   The narrator acknowledges that perhaps "my vision deceived me." But what he sees suggests as much as anything else that his imagination may in fact be playing tricks on him: The diamond-hilted dagger was in Poe's day a cliché of romantic fiction, as many contemporary readers would have recognized.

31   Compare Luke 9:57: "And it came to pass, that, as they went in the way, a certain *man* said unto him, Lord, I will follow thee whithersoever thou goest."

32   The narrator's familiarity with Broadway and City Hall Park reinforces the idea that he is an American in London. This passage also indicates why Poe set this story in London: he needed a city that was populous enough to create large street crowds. No American city would do.

curiosity, and I resolved to follow the stranger whithersoever he should go.[31]

It was now fully night-fall, and a thick humid fog hung over the city, soon ending in a settled and heavy rain. This change of weather had an odd effect upon the crowd, the whole of which was at once put into new commotion, and overshadowed by a world of umbrellas. The waver, the jostle, and the hum increased in a tenfold degree. For my own part I did not much regard the rain—the lurking of an old fever in my system rendering the moisture somewhat too dangerously pleasant. Tying a handkerchief about my mouth, I kept on. For half an hour the old man held his way with difficulty along the great thoroughfare; and I here walked close at his elbow through fear of losing sight of him. Never once turning his head to look back, he did not observe me. By and bye he passed into a cross street, which, although densely filled with people, was not quite so much thronged as the main one he had quitted. Here a change in his demeanor became evident. He walked more slowly and with less object than before—more hesitatingly. He crossed and re-crossed the way repeatedly without apparent aim; and the press was still so thick that, at every such movement, I was obliged to follow him closely. The street was a narrow and long one, and his course lay within it for nearly an hour, during which the passengers had gradually diminished to about that number which is ordinarily seen at noon in Broadway near the Park—so vast a difference is there between a London populace and that of the most frequented American city.[32] A second turn brought us into a square, brilliantly lighted, and overflowing with life. The old manner of the stranger re-appeared. His chin fell upon his breast, while his eyes rolled wildly from under his knit brows, in every direction, upon those who hemmed him in. He urged his way steadily and perseveringly. I was surprised, however, to find, upon his having made the circuit of the square, that he turned and retraced his steps. Still more was I astonished to see him repeat the same walk several times—once nearly detecting me as he came round with a sudden movement.

In this exercise he spent another hour, at the end of which we met with far less interruption from passengers than at first. The rain fell fast; the air grew cool; and the people were retiring to their homes. With a gesture of impatience, the wanderer passed into a bye-street comparatively deserted. Down this, some quarter of a mile long, he rushed with an activity I could not have dreamed of seeing in one so aged, and which put me to much trouble in pursuit. A few minutes brought us to a large and busy bazaar, with the localities of which the stranger appeared well acquainted, and where his original demeanor again became apparent, as he forced his way to and fro, without aim, among the host of buyers and sellers.

During the hour and a half, or thereabouts, which we passed in this place, it required much caution on my part to keep him within reach without attracting his observation. Luckily I wore a pair of caoutchouc over-shoes,[33] and could move about in perfect silence. At no moment did he see that I watched him. He entered shop after shop, priced nothing, spoke no word, and looked at all objects with a wild and vacant stare. I was now utterly amazed at his behaviour, and firmly resolved that we should not part until I had satisfied myself in some measure respecting him.

A loud-toned clock struck eleven, and the company were fast deserting the bazaar. A shop-keeper, in putting up a shutter, jostled the old man, and at the instant I saw a strong shudder come over his frame. He hurried into the street, looked anxiously around him for an instant, and then ran with incredible swiftness through many crooked and people-less lanes, until we emerged once more upon the great thoroughfare whence we had started—the street of the D——Hotel. It no longer wore, however, the same aspect. It was still brilliant with gas; but the rain fell fiercely, and there were few persons to be seen. The stranger grew pale. He walked moodily some paces up the once populous avenue, then, with a heavy sigh, turned in the direction of the river, and, plunging through a great variety of devious ways, came out, at length, in view of one of the principal theatres. It was about being closed, and the audience were thronging from the doors. I saw the old man gasp as if for breath while he threw himself amid the crowd; but I thought that the intense agony of his countenance had, in some measure, abated. His head again fell upon his breast; he appeared as I had seen him at first. I observed that he now took the course in which had gone the greater number of the audience—but, upon the whole, I was at a loss to comprehend the waywardness of his actions.[34]

As he proceeded, the company grew more scattered, and his old uneasiness and vacillation were resumed. For some time he fol-

33   In the 1840 version, the narrator wears "gum over-shoes." Both "gum" and "caoutchouc" were synonyms for rubber, which was becoming an increasingly important product since American inventor Charles Goodyear discovered the vulcanization process in 1839. A fashionable Londoner would likely sport patent leather shoes regardless of the weather; however, a practical-minded American might wear watertight rubber galoshes. The narrator's shoes also allow him to move undetected through the city streets. In *Poetic Justice* (1967), Ellery Queen calls Poe's narrator the earliest gumshoe detective in literary history. Patricia Merivale sees the tale as a "metaphysical gumshoe story" or "Gumshoe Gothic" for short: a genre that deals with "a Missing Person, a person sought for . . . gumshoe style, through endless, labyrinthine city streets, but never really Found—because he was never really There . . . One was, as postmodernist detective after postmodernist detective discovers, only following's one's own self" ("Gumshoe Gothics: Poe's 'The Man of the Crowd' and His Followers," *Detecting Texts: The Metaphysical Detective Story from Poe to Postmodernism*, ed. Patricia Merivale and Susan Elizabeth Sweeney [Philadelphia: University of Pennsylvania Press, 1999], 104). What *"er lasst sich nicht lessen"* means, then, is that we cannot understand *ourselves*, let alone others.

34   Poe's description of the old man's agitated restlessness anticipates the candid "street photography" of American photographer Lisette Model (1901–1983). Using a thirty-five millimeter camera, Model captured the movement of the modern city. Some of her most memorable work depicts people in a fragmented, depersonalized way—lower legs and feet—as they hurry through streets on their way to work or home or to appointments to which they feared being late.

Lisette Model, *Running Legs*, *New York*, *ca.* 1940–1941.

lowed closely a party of some ten or twelve roisterers;[35] but from this number one by one dropped off, until three only remained together, in a narrow and gloomy lane little frequented. The stranger paused, and, for a moment, seemed lost in thought; then, with every mark of agitation, pursued rapidly a route which brought us to the verge of the city, amid regions very different from those we had hitherto traversed. It was the most noisome quarter of London, where every thing wore the worst impress of the most deplorable poverty, and of the most desperate crime. By the dim light of an accidental lamp, tall, antique, worm-eaten, wooden tenements were seen tottering to their fall, in directions so many and capricious that scarce the semblance of a passage was discernible between them. The paving-stones lay at random, displaced from their beds by the rankly-growing grass. Horrible filth festered in the dammed-up gutters. The whole atmosphere teemed with desolation. Yet, as we proceeded, the sounds of human life revived by sure degrees, and at length large bands of the most abandoned of a London populace were seen reeling to and fro. The spirits of the old man again flickered up, as a lamp which is near its death-hour. Once more he strode onward with elastic tread. Suddenly a corner was turned, a blaze of light burst upon our sight, and we stood before one of the huge suburban temples of Intemperance—one of the palaces of the fiend, Gin.[36]

It was now nearly day-break; but a number of wretched inebriates still pressed in and out of the flaunting entrance. With a half shriek of joy the old man forced a passage within, resumed at once his original bearing, and stalked backward and forward, without apparent object, among the throng. He had not been thus long occupied, however, before a rush to the doors gave token that the host was closing them for the night. It was something even more intense than despair that I then observed upon the countenance of the singular being whom I had watched so pertinaciously. Yet he did not hesitate in his career, but, with a mad energy, retraced his steps at once, to the heart of the mighty London. Long and swiftly he fled, while I followed him in the wildest amazement, resolute not to abandon a scrutiny in which I now felt an interest all-absorbing. The sun arose while we proceeded, and, when we had once again reached that most thronged mart of the populous town, the street of the D——Hotel, it presented an appearance of human bustle and activity scarcely inferior to what I had seen on

35 Swaggering or noisy revelers.

36 Gin drinking was a much greater social problem in nineteenth-century Great Britain than the United States. Exposés against gin palaces recurred frequently in the contemporary British press. See, for example, [W. H. Leeds,] "A Chapter about Boutiques and Gin Palaces," *Fraser's Magazine* 20 (1839), 697–714.

37   In *The Arcades Project*, Walter Benjamin identifies Edward Bulwer-Lytton's *Eugene Aram* (1832) as Poe's source. In the novel, Bulwer-Lytton writes: "Through this crowd, self-absorbed as usual—with them—not one of them—Eugene Aram slowly wound his uncompanioned way. What an incalculable field of dread and sombre contemplation is opened to every man who, with his heart disengaged from himself, and his eyes accustomed to the sharp observance of his tribe, walks through the streets of a great city! What a world of dark and troublous secrets in the breast of every one who hurries by you! Goëthe has said somewhere, that each of us, the best as the worst, hides within him something—some feeling, some remembrance that, if known, would make you hate him. No doubt the saying is exaggerated; but still, what a gloomy and profound sublimity in the idea!—what a new insight it gives into the hearts of the common herd!—with what a strange interest it may inspire us for the humblest, the tritest passenger that shoulders us in the great thoroughfare of life!" (*Eugene Aram: A Tale*, 3 vols. [London: Henry Colburn and Richard Bentley, 1832], II, 276–277).

38   "The *Hortulus Animae cum Oratiunculis Aliquibus Superadditis* of Grünninger [Poe's note]." Poe added the note when he revised the story in 1845. The *Hortulus Animae* is a devotional manual illustrated with gruesome images, printed in Strassburg in the late fifteenth and early sixteenth centuries. See M. Consuelo Oldenbourg, *Hortulus Animae: (1494)-1523* (Hamburg: Hauswedell, 1973).

39   Bran Nicol argues that Poe's tale is a "parable" about its own refusal to be read: "'The Man of the Crowd' itself is a mystery which does not *permit itself* to be revealed. Poe's story *performs* a parallel version of what it tells us. Just as the old man's secret (if he has one) cannot be uncovered, so the point of the story itself remains obscure. The beauty of 'The Man of the Crowd' is that it both presents readers with what seems like a secret which cannot be told *and* itself figures as a text which cannot be read" ("Reading and Not Reading 'The Man of the Crowd,'" 483).

the evening before. And here, long, amid the momently increasing confusion, did I persist in my pursuit of the stranger. But, as usual, he walked to and fro, and during the day did not pass from out the turmoil of that street. And, as the shades of the second evening came on, I grew wearied unto death, and, stopping fully in front of the wanderer, gazed at him steadfastly in the face. He noticed me not, but resumed his solemn walk, while I, ceasing to follow, remained absorbed in contemplation. "This old man," I said at length, "is the type and the genius of deep crime. He refuses to be alone. *He is the man of the crowd*. It will be in vain to follow; for I shall learn no more of him, nor of his deeds.[37] The worst heart of the world is a grosser book than the *Hortulus Animae*,[38] and perhaps it is but one of the great mercies of God that '*er lasst sich nicht lesen*.'"[39]

The Murders in the Rue Morgue

What song the Syrens sang, or what name Achilles assumed when he hid himself among women, although puzzling questions, are not beyond *all* conjecture.

Sir Thomas Browne[1]

The mental features discoursed of as the analytical, are, in themselves, but little susceptible of analysis. We appreciate them only in their effects. We know of them, among other things, that they are always to their possessor, when inordinately possessed, a source of the liveliest enjoyment. As the strong man exults in his physical ability, delighting in such exercises as call his muscles into action, so glories the analyst in that moral activity which *disentangles.* He derives pleasure from even the most trivial occupations bringing his talent into play. He is fond of enigmas, of conundrums,[2] of hieroglyphics;[3] exhibiting in his solutions of each a degree of *acumen* which appears to the ordinary apprehension praeternatural. His results, brought about by the very soul and essence of method, have, in truth, the whole air of intuition.[4]

The faculty of re-solution is possibly much invigorated by mathematical study, and especially by that highest branch of it which, unjustly, and merely on account of its retrograde operations, has been called, as if *par excellence*, analysis. Yet to calculate is not in itself to analyse. A chess-player, for example, does the one without effort at the other. It follows that the game of chess, in its effects upon mental character, is greatly misunderstood. I am not now writing a treatise, but simply prefacing a somewhat peculiar narrative by observations very much at random; I will, therefore, take occasion to assert that the higher powers of the reflective intellect are more decidedly and more usefully tasked by the unostentatious game of draughts[5] than by all the elaborate frivolity of chess. In this latter, where the pieces have different and *bizarre* motions, with various and variable values, what is only complex is

With "The Murders in the Rue Morgue" (1841), Poe invented the modern detective story and introduced readers to sleuth C. Auguste Dupin, the original Sherlock Holmes. "The Murders in the Rue Morgue" proved to be popular with contemporary readers, and two more Dupin tales soon followed, giving weight to the claim sometimes made that Poe not only created the detective genre but developed the readership for it. Poe wrote his Dupin tales in an era when, as biographer Kenneth Silverman notes, crime was "much in the air, as its prevention became a pressing urban need." This was the dawn of scientific police work. The world's first professional police force had been created in London only a dozen years before the publication of "The Murders in the Rue Morgue." Though the word detective had not yet come into existence in English, Poe understood that he had created "something in a new key." His tale of "ratiocination," as he thought of it, anticipates nearly all of the important motifs of detective fiction: the astute consulting detective who operates by both logic and intuition; his dependable partner and foil; a plodding, largely ineffectual police force; the careful examination of the crime scene; the reliance on scientific methods; and the surprising solution to the mystery.

"The Murders in the Rue Morgue" debuted in the April 1841 issue of Graham's Magazine (the same issue that announced Poe's association with the magazine), when Poe and his family were still living in Philadelphia in what was proving to be the most productive period of his life. After "The Murders in the Rue Morgue" was set in type, the printer hired to see Graham's through press tossed the manuscript into the wastebasket, as was then common practice. J. M. Johnston, a boy working as a printer's apprentice, rescued it from the trash and asked if he might keep it. His quick thinking is responsible for the survival of one of the few complete manuscripts of Poe's fiction. The manuscript offers a fascinating picture of the author at work, as he adds and deletes materials, makes word substitutions, and changes punctuation and grammar. One of the alterations he made in manuscript was to change the title of the story from "The Murders in the Rue Trianon" to "The Murders in the Rue Trianon-Bas," before settling on "The Murders in the Rue Morgue." There is no Rue Morgue in Paris: the name is Poe' invention.

1 Sir Thomas Browne (1605–1682) published his eloquent meditation on death, *Hydriotaphia, Urn-Burial: or, A Discours of the Sepulchral Urns Lately Found in Norfolk*, in 1658. *Urn-Burial*, as it is usually called, is the original source for this story's epigraph, though Poe may have picked up the quotation secondhand; these words were often quoted as an instance of excellent English prose.

2   Poe was himself fond of riddles and puzzles. "Nothing intelligible can be written which, with time, I cannot decipher," he once boasted. In "Enigmatical and Conundrumical" (1839), the first of a series of articles on cryptology that Poe wrote for *Alexander's Weekly Messenger*, he famously dared readers to submit a cipher—"where, in place of alphabetical letters, any kind of marks are made use of at random"—that would stump him. Some of these challenges were later reprinted, along with Poe's solutions. In the same article, Poe presented twenty-five conundrums of his own composition. One of them, punning on his name, reads: "Why ought the author of the *Grotesque and Arabesque* to be a good writer of verses? Because he's a poet to a *t*. Add *t* to Poe makes it Poet."

3   Napoleon's invasion of Egypt in 1798 began a wholesale plundering of Egyptian antiquities and fueled a fascination with Egypt that spread across Western Europe and America. That fascination was stimulated in part by the mystery of the hieroglyphs that ancient Egyptians had left behind on their tombs, monuments, and temples. The discovery of the Rosetta Stone in 1799 by Napoleon's *corps de savants* did not immediately solve the riddle of the hieroglyphs. The eventual deciphering of hieroglyphics in the 1820s—revealing ancient Egyptian texts to be far more mundane than many people imagined—did not dissipate interest in Egypt. Rather, it reinforced the modern fascination for solving puzzles and mysteries, for reading the unreadable. Poe would spoof the Egyptian craze with his humorous short story "Some Words with a Mummy" (1845).

4   In "The Mystery of Marie Rogêt" (1842–1843), the first sequel to "The Murders in the Rue Morgue," Poe defines intuition as "the idiosyncrasy of the individual man of genius," a god-given ability, not a skill that can be mastered. Elsewhere, he emphasizes the value of intuition over analytical ability: "What I really say is this:—That there is no absolute *certainty* either in the Aristotelian [deductive] or Baconian [inductive] process—that, for this reason, neither Philosophy is so profound as it fancies itself—and that neither . . . has a right to sneer at that seemingly imaginative process called Intuition" (*Collected Letters of Edgar Allan Poe*, ed. John Ward Ostrom, Burton R. Pollin, and Jeffrey A. Savoye, 2 vols. [New York: Gordian Press, 2008], II, 688).

5   Checkers.

6   Various and complex.

mistaken (a not unusual error) for what is profound. The *attention* is here called powerfully into play. If it flag for an instant, an oversight is committed, resulting in injury or defeat. The possible moves being not only manifold but involute,[6] the chances of such oversights are multiplied; and in nine cases out of ten it is the more concentrative rather than the more acute player who conquers. In draughts, on the contrary, where the moves are *unique* and have but little variation, the probabilities of inadvertence are diminished, and the mere attention being left comparatively unemployed, what advantages are obtained by either party are obtained by superior *acumen*. To be less abstract—Let us suppose a game of draughts where the pieces are reduced to four kings, and where, of course, no oversight is to be expected. It is obvious that here the victory can be decided (the players being at all equal) only by some *recherché* movement, the result of some strong exertion of the intellect. Deprived of ordinary resources, the analyst throws himself into the spirit of his opponent, identifies himself therewith, and not unfrequently sees thus, at a glance, the sole methods (sometimes indeed absurdly simple ones) by which he may seduce into error or hurry into miscalculation.

Whist has long been noted for its influence upon what is termed the calculating power; and men of the highest order of intellect have been known to take an apparently unaccountable delight in it, while eschewing chess as frivolous.[7] Beyond doubt there is nothing of a similar nature so greatly tasking the faculty of analysis. The best chess-player in Christendom *may* be little more than the best player of chess; but proficiency in whist implies capacity for success in all those more important undertakings where mind struggles with mind. When I say proficiency, I mean that perfection in the game which includes a comprehension of *all* the sources whence legitimate advantage may be derived. These are not only manifold but multiform, and lie frequently among recesses of thought altogether inaccessible to the ordinary understanding. To observe attentively is to remember distinctly; and, so far, the concentrative chess-player will do very well at whist; while the rules of Hoyle[8] (themselves based upon the mere mechanism of the game) are sufficiently and generally comprehensible. Thus to have a retentive memory, and to proceed by "the book," are points commonly regarded as the sum total of good playing. But it

Stele of Zezen-nacht, stuccoed limestone with polychrome paint, *ca.* 2000 BCE. This gravestone from the village of Naga-ed-Dêr in Upper Egypt provides an excellent example of the ancient Egyptian hieroglyphics that so fascinated Poe and his contemporaries.

is in matters beyond the limits of mere rule that the skill of the analyst is evinced. He makes, in silence, a host of observations and inferences. So, perhaps, do his companions; and the difference in the extent of the information obtained, lies not so much in the validity of the inference as in the quality of the observation. The necessary knowledge is that of *what* to observe. Our player confines himself not at all; nor, because the game is the object, does he reject deductions from things external to the game. He examines the countenance of his partner, comparing it carefully with that of each of his opponents. He considers the mode of assorting the cards in each hand; often counting trump by trump, and honor by honor,[9] through the glances bestowed by their holders upon each. He notes every variation of face as the play progresses, gathering a fund of thought from the differences in the expression of certainty, of surprise, of triumph, or of chagrin. From the manner of gathering up a trick he judges whether the person taking it can

7 Enormously popular in the eighteenth and nineteenth centuries, Whist is a card game for four players working in two partnerships. The object is to win tricks, or rounds of play. One point is given for each trick in excess of six. Describing a particularly skillful play, Poe's contemporary Charles Barwell Coles remarks, "The following stroke at Whist (which, considering that cards are unseen, and their positions only presumed, equals a masterly move at chess,) is recorded as showing what first-rate play can do" (*Short Whist: Its Rise, Progress, and Laws* [London: Longman, Rees, Orme, Brown, Green, and Longman, 1835], 63).

8 Edmond Hoyle (1672–1769), the famed authority on the rules of card games and chess, published *A Short Treatise on the Game of Whist* in 1742. In his lifetime, Hoyle became a brand name as his *Treatise* went through numerous editions and was gradually expanded to contain rules for other games. After his death, countless books on card games invoked the authority of Edmond Hoyle. In Poe's era, the phrase "according to Hoyle" was already a common way to emphasize the authority of anything.

9   The honor cards are ace, king, queen, and jack.

10   Though the term "poker face" would not be coined until later in the nineteenth century, Poe is clearly familiar with the idea behind it. Like a detective, a successful card player must be a careful observer of other people—both their behavior and their facial expressions. In "A Scandal in Bohemia," Sherlock Holmes famously rebukes Watson: "You see but do not observe."

11   In *Biographia Literaria* (1817), Coleridge distinguishes fancy from imagination. Fancy resembles "ordinary memory," Coleridge says, because it "receive[s] all its materials ready made from the law of association," and then plays with, or rearranges, received sensory images to form new combinations. A higher faculty, imagination is not mechanical but "vital," echoing God's own creative powers.

12   The letter "C" may indicate the first initial of Dupin's name, or as E. D. Forgues suggests, it may stand for "chevalier" (I. M. Walker, *Edgar Allan Poe: The Critical Heritage* [New York: Routledge and Kegan Paul, 1986], 215). In 1840, Poe attempted to find a teaching position in Richmond for an acquaintance named C. Auguste Dubouchet. Poe most likely took the family name of his fictional detective from André-Marie-Jean-Jacques Dupin (1783–1865), an advocate, magistrate, and president of the French Chamber of Deputies. Mabbott notes that the French politician is "described as a person of antithetical qualities, a living encyclopedia, and a lover of legal methods, in *Sketches of Living Characters of France*, translated by R. M. Walsh (1841), a book reviewed by Poe in the issue of *Graham's* in which his story appeared" (Thomas Ollive Mabbott, ed., *Collected Works of Edgar Allan Poe*, 3 vols. [Cambridge, MA: The Belknap Press of Harvard University Press, 1969-1978], II, 525).

13   Rue Montmartre is an actual street in Paris. E. D. Forgues, though one of Poe's earliest and most enthusiastic French supporters, found his topographical descriptions of Paris incomprehensible. Discussing "The Murders in the Rue Morgue," Forgues remarks that the French reader "would be amazed to find the capital of France completely overturned" (Walker, *Edgar Allan Poe*, 214). Charles Baudelaire was less bothered by these inaccuracies. In a footnote to his translation of the story, Baudelaire asked his French readers, "Do I need to point out that Edgar Poe never came to Paris?" Poe either invented his topographical descriptions of Paris or borrowed them from other writers. As Borges explains, by setting his story in Paris,

make another in the suit. He recognises what is played through feint, by the air with which it is thrown upon the table. A casual or inadvertent word; the accidental dropping or turning of a card, with the accompanying anxiety or carelessness in regard to its concealment; the counting of the tricks, with the order of their arrangement; embarrassment, hesitation, eagerness or trepidation—all afford, to his apparently intuitive perception, indications of the true state of affairs.[10] The first two or three rounds having been played, he is in full possession of the contents of each hand, and thenceforward puts down his cards with as absolute a precision of purpose as if the rest of the party had turned outward the faces of their own.

The analytical power should not be confounded with simple ingenuity; for while the analyst is necessarily ingenious, the ingenious man is often remarkably incapable of analysis. The constructive or combining power, by which ingenuity is usually manifested, and to which the phrenologists (I believe erroneously) have assigned a separate organ, supposing it a primitive faculty, has been so frequently seen in those whose intellect bordered otherwise upon idiocy, as to have attracted general observation among writers on morals. Between ingenuity and the analytic ability there exists a difference far greater, indeed, than that between the fancy and the imagination,[11] but of a character very strictly analogous. It will be found, in fact, that the ingenious are always fanciful, and the *truly* imaginative never otherwise than analytic.

The narrative which follows will appear to the reader somewhat in the light of a commentary upon the propositions just advanced.

Residing in Paris during the spring and part of the summer of 18—, I there became acquainted with a Monsieur C. Auguste Dupin.[12] This young gentleman was of an excellent—indeed of an illustrious family, but, by a variety of untoward events, had been reduced to such poverty that the energy of his character succumbed beneath it, and he ceased to bestir himself in the world, or to care for the retrieval of his fortunes. By courtesy of his creditors, there still remained in his possession a small remnant of his patrimony; and, upon the income arising from this, he managed, by means of a rigorous economy, to procure the necessaries of life, without troubling himself about its superfluities. Books, indeed, were his sole luxuries, and in Paris these are easily obtained.

   Our first meeting was at an obscure library in the Rue Montmartre,[13] where the accident of our both being in search of the same very rare and very remarkable volume, brought us into closer communion. We saw each other again and again. I was deeply interested in the little family history which he detailed to me with all that candor which a Frenchman indulges whenever mere self is his theme. I was astonished, too, at the vast extent of his reading; and, above all, I felt my soul enkindled within me by the wild fervor, and the vivid freshness of his imagination. Seeking in Paris the objects I then sought, I felt that the society of such a man would be to me a treasure beyond price; and this feeling I frankly confided to him. It was at length arranged that we should live together during my stay in the city; and as my worldly circumstances were somewhat less embarrassed than his own, I was permitted to be at the expense of renting, and furnishing in a style which suited the rather fantastic gloom of our common temper, a time-eaten and grotesque mansion, long deserted through superstitions into which we did not inquire, and tottering to its fall in a retired and desolate portion of the Faubourg St. Germain.[14]

   Had the routine of our life at this place been known to the world, we should have been regarded as madmen—although, perhaps, as madmen of a harmless nature. Our seclusion was perfect. We admitted no visitors. Indeed the locality of our retirement had been carefully kept a secret from my own former associates; and it had been many years since Dupin had ceased to know or be known in Paris. We existed within ourselves alone.[15]

   It was a freak of fancy in my friend (for what else shall I call it?) to be enamored of the Night[16] for her own sake; and into this *bizarrerie*,[17] as into all his others, I quietly fell; giving myself up to his wild whims with a perfect *abandon*. The sable divinity would not herself dwell with us always; but we could counterfeit her presence. At the first dawn of the morning we closed all the massy shutters of our old building; lighting a couple of tapers which, strongly perfumed, threw out only the ghastliest and feeblest of rays.[18] By the aid of these we then busied our souls in dreams—reading, writing, or conversing, until warned by the clock of the advent of the true Darkness. Then we sallied forth into the streets, arm in arm, continuing the topics of the day, or roaming far and

André-Marie-Jean-Jacques Dupin, undated. Dupin the Elder, as he was commonly known, was a French advocate, magistrate, and president of the French Chamber of Deputies.

Poe allowed himself "more room for the imagination" ("The Detective Story," trans. Alberto Manguel, *Descant* 17 [1985], 20).

14   Poe's contemporary Elias Regnault calls the Faubourg St. Germain a "living image of the eighteenth century." He describes life there "as full of antiquated reminiscences as a faded beauty, as full of obstinate opinions as an elderly gentleman, and yet as full of preposterous delusions as the day-dream of a boy. The party is defeated one day—to anticipate a triumph on the next; and its hopes have already outlived a thousand disappointments" ("The Canoness," *Pictures of the French: A Series of Literary and Graphic Delineations of French Character* [London: William S. Orr, 1840], 209).

15   Not only did Poe anticipate Sherlock Holmes with the character of Dupin; his nameless narrator looks forward to Dr. Watson. In addition, the relationship between Dupin and the narrator foreshadows the relationship between Holmes and Watson. The narrator is both a sounding board and an audience for Dupin. Their shared interests

wide until a late hour, seeking, amid the wild lights and shadows of the populous city,[19] that infinity of mental excitement which quiet observation can afford.

At such times I could not help remarking and admiring (although from his rich ideality[20] I had been prepared to expect it) a peculiar analytic ability in Dupin. He seemed, too, to take an eager delight in its exercise—if not exactly in its display—and did not hesitate to confess the pleasure thus derived. He boasted to me, with a low chuckling laugh, that most men, in respect to himself, wore windows in their bosoms, and was wont to follow up such assertions by direct and very startling proofs of his intimate knowledge of my own. His manner at these moments was frigid and abstract; his eyes were vacant in expression; while his voice,

make them seem almost like doppelgangers, though there is no question regarding the hierarchy of their relationship. The narrator also serves as a stand-in for the reader. "The role of the narrator as Dupin's naive companion and confidante," J. A. Leo Lemay observes, "is a brilliant technical achievement, for Poe puts the reader into the story in the narrator's place, and the reader discovers that the narrator verbalizes his own thoughts and reactions" ("The Psychology of 'The Murders in the Rue Morgue,'" *American Literature* 54 [1982], 176).

16   Since Poe coined the phrase, it has been used by other American authors from Nathaniel Parker Willis to Cormac McCarthy. In "A Story I Am Inclined to Believe," which appeared in the June 1843 issue of *Graham's*, Willis writes: "The Freyherr, like himself, and like all who have outlived the effervescence of life, was enamored of the night. A moment of unfathomable moonlight was dearer to him than hours disenchanted with the sun." In *Suttree* (1979), McCarthy writes: "He wandered through the wastes like a jackal in the dark, in the keep of old warehouse walls and the quiet of gutted buildings. He was enamored of the night and those quiet regions on the city's inward edges too dismal for dwelling."

17   "Bizarrerie," in this context, means strangeness, oddness.

18   Borges observes: "To make [Dupin and the story's narrator] stranger, he makes them spend their days in a manner different from that of other men. When dawn rises, they draw the curtains, light the candles, and only at dusk do they go for a walk in the deserted Paris streets in search of that *infinite azur*, says Poe, only produced by a large sleeping city; to feel at the same time that which is multitudinous and that which is lonely, that which stirs the brain." In *Great Short Stories of Detection, Mystery and Horror* (1928), British crime writer Dorothy Sayers, whose amateur sleuth Lord Peter Wimsey is another of

Dupin's literary descendants, cites Dupin's habit of simulating nighttime during the day as an example of his eccentricity. She observes that eccentricity would become a defining feature of nearly all the great fictional detectives.

19   Typically, the phrase "wild lights" referred to either natural or supernatural illumination—lightning, St. Elmo's fire, the will-o'-the-wisp. Here, however, Poe means the street lights of the modern city, suggesting that gas illumination—then a still very new technology—might lend a wild, uncontrollable aspect to the nighttime city. As cinematographers and moviegoers in a later era would come to appreciate, the constant opposition of light and shadow can actually enhance anxiety and a sense of danger. Street lamps cast light on cobblestones, brick fronts, and passersby, but they also create shadows, where criminals might be hiding. The streets of Poe's Philadelphia began to be illuminated at night for the first time in 1836 as newly installed gas lamps were turned on.

20   According to phrenology, the study of the shape of the human head and its relation to intellect and character traits, creativity is represented by the organ of ideality, located on the upper forehead. "Speaking of heads," Poe wrote in a letter of October 27, 1841, "my own *has been* examined by several phrenologists—all of whom spoke of me in a species of extravaganza which I should be ashamed to repeat" (*Collected Letters*, I, 313). Having since become somewhat skeptical of the tenets of phrenology, however, Poe minimized his use of the pseudoscience when he revised "The Murders in the Rue Morgue" for republication in 1845, but it implicitly survives in the revised version. The language of phrenology influenced Poe's critical vocabulary, and its fundamental process—using external signs to read what lies hidden—forms an essential aspect of Dupin's detective process.

usually a rich tenor, rose into a treble which would have sounded petulantly but for the deliberateness and entire distinctness of the enunciation. Observing him in these moods, I often dwelt meditatively upon the old philosophy of the Bi-Part Soul,[21] and amused myself with the fancy of a double Dupin—the creative and the resolvent.[22]

Let it not be supposed, from what I have just said, that I am detailing any mystery, or penning any romance. What I have described in the Frenchman, was merely the result of an excited, or perhaps of a diseased intelligence. But of the character of his remarks at the periods in question an example will best convey the idea.

We were strolling one night down a long dirty street, in the vicinity of the Palais Royal.[23] Being both, apparently, occupied with thought, neither of us had spoken a syllable for fifteen minutes at least. All at once Dupin broke forth with these words:

"He is a very little fellow, that's true, and would do better for the *Théâtre des Variétés*."[24]

"There can be no doubt of that," I replied unwittingly, and not at first observing (so much had I been absorbed in reflection) the extraordinary manner in which the speaker had chimed in with my meditations. In an instant afterward I recollected myself, and my astonishment was profound.

"Dupin," said I, gravely, "this is beyond my comprehension. I do not hesitate to say that I am amazed, and can scarcely credit my senses. How was it possible you should know I was thinking of—?" Here I paused, to ascertain beyond a doubt whether he really knew of whom I thought.

—"of Chantilly," said he, "why do you pause? You were remarking to yourself that his diminutive figure unfitted him for tragedy."

This was precisely what had formed the subject of my reflections. Chantilly was a *quondam* cobbler of the Rue St. Denis, who, becoming stage-mad, had attempted the *rôle* of Xerxes, in Crébillon's tragedy[25] so called, and been notoriously Pasquinaded for his pains.[26]

"Tell me, for Heaven's sake," I exclaimed, "the method—if method there is—by which you have been enabled to fathom my soul in this matter." In fact I was even more startled than I would have been willing to express.

21 What Poe intended, exactly, by "the old philosophy of the Bi-Part Soul" is not clear. Nowhere in his critical writings, essays, and letters does he discuss the term. Perhaps reference should be understood as merely evocative. As George Stade observes, all of Poe's tales "depict bi-, tri- and poly-part souls at all angles of attraction and repulsion to each other" (*Literature, Moderns, Monsters, Popsters and Us* [Grosseto, Italy: Pari Publishing, 2007], 94).

The only other place Poe uses the term is in his humorous tale "Lionizing" (1835), when the narrator meets among other literary lions "a writer on ethics": "He talked of Fire, Unity, and Atoms—Bi-part, and Pre-existent soul—Affinity and Discord—primitive Intelligence and Homoomeria." Poe drew this odd lexicon directly from a dialogue by Edward Bulwer-Lytton: "What a waste of our power—what a mockery of our schemes—seemed the fabrics [the ancient sages] had erected—the Pythagorean unity, and the Heraclitan fire, to which that philosopher of woe, reduced the origin of all things. And the 'Homoomeria' and primitive 'intelligence' of Anaxagoras; and the affinity and discord of Empedocles, and the atoms of Epicurus, and the bipart and pre-existent soul which was evoked by Plato" ("Conversations with an Ambitious Student in Ill Health," *New Monthly Magazine* 31 [1831], 304–305). In *The Republic*, Plato divides the soul into three, not two, parts: the appetitive, the spirited, and the rational.

22 Here "resolvent" means analytical. As the narrator has already made clear, Dupin works by a combination of intuition and analytical method. "Though sometimes depicted as a reasoner," Richard Wilbur comments, "[Dupin] is the embodiment of an idea, strongly urged in *Eureka* and elsewhere, that poetic intuition is a supra-logical faculty, infallible in nature, which includes and obviates analytical genius" ("The Poe Mystery Case," *New York Review of Books* [July 13, 1967]).

23 Originally built in the 1630s for Cardinal Richelieu, the Palais Royal is a large, hollow rectangle enclosing a garden-filled park. It was a fashionable pleasure destination in Poe's day.

24 Erected in 1807 on the Boulevard Montmarte, the Théâtre des Variétés primarily featured burlesque drama.

25 Stories of unsophisticated laborers going stage mad circulated in the contemporary print and oral culture. *Xerxes*, a tragedy by Prosper Jolyot de Crébillon (1674–1762), was first performed in 1714.

26 A pasquinade is a published lampoon.

27   In Shakespeare's *Julius Caesar*, I.i.15, the cobbler defines himself as "a mender of bad soles." "Et id genus omne" means "and all that sort of thing."

28   In "The Adventures of the Creeping Man," Dr. Watson offers a picture of his partnership with the eccentric supersleuth Sherlock Holmes—but he might just as easily be talking about the narrator and Dupin: "The relations between us . . . were peculiar. He was a man of habits, narrow and concentrated habits, and I had become one of them. As an institution I was like the violin, the shag tobacco, the old black pipe, the index books, and others perhaps less excusable. When it was a case of active work and a comrade was needed upon whose nerve he could place some reliance, my role was obvious. But apart from this I had uses. I was a whetstone for his mind. I stimulated him. He liked to think aloud in my presence. His remarks could hardly be said to be made to me—many of them would have been as appropriately addressed to his bedstead—but none the less, having formed the habit, it had become in some way helpful that I should register and interject. If I irritated him by a certain methodical slowness in my mentality, that irritation served only to make his own flame-like intuitions and impressions flash up the more vividly and swiftly. Such was my humble role in our alliance."

29   More contemptuous than the term "charlatanism," charlatanry, as the word is typically spelled, indicates the action of a charlatan: quackery, imposture.

30   By naming a little alley after the French poet Alphonse de Lamartine (1790–1869), Poe expresses his disdain for him.

31   The art of stonecutting for the construction of roads and buildings.

32   Epicurus (341–270 BCE), an atomist, argued that the cosmos was constituted by small, indivisible bits of matter (atoms) and empty space. Being a material thing, the soul, Epicurus maintained, does not survive death.

33   In his review of T. Babington Macaulay's *Critical and Miscellaneous Essays*, Poe defines the theory of nebular cosmogony: "This cosmogony *demonstrates* that all existing bodies in the universe are formed of a nebular matter, a rare ethereal medium, pervading space—shows the mode and laws of formation—and *proves* that all things are in a perpetual state of progress—that nothing in nature is *perfected*" (*Essays and Reviews*, ed. G. R. Thompson [New York: Library of America, 1984], 323–324).

"It was the fruiterer," replied my friend, "who brought you to the conclusion that the mender of soles was not of sufficient height for Xerxes *et id genus omne*."[27]

"The fruiterer!—you astonish me—I know no fruiterer whomsoever."

"The man who ran up against you as we entered the street—it may have been fifteen minutes ago."

I now remembered that, in fact, a fruiterer, carrying upon his head a large basket of apples, had nearly thrown me down, by accident, as we passed from the Rue C——into the thoroughfare where we stood; but what this had to do with Chantilly I could not possibly understand.[28]

There was not a particle of *charlatanerie*[29] about Dupin. "I will explain," he said, "and that you may comprehend all clearly, we will first retrace the course of your meditations, from the moment in which I spoke to you until that of the *rencontre* with the fruiterer in question. The larger links of the chain run thus—Chantilly, Orion, Dr. Nichol, Epicurus, Stereotomy, the street stones, the fruiterer."

There are few persons who have not, at some period of their lives, amused themselves in retracing the steps by which particular conclusions of their own minds have been attained. The occupation is often full of interest; and he who attempts it for the first time is astonished by the apparently illimitable distance and incoherence between the starting-point and the goal. What, then, must have been my amazement when I heard the Frenchman speak what he had just spoken, and when I could not help acknowledging that he had spoken the truth. He continued:

"We had been talking of horses, if I remember aright, just before leaving the Rue C——. This was the last subject we discussed. As we crossed into this street, a fruiterer, with a large basket upon his head, brushing quickly past us, thrust you upon a pile of paving-stones collected at a spot where the causeway is undergoing repair. You stepped upon one of the loose fragments, slipped, slightly strained your ankle, appeared vexed or sulky, muttered a few words, turned to look at the pile, and then proceeded in silence. I was not particularly attentive to what you did; but observation has become with me, of late, a species of necessity.

"You kept your eyes upon the ground—glancing, with a petulant expression, at the holes and ruts in the pavement, (so that I saw you were still thinking of the stones,) until we reached the little alley called Lamartine,[30] which has been paved, by way of experiment, with the overlapping and riveted blocks. Here your countenance brightened up, and, perceiving your lips move, I could not doubt that you murmured the word 'stereotomy,' a term very affectedly applied to this species of pavement.[31] I knew that you could not say to yourself 'stereotomy' without being brought to think of atomies, and thus of the theories of Epicurus;[32] and since, when we discussed this subject not very long ago, I mentioned to you how singularly, yet with how little notice, the vague guesses of that noble Greek had met with confirmation in the late nebular cosmogony,[33] I felt that you could not avoid casting your eyes upward to the great *nebula* in Orion,[34] and I certainly expected that you would do so. You did look up; and I was now assured that I had correctly followed your steps. But in that bitter *tirade* upon Chantilly, which appeared in yesterday's *Musée*,[35] the satirist, making some disgraceful allusions to the cobbler's change of name upon assuming the buskin,[36] quoted a Latin line about which we have often conversed. I mean the line

Perdidit antiquum litera prima sonum[37]

I had told you that this was in reference to Orion, formerly written Urion; and, from certain pungencies connected with this explanation, I was aware that you could not have forgotten it. It was clear, therefore, that you would not fail to combine the two ideas of Orion and Chantilly. That you did combine them I saw by the character of the smile which passed over your lips. You thought of the poor cobbler's immolation. So far, you had been stooping in your gait; but now I saw you draw yourself up to your full height. I was then sure that you reflected upon the diminutive figure of Chantilly. At this point I interrupted your meditations to remark that as, in fact, he was a very little fellow—that Chantilly—he would do better at the *Théâtre des Variétés*."

Not long after this, we were looking over an evening edition of the *Gazette des Tribunaux*,[38] when the following paragraphs arrested our attention.

"EXTRAORDINARY MURDERS.—This morning, about three o'clock, the inhabitants of the Quartier St. Roch[39] were aroused from sleep by a succession of terrific shrieks, issuing, apparently, from the

34 Visible to the naked eye, the constellation Orion is named after the giant hunter of Greek mythology. Walter Benjamin was not the first but certainly one of the most prominent critics to observe the similarities in the way Natty Bumppo, James Fenimore Cooper's fabled woodsman and hunter, interprets the physical terrain of the American wilderness—a footprint, a broken twig—and the way the detective reads clues in the urban landscape: "Owing to the influence of Cooper, it becomes possible for the novelist in an urban setting to give scope to the experiences of the hunter. This has a bearing on the rise of the detective story" (*The Arcades Project* [Cambridge, MA: Harvard University Press, 1999], 439). Poe, however, may have been the first, at least implicitly, to draw the parallel between hunting and detective work.

35 *Musée des familles* was a popular monthly magazine in Paris, which Poe represents as a daily newspaper.

36 The buskin is a high, thick-soled boot worn by actors in ancient Greek tragedy. It had long since become a metonym for tragic drama. To put on the buskins means to assume a tragic style.

37 The quotation, which comes from Ovid's *Fastorum*, book V, line 536, can be translated: "The first letter has lost its original sound." According to Ovid, Orion sprang from the urine of Jupiter, Neptune, and Mercury. He was at first called Urion from "urina." The corruption of a letter changed his name. Contemporary medical literature often described the smell of urine as pungent; Dupin's reference to "certain pungencies" in the following sentence verifies that he and the narrator had indeed been talking about urine. The whole episode suggests another side of their relationship, making Dupin and the narrator resemble schoolboys chuckling over a tidbit of scatological humor they read in Latin class.

38 A daily Paris newspaper established in 1825 that reported current trials and the latest legal news.

39 Poe took his reference to this Parisian neighborhood from one of his key sources for "The Murders in the Rue Morgue": "The Scrap-Stall," a short story by Catherine Grace Frances Gore, which forms part of *Mary Raymond, and Other Tales* (1838). Mrs. Gore, as she was known to contemporaries, depicts the Quartier St. Roch as a poor, filthy part of the city (Kevin J. Hayes, "Mrs. Gore and 'The Murders in the Rue Morgue,'" *Notes and Queries* 58 [2011], 85–87).

40 A Napoleon is a twenty-franc gold coin.

41 Métal d'Alger is an inexpensive substitute for silver made from lead, tin, and antimony. Poe found this detail in Mrs. Gore's "Scrap-Stall," which depicts the eating utensils of a poor old man: "a wooden platter, with a knife and fork of *métal d'Alger*."

fourth story of a house in the Rue Morgue, known to be in the sole occupancy of one Madame L'Espanaye, and her daughter, Mademoiselle Camille L'Espanaye. After some delay, occasioned by a fruitless attempt to procure admission in the usual manner, the gateway was broken in with a crowbar, and eight or ten of the neighbors entered, accompanied by two *gendarmes.* By this time the cries had ceased; but, as the party rushed up the first flight of stairs, two or more rough voices, in angry contention, were distinguished, and seemed to proceed from the upper part of the house. As the second landing was reached, these sounds, also, had ceased, and everything remained perfectly quiet. The party spread themselves, and hurried from room to room. Upon arriving at a large back chamber in the fourth story, (the door of which, being found locked, with the key inside, was forced open,) a spectacle presented itself which struck every one present not less with horror than with astonishment.

"The apartment was in the wildest disorder—the furniture broken and thrown about in all directions. There was only one bedstead; and from this the bed had been removed, and thrown into the middle of the floor. On a chair lay a razor, besmeared with blood. On the hearth were two or three long and thick tresses of grey human hair, also dabbled in blood, and seeming to have been pulled out by the roots. On the floor were found four Napoleons,[40] an ear-ring of topaz, three large silver spoons, three smaller of *métal d'Alger,*[41] and two bags, containing nearly four thousand francs in gold. The drawers of a *bureau,* which stood in one corner, were open, and had been, apparently, rifled, although many articles still remained in them. A small iron safe was discovered under the *bed* (not under the bedstead). It was open, with the key still in the door. It had no contents beyond a few old letters, and other papers of little consequence.

"Of Madame L'Espanaye no traces were here seen; but an unusual quantity of soot being observed in the fire-place, a search was made in the chimney, and (horrible to relate!) the corpse of the daughter, head downward, was dragged therefrom; it having been thus forced up the narrow aperture for a considerable distance. The body was quite warm. Upon examining it, many excoriations were perceived, no doubt occasioned by the violence with which it had been thrust up and disengaged. Upon the face were many severe scratches, and, upon the throat, dark bruises, and deep indentations of finger nails, as if the deceased had been throttled to death.

"After a thorough investigation of every portion of the house, without farther discovery, the party made its way into a small paved yard in the rear of the building, where lay the corpse of the old lady, with her throat so entirely cut that, upon an attempt to raise her, the head fell off. The body, as well as the head, was fearfully mutilated—the former so much so as scarcely to retain any semblance of humanity.[42]

"To this horrible mystery there is not as yet, we believe, the slightest clew."

The next day's paper had these additional particulars.

"*The Tragedy in the Rue Morgue.* Many individuals have been examined in relation to this most extraordinary and frightful affair." (The word "*affaire*" has not yet, in France, that levity of import which it conveys with us,)[43] "but nothing whatever has transpired to throw light upon it. We give below all the material testimony elicited.

"*Pauline Dubourg,*[44] laundress, deposes that she has known both the deceased for three years, having washed for them during that period. The old lady and her daughter seemed on good terms—very affectionate towards each other. They were excellent pay. Could not speak in regard to their mode or means of living. Believed that Madame L. told fortunes for a living. Was reputed to have money put by. Never met any persons in the house when she called for the clothes or took them home. Was sure that they had no servant in employ. There appeared to be no furniture in any part of the building except in the fourth story.

"*Pierre Moreau,* tobacconist, deposes that he has been in the habit of selling small quantities of tobacco and snuff to Madame L'Espanaye for nearly four years. Was born in the neighborhood, and has always resided there. The deceased and her daughter had occupied the house in which the corpses were found, for more than six years. It was formerly occupied by a jeweller, who underlet the upper rooms to various persons. The house was the property of Madame L. She became dissatisfied with the abuse of the premises by her tenant, and moved into them herself, refusing to let any portion. The old lady was childish. Witness had seen the daughter some five or six times during the six years. The two lived an exceedingly retired life—were reputed to have money. Had

42 With the advent of steam-powered printing, many inexpensive, tabloid-style newspapers (penny press papers) sprang into existence in the 1830s in the United States, all vying to outdo each other in reporting the lurid details of criminal trials, suicides, and murders. Silverman notes: "Writing a story much concerned with newspapers, Poe picked up many hints from such articles" (*Edgar A. Poe: Mournful and Never-Ending Remembrance* [New York: HarperCollins, 1991], 171–172). Situating the description of the murders within a newspaper account, as Poe does, he lends the appearance of truth and impartiality to this depiction of "the facts." Of course, the penny papers were themselves hardly impartial. Poe's tale seems to suggest that horrific violence, or reading about it anyway, had become commonplace in the modern city.

43 Since the newspaper article is Poe's invention, it may seem odd that he would include in it a word that then requires bracketed explanation. But of course the parenthetical comment functions to increase the verisimilitude of the newspaper account. Used with levity, the word "affair" means something that is inferior or slipshod in quality: "a poor affair."

44 When he lived in London as a boy, Poe attended a grammar school run by the Misses Dubourg. Whether the names of all the other witnesses allude to people he knew personally is a good question. If so, the real-life equivalents of many of them have continued to escape detection.

Bishop William Henry Odenheimer, ca. 1855–1865.

heard it said among the neighbors that Madame L. told fortunes—did not believe it. Had never seen any person enter the door except the old lady and her daughter, a porter once or twice, and a physician some eight or ten times.

"Many other persons, neighbors, gave evidence to the same effect. No one was spoken of as frequenting the house. It was not known whether there were any living connexions of Madame L. and her daughter. The shutters of the front windows were seldom opened. Those in the rear were always closed, with the exception of the large back room, fourth story. The house was a good house—not very old.

"*Isidore Musèt, gendarme,* deposes that he was called to the house about three o'clock in the morning, and found some twenty or thirty persons at the gateway, endeavoring to gain admittance. Forced it open, at length, with a bayonet—not with a crowbar. Had but little difficulty in getting it open, on account of its being a double or folding gate, and bolted neither at bottom nor top. The shrieks were continued until the gate was forced—and then suddenly ceased. They seemed to be screams of some person (or persons) in great agony—were loud and drawn out, not short and quick. Witness led the way up stairs. Upon reaching the first landing, heard two voices in loud and angry contention—the one a gruff voice, the other much shriller—a very strange voice. Could distinguish some words of the former, which was that of a Frenchman. Was positive that it was not a woman's voice. Could distinguish the words '*sacré*' and '*diable*.' The shrill voice was that of a foreigner. Could not be sure whether it was the voice of a man or of a woman. Could not make out what was said, but believed the language to be Spanish. The state of the room and of the bodies was described by this witness as we described them yesterday.

"*Henri Duval,* a neighbor, and by trade a silver-smith, deposes that he was one of the party who first entered the house. Corroborates the testimony of Musèt in general. As soon as they forced an entrance, they reclosed the door, to keep out the crowd, which collected very fast, notwithstanding the lateness of the hour. The shrill voice, this witness thinks, was that of an Italian. Was certain it was not French. Could not be sure that it was a man's voice. It might have been a woman's. Was not acquainted with the Italian language. Could not distinguish the words, but was convinced by the intonation that the speaker was an Italian. Knew Madame L.

and her daughter. Had conversed with both frequently. Was sure that the shrill voice was not that of either of the deceased.

"———*Odenheimer,*[45] *restaurateur.* This witness volunteered his testimony. Not speaking French, was examined through an interpreter. Is a native of Amsterdam. Was passing the house at the time of the shrieks. They lasted for several minutes—probably ten. They were long and loud—very awful and distressing. Was one of those who entered the building. Corroborated the previous evidence in every respect but one. Was sure that the shrill voice was that of a man—of a Frenchman. Could not distinguish the words uttered. They were loud and quick—unequal—spoken apparently in fear as well as in anger. The voice was harsh—not so much shrill as harsh. Could not call it a shrill voice. The gruff voice said repeatedly '*sacré,*' '*diable,*' and once '*mon Dieu.*'

"*Jules Mignaud,* banker, of the firm of Mignaud et Fils, Rue Deloraine. Is the elder Mignaud. Madame L'Espanaye had some property. Had opened an account with his banking house in the spring of the year———(eight years previously). Made frequent deposits in small sums. Had checked for nothing until the third day before her death, when she took out in person the sum of 4000 francs. This sum was paid in gold, and a clerk went home with the money.

"*Adolphe Le Bon,* clerk to Mignaud et Fils, deposes that on the day in question, about noon, he accompanied Madame L'Espanaye to her residence with the 4000 francs, put up in two bags. Upon the door being opened, Mademoiselle L. appeared and took from his hands one of the bags, while the old lady relieved him of the other. He then bowed and departed. Did not see any person in the street at the time. It is a bye-street—very lonely.

"*William Bird,* tailor, deposes that he was one of the party who entered the house. Is an Englishman. Has lived in Paris two years. Was one of the first to ascend the stairs. Heard the voices in contention. The gruff voice was that of a Frenchman. Could make out several words, but cannot now remember all. Heard distinctly '*sacré*' and '*mon Dieu.*' There was a sound at the moment as if of several persons struggling—a scraping and scuffling sound. The shrill voice was very loud—louder than the gruff one. Is sure that it was not the voice of an Englishman. Appeared to be that of a German. Might have been a woman's voice. Does not understand German.

45 The Reverend William Henry Odenheimer (1817–1879) was appointed assistant rector of St. Peter's Church in 1840. Choosing to name his Paris restaurateur after a Philadelphia minister, Poe implies that organized religion is something to be dished out and served up. Writing in *Alexander's Weekly Messenger* about the current popularity of religious revivals in the year prior to the publication of "The Murders in the Rue Morgue," Poe says: "The chief subject of wonder, however, is that the principal recruits have been enlisted from the ranks of a party which is the last in the world a body would suspect of giving up its evil ways—we mean the jolly corporation of victuallers. These people we always thought worldly-minded individuals, hankerers after creature comforts, men of the *flesh,* rather than of the spirit."

46 Dorothy Sayers observes that Poe invented "the hermetically sealed death-chamber," which would become a favorite device of later detective writers. However, the sealed-room mystery does find a slightly earlier precedent in Joseph Sheridan Le Fanu's tale "Passages in the Secret History of an Irish Countess," which appeared in the *Dublin University Magazine* three years earlier (Patrick Diskin, "Poe, Le Fanu, and the Sealed Room Mystery," *Notes and Queries* 13 [1966], 337–339).

47 The mansarde, or mansard as it is usually spelled in English, is an apartment beneath a mansard roof, with a low ceiling and steeply sloping walls. It was typically a dwelling of the poor. Seven years before the release of his pioneering film *The Birth of a Nation*, D. W. Griffith portrayed an impoverished Poe and his wife, Virginia, living in a mansard apartment in the short drama *Edgar Allen Poe* (1909).

"Four of the above-named witnesses, being recalled, deposed that the door of the chamber in which was found the body of Mademoiselle L. was locked on the inside when the party reached it. Every thing was perfectly silent—no groans or noises of any kind. Upon forcing the door no person was seen. The windows, both of the back and front room, were down and firmly fastened from within.[46] A door between the two rooms was closed, but not locked. The door leading from the front room into the passage was locked, with the key on the inside. A small room in the front of the house, on the fourth story, at the head of the passage, was open, the door being ajar. This room was crowded with old beds, boxes, and so forth. These were carefully removed and searched. There was not an inch of any portion of the house which was not carefully searched. Sweeps were sent up and down the chimneys. The house was a four story one, with garrets *(mansardes.)*[47] A trap-door on the roof was nailed down very securely—did not appear to have been opened for years. The time elapsing between the hearing of the voices in contention and the breaking open of the room door, was variously stated by the witnesses. Some made it as short as three minutes—some as long as five. The door was opened with difficulty.

"*Alfonzo Garcio,* undertaker, deposes that he resides in the Rue Morgue. Is a native of Spain. Was one of the party who entered the house. Did not proceed up stairs. Is nervous, and was apprehensive of the consequences of agitation. Heard the voices in contention. The gruff voice was that of a Frenchman. Could not distinguish what was said. The shrill voice was that of an Englishman—is sure of this. Does not understand the English language, but judges by the intonation.

"*Alberto Montani*, confectioner, deposes that he was among the first to ascend the stairs. Heard the voices in question. The gruff voice was that of a Frenchman. Distinguished several words. The speaker appeared to be expostulating. Could not make out the words of the shrill voice. Spoke quick and unevenly. Thinks it the voice of a Russian. Corroborates the general testimony. Is an Italian. Never conversed with a native of Russia.

"Several witnesses, recalled, here testified that the chimneys of all the rooms on the fourth story were too narrow to admit the passage of a human being. By 'sweeps' were meant cylindrical sweeping-brushes, such as are employed by those who clean chim-

Screen shot from D. W. Griffith's short film *Edgar Allen Poe* (1909), starring Barry O'Moore (as Herbert Yost) and Virginia Arvidson. The misspelling of Poe's name may be due to Griffith's rush to get the film out in time for the centenary celebrations of Poe's birth.

neys. These brushes were passed up and down every flue in the house. There is no back passage by which any one could have descended while the party proceeded up stairs. The body of Mademoiselle L'Espanaye was so firmly wedged in the chimney that it could not be got down until four or five of the party united their strength.

"*Paul Dumas*, physician, deposes that he was called to view the bodies about day-break. They were both then lying on the sacking of the bedstead in the chamber where Mademoiselle L. was found. The corpse of the young lady was much bruised and excoriated. The fact that it had been thrust up the chimney would sufficiently account for these appearances. The throat was greatly chafed. There were several deep scratches just below the chin, together with a series of livid spots which were evidently the impression of fingers. The face was fearfully discolored, and the eyeballs protruded. The tongue had been partially bitten through. A large bruise was discovered upon the pit of the stomach, produced, apparently, by the pressure of a knee. In the opinion of M. Dumas, Mademoiselle L'Espanaye had been throttled to death by some person or persons unknown. The corpse of the mother was horribly mutilated. All the bones of the right leg and arm were more or less shattered. The left *tibia* much splintered, as well as all the ribs

48   "Adolphe Le Bon" means "Adolphe the good." Nothing incriminates this good man beyond purely circumstantial evidence, but that fact doesn't prevent him from being arrested and imprisoned on grounds of suspicion. Dorothy Sayers notes that the motif of the wrongly suspected man, like so many other aspects of this tale, would become standard in subsequent detective fiction.

49   Poe refers to Molière's *Le Bourgeois gentilhomme*, a comedy first performed in 1670. In Act I, scene 2, Monsieur Jourdain asks for his "robe de chambre," which, he imagines, will help him appreciate chamber music. Nicolas Gouin Dufief excerpted this hilarious scene in his French textbook *Nature Displayed in Her Mode of Teaching Language to Man*, which Poe borrowed from the University of Virginia library in 1826 when he was a student (Kevin J. Hayes, *Poe and the Printed Word* [New York: Cambridge University Press, 2000], 12–14).

of the left side. Whole body dreadfully bruised and discolored. It was not possible to say how the injuries had been inflicted. A heavy club of wood, or a broad bar of iron—a chair—any large, heavy, and obtuse weapon would have produced such results, if wielded by the hands of a very powerful man. No woman could have inflicted the blows with any weapon. The head of the deceased, when seen by witness, was entirely separated from the body, and was also greatly shattered. The throat had evidently been cut with some very sharp instrument—probably with a razor.

"*Alexandre Etienne*, surgeon, was called with M. Dumas to view the bodies. Corroborated the testimony, and the opinions of M. Dumas.

"Nothing farther of importance was elicited, although several other persons were examined. A murder so mysterious, and so perplexing in all its particulars, was never before committed in Paris—if indeed a murder has been committed at all. The police are entirely at fault—an unusual occurrence in affairs of this nature. There is not, however, the shadow of a clew apparent."

The evening edition of the paper stated that the greatest excitement still continued in the Quartier St. Roch—that the premises in question had been carefully re-searched, and fresh examinations of witnesses instituted, but all to no purpose. A postscript, however, mentioned that Adolphe Le Bon had been arrested and imprisoned—although nothing appeared to criminate him, beyond the facts already detailed.[48]

Dupin seemed singularly interested in the progress of this affair—at least so I judged from his manner, for he made no comments. It was only after the announcement that Le Bon had been imprisoned, that he asked me my opinion respecting the murders.

I could merely agree with all Paris in considering them an insoluble mystery. I saw no means by which it would be possible to trace the murderer.

"We must not judge of the means," said Dupin, "by this shell of an examination. The Parisian police, so much extolled for *acumen*, are cunning, but no more. There is no method in their proceedings, beyond the method of the moment. They make a vast parade of measures; but, not unfrequently, these are so ill adapted to the objects proposed, as to put us in mind of Monsieur Jourdain's calling for his *robe-de-chambre—pour mieux entendre la musique.*[49]

The results attained by them are not unfrequently surprising, but, for the most part, are brought about by simple diligence and activity. When these qualities are unavailing, their schemes fail. Vidocq, for example, was a good guesser, and a persevering man.[50] But, without educated thought, he erred continually by the very intensity of his investigations. He impaired his vision by holding the object too close. He might see, perhaps, one or two points with unusual clearness, but in so doing he, necessarily, lost sight of the matter as a whole. Thus there is such a thing as being too profound. Truth is not always in a well. In fact, as regards the more important knowledge, I do believe that she is invariably superficial. The depth lies in the valleys where we seek her, and not upon the mountain-tops where she is found. The modes and sources of this kind of error are well typified in the contemplation of the heavenly bodies. To look at a star by glances—to view it in a sidelong way, by turning toward it the exterior portions of the *retina* (more susceptible of feeble impressions of light than the interior), is to behold the star distinctly—is to have the best appreciation of its lustre—a lustre which grows dim just in proportion as we turn our vision *fully* upon it. A greater number of rays actually fall upon the eye in the latter case, but, in the former, there is the more refined capacity for comprehension. By undue profundity we perplex and enfeeble thought; and it is possible to make even Venus herself vanish from the firmanent by a scrutiny too sustained, too concentrated, or too direct.[51]

"As for these murders, let us enter into some examinations for ourselves, before we make up an opinion respecting them. An inquiry will afford us amusement," (I thought this an odd term, so applied, but said nothing) "and, besides, Le Bon once rendered me a service for which I am not ungrateful. We will go and see the premises with our own eyes. I know G——, the Prefect of Police,[52] and shall have no difficulty in obtaining the necessary permission."

The permission was obtained, and we proceeded at once to the Rue Morgue. This is one of those miserable thoroughfares which intervene between the Rue Richelieu and the Rue St. Roch. It was late in the afternoon when we reached it; as this quarter is at a great distance from that in which we resided. The house was readily found; for there were still many persons gazing up at the closed

50 François-Eugène Vidocq (1775–1857) was chief of the newly formed investigative branch of the French police department under Napoleon. Many of the agents Vidocq hired were, like himself, ex-criminals. Victor Hugo, Alexandre Dumas, and Honoré de Balzac all found literary inspiration in elements of Vidocq's colorful life story. Between 1838 and May 1839, just before Poe became co-editor at *Burton's Gentlemen's Magazine*, the magazine issued a series of stories titled "Unpublished Passages in the Life of Vidocq, the French Minister of Police," by "J. M. B." It's almost certain that Poe read these stories. "Vidocq" in the "Unpublished Passages" bears little resemblance either to his fascinating real-life antecedent or to Poe's Dupin. See Ian V. K. Ousby, "'The Murders in the Rue Morgue' and 'Doctor D'Arsac': A Poe Source," *Poe Studies* 5 [1972], 52).

51 See David Brewster's *Letters on Natural Magic* (1834): "It is a curious circumstance, that when we wish to obtain a sight of a very faint star, such as one of the satellites of Saturn, we can see it most distinctly by *looking away from it*, and when the eye is turned full upon it, it immediately disappears."

52 Poe's prefect has a real-life equivalent: Henri-Joseph Gisquet, who was prefect of the Paris police from 1831 to 1836.

53 Much of Poe's description in this paragraph also comes from Mrs. Gore's "Scrap-Stall."

54 "I humored him cautiously."

55 *Outré:* Eccentric, extreme, peculiar, unorthodox.

shutters, with an objectless curiosity, from the opposite side of the way. It was an ordinary Parisian house, with a gateway, on one side of which was a glazed watch-box, with a sliding panel in the window, indicating a *loge de concierge.*[53] Before going in we walked up the street, turned down an alley, and then, again turning, passed in the rear of the building—Dupin, meanwhile, examining the whole neighborhood, as well as the house, with a minuteness of attention for which I could see no possible object.

Retracing our steps, we came again to the front of the dwelling, rang, and, having shown our credentials, were admitted by the agents in charge. We went up stairs—into the chamber where the body of Mademoiselle L'Espanaye had been found, and where both the deceased still lay. The disorders of the room had, as usual, been suffered to exist. I saw nothing beyond what had been stated in the *Gazette des Tribunaux.* Dupin scrutinized every thing—not excepting the bodies of the victims. We then went into the other rooms, and into the yard; a *gendarme* accompanying us throughout. The examination occupied us until dark, when we took our departure. On our way home my companion stepped in for a moment at the office of one of the daily papers.

I have said that the whims of my friend were manifold, and that *Je les ménagais:*[54]—for this phrase there is no English equivalent. It was his humor, now, to decline all conversation on the subject of the murder, until about noon the next day. He then asked me, suddenly, if I had observed any thing *peculiar* at the scene of the atrocity.

There was something in his manner of emphasizing the word "peculiar," which caused me to shudder, without knowing why.

"No, nothing *peculiar,*" I said; "nothing more, at least, than we both saw stated in the paper."

"The *Gazette,*" he replied, "has not entered, I fear, into the unusual horror of the thing. But dismiss the idle opinions of this print. It appears to me that this mystery is considered insoluble, for the very reason which should cause it to be regarded as easy of solution—I mean for the *outré* character of its features.[55] The police are confounded by the seeming absence of motive—not for the murder itself—but for the atrocity of the murder. They are puzzled, too, by the seeming impossibility of reconciling the voices heard in contention, with the facts that no one was discovered up stairs but the assassinated Mademoiselle L'Espanaye, and that there were no means of egress without the notice of the party ascending. The wild disorder of the room; the corpse thrust, with the head downward, up the chimney; the frightful mutilation of the body of the old lady; these considerations, with those just mentioned, and others which I need not mention, have sufficed to paralyze the powers, by putting completely at fault the boasted *acumen*, of the government agents. They have fallen into the gross but common error of confounding the unusual with the abstruse. But it is by these deviations from the plane of the ordinary, that reason feels its way, if at all, in its search for the true. In investigations such as we are now pursuing, it should not be so much asked 'what has occurred,' as 'what has occurred that has never occurred before.'[56] In fact, the facility with which I shall arrive, or have arrived, at the solution of this mystery, is in the direct ratio of its apparent insolubility in the eyes of the police."[57]

I stared at the speaker in mute astonishment.

"I am now awaiting," continued he, looking toward the door of our apartment—"I am now awaiting a person who, although perhaps not the perpetrator of these butcheries, must have been in some measure implicated in their perpetration. Of the worst portion of the crimes committed, it is probable that he is innocent. I hope that I am right in this supposition; for upon it I build my expectation of reading the entire riddle. I look for the man here—in this room—every moment. It is true that he may not arrive; but the probability is that he will. Should he come, it will be necessary to detain him. Here are pistols; and we both know how to use them when occasion demands their use."[58]

I took the pistols, scarcely knowing what I did, or believing what I heard, while Dupin went on, very much as if in a soliloquy. I have already spoken of his abstract manner at such times. His discourse was addressed to myself; but his voice, although by no means loud, had that intonation which is commonly employed in speaking to some one at a great distance. His eyes, vacant in expression, regarded only the wall.

"That the voices heard in contention," he said, "by the party upon the stairs, were not the voices of the women themselves, was fully proved by the evidence. This relieves us of all doubt upon the question whether the old lady could have first destroyed

56   Dorothy Sayers offers this gloss: here we see "for the first time those two great aphorisms of detective science: first, that when you have eliminated all the impossibilities, then, whatever remains, *however improbable*, must be the truth; and, secondly, that the more *outré* a case may appear, the easier it is to solve. Indeed, take it all round," she continues, "'The Murders in the Rue Morgue' constitutes in itself almost a complete manual of detective theory and practice."

57   In his Preface to *The Adventures of Sherlock Holmes*, Arthur Conan Doyle writes that Poe "was the father of the detective tale, and covered its limits so completely that I fail to see how his followers can find any fresh ground which they can confidently call their own. For the secret of the thinness and also of the intensity of the detective story is, that the writer is left with only one quality, that of intellectual acuteness, with which to endow his hero. Everything else is outside the picture and weakens the effect. The problem and its solution must form the theme, and the character-drawing be limited and subordinate. On this narrow path the writer must walk, and he sees the footmarks of Poe always in front of him. He is happy if he ever finds the means of breaking away and striking out on some little side-track of his own" (*The Adventures of Sherlock Holmes* [New York: D. Appleton and Company, 1902], vi).

58   The introduction of the pistols creates a sense of tension as Dupin and the narrator await the arrival of the mysterious stranger, and thus helps to sustain the reader's interest through the long, detailed analytical section that follows. Either Dupin has a third pistol on his person or Poe forgets that Dupin has handed the pistols over to the narrator, because Dupin will later theatrically "draw a pistol from his bosom."

the daughter, and afterward have committed suicide. I speak of this point chiefly for the sake of method; for the strength of Madame L'Espanaye would have been utterly unequal to the task of thrusting her daughter's corpse up the chimney as it was found; and the nature of the wounds upon her own person entirely preclude the idea of self-destruction. Murder, then, has been committed by some third party; and the voices of this third party were those heard in contention. Let me now advert—not to the whole testimony respecting these voices—but to what was *peculiar* in that testimony. Did you observe any thing peculiar about it?"

I remarked that, while all the witnesses agreed in supposing the gruff voice to be that of a Frenchman, there was much disagreement in regard to the shrill, or, as one individual termed it, the harsh voice.

"That was the evidence itself," said Dupin, "but it was not the peculiarity of the evidence. You have observed nothing distinctive. Yet there *was* something to be observed. The witnesses, as you remark, agreed about the gruff voice; they were here unanimous. But in regard to the shrill voice, the peculiarity is—not that they disagreed—but that, while an Italian, an Englishman, a Spaniard, a Hollander, and a Frenchman attempted to describe it, each one spoke of it as that *of a foreigner.* Each is sure that it was not the voice of one of his own countrymen. Each likens it—not to the voice of an individual of any nation with whose language he is conversant—but the converse. The Frenchman supposes it the voice of a Spaniard, and 'might have distinguished some words *had he been acquainted with the Spanish.'* The Dutchman maintains it to have been that of a Frenchman; but we find it stated that '*not understanding French this witness was examined through an interpreter.'* The Englishman thinks it the voice of a German, and '*does not understand German.'* The Spaniard 'is sure' that it was that of an Englishman, but 'judges by the intonation' altogether, '*as he has no knowledge of the English.'* The Italian believes it the voice of a Russian, but '*has never conversed with a native of Russia.'* A second Frenchman differs, moreover, with the first, and is positive that the voice was that of an Italian; but, *not being cognizant of that tongue,* is, like the Spaniard, 'convinced by the intonation.' Now, how strangely unusual must that voice have really been, about which such testimony as this *could* have been elicited!—in whose *tones*, even, denizens of the five great divisions of Europe could recognise nothing familiar! You will say that it might have been the voice of an Asiatic—of an African. Neither Asiatics nor Africans abound in Paris; but, without denying the inference, I will now merely call your attention to three points. The voice is termed by one witness 'harsh rather than shrill.' It is represented by two others to have been 'quick and *unequal*.' No words—no sounds resembling words—were by any witness mentioned as distinguishable.

"I know not," continued Dupin, "what impression I may have made, so far, upon your own understanding; but I do not hesitate to say that legitimate deductions even from this portion of the testimony—the portion respecting the gruff and shrill voices—are in themselves sufficient to engender a suspicion which should give direction to all farther progress in the investigation of the mystery. I said 'legitimate deductions'; but my meaning is not thus fully expressed. I designed to imply that the deductions are the *sole* proper ones, and that the suspicion arises *inevitably* from them as the single result. What the suspicion is, however, I will not say just yet. I merely wish you to bear in mind that, with myself, it was sufficiently forcible to give a definite form—a certain tendency—to my inquiries in the chamber.

"Let us now transport ourselves, in fancy, to this chamber. What shall we first seek here? The means of egress employed by the murderers. It is not too much to say that neither of us believe in praeternatural events. Madame and Mademoiselle L'Espanaye were not destroyed by spirits.[59] The doers of the deed were material, and escaped materially. Then how? Fortunately, there is but one mode of reasoning upon the point, and that mode *must* lead us to a definite decision.—Let us examine, each by each, the possible means of egress. It is clear that the assassins were in the room where Mademoiselle L'Espanaye was found, or at least in the room adjoining, when the party ascended the stairs. It is then only from these two apartments that we have to seek issues. The police have laid bare the floors, the ceilings, and the masonry of the walls, in every direction. No *secret* issues could have escaped their vigilance. But, not trusting to *their* eyes, I examined with my own. There were, then, *no* secret issues. Both doors leading from the rooms into the passage were securely locked, with the keys in-

59   This sentence marks a crucial shift in Poe's work as a whole. Whereas his earlier writings often contain supernatural elements, Dupin denies the possibility of spirits. The general trajectory of Poe's fiction shifts from the supernatural to the natural.

side. Let us turn to the chimneys. These, although of ordinary width for some eight or ten feet above the hearths, will not admit, throughout their extent, the body of a large cat. The impossibility of egress, by means already stated, being thus absolute, we are reduced to the windows. Through those of the front room no one could have escaped without notice from the crowd in the street. The murderers *must* have passed, then, through those of the back room. Now, brought to this conclusion in so unequivocal a manner as we are, it is not our part, as reasoners, to reject it on account of apparent impossibilities. It is only left for us to prove that these apparent 'impossibilities' are, in reality, not such.

"There are two windows in the chamber. One of them is unobstructed by furniture, and is wholly visible. The lower portion of the other is hidden from view by the head of the unwieldy bedstead which is thrust close up against it. The former was found securely fastened from within. It resisted the utmost force of those who endeavored to raise it. A large gimlet-hole had been pierced in its frame to the left, and a very stout nail was found fitted therein, nearly to the head. Upon examining the other window, a similar nail was seen similarly fitted in it; and a vigorous attempt to raise this sash, failed also. The police were now entirely satisfied that egress had not been in these directions. And, *therefore,* it was thought a matter of supererogation to withdraw the nails and open the windows.

"My own examination was somewhat more particular, and was so for the reason I have just given—because here it was, I knew, that all apparent impossibilities *must* be proved to be not such in reality.

"I proceeded to think thus—*à posteriori.*[60] The murderers *did* escape from one of these windows. This being so, they could not have re-fastened the sashes from the inside, as they were found fastened;—the consideration which put a stop, through its obviousness, to the scrutiny of the police in this quarter. Yet the sashes *were* fastened. They *must,* then, have the power of fastening themselves. There was no escape from this conclusion. I stepped to the unobstructed casement, withdrew the nail with some difficulty, and attempted to raise the sash. It resisted all my efforts, as I had anticipated. A concealed spring must, I now knew, exist; and this corroboration of my idea convinced me that my premises, at least, were correct, however mysterious still appeared the circumstances attending the nails. A careful search soon brought to light the hidden spring. I pressed it, and, satisfied with the discovery, forbore to upraise the sash.

"I now replaced the nail and regarded it attentively. A person passing out through this window might have reclosed it, and the spring would have caught—but the nail could not have been replaced. The conclusion was plain, and again narrowed in the field of my investigations. The assassins *must* have escaped through the other window. Supposing, then, the springs upon each sash to be the same, as was probable, there *must* be found a difference between the nails, or at least between the modes of their fixture. Getting upon the sacking of the bedstead, I looked over the head-board minutely at the second casement. Passing my hand down behind the board, I readily discovered and pressed the spring, which was, as I had supposed, identical in character with its neighbor. I now looked at the nail. It was as stout as the other, and apparently fitted in the same manner—driven in nearly up to the head.

"You will say that I was puzzled; but, if you think so, you must have misunderstood the nature of the inductions. To use a sporting phrase, I had not been once 'at fault.'[61] The scent had never for an instant been lost. There was no flaw in any link of the chain. I had traced the secret to its ultimate result,—and that result was *the nail*. It had, I say, in every respect, the appearance of its fellow in the other window; but this fact was an absolute nullity (conclusive as it might seem to be) when compared with the consideration that here, at this point, terminated the clew. 'There *must* be something wrong,' I said, 'about the nail.' I touched it; and the head, with about a quarter of an inch of the shank, came off in my fingers. The rest of the shank was in the gimlet-hole, where it had been broken off. The fracture was an old one (for its edges were incrusted with rust), and had apparently been accomplished by the blow of a hammer, which had partially imbedded, in the top of the bottom sash, the head portion of the nail. I now carefully replaced this head portion in the indentation whence I had taken it, and the resemblance to a perfect nail was complete—the fissure was invisible. Pressing the spring, I gently raised the sash for a few inches; the head went up with it, remaining firm in its bed. I closed the window, and the semblance of the whole nail was again perfect.

"The riddle, so far, was now unriddled. The assassin had es-

61 This term comes from the sport of fox hunting. A contemporary sporting article relates: "The fox led them from covert to covert, and from jungle to jungle; and, after a run of about thirty minutes, in which they had not been one moment at fault, one of the huntsmen gave the view halloo!—at the same time declaring it to be a jet black fox" ("The Black Fox Hunt Described," *American Turf Register* 4 [1833], 236).

62 Poe seems mistaken in his terminology. "Ferrades" are bull-branding festivals that occur in the south of France.

caped through the window which looked upon the bed. Dropping of its own accord upon his exit (or perhaps purposely closed), it had become fastened by the spring; and it was the retention of this spring which had been mistaken by the police for that of the nail,—farther inquiry being thus considered unnecessary.

"The next question is that of the mode of descent. Upon this point I had been satisfied in my walk with you around the building. About five feet and a half from the casement in question there runs a lightning-rod. From this rod it would have been impossible for any one to reach the window itself, to say nothing of entering it. I observed, however, that the shutters of the fourth story were of the peculiar kind called by Parisian carpenters *ferrades*[62]— a kind rarely employed at the present day, but frequently seen upon very old mansions at Lyons and Bourdeaux. They are in the form of an ordinary door, (a single, not a folding door) except that the upper half is latticed or worked in open trellis—thus affording an excellent hold for the hands. In the present instance these shutters are fully three feet and a half broad. When we saw them from the rear of the house, they were both about half open—that is to say, they stood off at right angles from the wall. It is probable that the police, as well as myself, examined the back of the tenement; but, if so, in looking at these *ferrades* in the line of their breadth (as they must have done), they did not perceive this great breadth itself, or, at all events, failed to take it into due consideration. In fact, having once satisfied themselves that no egress could have been made in this quarter, they would naturally bestow here a very cursory examination. It was clear to me, however, that the shutter belonging to the window at the head of the bed, would, if swung fully back to the wall, reach to within two feet of the lightning-rod. It was also evident that, by exertion of a very unusual degree of activity and courage, an entrance into the window, from the rod, might have been thus effected.—By reaching to the distance of two feet and a half (we now suppose the shutter open to its whole extent) a robber might have taken a firm grasp upon the trellis-work. Letting go, then, his hold upon the rod, placing his feet securely against the wall, and springing boldly from it, he might have swung the shutter so as to close it, and, if we imagine the window open at the time, might even have swung himself into the room.

"I wish you to bear especially in mind that I have spoken of a very unusual degree of activity as requisite to success in so hazardous and so difficult a feat. It is my design to show you, first, that the thing might possibly have been accomplished:—but, secondly and *chiefly*, I wish to impress upon your understanding the *very extraordinary*—the almost praeternatural character of that agility which could have accomplished it.

"You will say, no doubt, using the language of the law, that 'to make out my case,' I should rather undervalue, than insist upon a full estimation of the activity required in this matter. This may be the practice in law, but it is not the usage of reason. My ultimate object is only the truth. My immediate purpose is to lead you to place in juxta-position, that *very unusual* activity of which I have just spoken, with that *very peculiar* shrill (or harsh) and *unequal* voice, about whose nationality no two persons could be found to agree, and in whose utterance no syllabification could be detected."

At these words a vague and half-formed conception of the meaning of Dupin flitted over my mind. I seemed to be upon the verge of comprehension, without power to comprehend—as men, at times, find themselves upon the brink of remembrance, without being able, in the end, to remember. My friend went on with his discourse.

"You will see," he said, "that I have shifted the question from the mode of egress to that of ingress. It was my design to suggest the idea that both were effected in the same manner, at the same point. Let us now revert to the interior of the room. Let us survey the appearances here. The drawers of the bureau, it is said, had been rifled, although many articles of apparel still remained within them. The conclusion here is absurd. It is a mere guess—a very silly one—and no more. How are we to know that the articles found in the drawers were not all these drawers had originally contained? Madame L'Espanaye and her daughter lived an exceedingly retired life—saw no company—seldom went out—had little use for numerous changes of habiliment. Those found were at least of as good quality as any likely to be possessed by these ladies. If a thief had taken any, why did he not take the best—why did he not take all?[63] In a word, why did he abandon four thousand francs in gold to encumber himself with a bundle of linen? The

63 Even Dupin has his blind spots. He seems not to consider the possibility that the thief might be a sexual pervert who steals women's used underclothing for auto-erotic purposes. Lemay explains: "Dupin believes that breaking-and-entering, theft, gruesome mutilations and murders might well be committed for a few pieces of new linen worth a few francs—but not for psychotic sexual drives. Dupin is an incredible egghead, an intellectual, blind to the facts of life" ("The Psychology of 'The Murders in the Rue Morgue,'" 178).

gold *was* abandoned. Nearly the whole sum mentioned by Monsieur Mignaud, the banker, was discovered, in bags, upon the floor. I wish you, therefore, to discard from your thoughts the blundering idea of *motive*, engendered in the brains of the police by that portion of the evidence which speaks of money delivered at the door of the house. Coincidences ten times as remarkable as this (the delivery of the money, and murder committed within three days upon the party receiving it), happen to all of us every hour of our lives, without attracting even momentary notice. Coincidences, in general, are great stumbling-blocks in the way of that class of thinkers who have been educated to know nothing of the theory of probabilities—that theory to which the most glorious objects of human research are indebted for the most glorious of illustration. In the present instance, had the gold been gone, the fact of its delivery three days before would have formed something more than a coincidence. It would have been corroborative of this idea of motive. But, under the real circumstances of the case, if we are to suppose gold the motive of this outrage, we must also imagine the perpetrator so vacillating an idiot as to have abandoned his gold and his motive together.

"Keeping now steadily in mind the points to which I have drawn your attention—that peculiar voice, that unusual agility, and that startling absence of motive in a murder so singularly atrocious as this—let us glance at the butchery itself. Here is a woman strangled to death by manual strength, and thrust up a chimney, head downward. Ordinary assassins employ no such modes of murder as this. Least of all, do they thus dispose of the murdered. In the manner of thrusting the corpse up the chimney, you will admit that there was something *excessively outré*—something altogether irreconcilable with our common notions of human action, even when we suppose the actors the most depraved of men. Think, too, how great must have been that strength which could have thrust the body up such an aperture so forcibly that the united vigor of several persons was found barely sufficient to drag it *down!*

"Turn, now, to other indications of the employment of a vigor most marvellous. On the hearth were thick tresses—very thick tresses—of grey human hair. These had been torn out by the roots. You are aware of the great force necessary in tearing thus from the head even twenty or thirty hairs together. You saw the locks in question as well as myself. Their roots (a hideous sight!) were clotted with fragments of the flesh of the scalp—sure token of the prodigious power which had been exerted in uprooting perhaps half a million of hairs at a time. The throat of the old lady was not merely cut, but the head absolutely severed from the body: the instrument was a mere razor. I wish you also to look at the *brutal* ferocity of these deeds. Of the bruises upon the body of Madame L'Espanaye I do not speak. Monsieur Dumas, and his worthy coadjutor Monsieur Etienne, have pronounced that they were inflicted by some obtuse instrument; and so far these gentlemen are very correct. The obtuse instrument was clearly the stone pavement in the yard, upon which the victim had fallen from the window which looked in upon the bed. This idea, however simple it may now seem, escaped the police for the same reason that the breadth of the shutters escaped them—because, by the affair of the nails, their perceptions had been hermetically sealed against the possibility of the windows having ever been opened at all.

"If now, in addition to all these things, you have properly reflected upon the odd disorder of the chamber, we have gone so far as to combine the ideas of an agility astounding, a strength superhuman, a ferocity brutal, a butchery without motive, a *grotesquerie* in horror absolutely alien from humanity, and a voice foreign in tone to the ears of men of many nations, and devoid of all distinct or intelligible syllabification. What result, then, has ensued? What impression have I made upon your fancy?"

I felt a creeping of the flesh as Dupin asked me the question. "A madman," I said, "has done this deed—some raving maniac, escaped from a neighboring *Maison de Santé.*"[64]

"In some respects," he replied, "your idea is not irrelevant. But the voices of madmen, even in their wildest paroxysms, are never found to tally with that peculiar voice heard upon the stairs. Madmen are of some nation, and their language, however incoherent in its words, has always the coherence of syllabification. Besides, the hair of a madman is not such as I now hold in my hand. I disentangled this little tuft from the rigidly clutched fingers of Madame L'Espanaye. Tell me what you can make of it."

"Dupin!" I said, completely unnerved; "this hair is most unusual—this is no *human* hair."

"I have not asserted that it is," said he; "but, before we decide this point, I wish you to glance at the little sketch I have here

64 The *Oxford English Dictionary* defines "maison de santé" as a nursing home, especially one for the mentally ill, citing "The Murders in the Rue Morgue" as the earliest known usage of this term in English. Poe's story has been largely responsible for associating the term "maison de santé" with mental patients. In actuality, these facilities attended to people with many different types of physical and mental ailments. After 1838, however, they no longer cared for the mentally ill.

65   Georges Cuvier (1769–1832) describes the orangutan in detail:

Of all animals, this Ourang is considered as approaching most nearly to Man in the form of his head, height of forehead, and volume of brain; but the exaggerated descriptions of some authors respecting this resemblance, are partly to be attributed to the fact of their being drawn from young individuals only; and there is every reason to believe, that with age, their muzzle becomes much more prominent. . . . After a strict and critical examination, I have ascertained that the Ourang-Outang inhabits the most eastern countries only, such as Malabar, Cochin China, and particularly the great island of Borneo, whence he has been occasionally brought to Europe by the way of Java. When young, and such as he appears to us in his captivity, he is a mild and gentle animal, easily rendered tame and affectionate, which is enabled by his conformation to imitate many of our actions, but whose intelligence does not appear to be as great as is reported, not much surpassing even that of the Dog.

A note to this passage explains the derivation of the animal's unusual name: "*Orang* is a Malay word signifying *reasonable being*, which is applied to man, the ourang-outang, and the elephant. *Outang* means *wild*, or *of the woods*, hence, Wild Man of the Woods" (*The Animal Kingdom Arranged in Conformity with Its Organization*, trans. Henry McMurtrie, 4 vols. [New York: Carvill, 1831], 1, 57–58).

66   Richard Wilbur links Dupin's two registers and the high and low voices of the sailor and the orangutan, seeing speech in the tale as a symbolic expression of identity. "Like Roderick Usher and the divided William Wilson, Dupin has two distinct speaking voices, one high and one low. The narrator makes much of this phenomenon, and toys with the thought that these voices express 'a double Dupin.' The narrator thus introduces, early on, the crucial idea that one person may contain several natures. . . . It appears that while Dupin may be regarded as 'double' or multiple, other figures in the story—the sailor and the orangutan—may be combined and considered as a single 'party.' The implication is that the mastermind Dupin, who can intuitively 'fathom' all the other characters of the narrative, is to be seen as including them all—that the other 'persons' of the tale are to be taken allegorically as elements of one person, whereof Dupin is the presiding faculty." Dupin's ultimate genius is his ability "to detect and

traced upon this paper. It is a *fac-simile* drawing of what has been described in one portion of the testimony as 'dark bruises, and deep indentations of finger nails,' upon the throat of Mademoiselle L'Espanaye, and in another, (by Messrs. Dumas and Etienne,) as a 'series of livid spots, evidently the impression of fingers.'

"You will perceive," continued my friend, spreading out the paper upon the table before us, "that this drawing gives the idea of a firm and fixed hold. There is no *slipping* apparent. Each finger has retained—possibly until the death of the victim—the fearful grasp by which it originally imbedded itself. Attempt, now, to place all your fingers, at the same time, in the respective impressions as you see them."

I made the attempt in vain.

"We are possibly not giving this matter a fair trial," he said. "The paper is spread out upon a plane surface; but the human throat is cylindrical. Here is a billet of wood, the circumference of which is about that of the throat. Wrap the drawing around it, and try the experiment again."

I did so; but the difficulty was even more obvious than before. "This," I said, "is the mark of no human hand."

"Read now," replied Dupin, "this passage from Cuvier."[65]

It was a minute anatomical and generally descriptive account of the large fulvous Ourang-Outang of the East Indian Islands. The gigantic stature, the prodigious strength and activity, the wild ferocity, and the imitative propensities of these mammalia are sufficiently well known to all. I understood the full horrors of the murder at once.

"The description of the digits," said I, as I made an end of reading, "is in exact accordance with this drawing. I see that no animal but an Ourang-Outang, of the species here mentioned, could have impressed the indentations as you have traced them. This tuft of tawny hair, too, is identical in character with that of the beast of Cuvier. But I cannot possibly comprehend the particulars of this frightful mystery. Besides, there were *two* voices heard in contention, and one of them was unquestionably the voice of a Frenchman."[66]

"True; and you will remember an expression attributed almost unanimously, by the evidence, to this voice,—the expression, '*mon Dieu!*' This, under the circumstances, has been justly characterized by one of the witnesses (Montani, the confectioner,) as an expression of remonstrance or expostulation. Upon these two words, therefore, I have mainly built my hopes of a full solution of the riddle. A Frenchman was cognizant of the murder. It is possible—indeed it is far more than probable—that he was innocent of all participation in the bloody transactions which took place. The Ourang-Outang may have escaped from him. He may have traced it to the chamber; but, under the agitating circumstances which ensued, he could never have re-captured it. It is still at large. I will not pursue these guesses—for I have no right to call them more—since the shades of reflection upon which they are based are scarcely of sufficient depth to be appreciable by my own intellect, and since I could not pretend to make them intelligible to the understanding of another. We will call them guesses then, and speak of them as such. If the Frenchman in question is indeed, as I suppose, innocent of this atrocity, this advertisement, which I left last night, upon our return home, at the office of *Le Monde*, (a paper devoted to the shipping interest, and much sought by sailors,) will bring him to our residence."

He handed me a paper, and I read thus:

Caught—*In the Bois de Boulogne,*[67] *early in the morning of the——inst.,* (the morning of the murder,) *a very large, tawny Ourang-Outang of the Bornese species. The owner, (who is ascertained to be a sailor, belonging to a Maltese vessel,) may have the animal again, upon identifying it satisfactorily, and paying a few charges arising from its capture and keeping. Call at No.——, Rue——, Faubourg St. Germain——au troisième.*[68]

"How was it possible," I asked, "that you should know the man to be a sailor, and belonging to a Maltese vessel?"

"I do *not* know it," said Dupin. "I am not *sure* of it. Here, however, is a small piece of ribbon, which from its form, and from its greasy appearance, has evidently been used in tying the hair in one of those long *queues* of which sailors are so fond.[69] Moreover, this knot is one which few besides sailors can tie, and is peculiar to the Maltese. I picked the ribbon up at the foot of the lightning-rod. It could not have belonged to either of the deceased. Now if, after all, I am wrong in my induction from this ribbon, that the Frenchman was a sailor belonging to a Maltese vessel, still I can have done no harm in saying what I did in the advertisement. If I am in error, he will merely suppose that I have been misled by some circumstance into which he will not take the trouble to inquire. But if

restrain the brute in himself" ("The Poe Mystery Case," *New York Review of Books* [July 13, 1967]).

67 Originally a forest and royal hunting ground on the eastern edge of Paris, the Bois de Boulogne had become a desolate wasteland covered with debris and ashes after Napoleon's defeat in 1814, thanks to English, Russian, and Prussian encampments. The Bois de Boulogne was ceded to the city of Paris in 1852 and was then transformed into the fashionable promenade we associate with its name today.

68 According to FBI criminal profiler John Douglas, "The Murders in the Rue Morgue" represents "the first use of a proactive technique by the profiler to flush out an unknown subject and vindicate an innocent man imprisoned for the killings" (John Douglas and Mark Olshaker, *Mindhunter: Inside the FBI's Elite Serial Crime Unit* [New York: Scribner, 1995], 32).

69 A pioneer in crime reconstruction, Edmond Locard (1877–1966) articulated the fundamental principle of forensic science—the so-called Locard Exchange Principle that "every contact leaves a trace." What this means is that criminals cannot commit crimes without leaving behind evidence of their passage. At the crime scene, "trace evidence" is gathered and then analyzed by experts. The piece of ribbon and the strands of orangutan hair would be examples of trace evidence, which Dupin uses to solve the murders. The similarities between Dupin's and Locard's methods of criminal investigation are not coincidental. In 1912, eight years before the appearance of his groundbreaking textbook of forensic science, *L'Enquête criminelle et les methodes scientifiques* (1920), Locard published a sixteen-page pamphlet offering an appreciation of the investigative methods Poe developed in his short fiction.

70 Poe's surviving daguerreotype portraits reveal his personal preferences when it came to facial hair. As a young man, he wore mutton chops but no moustache. After sitting for his first daguerreotype, however, he noticed how deep and unattractive the indentation in his upper lip was. He shaved the mutton chops and started growing a moustache (Kevin J. Hayes, "Poe, the Daguerreotype, and the Autobiographical Act," *Biography* 25 [2002], 486).

71 Poe coined this term, which is not in the *Oxford English Dictionary*. He uses the word to mean uncouth or countrified.

I am right, a great point is gained. Cognizant although innocent of the murder, the Frenchman will naturally hesitate about replying to the advertisement—about demanding the Ourang-Outang. He will reason thus:—'I am innocent; I am poor; my Ourang-Outang is of great value—to one in my circumstances a fortune of itself—why should I lose it through idle apprehensions of danger? Here it is, within my grasp. It was found in the Bois de Boulogne—at a vast distance from the scene of that butchery. How can it ever be suspected that a brute beast should have done the deed? The police are at fault—they have failed to procure the slightest clew. Should they even trace the animal, it would be impossible to prove me cognizant of the murder, or to implicate me in guilt on account of that cognizance. Above all, *I am known*. The advertiser designates me as the possessor of the beast. I am not sure to what limit his knowledge may extend. Should I avoid claiming a property of so great value, which it is known that I possess, I will render the animal at least, liable to suspicion. It is not my policy to attract attention either to myself or to the beast. I will answer the advertisement, get the Ourang-Outang, and keep it close until this matter has blown over.'"

At this moment we heard a step upon the stairs.

"Be ready," said Dupin, "with your pistols, but neither use them nor show them until at a signal from myself."

The front door of the house had been left open, and the visiter had entered, without ringing, and advanced several steps upon the staircase. Now, however, he seemed to hesitate. Presently we heard him descending. Dupin was moving quickly to the door, when we again heard him coming up. He did not turn back a second time, but stepped up with decision, and rapped at the door of our chamber.

"Come in," said Dupin, in a cheerful and hearty tone.

A man entered. He was a sailor, evidently,—a tall, stout, and muscular-looking person, with a certain dare-devil expression of countenance, not altogether unprepossessing. His face, greatly sunburnt, was more than half hidden by whisker and *mustachio*.[70] He had with him a huge oaken cudgel, but appeared to be otherwise unarmed. He bowed awkwardly, and bade us "good evening," in French accents, which, although somewhat Neufchatelish,[71] were still sufficiently indicative of a Parisian origin.

"Sit down, my friend," said Dupin. "I suppose you have called about the Ourang-Outang. Upon my word, I almost envy you the possession of him; a remarkably fine, and no doubt a very valuable animal. How old do you suppose him to be?"

The sailor drew a long breath, with the air of a man relieved of some intolerable burden, and then replied, in an assured tone:

"I have no way of telling—but he can't be more than four or five years old. Have you got him here?"

"Oh no; we had no conveniences for keeping him here. He is at a livery stable in the Rue Dubourg, just by. You can get him in the morning. Of course you are prepared to identify the property?"

"To be sure I am, sir."

"I shall be sorry to part with him," said Dupin.

"I don't mean that you should be at all this trouble for nothing, sir," said the man. "Couldn't expect it. Am very willing to pay a reward for the finding of the animal—that is to say, any thing in reason."

"Well," replied my friend, "that is all very fair, to be sure. Let me think!—what should I have? Oh! I will tell you. My reward shall be this. You shall give me all the information in your power about these murders in the Rue Morgue."

Dupin said the last words in a very low tone, and very quietly. Just as quietly, too, he walked toward the door, locked it, and put the key in his pocket. He then drew a pistol from his bosom and placed it, without the least flurry, upon the table.

The sailor's face flushed up as if he were struggling with suffocation. He started to his feet and grasped his cudgel; but the next moment he fell back into his seat, trembling violently, and with the countenance of death itself. He spoke not a word. I pitied him from the bottom of my heart.

"My friend," said Dupin, in a kind tone, "you are alarming yourself unnecessarily—you are indeed. We mean you no harm whatever. I pledge you the honor of a gentleman, and of a Frenchman, that we intend you no injury. I perfectly well know that you are innocent of the atrocities in the Rue Morgue. It will not do, however, to deny that you are in some measure implicated in them. From what I have already said, you must know that I have had means of information about this matter—means of which you could never have dreamed. Now the thing stands thus. You have done nothing which you could have avoided—nothing, certainly, which renders you culpable. You were not even guilty of robbery,

72   The large group of islands located between Australia and mainland Asia, the Indian Archipelago was also known as the East Indies. It is now called the Malay Archipelago. Borneo is the largest island of the group.

73   The splinter in the animal's foot is an allusion to Aesop's fable "Androcles and the Lion." In the fable Androcles, an escaped slave, removes a thorn from the lion's paw, and the two become friends. The lion's gratitude eventually secures life and freedom for both human and beast, thus proving the moral: gratitude is the sign of noble souls. Unfortunately, kindness and gratitude are not usually the result when man and beast come together. Again and again, we see Poe setting himself against a milieu he believed was concerned to a fault with the moral instruction of literature, an inclination he denounced as "the heresy of *The Didactic.*" Poe encountered *Aesop's Fables* as a child, as did many young readers in England and America in the nineteenth century.

74   Poe makes use of a popular folktale about a monkey. It goes basically as follows: A man grows increasingly annoyed by a monkey that imitates whatever he does. The man devises a scheme to get rid of the monkey. He shaves himself as the monkey watches, pretending to draw his razor across his throat. Once the man leaves, the monkey imitates the man by lathering his face, scraping off the lather with the razor, and then cutting its own throat. Poe likely encountered the story in the oral tradition, but he also knew David Humphreys's versification of it, "The Monkey Who Shaved Himself and His Friends: A Fable," which Samuel Kettell had included in *Specimens of American Poetry* (1829). Poe did not have much respect for Kettell's editorial judgment, but Humphreys's monkey apparently caught Poe's attention. Here's a snippet describing what the monkey did after watching the barber shave:

> He'd seen the barber shave himself;
> So by the glass, upon the table,
> He rubs with soap his visage sable,
> Then with left hand holds smooth his jaw,—
> The razor in his dexter paw;
> Around he flourishes and slashes,
> Till all his face is seam'd with gashes.
> His cheeks despatch'd—his visage thin
> He cock'd, to shave beneath his chin;
> Drew razor swift as he could pull it,
> And cut, from ear to ear, his gullet.

when you might have robbed with impunity. You have nothing to conceal. You have no reason for concealment. On the other hand, you are bound by every principle of honor to confess all you know. An innocent man is now imprisoned, charged with that crime of which you can point out the perpetrator."

The sailor had recovered his presence of mind, in a great measure, while Dupin uttered these words; but his original boldness of bearing was all gone.

"So help me God," said he, after a brief pause, "I *will* tell you all I know about this affair;—but I do not expect you to believe one half I say—I would be a fool indeed if I did. Still, I am innocent, and I will make a clean breast if I die for it."

What he stated was, in substance, this. He had lately made a voyage to the Indian Archipelago.[72] A party, of which he formed one, landed at Borneo, and passed into the interior on an excursion of pleasure. Himself and a companion had captured the Ourang-Outang. This companion dying, the animal fell into his own exclusive possession. After great trouble, occasioned by the intractable ferocity of his captive during the home voyage, he at length succeeded in lodging it safely at his own residence in Paris, where, not to attract toward himself the unpleasant curiosity of his neighbors, he kept it carefully secluded, until such time as it should recover from a wound in the foot, received from a splinter on board ship.[73] His ultimate design was to sell it.

Returning home from some sailors' frolic on the night, or rather in the morning of the murder, he found the beast occupying his own bed-room, into which it had broken from a closet adjoining, where it had been, as was thought, securely confined. Razor in hand, and fully lathered, it was sitting before a looking-glass, attempting the operation of shaving, in which it had no doubt previously watched its master through the key-hole of the closet.[74] Terrified at the sight of so dangerous a weapon in the possession of an animal so ferocious, and so well able to use it, the man, for some moments, was at a loss what to do. He had been accustomed, however, to quiet the creature, even in its fiercest moods, by the use of a whip, and to this he now resorted. Upon sight of it, the Ourang-Outang sprang at once through the door of the chamber, down the stairs, and thence, through a window, unfortunately open, into the street.

The Frenchman followed in despair; the ape, razor still in hand, occasionally stopping to look back and gesticulate at its pursuer, until the latter had nearly come up with it. It then again made off. In this manner the chase continued for a long time. The streets were profoundly quiet, as it was nearly three o'clock in the morning. In passing down an alley in the rear of the Rue Morgue, the fugitive's attention was arrested by a light gleaming from the open window of Madame L'Espanaye's chamber, in the fourth story of her house. Rushing to the building, it perceived the lightning-rod, clambered up with inconceivable agility, grasped the shutter, which was thrown fully back against the wall, and, by its means, swung itself directly upon the headboard of the bed. The whole feat did not occupy a minute. The shutter was kicked open again by the Ourang-Outang as it entered the room.[75]

The sailor, in the meantime, was both rejoiced and perplexed. He had strong hopes of now recapturing the brute, as it could scarcely escape from the trap into which it had ventured, except by the rod, where it might be intercepted as it came down. On the other hand, there was much cause for anxiety as to what it might do in the house. This latter reflection urged the man still to follow the fugitive. A lightning-rod is ascended without difficulty, especially by a sailor; but, when he had arrived as high as the window, which lay far to his left, his career was stopped; the most that he could accomplish was to reach over so as to obtain a glimpse of the interior of the room. At this glimpse he nearly fell from his hold through excess of horror. Now it was that those hideous shrieks arose upon the night, which had startled from slumber the inmates of the Rue Morgue. Madame L'Espanaye and her daughter, habited in their night clothes, had apparently been occupied in arranging some papers in the iron chest already mentioned, which had been wheeled into the middle of the room. It was open, and its contents lay beside it on the floor. The victims must have been sitting with their backs toward the window; and, from the time elapsing between the ingress of the beast and the screams, it seems probable that it was not immediately perceived. The flapping-to of the shutter would naturally have been attributed to the wind.

As the sailor looked in, the gigantic animal had seized Madame L'Espanaye by the hair, (which was loose, as she had been combing it,) and was flourishing the razor about her face, in imitation of the motions of a barber. The daughter lay prostrate and motionless; she had swooned. The screams and struggles of the old lady

75 In 1834, a British newspaper reported a story about a showman who had trained a baboon to commit nighttime robberies by scaling walls and entering bedroom windows. See "New Mode of Thieving," *The Annual Register, or A View of the History, Politics, and Literature of the Year 1834* (London: Baldwin and Cradock, 1835), 122.

76   Founded in 1626 as the Jardin Royal des Plantes Mé-
dicinales, the famed botanical garden in France also has on
its grounds a museum of natural history and a zoo.

77   Many of Poe's contemporary readers were eager to
confound Dupin's detective abilities with the author's own
uncanny skills, sometimes to Poe's annoyance. In a gush-
ing appreciation of 1846, the popular British poet Martin
Farquhar Tupper compares Poe to both François-Eugène
Vidocq and Joseph Fouché, the Minister of Police under
Napoleon Bonaparte:

> Induction, and a microscopic power of analysis,
> seem to be the pervading characteristics of the mind
> of Edgar Poe. Put him on any trail, and he traces it as
> keenly as a Blackfoot or Ojibbeway; give him any
> clue, and he unravels the whole web of mystery;
> never was blood hound more sagacious in scenting
> out a murderer; nor Oedipus himself more shrewd in
> solving an enigma. He would make a famous Trans-
> atlantic Vidocq, and is capable of more address and
> exploit than a Fouché, he has all his wits about him
> ready for use, and could calmly investigate the burst-
> ing of a bombshell; he is a hound never at fault, a
> moral tight-rope dancer never thrown from his equi-
> librium; a close keen reasoner, whom no sophistry
> distracts—nothing foreign or extraneous diverts him
> from his inquiry.
>
> (Walker, *Edgar Allan Poe*, 203)

Writing to Philip Pendleton Cooke on August 9, 1846, Poe
comments: "These tales of ratiocination owe most of their
popularity to being something in a new key. I do not mean
to say that they are not ingenious—but people think them
more ingenious than they are—on account of their method
and *air* of method. In the 'Murders in the Rue Morgue,' for
instance, where is the ingenuity of unravelling a web which
you yourself (the author) have woven for the express purpose of unravelling? The reader is made to confound the
ingenuity of the suppositious Dupin with that of the writer
of the story" (*Collected Letters*, I, 595).

78   Laverna, the Roman goddess of thieves and dishonest
persons, was generally represented by a head without a
body.

Harry Clarke, illustration for "The Murders in the Rue Morgue," from
Tales of Mystery and Imagination (London: George G. Harrap, 1919).

(during which the hair was torn from her head) had the effect
of changing the probably pacific purposes of the Ourang-Outang
into those of wrath. With one determined sweep of its muscular
arm it nearly severed her head from her body. The sight of blood
inflamed its anger into phrenzy. Gnashing its teeth, and flashing
fire from its eyes, it flew upon the body of the girl, and imbedded
its fearful talons in her throat, retaining its grasp until she expired.
Its wandering and wild glances fell at this moment upon the head
of the bed, over which the face of its master, rigid with horror, was
just discernible. The fury of the beast, who no doubt bore still in
mind the dreaded whip, was instantly converted into fear. Conscious of having deserved punishment, it seemed desirous of con-

cealing its bloody deeds, and skipped about the chamber in an agony of nervous agitation; throwing down and breaking the furniture as it moved, and dragging the bed from the bedstead. In conclusion, it seized first the corpse of the daughter, and thrust it up the chimney, as it was found; then that of the old lady, which it immediately hurled through the window headlong.

As the ape approached the casement with its mutilated burden, the sailor shrank aghast to the rod, and, rather gliding than clambering down it, hurried at once home—dreading the consequences of the butchery, and gladly abandoning, in his terror, all solicitude about the fate of the Ourang-Outang. The words heard by the party upon the staircase were the Frenchman's exclamations of horror and affright, commingled with the fiendish jabberings of the brute.

I have scarcely anything to add. The Ourang-Outang must have escaped from the chamber, by the rod, just before the breaking of the door. It must have closed the window as it passed through it. It was subsequently caught by the owner himself, who obtained for it a very large sum at the *Jardin des Plantes*.[76] Le Bon was instantly released, upon our narration of the circumstances (with some comments from Dupin) at the *bureau* of the Prefect of Police. This functionary, however well disposed to my friend, could not altogether conceal his chagrin at the turn which affairs had taken, and was fain to indulge in a sarcasm or two, about the propriety of every person minding his own business.

"Let him talk," said Dupin, who had not thought it necessary to reply. "Let him discourse; it will ease his conscience. I am satisfied with having defeated him in his own castle.[77] Nevertheless, that he failed in the solution of this mystery, is by no means that matter for wonder which he supposes it; for, in truth, our friend the Prefect is somewhat too cunning to be profound. In his wisdom is no *stamen*. It is all head and no body, like the pictures of the Goddess Laverna,[78]—or, at best, all head and shoulders, like a codfish. But he is a good creature after all. I like him especially for one master stroke of cant, by which he has attained his reputation for ingenuity. I mean the way he has '*de nier ce qui est, et d'expliquer ce qui n'est pas.*'"[79]

79 "Rousseau—*Nouvelle Heloise* [Poe's note]." This quotation—"To deny what is and explain what is not"—comes from *Julie; ou, La Nouvelle Héloise*, the popular epistolary novel by Jean-Jacques Rousseau (1712–1778). Poe's likely source, however, is one of his favorite writers, Edward Bulwer-Lytton, who explains that Rousseau "knew *mankind* in the general, but not *men* in the detail. Thus, when he makes an aphorism or reflection, it comes home at once to you as true; but when he would *analyze* that reflection, when he argues, reasons, and attempts to prove, you reject him as unnatural, or you refute him as false. It is then that he partakes of that *manie commune* [common mania] which he imputes to other philosophers, '*de nier ce qui est, et d'expliquer ce qui n'est pas*'" (*Pelham; or, The Adventures of a Gentleman*, 3 vols. [London: Henry Colburn, 1828], I, 210–211).

The word "maelstrom" (early modern Dutch, from maalen, to grind and whirl round, and stroom, stream) describes any powerful whirlpool but especially a tidal whirlpool in a bay or strait. Here, however, "the maelstrom," or Moskstraumen, refers to a series of tidal eddies and whirlpools in the Arctic Ocean, off the Norwegian coast near the Lofoten Islands. Poe himself had never witnessed the phenomenon, nor did he have any real nautical experience. In writing his tale, he therefore relied on several sources: "Maelstrom," in the Encyclopaedia Britannica (6th ed.), in turn drawn from Erich Pontoppidan's The Natural History of Norway (1755); The Mariner's Chronicle (1834), "containing narratives of the most remarkable disasters at sea"; and, most notably, Edward William Landor's "The Maelstrom: A Fragment," in Fraser's Magazine (1834), with which Poe's tale shares many particulars. All of these accounts exaggerate the size and power of the maelstrom, but in Poe's tale the giant vortex seems less the action of the tides than an almost supernatural phenomenon. Only recently have satellite images revealed massive vortexes in the South Atlantic Ocean, mathematical analogues to black holes in space. Not surprisingly Arthur C. Clarke was drawn to Poe's tale. His story "Maelstrom II," in The Wind from the Sun (1972), offers itself as a kind of sequel to Poe's tale.

By the early nineteenth century the word "maelstrom" was already being employed figuratively to mean anything in a state of turbulence or turmoil in which people might be caught. The figurative meanings of "maelstrom" make possible a variety of critical interpretations of Poe's story—of which there have been many. Some of the more interesting symbolic interpretations have focused on the role the old fisherman plays (or not) in orchestrating his own rescue.

Poe—the only known author to insist on placing an umlaut over the "o" in "Maelstrom"—first published the story in the May 1841 issue of Graham's. The story added to the magazine's growing prestige and Poe's growing reputation. "A Descent into the Maelström" was reprinted numerous times in English and translated into German and French during Poe's lifetime.

1 This quotation comes from Joseph Glanvill's Essays on Several Important Subjects in Philosophy and Religion (1676). Most likely, however, Poe took it from a secondary source: J. C. Colquhoun's Isis Revelata: An Inquiry into the Origin, Progress, and Present State of Animal Magnetism, 2 vols. (Edinburgh: MacLachlan and Stewart, 1836), I, xxviii.

2 Poe structures his narrative as a frame tale, a story within a story, though the end frame is only implied. The frame tale has a long literary pedigree that dates back at

A Descent into the Maelström

The ways of God in Nature, as in Providence, are not as *our* ways; nor are the models that we frame any way commensurate to the vastness, profundity, and unsearchableness of His works, *which have a depth in them greater than the well of Democritus.*

Joseph Glanville[1]

We had now reached the summit of the loftiest crag. For some minutes the old man seemed too much exhausted to speak.[2]

"Not long ago," said he at length, "and I could have guided you on this route as well as the youngest of my sons; but, about three years past, there happened to me an event such as never happened before to mortal man—or at least such as no man ever survived to tell of—and the six hours of deadly terror which I then endured have broken me up body and soul. You suppose me a *very* old man—but I am not. It took less than a single day to change these hairs from a jetty black to white,[3] to weaken my limbs, and to unstring my nerves, so that I tremble at the least exertion, and am frightened at a shadow. Do you know I can scarcely look over this little cliff without getting giddy?"

The "little cliff," upon whose edge he had so carelessly thrown himself down to rest that the weightier portion of his body hung over it, while he was only kept from falling by the tenure of his elbow on its extreme and slippery edge—this "little cliff" arose, a sheer unobstructed precipice of black shining rock, some fifteen or sixteen hundred feet from the world of crags beneath us.[4] Nothing would have tempted me to within half a dozen yards of its brink. In truth so deeply was I excited by the perilous position of my companion, that I fell at full length upon the ground, clung to the shrubs around me, and dared not even glance upward at the sky—while I struggled in vain to divest myself of the idea that the very foundations of the mountain were in danger from the fury of the winds. It was long before I could reason myself into sufficient courage to sit up and look out into the distance.[5]

"You must get over these fancies," said the guide, "for I have brought you here that you might have the best possible view of the scene of that event I mentioned—and to tell you the whole story with the spot just under your eye."[6]

"We are now," he continued, in that particularizing manner which distinguished him—"we are now close upon the Norwegian coast—in the sixty-eighth degree of latitude—in the great province of Nordland—and in the dreary district of Lofoden.[7] The mountain upon whose top we sit is Helseggen, the Cloudy.[8] Now raise yourself up a little higher—hold on to the grass if you feel giddy—so—and look out, beyond the belt of vapor beneath us, into the sea."

I looked dizzily, and beheld a wide expanse of ocean, whose waters wore so inky a hue as to bring at once to my mind the Nubian geographer's account of the *Mare Tenebrarum*.[9] A panorama more deplorably desolate no human imagination can conceive. To the right and left, as far as the eye could reach, there lay outstretched, like ramparts of the world, lines of horridly black and beetling cliff,[10] whose character of gloom was but the more forcibly illustrated by the surf which reared high up against its white and ghastly crest, howling and shrieking for ever. Just opposite the promontory upon whose apex we were placed, and at a distance of some five or six miles out at sea, there was visible a small, bleak-looking island; or, more properly, its position was discernible through the wilderness of surge in which it was enveloped. About two miles nearer the land, arose another of smaller size, hideously craggy and barren, and encompassed at various intervals by a cluster of dark rocks.[11]

The appearance of the ocean, in the space between the more distant island and the shore, had something very unusual about it. Although, at the time, so strong a gale was blowing landward that a brig in the remote offing lay to under a double-reefed trysail,[12] and constantly plunged her whole hull out of sight, still there was here nothing like a regular swell, but only a short, quick, angry cross dashing of water in every direction—as well in the teeth of the wind as otherwise. Of foam there was little except in the immediate vicinity of the rocks.

"The island in the distance," resumed the old man, "is called by the Norwegians Vurrgh. The one midway is Moskoe. That a mile to the northward is Ambaaren. Yonder are Iflesen, Hoeyholm,

least as far as Homer's *Odyssey*. But Poe may have taken inspiration from works far less removed in time. Many critics have noted the similarities in structure and numerous particulars between Poe's tale and Coleridge's "Rime of the Ancient Mariner" (1798; 1817), whose inner story is also related by the lone, white-haired survivor of a terrifying sea journey. Southwestern humorist Thomas Bangs Thorpe's "The Big Bear of Arkansas," one of the most popular frame tales of the nineteenth century, appeared in the *Spirit of the Times* only months before the publication of Poe's tale.

3   Hair turning white from terror is a motif frequently found in folk legends.

4   The old fisherman's position recalls the position of the title character of Friedrich Schiller's ballad "The Diver" (1797), stanza 5, as he gazes into a whirlpool from a cliff high above it:

> And as he hung over the craggy verge,
>   And cast on the deep his eye,
> Charybdis the floods was about to disgorge,
>   Ingulfed voraciously.

5   The foreign traveler is a tourist and thrill seeker at the dawn of modern tourism, when advances in transport technology made tour travel possible for those with sufficient time and money. We learn later in passing that the traveler has been to Niagara Falls and has seen the American prairies. Norway's maelstrom is another sublime wonder to be added to his growing collection of experiences—though he has no wish to put himself in harm's way (Kevin J. Hayes, *Edgar Allan Poe* [London: Reaktion, 2009], 108).

6   Like Poe's Norwegian guide, some Aboriginal storytellers have felt unable to relate a tale unless they can do so at a geographic site linked to the narrative (Stephen Mueke, "Ideology Reiterated: The Uses of Aboriginal Oral Narrative," *Southern Review* [Adelaide] 16 [1983], 94–95). Incidentally, South Australia's fondness for Poe's tale has persisted well into the twentieth century. In 1986, the Australian Dance Theatre premiered "The Descent into the Maelstrom" in Adelaide with music by Philip Glass and choreography by Molissa Fenley.

7   Poe took these geographical facts from an article in the *Encyclopaedia Britannica*, 6th ed., which is heavily indebted to Erich Pontoppidan, *The Natural History of Norway* (1755).

Keildholm, Suarven, and Buckholm. Farther off—between Moskoe and Vurrgh—are Otterholm, Flimen, Sandflesen, and Skarholm.[13] These are the true names of the places—but why it has been thought necessary to name them at all, is more than either you or I can understand. Do you hear any thing? Do you see any change in the water?"

We had now been about ten minutes upon the top of Helseggen, to which we had ascended from the interior of Lofoden, so that we had caught no glimpse of the sea until it had burst upon us from the summit. As the old man spoke, I became aware of a loud and gradually increasing sound, like the moaning of a vast herd of buffaloes upon an American prairie;[14] and at the same moment I perceived that what seamen term the *chopping* character of the ocean

8 Edward Wilson Landor, the author of one of Poe's key sources for this tale, places a group of people upon the shore just beneath the mountain of Helseggen, where they witness a doomed vessel caught within the Norway Maelstrom. After fainting, the only survivor of the wreck finds himself on shore, with no knowledge of how he survived ("The Maelstrom: A Fragment," *Fraser's Magazine* 10 [1834], 279–281). Commenting on Poe's indebtedness to Landor, Mabbott observes, "It was characteristic of Poe, in response to the magazinist's failure, to devise the machinery for the rescue" (Thomas Ollive Mabbott, ed., *Collected Works of Edgar Allan Poe*, 3 vols. [Cambridge, MA: The Belknap Press of Harvard University Press, 1969–1978], II, 575).

9 This reference marks the narrator as a scholar or bookish person. Abu 'Abd Allah Muhammad b. Muhammad al-Idrisi, a twelfth-century geographer, wrote *Nuzhat al-mushtaq fi ikhtiraq al-afaq*, which Gabriele Sionita and Joannes Hesronita abridged and translated into Latin from the original Arabic and published as *Geographia Nubiensis* (1619). With the publication of this Latin translation, Idrisi became known as the "Nubian geographer." Poe took his reference from Jacob Bryant's *New System; or, An Analysis of Antient Mythology*, 3rd ed., 6 vols. (London: for J. Walker, 1807), IV, 79–80.

10 The outside narrator's poetic diction shows him deliberately shaping his materials for literary effect. His simile comes from James Montgomery's "The Wanderer of Switzerland" (1813), part II, lines 13–16:

Where the Alpine summits rise,
Height o'er height stupendous hurl'd;
Like the pillars of the skies,
Like the ramparts of the world

Beetling means projecting or overhanging. The phrase "beetling cliff" comes from James Thomson's *The Seasons* (1744), lines 451–452: "where the Hawk, / High, in the beetling Cliff, his Airy builds."

11 A. S. Byatt adopted this paragraph for her novel, *The Biographer's Tale* (2000), which contains an episode relating a visit Linnaeus makes to Norway to see the Maelstrom. She told an interviewer: "I didn't know the Poe story when I had the idea of the maelstrom. I went and read it and then I snitched a bit of it." Byatt's process of borrowing is not dissimilar to Poe's. Phineas G. Nanson, Byatt's narrator, remarks, "I myself think that these lifted sentences, in their new contexts, are almost the purest and most beautiful parts of the transmission of scholarship" (*The Biographer's Tale* [London: Chatto and Windus, 2000], 51, 29; "A. S. Byatt in Conversation with Ignês Sodré," *On the Way Home: Conversations between Writers and Psychoanalysts*, ed. Marie Bridge [London: Karnac, 2007], 43).

12 A trysail is a small sail used by brigs and cutters in blustery weather. A double-reefed sail is one that has been rolled up considerably to reduce the amount of the sail's surface area exposed to the wind. A landlubber and city dweller, Poe may have borrowed these technical terms from Richard Henry Dana: "Again it was clew up and haul down, reef and furl, until we had got her down to close-reefed topsails, double-reefed trysail, and reefed fore-spenser" (*Two Years before the Mast* [New York: Harper and Brothers, 1840], 37).

13 These place names, with slight variations in spelling, come from the *Encyclopaedia Britannica*.

beneath us was rapidly changing into a current which set to the eastward. Even while I gazed, this current acquired a monstrous velocity. Each moment added to its speed—to its headlong impetuosity. In five minutes the whole sea, as far as Vurrgh, was lashed into ungovernable fury; but it was between Moskoe and the coast that the main uproar held its sway. Here the vast bed of the waters, seamed and scarred into a thousand conflicting channels, burst suddenly into phrensied convulsion—heaving, boiling, hissing— gyrating in gigantic and innumerable vortices, and all whirling and plunging on to the eastward with a rapidity which water never elsewhere assumes except in precipitous descents.[15]

In a few minutes more, there came over the scene another radical alteration. The general surface grew somewhat more smooth, and the whirlpools, one by one, disappeared, while prodigious streaks of foam became apparent where none had been seen before. These streaks, at length, spreading out to a great distance, and entering into combination, took unto themselves the gyratory motion of the subsided vortices, and seemed to form the germ of another more vast. Suddenly—very suddenly—this assumed a distinct and definite existence, in a circle of more than half a mile in diameter. The edge of the whirl was represented by a broad belt of gleaming spray; but no particle of this slipped into the mouth of the terrific funnel, whose interior, as far as the eye could fathom it, was a smooth, shining, and jet-black wall of water, inclined to the horizon at an angle of some forty-five degrees, speeding dizzily round and round with a swaying and sweltering motion, and sending forth to the winds an appalling voice, half shriek, half roar, such as not even the mighty cataract of Niagara[16] ever lifts up in its agony to Heaven.

The mountain trembled to its very base, and the rock rocked. I threw myself upon my face, and clung to the scant herbage in an excess of nervous agitation.

"This," said I at length, to the old man—"this *can* be nothing else than the great whirlpool of the Maelström."

"So it is sometimes termed," said he. "We Norwegians call it the Moskoe-ström, from the island of Moskoe in the midway."[17]

The ordinary accounts of this vortex had by no means prepared me for what I saw. That of Jonas Ramus,[18] which is perhaps the most circumstantial of any, cannot impart the faintest conception

14 Poe's comparison of the noise of the Maelstrom and that of a stampeding herd of buffalo inspired the boy genius Arthur Rimbaud, who in "Le Bateau ivre" ("The Drunken Boat," 1871) likens rough ocean swells to a hysteric herd—"vacheries hystériques"—as they crash against the reefs. "A Descent into the Maelström" is among the tales Charles Baudelaire translated into French in the 1850s.

15 Poe echoes an article about the Maelstrom that circulated widely in American newspapers and magazines from the mid-1820s through the 1830s. The earliest known instance of it is "The Maelstrom Whirlpool," *New-Hampshire Statesman* (July 18, 1825). The anonymous author says: "Imagine to yourself an immense circle, running round, of a diameter of one and a half miles, the velocity increasing as it approximated towards the centre, and gradually changing its dark blue colour to white—foaming, rushing, tumbling, to its vortex; very much concave, as much so as the water in a funnel when half run out; the noise too, hissing, roaring, dashing— all pressing on the mind at once, presented the most awful, grand, solemn sight, I ever experienced."

16 Poe's reference to Niagara Falls reinforces his parallel with the American West. Not only was Niagara Falls a standard Western reference, but also there was a famous whirlpool just a few miles from the falls (Edwin Fussell, *Frontier: American Literature and the American West* [Princeton: Princeton University Press, 1965], 163).

17 Following Pontoppidan's *Natural History*, *Encyclopaedia Britannica* gives "Moskoestrom" as another name for Maelstrom, an alternative that Landor reiterates ("The Maelstrom," 274).

18 A pastor in Norderhaug, Norway, Jonas Ramus (1649–1718) was a Norwegian antiquarian who theorized that Homer's story of Odysseus caught between the Scylla and Charybdis actually occurred between the Norwegian coast and the Maelstrom. Poe took Ramus's words in the following paragraph from the *Encyclopaedia Britannica*, which also borrows text from Pontoppidan's *Natural History*.

19 A Norway mile is equal to 6.92 English miles (James Hingston Tuckey, *Maritime Geography and Statistics,* 4 vols. [London: for Black, Parry, 1815], I, 519).

20 Poe abbreviated this sentence from the original in the *Encyclopaedia Britannica,* omitting a reference to sheep farming on the island and thus making the setting more rugged and untamed. These changes reinforce the parallel between the Norwegian fisherman's journey to the Maelstrom and the American frontiersman's journey into the wilderness of the West.

either of the magnificence, or of the horror of the scene—or of the wild bewildering sense of *the novel* which confounds the beholder. I am not sure from what point of view the writer in question surveyed it, nor at what time; but it could neither have been from the summit of Helseggen, nor during a storm. There are some passages of his description, nevertheless, which may be quoted for their details, although their effect is exceedingly feeble in conveying an impression of the spectacle.

"Between Lofoden and Moskoe," he says, "the depth of the water is between thirty-six and forty fathoms; but on the other side, toward Ver (Vurrgh) this depth decreases so as not to afford a convenient passage for a vessel, without the risk of splitting on the rocks, which happens even in the calmest weather. When it is flood, the stream runs up the country between Lofoden and Moskoe with a boisterous rapidity; but the roar of its impetuous ebb to the sea is scarce equalled by the loudest and most dreadful cataracts; the noise being heard several leagues off, and the vortices or pits are of such an extent and depth, that if a ship comes within its attraction, it is inevitably absorbed and carried down to the bottom, and there beat to pieces against the rocks; and when the water relaxes, the fragments thereof are thrown up again. But these intervals of tranquility are only at the turn of the ebb and flood, and in calm weather, and last but a quarter of an hour, its violence gradually returning. When the stream is most boisterous, and its fury heightened by a storm, it is dangerous to come within a Norway mile[19] of it. Boats, yachts, and ships have been carried away by not guarding against it before they were within its reach. It likewise happens frequently, that whales come too near the stream, and are overpowered by its violence; and then it is impossible to describe their howlings and bellowings in their fruitless struggles to disengage themselves. A bear once, attempting to swim from Lofoden to Moskoe, was caught by the stream and borne down, while he roared terribly, so as to be heard on shore.[20] Large stocks of firs and pine trees, after being absorbed by the current, rise again broken and torn to such a degree as if bristles grew upon them. This plainly shows the bottom to consist of craggy rocks, among which they are whirled to and fro. This stream is regulated by the flux and reflux of the sea—it being constantly high and low water every six hours. In the year 1645, early in the morning of

Sexagesima Sunday,[21] it raged with such noise and impetuosity that the very stones of the houses on the coast fell to the ground."

In regard to the depth of the water, I could not see how this could have been ascertained at all in the immediate vicinity of the vortex. The "forty fathoms" must have reference only to portions of the channel close upon the shore either of Moskoe or Lofoden. The depth in the centre of the Moskoe-ström must be immeasurably greater; and no better proof of this fact is necessary than can be obtained from even the sidelong glance into the abyss of the whirl which may be had from the highest crag of Helseggen. Looking down from this pinnacle upon the howling Phlegethon[22] below, I could not help smiling at the simplicity with which the honest Jonas Ramus records, as a matter difficult of belief, the anecdotes of the whales and the bears; for it appeared to me, in fact, a self-evident thing, that the largest ship of the line in existence, coming within the influence of that deadly attraction, could resist it as little as a feather the hurricane, and must disappear bodily and at once.

The attempts to account for the phenomenon—some of which, I remember, seemed to me sufficiently plausible in perusal—now wore a very different and unsatisfactory aspect. The idea generally received is that this, as well as three smaller vortices among the Ferroe islands, "have no other cause than the collision of waves rising and falling, at flux and reflux, against a ridge of rocks and shelves, which confines the water so that it precipitates itself like a cataract; and thus the higher the flood rises, the deeper must the fall be, and the natural result of all is a whirlpool or vortex, the prodigious suction of which is sufficiently known by lesser experiments."—These are the words of the *Encyclopaedia Britannica*.[23] Kircher and others imagine that in the centre of the channel of the Maelström is an abyss penetrating the globe, and issuing in some very remote part—the Gulf of Bothnia being somewhat decidedly named in one instance.[24] This opinion, idle in itself, was the one to which, as I gazed, my imagination most readily assented; and, mentioning it to the guide, I was rather surprised to hear him say that, although it was the view almost universally entertained of the subject by the Norwegians, it nevertheless was not his own. As to the former notion he confessed his inability to comprehend it; and here I agreed with him—for, however conclusive on paper, it be-

21 The second Sunday before Lent and therefore the eighth Sunday before Easter.

22 In the *Aeneid*, Virgil depicts Phlegethon, the burning river in Hell. John Milton, *Paradise Lost*, book II, lines 580–581, reiterates Virgil's imagery: "fierce *Phlegeton*, / Whose waves of torrent fire inflame with rage."

23 The outside narrator's explicit reference to his source is highly unusual for Poe, who much preferred to mask his sources. The fact that the source is the *Encyclopaedia Britannica* may have something to do with the explicitness of the reference. It serves as a reminder that the outside narrator, having since returned home, is now comfortably surrounded by his books as he writes up the story of his Norwegian experience. In its broadest sense, the word "encyclopaedia" means a circle of learning. Poe's reference thus provides another analogue for the Maelstrom. We may drown in information.

24 Athanasius Kircher (1601–1680), a prolific yet eccentric German scholar and mathematician, maintained that the Maelstrom was a sea vortex that drew the water beneath Norway and discharged it into the Gulf of Bothnia, the northernmost arm of the Baltic Sea.

25   Superstitious sailors believed that sailing on a ship with brothers aboard was bad luck.

26   A smack, or vessel, that is schooner-rigged contains two gaff sails (sails that can take wind from either side) and a head sail set on a bowsprit (a spar extending forward from the ship's bow).

27   The inside narrator's words echo the promises and language of early American promotion literature, suggesting a parallel between the old man and the American frontiersman. Compare what Captain John Smith says in *A Description of New England* (1616): "Who can desire more content, that hath small means; or but only his merit to advance his fortune, than to tread, and plant that ground he hath purchased by the hazard of his life?"

comes altogether unintelligible, and even absurd, amid the thunder of the abyss.

"You have had a good look at the whirl now," said the old man, "and if you will creep round this crag, so as to get in its lee, and deaden the roar of the water, I will tell you a story that will convince you I ought to know something of the Moskoe-ström."

I placed myself as desired, and he proceeded.

"Myself and my two brothers[25] once owned a schooner-rigged smack of about seventy tons burthen,[26] with which we were in the habit of fishing among the islands beyond Moskoe, nearly to Vurrgh. In all violent eddies at sea there is good fishing, at proper opportunities, if one has only the courage to attempt it; but among the whole of the Lofoden coastmen, we three were the only ones who made a regular business of going out to the islands, as I tell you. The usual grounds are a great way lower down to the southward. There fish can be got at all hours, without much risk, and therefore these places are preferred. The choice spots over here among the rocks, however, not only yield the finest variety, but in far greater abundance; so that we often got in a single day, what the more timid of the craft could not scrape together in a week. In fact, we made it a matter of desperate speculation—the risk of life standing instead of labor, and courage answering for capital.[27]

"We kept the smack in a cove about five miles higher up the coast than this; and it was our practice, in fine weather, to take advantage of the fifteen minutes' slack to push across the main channel of the Moskoe-ström, far above the pool, and then drop down upon anchorage somewhere near Otterholm, or Sandflesen, where the eddies are not so violent as elsewhere. Here we used to remain until nearly time for slack-water again, when we weighed and made for home. We never set out upon this expedition without a steady side wind for going and coming—one that we felt sure would not fail us before our return—and we seldom made a mis-calculation upon this point. Twice, during six years, we were forced to stay all night at anchor on account of a dead calm, which is a rare thing indeed just about here; and once we had to remain on the grounds nearly a week, starving to death, owing to a gale which blew up shortly after our arrival, and made the channel too boisterous to be thought of. Upon this occasion we should have been driven out to sea in spite of everything, (for the whirlpools threw us round and round so violently, that, at length, we fouled

Marcel Roux (1878–1922), woodcut from *Une descente dans le maelstrom* (Paris: Devambez, 1920). Roux, who primarily produced etchings before his experiences in World War I left him too injured to work in that medium, turned to woodcuts after the war. He is known for his dark, tortured works.

our anchor and dragged it) if it had not been that we drifted into one of the innumerable cross currents—here to-day and gone to-morrow—which drove us under the lee of Flimen, where, by good luck, we brought up.

"I could not tell you the twentieth part of the difficulties we encountered 'on the grounds'—it is a bad spot to be in, even in good weather—but we made shift always to run the gauntlet of the Moskoe-ström itself without accident; although at times my

28   This, the third proverbial phrase in a half dozen lines, recalls a technique Poe had used earlier in "Manuscript Found in a Bottle." The quick succession of proverbial phrases suggests that the narrator is struggling to find the right words to tell his story.

29   Sweeps, as Admiral William Henry Smyth defines them, are "large oars used on board ships of war in a calm, either to assist the rudder in turning them round, or to propel them ahead when chasing in light winds" (*The Sailor's Word-Book: An Alphabetical Digest of Nautical Terms* [London: Blackie and Son, 1867], 669).

30   The fact that the fishermen must rely on a watch, and must monitor the time they spend in the channel, conveys the danger they face.

31   Encyclopedist J. L. Blake describes one of the signs of a coming hurricane: "[A] copper colored cloud . . . [first] rises in a serene sky, and suddenly obscures the whole horizon, after which the tempest bursts forth, and the whole air is thrown into the most violent agitation" (*The Family Encyclopaedia of Useful Knowledge and General Literature* [New York: Peter Hill, 1834], 465).

heart has been in my mouth[28] when we happened to be a minute or so behind or before the slack. The wind sometimes was not as strong as we thought it at starting, and then we made rather less way than we could wish, while the current rendered the smack unmanageable. My eldest brother had a son eighteen years old, and I had two stout boys of my own. These would have been of great assistance at such times, in using the sweeps,[29] as well as afterward in fishing—but, somehow, although we ran the risk ourselves, we had not the heart to let the young ones get into the danger—for, after all is said and done, it *was* a horrible danger, and that is the truth.

"It is now within a few days of three years since what I am going to tell you occurred. It was on the tenth day of July, 18—, a day which the people of this part of the world will never forget—for it was one in which blew the most terrible hurricane that ever came out of the heavens. And yet all the morning, and indeed until late in the afternoon, there was a gentle and steady breeze from the south-west, while the sun shone brightly, so that the oldest seaman among us could not have foreseen what was to follow.

"The three of us—my two brothers and myself—had crossed over to the islands about two o'clock P.M., and had soon nearly loaded the smack with fine fish, which, we all remarked, were more plenty that day than we had ever known them. It was just seven, *by my watch,* when we weighed and started for home, so as to make the worst of the Ström at slack water, which we knew would be at eight.[30]

"We set out with a fresh wind on our starboard quarter, and for some time spanked along at a great rate, never dreaming of danger, for indeed we saw not the slightest reason to apprehend it. All at once we were taken aback by a breeze from over Helseggen. This was most unusual—something that had never happened to us before—and I began to feel a little uneasy, without exactly knowing why. We put the boat on the wind, but could make no headway at all for the eddies, and I was upon the point of proposing to return to the anchorage, when, looking astern, we saw the whole horizon covered with a singular copper-colored cloud that rose with the most amazing velocity.[31]

"In the meantime the breeze that had headed us off fell away, and we were dead becalmed, drifting about in every direction. This state of things, however, did not last long enough to give us time to think about it. In less than a minute the storm was upon us—in less than two the sky was entirely overcast—and what with this and the driving spray, it became suddenly so dark that we could not see each other in the smack.

"Such a hurricane as then blew it is folly to attempt describing. The oldest seaman in Norway never experienced any thing like it. We had let our sails go by the run[32] before it cleverly took us; but, at the first puff, both our masts went by the board as if they had been sawed off—the mainmast taking with it my youngest brother, who had lashed himself to it for safety.[33]

"Our boat was the lightest feather of a thing that ever sat upon water. It had a complete flush deck, with only a small hatch near the bow, and this hatch it had always been our custom to batten down when about to cross the Ström, by way of precaution against the chopping seas. But for this circumstance we should have foundered at once—for we lay entirely buried for some moments. How my elder brother escaped destruction I cannot say, for I never had an opportunity of ascertaining. For my part, as soon as I had let the foresail run, I threw myself flat on deck, with my feet against the narrow gunwale of the bow,[34] and with my hands grasping a ring-bolt near the foot of the foremast. It was mere instinct that prompted me to do this—which was undoubtedly the very best thing I could have done—for I was too much flurried to think.

"For some moments we were completely deluged, as I say, and all this time I held my breath, and clung to the bolt. When I could stand it no longer I raised myself upon my knees, still keeping hold with my hands, and thus got my head clear. Presently our little boat gave herself a shake, just as a dog does in coming out of the water, and thus rid herself, in some measure, of the seas.[35] I was now trying to get the better of the stupor that had come over me, and to collect my senses so as to see what was to be done, when I felt somebody grasp my arm. It was my elder brother, and my heart leaped for joy, for I had made sure that he was overboard—but the next moment all this joy was turned into horror—for he put his mouth close to my ear, and screamed out the word '*Moskoe-ström!*'

"No one ever will know what my feelings were at that moment. I shook from head to foot as if I had had the most violent fit of the ague.[36] I knew what he meant by that one word well enough—I knew what he wished to make me understand. With the wind that

32 To let go at once or entirely, instead of slackening the rope and tackle by which the sails were otherwise held fast.

33 In Homer's *Odyssey*, Odysseus has his men lash him to the mast to protect him from the lure of the Sirens' song. The younger brother's inability to save himself from the Maelstrom using a similar technique suggests that traditional methods do not work in the face of unprecedented danger.

34 A gunwale is a piece of timber that extends around the top side of the hull.

35 Poe's calculated figurative use of the verb "to shake," that is, comparing their boat to a dog shaking the water from its coat, gives readers a familiar, comfortable, even homey image, which creates a false, momentary sense of security. The shock that follows is intensified on a subliminal level by Poe's use of the verb again in the next paragraph, only now the old fisherman shakes in fear.

36 A violent fever marked by paroxysms alternating between a burning, feverish stage and a cold, shivering stage. Like King Lear, like all of us, Poe's narrator is not ague-proof. See *King Lear*, Act IV, scene VI.

37 A ninety-gun ship was the largest type of warship in the British fleet. Poe may have known William Falconer's poem "Description of a Ninety Gun Ship" (1759), lines 41–44:

> Full ninety brazen guns her port-holes fill,
> Ready with nitrous magazines to kill,
> From dread embrazures formidably peep,
> And seem to threaten ruin to the deep.

38 To scud means to move briskly or hurriedly.

39 A proverbial comparison, as is "pale as death" in the following paragraph.

40 In Norway in July, the moon would scarcely rise above the southern horizon, and, indeed, moonlight would be superfluous during the summertime in the Land of the Midnight Sun (Frank C. Jordan, "Astronomical Fiction," *Natural History* 36 [1935], 217–219).

41 While technology has provided the fisherman with the ability to precisely calculate the hour of the day, a pocket-watch is only as good as the all-too-frail human memory. It must be wound regularly if it's to continue keeping time. The fisherman throws away the watch in disgust, but this is also a heavily symbolic act: there are limits to what technology can achieve. Where the brothers are headed now, they will have no use for a timepiece.

42 The curved part of a ship's stern.

43 A narrow channel in which water is forced to turn a water wheel.

now drove us on, we were bound for the whirl of the Ström, and nothing could save us!

"You perceive that in crossing the Ström *channel,* we always went a long way up above the whirl, even in the calmest weather, and then had to wait and watch carefully for the slack—but now we were driving right upon the pool itself, and in such a hurricane as this! 'To be sure,' I thought, 'we shall get there just about the slack—there is some little hope in that'—but in the next moment I cursed myself for being so great a fool as to dream of hope at all. I knew very well that we were doomed, had we been ten times a ninety-gun ship.[37]

"By this time the first fury of the tempest had spent itself, or perhaps we did not feel it so much, as we scudded before it,[38] but at all events the seas, which at first had been kept down by the wind, and lay flat and frothing, now got up into absolute mountains. A singular change, too, had come over the heavens. Around in every direction it was still as black as pitch,[39] but nearly overhead there burst out, all at once, a circular rift of clear sky—as clear as I ever saw—and of a deep bright blue—and through it there blazed forth the full moon with a lustre that I never before knew her to wear.[40] She lit up every thing about us with the greatest distinctness—but, oh God, what a scene it was to light up!

"I now made one or two attempts to speak to my brother—but, in some manner which I could not understand, the din had so increased that I could not make him hear a single word, although I screamed at the top of my voice in his ear. Presently he shook his head, looking as pale as death, and held up one of his fingers, as if to say '*listen!*'

"At first I could not make out what he meant—but soon a hideous thought flashed upon me. I dragged my watch from its fob. It was not going. I glanced at its face by the moonlight, and then burst into tears as I flung it far away into the ocean.[41] *It had run down at seven o'clock! We were behind the time of the slack, and the whirl of the Ström was in full fury!*

"When a boat is well built, properly trimmed, and not deep laden, the waves in a strong gale, when she is going large, seem always to slip from beneath her—which appears very strange to a landsman—and this is what is called *riding,* in sea phrase. Well, so far we had ridden the swells very cleverly; but presently a gigantic sea happened to take us right under the counter,[42] and bore us

with it as it rose—up—up—as if into the sky. I would not have believed that any wave could rise so high. And then down we came with a sweep, a slide, and a plunge, that made me feel sick and dizzy, as if I was falling from some lofty mountain-top in a dream. But while we were up I had thrown a quick glance around—and that one glance was all sufficient. I saw our exact position in an instant. The Moskoe-ström whirlpool was about a quarter of a mile dead ahead—but no more like the every-day Moskoe-ström, than the whirl as you now see it is like a mill-race.[43] If I had not known where we were, and what we had to expect, I should not have recognised the place at all. As it was, I involuntarily closed my eyes in horror. The lids clenched themselves together as if in a spasm.

Paul Gauguin, *Dramas of the Sea: A Descent into the Maelstrom*, 1889. The influence of "Ligeia" and "The Raven" on Gauguin are well known. This zincograph, now recognized as a key proto-modernist work, shows Gauguin's appreciation of another one of Poe's major tales.

44   This stunningly modern comparison not only demonstrates an awareness of recent technology but also suggests the frightening potential of that technology. Humans had yet to invent a method of coordinating thousands of steam engines. Technology, too, can be a maelstrom.

"It could not have been more than two minutes afterward until we suddenly felt the waves subside, and were enveloped in foam. The boat made a sharp half turn to larboard, and then shot off in its new direction like a thunderbolt. At the same moment the roaring noise of the water was completely drowned in a kind of shrill shriek—such a sound as you might imagine given out by the waste-pipes of many thousand steam-vessels, letting off their steam all together.[44] We were now in the belt of surf that always surrounds the whirl; and I thought, of course, that another moment would plunge us into the abyss—down which we could only see indistinctly on account of the amazing velocity with which we were borne along. The boat did not seem to sink into the water at all, but to skim like an air-bubble upon the surface of the surge. Her starboard side was next the whirl, and on the larboard arose the world of ocean we had left. It stood like a huge writhing wall between us and the horizon.

"It may appear strange, but now, when we were in the very jaws of the gulf, I felt more composed than when we were only approaching it. Having made up my mind to hope no more, I got rid of a great deal of that terror which unmanned me at first. I suppose it was despair that strung my nerves.

"It may look like boasting—but what I tell you is truth—I began to reflect how magnificent a thing it was to die in such a manner, and how foolish it was in me to think of so paltry a consideration as my own individual life, in view of so wonderful a manifestation of God's power. I do believe that I blushed with shame when this idea crossed my mind. After a little while I became possessed with the keenest curiosity about the whirl itself. I positively felt a *wish* to explore its depths, even at the sacrifice I was going to make; and my principal grief was that I should never be able to tell my old companions on shore about the mysteries I should see. These, no doubt, were singular fancies to occupy a man's mind in such extremity—and I have often thought since, that the revolutions of the boat around the pool might have rendered me a little light-headed.

"There was another circumstance which tended to restore my self-possession; and this was the cessation of the wind, which could not reach us in our present situation—for, as you saw yourself, the belt of surf is considerably lower than the general bed of the ocean, and this latter now towered above us, a high, black,

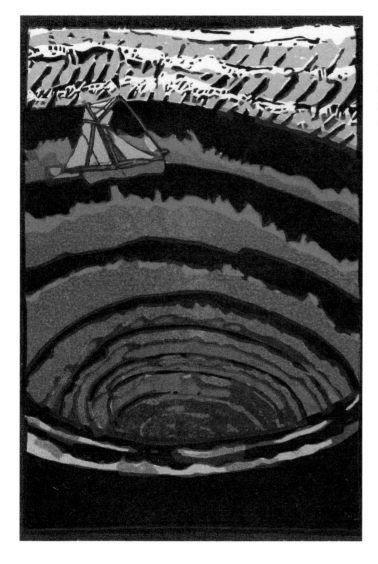

Marcel Roux, woodcut from *Une descente dans le maelstrom*, illustrating the "wild gyrations" of the maelstrom as the mariner's ship descends into its depths.

mountainous ridge. If you have never been at sea in a heavy gale, you can form no idea of the confusion of mind occasioned by the wind and spray together. They blind, deafen, and strangle you, and take away all power of action or reflection. But we were now, in a great measure, rid of these annoyances—just as death-condemned felons in prison are allowed petty indulgences, forbidden them while their doom is yet uncertain.

"How often we made the circuit of the belt it is impossible to say. We careered round and round for perhaps an hour, flying rather than floating, getting gradually more and more into the

45   A basket used to catch fish.

46   The German philosopher and critical theorist The-
odor W. Adorno (1903–1969) finds in Poe's image of the
maelstrom a powerful metaphor for capitalist culture's
perpetual, insatiable appetite for everything and anything
new: "In central passages of Poe . . . the concept of newness emerges. . . . in the description of the maelstrom
and the shudder it inspires—equated with 'the novel'—of
which none of the traditional reports is said to give an adequate idea. . . . it is an unknown threat that the subject em-
braces and which, in a dizzy reversal, promises joy. The
new, a blank place in consciousness, awaited as if with shut
eyes, seems the formula by means of which a stimulus is
extracted from dread and despair. . . . Poe's allegory of the
'novel' is that of the breathlessly spinning yet in a sense sta-
tionary movement of the helpless boat in the eye of the
maelstrom" (*Minima Moralia: Reflections on a Damaged
Life* [New York: Verso, 2005], 235–236).

middle of the surge, and then nearer and nearer to its horrible inner edge. All this time I had never let go of the ring-bolt. My
brother was at the stern, holding on to a large empty watercask
which had been securely lashed under the coop[45] of the counter,
and was the only thing on deck that had not been swept overboard
when the gale first took us. As we approached the brink of the pit
he let go his hold upon this, and made for the ring, from which,
in the agony of his terror, he endeavored to force my hands, as it
was not large enough to afford us both a secure grasp. I never
felt deeper grief than when I saw him attempt this act—although
I thought he was a madman when he did it—a raving maniac
through sheer fright. I did not care, however, to contest the point
with him. I knew it could make no difference whether either of us
held on at all; so I let him have the bolt, and went astern to the
cask. This there was no great difficulty in doing; for the smack
flew round steadily enough, and upon an even keel—only swaying to and fro, with the immense sweeps and swelters of the whirl.
Scarcely had I secured myself in my new position, when we gave a
wild lurch to starboard, and rushed headlong into the abyss. I muttered a hurried prayer to God, and thought all was over.

"As I felt the sickening sweep of the descent, I had instinctively
tightened my hold upon the barrel, and closed my eyes. For some
seconds I dared not open them—while I expected instant destruction, and wondered that I was not already in my death-struggles
with the water. But moment after moment elapsed. I still lived.
The sense of falling had ceased; and the motion of the vessel
seemed much as it had been before while in the belt of foam, with
the exception that she now lay more along. I took courage, and
looked once again upon the scene.

"Never shall I forget the sensations of awe, horror, and admiration with which I gazed about me. The boat appeared to be hanging, as if by magic, midway down, upon the interior surface of a
funnel vast in circumference, prodigious in depth, and whose perfectly smooth sides might have been mistaken for ebony, but for
the bewildering rapidity with which they spun around, and for the
gleaming and ghastly radiance they shot forth, as the rays of the
full moon, from that circular rift amid the clouds which I have
already described, streamed in a flood of golden glory along the
black walls, and far away down into the inmost recesses of the
abyss.[46]

"At first I was too much confused to observe anything accurately. The general burst of terrific grandeur was all that I beheld. When I recovered myself a little, however, my gaze fell instinctively downward. In this direction I was able to obtain an unobstructed view, from the manner in which the smack hung on the inclined surface of the pool. She was quite upon an even keel—that is to say, her deck lay in a plane parallel with that of the water—but this latter sloped at an angle of more than forty-five degrees, so that we seemed to be lying upon our beam-ends. I could not help observing, nevertheless, that I had scarcely more difficulty in maintaining my hold and footing in this situation, than if we had been upon a dead level; and this, I suppose, was owing to the speed at which we revolved.

"The rays of the moon seemed to search the very bottom of the profound gulf; but still I could make out nothing distinctly, on account of a thick mist in which everything there was enveloped, and over which there hung a magnificent rainbow, like that narrow and tottering bridge which Mussulmen say is the only pathway between Time and Eternity.[47] This mist, or spray, was no doubt occasioned by the clashing of the great walls of the funnel, as they all met together at the bottom—but the yell that went up to the Heavens from out of that mist, I dare not attempt to describe.

"Our first slide into the abyss itself, from the belt of foam above, had carried us a great distance down the slope; but our farther descent was by no means proportionate. Round and round we swept—not with any uniform movement—but in dizzying swings and jerks, that sent us sometimes only a few hundred feet—sometimes nearly the complete circuit of the whirl. Our progress downward, at each revolution, was slow, but very perceptible.

"Looking about me upon the wide waste of liquid ebony on which we were thus borne, I perceived that our boat was not the only object in the embrace of the whirl. Both above and below us were visible fragments of vessels, large masses of building timber and trunks of trees, with many smaller articles, such as pieces of house furniture, broken boxes, barrels and staves.[48] I have already described the unnatural curiosity which had taken the place of my original terrors. It appeared to grow upon me as I drew nearer and nearer to my dreadful doom. I now began to watch, with a strange interest, the numerous things that floated in our company. I *must* have been delirious—for I even sought *amusement* in speculating

47   In his introduction to the *The Koran*, George Sale explains: "The Mohammedans hold, that those who are to be admitted into paradise will take the right hand way, and those who are destined to hell-fire will take the left, but both of them must first pass the bridge, called in Arabic, al Sirât, which they say is laid over the midst of hell, and describe to be finer than a hair, and sharper than the edge of a sword" (*The Koran*, 2 vols. [Philadelphia: Thomas Wardle, 1833], I, 102).

48   The inside narrator's behavior within the Maelstrom echoes both "The Philosophy of Furniture" and "The Man of the Crowd." Much like the urban observer strolling the streets of the modern city—the flaneur—the narrator observes house furniture and other objects of the material culture, contemplates their meaning, and makes conclusions regarding their significance (Kevin J. Hayes, "The Flaneur in the Parlor: Poe's 'Philosophy of Furniture,'" *Prospects* 27 [2002], 103–119).

49 "See Archimedes, *De Incidentibus in Fluido.*—lib. 2 [Poe's note]." Poe added this note when he revised "A Descent into the Maelström" for *Tales* (1845). Archimedes's two-book study of hydrodynamics is actually titled *De insidentibus aquae*, the second book of which is titled *De insidentibus in humido*. Poe follows a common error, mistranscribing the word "fluido" for "humido." The first book offers propositions pertaining to bodies floating on liquids, or sinking or rising in them. The second book posits several propositions designed to ascertain the position of different bodies within a whirlpool. Speaking as one "Walter G. Bowen" in "A Reviewer Reviewed," a self-parody he left unpublished at the end of his life, Poe accuses himself of making up this detail and asserts that there is no such passage in Archimedes.

50 The ingenuity of the narrator's solution—his decision to leap overboard while lashed to a cylindrical cask—suggests that the story may also be read as a parable about one of Poe's key aesthetic concepts: originality. In an unsigned review of his own *Tales* that appeared in the October 1845 issue of the *Aristidean*, Poe declares: "The great fault of American and British authors is imitation of the peculiarities of thought and diction of those who have gone before them. . . . To produce something which has not been produced before, in their estimation, is equal to six, at least, of the seven deadly sins—perhaps, the unpardonable sin itself—and for this crime they think the author should atone here in the purgatory of false criticism, and hereafter by the hell of oblivion." It is imitation that is the real crime. Poe holds himself up as an exemplar of originality: "The evident and most prominent aim of Mr. POE is originality, either of idea, or the combination of ideas. . . . Most writers get their subjects first, and write to develop it. The first inquiry of Mr. POE is for a novel effect—then for a subject; that is, a new arrangement of circumstance, or a new application of tone, by which the effect shall be developed. And he evidently holds whatever tends to the furtherance of the effect, to be legitimate material. Thus it is that he has produced works of the most notable character, and elevated the mere 'tale,' in this country, over the larger 'novel'—conventionally so termed."

upon the relative velocities of their several descents toward the foam below. 'This fir tree,' I found myself at one time saying, 'will certainly be the next thing that takes the awful plunge and disappears,'—and then I was disappointed to find that the wreck of a Dutch merchant ship overtook it and went down before. At length, after making several guesses of this nature, and being deceived in all—this fact—the fact of my invariable miscalculation—set me upon a train of reflection that made my limbs again tremble, and my heart beat heavily once more.

"It was not a new terror that thus affected me, but the dawn of a more exciting *hope*. This hope arose partly from memory, and partly from present observation. I called to mind the great variety of buoyant matter that strewed the coast of Lofoden, having been absorbed and then thrown forth by the Moskoe-ström. By far the greater number of the articles were shattered in the most extraordinary way—so chafed and roughened as to have the appearance of being stuck full of splinters—but then I distinctly recollected that there were *some* of them which were not disfigured at all. Now I could not account for this difference except by supposing that the roughened fragments were the only ones which had been *completely absorbed*—that the others had entered the whirl at so late a period of the tide, or, for some reason, had descended so slowly after entering, that they did not reach the bottom before the turn of the flood came, or of the ebb, as the case might be. I conceived it possible, in either instance, that they might thus be whirled up again to the level of the ocean, without undergoing the fate of those which had been drawn in more early, or absorbed more rapidly. I made, also, three important observations. The first was, that, as a general rule, the larger the bodies were, the more rapid their descent;—the second, that, between two masses of equal extent, the one spherical, and the other *of any other shape*, the superiority in speed of descent was with the sphere;—the third, that, between two masses of equal size, the one cylindrical, and the other of any other shape, the cylinder was absorbed the more slowly. Since my escape, I have had several conversations on this subject with an old school-master of the district; and it was from him that I learned the use of the words 'cylinder' and 'sphere.' He explained to me—although I have forgotten the explanation—how what I observed was, in fact, the natural consequence of the forms of the floating fragments—and showed me how it happened that a cylinder, swimming in a vortex, offered more resistance to its suction, and was drawn in with greater difficulty than an equally bulky body, of any form whatever.[49]

"There was one startling circumstance which went a great way in enforcing these observations, and rendering me anxious to turn them to account, and this was that, at every revolution, we passed something like a barrel, or else the broken yard or the mast of a vessel, while many of these things, which had been on our level when I first opened my eyes upon the wonders of the whirlpool, were now high up above us, and seemed to have moved but little from their original station.

"I no longer hesitated what to do. I resolved to lash myself securely to the water cask upon which I now held, to cut it loose from the counter, and to throw myself with it into the water. I attracted my brother's attention by signs, pointed to the floating barrels that came near us, and did everything in my power to make him understand what I was about to do. I thought at length that he comprehended my design—but, whether this was the case or not, he shook his head despairingly, and refused to move from his station by the ring-bolt. It was impossible to force him; the emergency admitted no delay; and so, with a bitter struggle, I resigned him to his fate, fastened myself to the cask by means of the lashings which secured it to the counter, and precipitated myself with it into the sea, without another moment's hesitation.[50]

"The result was precisely what I had hoped it might be. As it is myself who now tells you this tale—as you see that I *did* escape—and as you are already in possession of the mode in which this escape was effected, and must therefore anticipate all that I have farther to say—I will bring my story quickly to conclusion.[51] It might have been an hour, or thereabout, after my quitting the smack, when, having descended to a vast distance beneath me, it made three or four wild gyrations in rapid succession, and, bearing my loved brother with it, plunged headlong, at once and forever, into the chaos of foam[52] below. The cask to which I was attached sank very little farther than half the distance between the bottom of the gulf and the spot at which I leaped overboard, before a great change took place in the character of the whirlpool. The slope of the sides of the vast funnel became momently less and less steep. The gyrations of the whirl grew, gradually, less and less violent. By degrees, the froth and the rainbow disappeared, and the bottom

51 The Canadian communications theorist Marshall McLuhan (1911–1980) finds in the tale's memorable imagery a useful metaphor for coping with the onslaught of information in the age of modern media: "It's inevitable that the world-pool of electronic information movement will toss us all about like corks on a stormy sea, but if we keep our cool during the descent into the maelstrom, studying the process as it happens to us and what we can do about it, we can come through." Elsewhere, he says, "A whirling phantasmagoria can be grasped only when arrested for contemplation. And this very arrest is also a release from the usual participation" (Eric Norden, "The Playboy Interview: Marshall McLuhan," *Playboy* [March 1969], 158; Marshall McLuhan, *The Mechanical Bride: Folklore of Industrial Man* [Boston: Beacon, 1968], v).

52 Percy Bysshe Shelley coined the phrase "a chaos of foam." See *History of a Six Weeks' Tour through a Part of France, Switzerland, Germany and Holland with Letters Descriptive of a Sail Round the Lake of Geneva, and of the Glaciers of Chamouni* (London: T. Hookham, Jr., 1817), 120.

Marcel Roux, woodcut from *Une descente dans le maelstrom,* illustrating the mariner once he has fastened himself to a water cask and jumped into the maelstrom.

of the gulf seemed slowly to uprise. The sky was clear, the winds had gone down, and the full moon was setting radiantly in the west, when I found myself on the surface of the ocean, in full view of the shores of Lofoden, and above the spot where the pool of the Moskoe-ström *had been*. It was the hour of the slack—but the sea still heaved in mountainous waves from the effects of the hurricane. I was borne violently into the channel of the Ström, and in a few minutes was hurried down the coast into the 'grounds' of the fishermen. A boat picked me up—exhausted from fatigue—and (now that the danger was removed) speechless from the memory of its horror. Those who drew me on board were my old mates and daily companions—but they knew me no more than they would have known a traveller from the spirit-land. My hair which had been raven-black the day before, was as white as you see it now. They say too that the whole expression of my countenance had changed. I told them my story. They did not believe it. I now tell it to *you*—and I can scarcely expect you to put more faith in it than did the merry fishermen of Lofoden."[53]

53 One New York editor found this tale "so full of improbabilities that we can fully appreciate the sageness of the sentence with which it closes—that 'you will put no more faith in it than did the merry fishermen of Lofoden'" (*New-York Spectator,* April 28, 1841). Poe's good friend Joseph Evans Snodgrass, on the other hand, enjoyed the story very much and wrote to compliment Poe. Poe replied with a self-effacing letter: "You flatter me about the Maelström. It was finished in a hurry, and therefore its conclusion is imperfect. Upon the whole it is neither so good, nor has it been ½ so popular as 'The Murders in the Rue Morgue'" (*Collected Letters of Edgar Allan Poe,* ed. John Ward Ostrom, Burton R. Pollin, and Jeffrey A. Savoye, 2 vols. [New York: Gordian Press, 2008], I, 297).

The Oval Portrait

"The Oval Portrait," or "Life in Death," as it was first called, appeared in the April 1842 issue of Graham's along with Poe's short laudatory review of Hawthorne's Twice-Told Tales (a much longer, equally laudatory review by Poe would appear in the next issue). The similarities between Poe's "The Oval Portrait" and Hawthorne's "The Birthmark" (1843)— both concern ambitious, creative men who with tragic consequences attempt to perfect the women they love—have suggested to some critics that Hawthorne was influenced by Poe's earlier tale. It's equally likely that "The Birthmark" inspired the extensive revisions Poe would make when he republished "The Oval Portrait" in 1845, in which case the influence ran in two directions. Besides changing the title of his tale, Poe would cut more than six hundred words, sharpening and perfecting the tale while generally making it less literal. One of the most significant cuts was the elimination of a lengthy introductory paragraph, in which the narrator details his consumption of opium, which had created in the reader's mind the idea that the tale might be explained, or explained away, as a drug-addled hallucination.

"The Oval Portrait" has resonated strongly with modern filmmakers. Toward the end of Jean-Luc Godard's Vivre sa vie (My Life to Live, 1962), close-up shots of the Young Man reading from Charles Baudelaire's translation of Poe's tale are intercut with close-ups of Nana, who is played by Anna Karina, Godard's wife. The voice that reads the text aloud is not the actor's but the director's. At one point, Godard interrupts the written text to call Poe's tale "our story . . . a painter portraying his love." As an artist, Godard, too, attempts to capture his wife's beauty in a lasting work of art. The Argentinian filmmaker Edgardo Cozarinsky went Godard one better in his appreciation. Speaking about his documentary film One Man's War (1982), which uses freeze frames to capture faces of people who would fall victim to the Holocaust, Cozarinsky mentions his desire to "rescue the faces of these people and preserve them." Asked if cinema generally reflects this impulse, Cozarinsky said, "For me its best expression is to be found in 'The Oval Portrait,' the Poe story. In a sense that is the most extraordinary thing ever to be written about the cinema" ("Discourse and History: One Man's War—An Interview with Edgardo Cozarinsky," in Thomas Elsaesser, European Cinema: Face to Face with Hollywood [Amsterdam: Amsterdam University Press, 2005], 404).

The chateau into which my valet had ventured to make forcible entrance, rather than permit me, in my desperately wounded condition, to pass a night in the open air, was one of those piles of commingled gloom and grandeur which have so long frowned among the Appenines, not less in fact than in the fancy of Mrs. Radcliffe.[1] To all appearance it had been temporarily and very lately abandoned. We established ourselves in one of the smallest and least sumptuously furnished apartments. It lay in a remote turret of the building. Its decorations were rich, yet tattered and antique. Its walls were hung with tapestry and bedecked with manifold and multiform armorial trophies, together with an unusually great number of very spirited modern paintings in frames of rich golden arabesque. In these paintings, which depended from the walls not only in their main surfaces, but in very many nooks which the bizarre architecture of the chateau rendered necessary—in these paintings my incipient delirium, perhaps, had caused me to take deep interest; so that I bade Pedro to close the heavy shutters of the room—since it was already night—to light the tongues of a tall candelabrum which stood by the head of my bed—and to throw open far and wide the fringed curtains of black velvet which enveloped the bed itself.[2] I wished all this done that I might resign myself, if not to sleep, at least alternately to the contemplation of these pictures, and the perusal of a small volume which had been found upon the pillow, and which purported to criticise and describe them.

Long—long I read—and devoutly, devotedly I gazed.[3] Rapidly and gloriously the hours flew by, and the deep midnight came. The position of the candelabrum displeased me, and outreaching

1   The Apennines, a rugged mountain range running the length of peninsular Italy, was a popular tourist destination. The British novelist Ann Radcliffe (1764–1824) published a series of popular Gothic romances in the 1790s, including The Mysteries of Udolpho (1794), which is set in a remote and moldering castle in the Apennines. Radcliffe's

novels inspired numerous, lesser imitations, replete with castles, mountainous landscapes, fainting heroines, and villainous characters. Poe's tale is itself a parade of Gothic clichés—though put to far different purposes than the fictions of Radcliffe's imitators—and announces itself as such by invoking the name of the writer most closely associated with the Gothic craze.

2   Poe closely parallels narrator and reader. Mary Ann Caws explains: "The reader's gaze is trained in the same way as that of the narrator, within a range progressively narrower, moving in from dark corridors to dark room to dark-curtained bed, the latter providing an imaginatively suggestive, if gloomy, position from which to contemplate the portrait of the young bride upon the wall" ("Insertion in an Oval Frame: Poe Circumscribed by Baudelaire," *French Review* 56 [1983], 680).

3   As in "The Man of the Crowd," where the narrator gazes back and forth from his newspaper to the crowd outside the coffeehouse window, Poe parallels the acts of reading and looking. In "Prophetic Principle," another tale in *Twice-Told Tales*, Hawthorne tells the parable of a painter endowed with magical powers. Here, too, Hawthorne connects the activities of reading and looking, and suggests the inherent danger of close scrutiny: "It is not good for man to cherish a solitary ambition. Unless there be those around him by whose example he may regulate himself, his thoughts, desires, and hopes will become extravagant, and he the semblance, perhaps the reality, of a madman. Reading other bosoms with an acuteness almost preternatural, the painter failed to see the disorder of his own" (*Tales and Sketches*, ed. Roy Harvey Pearce [New York: Library of America, 1982], 467).

4   The theme of distorted perception, especially the distortion of the sense of sight, runs through Poe's work. The effort to see through the distortions—to see "aright," as Poe phrases it in the following paragraph—is a frequent activity of his narrators.

5   The narrator never says what, exactly, startles him about the expression of the portrait. In the longer, earlier version of the tale, Poe refers to "the sad meaning smile of the half-parted lips" and "the too real luster of the wild eye." Left unstated, the possibilities play more freely in the reader's imagination. Did the bride smile, did her eyes move?

The Young Man (Peter Kassovitz) reads "The Oval Portrait" in the film *Vivre sa vie (My Life to Live)*, 1962.

my hand with difficulty, rather than disturb my slumbering valet, I placed it so as to throw its rays more fully upon the book.

But the action produced an effect altogether unanticipated.[4] The rays of the numerous candles (for there were many) now fell within a niche of the room which had hitherto been thrown into deep shade by one of the bed-posts. I thus saw in vivid light a picture all unnoticed before. It was the portrait of a young girl just ripening into womanhood. I glanced at the painting hurriedly, and then closed my eyes. Why I did this was not at first apparent even to my own perception. But while my lids remained thus shut, I ran over in my mind my reason for so shutting them. It was an impulsive movement to gain time for thought—to make sure that my vision had not deceived me—to calm and subdue my fancy for a more sober and more certain gaze. In a very few moments I again looked fixedly at the painting.

That I now saw aright I could not and would not doubt; for the first flashing of the candles upon that canvass had seemed to dissipate the dreamy stupor which was stealing over my senses, and to startle me at once into waking life.[5]

The portrait, I have already said, was that of a young girl. It was a mere head and shoulders, done in what is technically termed a *vignette*[6] manner; much in the style of the favorite heads of Sully.

Nana (Anna Karina) listening as Luigi reads Poe in *Vivre sa vie*.

6   A vignette is "any embellishment, illustration, or picture uninclosed in a border, or having the edges shading off into the surrounding paper" *(OED)*.

7   Moorish in style or ornamental design.

8   Though the narrator quickly discounts the painting as a "thing of art," Poe does not necessarily expect readers to discount it so quickly. In his review of Hawthorne's *Twice-Told Tales*, Poe writes: "Of Mr. Hawthorne's Tales we would say, emphatically, that they belong to the highest region of Art—an Art subservient to genius of a very lofty order. We had supposed, with good reason for so supposing, that he had been thrust into his present position by one of the impudent *cliques* which beset our literature, and whose pretensions it is our full purpose to expose at the earliest opportunity; but we have been most agreeably mistaken. We Know of few compositions which the critic can more honestly commend than these 'Twice-Told Tales.' As Americans, we feel proud of the book."

9   In light of the fate of the artist's young wife, this sentence is heavily ironic.

10   Poe creates a situation in which the reader looks over the narrator's shoulder as he reads from the guidebook, both of them trying to find within its pages some explanation for the narrator's unusual response to the painting (Emma Kafalenos, "Effects of Sequence, Embedding, and Ekphrasis in Poe's 'The Oval Portrait,'" *A Companion to Narrative Theory*, ed. James Phelan and Peter J. Rabinowitz [Malden, MA: Blackwell, 2005], 261).

The arms, the bosom and even the ends of the radiant hair, melted imperceptibly into the vague yet deep shadow which formed the back ground of the whole. The frame was oval, richly gilded and filagreed in *Moresque*.[7] As a thing of art[8] nothing could be more admirable than the painting itself. But it could have been neither the execution of the work, nor the immortal beauty of the countenance, which had so suddenly and so vehemently moved me. Least of all, could it have been that my fancy, shaken from its half slumber, had mistaken the head for that of a living person.[9] I saw at once that the peculiarities of the design, of the *vignetting*, and of the frame, must have instantly dispelled such idea—must have prevented even its momentary entertainment. Thinking earnestly upon these points, I remained, for an hour perhaps, half sitting, half reclining, with my vision riveted upon the portrait. At length, satisfied with the true secret of its effect, I fell back within the bed. I had found the spell of the picture in an absolute *life-likeliness* of expression, which, at first startling, finally confounded, subdued and appalled me. With deep and reverent awe I replaced the candelabrum in its former position. The cause of my deep agitation being thus shut from view, I sought eagerly the volume which discussed the paintings and their histories. Turning to the number which designated the oval portrait, I there read the vague and quaint words which follow:[10]

11   In mid January 1842, a few months before the publication of "Life in Death," Virginia Poe ruptured a blood vessel while singing and remained dangerously ill for weeks. The hemorrhaging was a tell-tale sign of consumption (tuberculosis), the illness that would eventually claim her life in 1847. Kenneth Silverman notes that consumption, a wasting disease, was commonly called "death-in-life." In a letter of February 4, 1842, Poe apologized to a friend for neglecting his correspondence: "My dear little wife has been dangerously ill. About a fortnight since, in singing, she ruptured a blood-vessel, and it was only on yesterday that the physicians gave me any hope of her recovery. You might imagine the agony I have suffered, for you know how devotedly I love her. But to-day the prospect brightens, and I trust that this cup of misery will not be my portion (*Collected Letters of Edgar Allan Poe*, ed. John Ward Ostrom, Burton R. Pollin, and Jeffrey A. Savoye, 2 vols. [New York: Gordian Press, 2008], I, 324).

12   Mabbott observes that the tale's "central idea is the very ancient one that the spirit may take up residence in a facsimile. This was doctrinal to the Ancient Egyptians, who made statues for the *ka* (what modern Occultists call the astral body), and to modern primitive people who are afraid of photography." Similarly, Patrick Quinn has argued that the life force, drained from the artist's young wife, does not dissipate but is *transferred* to the painting: The "quantity of life" must remain constant. See Thomas Ollive Mabbott, ed., *Collected Works of Edgar Allan Poe*, 3 vols. (Cambridge, MA: The Belknap Press of Harvard University Press, 1969-1978), II, 660-661.

13   In "Metzengerstein," Poe portrays the artist's devotion to his work as a kind of suicide. Here, in another allegory about the vexed relationship between life and art, Poe depicts the artist not as a suicide but as a murderer. In "Life in Death," the much longer, earlier version of this tale, Poe concludes with this further, unnecessary sentence: "The painter then added—'But is this indeed Death?'" The idea that a great work of art may outlive its subject is of course an ancient one, as Daniel Hoffman observes, "but Poe makes the artist a cannibal or vampire whose subject *must die* so that there may be art" (*Poe Poe Poe Poe Poe Poe Poe* [Garden City, NY: Doubleday, 1972], 310–311).

"She was a maiden of rarest beauty, and not more lovely than full of glee. And evil was the hour when she saw, and loved, and wedded the painter. He, passionate, studious, austere, and having already a bride in his Art; she a maiden of rarest beauty, and not more lovely than full of glee: all light and smiles, and frolicsome as the young fawn: loving and cherishing all things: hating only the Art which was her rival: dreading only the pallet and brushes and other untoward instruments which deprived her of the countenance of her lover. It was thus a terrible thing for this lady to hear the painter speak of his desire to portray even his young bride. But she was humble and obedient, and sat meekly for many weeks in the dark high turret-chamber where the light dripped upon the pale canvass only from overhead. But he, the painter, took glory in his work, which went on from hour to hour, and from day to day. And he was a passionate, and wild, and moody man, who became lost in reveries; so that he *would* not see that the light which fell so ghastlily in that lone turret withered the health and the spirits of his bride, who pined visibly to all but him.[11] Yet she smiled on and still on, uncomplainingly, because she saw that the painter, (who had high renown,) took a fervid and burning pleasure in his task, and wrought day and night to depict her who so loved him, yet who grew daily more dispirited and weak. And in sooth some who beheld the portrait spoke of its resemblance in low words, as of a mighty marvel, and a proof not less of the power of the painter than of his deep love for her whom he depicted so surpassingly well. But at length, as the labor drew nearer to its conclusion, there were admitted none into the turret; for the painter had grown wild with the ardor of his work, and turned his eyes from the canvass rarely, even to regard the countenance of his wife. And he *would* not see that the tints which he spread upon the canvass were drawn from the cheeks of her who sat beside him.[12] And when many weeks had passed, and but little remained to do, save one brush upon the mouth and one tint upon the eye, the spirit of the lady again flickered up as the flame within the socket of the lamp. And then the brush was given, and then the tint was placed; and, for one moment, the painter stood entranced before the work which he had wrought; but in the next, while he yet gazed, he grew tremulous and very pallid, and aghast, and crying with a loud voice, 'This is indeed *Life* itself!' turned suddenly to regard his beloved:—*She was dead!*"[13]

The Masque of the Red Death

The "Red Death" had long devastated the country.[1] No pestilence had ever been so fatal, or so hideous. Blood was its Avatar[2] and its seal—the redness and the horror of blood. There were sharp pains, and sudden dizziness, and then profuse bleeding at the pores, with dissolution. The scarlet stains upon the body and especially upon the face of the victim, were the pest ban which shut him out from the aid and from the sympathy of his fellow-men. And the whole seizure, progress and termination of the disease, were the incidents of half an hour.

But the Prince Prospero[3] was happy and dauntless and sagacious. When his dominions were half depopulated, he summoned to his presence a thousand hale and light-hearted friends from among the knights and dames of his court, and with these retired to the deep seclusion of one of his castellated abbeys.[4] This was an extensive and magnificent structure, the creation of the prince's own eccentric yet august taste. A strong and lofty wall girdled it in. This wall had gates of iron. The courtiers, having entered, brought furnaces and massy hammers[5] and welded the bolts. They resolved to leave means neither of ingress or egress to the sudden impulses of despair or of frenzy from within. The abbey was amply provisioned. With such precautions the courtiers might bid defiance to contagion. The external world could take care of itself. In the meantime it was folly to grieve, or to think. The prince had provided all the appliances of pleasure. There were buffoons, there were improvisatori,[6] there were ballet-dancers, there were musicians, there was Beauty, there was wine. All these and security were within. Without was the "Red Death."

In Tom Wolfe's society novel, The Bonfire of the Vanities (1987), Lord Buffing pontificates on "The Masque of the Red Death" at a swank Manhattan cocktail party. Buffing asserts that Poe "wrote a story that tells all we need to know about the moment we live in now," meaning that the end of Poe's tale foreshadows the disastrous end of New York's wealthy elite toward the close of the twentieth century (The Bonfire of the Vanities [1987; New York: Picador, 2002], 367). Poe's tale is an indictment of the social elite of his own day, when masquerade balls were fashionable. Mabbott identifies a historical antecedent for the imaginary Red Death: the 1832 cholera epidemic that struck Paris especially hard. Many in the city, convinced they would die soon, chose to live as merrily, or recklessly, as possible, hosting and attending masquerade balls. In The American Plague (2006), Molly Caldwell Crosby identifies a different historical precedent, suggesting that the Red Death symbolizes the yellow fever epidemics that struck the United States from the late eighteenth to the mid-nineteenth century. Bleeding from the mouth, nose, and eyes was a symptom of the often fatal disease, caused by a virus spread through mosquito bites. Poe published the story in 1842 as "The Mask of the Red Death." He changed the title to "The Masque of the Red Death" when he republished it three years later. Slight as it is, the change turns the title into a double entendre, inviting us to see Prince Prospero's great fête not only as a masquerade but also as a masque, a short, lavish dramatic entertainment typically performed at court, incorporating music, dance, and visual spectacle. A Renaissance form, the masque is always allegorical in its import, its emblematic characters appealing directly to the audience for its intervention or judgment. The revision shifts the emphasis from the deadly intruder to the revelers themselves—and the reader.

1   The term "red death" usually refers to violent death on the battlefield. *The Meeting of Gallants at an Ordinarie* (1604), an anonymous work possibly by the English dramatist and pamphleteer Thomas Dekker (1572–1632), presents a dialogue between three personified figures: Warre, Famine, and Pestilence. Pestilence emphasizes its own power over Warre, whose "red death" is no match for the plague. Though Poe uses "Red Death" in a different sense, associating it with the Black Death—the fourteenth-century plague that devastated Europe—the figure of Pestilence in this Elizabethan dialogue, reprinted in 1841, may have influenced him.

2   In Hindu myth, an Avatar is a deity that descends to earth in an incarnate form. The word "avatar" was introduced to English in the late eighteenth century. As its

B. Smith after George Romney, "Shakespeare, *Tempest*, Act 1, Scene 1," 1797.

meaning became more general, it could refer to any idea or thing that manifested itself in human or other physical form.

3   Prince Prospero, Mabbott notes, "like his namesake in *The Tempest*, fled from the world, but ironically Poe's Prince ceased to prosper" (Thomas Ollive Mabbott, ed., *Collected Works of Edgar Allan Poe*, 3 vols. [Cambridge, MA: The Belknap Press of Harvard University Press, 1969–1978], II, 677).

4   The situation recalls Boccaccio's *Decameron*, in which several men and women flee the Black Plague in Florence to take refuge in a secluded villa near Fiesole, where they spend their afternoons telling stories. The Russian philosopher and literary theorist M. M. Bakhtin (1895–1975) argues that at the heart of Poe's tale lies a "Boccaccian matrix": "the *plague* (death, the grave)—a *holiday* (gaiety, laughter, wine, eroticism)." Whereas Boccaccio softens the contrast between these two plot elements in what is ultimately a grand celebration of life, Poe allows the contrast to remain stark, and the matrix is therefore "oriented toward death" (*The Dialogic Imagination: Four Essays*, ed. and trans. Caryl Emerson and Michael Holquist [Austin: University of Texas Press, 1981], 200).

5   "Massy" is a variation of the word "massive." The phrase "massy hammers" comes from Erasmus Darwin's *Botanic Garden* (1791): "Hard dies of steel the cupreous circles cramp, / And with quick fall his massy hammers stamp."

6   Poe's contemporary Peter Parley defines improvisatori as "poets who compose and recite, with great rapidity and beauty, verses on any subject given to them" (*Tales about Rome and Modern Italy* [London: Thomas Tegg, 1839], 350).

It was toward the close of the fifth or sixth month of his seclusion, and while the pestilence raged most furiously abroad, that the Prince Prospero entertained his thousand friends at a masked ball of the most unusual magnificence.

It was a voluptuous scene, that masquerade. But first let me tell of the rooms in which it was held.[7] There were seven—an imperial suite.[8] In many palaces, however, such suites form a long and straight vista, while the folding doors slide back nearly to the walls on either hand, so that the view of the whole extent is scarcely impeded. Here the case was very different; as might have been expected from the duke's love of the *bizarre*. The apartments were so irregularly disposed that the vision embraced but little more than one at a time. There was a sharp turn at every twenty or thirty yards, and at each turn a novel effect. To the right and left, in the middle of each wall, a tall and narrow Gothic window looked out upon a closed corridor which pursued the windings of the suite. These windows were of stained glass whose color varied in accordance with the prevailing hue of the decorations of the chamber into which it opened. That at the eastern extremity was hung, for example in blue—and vividly blue were its windows. The second chamber was purple in its ornaments and tapestries, and here the panes were purple. The third was green throughout, and so were the casements. The fourth was furnished and lighted with orange—the fifth with white—the sixth with violet. The seventh apartment was closely shrouded in black velvet tapestries that hung all over the ceiling and down the walls, falling in heavy folds upon a carpet of the same material and hue. But in this chamber only, the color of the windows failed to correspond with the decorations. The panes here were scarlet—a deep blood color.[9] Now in no one of the seven apartments was there any lamp or candelabrum, amid the profusion of golden ornaments that lay scattered to and fro or depended from the roof. There was no light of any kind emanating from lamp or candle within the suite of chambers. But in the corridors that followed the suite, there stood, opposite to each window, a heavy tripod, bearing a brazier of fire that projected its rays through the tinted glass and so glaringly illumined the room. And thus were produced a multitude of gaudy and fantastic appearances. But in the western or black chamber the effect of the fire-light that streamed upon the dark hangings through

7 This sentence exemplifies Poe's use of what critical theorists call the "dramatized author," that is, a narrator that does not function as a character in a story but instead hovers over the tale and becomes visible through the narration. Poe's narrator becomes visible in this instance through the use of a first-person pronoun, "me" (Luc Herman and Bart Vervaeck, *Handbook of Narrative Analysis* [Lincoln: University of Nebraska Press, 2005], 18–19).

8 The number seven traditionally symbolizes completeness or perfection—and thus Poe uses it ironically. Seven sacraments, seven pillars of wisdom, seven deadly sins, seven ages of man: all deserve consideration in relation to the story's symbolism.

9 Creating a sequence of colors that resembles yet deviates from the visible spectrum, Poe teasingly invites speculation. In any case, the motley-colored suite of rooms offers numerous possible interpretations, and critics have been happy to supply them.

10   Robert Louis Stevenson admired Poe's use of the ebony clock to create tension: "Each time the clock struck
(the reader will remember), it struck so loudly that the music and the dancing must cease perforce until it had made
an end; as the hours ran on towards midnight, these pauses
grew naturally longer; the maskers had the more time to
think and look at one another, and their thoughts were
none the more pleasant. Thus, as each hour struck, there
went a jar about the assemblage; until, as the reader will
remember, the end comes suddenly. Now, this is quite legitimate; no one need be ashamed of being frightened or
excited by such means; the rules of the game have been
respected; only, by the true instinct of the story-teller he
has told his story to the best advantage, and got full value
for his imaginations" ("Literature," *Academy*, January 2,
1875, 1).

11   Beauty (Latin).

12   *Hernani* (1830), Victor Hugo's early verse play involving intrigue, romance, and suicide in the sixteenth-century
Spanish court, premiered at the Comédie Française on
February 25, 1830. The drama sparked a heated literary
war—and sometimes physical fights inside the theater during its initial run—between its young Romantic advocates
and defenders of neoclassical principles offended by the
play's expression of Romantic sentiments and mixing of in-
compatible elements (such as comedy and tragedy, the grotesque and the sublime).

the blood-tinted panes, was ghastly in the extreme, and produced
so wild a look upon the countenances of those who entered, that
there were few of the company bold enough to set foot within its
precincts at all.

It was in this apartment, also, that there stood against the western wall, a gigantic clock of ebony. Its pendulum swung to and fro
with a dull, heavy, monotonous clang; and when the minute-hand
made the circuit of the face, and the hour was to be stricken, there
came from the brazen lungs of the clock a sound which was clear
and loud and deep and exceedingly musical, but of so peculiar a
note and emphasis that, at each lapse of an hour, the musicians of
the orchestra were constrained to pause, momentarily, in their performance, to harken to the sound; and thus the waltzers perforce
ceased their evolutions; and there was a brief disconcert of the
whole gay company; and, while the chimes of the clock yet rang, it
was observed that the giddiest grew pale, and the more aged and
sedate passed their hands over their brows as if in confused revery
or meditation. But when the echoes had fully ceased, a light laughter at once pervaded the assembly; the musicians looked at each
other and smiled as if at their own nervousness and folly, and made
whispering vows, each to the other, that the next chiming of the
clock should produce in them no similar emotion; and then, after
the lapse of sixty minutes, (which embrace three thousand and six
hundred seconds of the Time that flies,) there came yet another
chiming of the clock, and then were the same disconcert and trem-
ulousness and meditation as before.[10]

But, in spite of these things, it was a gay and magnificent revel.
The tastes of the duke were peculiar. He had a fine eye for colors
and effects. He disregarded the *decora*[11] of mere fashion. His plans
were bold and fiery, and his conceptions glowed with barbaric lustre. There are some who would have thought him mad. His followers felt that he was not. It was necessary to hear and see and
touch him to be *sure* that he was not.

He had directed, in great part, the moveable embellishments of
the seven chambers, upon occasion of this great fête; and it was his
own guiding taste which had given character to the masqueraders.
Be sure they were grotesque. There were much glare and glitter
and piquancy and phantasm—much of what has been since seen
in *Hernani*.[12] There were arabesque figures with unsuited limbs
and appointments. There were delirious fancies such as the mad-

man fashions. There were much of the beautiful, much of the wanton, much of the *bizarre*, something of the terrible, and not a little of that which might have excited disgust. To and fro in the seven chambers there stalked, in fact, a multitude of dreams. And these—the dreams—writhed in and about, taking hue from the rooms, and causing the wild music of the orchestra to seem as the echo of their steps. And, anon, there strikes the ebony clock which stands in the hall of the velvet. And then, for a moment, all is still, and all is silent save the voice of the clock. The dreams are stiff-frozen as they stand. But the echoes of the chime die away —they have endured but an instant—and a light, half-subdued laughter floats after them as they depart. And now again the music swells, and the dreams live, and writhe to and fro more merrily than ever, taking hue from the many tinted windows through

Charles Demuth, *Illustration for Poe's Masque of Red Death*, 1918. Demuth (1883–1935) was an American watercolorist whose works captured the bohemian, avant-garde lifestyle he followed. In addition to Poe, he illustrated the work of Henry James and Emile Zola, among others.

13   In his landmark essay "Chiastic Structures in Literature: Some Forms and Functions," Swiss critic Max Nänny
(1932–2006) calls attention to the way Poe uses syntax
to achieve psychological and aesthetic effects. More particularly, he cites Poe's use of chiastic structure—a "crossing," or parallel inversion, of the order of words—in this
and the preceding six sentences to render "the to and fro
movement of the dancing dreams in the *seven* chambers of
Prince Prospero's abbey . . . [and] to mime how the dance
and the music come to a sudden stop at the striking of the
ebony clock and how they begin again when the echoes of
the chime die away." Nänny helpfully marks the *seven* sentences to illustrate the key repeated words in the structure,
centered "around the fourth or middle sentence which itself has its fulcrum in 'all'—'still'—'all.'":

> | *To and fro* in the seven chambers there stalked, in
> fact, a multitude of dreams. | And these—the
> dreams—*writhed* in and about, taking hue from the
> rooms, and causing the wild *music* of the orchestra to
> seem as the *echo* of their steps. | And, anon, there
> strikes the ebony *clock* which stands in the hall of the
> velvet. || And then, for a moment, *all* is *still*, and *all*
> is silent save the voice of the *clock*. || The dreams
> are stiff-frozen as they stand. | But the *echoes* of the
> chime die away—they have endured but an in-
> stant—and a light, half-subdued laughter floats after
> them as they depart. | And now again the *music*
> swells, and the dreams live, and *writhe to and fro* more
> merrily than ever, taking hue from the many-tinted
> windows through which stream the rays from the tri-
> pods. |

See "Chiastic Structures in Literature: Some Forms and
Functions," *The Structure of Texts*, ed. Udo Fries (Tübin-
gen: Gunter Narr, 1987), 83.

14   The cholera epidemic of 1832 arrived on North American shores first in the form of news stories before it arrived
in fact in the summer. The June 2, 1832, issue of the New
York *Mirror* carried this chilling description of a masquerade ball in plague-ridden Paris: "At a masque ball at the
Théâtre des Varietés . . . one man, immensely tall, dressed
as a personification of the *Cholera* itself, with skeleton ar-
mor, bloodshot eyes, and other horrible appurtenances of a
walking pestilence" Mabbott notes that "there can be little
doubt that Poe was familiar with it" (Mabbott II, 668). The
disease moved quickly through major East Coast cities like
New York, Philadelphia, and Baltimore (where Poe was
living at the time), causing widespread panic.

which stream the rays from the tripods.[13] But to the chamber which
lies most westwardly of the seven, there are now none of the maskers who venture; for the night is waning away; and there flows
a ruddier light through the blood-colored panes; and the blackness of the sable drapery appals; and to him whose foot falls upon
the sable carpet, there comes from the near clock of ebony a muffled peal more solemnly emphatic than any which reaches *their*
ears who indulge in the more remote gaieties of the other apartments.

But these other apartments were densely crowded, and in them
beat feverishly the heart of life. And the revel went whirlingly on,
until at length there commenced the sounding of midnight upon
the clock. And then the music ceased, as I have told; and the evolutions of the waltzers were quieted; and there was an uneasy cessation of all things as before. But now there were twelve strokes to
be sounded by the bell of the clock; and thus it happened, perhaps,
that more of thought crept, with more of time, into the meditations of the thoughtful among those who revelled. And thus too,
it happened, perhaps, that before the last echoes of the last chime
had utterly sunk into silence, there were many individuals in the
crowd who had found leisure to become aware of the presence of a
masked figure which had arrested the attention of no single individual before. And the rumor of this new presence having spread
itself whisperingly around, there arose at length from the whole
company a buzz, or murmur, expressive of disapprobation and
surprise—then, finally, of terror, of horror, and of disgust.

In an assembly of phantasms such as I have painted, it may well
be supposed that no ordinary appearance could have excited such
sensation. In truth the masquerade license of the night was nearly
unlimited; but the figure in question had out-Heroded Herod, and
gone beyond the bounds of even the prince's indefinite decorum.
There are chords in the hearts of the most reckless which cannot
be touched without emotion. Even with the utterly lost, to whom
life and death are equally jests, there are matters of which no jest
can be made. The whole company, indeed, seemed now deeply to
feel that in the costume and bearing of the stranger neither wit
nor propriety existed. The figure was tall and gaunt, and shrouded
from head to foot in the habiliments of the grave. The mask which
concealed the visage was made so nearly to resemble the countenance of a stiffened corpse that the closest scrutiny must have had

In a Technicolor segment of *The Phantom of the Opera* (1925), the Phantom (Lon Chaney) attends a grand masquerade ball as Red Death, an homage to Poe's tale.

difficulty in detecting the cheat. And yet all this might have been endured, if not approved, by the mad revellers around. But the mummer had gone so far as to assume the type of the Red Death.[14] His vesture was dabbled in *blood*[15]—and his broad brow, with all the features of the face, was besprinkled with the scarlet horror.[16]

When the eyes of Prince Prospero fell upon this spectral image (which with a slow and solemn movement, as if more fully to sustain its *role*, stalked to and fro among the waltzers) he was seen to be convulsed, in the first moment with a strong shudder either of terror or distaste; but, in the next, his brow reddened with rage.

"Who dares?" he demanded hoarsely of the courtiers who stood near him—"who dares insult us with this blasphemous mockery? Seize him and unmask him—that we may know whom we have to hang at sunrise, from the battlements!"

It was in the eastern or blue chamber in which stood the Prince Prospero as he uttered these words. They rang throughout the seven rooms loudly and clearly—for the prince was a bold and robust man, and the music had become hushed at the waving of his hand.

15 Revelation 19:13: "And he was clothed with a vesture dipped in blood: and his name is called The Word of God."

16 To the annoyance of Poe and many American writers, the American periodical press began to issue cheap paperbound editions of popular British and French novels in the 1840s, when steam-powered papermaking and printing made their mass production possible. Nor was copyright an obstacle to their proliferation, since there was then no international copyright agreement. The influential New York editor Evert Duyckinck (1816–1878), a champion of Poe's work, once disparagingly referred to these popular pamphlet novels as "the crimson and yellow literature." "These were the colors under which it sailed," he explains, "under which this vile craft went forth from the booksellers' counters—the hues of blood and the plague." It is tempting to read the Red Death as the sudden plague of crimson and yellow literature on American publishing (Kevin J. Hayes, *Poe and the Printed Word* [New York: Cambridge University Press, 2000], 88).

17 In *The Bonfire of the Vanities*, Lord Buffing observes: "The exquisite part of [Poe's tale] is that somehow the guests have known all along what awaits them in this room, and yet they are drawn irresistibly toward it, because the excitement is so intense and the pleasure is so unbridled and the gowns and the food and the drink and the flesh are so sumptuous—and that is all they have. Families, homes, children, the great chain of being, the eternal tide of chromosomes mean nothing to them any longer. They are bound together, and they whirl about one another, endlessly, particles in a doomed atom—and what else could the Red Death be but some sort of final stimulation, the *ne plus ultra?*" (367–368).

18 Roger Corman, who directed *The Masque of the Red Death* (1964) starring Vincent Price as Prince Prospero, argues that Ingmar Bergman's inspiration for the personified figure of Death in *The Seventh Seal* (1957) was Poe's tale.

19 1 Thessalonians 5:1–2: "But of the times and the seasons, brethren, ye have no need that I write unto you. For yourselves know perfectly that the day of the Lord so cometh as a thief in the night."

20 Patrick Cheney calls attention to allusions, cadences, and syntax in the tale's concluding paragraph that are clearly biblical. But where the Bible "depicts man's victory over sin, death, and time, Poe's mythic pattern depicts the triumph of these agents over the destruction of man." The Red Death is an anti-Christ: "In Poe's mythology, the Red Death replaces Christ as the reigning force in the universe. Hence, the Red Death is said to have 'dominion over all'— a reversal of Paul's statement in Romans 6:9, in which 'death hath no more dominion' because of Christ's resurrection. Moreover, the halls of Poe's earthly paradise become 'blood-bedewed'—suggesting a conflation of two familiar Biblical images, blood and dew: the blood of Christ's resurrection that redeems man, and the drops of dew that fall from heaven to save man from the harshness of nature (Deuteronomy 33:28). In Poe, the blood and dew of the Red Death replace the blood of Christ and the dew of heaven" (Patrick Cheney, "Poe's Use of *The Tempest* and the Bible in 'The Masque of the Red Death,'" *English Language Notes* 20 [1983], 32, 34). Similarly, Hubert Zapf sees the plague "as a metaphor in the story for the destruction of human hopes and illusions by the agency of a superhuman fate, and which is personified and becomes the 'spectral image' for the final emptiness and futility of earthly life" (Hubert Zapf, "Entropic Imagination in Poe's 'The Masque of the Red Death,'" *College Literature* 16 [1989], 211).

It was in the blue room where stood the prince, with a group of pale courtiers by his side. At first, as he spoke, there was a slight rushing movement of this group in the direction of the intruder, who, at the moment was also near at hand, and now, with deliberate and stately step, made closer approach to the speaker. But from a certain nameless awe with which the mad assumptions of the mummer had inspired the whole party, there were found none who put forth hand to seize him; so that, unimpeded, he passed within a yard of the prince's person; and, while the vast assembly, as if with one impulse, shrank from the centres of the rooms to the walls, he made his way uninterruptedly, but with the same solemn and measured step which had distinguished him from the first, through the blue chamber to the purple—through the purple to the green—through the green to the orange—through this again to the white—and even thence to the violet, ere a decided movement had been made to arrest him. It was then, however, that the Prince Prospero, maddening with rage and the shame of his own momentary cowardice, rushed hurriedly through the six chambers, while none followed him on account of a deadly terror that had seized upon all. He bore aloft a drawn dagger, and had approached, in rapid impetuosity, to within three or four feet of the retreating figure, when the latter, having attained the extremity of the velvet apartment, turned suddenly and confronted his pursuer. There was a sharp cry—and the dagger dropped gleaming upon the sable carpet, upon which, instantly afterwards, fell prostrate in death the Prince Prospero. Then, summoning the wild courage of despair, a throng of the revellers at once threw themselves into the black apartment, and, seizing the mummer, whose tall figure stood erect and motionless within the shadow of the ebony clock, gasped in unutterable horror at finding the grave cerements and corpselike mask which they handled with so violent a rudeness, untenanted by any tangible form.[17]

And now was acknowledged the presence of the Red Death.[18] He had come like a thief in the night.[19] And one by one dropped the revellers in the blood-bedewed halls of their revel, and died each in the despairing posture of his fall. And the life of the ebony clock went out with that of the last of the gay. And the flames of the tripods expired. And Darkness and Decay and the Red Death held illimitable dominion over all.[20]

The Pit and the Pendulum

Impia tortorum longas hic turba furores
Sanguinis innocui, non satiata, aluit.
Sospite nunc patriâ, fracto nunc funeris antro,
Mors ubi dira fuit, vita salusque patent.[1]

*(Quatrain composed for the gates of a market to be erected
upon the site of the Jacobin Club House at Paris.)*[2]

I was sick—sick unto death[3] with that long agony; and when they at length unbound me, and I was permitted to sit, I felt that my senses were leaving me. The sentence—the dread sentence of death—was the last of distinct accentuation which reached my ears. After that, the sound of the inquisitorial voices seemed merged in one dreamy indeterminate hum. It conveyed to my soul the idea of *revolution*—perhaps from its association in fancy with the burr of a mill-wheel.[4] This only for a brief period; for presently I heard no more. Yet, for a while, I saw; but with how terrible an exaggeration! I saw the lips of the black-robed judges. They appeared to me white—whiter than the sheet upon which I trace these words—and thin even to grotesqueness; thin with the intensity of their expression of firmness—of immoveable resolution—of stern contempt of human torture. I saw that the decrees of what to me was Fate, were still issuing from those lips. I saw them writhe with a deadly locution. I saw them fashion the syllables of my name; and I shuddered because no sound succeeded. I saw, too, for a few moments of delirious horror, the soft and nearly imperceptible waving of the sable draperies which enwrapped the walls of the apartment. And then my vision fell upon the seven tall candles upon the table.[5] At first they wore the aspect of charity, and seemed white and slender angels who would save me; but then, all at once, there came a most deadly nausea over my spirit, and I felt every fibre in my frame thrill as if I had touched the wire of a galvanic battery,[6] while the angel forms became meaningless spectres, with heads of flame, and I saw that from them there would be no help. And then there stole into my fancy, like a rich musical note,

"The Pit and the Pendulum" is on its simplest level a story of torments endured at the hands of the Inquisition. The mere mention of the Spanish Inquisition conjures up for many readers images of extraordinary horror. Authorized by Pope Sixtus IV in 1478 and organized under Ferdinand II and Isabella I, the Spanish Inquisition sought to combat heresy, mainly targeting converted Jews, Muslims, and those accused of witchcraft, but it was also used against political enemies. The organization remained in force for centuries, accumulating additional power and spreading throughout the Spanish colonies. Remarkably, it was not abolished until the early nineteenth century. The stories about the horrors of the Spanish Inquisition that appeared in early nineteenth-century English-language newspapers and magazines fueled contemporary anti-Catholic sentiments.

Poe's primary inspiration for "The Pit and the Pendulum," which first appeared in 1842, was "Anecdote towards the History of the Spanish Inquisition," a magazine article initially published in London in the August 26, 1820, issue of the Literary Gazette. *Dozens of American newspapers and magazines from the Albany* Plough Boy *to the* New-England Galaxy *reprinted and recirculated this article over the next two decades. It concerns an episode that supposedly took place during the Peninsular War (1807–1814), the conflict between France and Great Britain on the Iberian Peninsula. Though the British public largely condemned Napoleon's incursions into Spain, some believed his actions might finally liberate the Spanish from the terror of the Inquisition. Poe took this contemporary anti-Catholic anecdote and turned it into a timeless tale of despair and alienation. Mabbott observes that the central idea of the story "is that the fear of the unknown exceeds the fear of anything known" (Thomas Ollive Mabbott, ed.,* Collected Works of Edgar Allan Poe, *3 vols. [Cambridge, MA: The Belknap Press of Harvard University Press, 1969–1978], II, 678).*

1 "Here the wicked mob, unappeased, long cherished a hatred of innocent blood. Now that the fatherland is saved, and the cave of death demolished; where grim death has been, life and health appear." Poe added this motto when he published a revised version of "The Pit and the Pendulum" in 1845. He took these lines from a note in *Mooriana* (1803), a posthumous collection of Dr. John Moore's writings (Kevin J. Hayes, "Poe's Motto to 'The Pit and the Pendulum,'" *Notes and Queries* 58 [2011], 88).

2 In his translation of "The Pit and the Pendulum," Charles Baudelaire noted that the Marché St. Honoré, the marketplace erected on the site of the Jacobin Club, has neither gates nor inscription.

3   Isaiah 38:1: "In those days was Hezekiah sick unto death. And Isaiah the prophet the son of Amoz came unto him, and said unto him, Thus saith the Lord, Set thine house in order: for thou shalt die, and not live." In Isaiah 38:17, after his miraculous recovery from the unnamed illness (Jehovah extends Hezekiah's life by another fifteen years), Hezekiah gives thanks to Jehovah for his deliverance from "the pit of corruption": "Behold, for peace I had great bitterness: but thou hast in love to my soul delivered it from the pit of corruption: for thou hast cast all my sins behind thy back."

Richard Wilber comments that the biblical allusion to Isaiah 38 shows the tale must be understood as "an allegory of near-damnation and divine mercy" ("The Poe Mystery Case," *New York Review of Books* [July 13, 1967]).

4   Robert Louis Stevenson, not an uncritical admirer of Poe, objected to this description, commenting: "It wants but a moment's reflection to prove how much too clever Poe has been here, how far from true reason he has been carried by this *nimium acumen* [excessive acumen]. For—the man being giddy—the 'idea of revolution' must have preceded the merging of the inquisitorial voices into an indeterminate hum, and most certainly could not have followed it as any fanciful deduction." Richard Wilbur suggests that Poe uses the buzz of a mill wheel to symbolize the transition to a dream state, as he had done earlier in "Manuscript Found in a Bottle" (Robert Louis Stevenson, "Literature," *The Academy*, January 2, 1875, 2; Richard Wilbur, "Edgar Allan Poe," *Major Writers of America*, ed. Perry Miller [New York: Harcourt, Brace, 1962], 438).

5   Revelation 1:12–13: "And I turned to see the voice that spake with me. And being turned, I saw seven golden candlesticks; And in the midst of the seven candlesticks one like unto the Son of man, clothed with a garment down to the foot, and girt about the paps with a golden girdle."

6   Named for Luigi Galvani (1737–1798), the Italian physiologist who invented it to carry out experiments to determine the relationship between electricity and animal tissue, the galvanic battery initially seems out of place in this tale, which may otherwise appear to be set in a remote past, when religious superstition was used to justify all sorts of cruelty. It is chilling to think that the electric battery—an icon of the Enlightenment—and the Spanish Inquisition coexisted for a time. The narrator's cognizance of galvanic batteries marks him as a representative of rational, scientific thought—in stark contrast to his tormentors.

Arthur Rackham, illustration from "The Pit and the Pendulum," published in Poe's *Tales of Mystery and Imagination* (1935). A British painter and illustrator, Arthur Rackham (1867–1939) established his reputation as a book illustrator in the heyday of the English illustrated book. He was especially drawn to German subjects, and his images for Grimm's fairy tales and Wagner's *Ring* cycle were among his favorites. Coming to Poe toward the end of his life, Rackham recaptured the style of his Grimm and Wagner illustrations to create some of his most lasting images.

the thought of what sweet rest there must be in the grave. The thought came gently and stealthily, and it seemed long before it attained full appreciation; but just as my spirit came at length properly to feel and entertain it, the figures of the judges vanished, as if magically, from before me; the tall candles sank into nothingness; their flames went out utterly; the blackness of darkness[7] supervened; all sensations appeared swallowed up in a mad rushing descent as of the soul into Hades. Then silence, and stillness, and night were the universe.[8]

I had swooned; but still will not say that all of consciousness was lost. What of it there remained I will not attempt to define, or even to describe; yet all was not lost. In the deepest slumber—no! In delirium—no! In a swoon—no! In death—no! even in the grave all is *not* lost. Else there is no immortality for man. Arousing from the most profound of slumbers, we break the gossamer web of *some* dream.[9] Yet in a second afterward, (so frail may that web have been) we remember not that we have dreamed. In the return to life from the swoon there are two stages; first, that of the sense of mental or spiritual; secondly, that of the sense of physical, existence. It seems probable that if, upon reaching the second stage, we could recall the impressions of the first, we should find these impressions eloquent in memories of the gulf beyond. And that gulf is—what? How at least shall we distinguish its shadows from those of the tomb? But if the impressions of what I have termed the first stage, are not, at will, recalled, yet, after long interval, do they not come unbidden, while we marvel whence they come? He who has never swooned, is not he who finds strange palaces and wildly familiar faces in coals that glow; is not he who beholds floating in mid-air the sad visions that the many may not view; is not he who ponders over the perfume of some novel flower—is not he whose brain grows bewildered with the meaning of some musical cadence which has never before arrested his attention.[10]

Amid frequent and thoughtful endeavors to remember; amid earnest struggles to regather some token of the state of seeming nothingness into which my soul had lapsed, there have been moments when I have dreamed of success; there have been brief, very brief periods when I have conjured up remembrances which the lucid reason of a later epoch assures me could have had reference only to that condition of seeming unconsciousness. These shadows of memory tell, indistinctly, of tall figures that lifted and bore me in silence down—down—still down—till a hideous dizziness oppressed me at the mere idea of the interminableness of the descent. They tell also of a vague horror at my heart on account of that heart's unnatural stillness. Then comes a sense of sudden

7 Jude 1:13: "Raging waves of the sea, foaming out their own shame; wandering stars, to whom is reserved the blackness of darkness for ever."

8 In his critical writings, Poe stresses what he calls variously the "totality of impression," "unity of effect," or "single effect" a writer must strive for in any work of art. In his review of Hawthorne's *Twice-Told Tales*, published in *Graham's Magazine* only months before the appearance of "The Pit and the Pendulum" in *The Gift: A Christmas and New Year's Present*, Poe explains the principle: "If wise, [the short story writer] has not fashioned his thoughts to accommodate his incidents; but having conceived with deliberate care, a certain unique or single *effect* to be wrought out, he then invents such incidents—he then combines such events as may best aid him in establishing this preconceived effect. If his very initial sentence tend not to the outbringing of this effect, then he has failed in his first step. In the whole composition there should be no word written, of which tendency, direct or indirect, is not to the pre-established design."

9 Poe was fascinated with the transition state between dreaming and waking. How can the dreamer discern the difference between dream and reality? He never really had a satisfactory answer to that question until he encountered a passage by the German Romantic poet Novalis: "We are near waking when we dream that we dream" (*Fragments from German Prose Writers*, trans. Sarah Austin [New York: D. Appleton, 1841], 21).

10 Poe was especially fascinated with hypnagogic hallucinations, those illusions that occur during that transition state between wakefulness and sleep, a skimble-skamble world where confusion is king, the logic of cause and effect no longer applies, and random images drift in and fade out, perhaps never to return.

11   The way the narrator understands his situation anticipates Joseph K's predicament in Franz Kafka's novel *The
Trial* (1925). Like Joseph K, Poe's narrator is "condemned
not only in innocence but also in ignorance."

12   "The Pit and the Pendulum" can be read as a transcript of a dream. Our physical positions during sleep can
often shape the contents of our dreams. Consider how
many times the narrator mentions reaching out his hand or
stretching out his arm. These physical movements, a nor-
mal part of sleep, could find their way into his dream.

13   The term *auto da fe*—"act of faith" in Portuguese—
refers to the ritual during which the Inquisition pronounced judgment against heretics, which was followed by
the execution of sentence by secular authorities, including
death by fire. More broadly, the term came to mean burning at the stake.

motionlessness throughout all things; as if those who bore me (a
ghastly train!) had outrun, in their descent, the limits of the limitless, and paused from the wearisomeness of their toil. After this I
call to mind flatness and dampness; and then all is *madness*—the
madness of a memory which busies itself among forbidden things.

Very suddenly there came back to my soul motion and sound—
the tumultuous motion of the heart, and, in my ears, the sound of
its beating. Then a pause in which all is blank. Then again sound,
and motion, and touch—a tingling sensation pervading my frame.
Then the mere consciousness of existence, without thought—a
condition which lasted long. Then, very suddenly, *thought,* and
shuddering terror, and earnest endeavor to comprehend my true
state. Then a strong desire to lapse into insensibility. Then a rushing revival of soul and a successful effort to move. And now a full
memory of the trial, of the judges, of the sable draperies, of the
sentence, of the sickness, of the swoon. Then entire forgetfulness
of all that followed; of all that a later day and much earnestness of
endeavor have enabled me vaguely to recall.[11]

So far, I had not opened my eyes. I felt that I lay upon my back,
unbound. I reached out my hand, and it fell heavily upon something damp and hard.[12] There I suffered it to remain for many minutes, while I strove to imagine where and *what* I could be. I longed,
yet dared not to employ my vision. I dreaded the first glance at
objects around me. It was not that I feared to look upon things
horrible, but that I grew aghast lest there should be *nothing* to see.
At length, with a wild desperation at heart, I quickly unclosed my
eyes. My worst thoughts, then, were confirmed. The blackness of
eternal night encompassed me. I struggled for breath. The intensity of the darkness seemed to oppress and stifle me. The atmosphere was intolerably close. I still lay quietly, and made effort to
exercise my reason. I brought to mind the inquisitorial proceedings, and attempted from that point to deduce my real condition.
The sentence had passed; and it appeared to me that a very long
interval of time had since elapsed. Yet not for a moment did I suppose myself actually dead. Such a supposition, notwithstanding
what we read in fiction, is altogether inconsistent with real existence;—but where and in what state was I? The condemned to
death, I knew, perished usually at the *autos-da-fé*,[13] and one of
these had been held on the very night of the day of my trial. Had I
been remanded to my dungeon, to await the next sacrifice, which

would not take place for many months? This I at once saw could not be. Victims had been in immediate demand. Moreover, my dungeon, as well as all the condemned cells at Toledo,[14] had stone floors, and light was not altogether excluded.

A fearful idea now suddenly drove the blood in torrents upon my heart, and for a brief period, I once more relapsed into insensibility. Upon recovering, I at once started to my feet, trembling convulsively in every fibre. I thrust my arms wildly above and around me in all directions. I felt nothing; yet dreaded to move a step, lest I should be impeded by the walls of a *tomb*. Perspiration burst from every pore, and stood in cold big beads upon my forehead. The agony of suspense, grew at length intolerable, and I cautiously moved forward, with my arms extended, and my eyes straining from their sockets, in the hope of catching some faint ray of light. I proceeded for many paces; but still all was blackness and vacancy. I breathed more freely. It seemed evident that mine was not, at least, the most hideous of fates.

And now, as I still continued to step cautiously onward, there came thronging upon my recollection a thousand vague rumors of the horrors of Toledo. Of the dungeons there had been strange things narrated—fables I had always deemed them—but yet strange, and too ghastly to repeat, save in a whisper. Was I left to perish of starvation in this subterranean world of darkness;[15] or what fate, perhaps even more fearful, awaited me? That the result would be death, and a death of more than customary bitterness,[16] I knew too well the character of my judges to doubt. The mode and the hour were all that occupied or distracted me.

My outstretched hands at length encountered some solid obstruction. It was a wall, seemingly of stone masonry—very smooth, slimy, and cold. I followed it up; stepping with all the careful distrust with which certain antique narratives had inspired me.[17] This process, however, afforded me no means of ascertaining the dimensions of my dungeon; as I might make its circuit, and return to the point whence I set out, without being aware of the fact; so perfectly uniform seemed the wall. I therefore sought the knife which had been in my pocket, when led into the inquisitorial chamber; but it was gone; my clothes had been exchanged for a wrapper of coarse serge.[18] I had thought of forcing the blade in some minute crevice of the masonry, so as to identify my point of departure. The difficulty, nevertheless, was but trivial; although,

14   In the eleventh century, the Moors made Toledo the capital of an independent kingdom, fortified the city, and established its reputation for sword making. The place became so renowned for its swords that the name Toledo was sometimes used as a synonym for sword. In the sixteenth century, Toledo became the center of the Spanish Inquisition. Poe's choice of Toledo as the location for this tale largely stems from his key source, "Anecdote Towards the History of the Spanish Inquisition," which is set in Toledo, Spain. The city's reputation for swords may have inspired his invention of the scythe-like pendulum—a Toledo blade—that figures so memorably later on in the story.

15   The phrase can be taken both figuratively and literally. It is a circumlocution for hell as well as a description of the dungeons beneath Toledo. Its presence in this story reinforces Poe's fascination with dark, scary underground spaces—basements, catacombs, crypts, graves—that occur in many of his tales.

16   1 Samuel 15:32: "Then said Samuel, Bring ye hither to me Agag the king of the Amalekites. And Agag came unto him delicately. And Agag said, Surely the bitterness of death is past."

17   An intelligent, educated man, the narrator knows enough about the Inquisition to cause him considerable worry. Having read earlier stories about its devilish tortures, he is understandably fearful of what is to come.

18   The term "serge" generally refers to a woollen fabric, but its precise meaning varies. "Coarse serge" was typically associated with a monk's garb. In *Rienzi* (1835), Edward Bulwer-Lytton refers to "a friar's coarse serge, the parade of humility."

in the disorder of my fancy, it seemed at first insuperable. I tore a part of the hem from the robe and placed the fragment at full length, and at right angles to the wall. In groping my way around the prison, I could not fail to encounter this rag upon completing the circuit. So, at least I thought: but I had not counted upon the extent of the dungeon, or upon my own weakness. The ground was moist and slippery. I staggered onward for some time, when I stumbled and fell. My excessive fatigue induced me to remain prostrate; and sleep soon overtook me as I lay.

Upon awaking, and stretching forth an arm, I found beside me a loaf and a pitcher with water. I was too much exhausted to reflect upon this circumstance, but ate and drank with avidity. Shortly afterward, I resumed my tour around the prison, and with much toil, came at last upon the fragment of the serge. Up to the period when I fell, I had counted fifty-two paces, and, upon resuming my walk, I had counted forty-eight more—when I arrived at the rag. There were in all, then, a hundred paces; and, admitting two paces to the yard, I presumed the dungeon to be fifty yards in circuit. I had met, however, with many angles in the wall, and thus I could form no guess at the shape of the vault; for vault I could not help supposing it to be.

I had little object—certainly no hope—in these researches; but a vague curiosity prompted me to continue them. Quitting the wall, I resolved to cross the area of the enclosure. At first, I proceeded with extreme caution, for the floor, although seemingly of solid material, was treacherous with slime. At length, however, I took courage, and did not hesitate to step firmly—endeavoring to cross in as direct a line as possible. I had advanced some ten or twelve paces in this manner, when the remnant of the torn hem of my robe became entangled between my legs. I stepped on it, and fell violently on my face.

In the confusion attending my fall, I did not immediately apprehend a somewhat startling circumstance, which yet, in a few seconds afterward, and while I still lay prostrate, arrested my attention. It was this: my chin rested upon the floor of the prison, but my lips, and the upper portion of my head, although seemingly at a less elevation than the chin, touched nothing. At the same time, my forehead seemed bathed in a clammy vapor, and the peculiar smell of decayed fungus arose to my nostrils. I put forward my arm, and shuddered to find that I had fallen at the very brink of a circular pit, whose extent, of course, I had no means of ascertaining at the moment.[19] Groping about the masonry just below the margin, I succeeded in dislodging a small fragment, and let it fall into the abyss. For many seconds I hearkened to its reverberations as it dashed against the sides of the chasm in its descent: at length, there was a sullen plunge into water, succeeded by loud echoes. At the same moment, there came a sound resembling the quick opening, and as rapid closing of a door overhead, while a faint gleam of light flashed suddenly through the gloom, and as suddenly faded away.

I saw clearly the doom which had been prepared for me, and congratulated myself upon the timely accident by which I had escaped. Another step before my fall, and the world had seen me no more. And the death just avoided, was of that very character which I had regarded as fabulous and frivolous in the tales respecting the Inquisition. To the victims of its tyranny, there was the choice of death with its direst physical agonies, or death with its most hideous moral horrors. I had been reserved for the latter. By long suffering my nerves had been unstrung, until I trembled at the sound of my own voice, and had become in every respect a fitting subject for the species of torture which awaited me.

Shaking in every limb, I groped my way back to the wall—resolving there to perish rather than risk the terrors of the wells, of which my imagination now pictured many in various positions about the dungeon. In other conditions of mind, I might have had courage to end my misery at once, by a plunge into one of these abysses; but now I was the veriest of cowards. Neither could I forget what I had read of these pits—that the *sudden* extinction of life formed no part of their most horrible plan.

Agitation of spirit kept me awake for many long hours; but at length I again slumbered. Upon arousing, I found by my side, as before, a loaf and a pitcher of water. A burning thirst consumed me, and I emptied the vessel at a draught. It must have been drugged—for scarcely had I drunk, before I became irresistibly drowsy. A deep sleep fell upon me[20]—a sleep like that of death. How long it lasted, of course, I know not; but when, once again, I unclosed my eyes, the objects around me were visible. By a wild, sulphurous lustre,[21] the origin of which I could not at first determine, I was enabled to see the extent and aspect of the prison.

In its size I had been greatly mistaken. The whole circuit of

19 For the motif of the pit, Poe may have been influenced by Sir Walter Scott's *Anne of Geierstein* (1829), in which Arthur Philipson, a young English traveler, is captured and thrown into a dungeon with a large pit in the middle into which he almost falls (Donald A. Ringe, "Poe's Debt to Scott in 'The Pit and the Pendulum,'" *English Language Notes* 18 [1981], 281–283).

20 Genesis 15:12: "And when the sun was going down, a deep sleep fell upon Abram; and, lo, an horror of great darkness fell upon him."

21 As it is used here, the word "sulphurous" means hellish or satanic.

22   The narrator experiences a double horror: the horrors themselves and the fearful representations of them. The violence and gruesomeness of the images, faded somewhat in their colors, suggests that the narrator finds himself in a place where horror has become conventional for the punishers.

23   The word "surcingle" has two meanings. It is the term for a strap that attaches a burden to a packhorse, but it also refers to the belt around a monk's cassock. The former suggests the narrator's body is the burden that the implement of torture must bear. But the latter closely identifies the narrator with his torturers, suggesting perhaps that the Church's acts of torture are acts of self-mutilation.

its walls did not exceed twenty-five yards. For some minutes this fact occasioned me a world of vain trouble; vain indeed—for what could be of less importance, under the terrible circumstances which environed me, then the mere dimensions of my dungeon? But my soul took a wild interest in trifles, and I busied myself in endeavors to account for the error I had committed in my measurement. The truth at length flashed upon me. In my first attempt at exploration, I had counted fifty-two paces, up to the period when I fell: I must then have been within a pace or two of the fragment of serge; in fact, I had nearly performed the circuit of the vault. I then slept—and, upon awaking, I must have returned upon my steps—thus supposing the circuit nearly double what it actually was. My confusion of mind prevented me from observing that I began my tour with the wall to the left, and ended it with the wall to the right.

I had been deceived, too, in respect to the shape of the enclosure. In feeling my way, I had found many angles, and thus deduced an idea of great irregularity; so potent is the effect of total darkness upon one arousing from lethargy or sleep! The angles were simply those of a few slight depressions, or niches, at odd intervals. The general shape of the prison was square. What I had taken for masonry seemed now to be iron, or some other metal, in huge plates, whose sutures or joints occasioned the depressions. The entire surface of this metallic enclosure was rudely daubed in all the hideous and repulsive devices to which the charnel superstition of the monks has given rise. The figures of fiends in aspects of menace, with skeleton forms, and other more really fearful images, overspread and disfigured the walls. I observed that the outlines of these monstrosities were sufficiently distinct, but that the colors seemed faded and blurred, as if from the effects of a damp atmosphere.[22] I now noticed the floor, too, which was of stone. In the centre yawned the circular pit from whose jaws I had escaped; but it was the only one in the dungeon.

All this I saw indistinctly and by much effort—for my personal condition had been greatly changed during slumber. I now lay upon my back, and at full length, on a species of low framework of wood. To this I was securely bound by a long strap resembling a surcingle.[23] It passed in many convolutions about my limbs and body, leaving at liberty only my head, and my left arm to such extent, that I could, by dint of much exertion, supply myself with

PUCK

THE PIT AND THE PENDULUM.

"The Pit and The Pendulum," by Edgar Allan Poe, Tells of a Victim of the Spanish Inquisition Doomed to Watch a Knife-Like Pendulum That Swung Nearer and Nearer to His Heart.

"The Pit and the Pendulum," a political cartoon from *Puck*, vol. 65, no. 1682 (May 26, 1909). As pertinent today as it was over a hundred years ago, this political cartoon uses Poe's tale to illustrate the consumer's inability to cope with the increasing cost of living because of restrictive government regulations.

24 In Western art, time is characteristically personified as a winged old man carrying an hourglass and a scythe. Here the pendulum replaces the scythe, turning Father Time into a deadly timepiece—and literalizing the struggle against time. Glossing the story, Harry Levin writes, "Time is the pendulum, the sword of Damocles, that hangs over every man, while space is the pit to which a smouldering and ever-contracting existence condemns him" (*The Power of Blackness: Hawthorne, Poe, Melville* [New York: Knopf, 1958], 153).

25 When Roger Corman brought Poe's tale to the cinema as *The Pit and the Pendulum* (1961), he took many liberties with the story but retained its central image. Corman's re-creation of the scythelike pendulum remains powerful and disturbing.

food from an earthen dish which lay by my side on the floor. I saw, to my horror, that the pitcher had been removed. I say, to my horror—for I was consumed with intolerable thirst. This thirst it appeared to be the design of my persecutors to stimulate—for the food in the dish was meat pungently seasoned.

Looking upward, I surveyed the ceiling of my prison. It was some thirty or forty feet overhead, and constructed much as the side walls. In one of its panels a very singular figure riveted my whole attention. It was the painted figure of Time[24] as he is commonly represented, save that, in lieu of a scythe, he held what, at a casual glance, I supposed to be the pictured image of a huge pendulum, such as we see on antique clocks. There was something, however, in the appearance of this machine which caused me to regard it more attentively. While I gazed directly upward at it, (for its position was immediately over my own,) I fancied that I saw it in motion. In an instant afterward the fancy was confirmed. Its sweep was brief, and of course slow. I watched it for some minutes, somewhat in fear, but more in wonder. Wearied at length with observing its dull movement, I turned my eyes upon the other objects in the cell.

A slight noise attracted my notice, and, looking to the floor, I saw several enormous rats traversing it. They had issued from the well, which lay just within view to my right. Even then, while I gazed, they came up in troops, hurriedly, with ravenous eyes, allured by the scent of the meat. From this it required much effort and attention to scare them away.

It might have been half an hour, perhaps even an hour, (for I could take but imperfect note of time) before I again cast my eyes upward. What I then saw, confounded and amazed me. The sweep of the pendulum had increased in extent by nearly a yard. As a natural consequence, its velocity was also much greater. But what mainly disturbed me was the idea that it had perceptibly *descended*. I now observed—with what horror it is needless to say—that its nether extremity was formed of a crescent of glittering steel, about a foot in length from horn to horn; the horns upward, and the under edge evidently as keen as that of a razor. Like a razor also, it seemed massy and heavy, tapering from the edge into a solid and broad structure above. It was appended to a weighty rod of brass, and the whole *hissed* as it swung through the air.[25]

I could no longer doubt the doom prepared for me by monkish

ingenuity in torture. My cognizance of the pit had become known to the inquisitorial agents—*the pit,* whose horrors had been destined for so bold a recusant[26] as myself—*the pit,* typical of hell, and regarded by rumor as the Ultima Thule[27] of all their punishments. The plunge into this pit I had avoided by the merest of accidents, and I knew that surprise, or entrapment into torment, formed an important portion of all the grotesquerie of these dungeon deaths. Having failed to fall, it was no part of the demon plan to hurl me into the abyss; and thus (there being no alternative) a different and a milder destruction awaited me. Milder! I half smiled in my agony as I thought of such application of such a term.

What boots it[28] to tell of the long, long hours of horror more than mortal, during which I counted the rushing oscillations of the steel! Inch by inch—line by line—with a descent only appreciable at intervals that seemed ages—down and still down it came! Days passed—it might have been that many days passed—ere it swept so closely over me as to fan me with its acrid breath. The odor of the sharp steel forced itself into my nostrils.[29] I prayed—I wearied heaven with my prayer for its more speedy descent. I grew frantically mad, and struggled to force myself upward against the sweep of the fearful scimitar.[30] And then I fell suddenly calm, and lay smiling at the glittering death, as a child at some rare bauble.

There was another interval of utter insensibility; it was brief; for, upon again lapsing into life, there had been no perceptible descent in the pendulum. But it might have been long—for I knew there were demons who took note of my swoon, and who could have arrested the vibration at pleasure. Upon my recovery, too, I felt very—oh, inexpressibly—sick and weak, as if through long inanition.[31] Even amid the agonies of that period, the human nature craved food. With painful effort I outstretched my left arm as far as my bonds permitted, and took possession of the small remnant which had been spared me by the rats. As I put a portion of it within my lips, there rushed to my mind a half-formed thought of joy—of hope. Yet what business had *I* with hope? It was, as I say, a half-formed thought—man has many such, which are never completed. I felt that it was of joy—of hope; but I felt also that it had perished in its formation. In vain I struggled to perfect—to regain it. Long suffering had nearly annihilated all my ordinary powers of mind. I was an imbecile—an idiot.

The vibration of the pendulum was at right angles to my length.

26 A "recusant" was a Roman Catholic who did not attend the services of the Church of England, as required by English penal laws until the middle of the seventeenth century. Using a term that historically refers to Catholics to describe the victim of inquisitorial torture, Poe turns the concept on its head.

27 A favorite concept for Poe, "Ultima Thule" means the utmost point that can be attained.

28 What good would it do.

29 Poe employs the details of sensation to create terror, emphasizing the blade's sight and sound—and smell. His use of onomatopoeia reinforces the *hissing* sound of the deadly blade as it passes above the narrator and also keeps it present in a frightening-because-subliminal way in the reader's mind. Listen to the sibilants: cessation, crescent, scimitar, surcingle.

30 Poe puns on William Blake, "The Tiger," lines 3–4:

> What immortal hand or eye
> Could frame thy fearful symmetry?

Though Blake's poetry was not widely known, "The Tiger" was reprinted frequently during Poe's lifetime. In case readers missed the punning reference to Blake's poem, Poe reiterates it a few paragraphs later by comparing the movement of the blade to the pace of a tiger. Poe's clever pun has a serious purpose. A tiger's ferocity, he implies, is nothing compared with man's innate capacity to elicit fear or inflict carnage on his fellow man. See Kevin J. Hayes, "Poe's Knowledge of William Blake," *Notes and Queries* 61 (2014), 83-84.

31 Exhaustion resulting from extreme hunger.

I saw that the crescent was designed to cross the region of the heart. It would fray the serge of my robe—it would return and repeat its operations—again—and again. Notwithstanding its terrifically wide sweep, (some thirty feet or more,) and the hissing vigor of its descent, sufficient to sunder these very walls of iron, still the fraying of my robe would be all that, for several minutes, it would accomplish. And at this thought I paused. I dared not go farther than this reflection. I dwelt upon it with a pertinacity of attention—as if, in so dwelling, I could arrest *here* the descent of the steel. I forced myself to ponder upon the sound of the crescent as it should pass across the garment—upon the peculiar thrilling sensation which the friction of cloth produces on the nerves. I pondered upon all this frivolity until my teeth were on edge.

Down—steadily down it crept. I took a frenzied pleasure in contrasting its downward with its lateral velocity. To the right—to the left—far and wide—with the shriek of a damned spirit! to my heart, with the stealthy pace of the tiger! I alternately laughed and howled, as the one or the other idea grew predominant.

Down—certainly, relentlessly down! It vibrated within three inches of my bosom! I struggled violently—furiously—to free my left arm. This was free only from the elbow to the hand. I could reach the latter, from the platter beside me, to my mouth, with great effort, but no farther. Could I have broken the fastenings above the elbow, I would have seized and attempted to arrest the pendulum. I might as well have attempted to arrest an avalanche!

Down—still unceasingly—still inevitably down! I gasped and struggled at each vibration. I shrunk convulsively at its every sweep. My eyes followed its outward or upward whirls with the eagerness of the most unmeaning despair; they closed themselves spasmodically at the descent, although death would have been a relief, oh, how unspeakable! Still I quivered in every nerve to think how slight a sinking of the machinery would precipitate that keen, glistening axe upon my bosom. It was *hope* that prompted the nerve to quiver—the frame to shrink. It was *hope*—the hope that triumphs on the rack—that whispers to the death-condemned even in the dungeons of the Inquisition.

I saw that some ten or twelve vibrations would bring the steel in actual contact with my robe—and with this observation there suddenly came over my spirit all the keen, collected calmness of despair. For the first time during many hours—or perhaps days—

I *thought*. It now occurred to me, that the bandage, or surcingle, which enveloped me, was *unique*. I was tied by no separate cord. The first stroke of the razor-like crescent athwart any portion of the band, would so detach it that it might be unwound from my person by means of my left hand. But how fearful, in that case, the proximity of the steel! The result of the slightest struggle, how deadly! Was it likely, moreover, that the minions of the torturer had not foreseen and provided for this possibility? Was it probable that the bandage crossed my bosom in the track of the pendulum? Dreading to find my faint, and, as it seemed, my last hope frustrated, I so far elevated my head as to obtain a distinct view of my breast. The surcingle enveloped my limbs and body close in all directions—*save in the path of the destroying crescent.*

Scarcely had I dropped my head back into its original position, when there flashed upon my mind what I cannot better describe than as the unformed half of that idea of deliverance to which I have previously alluded, and of which a moiety[32] only floated indeterminately through my brain when I raised food to my burning lips. The whole thought was now present—feeble, scarcely sane, scarcely definite—but still entire. I proceeded at once, with the nervous energy of despair, to attempt its execution.

For many hours the immediate vicinity of the low framework upon which I lay, had been literally swarming with rats. They were wild, bold, ravenous—their red eyes glaring upon me as if they waited but for motionlessness on my part to make me their prey. "To what food," I thought, "have they been accustomed in the well?"

They had devoured, in spite of all my efforts to prevent them, all but a small remnant of the contents of the dish. I had fallen into an habitual see-saw, or wave of the hand about the platter; and, at length, the unconscious uniformity of the movement deprived it of effect. In their voracity, the vermin frequently fastened their sharp fangs in my fingers. With the particles of the oily and spicy viand which now remained, I thoroughly rubbed the bandage wherever I could reach it; then, raising my hand from the floor, I lay breathlessly still.

At first, the ravenous animals were startled and terrified at the change—at the cessation of movement. They shrank alarmedly back; many sought the well. But this was only for a moment. I had not counted in vain upon their voracity. Observing that I remained

32   A small amount.

33 Adapting Poe's tale as *The Pit and the Pendulum*
(1913), director Alice Guy sought to make this scene as realistic and as true to the original as she could. Consequently, she tied the arms and legs of Darwin Karr, her
leading man, with rope, smeared the rope with food, and
then filmed the scene as real rats crawled over the actor's
body and slowly ate through the ropes. Once the ropes
broke, Karr jumped to his feet, swearing there would be no
retakes!

without motion, one or two of the boldest leaped upon the framework, and smelt at the surcingle. This seemed the signal for a general rush. Forth from the well they hurried in fresh troops. They
clung to the wood—they overran it, and leaped in hundreds upon
my person. The measured movement of the pendulum disturbed
them not at all. Avoiding its strokes, they busied themselves with
the anointed bandage. They pressed—they swarmed upon me in
ever accumulating heaps. They writhed upon my throat; their cold
lips sought my own; I was half stifled by their thronging pressure;
disgust, for which the world has no name, swelled my bosom, and
chilled, with a heavy clamminess, my heart. Yet one minute, and I
felt that the struggle would be over. Plainly I perceived the loosen-
ing of the bandage. I knew that in more than one place it must be
already severed. With a more than human resolution I lay *still*.

Nor had I erred in my calculations—nor had I endured in vain.
I at length felt that I was *free*. The surcingle hung in ribands from
my body. But the stroke of the pendulum already pressed upon my
bosom. It had divided the serge of the robe. It had cut through the
linen beneath. Twice again it swung, and a sharp sense of pain shot
through every nerve. But the moment of escape had arrived. At a
wave of my hand my deliverers hurried tumultuously away. With
a steady movement—cautious, sidelong, shrinking, and slow—I
slid from the embrace of the bandage and beyond the reach of the
scimitar. For the moment, at least, *I was free*.[33]

Free!—and in the grasp of the Inquisition! I had scarcely
stepped from my wooden bed of horror upon the stone floor of
the prison, when the motion of the hellish machine ceased, and I
beheld it drawn up, by some invisible force, through the ceiling.
This was a lesson which I took desperately to heart. My every
motion was undoubtedly watched. Free!—I had but escaped death
in one form of agony, to be delivered unto worse than death in
some other. With that thought I rolled my *eyes* nervously around
on the barriers of iron that hemmed me in. Something unusual—
some change which, at first, I could not appreciate distinctly—
it was obvious, had taken place in the apartment. For many minutes of a dreamy and trembling abstraction, I busied myself in
vain, unconnected conjecture. During this period, I became aware,
for the first time, of the origin of the sulphurous light which illumined the cell. It proceeded from a fissure, about half an inch
in width, extending entirely around the prison at the base of the

Byam Shaw, "The Pit and the Pendulum," from *Selected Tales of Mystery* (London: Sidgwick & Jackson, 1909).

34   The mysterious light implicitly comes from the infernal regions. Poe uses the motif in other tales. See Oliver Evans, "Infernal Illumination in Poe," *Modern Language Notes* 75 (1960), 295–297.

35   Poe borrowed this phrase from a popular ballad by Margaret Harries Baron-Wilson, "I Watch for Thee," lines 1–4:

> I watch for Thee!—When parting day
> Sheds on the earth a ling'ring ray;
> When his last blushes, o'er the rose,
> A richer tint of crimson throws

The phrase provides a good example of his use of literary source material. Believing, as he did, that all poets work toward the same end, that is, to create works that strive for eternal beauty, Poe felt free to plunder the works of previous writers, as long as he made better what he borrowed. Baron-Wilson had cast her richer tint of crimson over a conventional romantic symbol, the red rose. Poe casts his over an image of bloodshed. Baron-Wilson's light imagery intensifies the beauty of the rose, but Poe understood that beauty, in absolute terms, did not need to be strictly beautiful. As he said elsewhere, the pure imagination, on selecting its materials, can choose "from either beauty or deformity" (*Essays and Reviews*, ed. G. R. Thompson [New York: Library of America, 1984], 1126). Here, the rich tint of crimson enhances the gory imagery.

36   Job 18:14: "His confidence shall be rooted out of his tabernacle, and it shall bring him to the king of terrors."

walls, which thus appeared, and were completely separated from the floor.[34] I endeavored, but of course in vain, to look through the aperture.

As I arose from the attempt, the mystery of the alteration in the chamber broke at once upon my understanding. I have observed that, although the outlines of the figures upon the walls were sufficiently distinct, yet the colors seemed blurred and indefinite. These colors had now assumed, and were momentarily assuming, a startling and most intense brilliancy, that gave to the spectral and fiendish portraitures an aspect that might have thrilled even firmer nerves than my own. Demon eyes, of a wild and ghastly vivacity, glared upon me in a thousand directions, where none had been visible before, and gleamed with the lurid lustre of a fire that I could not force my imagination to regard as unreal.

Unreal!—Even while I breathed there came to my nostrils the breath of the vapor of heated iron! A suffocating odor pervaded the prison! A deeper glow settled each moment in the eyes that glared at my agonies! A richer tint of crimson[35] diffused itself over the pictured horrors of blood. I panted! I gasped for breath! There could be no doubt of the design of my tormentors—oh! most unrelenting! oh! most demoniac of men! I shrank from the glowing metal to the centre of the cell. Amid the thought of the fiery destruction that impended, the idea of the coolness of the well came over my soul like balm. I rushed to its deadly brink. I threw my straining vision below. The glare from the enkindled roof illumined its inmost recesses. Yet, for a wild moment, did my spirit refuse to comprehend the meaning of what I saw. At length it forced—it wrestled its way into my soul—it burned itself in upon my shuddering reason. Oh! for a voice to speak!—oh! horror!—oh! any horror but this! With a shriek, I rushed from the margin, and buried my face in my hands—weeping bitterly.

The heat rapidly increased, and once again I looked up, shuddering as with a fit of the ague. There had been a second change in the cell—and now the change was obviously in the *form*. As before, it was in vain that I at first endeavored to appreciate or understand what was taking place. But not long was I left in doubt. The Inquisitorial vengeance had been hurried by my two-fold escape, and there was to be no more dallying with the King of Terrors.[36] The room had been square. I saw that two of its iron angles were now acute—two, consequently, obtuse. The fearful differ-

Henri Guvedon, *Le Général La-salle*, 1825.

ence quickly increased with a low rumbling or moaning sound. In an instant the apartment had shifted its form into that of a lozenge.[37] But the alteration stopped not here—I neither hoped nor desired it to stop. I could have clasped the red walls to my bosom as a garment of eternal peace. "Death," I said, "any death but that of the pit!" Fool! might I not have known that *into the pit* it was the object of the burning iron to urge me? Could I resist its glow? or if even that, could I withstand its pressure? And now, flatter and flatter grew the lozenge, with a rapidity that left me no time for contemplation. Its centre, and of course, its greatest width, came just over the yawning gulf. I shrank back—but the closing walls pressed me resistlessly onward. At length for my seared and writhing body there was no longer an inch of foothold on the firm floor

37 Poe borrowed the device of contracting prison walls from "The Iron Shroud," a tale William Mudford published in the August 1830 issue of *Blackwood's*. Contemporary readers recognized the similarity. In the April 1843 issue of the *Foreign and Colonial Quarterly Review*, a contributor observes, "'The Pit and the Pendulum,' which, although a palpable imitation of Mr. Mudford's powerful tale of the 'Iron Shroud,' is nevertheless, both clever and effective." In *Scenes of Life at the Capital* (1971), Beat poet Philip Whalen recalls Poe's tale with the following lines:

> Edgar Allan Poe saw the walls of Plato's cave
> Slowly moving inwards to crush us

And in *Couples* (1968), John Updike mentions "The Pit and the Pendulum" in reference to an old woman who hoards back issues of *National Geographic*, which she has stacked up along the walls of her home. Her collection has grown so huge that, like the walls of the torture chamber in "The Pit and the Pendulum," it closes in around her, threatening to crush her.

38   "Anecdote towards the History of the Spanish Inquisition," the article that inspired "The Pit and the Pendulum," concerns Antoine Charles Louis, Comte de Lasalle (1775–1809), one of Napoleon's greatest generals. It begins: "When General Lasalle entered Toledo, he immediately visited the Palace of the Inquisition." The article describes one particular implement of torture, a statue of the Virgin Mary covered with spikes and razor-sharp blades with moving arms that would clasp a victim to its breast. In the article, Lasalle and his men test the device using one of the soldier's knapsacks, which is soon punctured with numerous holes. Though fascinated by the story, Poe nevertheless recognized what was wrong with it, at least from a dramatic point of view: it was backwards. By having Lasalle arrive in the first sentence, the article destroys all possibilities for tension and terror. Poe turned the story around, describing what happens to one particular prisoner while saving Lasalle's timely intervention for the final paragraph.

of the prison. I struggled no more, but the agony of my soul found vent in one loud, long, and final scream of despair. I felt that I tottered upon the brink—I averted my eyes—

There was a discordant hum of human voices! There was a loud blast as of many trumpets! There was a harsh grating as of a thousand thunders! The fiery walls rushed back! An outstretched arm caught my own as I fell, fainting, into the abyss. It was that of General Lasalle. The French army had entered Toledo. The Inquisition was in the hands of its enemies.[38]

The Tell-Tale Heart

Alongside his detective tales, Poe developed another genre of crime fiction—"noir killer fiction"—stories of depravity narrated by psychopaths who seduce readers into responding sympathetically. Though the narrator of "The Tell-Tale Heart" is a murderer, Poe attempts to establish, and even to understand, the criminal's humanity and rationality and thus to establish the bond he shares with his fellow man. "The Tell-Tale Heart" is a story of both the victim as well as the killer. Poe does not explicitly define the relationship between the two men. When D. W. Griffith adapted "The Tell-Tale Heart" for the cinema as The Avenging Conscience *(1914), he made the men an uncle and his nephew. In Poe's story, they could be uncle and nephew, father and son, tenant and boarder, boarder and tenant, or mentor and pupil. Though there may be no family relationship between the two, there seems little doubt that the older man is a father figure to the younger, who resents the old man's surveillance of him to such an extent that he becomes obsessed with his all-seeing eye. Repressed beneath its gaze, the younger man sees no way to escape save for destroying the life of the man who keeps him under surveillance.*

When it appeared in January 1843, "The Tell-Tale Heart" proved to be a sensation. Many of its first readers recognized the story's power but were nonetheless repulsed. Reviewing the story for the New York Tribune *(July 13, 1843), Horace Greeley called it "a strong and skilful, but to our minds overstrained and repulsive, analysis of the feelings and promptings of an insane homicide. The painting of the terror of the victim while he sat upright in his bed feeling that death was near him is most powerful and fearfully vivid." During Poe's lifetime, "The Tell-Tale Heart" was reprinted in the United States, Canada, and Great Britain. Some editors found Poe's title a little too vague. The new titles they substituted reflect how they interpreted the story and its narrator. The* Cleaves Penny Gazette, *a London weekly, added the subtitle "The Unconscious Madman." And the* Literary Garland, *a Montreal monthly, retitled the story "Confession of a Maniac."*

True!—nervous—very, very dreadfully nervous I had been and am; but why *will* you say that I am mad? The disease had sharpened my senses—not destroyed—not dulled them.[1] Above all was the sense of hearing acute. I heard all things in the heaven and in the earth.[2] I heard many things in hell. How, then, am I mad? Hearken! and observe how healthily—how calmly I can tell you the whole story.

It is impossible to say how first the idea[3] entered my brain; but, once conceived, it haunted me day and night. Object there was none. Passion there was none. I loved the old man. He had never wronged me. He had never given me insult. For his gold I had no desire. I think it was his eye![4] yes, it was this! One of his eyes resembled that of a vulture—a pale blue eye, with a film over it.[5] Whenever it fell upon me, my blood ran cold; and so by degrees—very gradually—I made up my mind to take the life of the old man, and thus rid myself of the eye forever.

Now this is the point. You fancy me mad. Madmen know nothing. But you should have seen *me*. You should have seen how wisely I proceeded—with what caution—with what foresight—with what dissimulation I went to work! I was never kinder to the old man than during the whole week before I killed him. And every night, about midnight, I turned the latch of his door and opened it—oh, so gently! And then, when I had made an opening sufficient for my head, I put in a dark lantern, all closed, closed, so that no light shone out, and then I thrust in my head. Oh, you would have laughed to see how cunningly I thrust it in! I moved it slowly—very, very slowly, so that I might not disturb the old

1 Like the opening of any dramatic monologue, this initial paragraph implies a concrete dramatic context. Apparently, the narrator and the "you" he addresses have already spoken about his physiological and psychological condition. The "you" has suggested that the narrator is mad; the narrator replies that the disease that had afflicted him now served to heighten his senses, meaning his perception and, perhaps, his sense of reason. These auditory hallucinations may suggest paranoid schizophrenia, but the disease need not be pinpointed so precisely.

2 Philippians 2:10: "That at the name of Jesus every knee should bow, of things in heaven, and things in earth, and things under the earth."

3   The term "idea" seems innocuous enough at first, but as the story develops, it becomes clear that the *idea* the narrator is talking about is murder: a nerve-deadening abstraction that names something without the narrator's having to picture it. It is symptomatic of the narrator's dispassionate and wholly intellectual approach to premeditated murder—and thus monstrous. But one senses too in the creation of a credible psychopath some of the author's necessary admiration and amazement for the criminal's chilling rationality, as it unfolds in the narrator's telling of his own tale. In his essay "On Murder Considered as One of the Fine Arts," Thomas DeQuincey says that murder "may be laid hold of by its moral handle (as it generally is in the pulpit and at the Old Bailey), and *that*, I confess, is its weak side; or it may also be treated *aesthetically*, as the Germans call it, that is, in relation to good taste" (*Blackwood's* 21 [1827], 200).

4   According to superstition, people with the Evil Eye had the power to harm or even kill another person simply by looking at them. The old man's Evil Eye helps reveal one possible reason the narrator would hurt someone who meant him no harm. Some legends of people using the power of the Evil Eye with deliberate malevolence exist, but the person possessing the Evil Eye does not necessarily have to have evil intentions (James Kirkland, "'The Tell-Tale Heart' as Evil Eye Event," *Southern Folklore* 56 [1999], 135, 137).

5   Job 28:7: "There is a path which no fowl knoweth, and which the vulture's eye hath not seen." In Poe's day, the term "film" could mean any sort of morbid growth on the eye. It also applied to the growing dimness in the eyes of a dying person, often referred to as the "film of death" *(OED)*. Compare the following line from Alaric A. Watts's popular sentimental poem "The Death of the First-Born" (1824): "It came at length;—o'er thy bright blue eye the film was gathering fast."

6   Job 38:9: "I made the cloud the garment thereof, and thick darkness a swaddling band for it."

7   "Death watch" is the popular name for several beetles that make a noise that sounds like the ticking of a watch and that, according to superstition, portends death. Herman Melville would make use of death watch beetles in his short story "The Apple-Tree Table" (1856), in which he describes their sound as a "faint sort of inward rapping or rasping—a strange, inexplicable sound, mixed with a slight kind of wood-pecking or ticking."

man's sleep. It took me an hour to place my whole head within the opening so far that I could see him as he lay upon his bed. Ha!—would a madman have been so wise as this? And then, when my head was well in the room, I undid the lantern cautiously—oh, so cautiously—cautiously (for the hinges creaked)—I undid it just so much that a single thin ray fell upon the vulture eye. And this I did for seven long nights—every night just at midnight—but I found the eye always closed; and so it was impossible to do the work; for it was not the old man who vexed me, but his Evil Eye. And every morning, when the day broke, I went boldly into the chamber, and spoke courageously to him, calling him by name in a hearty tone, and inquiring how he had passed the night. So you see he would have been a very profound old man, indeed, to suspect that every night, just at twelve, I looked in upon him while he slept.

Upon the eighth night I was more than usually cautious in opening the door. A watch's minute hand moves more quickly than did mine. Never before that night had I *felt* the extent of my own powers—of my sagacity. I could scarcely contain my feelings of triumph. To think that there I was, opening the door, little by little, and he not even to dream of my secret deeds or thoughts. I fairly chuckled at the idea; and perhaps he heard me; for he moved on the bed suddenly, as if startled. Now you may think that I drew back—but no. His room was as black as pitch with the thick darkness,[6] (for the shutters were close fastened, through fear of robbers,) and so I knew that he could not see the opening of the door, and I kept pushing it on steadily, steadily.

I had my head in, and was about to open the lantern, when my thumb slipped upon the tin fastening, and the old man sprang up in the bed, crying out—"Who's there?"

I kept quite still and said nothing. For a whole hour I did not move a muscle, and in the meantime I did not hear him lie down. He was still sitting up in the bed listening;—just as I have done, night after night, hearkening to the death watches in the wall.[7]

Presently I heard a slight groan, and I knew it was the groan of mortal terror. It was not a groan of pain or of grief—oh, no!—it was the low stifled sound that arises from the bottom of the soul when overcharged with awe. I knew the sound well. Many a night, just at midnight, when all the world slept, it has welled up from my own bosom, deepening, with its dreadful echo, the terrors that dis-

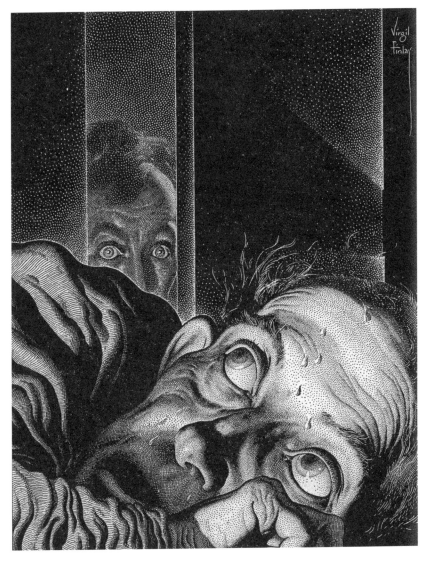

Virgil Finlay, illustration for "The Tell-Tale Heart," *Fantastic* 1 (Fall 1952), 154. Finlay (1914–1971) was a pulp artist who specialized in fantasy, science fiction, and horror. He produced more than 2,600 works of graphic art despite the abundance of detail that characterized his work.

tracted me.[8] I say I knew it well. I knew what the old man felt, and pitied him, although I chuckled at heart. I knew that he had been lying awake ever since the first slight noise, when he had turned in the bed. His fears had been ever since growing upon him. He had been trying to fancy them causeless, but could not. He had been saying to himself—"It is nothing but the wind in the chimney— it is only a mouse crossing the floor," or "it is merely a cricket which has made a single chirp." Yes, he has been trying to comfort himself with these suppositions: but he had found all in vain. *All in vain;* because Death, in approaching him, had stalked with

8   As in so many of Poe's works, he seems fascinated with the auditory sense, offering here what amounts to an anatomy of sounds that terrify.

9 *Macbeth*, V.i.35: "Out, damn'd spot!"

10 The word "tattoo" originally meant a drumbeat, but its meaning had become more generalized, and it could refer to any sort of repetitive, drumlike beating or thumping or rapping. The phrase "the devil's tattoo" refers to idly tapping or drumming with the fingers or other object in an irritating manner or as a sign of vexation or impatience. For *The Avenging Conscience*, a silent film, D. W. Griffith sought visual ways to represent the sound of the beating heart, and, at one point during the interrogation scene, the detective pounds out the devil's tattoo with his pencil.

11 John 13:1: "Now before the feast of the passover, when Jesus knew that his hour was come that he should depart out of this world unto the Father, having loved his own which were in the world, he loved them unto the end."

John Raphael Smith after Henry Fuseli, "Lady Macbeth," 1784, mezzotint.

his black shadow before him, and enveloped the victim. And it was the mournful influence of the unperceived shadow that caused him to feel—although he neither saw nor heard—to *feel* the presence of my head within the room.

When I had waited a long time, very patiently, without hearing him lie down, I resolved to open a little—a very, very little crevice in the lantern. So I opened it—you cannot imagine how stealthily, stealthily—until, at length a single dim ray, like the thread of the spider, shot from out the crevice and fell upon the vulture eye.

It was open—wide, wide open—and I grew furious as I gazed upon it. I saw it with perfect distinctness—all a dull blue, with a hideous veil over it that chilled the very marrow in my bones; but I could see nothing else of the old man's face or person: for I had directed the ray as if by instinct, precisely upon the damned spot.[9]

And now—have I not told you that what you mistake for madness is but over acuteness of the senses?—now, I say, there came to my ears a low, dull, quick sound, such as a watch makes when enveloped in cotton. I knew *that* sound well, too. It was the beating of the old man's heart. It increased my fury, as the beating of a drum stimulates the soldier into courage.

But even yet I refrained and kept still. I scarcely breathed. I held the lantern motionless. I tried how steadily I could maintain the ray upon the eye. Meantime the hellish tattoo[10] of the heart increased. It grew quicker and quicker, and louder and louder every instant. The old man's terror *must* have been extreme! It grew louder, I say, louder every moment!—do you mark me well? I have told you that I am nervous: so I am. And now at the dead hour of the night, amid the dreadful silence of that old house, so strange a noise as this excited me to uncontrollable terror. Yet, for some minutes longer I refrained and stood still. But the beating grew louder, louder! I thought the heart must burst. And now a new anxiety seized me—the sound would be heard by a neighbor! The old man's hour had come![11] With a loud yell, I threw open the lantern and leaped into the room. He shrieked once—once only. In an instant I dragged him to the floor, and pulled the heavy bed over him. I then smiled gaily, to find the deed so far done. But, for many minutes, the heart beat on with a muffled sound. This, however, did not vex me; it would not be heard through the wall. At length it ceased. The old man was dead. I removed the bed and examined the corpse. Yes, he was stone, stone dead. I placed my

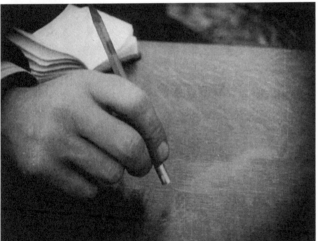

In a sequence from D. W. Griffith's film *The Avenging Conscience* (1914), the Detective (Ralph Lewis, top) confronts the Nephew (Henry B. Walthall, bottom), who apparently has murdered his uncle.

12   Wendy Lesser notes that Poe's madmen "retain a strange sort of innocence by virtue of their failure to understand their own power" (*Pictures at an Execution* [Cambridge, MA: Harvard University Press, 1993], 60).

13   Small beams or pieces of wood. Apparently, it has not occurred to the acutely sensitive narrator that the body parts hidden beneath the floor boards will soon begin to reek.

14   In *The Avenging Conscience*, D. W. Griffith depicts the house the two men share as a rural cottage, but the phrase "street door" clearly gives "The Tell-Tale Heart" an urban setting. To Poe's contemporary readers the tale suggested that in the anonymity of the modern city, people are unaware of the horrors that may be occurring behind their neighbors' doors.

hand upon the heart and held it there many minutes.[12] There was no pulsation. He was stone dead. His eye would trouble me no more.

If still you think me mad, you will think so no longer when I describe the wise precautions I took for the concealment of the body. The night waned, and I worked hastily, but in silence. First of all I dismembered the corpse. I cut off the head and the arms and the legs.

I then took up three planks from the flooring of the chamber, and deposited all between the scantlings.[13] I then replaced the boards so cleverly, so cunningly, that no human eye—not even *his*—could have detected anything wrong. There was nothing to wash out—no stain of any kind—no blood-spot whatever. I had been too wary for that. A tub had caught all—ha! ha!

When I had made an end of these labors, it was four o'clock—still dark as midnight. As the bell sounded the hour, there came a knocking at the street door.[14] I went down to open it with a light heart,—for what had I *now* to fear? There entered three men, who introduced themselves, with perfect suavity, as officers of the police. A shriek had been heard by a neighbor during the night; suspicion of foul play had been aroused; information had been lodged at the police office, and they (the officers) had been deputed to search the premises.

I smiled,—for *what* had I to fear? I bade the gentlemen welcome. The shriek, I said, was my own in a dream. The old man, I mentioned, was absent in the country. I took my visiters all over the house. I bade them search—search *well*. I led them, at length, to *his* chamber. I showed them his treasures, secure, undisturbed. In the enthusiasm of my confidence, I brought chairs into the room, and desired them *here* to rest from their fatigues, while I myself, in the wild audacity of my perfect triumph, placed my own seat upon the very spot beneath which reposed the corpse of the victim.

The officers were satisfied. My *manner* had convinced them. I was singularly at ease. They sat, and while I answered cheerily, they chatted of familiar things. But, ere long, I felt myself getting pale and wished them gone. My head ached, and I fancied a ringing in my ears: but still they sat and still chatted. The ringing became more distinct:—it continued and became more distinct: I talked more freely to get rid of the feeling: but it continued and gained definitiveness—until, at length, I found that the noise was *not* within my ears.

No doubt I now grew *very* pale;—but I talked more fluently, and with a heightened voice. Yet the sound increased—and what could I do? It was a low, dull, quick sound—*much such a sound as a watch makes when enveloped in cotton*. I gasped for breath—and yet the officers heard it not. I talked more quickly—more vehemently; but the noise steadily increased. I arose and argued about trifles, in a high key and with violent gesticulations; but the noise steadily increased. Why *would* they not be gone? I paced the floor to and fro with heavy strides, as if excited to fury by the observations of the men—but the noise steadily increased. Oh God! what *could* I do? I foamed—I raved—I swore! I swung the chair upon which I had been sitting, and grated it upon the boards, but the noise arose over all and continually increased. It grew louder—louder—louder! And still the men chatted pleasantly, and smiled. Was it possible they heard not? Almighty God!—no, no! They heard!—they suspected!—they *knew!*—they were making a mockery of my horror!—this I thought, and this I think.[15] But anything was better than this agony! Anything was more tolerable than this derision! I could bear those hypocritical smiles no longer! I felt that I must scream or die!—and now—again!—hark! louder! louder! louder! *louder!*—

"Villains!" I shrieked, "dissemble no more! I admit the deed!—tear up the planks!—here, here!—it is the beating of his hideous heart!"[16]

15 "The Tell-Tale Heart" provides a good example of what behavioral psychologists call "the illusion of transparency," that is, the tendency to overestimate the extent to which our thoughts, feelings, and sensations can be read by others.

16 We may suppose the narrator either imagines he hears the beating of the old man's heart or confuses the sound of his own pulsing heart with that of his victim. Pulsatile tinnitus, or hearing one's own heartbeat in one or both ears, can have many causes. But Poe's intent is clear enough: the narrator's paranoid imagination or confusion dramatizes a guilty conscience.

The Gold-Bug

What ho! what ho! this fellow is dancing mad!
He hath been bitten by the Tarantula.

All in the Wrong[1]

Many years ago, I contracted an intimacy with a Mr. William Legrand.[2] He was of an ancient Huguenot family,[3] and had once been wealthy; but a series of misfortunes had reduced him to want. To avoid the mortification consequent upon his disasters, he left New Orleans, the city of his forefathers, and took up his residence at Sullivan's Island, near Charleston, South Carolina.[4]

This Island is a very singular one. It consists of little else than the sea sand, and is about three miles long. Its breadth at no point exceeds a quarter of a mile. It is separated from the main land by a scarcely perceptible creek, oozing its way through a wilderness of reeds and slime, a favorite resort of the marsh-hen.[5] The vegetation, as might be supposed, is scant, or at least dwarfish. No trees of any magnitude are to be seen. Near the western extremity, where Fort Moultrie stands, and where are some miserable frame buildings, tenanted, during summer, by the fugitives from Charleston dust and fever, may be found, indeed, the bristly palmetto;[6] but the whole island, with the exception of this western point, and a line of hard, white beach on the seacoast, is covered with a dense undergrowth of the sweet myrtle, so much prized by the horticulturists of England.[7] The shrub here often attains the height of fifteen or twenty feet, and forms an almost impenetrable coppice, burthening the air with its fragrance.[8]

In the inmost recesses of this coppice, not far from the eastern or more remote end of the island, Legrand had built himself a small hut, which he occupied when I first, by mere accident, made his acquaintance. This soon ripened into friendship—for there was much in the recluse to excite interest and esteem. I found

A. Vizitelly, *Fort Moultrie, Charleston Harbor*, 1861.

about the world as if he was bit by a tarantula." According to superstition, the bite of a tarantula makes a person mad for dancing.

2   Many commentators have noted the similarities between William Legrand and Poe's sleuth C. Auguste Dupin. Like Dupin, Legrand is "fond of enigmas, of conundrums, of hieroglyphics; exhibiting in his solutions of each a degree of *acumen* which appears to the ordinary apprehension praeternatural" ("The Murders in the Rue Morgue," see page 175). Both operate by a combination of analytical reasoning and intuition. Poe thought of "The Gold-Bug" as another of his "tales of ratiocination," a category he did not limit to the three detective tales featuring Dupin. Jorge Luis Borges writes that Poe's signal achievement with the tales of ratiocination was to demonstrate that literature may be "an operation of the mind, not the spirit" (Jorge Luis Borges, "The Detective Story," *Jorge Luis Borges: On Writing*, ed. Suzanne Jill Levine [New York: Penguin Books, 2010], 127).

3   Huguenots were French Protestants of the sixteenth and seventeenth centuries. When the Edict of Nantes, granting rights to Protestants, was revoked in 1685, many Huguenots emigrated to British North America. Legrand's ancestry provides a cultural and geographical perspective different from that found in much American literature of Poe's time, derived from the Puritan New England heritage. Poe, whose great ambition was to edit and publish a magazine of his own, understood that there were many potential readers in the South and West, a region stretching from Charleston to New Orleans.

4   Setting the story on Sullivan's Island, Poe chose a location he knew well. When he was a young private in the U.S. Army, he was stationed on the island at Fort Moultrie from November 1827 to December 1828. For an excellent discussion of his military service at Fort Moultrie, see William F. Hecker, *Private Perry and Mister Poe: The West Point Poems, 1831* (Baton Rouge: Louisiana State University Press, 2005), xvii–xli.

5   The great red-breasted rail or freshwater marsh hen *(Rallus elegans)*. The American ornithologist John James Audubon (1785–1851) found the freshwater marsh hen abundant in South Carolina but observed, "These birds are rarely shot by common gunners, on account of the difficulty of raising them, and because they generally confine themselves to places so swampy and covered with briars, smilaxes, and rough weeds, that they are scarcely accessible" (*Ornithological Biography: or, An Account of the Habits of the Birds of the United States of America*, 5 vols. [Edinburgh: Adam and Charles Black, 1835], III, 28–29).

6   The cabbage palm (*Sabal palmetto* or *Serenoa repens*).

7   *Myrica cerifera*. Linking a plant species that flourishes in the American South with England, Poe implicitly associates the two at a cultural as well as a horticultural level.

8   Botanists Richard Stalter and Eric E. Lamont quote this passage to indicate that the woody vegetation on Sullivan's Island in the early nineteenth century was similar to the vegetation there today ("The Vascular Flora of Fort Sumter and Fort Moultrie, South Carolina, One Year after Hurricane Hugo," *Castanea* 58 [1993], 142).

9   Psychology as a professional discipline would not emerge until the late nineteenth century, but many of Poe's descriptions of his characters' mental states shrewdly anticipate certain psychological conditions that had yet to be diagnosed or even named. His identification of a mental state that oscillates between enthusiasm and melancholy suggests that Legrand suffers from bipolar disorder.

10   Jan Swammerdamm (1637–1680), a Dutch naturalist and microscopist, may be best known for his discovery of red blood corpuscles, but he performed pioneering entomological work, collecting over three thousand different species of insects. Swammerdamm's work on insects forms the basis of modern entomology.

11   The character of Jupiter owes something to various sources: antebellum plantation romances that idealized plantation life; the humorous tales of the Old Southwest such as A. B. Longstreet's *Georgia Scenes* (1835), characterized by exaggeration, colloquial speech, and provincial manners; and minstrel shows, in which blackface characters were portrayed on stage by white actors such as Edwin Forrest and Thomas Dartmouth "Daddy" Rice. Interpretations of race in literature are more nuanced today than they were in the 1980s and 1990s but are still frequently anachronistic. From our twenty-first century perspective, all of antebellum culture is racist. J. Gerald Kennedy acknowledges this difficulty, speculating that Poe "understood and presumably shared widespread white attitudes about the racial inferiority of blacks. Such assumptions so thoroughly pervaded American culture in that era as to render superfluous current efforts to identify and castigate individual purveyors of literary racism" (J. Gerald Kennedy, "'Trust No Man': Poe, Douglass, and the Culture of Slavery," *Romancing the Shadow: Poe and Race*, ed. J. Gerald Kennedy and Liliane Weissberg [New York: Oxford University Press, 2001], 236). Terence Whalen argues that Poe, the magazinist, strategically cultivated an "average racism," that is, his views on race and slavery were "designed to overcome political dissension in the emerging mass audience" (*Edgar Allan Poe and the Masses: The Political Economy of Literature in Antebellum America* [Princeton: Princeton University Press, 1999], 112).

him well educated, with unusual powers of mind, but infected with misanthropy, and subject to perverse moods of alternate enthusiasm and melancholy.[9] He had with him many books, but rarely employed them. His chief amusements were gunning and fishing, or sauntering along the beach and through the myrtles, in quest of shells or entomological specimens;—his collection of the latter might have been envied by a Swammerdamm.[10] In these excursions he was usually accompanied by an old negro, called Jupiter, who had been manumitted before the reverses of the family, but who could be induced, neither by threats nor by promises, to abandon what he considered his right of attendance upon the footsteps of his young "Massa Will."[11] It is not improbable that the relatives of Legrand, conceiving him to be somewhat unsettled in intellect, had contrived to instil this obstinacy into Jupiter, with a view to the supervision and guardianship of the wanderer.[12]

The winters in the latitude of Sullivan's Island are seldom very severe, and in the fall of the year it is a rare event indeed when a fire is considered necessary. About the middle of October, 18—, there occurred, however, a day of remarkable chilliness. Just before sunset I scrambled my way through the evergreens to the hut of my friend, whom I had not visited for several weeks—my residence being, at that time, in Charleston, a distance of nine miles from the Island, while the facilities of passage and re-passage were very far behind those of the present day. Upon reaching the hut I rapped, as was my custom, and getting no reply, sought for the key where I knew it was secreted, unlocked the door and went in. A fine fire was blazing upon the hearth. It was a novelty, and by no means an ungrateful one. I threw off an overcoat, took an armchair by the crackling logs, and awaited patiently the arrival of my hosts.

Soon after dark they arrived, and gave me a most cordial welcome. Jupiter, grinning from ear to ear, bustled about to prepare some marsh-hens for supper.[13] Legrand was in one of his fits—how else shall I term them?—of enthusiasm. He had found an unknown bivalve,[14] forming a new genus, and, more than this, he had hunted down and secured, with Jupiter's assistance, a *scarabaeus*[15] which he believed to be totally new, but in respect to which he wished to have my opinion on the morrow.

"And why not to-night?" I asked, rubbing my hands over the blaze, and wishing the whole tribe of *scarabaei* at the devil.

G. C. Widney, illustration for *The Gold-Bug* (Chicago: Rand McNally, 1901). Reflecting the prejudices of the early twentieth century, Widney depicts Jupiter as the stereotypical wide-eyed plantation darkie.

"Ah, if I had only known you were here!" said Legrand, "but it's so long since I saw you; and how could I foresee that you would pay me a visit this very night of all others? As I was coming home I met Lieutenant G———,[16] from the fort, and, very foolishly,

12   The relationship between Legrand and Jupiter, the younger, uncontrollable white man and the cautious, conservative, doting black man, establishes a model that would have a long history in American literature and popular culture. Mark Twain's Huck Finn and Jim provide only the most famous of numerous examples. In the cinema, the character types frequently appear in such buddy comedies as *Lethal Weapon*.

13   Poe wrote "The Gold-Bug" while living in a small row house on Coates Street in the Fairmount district of Philadelphia. Located on the edge of town, the house was near the Wissahickon River, which provided opportunities for sport and sustenance. Poe's military training had made him a crack shot. The boy next door remembered, "When Poe asked me to go with him for reed birds I went. I was an active boy. We got into a boat and paddled down to about Gray's Ferry. I rowed while he loaded and shot. For many of the birds I waded in water up to my chin. We brought home a big bag" (quoted in Mary E. Phillips, *Edgar Allan Poe: The Man*, 2 vols. [Chicago: John C. Winston, 1926], I, 749).

14   In *The Conchologist's First Book: A System of Testaceous Malacology*, 2nd ed. (Philadelphia: Haswell, Barrington, and Haswell, 1840), 10, Poe defines this term: "Bivalve shells consist of two parts or valves, connected by a cartilage, and a hinge which is generally composed of teeth; those of the one valve locking into a cavity in the other. The valves of some bivalve shells are formed exactly alike, and others are very different; the one being smooth, the other rugose; one flat and another convex; and often one is shorter than the other." In other words, the bivalve provided a natural manifestation of one of Poe's favorite literary motifs: the doppelganger.

15   A beetle of the genus *Scarabaeus*, sacred to the Ancient Egyptians. Poe's use of the scarabaeus is consistent with the contemporary fascination with Egyptology. J. Gardner Wilkinson explains that in ancient Egyptian culture, the scarabaeus symbolized not only the sun but also the world, creative power, manly force, and virility (*A Second Series of the Manners and Customs of the Ancient Egyptians*, 3 vols. [London: John Murray, 1841], II, 256).

16   This may be a private reference: one of Poe's officers at Fort Moultrie was Captain Henry W. Griswold. If so, Griswold did not survive to appreciate it. He perished of yellow fever on October 23, 1834, while stationed at Fort Moultrie.

17   This is the first mention of "the bug." The New York correspondent of the Charleston *Southern Patriot* (October 11, 1845) reported that the British could not bring themselves to read the 1845 Wiley and Putnam edition of Poe's *Tales* because of "the word '*Bug*' being *tabooed* by English delicacy!" Mabbott notes that in England the word "bug" was synonymous with "bedbug" (Thomas Ollive Mabbott, ed., *Collected Works of Edgar Allan Poe*, 3 vols. [Cambridge, MA: The Belknap Press of Harvard University Press, 1969–1978], III, 844).

When London publisher Henry Vizetelly issued *Tales of Mystery, Imagination, and Humour* in 1852, he retitled the story "The Gold-Beetle." It was known by this title in Great Britain through the nineteenth century. The small change helped make Poe's tale more acceptable and comprehensible to British readers. When first translated into Chinese in the early twentieth century, Poe's tale was titled "The Story of a Jade-Bug."

18   The narrator is making a joke at Legrand's expense— not about unclear pronoun usage, since he knows quite well to what Legrand refers, but about his friend's exuberance for an insect specimen.

19   In the rural South, the short "e" is often pronounced as a short "i," so Jupiter hears the middle syllable of "antennae" as "tin." But Jupiter's words do more than capture his dialect. They also form a double entendre. Elsewhere he uses "notin" to mean "nothing." That meaning is implicit here, as well: "There is nothing to the gold bug." Thomas Dunn English observes: "The bug, which gives title to the story, is used only in the way of mystification, having throughout a seeming and no real connection with the subject. Its purpose is to seduce the reader into the idea of supernatural machinery, and keeping him so mystified until the last moment" (I. M. Walker, ed., *Edgar Allan Poe: The Critical Heritage* [New York: Routledge and Kegan Paul, 1986], 194).

20   In alchemy, the pseudoscience that attempted to change base metals into gold, "Jupiter" was the symbolic name for tin, one of seven planetary metals. For Poe's playful incorporation of alchemy in this tale, see Barton Levi St. Armand, "Poe's 'Sober Mystification': The Uses of Alchemy in 'The Gold-Bug,'" *Poe Studies* 4 (1971), 1–7.

21   A colorful, fantastically shaped hat adorned with bells and worn by fools or jesters, the fool's cap became associated with paper once it started being used as a watermark. By Poe's time, the term "foolscap" had come to mean simply a long sheet of writing paper.

I lent him the bug;[17] so it will be impossible for you to see it until the morning. Stay here to-night, and I will send Jup down for it at sunrise. It is the loveliest thing in creation!"

"What?—sunrise?"[18]

"Nonsense! no!—the bug. It is of a brilliant gold color—about the size of a large hickory-nut—with two jet black spots near one extremity of the back, and another, somewhat longer, at the other. The *antennae* are—"

"Dey aint *no* tin[19] in him, Massa Will, I keep a tellin on you," here interrupted Jupiter; "de bug is a goole bug, solid, ebery bit of him, inside and all, sep him wing—neber feel half so hebby a bug in my life."[20]

"Well, suppose it is, Jup," replied Legrand, somewhat more earnestly, it seemed to me, than the case demanded, "is that any reason for your letting the birds burn? The color"—here he turned to me—"is really almost enough to warrant Jupiter's idea. You never saw a more brilliant metallic lustre than the scales emit—but of this you cannot judge till to-morrow. In the mean time I can give you some idea of the shape." Saying this, he seated himself at a small table, on which were a pen and ink, but no paper. He looked for some in a drawer, but found none.

"Never mind," said he at length, "this will answer"; and he drew from his waistcoat pocket a scrap of what I took to be very dirty foolscap,[21] and made upon it a rough drawing with the pen. While he did this, I retained my seat by the fire, for I was still chilly. When the design was complete, he handed it to me without rising. As I received it, a loud growl was heard, succeeded by a scratching at the door. Jupiter opened it, and a large Newfoundland, belonging to Legrand, rushed in, leaped upon my shoulders, and loaded me with caresses; for I had shown him much attention during previous visits. When his gambols were over, I looked at the paper, and, to speak the truth, found myself not a little puzzled at what my friend had depicted.

"Well!" I said, after contemplating it for some minutes, "this *is* a strange *scarabaeus*, I must confess: new to me: never saw anything like it before—unless it was a skull, or a death's-head[22]— which it more nearly resembles than anything else that has come under *my* observation."

"A death's-head!" echoed Legrand—"Oh—yes—well, it has something of that appearance upon paper, no doubt. The two up-

J. W. Kennedy, illustration for *The Gold-Bug* (Boston: Dana Estes, 1899). Kennedy captures another racial stereotype, the African-American male dressed up in his finest, the kind of fancy dress associated with cake-walks, or dances held on slave plantations. Stephen Crane made creative use of the stereotype in "The Monster," published the same year as the Dana Estes edition of *The Gold-Bug*.

per black spots look like eyes, eh? and the longer one at the bottom like a mouth—and then the shape of the whole is oval."

"Perhaps so," said I; "but, Legrand, I fear you are no artist. I must wait until I see the beetle itself, if I am to form any idea of its personal appearance."

"Well, I don't know," said he, a little nettled, "I draw tolerably—*should* do it at least—have had good masters, and flatter myself that I am not quite a blockhead."[23]

"But, my dear fellow, you are joking then," said I, "this is a very passable *skull*—indeed, I may say that it is a very *excellent* skull, according to the vulgar notions about such specimens of physiol-

22 In Western culture, the skull was a prominent icon in the tradition of *memento mori*, Latin for "remember death."

23 Legrand's boast about his drawing ability may be read as an invitation to see him as another of Poe's stand-ins for the artist.

24 "Caput hominis" means a man's head.

25 The term "cut" refers to any kind of printed illustration that had been cut or engraved into copper, steel, or wood.

ogy—and your *scarabaeus* must be the queerest *scarabaeus* in the world if it resembles it. Why, we may get up a very thrilling bit of superstition upon this hint. I presume you will call the bug *scarabaeus caput hominis*,[24] or something of that kind—there are many similar titles in the Natural Histories. But where are the *antennae* you spoke of?"

"The *antennae!*" said Legrand, who seemed to be getting unaccountably warm upon the subject; "I am sure you must see the *antennae*. I made them as distinct as they are in the original insect, and I presume that is sufficient."

"Well, well," I said, "perhaps you have—still I don't see them;" and I handed him the paper without additional remark, not wishing to ruffle his temper; but I was much surprised at the turn affairs had taken; his ill humor puzzled me—and, as for the drawing of the beetle, there were positively *no antennae* visible, and the whole *did* bear a very close resemblance to the ordinary cuts of a death's-head.[25]

He received the paper very peevishly, and was about to crumple it, apparently to throw it in the fire, when a casual glance at the design seemed suddenly to rivet his attention. In an instant his face grew violently red—in another as excessively pale. For some minutes he continued to scrutinize the drawing minutely where he sat. At length he arose, took a candle from the table, and proceeded to seat himself upon a sea-chest in the farthest corner of the room. Here again he made an anxious examination of the paper; turning it in all directions. He said nothing, however, and his conduct greatly astonished me; yet I thought it prudent not to exacerbate the growing moodiness of his temper by any comment. Presently he took from his coat pocket a wallet, placed the paper carefully in it, and deposited both in a writing-desk, which he locked. He now grew more composed in his demeanor; but his original air of enthusiasm had quite disappeared. Yet he seemed not so much sulky as abstracted. As the evening wore away he became more and more absorbed in reverie, from which no sallies of mine could arouse him. It had been my intention to pass the night at the hut, as I had frequently done before, but, seeing my host in this mood, I deemed it proper to take leave. He did not press me to remain, but, as I departed, he shook my hand with even more than his usual cordiality.

It was about a month after this (and during the interval I had seen nothing of Legrand) when I received a visit, at Charleston, from his man, Jupiter. I had never seen the good old negro look so dispirited, and I feared that some serious disaster had befallen my friend.

"Well, Jup," said I, "what is the matter now?—how is your master?"

"Why, to speak de troof, massa, him not so berry well as mought be."

"Not well! I am truly sorry to hear it. What does he complain of?"

"Dar! dat's it!—him neber plain of notin—but him berry sick for all dat."[26]

"*Very* sick, Jupiter!—why didn't you say so at once? Is he confined to bed?"

"No, dat he aint!—he aint find nowhar—dat's just whar de shoe pinch[27]—my mind is got to be berry hebby bout poor Massa Will."

"Jupiter, I should like to understand what it is you are talking about. You say your master is sick. Hasn't he told you what ails him?"

"Why, massa, taint worf while for to git mad about de matter—Massa Will say noffin at all aint de matter wid him—but den what make him go about looking dis here way, wid he head down and he soldiers up, and as white as a gose?[28] And den he keep a syphon all de time—"[29]

"Keeps a what, Jupiter?"

"Keeps a syphon wid de figgurs on de slate—de queerest figgurs I ebber did see. Ise gittin to be skeered, I tell you.[30] Hab for to keep mighty tight eye pon him noovers.[31] Todder day he gib me slip fore de sun up and was gone de whole ob de blessed day. I had a big stick ready cut for to gib him d——d good beating when he did come—but Ise sich a fool dat I hadn't de heart arter all—he look so berry poorly."

"Eh?—what?—ah yes!—upon the whole I think you had better not be too severe with the poor fellow—don't flog him, Jupiter—he can't very well stand it—but can you form no idea of what has occasioned this illness, or rather this change of conduct? Has anything unpleasant happened since I saw you?"

"No, massa, dey aint bin noffin onpleasant *since* den—'twas *fore* den I'm feared—'twas de berry day you was dare."

26 As Jupiter speaks, he often drops the first syllable from multisyllabic words. "Complain" becomes "plain." Later, he would say "sis pon" for "insist upon." Jupiter also pronounces the v-sound as a b-sound. Poe's use of dialect and humor in this tale is similar to that of his contemporaries Augustus B. Longstreet, George Washington Harris, and Johnson Jones Hooper, among other humorists of the Old Southwest, important forerunners of Mark Twain.

27 A proverbial expression, meaning where the trouble lies, or the real cause for worry.

28 White as a ghost: a proverbial comparison.

29 Jupiter confuses "cipher"—an algorithm for performing encryption or decryption—with "siphon."

30 The illiterate traditionally attributed supernatural powers to any sort of writing. In "King Pest" (1835), a short story set in London centuries earlier, Poe says of his two tipsy sailor-protagonists: "They were eyeing, from behind a huge flagon of unpaid-for 'humming-stuff,' the portentous words, 'No Chalk,' which to their indignation and astonishment were scored over the doorway by means of that very mineral whose presence they purported to deny. Not that the gift of deciphering written characters—a gift among the commonality of that day considered little less cabalistical than the art of indicting—could, in strict justice, have been laid to the charge of either disciple of the sea."

31 Maneuvers.

32   Jupiter attributes Legrand's strange behavior to an illness transmitted by the bite of the bug. "The Gold-Bug"
gave rise to the proverbial expression bitten by the gold
bug. When gold was discovered in California in 1848,
five years after the story's publication, many people remembered Poe's tale. The thousands of gold-seekers who
pulled up stakes and made the hazardous journey by land
or sea to California were said to be "bitten by the gold
bug." Later in the nineteenth century, the term "gold bug"
came to mean a person in favor of the free circulation of
gold as well as a gold speculator (*The Oxford Dictionary
of American Political Slang*, ed. Grant Barrett [New York:
Oxford University Press, 2004], 119).

33   Bluntness of manner.

34   Alone.

35   The term "cabinet" refers to a private collection of curiosities, often but not always curiosities of natural history. By Poe's day, the cabinet of curiosities already had a
long tradition. In *Gesta Grayorum* (1594), Francis Bacon
briefly delineated its ideal contents. He recommended "a
goodly huge cabinet" to hold "whatsoever the hand of man
by exquisite art or engine hath made rare in stuff, form or
motion; whatsoever singularity chance and the shuffle of
things hath produced; whatsoever Nature hath wrought
in things that want life and may be kept." No matter how
capacious the cabinet, a collection of curiosities would in
time typically grow beyond its confines and spill over into
the collector's living quarters. Even then, the collection as
a whole was still called a "cabinet of curiosities."

"How? what do you mean?"

"Why, massa, I mean de bug—dare now."

"The what?"

"De bug,—I'm berry sartain dat Massa Will bin bit somewhere bout de head by dat goole-bug."[32]

"And what cause have you, Jupiter, for such a supposition?"

"Claws enuff, massa, and mouff too. I nebber did see sich a d——d bug—he kick and he bite ebery ting what cum near him. Massa Will cotch him fuss, but had for to let him go gin mighty quick, I tell you—den was de time he must ha got de bite. I didn't like de look ob de bug mouff, myself, no how, so I wouldn't take hold ob him wid my finger, but I cotch him wid a piece ob paper dat I found. I rap him up in de paper and stuff piece ob it in he mouff—dat was de way."

"And you think, then, that your master was really bitten by the beetle, and that the bite made him sick?"

"I don't tink noffin about it—I nose it. What make him dream bout de goole so much, if taint cause he bit by de goole-bug? Ise heerd bout dem goole-bugs fore dis."

"But how do you know he dreams about gold?"

"How I know? why cause he talk about it in he sleep—dat's how I nose."

"Well, Jup, perhaps you are right; but to what fortunate circumstance am I to attribute the honor of a visit from you to-day?"

"What de matter, massa?"

"Did you bring any message from Mr. Legrand?"

"No, massa, I bring dis here pissel"; and here Jupiter handed me a note which ran thus:

My Dear——
Why have I not seen you for so long a time? I hope you have not been so foolish as to take offence at any little *brusquerie*[33] of mine; but no, that is improbable.

Since I saw you I have had great cause for anxiety. I have something to tell you, yet scarcely know how to tell it, or whether I should tell it at all.

I have not been quite well for some days past, and poor old Jup annoys me, almost beyond endurance, by his well-meant attentions. Would you believe it?—he had prepared a huge stick, the other day, with which to chastise me for giv-

Jupiter (Geoffrey Holder) and Boy (Anthony Michael Hall), a character introduced to the story for "The Gold Bug," an episode of the children's program *ABC Weekend Special* that premiered on February 2, 1980. The six-foot, six-inch Holder, best known as Baron Samedi in *Live and Let Die* (1973), turns Jupiter into a much more imposing figure than earlier readers perceived.

ing him the slip, and spending the day, *solus*,[34] among the hills on the main land. I verily believe that my ill looks alone saved me a flogging.

I have made no addition to my cabinet[35] since we met.

If you can, in any way, make it convenient, come over with Jupiter. *Do* come. I wish to see you *to-night*, upon business of importance. I assure you that it is of the *highest* importance.

Ever yours,   William Legrand.

36 Only later in the story does it become fully clear that Legrand's letter and subsequent behavior are themselves a kind of performance. Legrand's ability to disguise or vary the tone and style of his writing indicates his literary skill. Reviewing John Pendleton Kennedy's *Horse-Shoe Robinson*, a historical novel set in Revolutionary times, Poe praises its author's style: "It varies gracefully and readily with the nature of his subject, never sinking, even in the low comedy of some parts of the book, into the insipid or the vulgar; and often, very often rising into the energetic and sublime" (*Essays and Reviews*, ed. G. R. Thompson [New York: Library of America, 1984], 651).

37 "A whimsical fancy; a perverse conceit; a peculiar notion on some point (usually considered unimportant) held by an individual in opposition to common opinion" *(OED)*.

38 "The devil's own" is another proverbial phrase, less common than it once was. It often occurs as "the devil's own luck" but has numerous variations. Here it means expensive or high-priced.

39 Eagerness; an animated display of cordiality.

There was something in the tone of this note which gave me great uneasiness. Its whole style differed materially from that of Legrand.[36] What could he be dreaming of? What new crotchet[37] possessed his excitable brain? What "business of the highest importance" could *he* possibly have to transact? Jupiter's account of him boded no good. I dreaded lest the continued pressure of misfortune had, at length, fairly unsettled the reason of my friend. Without a moment's hesitation, therefore, I prepared to accompany the negro.

Upon reaching the wharf, I noticed a scythe and three spades, all apparently new, lying in the bottom of the boat in which we were to embark.

"What is the meaning of all this, Jup?" I inquired.

"Him syfe, massa, and spade."

"Very true; but what are they doing here?"

"Him de syfe and de spade what Massa Will sis pon my buying for him in de town, and de debbils own lot of money[38] I had to gib for em."

"But what, in the name of all that is mysterious, is your 'Massa Will' going to do with scythes and spades?"

"Dat's more dan *I* know, and debbil take me if I don't blieve 'tis more dan he know, too. But it's all cum ob de bug."

Finding that no satisfaction was to be obtained of Jupiter, whose whole intellect seemed to be absorbed by "de bug," I now stepped into the boat and made sail. With a fair and strong breeze we soon ran into the little cove to the northward of Fort Moultrie, and a walk of some two miles brought us to the hut. It was about three in the afternoon when we arrived. Legrand had been awaiting us in eager expectation. He grasped my hand with a nervous *empressement*[39] which alarmed me and strengthened the suspicions already entertained. His countenance was pale even to ghastliness, and his deep-set eyes glared with unnatural lustre. After some inquiries respecting his health, I asked him, not knowing what better to say, if he had yet obtained the *scarabaeus* from Lieutenant G———.

"Oh, yes," he replied, coloring violently, "I got it from him the next morning. Nothing should tempt me to part with that *scarabaeus*. Do you know that Jupiter is quite right about it?"

"In what way?" I asked, with a sad foreboding at heart.

"In supposing it to be a bug of *real gold*." He said this with an air of profound seriousness, and I felt inexpressibly shocked.

"This bug is to make my fortune," he continued, with a triumphant smile, "to reinstate me in my family possessions. Is it any wonder, then, that I prize it? Since Fortune has thought fit to bestow it upon me, I have only to use it properly and I shall arrive at the gold of which it is the index. Jupiter, bring me that *scarabaeus!*"

"What! de bug, massa? I'd rudder not go fer trubble dat bug— you mus git him for your own self." Hereupon Legrand arose, with a grave and stately air, and brought me the beetle from a glass case in which it was enclosed. It was a beautiful *scarabaeus*, and, at that time, unknown to naturalists—of course a great prize in a scientific point of view. There were two round, black spots near one extremity of the back, and a long one near the other. The scales were exceedingly hard and glossy, with all the appearance of burnished gold. The weight of the insect was very remarkable, and, taking all things into consideration, I could hardly blame Jupiter for his opinion respecting it; but what to make of Legrand's agreement with that opinion, I could not, for the life of me, tell.

"I sent for you," said he, in a grandiloquent tone, when I had completed my examination of the beetle, "I sent for you, that I might have your counsel and assistance in furthering the views of Fate and of the bug"—

"My dear Legrand," I cried, interrupting him, "you are certainly unwell, and had better use some little precautions. You shall go to bed, and I will remain with you a few days, until you get over this. You are feverish and"—

"Feel my pulse," said he.

I felt it, and, to say the truth, found not the slightest indication of fever.

"But you may be ill and yet have no fever. Allow me this once to prescribe for you. In the first place, go to bed. In the next"—

"You are mistaken," he interposed, "I am as well as I can expect to be under the excitement which I suffer. If you really wish me well, you will relieve this excitement."

"And how is this to be done?"

"Very easily. Jupiter and myself are going upon an expedition, into the hills, upon the main land, and, in this expedition we shall need the aid of some person in whom we can confide. You are the only one we can trust. Whether we succeed or fail, the excitement which you now perceive in me will be equally allayed."

"I am anxious to oblige you in any way," I replied; "but do you

40 Magician.

mean to say that this infernal beetle has any connection with your expedition into the hills?"

"It has."

"Then, Legrand, I can become a party to no such absurd proceeding."

"I am sorry—very sorry—for we shall have to try it by ourselves."

"Try it by yourselves! The man is surely mad!—but stay!—how long do you propose to be absent?"

"Probably all night. We shall start immediately, and be back, at all events, by sunrise."

"And will you promise me, upon your honor, that when this freak of yours is over, and the bug business (good God!) settled to your satisfaction, you will then return home and follow my advice implicitly, as that of your physician?"

"Yes; I promise; and now let us be off, for we have no time to lose."

With a heavy heart I accompanied my friend. We started about four o'clock—Legrand, Jupiter, the dog, and myself. Jupiter had with him the scythe and spades—the whole of which he insisted upon carrying—more through fear, it seemed to me, of trusting either of the implements within reach of his master, than from any excess of industry or complaisance. His demeanor was dogged in the extreme, and "dat deuced bug" were the sole words which escaped his lips during the journey. For my own part, I had charge of a couple of dark lanterns, while Legrand contented himself with the *scarabaeus*, which he carried attached to the end of a bit of whip-cord; twirling it to and fro, with the air of a conjuror,[40] as he went. When I observed this last, plain evidence of my friend's aberration of mind, I could scarcely refrain from tears. I thought it best, however, to humor his fancy, at least for the present, or until I could adopt some more energetic measures with a chance of success. In the mean time I endeavored, but all in vain, to sound him in regard to the object of the expedition. Having succeeded in inducing me to accompany him, he seemed unwilling to hold conversation upon any topic of minor importance, and to all my questions vouchsafed no other reply than "we shall see!"

We crossed the creek at the head of the island by means of a skiff, and, ascending the high grounds on the shore of the main land, proceeded in a northwesterly direction, through a tract of country excessively wild and desolate, where no trace of a human footstep was to be seen. Legrand led the way with decision; pausing only for an instant, here and there, to consult what appeared to be certain landmarks of his own contrivance upon a former occasion.

In this manner we journeyed for about two hours, and the sun was just setting when we entered a region infinitely more dreary than any yet seen. It was a species of table land,[41] near the summit of an almost inaccessible hill, densely wooded from base to pinnacle, and interspersed with huge crags that appeared to lie loosely upon the soil, and in many cases were prevented from precipitating themselves into the valleys below, merely by the support of the trees against which they reclined. Deep ravines, in various directions, gave an air of still sterner solemnity to the scene.

The natural platform to which we had clambered was thickly overgrown with brambles, through which we soon discovered that it would have been impossible to force our way but for the scythe; and Jupiter, by direction of his master, proceeded to clear for us a path to the foot of an enormously tall tulip-tree, which stood, with some eight or ten oaks, upon the level, and far surpassed them all, and all other trees which I had then ever seen, in the beauty of its foliage and form, in the wide spread of its branches, and in the general majesty of its appearance. When we reached this tree, Legrand turned to Jupiter, and asked him if he thought he could climb it. The old man seemed a little staggered by the question, and for some moments made no reply. At length he approached the huge trunk, walked slowly around it, and examined it with minute attention. When he had completed his scrutiny, he merely said,

"Yes, massa, Jup climb any tree he ebber see in he life."

"Then up with you as soon as possible, for it will soon be too dark to see what we are about."

"How far mus go up, massa?" inquired Jupiter.

"Get up the main trunk first, and then I will tell you which way to go—and here—stop! take this beetle with you."

"De bug, Massa Will!—de goole bug!" cried the negro, drawing back in dismay—"what for mus tote de bug way up de tree?— d—n if I do!"

"If you are afraid, Jup, a great big negro like you, to take hold of a harmless little dead beetle, why you can carry it up by this

41   An elevated region of comparatively flat land.

string—but, if you do not take it up with you in some way, I shall
be under the necessity of breaking your head with this shovel."

"What de matter now, massa?" said Jup, evidently shamed into
compliance; "always want for to raise fuss wid old nigger. Was
only funnin any how. Me feered de bug! what I keer for de bug?"
Here he took cautiously hold of the extreme end of the string,
and, maintaining the insect as far from his person as circumstances
would permit, prepared to ascend the tree.

In youth, the tulip-tree, or *Liriodendron Tulipiferum*, the most
magnificent of American foresters, has a trunk peculiarly smooth,
and often rises to a great height without lateral branches; but, in its
riper age, the bark becomes gnarled and uneven, while many short
limbs make their appearance on the stem. Thus the difficulty of
ascension, in the present case, lay more in semblance than in reality. Embracing the huge cylinder, as closely as possible, with his
arms and knees, seizing with his hands some projections, and resting his naked toes upon others, Jupiter, after one or two narrow
escapes from falling, at length wriggled himself into the first great
fork, and seemed to consider the whole business as virtually accomplished. The *risk* of the achievement was, in fact, now over,
although the climber was some sixty or seventy feet from the
ground.

"Which way mus go now, Massa Will?" he asked.

"Keep up the largest branch—the one on this side," said Legrand. The negro obeyed him promptly, and apparently with but
little trouble; ascending higher and higher, until no glimpse of his
squat figure could be obtained through the dense foliage which enveloped it. Presently his voice was heard in a sort of halloo.[42]

"How much fudder is got for go?"

"How high up are you?" asked Legrand.

"Ebber so fur," replied the negro; "can see de sky fru de top ob
de tree."

"Never mind the sky, but attend to what I say. Look down the
trunk and count the limbs below you on this side. How many limbs
have you passed?"

"One, two, tree, four, fibe—I done pass fibe big limb, massa,
pon dis side."

"Then go one limb higher."

In a few minutes the voice was heard again, announcing that the
seventh limb was attained.

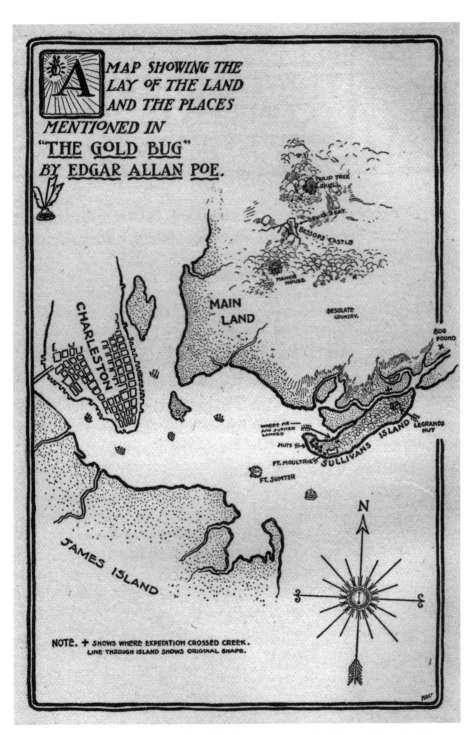

"A Map Showing the Lay of the Land and the Places Mentioned in 'The Gold Bug' by Edgar Allan Poe," illustration for Rand McNally's 1901 edition of the tale.

43   In *A Christmas Carol*, published the same year as "The Gold-Bug," Charles Dickens meditates amusingly on this idiomatic expression:

> "Old Marley was as dead as a door-nail.
> Mind! I don't mean to say that I know, of my own knowledge, what there is particularly dead about a door-nail. I might have been inclined, myself, to regard a coffin-nail as the deadest piece of ironmongery in the trade. But the wisdom of our ancestors is in the simile; and my unhallowed hands shall not disturb it, or the Country's done for. You will therefore permit me to repeat, emphatically, that Marley was as dead as a door-nail" (Charles Dickens, *A Christmas Carol in Prose, Being a Ghost Story of Christmas* [London: Bradbury and Evans, 1858], 1)

"Now, Jup," cried Legrand, evidently much excited, "I want you to work your way out upon that limb as far as you can. If you see anything strange, let me know."

By this time what little doubt I might have entertained of my poor friend's insanity, was put finally at rest. I had no alternative but to conclude him stricken with lunacy, and I became seriously anxious about getting him home. While I was pondering upon what was best to be done, Jupiter's voice was again heard.

"Mos feerd for to venture pon dis limb berry far—tis dead limb putty much all de way."

"Did you say it was a *dead* limb, Jupiter?" cried Legrand in a quavering voice.

"Yes, massa, him dead as de door-nail[43]—done up for sartain—done departed dis here life."

"What in the name of heaven shall I do?" asked Legrand, seemingly in the greatest distress.

"Do!" said I, glad of an opportunity to interpose a word, "why come home and go to bed. Come now!—that's a fine fellow. It's getting late, and, besides, you remember your promise."

"Jupiter," cried he, without heeding me in the least, "do you hear me?"

"Yes, Massa Will, hear you ebber so plain."

"Try the wood well, then, with your knife, and see if you think it *very* rotten."

"Him rotten, massa, sure nuff," replied the negro in a few moments, "but not so berry rotten as mought be. Mought ventur out leetle way pon de limb by myself, dat's true."

"By yourself!—what do you mean?"

"Why I mean de bug. 'Tis *berry* hebby bug. Spose I drop him down fuss, and den de limb won't break wid just de weight ob one nigger."

"You infernal scoundrel!" cried Legrand, apparently much relieved, "what do you mean by telling me such nonsense as that? As sure as you drop that beetle I'll break your neck. Look here, Jupiter, do you hear me?"

"Yes, massa, needn't hollo at poor nigger dat style."

"Well! now listen!—if you will venture out on the limb as far as you think safe, and not let go the beetle, I'll make you a present of a silver dollar as soon as you get down."

"I'm gwine, Massa Will—deed I is," replied the negro very promptly—"mos out to the eend now."

"Out to the end!" here fairly screamed Legrand, "do you say you are out to the end of that limb?"

"Soon be to de eend, massa,—o-o-o-o-oh! Lor-gol-a-marcy! what is dis here pon de tree?"

"Well!" cried Legrand, highly delighted, "what is it?"

"Why taint noffin but a skull—somebody bin lef him head up de tree, and de crows done gobble ebery bit ob de meat off."[44]

"A skull, you say!—very well!—how is it fastened to the limb?—what holds it on?"

"Sure nuff, massa; mus look. Why dis berry curous sarcum-stance, pon my word—dare's a great big nail in de skull, what fastens ob it on to de tree."

"Well now, Jupiter, do exactly as I tell you—do you hear?"

"Yes, massa."

"Pay attention, then!—find the left eye of the skull."

"Hum! hoo! dat's good! why dar aint no eye lef at all."

"Curse your stupidity! do you know your right hand from your left?"[45]

"Yes, I nose dat—nose all bout dat—tis my lef hand what I chops de wood wid."

"To be sure! you are left-handed; and your left eye is on the same side as your left hand.[46] Now, I suppose, you can find the left eye of the skull, or the place where the left eye has been. Have you found it?"

Here was a long pause. At length the negro asked,

"Is de lef eye of de skull pon de same side as de lef hand of de skull, too?—cause de skull aint got not a bit ob a hand at all—nebber mind! I got de lef eye now—here de lef eye! what mus do wid it?"

"Let the beetle drop through it, as far as the string will reach—but be careful and not let go your hold of the string."

"All dat done, Massa Will; mighty easy ting for to put de bug fru de hole—look out for him dare below!"

During this colloquy no portion of Jupiter's person could be seen; but the beetle, which he had suffered to descend, was now visible at the end of the string, and glistened, like a globe of burnished gold, in the last rays of the setting sun, some of which still faintly illumined the eminence upon which we stood. The *scarabaeus* hung quite clear of any branches, and, if allowed to fall, would have fallen at our feet. Legrand immediately took the scythe, and cleared with it a circular space, three or four yards

44 Jupiter's theory—that a human head had been placed intact on the tree limb and picked clean by scavengers—is meant to be comically absurd. But Jupiter's words cannot be dismissed out of hand. His assumption—the assumption of a former slave—that cruel violence has been perpetrated here, will be proven to be correct. Jupiter's imagery recalls a disturbing passage from Crèvecoeur's *Letters from an American Farmer* (1782), which describes a slave who has been caged, hung in a tree, and subjected to severe mutilation at the hands of nature: "I shudder when I recollect that the birds had already picked out his eyes, his cheek bones were bare; his arms had been attacked in several places, and his body seemed covered with a multitude of wounds."

45 Jonah 4:11: "And should not I spare Nineveh, that great city, wherein are more than sixscore thousand persons that cannot discern between their right hand and their left hand; and also much cattle?"

46 According to one superstition that circulated widely in the South, if your left hand itches, you are going to get some money (*The Frank C. Brown Collection of North Carolina Folklore*, ed. Newman Ivey White, 7 vols. [Durham: Duke University Press, 1952–1964], no. 8536).

47 Poe means legends of buried treasure, but these superstition-filled narratives were not unique to the Southern United States.

48 A proverbial expression meaning "to do with apparent willingness, or as if performing a meritorious action, what one in reality cannot help doing; to submit to circumstances with a good grace" *(OED)*.

in diameter, just beneath the insect, and, having accomplished this, ordered Jupiter to let go the string and come down from the tree.

Driving a peg, with great nicety, into the ground, at the precise spot where the beetle fell, my friend now produced from his pocket a tape-measure. Fastening one end of this at that point of the trunk of the tree which was nearest the peg, he unrolled it till it reached the peg, and thence farther unrolled it, in the direction already established by the two points of the tree and the peg, for the distance of fifty feet—Jupiter clearing away the brambles with the scythe. At the spot thus attained a second peg was driven, and about this, as a centre, a rude circle, about four feet in diameter, described. Taking now a spade himself, and giving one to Jupiter and one to me, Legrand begged us to set about digging as quickly as possible.

To speak the truth, I had no especial relish for such amusement at any time, and, at that particular moment, would most willingly have declined it; for the night was coming on, and I felt much fatigued with the exercise already taken; but I saw no mode of escape, and was fearful of disturbing my poor friend's equanimity by a refusal. Could I have depended, indeed, upon Jupiter's aid, I would have had no hesitation in attempting to get the lunatic home by force; but I was too well assured of the old negro's disposition, to hope that he would assist me, under any circumstances, in a personal contest with his master. I made no doubt that the latter had been infected with some of the innumerable Southern superstitions about money buried,[47] and that his phantasy had received confirmation by the finding of the *scarabaeus*, or, perhaps, by Jupiter's obstinacy in maintaining it to be "a bug of real gold." A mind disposed to lunacy would readily be led away by such suggestions—especially if chiming in with favorite preconceived ideas—and then I called to mind the poor fellow's speech about the beetle's being "the index of his fortune." Upon the whole, I was sadly vexed and puzzled, but, at length, I concluded to make a virtue of necessity[48]—to dig with a good will, and thus the sooner to convince the visionary, by ocular demonstration, of the fallacy of the opinions he entertained.

The lanterns having been lit, we all fell to work with a zeal worthy a more rational cause; and, as the glare fell upon our persons and implements, I could not help thinking how picturesque a group we composed, and how strange and suspicious our labors must have appeared to any interloper who, by chance, might have stumbled upon our whereabouts.

We dug very steadily for two hours. Little was said; and our chief embarrassment lay in the yelpings of the dog, who took exceeding interest in our proceedings. He, at length, became so obstreperous that we grew fearful of his giving the alarm to some stragglers in the vicinity;—or, rather, this was the apprehension of Legrand;—for myself, I should have rejoiced at any interruption which might have enabled me to get the wanderer home. The noise was, at length, very effectually silenced by Jupiter, who, getting out of the hole with a dogged air of deliberation, tied the brute's mouth up with one of his suspenders, and then returned, with a grave chuckle, to his task.

When the time mentioned had expired, we had reached a depth of five feet, and yet no signs of any treasure became manifest. A general pause ensued, and I began to hope that the farce was at an end. Legrand, however, although evidently much disconcerted, wiped his brow thoughtfully and recommenced. We had excavated the entire circle of four feet diameter, and now we slightly enlarged the limit, and went to the farther depth of two feet. Still nothing appeared. The gold-seeker, whom I sincerely pitied, at length clambered from the pit, with the bitterest disappointment imprinted upon every feature, and proceeded, slowly and reluctantly, to put on his coat, which he had thrown off at the beginning of his labor. In the mean time I made no remark. Jupiter, at a signal from his master, began to gather up his tools. This done, and the dog having been unmuzzled, we turned in profound silence towards home.

We had taken, perhaps, a dozen steps in this direction, when, with a loud oath, Legrand strode up to Jupiter, and seized him by the collar. The astonished negro opened his eyes and mouth to the fullest extent, let fall the spades, and fell upon his knees.

"You scoundrel," said Legrand, hissing out the syllables from between his clenched teeth—"you infernal black villain!—speak, I tell you!—answer me this instant, without prevarication!—which—which is your left eye?"

"Oh, my golly, Massa Will! aint dis here my lef eye for sartain?" roared the terrified Jupiter, placing his hand upon his *right* organ of vision, and holding it there with a desperate pertinacity, as if in immediate dread of his master's attempt at a gouge.[49]

49   Eye gouging is a commonplace motif among the tales of the Southwestern humorists. In his appreciative review of Augustus Baldwin Longstreet's *Georgia Scenes* (1835), Poe paraphrased an incident from "Georgia Theatrics," the first sketch in Longstreet's collection: "Having overcome about half the space which separated him from the combatants, our friend Hall is horror-stricken at seeing 'the uppermost make a heavy plunge with both his thumbs, and hearing, at the same instant, a cry in the accent of keenest torture, "Enough! My eye's out!"'" (*Essays and Reviews*, 780).

50 A curvet is the leap of a horse in which the fore legs are first raised together and then the hind legs are raised with a spring before the fore legs can touch the ground, but the term often refers to any kind of leaping motion. A caracol occurs when a rider executes a half-turn to the right or left.

51 *Hamlet*, II.ii.203–204: "Though this be madness, yet there is method in't."

"I thought so!—I knew it! hurrah!" vociferated Legrand, letting the negro go, and executing a series of curvets and caracols,[50] much to the astonishment of his valet, who, arising from his knees, looked, mutely, from his master to myself, and then from myself to his master.

"Come! we must go back," said the latter, "the game's not up yet"; and he again led the way to the tulip-tree.

"Jupiter," said he, when we reached its foot, "come here! was the skull nailed to the limb with the face outwards, or with the face to the limb?"

"De face was out, massa, so dat de crows could get at de eyes good, widout any trouble."

"Well, then, was it this eye or that through which you let fall the beetle?"—here Legrand touched each of Jupiter's eyes.

"Twas dis eye, massa—de lef eye—jis as you tell me," and here it was his right eye that the negro indicated.

"That will do—we must try it again."

Here my friend, about whose madness I now saw, or fancied that I saw, certain indications of method,[51] removed the peg which marked the spot where the beetle fell, to a spot about three inches to the westward of its former position. Taking, now, the tape-measure from the nearest point of the trunk to the peg, as before, and continuing the extension in a straight line to the distance of fifty feet, a spot was indicated, removed, by several yards, from the point at which we had been digging.

Around the new position a circle, somewhat larger than in the former instance, was now described, and we again set to work with the spades. I was dreadfully weary, but, scarcely understanding what had occasioned the change in my thoughts, I felt no longer any great aversion from the labor imposed. I had become most unaccountably interested—nay, even excited. Perhaps there was something, amid all the extravagant demeanor of Legrand—some air of forethought, or of deliberation, which impressed me. I dug eagerly, and now and then caught myself actually looking, with something that very much resembled expectation, for the fancied treasure, the vision of which had demented my unfortunate companion. At a period when such vagaries of thought most fully possessed me, and when we had been at work perhaps an hour and a half, we were again interrupted by the violent howlings of the dog. His uneasiness, in the first instance, had been, evidently, but the result of playfulness or caprice, but he now assumed a bitter and serious tone. Upon Jupiter's again attempting to muzzle him, he made furious resistance, and, leaping into the hole, tore up the mould frantically with his claws. In a few seconds he had uncovered a mass of human bones, forming two complete skeletons, intermingled with several buttons of metal, and what appeared to be the dust of decayed woollen. One or two strokes of a spade upturned the blade of a large Spanish knife, and, as we dug farther, three or four loose pieces of gold and silver coin came to light.

At sight of these the joy of Jupiter could scarcely be restrained, but the countenance of his master wore an air of extreme disappointment. He urged us, however, to continue our exertions, and the words were hardly uttered when I stumbled and fell forward, having caught the toe of my boot in a large ring of iron that lay half buried in the loose earth.

We now worked in earnest, and never did I pass ten minutes of more intense excitement. During this interval we had fairly unearthed an oblong chest of wood, which, from its perfect preservation and wonderful hardness, had plainly been subjected to some mineralizing process—perhaps that of the Bi-chloride of Mercury.[52] This box was three feet and a half long, three feet broad, and two and a half feet deep. It was firmly secured by bands of wrought iron, riveted, and forming a kind of open trellis-work over the whole. On each side of the chest, near the top, were three rings of iron—six in all—by means of which a firm hold could be obtained by six persons. Our utmost united endeavors served only to disturb the coffer very slightly in its bed. We at once saw the impossibility of removing so great a weight. Luckily, the sole fastenings of the lid consisted of two sliding bolts. These we drew back—trembling and panting with anxiety. In an instant, a treasure of incalculable value lay gleaming before us. As the rays of the lanterns fell within the pit, there flashed upwards from a confused heap of gold and of jewels, a glow and a glare that absolutely dazzled our eyes.

I shall not pretend to describe the feelings with which I gazed. Amazement was, of course, predominant. Legrand appeared exhausted with excitement, and spoke very few words. Jupiter's countenance wore, for some minutes, as deadly a pallor as it is possible, in nature of things, for any negro's visage to assume. He

52 Poe elsewhere mentions the use of this same chemical compound as a preservative agent. In "The Mystery of Marie Rogêt," for instance, he explains: "There are chemical infusions by which the animal frame can be preserved *forever* from corruption; the Bi-chloride of Mercury is one" (Mabbott, III, 742).

seemed stupified—thunderstricken. Presently he fell upon his knees in the pit, and, burying his naked arms up to the elbows in gold, let them there remain, as if enjoying the luxury of a bath. At length, with a deep sigh, he exclaimed, as if in a soliloquy,

"And dis all cum ob de goole-bug! de putty goole bug! de poor little goole-bug, what I boosed in dat sabage kind ob style! Aint you shamed ob yourself, nigger?—answer me dat!"

It became necessary, at last, that I should arouse both master and valet to the expediency of removing the treasure. It was growing late, and it behooved us to make exertion, that we might get every thing housed before daylight. It was difficult to say what should be done; and much time was spent in deliberation—so confused were the ideas of all. We, finally, lightened the box by removing two thirds of its contents, when we were enabled, with some trouble, to raise it from the hole. The articles taken out were deposited among the brambles, and the dog left to guard them, with strict orders from Jupiter neither, upon any pretence, to stir from the spot, nor to open his mouth until our return. We then hurriedly made for home with the chest; reaching the hut in safety, but after excessive toil, at one o'clock in the morning. Worn out as we were, it was not in human nature to do more just then. We rested until two, and had supper; starting for the hills immediately afterwards, armed with three stout sacks, which, by good luck, were upon the premises. A little before four we arrived at the pit, divided the remainder of the booty, as equally as might be, among us, and, leaving the holes unfilled, again set out for the hut, at which, for the second time, we deposited our golden burthens, just as the first streaks of the dawn gleamed from over the tree-tops in the East.

We were now thoroughly broken down; but the intense excitement of the time denied us repose. After an unquiet slumber of some three or four hours' duration, we arose, as if by preconcert,[53] to make examination of our treasure.

The chest had been full to the brim, and we spent the whole day, and the greater part of the next night, in a scrutiny of its contents. There had been nothing like order or arrangement. Every thing had been heaped in promiscuously. Having assorted all with care, we found ourselves possessed of even vaster wealth than we had at first supposed. In coin there was rather more than four hundred and fifty thousand dollars—estimating the value of the pieces, as accurately as we could, by the tables of the period. There was not a particle of silver. All was gold of antique date and of great variety—French, Spanish, and German money, with a few English guineas, and some counters,[54] of which we had never seen specimens before. There were several very large and heavy coins, so worn that we could make nothing of their inscriptions. There was no American money. The value of the jewels we found more difficulty in estimating. There were diamonds—some of them exceedingly large and fine—a hundred and ten in all, and not one of them small; eighteen rubies of remarkable brilliancy;—three hundred and ten emeralds, all very beautiful; and twenty-one sapphires, with an opal. These stones had all been broken from their settings and thrown loose in the chest. The settings themselves, which we picked out from among the other gold, appeared to have been beaten up with hammers, as if to prevent identification. Besides all this, there was a vast quantity of solid gold ornaments;—nearly two hundred massive finger and ear rings;—rich chains—thirty of these, if I remember;—eighty-three very large and heavy crucifixes;—five gold censers of great value;—a prodigious golden punch-bowl, ornamented with richly chased vine-leaves and Bacchanalian figures;[55] with two sword-handles exquisitely embossed, and many other smaller articles which I cannot recollect. The weight of these valuables exceeded three hundred and fifty pounds avoirdupois;[56] and in this estimate I have not included one hundred and ninety-seven superb gold watches; three of the number being worth each five hundred dollars, if one. Many of them were very old, and as time keepers valueless; the works having suffered, more or less, from corrosion—but all were richly jewelled and in cases of great worth. We estimated the entire contents of the chest, that night, at a million and a half of dollars; and, upon the subsequent disposal of the trinkets and jewels (a few being retained for our own use), it was found that we had greatly undervalued the treasure.[57]

When, at length, we had concluded our examination, and the intense excitement of the time had, in some measure, subsided, Legrand, who saw that I was dying with impatience for a solution of this most extraordinary riddle, entered into a full detail of all the circumstances connected with it.[58]

54 The term "counter" means an imitation coin most often made of brass or some other inferior metal, but the contemporary literature also mentions gold counters.

55 Figures from antiquity celebrating the love of drink and characterized by drunken revelry.

56 The avoirdupois weight system, based on the sixteen-ounce pound, was the standard system of weights used in Great Britain until it was repealed by the Weights and Measure Act of 1824. It continues to be used in the United States.

57 David Kahn observes that we can get some sense of how the treasure plot may have struck Poe's contemporary readers by looking at Baudelaire's response: "'How beautiful is the description of the treasure, and how good a feeling of warmth and dazzlement one gets from it! For they find treasure! *it is not a dream*, as generally happens in all these novels, where the author awakens us brutally after having excited our minds with appetizing hopes; this time, it is a *real* treasure, and the decipherer has really won it'" (*The Codebreakers: The Comprehensive History of Secret Communication from Ancient Times to the Internet* [New York: Scribner, 1996], 791).

58 The first of the two installments of "The Gold-Bug" that were published in the *Dollar Newspaper* concludes here. This point marks a shift in the tale. Now that the treasure has been recovered, Legrand describes his process of discovery. Poe reverses the structure of the traditional story of buried treasure, in which the first part tells how the pirates hid their treasure and the second part relates the story of the search for it. The reversal underscores Poe's interest in deductive reasoning and the narrative possibilities it provides. See Gerard T. Hurley, "Buried Treasure Tales in America," *Western Folklore* 10 (1951), 197–216.

59   Parchment is an animal skin, usually from a sheep or a goat, that has been prepared as a writing surface. Vellum is an especially fine parchment prepared from the skins of calves, lambs, or kids.

"You remember," said he, "the night when I handed you the rough sketch I had made of the *scarabaeus*. You recollect also, that I became quite vexed at you for insisting that my drawing resembled a death's-head. When you first made this assertion I thought you were jesting; but afterwards I called to mind the peculiar spots on the back of the insect, and admitted to myself that your remark had some little foundation in fact. Still, the sneer at my graphic powers irritated me—for I am considered a good artist—and, therefore, when you handed me the scrap of parchment, I was about to crumple it up and throw it angrily into the fire."

"The scrap of paper, you mean," said I.

"No; it had much of the appearance of paper, and at first I supposed it to be such, but when I came to draw upon it, I discovered it, at once, to be a piece of very thin parchment.[59] It was quite dirty, you remember. Well, as I was in the very act of crumpling it up, my glance fell upon the sketch at which you had been looking, and you may imagine my astonishment when I perceived, in fact, the figure of a death's-head just where, it seemed to me, I had made the drawing of the beetle. For a moment I was too much amazed to think with accuracy. I knew that my design was very different in detail from this—although there was a certain similarity in general outline. Presently I took a candle, and seating myself at the other end of the room, proceeded to scrutinize the parchment more closely. Upon turning it over, I saw my own sketch upon the reverse, just as I had made it. My first idea, now, was mere surprise at the really remarkable similarity of outline—at the singular coincidence involved in the fact, that unknown to me, there should have been a skull upon the other side of the parchment, immediately beneath my figure of the *scarabaeus,* and that this skull, not only in outline, but in size, should so closely resemble my drawing. I say the singularity of this coincidence absolutely stupified me for a time. This is the usual effect of such coincidences. The mind struggles to establish a connexion—a sequence of cause and effect—and, being unable to do so, suffers a species of temporary paralysis. But, when I recovered from this stupor, there dawned upon me gradually a conviction which startled me even far more than the coincidence. I began distinctly, positively, to remember that there had been no drawing on the parchment when I made my sketch of the *scarabaeus*. I became perfectly certain of this; for I recollected turning up first one side and then the other, in search of the cleanest spot. Had the skull been then there, of course I could not have failed to notice it. Here was indeed a mystery which I felt it impossible to explain; but, even at that early moment, there seemed to glimmer, faintly, within the most remote and secret chambers of my intellect, a glow-worm-like conception of that truth which last night's adventure brought to so magnificent a demonstration. I arose at once, and putting the parchment securely away, dismissed all farther reflection until I should be alone.

"When you had gone, and when Jupiter was fast asleep, I betook myself to a more methodical investigation of the affair. In the first place I considered the manner in which the parchment had come into my possession. The spot where we discovered the *scarabaeus* was on the coast of the main land, about a mile eastward of the island, and but a short distance above high water mark. Upon my taking hold of it, it gave me a sharp bite, which caused me to let it drop. Jupiter, with his accustomed caution, before seizing the insect, which had flown towards him, looked about him for a leaf, or something of that nature, by which to take hold of it. It was at this moment that his eyes, and mine also, fell upon the scrap of parchment, which I then supposed to be paper. It was lying half buried in the sand, a corner sticking up. Near the spot where we found it, I observed the remnants of the hull of what appeared to have been a ship's long boat.[60] The wreck seemed to have been there for a very great while; for the resemblance to boat timbers could scarcely be traced.

"Well, Jupiter picked up the parchment, wrapped the beetle in it, and gave it to me. Soon afterwards we turned to go home, and on the way met Lieutenant G———. I showed him the insect, and he begged me to let him take it to the fort. On my consenting, he thrust it forthwith into his waistcoat pocket, without the parchment in which it had been wrapped, and which I had continued to hold in my hand during his inspection. Perhaps he dreaded my changing my mind, and thought it best to make sure of the prize at once—you know how enthusiastic he is on all subjects connected with Natural History. At the same time, without being conscious of it, I must have deposited the parchment in my own pocket.

"You remember that when I went to the table, for the purpose of making a sketch of the beetle, I found no paper where it was

60 A large open boat belonging to a sailing vessel, to be rowed by several men and capable of transporting heavy objects.

61   The "Jolly Roger," that is, the black flag adorned with the death's head, had been a symbol of the pirate's ship since at least the mid-eighteenth century. Naval historian John Campbell relates, "Captain *Ogle* returned then to the Bay, hoisting the King's Colours, under the Pirates black Flag with a Death's Head in it. This prudent Stratagem, had the desired Effect; for the Pirates, seeing the black Flag uppermost, concluded the King's Ship had been taken, and came out full of Joy to congratulate their Consort on the Victory" (*Lives of the Admirals and Other Eminent British Seamen*, 4 vols. [London: John Applebee, 1742–1744], IV, 472–473).

usually kept. I looked in the drawer, and found none there. I searched my pockets, hoping to find an old letter—and then my hand fell upon the parchment. I thus detail the precise mode in which it came into my possession; for the circumstances impressed me with peculiar force.

"No doubt you will think me fanciful—but I had already established a kind of *connexion*. I had put together two links of a great chain. There was a boat lying upon a sea-coast, and not far from the boat was a parchment—*not a paper*—with a skull depicted on it. You will, of course, ask 'where is the connexion?' I reply that the skull, or death's-head, is the well-known emblem of the pirate. The flag of the death's-head is hoisted in all engagements.[61]

"I have said that the scrap was parchment, and not paper. Parchment is durable—almost imperishable. Matters of little moment are rarely consigned to parchment; since, for the mere ordinary purposes of drawing or writing, it is not nearly so well adapted as paper. This reflection suggested some meaning—some relevancy—in the death's-head. I did not fail to observe, also, the *form* of the parchment. Although one of its corners had been, by some accident, destroyed, it could be seen that the original form was oblong. It was just such a slip, indeed, as might have been chosen for a memorandum—for a record of something to be long remembered and carefully preserved."

"But," I interposed, "you say that the skull was *not* upon the parchment when you made the drawing of the beetle. How then do you trace any connexion between the boat and the skull—since this latter, according to your own admission, must have been designed (God only knows how or by whom) at some period subsequent to your sketching the *scarabaeus?*"

"Ah, hereupon turns the whole mystery; although the secret, at this point, I had comparatively little difficulty in solving. My steps were sure, and could afford but a single result. I reasoned, for example, thus: When I drew the *scarabaeus*, there was no skull apparent on the parchment. When I had completed the drawing, I gave it to you, and observed you narrowly until you returned it. *You*, therefore, did not design the skull, and no one else was present to do it. Then it was not done by human agency. And nevertheless it was done.

"At this stage of my reflections I endeavored to remember, and *did* remember, with entire distinctness, every incident which occurred about the period in question. The weather was chilly (oh rare and happy accident!),[62] and a fire was blazing on the hearth. I was heated with exercise and sat near the table. You, however, had drawn a chair close to the chimney. Just as I placed the parchment in your hand, and as you were in the act of inspecting it, Wolf, the Newfoundland, entered, and leaped upon your shoulders. With your left hand you caressed him and kept him off, while your right, holding the parchment, was permitted to fall listlessly between your knees, and in close proximity to the fire. At one moment I thought the blaze had caught it, and was about to caution you, but, before I could speak, you had withdrawn it, and were engaged in its examination. When I considered all these particulars, I doubted not for a moment that *heat* had been the agent in bringing to light, on the parchment, the skull which I saw designed on it. You are well aware that chemical preparations exist, and have existed time out of mind, by means of which it is possible to write upon either paper or vellum, so that the characters shall become visible only when subjected to the action of fire. Zaffre, digested in *aqua regia*, and diluted with four times its weight of water, is sometimes employed; a green tint results. The regulus of cobalt, dissolved in spirit of nitre, gives a red. These colors disappear at longer or shorter intervals after the material written on cools, but again become apparent upon the reapplication of heat.[63]

"I now scrutinized the death's-head with care. Its outer edges—the edges of the drawing nearest the edge of the vellum—were far more *distinct* than the others. It was clear that the action of the caloric had been imperfect or unequal. I immediately kindled a fire, and subjected every portion of the parchment to a glowing heat. At first, the only effect was the strengthening of the faint lines in the skull; but, on persevering in the experiment, there became visible, at the corner of the slip, diagonally opposite to the spot in which the death's-head was delineated, the figure of what I at first supposed to be a goat. A closer scrutiny, however, satisfied me that it was intended for a kid."

"Ha! ha!" said I, "to be sure I have no right to laugh at you—a million and a half of money is too serious a matter for mirth—but you are not about to establish a third link in your chain—you will not find any especial connexion between your pirates and a goat—pirates, you know, have nothing to do with goats; they appertain to the farming interest."

62 Much as the random tar-brush daubings of the narrator in "Manuscript Found in the Bottle" lead to DISCOVERY, accident or chance leads to the discovery of the treasure map. Seen as an analogue of the creative process, Legrand's behavior emphasizes the important role that chance can play in art.

63 Poe's description of sympathetic inks—colorless fluids used to write invisible messages that can be made visible through a variety of different processes, but typically involving the application of heat—is drawn from *Ree's Cyclopedia* (Mabbott, III, 847). Zaffre is an impure oxide of cobalt. Aqua regia is a mixture of nitric and hydrochloric acid; its name derives from the fact that it can dissolve "noble" or corrosion-resistant metals, such as silver, gold, and platinum. The term "regulus" means metal separated from a mineral or ore by smelting. Nitre, another name for saltpetre, was sometimes used as a cleansing agent. See Jeremiah 2:22: "For though thou wash thee with nitre, and take thee much soap, yet thine iniquity is marked before me, saith the Lord God."

64   Born in Scotland, Captain William Kidd (*ca.* 1645–1701) was one of the most infamous pirates of the seventeenth century. He came to prominence in 1696 when a syndicate of powerful Londoners backed his request to pursue and capture marauding pirates in the Indian Ocean. Kidd received a commission as a privateer, but once he reached the Indian Ocean, he and his men turned to piracy themselves. After being lured to Boston upon false promises of clemency, Kidd was arrested and imprisoned. He was then sent to London, where he was tried on charges of piracy and murder. Found guilty on all counts, he was sentenced to death and hung at London's "Execution Dock." The rumor that prior to his capture Kidd had buried his plunder somewhere on the Atlantic seaboard contributed considerably to the legend of Captain Kidd.

65   Poe was a great lover of puns. Like hieroglyphics, he suggests, the language of puns requires ingenuity to unravel.

"But I have just said that the figure was *not* that of a goat."

"Well, a kid then—pretty much the same thing."

"Pretty much, but not altogether," said Legrand. "You may have heard of one *Captain* Kidd.[64] I at once looked upon the figure of the animal as a kind of punning or hieroglyphical signature.[65] I say signature; because its position on the vellum suggested this idea. The death's-head at the corner diagonally opposite, had, in the same manner, the air of a stamp, or seal. But I was sorely put out by the absence of all else—of the body to my imagined instrument—of the text for my context."

"I presume you expected to find a letter between the stamp and the signature."

"Something of that kind. The fact is, I felt irresistibly impressed with a presentiment of some vast good fortune impending. I can scarcely say why. Perhaps, after all, it was rather a desire than an actual belief;—but do you know that Jupiter's silly words, about the bug being of solid gold, had a remarkable effect on my fancy? And then the series of accidents and coincidences—these were so *very* extraordinary. Do you observe how mere an accident it was that these events should have occurred upon the *sole* day of all the year in which it has been, or may be, sufficiently cool for fire, and that without the fire, or without the intervention of the dog at the precise moment in which he appeared, I should never have become aware of the death's-head, and so never the possessor of the treasure?"

"But proceed—I am all impatience."

"Well; you have heard, of course, the many stories current—the thousand vague rumors afloat about money buried, somewhere on the Atlantic coast, by Kidd and his associates. These rumors must have had some foundation in fact. And that the rumors have existed so long and so continuously, could have resulted, it appeared to me, only from the circumstance of the buried treasure still *remaining* entombed. Had Kidd concealed his plunder for a time, and afterwards reclaimed it, the rumors would scarcely have reached us in their present unvarying form. You will observe that the stories told are all about money-seekers, not about money-finders. Had the pirate recovered his money, there the affair would have dropped. It seemed to me that some accident—say the loss of a memorandum indicating its locality—had deprived him of the means of recovering it, and that this accident had become known to his followers, who otherwise might never have heard that treasure had been concealed at all, and who, busying themselves in vain, because unguided attempts, to regain it, had given first birth, and then universal currency, to the reports which are now so common. Have you ever heard of any important treasure being unearthed along the coast?"

"Never."

"But that Kidd's accumulations were immense, is well known. I took it for granted, therefore, that the earth still held them; and you will scarcely be surprised when I tell you that I felt a hope, nearly amounting to certainty, that the parchment so strangely found, involved a lost record of the place of deposit."[66]

"But how did you proceed?"

"I held the vellum again to the fire, after increasing the heat; but nothing appeared. I now thought it possible that the coating of dirt might have something to do with the failure; so I carefully rinsed the parchment by pouring warm water over it, and, having done this, I placed it in a tin pan, with the skull downwards, and put the pan upon a furnace of lighted charcoal. In a few minutes, the pan having become thoroughly heated, I removed the slip, and, to my inexpressible joy, found it spotted, in several places, with what appeared to be figures arranged in lines. Again I placed it in the pan, and suffered it to remain another minute. On taking it off, the whole was just as you see it now."

Here Legrand, having re-heated the parchment, submitted it to my inspection. The following characters were rudely traced, in a red tint, between the death's-head and the goat:

53‡‡†305))6*;4826)4‡.)4‡);806*;48†8¶60))85; > > 1‡
< < <;]8*> (;:‡*8†83(88)5*†;46(;88*96*?;8)*‡(;485
);5*†2:*‡(;4956*2(5*—4)8¶8*;4069285);)6†8)4‡‡;1(‡
9;48081;8:8‡1;48†85;4)485†528806*81(‡9;48;(88;4(‡?
34;48)4‡;161;:188;‡?;

"But," said I, returning him the slip, "I am as much in the dark as ever. Were all the jewels of Golconda[67] awaiting me on my solution of this enigma, I am quite sure that I should be unable to earn them."

"And yet," said Legrand, "the solution is by no means so difficult as you might be led to imagine from the first hasty inspec-

66 David Kahn notes that Poe's tale abounds in errors and absurdities. Would the parchment, for example, have remained in the same place for so many years? And even if it had, wouldn't it have suffered from the elements? But "Poe was less concerned with accuracy than with the appearance of accuracy. . . . Beyond that, and to the reader, none of them matters. For no one thinks of these problems when caught up in the powerful narrative current of the story. The tale perhaps owes some of its force to Poe's using it to vent some of his frustrated desires. 'I cannot keep from thinking with sadness how the unfortunate E. Poe must have dreamed more than once about how to discover such treasures,' wrote Baudelaire" (*The Codebreakers*, 791).

67 Famous for its diamonds, the ancient city of Golconda in southern India has become synonymous with any source of great wealth or happiness.

68   In "A Few Words on Secret Writing," the longest of his popular journalistic pieces on cryptography, published in *Graham's Magazine* (July 1841), Poe opines on the vocation of cryptography: "It is not to be supposed that Cryptography, as a serious thing, as the means of imparting important information, has gone out of use at the present day. It is still commonly practised in diplomacy; and there are individuals, even now, holding office in the eye of various foreign governments, whose real business is that of deciphering. We have already said that a peculiar mental action is called into play in the solution of cryptographical problems, at least in those of the higher order. Good cryptographists are rare indeed; and thus their services, although seldom required, are necessarily well requited."

Interestingly, "The Gold-Bug" has inspired both amateur and professional cryptographers. Leo Marks, the head of agents' codes and ciphers at Special Operations Executive (SOE) during World War II, decided to become a cryptographer after he encountered "The Gold-Bug" as a boy at his father's antiquarian bookshop at 84 Charing Cross Road. When he was with the SOE, he revolutionized its primitive code systems. His peacetime career reveals that he was also indebted to Poe's tales of terror: Marks would subsequently write the screenplay for Michael Powell's psychological thriller *Peeping Tom* (Leo Marks, *Between Silk and Cyanide: A Codemaker's War, 1941–1945* [New York: Free Press, 1998], 151).

tion of the characters. These characters, as any one might readily guess, form a cipher—that is to say, they convey a meaning; but then, from what is known of Kidd, I could not suppose him capable of constructing any of the more abstruse cryptographs.[68] I made up my mind, at once, that this was of a simple species—such, however, as would appear, to the crude intellect of the sailor, absolutely insoluble without the key."

"And you really solved it?"

"Readily; I have solved others of an abstruseness ten thousand times greater. Circumstances, and a certain bias of mind, have led me to take interest in such riddles, and it may well be doubted whether human ingenuity can construct an enigma of the kind which human ingenuity may not, by proper application, resolve. In fact, having once established connected and legible characters, I scarcely gave a thought to the mere difficulty of developing their import.

"In the present case—indeed in all cases of secret writing—the first question regards the *language* of the cipher; for the principles of solution, so far, especially, as the more simple ciphers are concerned, depend upon, and are varied by, the genius of the particular idiom. In general, there is no alternative but experiment (directed by probabilities) of every tongue known to him who attempts the solution, until the true one be attained. But, with the cipher now before us, all difficulty is removed by the signature. The pun on the word 'Kidd' is appreciable in no other language than the English. But for this consideration I should have begun my attempts with the Spanish and French, as the tongues in which a secret of this kind would most naturally have been written by a pirate of the Spanish main. As it was, I assumed the cryptograph to be English.

"You observe there are no divisions between the words. Had there been divisions, the task would have been comparatively easy. In such case I should have commenced with a collation and analysis of the shorter words, and, had a word of a single letter occurred, as is most likely, (*a* or I, for example,) I should have considered the solution as assured. But, there being no division, my first step was to ascertain the predominant letters, as well as the least frequent. Counting all, I constructed a table, thus:

Of the character 8 there are 33.

;	"	26.
4	"	19.
‡)	"	16.
*	"	13.
5	"	12.
6	"	11.
† 1	"	8.
o	"	6.
9 2	"	5.
: 3	"	4.
?	"	3.
¶	"	2.
] - .	"	1.

"Now, in English, the letter which most frequently occurs is *e*. Afterwards, the succession runs thus: *a o i d h n r s t u y c f g l m w b k p q x z*. E, however, predominates so remarkably that an individual sentence of any length is rarely seen, in which it is not the prevailing character.

"Here, then, we have, in the very beginning, the groundwork for something more than a mere guess. The general use which may be made of the table is obvious—but, in this particular cipher, we shall only very partially require its aid. As our predominant character is 8, we will commence by assuming it as the *e* of the natural alphabet. To verify the supposition, let us observe if the 8 be seen often in couples—for *e* is doubled with great frequency in English—in such words, for example, as 'meet,' 'fleet,' 'speed,' 'seen,' 'been,' 'agree,' etc. In the present instance we see it doubled no less than five times, although the cryptograph is brief.

"Let us assume 8, then, as *e*. Now, of all *words* in the language, 'the' is most usual; let us see, therefore, whether there are not repetitions of any three characters, in the same order of collocation, the last of them being 8. If we discover repetitions of such letters, so arranged, they will most probably represent the word 'the.' On inspection, we find no less than seven such arrangements, the characters being ;48. We may, therefore, assume that the semicolon represents *t*, 4 represents *h*, and 8 represents *e*—the last being now well confirmed. Thus a great step has been taken.

"But, having established a single word, we are enabled to establish a vastly important point; that is to say, several commence-ments and terminations of other words. Let us refer, for example, to the last instance but one, in which the combination ;48 occurs—not far from the end of the cipher. We know that the semicolon immediately ensuing is the commencement of a word, and, of the six characters succeeding this 'the,' we are cognizant of no less than five. Let us set these characters down, thus, by the letters we know them to represent, leaving a space for the unknown—

t eeth.

"Here we are enabled, at once, to discard the '*th*,' as forming no portion of the word commencing with the first *t;* since, by experiment of the entire alphabet for a letter adapted to the vacancy, we perceive that no word can be formed of which this *th* can be a part. We are thus narrowed into

t ee,

and, going through the alphabet, if necessary, as before, we arrive at the word 'tree,' as the sole possible reading. We thus gain another letter, *r*, represented by (, with the words 'the tree' in juxtaposition.

"Looking beyond these words, for a short distance, we again see the combination ;48, and employ it by way of *termination* to what immediately precedes. We have thus this arrangement:

the tree ;4(‡?34 the,

or, substituting the natural letters, where known, it reads thus:

the tree thr‡?3h the.

"Now, if, in place of the unknown characters, we leave blank spaces, or substitute dots, we read thus:

the tree thr . . . h the,

when the word '*through*' makes itself evident at once. But this discovery gives us three new letters, *o, u* and *g*, represented by ‡ ? and 3.

"Looking now, narrowly, through the cipher for combinations of known characters, we find, not very far from the beginning, this arrangement,

83(88, or egree,

which, plainly, is the conclusion of the word 'degree,' and gives us another letter, *d,* represented by †.

"Four letters beyond the word 'degree,' we perceive the combination

;46(;88*

"Translating the known characters, and representing the unknown by dots, as before, we read thus:

th.rtee.

an arrangement immediately suggestive of the word 'thirteen,' and again furnishing us with two new characters, *i* and *n,* represented by 6 and *.

"Referring, now, to the beginning of the cryptograph, we find the combination,

53‡‡†.

"Translating, as before, we obtain

. good,

which assures us that the first letter is *A,* and that the first two words are 'A good.'

"To avoid confusion, it is now time that we arrange our key, as far as discovered, in a tabular form. It will stand thus:

5	represents	a
†	"	d
8	"	e
3	"	g
4	"	h
6	"	i
*	"	n
‡	"	o
(	"	r
;	"	t

"We have, therefore, no less than ten of the most important letters represented, and it will be unnecessary to proceed with the details of the solution. I have said enough to convince you that ciphers of this nature are readily soluble, and to give you some in-

69 Though the word "hostel" was still used in Great Britain during Poe's day, it had largely fallen from usage in the United States. Not until the emergence of the Youth Hostel movement in the twentieth century would the word regain currency.

sight into the *rationale* of their development. But be assured that the specimen before us appertains to the very simplest species of cryptograph. It now only remains to give you the full translation of the characters upon the parchment, as unriddled. Here it is:

'*A good glass in the bishop's hostel in the devil's seat twenty-one degrees and thirteen minutes northeast and by north main branch seventh limb east side shoot from the left eye of the death's-head a bee line from the tree through the shot fifty feet out.*'"

"But," said I, "the enigma seems still in as bad a condition as ever. How is it possible to extort a meaning from all this jargon about 'devil's seats,' 'death's heads,' and 'bishop's hotels?'"

"I confess," replied Legrand, "that the matter still wears a serious aspect, when regarded with a casual glance. My first endeavor was to divide the sentence into the natural division intended by the cryptographist."

"You mean, to punctuate it?"

"Something of that kind."

"But how was it possible to effect this?"

"I reflected that it had been a *point* with the writer to run his words together without division, so as to increase the difficulty of solution. Now, a not over-acute man, in pursuing such an object, would be nearly certain to overdo the matter. When, in the course of his composition, he arrived at a break in his subject which would naturally require a pause, or a point, he would be exceedingly apt to run his characters, at this place, more than usually close together. If you will observe the MS., in the present instance, you will easily detect five such cases of unusual crowding. Acting on this hint, I made the division thus:

'*A good glass in the Bishop's hostel in the Devil's seat—twenty-one degrees and thirteen minutes—northeast and by north—main branch seventh limb east side—shoot from the left eye of the death's-head—a bee-line from the tree through the shot fifty feet out.*'"

"Even this division," said I, "leaves me still in the dark."

"It left me also in the dark," replied Legrand, "for a few days; during which I made diligent inquiry, in the neighborhood of Sullivan's Island, for any building which went by the name of the 'Bishop's Hotel;' for, of course, I dropped the obsolete word 'hostel.'[69] Gaining no information on the subject, I was on the point of extending my sphere of search, and proceeding in a more systematic manner, when, one morning, it entered into my head, quite suddenly, that this 'Bishop's Hostel' might have some reference to an old family, of the name of Bessop, which, time out of mind, had held possession of an ancient manor-house, about four miles to the northward of the Island. I accordingly went over to the plantation, and re-instituted my inquiries among the older negroes of the place.[70] At length one of the most aged of the women said that she had heard of such a place as *Bessop's Castle*, and thought that she could guide me to it, but that it was not a castle, nor a tavern, but a high rock.

"I offered to pay her well for her trouble, and, after some demur, she consented to accompany me to the spot. We found it without much difficulty, when, dismissing her, I proceeded to examine the place. The 'castle' consisted of an irregular assemblage of cliffs and rocks—one of the latter being quite remarkable for its height as well as for its insulated and artificial appearance. I clambered to its apex, and then felt much at a loss as to what should be next done.

"While I was busied in reflection, my eyes fell upon a narrow ledge in the eastern face of the rock, perhaps a yard below the summit on which I stood. This ledge projected about eighteen inches, and was not more than a foot wide, while a niche in the cliff just above it, gave it a rude resemblance to one of the hollow-backed chairs used by our ancestors. I made no doubt that here was the 'devil's seat' alluded to in the manuscript, and now I seemed to grasp the full secret of the riddle.

"The 'good glass,' I knew, could have reference to nothing but a telescope; for the word 'glass' is rarely employed in any other sense by seamen.[71] Now here, I at once saw, was a telescope to be used, and a definite point of view, *admitting no variation*, from which to use it. Nor did I hesitate to believe that the phrases, 'twenty-one degrees and thirteen minutes,' and 'northeast and by north,' were intended as directions for the levelling of the glass. Greatly excited by these discoveries, I hurried home, procured a telescope, and returned to the rock.

"I let myself down to the ledge, and found that it was impossible to retain a seat on it unless in one particular position. This fact confirmed my preconceived idea. I proceeded to use the glass. Of course, the 'twenty-one degrees and thirteen minutes' could allude to nothing but elevation above the visible horizon, since the horizontal direction was clearly indicated by the words, 'northeast and

70 Poe seems to acknowledge the important role memory plays in African-American culture. Memory, and its perpetuation from one person to another, indeed, from one generation to the next, can register places and events that escape written history.

71 "The Maelstrom Whirlpool," the widely reprinted newspaper article that influenced "A Descent into the Maelström," used the phrase "good glass" to mean a powerful, handheld telescope: "I went on the main topsail yard with a good glass. I had been seated but a few moments, when my ship entered the dish of the whirlpool" ("The Maelstrom Whirlpool," *New England Farmer and Horticultural Register*, July 29, 1825).

G. C. Widney, illustration for *The Gold-Bug*, 1901. Widney gives Legrand the aura of a great explorer.

by north.' This latter direction I at once established by means of a pocket-compass; then, pointing the glass as nearly at an angle of twenty-one degrees of elevation as I could do it by guess, I moved it cautiously up or down, until my attention was arrested by a circular rift or opening in the foliage of a large tree that overtopped its fellows in the distance. In the centre of this rift I perceived a white spot, but could not, at first, distinguish what it was. Adjusting the focus of the telescope, I again looked, and now made it out to be a human skull.

"On this discovery I was so sanguine as to consider the enigma solved; for the phrase 'main branch, seventh limb, east side,' could refer only to the position of the skull on the tree, while 'shoot from the left eye of the death's-head' admitted, also, of but one interpretation, in regard to a search for buried treasure. I perceived that the design was to drop a bullet from the left eye of the skull, and that a bee-line, or, in other words, a straight line, drawn from the nearest point of the trunk through 'the shot,' (or the spot where the bullet fell,) and thence extended to a distance of fifty feet, would indicate a definite point—and beneath this point I thought it at least *possible* that a deposit of value lay concealed."

"All this," I said, "is exceedingly clear, and, although ingenious, still simple and explicit. When you left the Bishop's Hotel, what then?"

"Why, having carefully taken the bearings of the tree, I turned homewards. The instant that I left 'the devil's seat,' however, the circular rift vanished; nor could I get a glimpse of it afterwards, turn as I would. What seems to me the chief ingenuity in this whole business, is the fact (for repeated experiment has convinced me it *is* a fact) that the circular opening in question is visible from no other attainable point of view than that afforded by the narrow ledge on the face of the rock.

"In this expedition to the 'Bishop's Hotel' I had been attended by Jupiter, who had, no doubt, observed, for some weeks past, the abstraction of my demeanor, and took especial care not to leave me alone. But, on the next day, getting up very early, I contrived to give him the slip, and went into the hills in search of the tree. After much toil I found it. When I came home at night my valet proposed to give me a flogging. With the rest of the adventure I believe you are as well acquainted as myself."

"I suppose," said I, "you missed the spot, in the first attempt at digging, through Jupiter's stupidity in letting the bug fall through the right instead of through the left eye of the skull."

"Precisely. This mistake made a difference of about two inches and a half in the 'shot'—that is to say, in the position of the peg nearest the tree; and had the treasure been *beneath* the 'shot,' the error would have been of little moment; but 'the shot,' together with the nearest point of the tree, were merely two points for the establishment of a line of direction; of course the error, however trivial in the beginning, increased as we proceeded with the line, and by the time we had gone fifty feet, threw us quite off the scent. But for my deep-seated conviction points that treasure was here somewhere actually buried, we might have had all our labor in vain."

"I presume the fancy of *the skull*—of letting fall a bullet through the skull's-eye—was suggested to Kidd by the piratical flag. No doubt he felt a kind of poetical consistency in recovering his money through this ominous insignium."

"Perhaps so; still I cannot help thinking that common-sense had quite as much to do with the matter as poetical consistency. To be visible from the Devil's seat, it was necessary that the object, if small, should be *white;* and there is nothing like your human skull for retaining and even increasing its whitenss under exposure to all vissitudes of weather.

"But your grandiloquence, and your conduct in swinging the beetle—how excessively odd! I was sure you were mad. And why did you insist on letting fall the bug, instead of a bullet, from the skull?"

"Why, to be frank, I felt somewhat annoyed by your evident suspicions touching my sanity, and so resolved to punish you quietly, in my own way, by a little bit of sober mystification. For this reason I swung the beetle, and for this reason I let it fall from the tree. An observation of yours about its great weight suggested the latter idea."

"Yes, I perceive; and now there is only one point which puzzles me. What are we to make of the skeletons found in the hole?"

"That is a question I am no more able to answer than yourself. There seems, however, only one plausible way of accounting for them—and yet it is dreadful to believe in such atrocity as my suggestion would imply. It is clear that Kidd—if Kidd indeed secreted this treasure, which I doubt not—it is clear that he must have had assistance in the labor. But, the worst of this labor concluded, he may have thought it expedient to remove all participants in his secret. Perhaps a couple of blows with a mattock were sufficient, while his coadjutors were busy in the pit; perhaps it required a dozen—who shall tell?"[72]

72 "The literal and obvious reply to Legrand's question 'Who shall tell?' is 'You can tell!'" observes J. A. Leo Lemay. Lemay suggests that the treasure was buried not by the legendary Captain Kidd but much more recently by Legrand himself. Lemay continues: "Throughout the story the reader is provided with clues that Legrand is Captain Kidd. Legrand/Kidd had murdered his collaborators who helped him bury the treasure—and the reader has, during the digging up of the treasure, constantly feared that Legrand would kill his present assistants, Jupiter and the narrator. In his explanations Legrand moves from the present back into the past when Captain Kidd buried the treasure—and Legrand frequently enters Kidd's mind to account for his actions." Of course, Poe's sleuth Auguste Dupin similarly possesses the ability to inhabit the criminal mind. Lemay's provocative comments appear in a brief book review in the September 1989 issue of *Nineteenth-Century Literature*. Privately, he communicated his desire to develop his thesis further, but he never did.

Poe continually challenged himself to create a body of fiction characterized by both originality and variety. In a letter of August 9, 1846, to Phillip P. Cooke, Poe explains what such variety means: "One of my chief aims has been the widest diversity of subject, thought, & especially tone and manner of handling. Were all my tales now before me in a large volume and as the composition of another—the merit which would principally arrest my attention would be the wide diversity and variety" (Collected Letters of Edgar Allan Poe, ed. John Ward Ostrom, Burton R. Pollin, and Jeffrey A. Savoye, 2 vols. [New York: Gordian Press, 2008], I, 596). Like "The Tell-Tale Heart," "The Black Cat" is narrated by a killer motivated by perverse impulses—but Poe does not simply repeat himself. He introduces a new subject: alcoholism. In the 1820s alcohol consumption in America exceeded five gallons of hard liquor per capita per annum. It was a problem Poe understood intimately: we know by his own admission that he sometimes drank to excess, and his often repeated promises to be "done with drinking forever" echo the refrain of the alcoholic (Paul Fisher, "Alcohol, Addiction, and Rehabilitation," Edgar Allan Poe in Context, ed. Kevin J. Hayes [New York: Cambridge University Press, 2013], 96–106). In 1849, Poe would take the step of joining the Shockoe Hill Division of the Sons of Temperance in Richmond, a fraternal organization that according to its constitution was created to shield members from "the evils of Intemperance, to afford mutual assistance in case of sickness, and elevate our characters as men."

In the antebellum era the printed word played a large role in the temperance reform message. Songs, poems, sermons, essays, and tales found their way into print in journals and leaflets. The temperance tale constituted it own genre, which portrayed the damaging consequences of excess consumption and the joys of a life of sobriety. Poe drew on the temperance tale in writing "The Black Cat" but created something far different, and therein lies the tale's originality ("the truest and surest test of originality," Poe once wrote, "is the manner of handling a hackneyed subject"). The tale first appeared in 1843 in the United States Saturday Post.

1   Like so many of today's horror films preoccupied with domesticity, Poe's "homely narrative" invokes the ideal of the sacrosanct, peaceful American home, only to turn it on its head.

2   "Barroques," or "baroques," as the word is usually spelled, is French for baroque pearls: misshapen pearls that had become unfashionable in Poe's day. In other words, the narrator likens his murderous actions to someone else's fashion faux pas. The narrator of "The Black Cat" uses several intricate rhetorical devices as a way of justifying his behavior to the reader. As Humbert Humbert says in Vlad-

The Black Cat

For the most wild, yet most homely narrative which I am about to pen, I neither expect nor solicit belief.[1] Mad indeed would I be to expect it, in a case where my very senses reject their own evidence. Yet, mad am I not—and very surely do I not dream. But to-morrow I die, and to-day I would unburthen my soul. My immediate purpose is to place before the world, plainly, succinctly, and without comment, a series of mere household events. In their consequences, these events have terrified—have tortured—have destroyed me. Yet I will not attempt to expound them. To me, they have presented little but Horror—to many they will seem less terrible than *barroques*.[2] Hereafter, perhaps, some intellect may be found which will reduce my phantasm to the common-place—some intellect more calm, more logical, and far less excitable than my own, which will perceive, in the circumstances I detail with awe, nothing more than an ordinary succession of very natural causes and effects.[3]

From my infancy I was noted for the docility and humanity of my disposition. My tenderness of heart was even so conspicuous as to make me the jest of my companions.[4] I was especially fond of animals, and was indulged by my parents with a great variety of pets. With these I spent most of my time, and never was so happy as when feeding and caressing them. This peculiarity of character grew with my growth, and, in my manhood, I derived from it one of my principal sources of pleasure. To those who have cherished an affection for a faithful and sagacious dog, I need hardly be at the trouble of explaining the nature or the intensity of the gratification thus derivable. There is something in the unselfish and self-sacrificing love of a brute, which goes directly to the heart of him who has had frequent occasion to test the paltry friendship and gossamer fidelity of mere *Man*.

I married early, and was happy to find in my wife a disposition not uncongenial with my own. Observing my partiality for domestic pets, she lost no opportunity of procuring those of the most agreeable kind. We had birds, gold-fish, a fine dog, rabbits, a small monkey, and *a cat*.[5]

This latter was a remarkably large and beautiful animal, entirely black, and sagacious to an astonishing degree.[6] In speaking of his intelligence, my wife, who at heart was not a little tinctured with superstition, made frequent allusion to the ancient popular notion, which regarded all black cats as witches in disguise.[7] Not that she was ever *serious* upon this point—and I mention the matter at all for no better reason than that it happens, just now, to be remembered.

Pluto—this was the cat's name—was my favorite pet and playmate.[8] I alone fed him, and he attended me wherever I went about the house. It was even with difficulty that I could prevent him from following me through the streets.

Our friendship lasted, in this manner, for several years, during which my general temperament and character—through the instrumentality of the Fiend Intemperance[9]—had (I blush to confess it) experienced a radical alteration for the worse. I grew, day by day, more moody, more irritable, more regardless of the feelings of others. I suffered myself to use intemperate language to my wife. At length, I even offered her personal violence. My pets, of course, were made to feel the change in my disposition. I not only neglected, but ill-used them. For Pluto, however, I still retained sufficient regard to restrain me from maltreating him, as I made no scruple of maltreating the rabbits, the monkey, or even the dog, when by accident, or through affection, they came in my way. But my disease grew upon me—for what disease is like Alcohol![10]—and at length even Pluto, who was now becoming old, and consequently somewhat peevish—even Pluto began to experience the effects of my ill temper.

One night, returning home, much intoxicated, from one of my haunts about town, I fancied that the cat avoided my presence. I seized him; when, in his fright at my violence, he inflicted a slight wound upon my hand with his teeth. The fury of a demon in-

imir Nabokov's *Lolita* (1955), "You can always count on a murderer for a fancy prose style."

3   Excluded from such a cold, logical account of merely "natural causes and effects," presumably, would be human agency and freedom.

4   Poe perhaps suggests that there is no fundamental *human* contradiction between the narrator's docility and tenderness and his subsequent drunken, violent impulses.

5   The only thing missing from this happy American household is a child: we can only imagine what kind of father the narrator would be. Walter Benjamin observes that the criminals in "The Black Cat," "The Tell-Tale Heart," and "William Wilson" are all "simple private citizens of the middle class" (Walter Benjamin, *The Arcades Project*, trans. Howard Eiland and Kevin McLaughlin [Cambridge, MA: The Belknap Press of Harvard University Press, 1999], 20). The narrator's ability to keep so many pets suggests a certain level of financial comfort.

6   Poe and his wife, Virginia, were cat owners. In "Instinct versus Reason—A Black Cat" (1840), Poe describes the family pet: "The writer of this article is the owner of one of the most remarkable black cats in the world—and this is saying much; for it will be remembered that black cats are all of them witches. The one in question has not a white hair about her, and is of a most demur and sanctified nature." Poe details the cat's cleverness in opening the kitchen door thumb-latch. "We have witnessed this singular feat a hundred times at least," he writes, "and never without being impressed with the truth of the remark with which we commenced this article—that the boundary between instinct and reason is of a very shadowy nature." Later, Poe and Virginia would own another cat, a large tortoiseshell they named "Catterina."

7   The Italian film director Dario Argento, who paid homage to Poe with "The Black Cat," an adaptation that forms the second segment of the feature film *Two Evil Eyes* (1990), explains: "For centuries cats, and especially black cats, were treated as incarnations of witches. Black cats have been haunted by these beliefs; for centuries they were hanged and burned and drowned. So they're different from other cats. They're more secretive, they keep to themselves. You look at them and you know something goes on in there" (quoted in Maitland McDonagh, *Broken Mirrors, Broken Minds: The Dark Dreams of Dario Argento* [Minneapolis: University of Minnesota Press, 2010], 247–248).

8   Pluto is god of the underworld in Greek mythology.

9   Intemperance, that is, immoderate indulgence in alcohol, is frequently personified as a fiend in the contemporary temperance literature. In an autobiographical confession that appeared in the August 1837 issue of—get this magazine title—the *Rum-Seller's Mirror, and Drunkard's Looking Glass*, J. Anthony admits, "I, who could once say from joyous experience, 'Religion is good,' have fallen by that accursed fiend, Intemperance."

10 Discussing the links between Poe's story and temperance literature, David S. Reynolds observes: "'The Black Cat' is a tale fully in the dark-temperance tradition, with reform images retained but an explicit moral message eclipsed. Many dark-temperance tales of the day dramatized the shattering of a happy family after the husband takes up the bottle. By exaggerating both the happy prologue and the horrific aftermath of the husband's tippling, Poe converts a popular reform formula into an intriguing study of the subversive forces unleashed by alcohol" ("Black Cats and Delerium Tremens: Temperance and the American Renaissance," *The Serpent in the Cup: Temperance in American Literature*, ed. David S. Reynolds and Debra J. Rosenthal [Amherst: University of Massachusetts Press, 1997], 34).

11 In *Inside the Whale* (1940), George Orwell discusses his somewhat disturbing reaction to Poe's tales in general and this episode in particular: "Their maniacal logic, in its own setting, is quite convincing. When, for instance, the drunkard seizes the black cat and cuts its eye out with his penknife, one knows exactly *why* he did it, even to the point of feeling that one would have done the same oneself."

12 Isaiah 19:14: "The Lord hath mingled a perverse spirit in the midst thereof: and they have caused Egypt to err in every work thereof, as a drunken man staggereth in his vomit." In "The Imp of the Perverse" (1845), Poe would figure this impulse that tempts us to do things "merely because we should *not*" as an impish agent: "In the sense I intend, it is, in fact, a *mobile* without motive, a motive not *motivirt*. Through its promptings we act without comprehensible object; or, if this shall be understood as a contradiction in terms, we may so far modify the proposition as to say, that through its promptings we act, for the reason that we should *not*. In theory, no reason can be more unreasonable, but, in fact, there is none more strong. With certain minds, under certain conditions, it becomes absolutely

Aubrey Beardsley, illustration for *The Black Cat*, 1901. An English decadent artist, Beardsley illustrated several of Poe's works. The stark contrast of this pen-and-ink illustration is characteristic of his work. Beardsley's daring illustrations challenged the mores of late Victorian society and earned the artist the Poe-esque moniker "Imp of the Perverse."

stantly possessed me. I knew myself no longer. My original soul seemed, at once, to take its flight from my body; and a more than fiendish malevolence, gin-nurtured, thrilled every fibre of my frame. I took from my waistcoat-pocket a pen-knife, opened it,

Seated at their kitchen table with a bottle of mescal, which casts a shadow on his chest, Rod Usher (Harvey Keitel) accosts his girl-friend in Dario Argento's "The Black Cat," one of two tales from the film *Two Evil Eyes* (1990). The theme of alcoholism pervades the tale and, through Keitel's powerful performance, indicates its ongoing relevance.

grasped the poor beast by the throat, and deliberately cut one of its eyes from the socket![11] I blush, I burn, I shudder, while I pen the damnable atrocity.

When reason returned with the morning—when I had slept off the fumes of the night's debauch—I experienced a sentiment half of horror, half of remorse, for the crime of which I had been guilty; but it was, at best, a feeble and equivocal feeling, and the soul remained untouched. I again plunged into excess, and soon drowned in wine all memory of the deed.

In the meantime the cat slowly recovered. The socket of the lost eye presented, it is true, a frightful appearance, but he no longer appeared to suffer any pain. He went about the house as usual, but, as might be expected, fled in extreme terror at my approach. I had so much of my old heart left, as to be at first grieved by this evident dislike on the part of a creature which had once so loved me. But this feeling soon gave place to irritation. And then came, as if to my final and irrevocable overthrow, the spirit of PERVERSENESS.[12] Of this spirit philosophy takes no account. Yet I am not more sure that my soul lives, than I am that perverseness is one of the primitive impulses of the human heart—one of the indivisible primary faculties, or sentiments, which give direction to the character of Man. Who has not, a hundred times, found himself committing a vile or a silly action, for no other reason than because he knows he should *not?* Have we not a perpetual inclination, in the teeth of our best judgment, to violate that which is *Law,* merely because we understand it to be such? This spirit of perverseness, I say, came to

irresistible. I am not more certain that I breathe, than that the assurance of the wrong or error of any action is often the one unconquerable *force* which impels us, and alone impels us to its prosecution. Nor will this overwhelming tendency to do wrong for the wrong's sake, admit of analysis, or resolution into ulterior elements. It is a radical, a primitive impulse—elementary" (Thomas Ollive Mabbott, ed., *Collected Works of Edgar Allan Poe,* 3 vols. [Cambridge, MA: The Belknap Press of Harvard University Press, 1969–1978], III, 1220–1221).

Poe's interest in perverse psychology presents another aspect of his work that marks him as distinctly modern and out-of-step with many of his contemporaries. Poe's champion Evert Duyckinck, a devout Episcopalian, recognized "The Black Cat" as a powerful tale but refused to accept the idea that perverseness is inherent to man's moral character: "The perverseness, to which the author refers, seems to us to be rightly classed, not among the original impulses of human nature, but among the phenomena of insanity. In its lighter manifestations in human character, we think that it would be possible to show that it is one of those secondary feelings, produced by the moral discord of the mind, and to be classed among the other frailties or sins of human nature. It is a moral disease, not a primitive impulse" (I. M. Walker, *Edgar Allan Poe: The Critical Heritage* [New York: Routledge and Kegan Paul, 1986], 190).

13 Poe's words anticipate *The Ballad of Reading Jail* (1898), Oscar Wilde's poetic rendering about a drunken wife-murderer who accepts his penalty with calmness, explaining that "each man kills the thing he loves."

14   This sentence presents the only irruption of Christian piety in the tale (and a rare instance in Poe's work as a whole), but it may be a rote invocation on the part of the narrator. Or is it a sop for Poe's pious readership, to offset the shockingly outrageous rationale for the killing?

15   That the narrator can be quickly roused from sleep by the cries of neighbors indicates the close proximity of other homes. Filming his adaptation of "The Black Cat" in co-director George Romero's Pittsburgh, Dario Argento reinforces the story's urban setting, finding the protagonist's abuse of the cat to be one of many "metropolitan horrors."

my final overthrow. It was this unfathomable longing of the soul *to vex itself*—to offer violence to its own nature—to do wrong for the wrong's sake only—that urged me to continue and finally to consummate the injury I had inflicted upon the unoffending brute. One morning, in cool blood, I slipped a noose about its neck and hung it to the limb of a tree;—hung it with the tears streaming from my eyes, and with the bitterest remorse at my heart;—hung it *because* I knew that it had loved me,[13] and *because* I felt it had given me no reason of offence;—hung it *because* I knew that in so doing I was committing a sin—a deadly sin that would so jeopardize my immortal soul as to place it—if such a thing were possible—even beyond the reach of the infinite mercy of the Most Merciful and Most Terrible God.[14]

On the night of the day on which this cruel deed was done, I was aroused from sleep by the cry of fire.[15] The curtains of my bed were in flames. The whole house was blazing. It was with great difficulty that my wife, a servant, and myself, made our escape from the conflagration. The destruction was complete. My entire worldly wealth was swallowed up, and I resigned myself thenceforward to despair.

I am above the weakness of seeking to establish a sequence of cause and effect, between the disaster and the atrocity. But I am detailing a chain of facts—and wish not to leave even a possible link imperfect. On the day succeeding the fire, I visited the ruins. The walls, with one exception, had fallen in. This exception was

Rod Usher's book *Metropolitan Horrors*, whose cover features his murder of the black cat, as displayed in a bookstore window in Dario Argento's "The Black Cat" from the feature film *Two Evil Eyes* (1990).

found in a compartment wall, not very thick, which stood about the middle of the house, and against which had rested the head of my bed. The plastering had here, in great measure, resisted the action of the fire—a fact which I attributed to its having been recently spread. About this wall a dense crowd were collected, and many persons seemed to be examining a particular portion of it with very minute and eager attention. The words "strange!" "singular!" and other similar expressions, excited my curiosity. I approached and saw, as if graven *in bas relief* upon the white surface, the figure of a gigantic *cat*.[16] The impression was given with an accuracy truly marvellous. There was a rope about the animal's neck.

When I first beheld this apparition—for I could scarcely regard it as less—my wonder and my terror were extreme. But at length reflection came to my aid. The cat, I remembered, had been hung in a garden adjacent to the house. Upon the alarm of fire, this garden had been immediately filled by the crowd—by some one of whom the animal must have been cut from the tree and thrown, through an open window, into my chamber. This had probably been done with the view of arousing me from sleep.[17] The falling of other walls had compressed the victim of my cruelty into the substance of the freshly-spread plaster; the lime of which, with the flames, and the *ammonia* from the carcass, had then accomplished the portraiture as I saw it.

Although I thus readily accounted to my reason, if not altogether to my conscience, for the startling fact just detailed, it did not the less fail to make a deep impression upon my fancy. For months I could not rid myself of the phantasm of the cat; and, during this period, there came back into my spirit a half-sentiment that seemed, but was not, remorse. I went so far as to regret the loss of the animal, and to look about me, among the vile haunts which I now habitually frequented, for another pet of the same species, and of somewhat similar appearance, with which to supply its place.

One night as I sat, half stupified, in a den of more than infamy, my attention was suddenly drawn to some black object, reposing upon the head of one of the immense hogsheads of Gin, or of Rum, which constituted the chief furniture of the apartment. I had been looking steadily at the top of this hogshead for some minutes, and what now caused me surprise was the fact that I had

16 The term "bas relief" refers to carved work in which the figures project "less than one half of their true proportions from the surface on which they are carved" *(OED)*.

17 While the act of throwing a dead cat through the window to awaken a sleeper may seem like bizarre behavior, similar activities were not unprecedented in the folk tradition. To remove warts, take a dead black cat into a graveyard at midnight, grab hold of it by the tail, and throw it toward the first noise you hear (*The Frank C. Brown Collection of North Carolina Folklore*, ed. Newman Ivey White, 7 vols. [Durham: Duke University Press, 1952–1964], no. 2451).

18   The narrator comes into possession of this mysterious cat in much the same way that Metzengerstein comes into possession of the mysterious horse in Poe's first published tale. Both animals appear as if out of nowhere. The key difference between the two provides an indication of the general shift Poe's work took over the course of his career: whereas Metzengerstein's horse is a supernatural manifestation—the Count Berlifitzing reincarnated—the new cat's uncanny resemblance to Pluto seems coincidental or delusional.

19   Though black cats are traditionally associated with bad luck, one folk belief suggests that if a black cat voluntarily comes to a person's home, then it is a sign of good luck (*Frank C. Brown Collection of North Carolina Folklore*, no. 3362). If Poe is making use of this traditional superstition, then he is using it ironically, given the way events unfold.

not sooner perceived the object thereupon. I approached it, and touched it with my hand. It was a black cat—a very large one—fully as large as Pluto, and closely resembling him in every respect but one. Pluto had not a white hair upon any portion of his body; but this cat had a large, although indefinite splotch of white, covering nearly the whole region of the breast.

Upon my touching him, he immediately arose, purred loudly, rubbed against my hand, and appeared delighted with my notice. This, then, was the very creature of which I was in search. I at once offered to purchase it of the landlord; but this person made no claim to it—knew nothing of it—had never seen it before.[18]

I continued my caresses, and, when I prepared to go home, the animal evinced a disposition to accompany me. I permitted it to do so; occasionally stooping and patting it as I proceeded. When it reached the house it domesticated itself at once, and became immediately a great favorite with my wife.[19]

For my own part, I soon found a dislike to it arising within me. This was just the reverse of what I had anticipated; but—I know not how or why it was—its evident fondness for myself rather disgusted and annoyed. By slow degrees, these feelings of disgust and annoyance rose into the bitterness of hatred. I avoided the creature; a certain sense of shame, and the remembrance of my former deed of cruelty, preventing me from physically abusing it. I did not, for some weeks, strike, or otherwise violently ill use it; but gradually—very gradually—I came to look upon it with unutterable loathing, and to flee silently from its odious presence, as from the breath of a pestilence.

What added, no doubt, to my hatred of the beast, was the discovery, on the morning after I brought it home, that, like Pluto, it also had been deprived of one of its eyes. This circumstance, however, only endeared it to my wife, who, as I have already said, possessed, in a high degree, that humanity of feeling which had once been my distinguishing trait, and the source of many of my simplest and purest pleasures.

With my aversion to this cat, however, its partiality for myself seemed to increase. It followed my footsteps with a pertinacity which it would be difficult to make the reader comprehend. Whenever I sat, it would crouch beneath my chair, or spring upon my knees, covering me with its loathsome caresses. If I arose to walk it would get between my feet and thus nearly throw me down, or,

John Caspar Wild, *Moyamensing Prison, Philadelphia*, 1840. The elaborate, Egyptian-style entrance to this large fortresslike prison complex provides further evidence of the Egyptian craze affecting America during Poe's lifetime. By his own account, Poe was detained in the prison on a charge of public drunkenness in July 1849.

fastening its long and sharp claws in my dress, clamber, in this manner, to my breast. At such times, although I longed to destroy it with a blow, I was yet withheld from so doing, partly by a memory of my former crime, but chiefly—let me confess it at once—by absolute *dread* of the beast.

This dread was not exactly a dread of physical evil—and yet I should be at a loss how otherwise to define it. I am almost ashamed to own—yes, even in this felon's cell, I am almost ashamed to own—that the terror and horror with which the animal inspired me, had been heightened by one of the merest chimaeras[20] it would be possible to conceive. My wife had called my attention, more than once, to the character of the mark of white hair, of which I have spoken, and which constituted the sole visible difference between the strange beast and the one I had destroyed. The reader

20 In Greek mythology, a fire-breathing creature, with a lion's head, a goat's body, and a serpent's tail; or, more generally, any fanciful conception.

21   The narrator relates his "homely narrative" from a felon's cell; he has already been convicted of a capital crime—and apparently sentenced as well, to death by hanging. In 1861, in his magazine *Vremia*, Fyodor Dostoevski introduced Russian readers to three newly translated tales by Poe—"The Tell-Tale Heart," "The Black Cat," and "The Devil in the Belfry." In his introduction to the tales, Dostoevski praises Poe for his "marvelous acumen," "amazing realism," and especially his "power of details." Richard Wilbur points out that it is "interesting" that two of the three tales published in Dostoevski's magazine "are accounts of murder, conscience, and confession" ("The Poe Mystery Case," *New York Review of Books* [July 13, 1967]). *Crime and Punishment* would appear five years later.

22   Genesis 1:27: "So God created man in his own image, in the image of God created he him; male and female created he them."

23   *The Witch of Edmonton* (1658), a drama by William Rowley, Thomas Dekker, and John Ford, is one possible source for Poe's tale. In Act III, a possessed familiar—a black dog—rubs against a character who soon murders his wife. Mabbott suggests *The Witch of Edmonton* as a possible source but doubts whether Poe read the play. He may have. His employer William Burton had a copy of *The Witch of Edmonton* in his library (*Bibliotheca Dramatica: Catalogue of the Theatrical and Miscellaneous Library of the Late William E. Burton* [New York: J. Sabin, 1860], lot 1040).

24   The Pulitzer Prize–winning novelist Marilynne Robinson argues that "Poe's great tales turn on guilt concealed or denied, then abruptly and shockingly exposed. He has always been reviled or celebrated for the absence of moral content in his work, despite the fact that these tales are all straightforward moral parables. For a writer so intrigued by the operations of the mind as Poe was, an interest in conscience leads to an interest in concealment and self-deception, things that are secretive and highly individual and at the same time so universal they shape civilizations" ("On Edgar Allan Poe," *New York Review of Books* [February 5, 2015], 6).

will remember that this mark, although large, had been originally very indefinite; but, by slow degrees—degrees nearly imperceptible, and which for a long time my Reason struggled to reject as fanciful—it had, at length, assumed a rigorous distinctness of outline. It was now the representation of an object that I shudder to name—and for this, above all, I loathed, and dreaded, and would have rid myself of the monster *had I dared*—it was now, I say, the image of a hideous—of a ghastly thing—of the GALLOWS!—oh, mournful and terrible engine of Horror and of Crime—of Agony and of Death![21]

And now was I indeed wretched beyond the wretchedness of mere Humanity. And *a brute beast*—whose fellow I had contemptuously destroyed—*a brute beast* to work out for *me*—for me a man, fashioned in the image of the High God[22]—so much of insufferable wo! Alas! neither by day nor by night knew I the blessing of Rest any more! During the former the creature left me no moment alone; and, in the latter, I started, hourly, from dreams of unutterable fear, to find the hot breath of *the thing* upon my face, and its vast weight—an incarnate Night-Mare that I had no power to shake off—incumbent eternally upon my *heart!*

Beneath the pressure of torments such as these, the feeble remnant of the good within me succumbed. Evil thoughts became my sole intimates—the darkest and most evil of thoughts. The moodiness of my usual temper increased to hatred of all things and of all mankind; while, from the sudden, frequent, and ungovernable outbursts of a fury to which I now blindly abandoned myself, my uncomplaining wife, alas! was the most usual and the most patient of sufferers.

One day she accompanied me, upon some household errand, into the cellar of the old building which our poverty compelled us to inhabit. The cat followed me down the steep stairs, and, nearly throwing me headlong, exasperated me to madness.[23] Uplifting an axe, and forgetting, in my wrath, the childish dread which had hitherto stayed my hand, I aimed a blow at the animal which, of course, would have proved instantly fatal had it descended as I wished. But this blow was arrested by the hand of my wife. Goaded, by the interference, into a rage more than demoniacal, I withdrew my arm from her grasp and buried the axe in her brain. She fell dead upon the spot, without a groan.[24]

This hideous murder accomplished, I set myself forthwith, and with entire deliberation, to the task of concealing the body. I knew that I could not remove it from the house, either by day or by night, without the risk of being observed by the neighbors. Many projects entered my mind. At one period I thought of cutting the corpse into minute fragments, and destroying them by fire. At another, I resolved to dig a grave for it in the floor of the cellar. Again, I deliberated about casting it in the well in the yard—about packing it in a box, as if merchandize, with the usual arrangements, and so getting a porter to take it from the house. Finally I hit upon what I considered a far better expedient than either of these. I determined to wall it up in the cellar—as the monks of the middle ages are recorded to have walled up their victims.[25]

For a purpose such as this the cellar was well adapted. Its walls were loosely constructed, and had lately been plastered throughout with a rough plaster, which the dampness of the atmosphere had prevented from hardening. Moreover, in one of the walls was a projection, caused by a false chimney, or fireplace, that had been filled up, and made to resemble the rest of the cellar. I made no doubt that I could readily displace the bricks at this point, insert the corpse, and wall the whole up as before, so that no eye could detect any thing suspicious.

And in this calculation I was not deceived. By means of a crowbar I easily dislodged the bricks, and, having carefully deposited the body against the inner wall, I propped it in that position, while, with little trouble, I re-laid the whole structure as it originally stood. Having procured mortar, sand, and hair, with every possible precaution, I prepared a plaster which could not be distinguished from the old, and with this I very carefully went over the new brick-work. When I had finished, I felt satisfied that all was right. The wall did not present the slightest appearance of having been disturbed. The rubbish on the floor was picked up with the minutest care. I looked around triumphantly, and said to myself—"Here at least, then, my labor has not been in vain."

My next step was to look for the beast which had been the cause of so much wretchedness; for I had, at length, firmly resolved to put it to death. Had I been able to meet with it, at the moment, there could have been no doubt of its fate; but it appeared that the crafty animal had been alarmed at the violence of my previous anger, and forebore to present itself in my present mood. It is impossible to describe, or to imagine, the deep, the blissful sense of relief

25 A real-life precedent for the denouement of "The Black Cat" appeared in the contemporary press. On July 16, 1842, the Philadelphia *Public Ledger* reprinted an item from the Greenfield, Massachusetts, *Democrat*, which reported the story of a Massachusetts man who took down a cellar wall while in the process of remodeling his home. Behind the wall, he found a fairly well preserved skeleton. By its position, the skeleton indicated that part of the wall had been taken down, the body placed behind it, and the removed part replaced. Examining the remains, physicians concluded that they belonged to a female in her late teens. She had a hole about the size of a bullet in the back of her skull. According to local tradition, a young woman who lived nearby about twenty-five years earlier had mysteriously disappeared (John E. Reilly, "A Source for the Immuration in 'The Black Cat,'" *Nineteenth-Century Literature* 48 [1993], 93–95).

26   Deuteronomy 13:6, 8: "If thy brother, the son of thy mother, or thy son, or thy daughter, or the wife of thy bosom, or thy friend, which is as thine own soul, entice thee secretly, saying, Let us go and serve other gods, which thou hast not known, thou, nor thy fathers . . . Thou shalt not consent unto him."

which the absence of the detested creature occasioned in my bosom. It did not make its appearance during the night—and thus for one night at least, since its introduction into the house, I soundly and tranquilly slept; aye, *slept* even with the burden of murder upon my soul!

The second and the third day passed, and still my tormentor came not. Once again I breathed as a freeman. The monster, in terror, had fled the premises forever! I should behold it no more! My happiness was supreme! The guilt of my dark deed disturbed me but little. Some few inquiries had been made, but these had been readily answered. Even a search had been instituted—but of course nothing was to be discovered. I looked upon my future felicity as secured.

Upon the fourth day of the assassination, a party of the police came, very unexpectedly, into the house, and proceeded again to make rigorous investigation of the premises. Secure, however, in the inscrutability of my place of concealment, I felt no embarrassment whatever. The officers bade me accompany them in their search. They left no nook or corner unexplored. At length, for the third or fourth time, they descended into the cellar. I quivered not in a muscle. My heart beat calmly as that of one who slumbers in innocence. I walked the cellar from end to end. I folded my arms upon my bosom, and roamed easily to and fro. The police were thoroughly satisfied and prepared to depart. The glee at my heart was too strong to be restrained. I burned to say if but one word, by way of triumph, and to render doubly sure their assurance of my guiltlessness.

"Gentlemen," I said at last, as the party ascended the steps, "I delight to have allayed your suspicions. I wish you all health, and a little more courtesy. By the bye, gentlemen, this—this is a very well constructed house." (In the rabid desire to say something easily, I scarcely knew what I uttered at all.)—"I may say an *excellently* well constructed house. These walls—are you going, gentlemen?—these walls are solidly put together"; and here, through the mere phrenzy of bravado, I rapped heavily, with a cane which I held in my hand, upon that very portion of the brick-work behind which stood the corpse of the wife of my bosom.[26]

But may God shield and deliver me from the fangs of the Arch-Fiend! No sooner had the reverberation of my blows sunk into silence, than I was answered by a voice from within the tomb!—by

H. Meyer, depiction of the policemen discovering the corpse beyond the wall, from *The Tales and Poems of Edgar Allan Poe* (Philadelphia: George Barrie, 1895).

a cry, at first muffled and broken, like the sobbing of a child, and then quickly swelling into one long, loud, and continuous scream, utterly anomalous and inhuman—a howl—a wailing shriek, half of horror and half of triumph, such as might have arisen only out of hell, conjointly from the throats of the damned in their agony and of the demons that exult in the damnation.

Of my own thoughts it is folly to speak. Swooning, I staggered to the opposite wall. For one instant the party upon the stairs remained motionless, through extremity of terror and of awe. In the next, a dozen stout arms were toiling at the wall. It fell bodily. The corpse, already greatly decayed and clotted with gore, stood erect before the eyes of the spectators. Upon its head, with red extended mouth and solitary eye of fire, sat the hideous beast whose craft had seduced me into murder, and whose informing voice had consigned me to the hangman. I had walled the monster up within the tomb![27]

27 In an essay entitled "On Reading," the French post-Impressionist painter Paul Gauguin recalls a frightening experience with Poe's tale. Seated together one winter evening before the fireplace in a home they had rented from a fellow artist, Paul and Sophie Gauguin were reading "The Black Cat" in a collection of Poe's tales. Sophie interrupted her reading to get some coal from the cellar. As she descended the steps, a black cat leapt in front of her, prompting her to jump back in fear. Sophie steeled herself and continued down the stairs only to discover a human skull buried beneath the coal. She rushed back upstairs and fainted. Once she recovered, Paul went down to the cellar himself and found other human remains in the pile of coal. He later learned that his artist friend had an articulated skeleton that he used as a model, which he threw into the cellar once it started falling apart. It was all a bizarre coincidence, but it did not stop Gauguin from cautioning readers: "Beware of Edgar Poe."

"The Purloined Letter" is a detective story that revolves around the theft and possession of an incriminating letter: both the criminal and his motivations, however, are completely transparent at the outset. All parties involved, including the police and the victim of the crime, know how, when, and why the theft was committed. And the criminal himself knows that everyone else knows he has perpetrated the crime. Much like the popular television show Columbo, *which reveals to the audience both the crime and the criminal at the start of each episode, "The Purloined Letter" engages our interest by the method of detection. Another important aspect of the tale is that the exact contents of the letter are never revealed. No tale in the Poe canon has been the subject of such intense scholarly debate as "The Purloined Letter." Readings by clinical psychologists, linguists, philosophers, and psychoanalysts—notably Jacques Lacan, Jacques Derrida, and Barbara Johnson—have revealed the tale's linguistic play and ingenuity, and its ability to sustain theoretically sophisticated enquiry. Taken together, they suggest a seemingly infinite number of possible interpretations (like the significance of the stolen letter, the meaning of "The Purloined Letter" depends on who possesses it). Critic John T. Irwin points out that what these psychoanalytic and other methodologically self-conscious readings tend to ignore is that "The Purloined Letter" is itself a canny parable about the interpretive effects it produces on its readers ("Mysteries We Reread, Mysteries of Rereading: Poe, Borges, and the Analytic Detective Story; Also Lacan, Derrida, and Johnson,"* Modern Language Notes *101 [1986], 1201).*

The third and final story to feature Poe's super sleuth C. Auguste Dupin, "The Purloined Letter" appeared in late September 1844 in The Gift: A Christmas, New Year, and Birthday Present, *an annual publication that was part of the nineteenth-century phenomenon of lavishly produced gift books that came out in advance of the holiday season. Henry Wadsworth Longfellow and Ralph Waldo Emerson also appear in the book's table of contents. Poe wrote "The Purloined Letter" in Philadelphia, shortly before he, Virginia, and Maria Clemm moved once again, this time back to New York City. Poe called it "perhaps, the best of my tales of ratiocination"* (Collected Letters of Edgar Allan Poe, *ed. John Ward Ostrom, Burton R. Pollin, and Jeffrey A. Savoye, 2 vols. [New York: Gordian Press, 2008], I, 450).*

1 "Nothing is more odious to true wisdom than too acute sharpness." There's no evidence that Seneca (4 BCE–65 CE), the Roman dramatist, wrote these words. Poe, a shameless magpie, took the Latin saying from a novel he had reviewed earlier, Samuel Warren's *Ten Thousand a-Year* (Philadelphia: Carey and Hart, 1841), which attributes the saying to Seneca.

The Purloined Letter

Nil sapientiae odiosius acumine nimio.
Seneca[1]

At Paris, just after dark one gusty evening in the autumn of 18——, I was enjoying the twofold luxury of meditation and a meerschaum,[2] in company with my friend C. Auguste Dupin, in his little back library, or book-closet,[3] *au troisième, No. 33, Rue Dunôt, Faubourg St. Germain.*[4] For one hour at least we had maintained a profound silence; while each, to any casual observer, might have seemed intently and exclusively occupied with the curling eddies of smoke that oppressed the atmosphere of the chamber. For myself, however, I was mentally discussing certain topics which had formed matter for conversation between us at an earlier period of the evening; I mean the affair of the Rue Morgue, and the mystery attending the murder of Marie Rogêt.[5] I looked upon it, therefore, as something of a coincidence, when the door of our apartment was thrown open and admitted our old acquaintance, Monsieur G——, the Prefect of the Parisian police.[6]

We gave him a hearty welcome; for there was nearly half as much of the entertaining as of the contemptible about the man, and we had not seen him for several years. We had been sitting in the dark, and Dupin now arose for the purpose of lighting a lamp, but sat down again, without doing so, upon G.'s saying that he had called to consult us, or rather to ask the opinion of my friend, about some official business which had occasioned a great deal of trouble.

"If it is any point requiring reflection," observed Dupin, as he forebore to enkindle the wick, "we shall examine it to better purpose in the dark."[7]

"That is another of your odd notions," said the Prefect, who had a fashion of calling every thing "odd" that was beyond his comprehension, and thus lived amid an absolute legion of "oddities."[8]

"Very true," said Dupin, as he supplied his visiter with a pipe, and rolled towards him a comfortable chair.

"And what is the difficulty now?" I asked. "Nothing more in the assassination way, I hope?"

"Oh no; nothing of that nature. The fact is, the business is *very* simple indeed, and I make no doubt that we can manage it sufficiently well ourselves; but then I thought Dupin would like to hear the details of it, because it is so excessively *odd*."

"Simple and odd," said Dupin.

"Why, yes; and not exactly that, either. The fact is, we have all been a good deal puzzled because the affair *is* so simple, and yet baffles us altogether."

"Perhaps it is the very simplicity of the thing which puts you at fault," said my friend.

"What nonsense you *do* talk!" replied the Prefect, laughing heartily.

"Perhaps the mystery is a little too plain," said Dupin.

"Oh, good heavens! who ever heard of such an idea?"

"A little *too* self-evident."

"Ha! ha! ha!—ha! ha! ha!—ho! ho! ho!" roared our visiter, profoundly amused, "oh, Dupin, you will be the death of me yet!"

"And what, after all, is the matter on hand?" I asked.

"Why, I will tell you," replied the Prefect, as he gave a long, steady, and contemplative puff, and settled himself in his chair. "I will tell you in a few words; but, before I begin, let me caution you that this is an affair demanding the greatest secrecy, and that I should most probably lose the position I now hold, were it known that I confided it to any one."

"Proceed," said I.

"Or not," said Dupin.

"Well, then; I have received personal information, from a very high quarter, that a certain document of the last importance, has been purloined from the royal apartments. The individual who purloined it is known; this beyond a doubt; he was seen to take it. It is known, also, that it still remains in his possession."

"How is this known?" asked Dupin.

"It is clearly inferred," replied the Prefect, "from the nature

2   The meerschaum pipe has a bowl made from an extremely lightweight type of white clay. The name meerschaum—literally sea-froth—pertains to both its color and its weight. The charm of a meerschaum comes from the way the bowl changes color through use. As it is smoked, the white bowl gradually assumes a mottled brown color. After use, no two meerschaum pipes are alike. Dupin's attraction to meerschaum makes sense: it offers an analogy to detection. Much as the clues at a crime scene lead to an understanding of what has happened there, the patina of a meerschaum bowl indicates how frequently and intensely the pipe has been smoked. Dupin's meerschaum prefigures Sherlock Holmes's calabash pipe—the detective's pipe is a trope for stillness and analysis.

3   Poe himself could never afford a home with a library. Apparently, Dupin's home has two: that it has a secluded *back* library implies that it also has a front library. This cozy back library is an intimate space, where Dupin and the narrator can share their thoughts and ideas. Virtually all the direct action, such as it is, occurs in this tiny library.

4   Dupin lives on the fourth floor, that is, three flights up. The address given here is more specific than the one provided in "The Murders in the Rue Morgue." Rue Dunôt, however, is fictional.

5   In "The Murders in the Rue Morgue," the narrator describes how he first met Dupin "at an obscure library in the Rue Montmartre, where the accident of our both being in search of the same very rare and very remarkable volume, brought us into closer communion. . . . [and] at length arranged that we should live together." In the intervening years, the two men have continued their housekeeping arrangement. Some modern readers have supposed their nocturnal habits and secrecy suggest a homosexual relationship. It has been several years since the narrator and Dupin last saw Monsieur G——, who also figures in "The Mystery of Marie Rogêt" (1842). "The Mystery of Marie Rogêt" originally carried the subtitle "A Sequel to 'The Murders in the Rue Morgue.'"

6   The Prefect barges in without knocking or being announced. Later, we learn that the Prefect possesses keys that "can open any chamber or cabinet in Paris." It seems at least possible, therefore, that he has let himself inside Dupin's home. Poe's Paris is a modern city where citizens are subject to intrusive surveillance.

7   Darkness enables Dupin to focus his mental faculties, both the intuitive and the analytic, on the mystery. The de-

tective must be able to enter the mind of the criminal. The plodding Prefect, by contrast, prefers the clear light of day.

8   The bungling and inept police of modern crime fiction are all Monsieur G's progeny. The "obtuse and resolute" G. Lestrade of Scotland Yard, who appears in several of Conan Doyle's Sherlock Holmes stories, is one example. In "The Adventures of the Empty House," Holmes offers Lestrade this back-handed compliment: "Three undetected murders in one year won't do, Lestrade. But you handled the Molesey Mystery with less than your usual—that's to say, you handled it fairly well."

9   The reader is lead to believe this "illustrious person-age" is the Queen. The real-life royal who inspired Poe's tale is Caroline, Princess of Wales (1768–1821). In her life-time, a letter she wrote to her estranged husband, the Prince Regent and later King George IV, came to symbol-ize their marital difficulties. Poe was less interested in Car-oline's real story than in a fanciful version of it that ap-peared in a popular book of scandal, which gave him the title for his tale: "The man in office met that day his *con-freres* at——, and, after dinner, amused them with an ac-count of the purloined letter" (*Death-Bed Confessions of the Late Countess of Guernsey to Lady Anne Hamilton* [Philadel-phia: James E. Moore, 1822], 74).

10   A proverbial comparison meaning keen-sighted.

11   Many critics have recognized that the stolen letter's function is far more important than its (sensitive) contents. In his seminar on "The Purloined Letter," the French psy-choanalyst Jacques Lacan (1901–1981) observes: "As for the letter's import, we know only the dangers it would bring with it were it to fall into the hands of a certain third party, and that its possession has allowed the Minister to wield, 'for political purposes, to a very dangerous extent,' the power it assures him over the person concerned. But this tells us nothing about the message it carries.

   "Love letter or conspiratorial letter, informant's letter or directive, demanding letter or letter of distress, we can rest assured of but one thing: the Queen cannot let her lord and master know of it" ("Seminar on 'The Purloined Let-ter,'" *Écrits: The First Complete Edition in English*, trans. Bruce Fink [New York: W. W. Norton, 2006], 19).

of the document, and from the non-appearance of certain results which would at once arise from its passing *out* of the robber's pos-session;—that is to say, from his employing it as he must design in the end to employ it."

"Be a little more explicit," I said.

"Well, I may venture so far as to say that the paper gives its holder a certain power in a certain quarter where such power is im-mensely valuable." The Prefect was fond of the cant of diplomacy.

"Still I do not quite understand," said Dupin.

"No? Well; the disclosure of the document to a third person, who shall be nameless, would bring in question the honor of a per-sonage of most exalted station; and this fact gives the holder of the document an ascendancy over the illustrious personage whose honor and peace are so jeopardized."[9]

"But this ascendancy," I interposed, "would depend upon the robber's knowledge of the loser's knowledge of the robber. Who would dare—"

"The thief," said G., "is the Minister D——, who dares all things, those unbecoming as well as those becoming a man. The method of the theft was not less ingenious than bold. The docu-ment in question—a letter, to be frank—had been received by the personage robbed while alone in the royal *boudoir*. During its perusal she was suddenly interrupted by the entrance of the other exalted personage from whom especially it was her wish to conceal it. After a hurried and vain endeavor to thrust it in a drawer, she was forced to place it, open as it was, upon a table. The address, however, was uppermost, and, the contents thus un-exposed, the letter escaped notice. At this juncture enters the Min-ister D——. His lynx eye[10] immediately perceives the paper, rec-ognises the handwriting of the address, observes the confusion of the personage addressed, and fathoms her secret. After some busi-ness transactions, hurried through in his ordinary manner, he pro-duces a letter somewhat similar to the one in question, opens it, pretends to read it, and then places it in close juxtaposition to the other. Again he converses, for some fifteen minutes, upon the pub-lic affairs. At length, in taking leave, he takes also from the table the letter to which he had no claim. Its rightful owner saw, but, of course, dared not call attention to the act, in the presence of the third personage who stood at her elbow. The minister decamped; leaving his own letter—one of no importance—upon the table."[11]

Samuel Osgood, *Edgar Allan Poe*, 1845. This is the only known oil portrait of Poe painted during his lifetime.

"Here, then," said Dupin to me, "you have precisely what you demand to make the ascendancy complete—the robber's knowledge of the loser's knowledge of the robber."

"Yes," replied the Prefect; "and the power thus attained has, for some months past, been wielded, for political purposes, to a very dangerous extent. The personage robbed is more thoroughly convinced, every day, of the necessity of reclaiming her letter. But

12   The phrase "perfect whirlwind"—another name for a tornado—was often used figuratively.

13   Townhouse.

14   To be *"au fait"* with a subject means to be familiar with it or even possess a mastery of it.

this, of course, cannot be done openly. In fine, driven to despair, she has committed the matter to me."

"Than whom," said Dupin, amid a perfect whirlwind of smoke,[12] "no more sagacious agent could, I suppose, be desired, or even imagined."

"You flatter me," replied the Prefect; "but it is possible that some such opinion may have been entertained."

"It is clear," said I, "as you observe, that the letter is still in possession of the minister; since it is this possession, and not any employment of the letter, which bestows the power. With the employment the power departs."

"True," said G——; "and upon this conviction I proceeded. My first care was to make thorough search of the minister's hotel;[13] and here my chief embarrassment lay in the necessity of searching without his knowledge. Beyond all things, I have been warned of the danger which would result from giving him reason to suspect our design."

"But," said I, "you are quite *au fait*[14] in these investigations. The Parisian police have done this thing often before."

"O yes; and for this reason I did not despair. The habits of the minister gave me, too, a great advantage. He is frequently absent from home all night. His servants are by no means numerous. They sleep at a distance from their master's apartment, and, being chiefly Neapolitans, are readily made drunk. I have keys, as you know, with which I can open any chamber or cabinet in Paris. For three months a night has not passed, during the greater part of which I have not been engaged, personally, in ransacking the D——Hotel. My honor is interested, and, to mention a great secret, the reward is enormous. So I did not abandon the search until I had become fully satisfied that the thief is a more astute man than myself. I fancy that I have investigated every nook and corner of the premises in which it is possible that the paper can be concealed."

"But is it not possible," I suggested, "that although the letter may be in possession of the minister, as it unquestionably is, he may have concealed it elsewhere than upon his own premises?"

"This is barely possible," said Dupin. "The present peculiar condition of affairs at court, and especially of those intrigues in which D——is known to be involved, would render the instant availability of the document—its susceptibility of being produced at a moment's notice—a point of nearly equal importance with its possession."

"Its susceptibility of being produced?" said I.

"That is to say, of being *destroyed*," said Dupin.

"True," I observed; "the paper is clearly then upon the premises. As for its being upon the person of the minister, we may consider that as out of the question."

"Entirely," said the Prefect. "He has been twice waylaid, as if by footpads,[15] and his person rigorously searched under my own inspection."

"You might have spared yourself this trouble," said Dupin. "D——, I presume, is not altogether a fool, and, if not, must have anticipated these waylayings, as a matter of course."

"Not *altogether* a fool," said G., "but then he's a poet, which I take to be only one remove from a fool."

"True," said Dupin, after a long and thoughtful whiff from his meerschaum, "although I have been guilty of certain doggrel myself."[16]

"Suppose you detail," said I, "the particulars of your search."

"Why the fact is, we took our time, and we searched *everywhere*. I have had long experience in these affairs. I took the entire building, room by room; devoting the nights of a whole week to each. We examined, first, the furniture of each apartment. We opened every possible drawer; and I presume you know that, to a properly trained police agent, such a thing as a *secret* drawer is impossible. Any man is a dolt who permits a 'secret' drawer to escape him in a search of this kind. The thing is *so* plain. There is a certain amount of bulk—of space—to be accounted for in every cabinet. Then we have accurate rules. The fiftieth part of a line could not escape us. After the cabinets we took the chairs. The cushions we probed with the fine long needles you have seen me employ.[17] From the tables we removed the tops."

"Why so?"

"Sometimes the top of a table, or other similarly arranged piece of furniture, is removed by the person wishing to conceal an article; then the leg is excavated, the article deposited within the cavity, and the top replaced. The bottoms and tops of bedposts are employed in the same way."

15 Highwaymen who rob on foot.

16 Dupin's expression of sympathy with another poet is the first indication that Dupin and Minister D—— have much in common. Later we learn that, like Dupin himself, his adversary is not just a poet but also a mathematician: "As poet *and* mathematician, he would reason well; as mere mathematician, he could not have reasoned at all, and thus would have been at the mercy of the Prefect." In "The Murders in the Rue Morgue," the narrator fancies that Dupin's combination of imagination and analytic skill make his friend "a double Dupin—the creative and the resolvent." Minister D——is therefore a double of the "double Dupin."

17 The image of the Prefect manipulating "the fine long needles" is more unsettling for the association we make between seat cushions and the body, which leaves its imprint on the cushion. Walter Benjamin, for whom seat cushions exemplify his notion of the householder imprinting him or herself on the domestic interior, understood this association. Poe lived and wrote in an era that saw the birth of modern police work and detection.

18   Here the word "microscope" means a magnifying glass. The magnifying glass would become so prevalent in later detective fiction that it would also feature in parodies of detective stories, as in Buster Keaton's *Sherlock, Jr.* (1924).

19   A gimlet is a tool used for boring holes in wood.

20   Poe anticipates another method of forensic science, the grid search.

"But could not the cavity be detected by sounding?" I asked.

"By no means, if, when the article is deposited, a sufficient wadding of cotton be placed around it. Besides, in our case, we were obliged to proceed without noise."

"But you could not have removed—you could not have taken to pieces *all* articles of furniture in which it would have been possible to make a deposit in the manner you mention. A letter may be compressed into a thin spiral roll, not differing much in shape or bulk from a large knitting-needle, and in this form it might be inserted into the rung of a chair, for example. You did not take to pieces all the chairs?"

"Certainly not; but we did better—we examined the rungs of every chair in the hotel, and, indeed the jointings of every description of furniture, by the aid of a most powerful microscope.[18] Had there been any traces of recent disturbance we should not have failed to detect it instantly. A single grain of gimlet-dust,[19] for example, would have been as obvious as an apple. Any disorder in the glueing—any unusual gaping in the joints—would have sufficed to insure detection."

"I presume you looked to the mirrors, between the boards and the plates, and you probed the beds and the bed-clothes, as well as the curtains and carpets."

"That of course; and when we had absolutely completed every particle of the furniture in this way, then we examined the house itself. We divided its entire surface into compartments, which we numbered, so that none might be missed; then we scrutinized each individual square inch throughout the premises, including the two houses immediately adjoining, with the microscope, as before."[20]

"The two houses adjoining!" I exclaimed; "you must have had a great deal of trouble."

"We had; but the reward offered is prodigious."

"You include the *grounds* about the houses?"

"All the grounds are paved with brick. They gave us comparatively little trouble. We examined the moss between the bricks, and found it undisturbed."

"You looked among D——'s papers, of course, and into the books of the library?"

"Certainly; we opened every package and parcel; we not only opened every book, but we turned over every leaf in each volume, not contenting ourselves with a mere shake, according to the fashion of some of our police officers. We also measured the thickness of every book-*cover,* with the most accurate admeasurement, and applied to each the most jealous scrutiny of the microscope. Had any of the bindings been recently meddled with, it would have been utterly impossible that the fact should have escaped observation. Some five or six volumes, just from the hands of the binder, we carefully probed, longitudinally, with the needles."

"You explored the floors beneath the carpets?"

"Beyond doubt. We removed every carpet, and examined the boards with the microscope."

"And the paper on the walls?"

"Yes."

"You looked into the cellars?"

"We did."

"Then," I said, "you have been making a miscalculation, and the letter is *not* upon the premises, as you suppose."

"I fear you are right there," said the Prefect. "And now, Dupin, what would you advise me to do?"

"To make a thorough re-search of the premises."

"That is absolutely needless,"[21] replied G———. "I am not more sure that I breathe than I am that the letter is not at the Hotel."

"I have no better advice to give you," said Dupin. "You have, of course, an accurate description of the letter?"

"Oh yes!"—And here the Prefect, producing a memorandum-book proceeded to read aloud a minute account of the internal, and especially of the external appearance of the missing document. Soon after finishing the perusal of this description, he took his departure, more entirely depressed in spirits than I had ever known the good gentleman before.

In about a month afterwards he paid us another visit, and found us occupied very nearly as before. He took a pipe and a chair and entered into some ordinary conversation. At length I said,—

"Well, but G———, what of the purloined letter? I presume you have at last made up your mind that there is no such thing as over-reaching the Minister?"

"Confound him, say I—yes; I made the re-examination, however, as Dupin suggested—but it was all labor lost, as I knew it would be."

"How much was the reward offered, did you say?" asked Dupin.

21 Another one of Poe's characteristic puns: given the Prefect's methodical use of long, probing needles, another search would be absolutely needles(s).

22 John Abernethy (1764–1831) was a famous British surgeon and lecturer on anatomy and physiology. By 1844, the "story about Abernethy" had been in circulation for decades, though it did not always feature Abernethy. For the earliest known version, see "Medical Anecdote," *European Magazine, and London Review* 2 (1782), 255.

23 A writing desk constructed to contain stationery and documents.

"Why, a very great deal—a *very* liberal reward—I don't like to say how much, precisely; but one thing I *will* say, that I wouldn't mind giving my individual check for fifty thousand francs to any one who could obtain me that letter. The fact is, it is becoming of more and more importance every day; and the reward has been lately doubled. If it were trebled, however, I could do no more than I have done."

"Why, yes," said Dupin, drawlingly, between the whiffs of his meerschaum, "I really—think, G——, you have not exerted yourself—to the utmost in this matter. You might—do a little more, I think, eh?"

"How?—in what way?"

"Why—puff, puff—you might—puff, puff—employ counsel in the matter, eh?—puff, puff, puff. Do you remember the story they tell of Abernethy?"[22]

"No; hang Abernethy!"

"To be sure! hang him and welcome. But, once upon a time, a certain rich miser conceived the design of spunging upon this Abernethy for a medical opinion. Getting up, for this purpose, an ordinary conversation in a private company, he insinuated his case to the physician, as that of an imaginary individual.

"'We will suppose,' said the miser, 'that his symptoms are such and such; now, doctor, what would *you* have directed him to take?'

"'Take!' said Abernethy, 'why, take *advice*, to be sure.'"

"But," said the Prefect, a little discomposed, "I am *perfectly* willing to take advice, and to pay for it. I would really give fifty thousand francs to any one who would aid me in the matter."

"In that case," replied Dupin, opening a drawer, and producing a check-book, "you may as well fill me up a check for the amount mentioned. When you have signed it, I will hand you the letter."

I was astounded. The Prefect appeared absolutely thunder-stricken. For some minutes he remained speechless and motionless, looking incredulously at my friend with open mouth, and eyes that seemed starting from their sockets; then, apparently recovering himself in some measure, he seized a pen, and after several pauses and vacant stares, finally filled up and signed a check for fifty thousand francs, and handed it across the table to Dupin. The latter examined it carefully and deposited it in his pocket-book; then, unlocking an *escritoire*,[23] took thence a letter and gave it to the Prefect. This functionary grasped it in a perfect agony of joy, opened it with a trembling hand, cast a rapid glance at its contents, and then, scrambling and struggling to the door, rushed at length unceremoniously from the room and from the house, without having uttered a syllable since Dupin had requested him to fill up the check.

When he had gone, my friend entered into some explanations.[24]

"The Parisian police," he said, "are exceedingly able in their way. They are persevering, ingenious, cunning, and thoroughly versed in the knowledge which their duties seem chiefly to demand. Thus, when G——detailed to us his mode of searching the premises at the Hotel D——, I felt entire confidence in his having made a satisfactory investigation—so far as his labors extended."

"So far as his labors extended?" said I.

"Yes," said Dupin. "The measures adopted were not only the best of their kind, but carried out to absolute perfection. Had the letter been deposited within the range of their search, these fellows would, beyond a question, have found it."

I merely laughed—but he seemed quite serious in all that he said.

"The measures, then," he continued, "were good in their kind, and well executed; their defect lay in their being inapplicable to the case, and to the man. A certain set of highly ingenious resources are, with the Prefect, a sort of Procrustean bed,[25] to which he forcibly adapts his designs. But he perpetually errs by being too deep or too shallow, for the matter in hand; and many a schoolboy is a better reasoner than he. I knew one about eight years of age, whose success at guessing in the game of 'even and odd' attracted universal admiration. This game is simple, and is played with marbles. One player holds in his hand a number of these toys, and demands of another whether that number is even or odd. If the guess is right, the guesser wins one; if wrong, he loses one.[26] The boy to whom I allude won all the marbles of the school. Of course he had some principle of guessing; and this lay in mere observation and admeasurement of the astuteness of his opponents. For example, an arrant simpleton is his opponent, and, holding up his closed hand, asks, 'are they even or odd?' Our schoolboy replies, 'odd,' and loses; but upon the second trial he wins, for he then says to himself, 'the simpleton had them even upon the first trial, and his

24 Amusingly, the Prefect of the Paris police department expresses no interest in learning *how* Dupin has recovered the purloined letter. The abrupt departure of the "functionary" restores the privacy and relaxed intimacy enjoyed by the two men before his intrusion. Like the narrator, the reader, too, is now brought into Dupin's confidence, as he explains how he has outwitted the Minister. The reader, too, is present in the intimate space of Dupin's back library or book closet.

25 In Greek mythology Procrustes, a son of Poseidon, tortured his overnight guests by making them conform to the size of an iron bed. If they proved to be too short, he stretched their limbs. If they were too tall, he lopped off their feet. "Procrustes's bed" is a proverbial expression for any uniformity by forceful or arbitrary methods. Thomas Jefferson uses the phrase to refute the desirability of uniform opinion: "But is uniformity of opinion desirable? No more than of face and stature. Introduce the bed of Procrustes then, and as there is danger that the large men may beat the small, make us all of a size, by lopping the former and stretching the latter" (*Notes on the State of Virginia*, ed. William Peden [1954; reprinted, New York: Norton, 1972], 160).

26 The game of "even and odd" has been played since ancient times. Marbles are unnecessary. Beans, almonds, coins: anything that can be easily concealed in the hand suffices.

27   The discovery of this phenomenon, which is known as neural mirroring, is generally attributed to Tommaso Campanella (1568–1639). Poe may have read about it in Horace Binney Wallace's novel *Stanley; or the Recollections of a Man of the World* (1838), which mentions Campanella and describes the phenomenon. Associating imitation with the ability to empathize and understand other minds, Poe anticipates twenty-first-century developments in cognitive psychology. Marco Iacobini has recently demonstrated a link between neural mirroring and psychological theories of imitation ("Imitation, Empathy, and Mirror Neurons," *Annual Review of Psychology* 60 [2009], 653–670).

28   In addition to Campanella, the other authors Poe mentions are François de la Rochefoucauld (1613–1680), remembered for his *Memoirs* and the *Maximes;* the French moralist Jean de La Bruyère (1645–1696); and the Florentine historian, politician, and philosopher Niccolò Machiavelli (1469–1527).

amount of cunning is just sufficient to make him have them odd upon the second; I will therefore guess odd;'—he guesses odd, and wins. Now, with a simpleton a degree above the first, he would have reasoned thus: 'This fellow finds that in the first instance I guessed odd, and, in the second, he will propose to himself, upon the first impulse, a simple variation from even to odd, as did the first simpleton; but then a second thought will suggest that this is too simple a variation, and finally he will decide upon putting it even as before. I will therefore guess even';—he guesses even, and wins. Now this mode of reasoning in the schoolboy, whom his fellows termed 'lucky,'—what, in its last analysis, is it?"

"It is merely," I said, "an identification of the reasoner's intellect with that of his opponent."

"It is," said Dupin; "and, upon inquiring of the boy by what means he effected the *thorough* identification in which his success consisted, I received answer as follows: 'When I wish to find out how wise, or how stupid, or how good, or how wicked is any one, or what are his thoughts at the moment, I fashion the expression of my face, as accurately as possible, in accordance with the expression of his, and then wait to see what thoughts or sentiments arise in my mind or heart, as if to match or correspond with the expression.'[27] This response of the schoolboy lies at the bottom of all the spurious profundity which has been attributed to Rochefoucault, to La Bruyère, to Machiavelli, and to Campanella."[28]

"And the identification," I said, "of the reasoner's intellect with that of his opponent, depends, if I understand you aright, upon the accuracy with which the opponent's intellect is admeasured."

"For its practical value it depends upon this," replied Dupin; "and the Prefect and his cohort fail so frequently, first, by default of this identification, and, secondly, by ill-admeasurement, or rather through non-admeasurement, of the intellect with which they are engaged. They consider only their *own* ideas of ingenuity; and, in searching for anything hidden, advert only to the modes in which *they* would have hidden it. They are right in this much— that their own ingenuity is a faithful representative of that of *the mass;* but when the cunning of the individual felon is diverse in character from their own, the felon foils them, of course. This always happens when it is above their own, and very usually when it is below. They have no variation of principle in their investigations; at best, when urged by some unusual emergency—by some extraordinary reward—they extend or exaggerate their old modes of *practice,* without touching their principles. What, for example, in this case of D——, has been done to vary the principle of action? What is all this boring, and probing, and sounding, and scrutinizing with the microscope, and dividing the surface of the building into registered square inches—what is it all but an exaggeration *of the application* of the one principle or set of principles of search, which are based upon the one set of notions regarding human ingenuity, to which the Prefect, in the long routine of his duty, has been accustomed? Do you not see he has taken it for granted that *all* men proceed to conceal a letter,—not exactly in a gimlet-hole bored in a chair-leg—but, at least, in *some* out-of-the-way hole or corner suggested by the same tenor of thought which would urge a man to secrete a letter in a gimlet-hole bored in a chair-leg? And do you not see also, that such *recherchés*[29] nooks for concealment are adapted only for ordinary occasions, and would be adopted only by ordinary intellects; for, in all cases of concealment, a disposal of the article concealed—a disposal of it in this *recherché* manner,—is, in the very first instance, presumable and presumed; and thus its discovery depends, not at all upon the acumen, but altogether upon the mere care, patience, and determination of the seekers; and where the case is of importance—or, what amounts to the same thing in the policial eyes, when the reward is of magnitude,—the qualities in question have *never* been known to fail. You will now understand what I meant in suggesting that, had the purloined letter been hidden any where within the limits of the Prefect's examination—in other words, had the principle of its concealment been comprehended within the principles of the Prefect—its discovery would have been a matter altogether beyond question. This functionary, however, has been thoroughly mystified; and the remote source of his defeat lies in the supposition that the Minister is a fool, because he has acquired renown as a poet. All fools are poets; this the Prefect *feels;* and he is merely guilty of a *non distributio medii* in thence inferring that all poets are fools."[30]

"But is this really the poet?" I asked. "There are two brothers, I know; and both have attained reputation in letters. The Minister I believe has written learnedly on the Differential Calculus. He is a mathematician, and no poet."[31]

29 Obscure.

30 *Non distributio medii* is a logical fallacy known as the fallacy of the undistributed middle, in which the middle term in a syllogism is not distributed. Poe encountered the term, and this example, in Wallace's *Stanley:* "He has reached the conclusion that all good books are unpopular, and by a very harmless *non distributio medii,* resolved therefrom that all unpopular books, like his own, are good" (I, 132–133).

31 When he was at West Point, then the finest engineering school in America, Poe excelled at both mathematics and languages.

32   "It is safe to wager that every idea that is public property, every accepted convention, is a bit of stupidity, for it has suited the majority." The French dramatist and essayist Sébastien-Roch Nicolas, known as Chamfort (1740–1794), whose *Maximes, pensées, caractères et anecdotes* (1795) was published posthumously, is the original source for this quotation. Poe most likely took the quotation not directly from Chamfort but from a secondary source, probably T. C. Morgan, a frequent contributor to the *New Monthly Magazine* who used the same quotation in several contributions to the magazine. Simultaneously dependent upon, and deeply resentful of, the popular culture of Jacksonian America, Poe was quite taken with the quote and employed it multiple times.

33   In other words, the English cognates for these Latin words do not indicate their precise meanings. *Ambitus* refers to seeking office; *religio* means superstition; and *homines honesti* is Cicero's term for men who belong to his party (Thomas Ollive Mabbott, ed., *Collected Works of Edgar Allan Poe*, 3 vols. [Cambridge, MA: The Belknap Press of Harvard University Press, 1969–1978], III, 995).

"You are mistaken; I know him well; he is both. As poet *and* mathematician, he would reason well; as mere mathematician, he could not have reasoned at all, and thus would have been at the mercy of the Prefect."

"You surprise me," I said, "by these opinions, which have been contradicted by the voice of the world. You do not mean to set at naught the well-digested idea of centuries. The mathematical reason has long been regarded as *the* reason *par excellence*."

"'*Il y a à parier,*'" replied Dupin, quoting from Chamfort, "'*que toute idée publique, toute convention reçue est une sottise, car elle a convenue au plus grand nombre.*'[32] The mathematicians, I grant you, have done their best to promulgate the popular error to which you allude, and which is none the less an error for its promulgation as truth. With an art worthy a better cause, for example, they have insinuated the term 'analysis' into application to algebra. The French are the originators of this particular deception; but if a term is of any importance—if words derive any value from applicability—then 'analysis' conveys 'algebra' about as much as, in Latin, '*ambitus*' implies 'ambition,' '*religio*' 'religion,' or '*homines honesti,*' a set of *honorable* men."[33]

"You have a quarrel on hand, I see," said I, "with some of the algebraists of Paris; but proceed."

"I dispute the availability, and thus the value, of that reason which is cultivated in any especial form other than the abstractly logical. I dispute, in particular, the reason educed by mathematical study. The mathematics are the science of form and quantity; mathematical reasoning is merely logic applied to observation upon form and quantity. The great error lies in supposing that even the truths of what is called *pure* algebra, are abstract or general truths. And this error is so egregious that I am confounded at the universality with which it has been received. Mathematical axioms are *not* axioms of general truth. What is true of *relation*—of form and quantity—is often grossly false in regard to morals, for example. In this latter science it is very usually *un*true that the aggregated parts are equal to the whole. In chemistry also the axiom fails. In the consideration of motive it fails; for two motives, each of a given value, have not, necessarily, a value when united, equal to the sum of their values apart. There are numerous other mathematical truths which are only truths within the limits of *relation*. But the mathematician argues, from his *finite truths*, through habit, as if they were of an absolutely general applicability—as the world indeed imagines them to be. Bryant, in his very learned *Mythology,* mentions an analogous source of error, when he says that 'although the Pagan fables are not believed, yet we forget ourselves continually, and make inferences from them as existing realities.'[34] With the algebraists, however, who are Pagans themselves, the 'Pagan fables' *are* believed, and the inferences are made, not so much through lapse of memory, as through an unaccountable addling of the brains. In short, I never yet encountered the mere mathematician who could be trusted out of equal roots, or one who did not clandestinely hold it as a point of his faith that $x^2 + px$ was absolutely and unconditionally equal to q. Say to one of these gentlemen, by way of experiment, if you please, that you believe occasions may occur where $x^2 + px$ is *not* altogether equal to q, and, having made him understand what you mean, get out of his reach as speedily as convenient, for, beyond doubt, he will endeavor to knock you down.

"I mean to say," continued Dupin, while I merely laughed at his last observations, "that if the Minister had been no more than a mathematician, the Prefect would have been under no necessity of giving me this check. I knew him, however, as both mathematician and poet, and my measures were adapted to his capacity, with reference to the circumstances by which he was surrounded. I knew him as a courtier, too, and as a bold *intriguant*.[35] Such a man, I considered, could not fail to be aware of the ordinary policial modes of action. He could not have failed to anticipate—and events have proved that he did not fail to anticipate—the waylayings to which he was subjected. He must have foreseen, I reflected, the secret investigations of his premises. His frequent absences from home at night, which were hailed by the Prefect as certain aids to his success, I regarded only as *ruses,* to afford opportunity for thorough search to the police, and thus the sooner to impress them with the conviction to which G——, in fact, did finally arrive—the conviction that the letter was not upon the premises. I felt, also, that the whole train of thought, which I was at some pains in detailing to you just now, concerning the invariable principle of policial action in searches for articles concealed—I felt that this whole train of thought would necessarily pass through the mind of the Minister. It would imperatively lead him to despise all the ordinary *nooks* of concealment. *He* could not, I reflected, be so weak

34 Poe quotes not Jacob Bryant but his own paraphrase of Bryant that appears in his early collection of sententiae, "Pinakidia," in the August 1836 issue of the *Southern Literary Messenger.* The original source reads: "We are so imbued in our childhood with notions of Mars, Hercules, and the rest of the celestial outlaws, that we scarce ever can lay them aside. We absolutely argue upon Pagan principles: and though we cannot believe the fables, which have been transmitted to us; yet we forget ourselves continually; and make inferences from them, as if they were real" (*A New System; or, An Analysis of Antient Mythology,* 3rd ed., 6 vols. [London: for J. Walker, 1807], II, 173).

35 A schemer.

36   With Dupin's seemingly offhand remarks at the beginning of the tale that "perhaps the mystery is a little too plain . . . [a] little too self-evident," Poe hides the solution to his own tale "in the open in the same manner that the Minister fools the Prefect. . . . Moreover, Poe manages to approximate the feat attributed to the famous showman by one of his ticket sellers, 'First he humbugs them, and then they pay to hear him tell how he did it,' by devoting roughly half of the tale to the detective's explanation of how he undoes (but also redoes) what the Minister has done" (John Gruesser, "Never Bet the Detective (or His Creator) Your Head: Character Rivalry, Authorial Sleight of Hand, and Generic Fluidity in Detective Fiction," *Edgar Allan Poe Review* 9 [2008], 16).

37   The force of inertia.

38   The extensive use of written signs in major American cities, whose populations were increasingly literate, was a fairly recent phenomenon. In Manhattan, for example, there was a major proliferation of verbal signs during the 1830s (David M. Henkin, *City Reading: Written Words and Public Spaces in Antebellum New York* [New York: Columbia University Press, 1998], 50).

as not to see that the most intricate and remote recess of his hotel would be as open as his commonest closets to the eyes, to the probes, to the gimlets, and to the microscopes of the Prefect. I saw, in fine, that he would be driven, as a matter of course, to *simplicity,* if not deliberately induced to it as a matter of choice. You will remember, perhaps, how desperately the Prefect laughed when I suggested, upon our first interview, that it was just possible this mystery troubled him so much on account of its being so *very* self-evident."[36]

"Yes," said I, "I remember his merriment well. I really thought he would have fallen into convulsions."

"The material world," continued Dupin, "abounds with very strict analogies to the immaterial; and thus some color of truth has been given to the rhetorical dogma, that metaphor, or simile, may be made to strengthen an argument, as well as to embellish a description. The principle of the *vis inertiae*,[37] for example, seems to be identical in physics and metaphysics. It is not more true in the former, that a large body is with more difficulty set in motion than a smaller one, and that its subsequent *momentum* is commensurate with this difficulty, than it is, in the latter, that intellects of the vaster capacity, while more forcible, more constant, and more eventful in their movements than those of inferior grade, are yet the less readily moved, and more embarrassed and full of hesitation in the first few steps of their progress. Again: have you ever noticed which of the street signs, over the shop-doors, are the most attractive of attention?"

"I have never given the matter a thought," I said.

"There is a game of puzzles," he resumed, "which is played upon a map. One party playing requires another to find a given word—the name of town, river, state or empire—any word, in short, upon the motley and perplexed surface of the chart. A novice in the game generally seeks to embarrass his opponents by giving them the most minutely lettered names; but the adept selects such words as stretch, in large characters, from one end of the chart to the other. These, like the over-largely lettered signs and placards of the street,[38] escape observation by dint of being excessively obvious; and here the physical oversight is precisely analogous with the moral inapprehension by which the intellect suffers to pass unnoticed those considerations which are too obtrusively and too palpably self-evident. But this is a point, it appears, somewhat above or beneath the understanding of the Prefect. He never once thought it probable, or possible, that the Minister had deposited the letter immediately beneath the nose of the whole world, by way of best preventing any portion of that world from perceiving it.

"But the more I reflected upon the daring, dashing, and discriminating ingenuity of D——; upon the fact that the document must always have been *at hand,* if he intended to use it to good purpose; and upon the decisive evidence, obtained by the Prefect, that it was not hidden within the limits of that dignitary's ordinary search—the more satisfied I became that, to conceal this letter, the Minister had resorted to the comprehensive and sagacious expedient of not attempting to conceal it at all.

"Full of these ideas, I prepared myself with a pair of green spectacles, and called one fine morning, quite by accident, at the Ministerial hotel. I found D——at home, yawning, lounging, and dawdling, as usual, and pretending to be in the last extremity of *ennui.* He is, perhaps, the most really energetic human being now alive—but that is only when nobody sees him.

"To be even with him, I complained of my weak eyes, and lamented the necessity of the spectacles, under cover of which I cautiously and thoroughly surveyed the apartment, while seemingly intent only upon the conversation of my host.

"I paid especial attention to a large writing-table near which he sat, and upon which lay confusedly, some miscellaneous letters and other papers, with one or two musical instruments and a few books. Here, however, after a long and very deliberate scrutiny, I saw nothing to excite particular suspicion.

"At length my eyes, in going the circuit of the room, fell upon a trumpery filagree card-rack of pasteboard, that hung dangling by a dirty blue ribbon, from a little brass knob just beneath the middle of the mantel-piece.[39] In this rack, which had three or four compartments, were five or six visiting cards and a solitary letter. This last was much soiled and crumpled. It was torn nearly in two, across the middle—as if a design, in the first instance, to tear it entirely up as worthless, had been altered, or stayed, in the second. It had a large black seal, bearing the D——cipher *very* conspicuously, and was addressed, in a diminutive female hand, to D——,

39 Filagree was originally jewel work of an intricate kind constructed with beads and twisted thread usually of gold and silver, but in Poe's day the term started being used to mean decorative objects formed from paper to resemble filagree. Figuratively, filagree and pasteboard came to symbolize both the artificial and the superficial. In "The Divinity School Address" (1838), Ralph Waldo Emerson observes: "I confess, all attempts to project and establish a Cultus with new rites and forms, seem to me vain. Faith makes us, and not we it; and faith makes its own forms. All attempts to contrive a system are as cold as the new worship introduced by the French to the goddess of Reason,—to-day, pasteboard and filagree; and ending, to-morrow, in madness and murder."

40 Thomas Raikes's short story "The Bibliophilist" (1838) is one possible source for Poe's hidden-in-plain-sight idea. The motif would become a standard of detective fiction. Dorothy Sayers credits "The Purloined Letter" for establishing "the formula of the *most obvious place*" (*Great Short Stories of Detection, Mystery and Horror* [London: Gollancz, 1928], 18).

the minister, himself. It was thrust carelessly, and even, as it seemed, contemptuously, into one of the upper divisions of the rack.

"No sooner had I glanced at this letter, than I concluded it to be that of which I was in search.[40] To be sure, it was, to all appearance, radically different from the one of which the Prefect had read us so minute a description. Here the seal was large and black, with the D——cipher; there it was small and red, with the ducal arms of the S——family. Here, the address, to the Minister, was diminutive and feminine; there the superscription, to a certain royal personage, was markedly bold and decided; the size alone formed a point of correspondence. But, then, the *radicalness* of these differences, which was excessive; the dirt; the soiled and torn condition of the paper, so inconsistent with the *true* methodical habits of D——, and so suggestive of a design to delude the beholder into an idea of the worthlessness of the document; these things, together with the hyperobtrusive situation of this document, full in the view of every visiter, and thus exactly in accordance with the conclusions to which I had previously arrived; these things, I say, were strongly corroborative of suspicion, in one who came with the intention to suspect.

"I protracted my visit as long as possible, and, while I maintained a most animated discussion with the Minister, on a topic which I knew well had never failed to interest and excite him, I kept my attention really riveted upon the letter. In this examination, I committed to memory its external appearance and arrangement in the rack; and also fell, at length, upon a discovery which set at rest whatever trivial doubt I might have entertained. In scrutinizing the edges of the paper, I observed them to be more *chafed* than seemed necessary. They presented the *broken* appearance which is manifested when a stiff paper, having been once folded and pressed with a folder, is refolded in a reversed direction, in the same creases or edges which had formed the original fold. This discovery was sufficient. It was clear to me that the letter had been turned, as a glove, inside out, re-directed, and resealed. I bade the Minister good morning, and took my departure at once, leaving a gold snuff-box upon the table.

"The next morning I called for the snuff-box, when we resumed, quite eagerly, the conversation of the preceding day. While thus engaged, however, a loud report, as if of a pistol, was heard immediately beneath the windows of the hotel, and was succeeded by a series of fearful screams, and the shoutings of a mob. D——— rushed to a casement, threw it open, and looked out. In the meantime, I stepped to the card-rack, took the letter, put it in my pocket, and replaced it by a *fac-simile,* (so far as regards externals,) which I had carefully prepared at my lodgings; imitating the D———cipher, very readily, by means of a seal formed of bread.[41]

"The disturbance in the street had been occasioned by the frantic behavior of a man with a musket. He had fired it among a crowd of women and children. It proved, however, to have been without ball, and the fellow was suffered to go his way as a lunatic or a drunkard. When he had gone, D———came from the window, whither I had followed him immediately upon securing the object in view. Soon afterwards I bade him farewell. The pretended lunatic was a man in my own pay."

"But what purpose had you," I asked, "in replacing the letter by a *fac-simile?* Would it not have been better, at the first visit, to have seized it openly, and departed?"

"D———," replied Dupin, "is a desperate man, and a man of nerve. His hotel, too, is not without attendants devoted to his interests. Had I made the wild attempt you suggest, I might never have left the Ministerial presence alive. The good people of Paris might have heard of me no more. But I had an object apart from these considerations. You know my political prepossessions. In this matter, I act as a partisan of the lady concerned. For eighteen months the Minister has had her in his power. She has now him in hers; since, being unaware that the letter is not in his possession, he will proceed with his exactions as if it was. Thus will he inevitably commit himself, at once, to his political destruction. His downfall, too, will not be more precipitate than awkward.[42] It is all very well to talk about the *facilis descensus Averni;*[43] but in all kinds of climbing, as Catalani[44] said of singing, it is far more easy to get up than to come down. In the present instance I have no sympathy—at least no pity—for him who descends. He is that *monstrum horrendum,*[45] an unprincipled man of genius. I confess, however, that I should like very well to know the precise character of his thoughts, when, being defied by her whom the Prefect terms 'a certain personage,' he is reduced to opening the letter which I left for him in the card-rack."[46]

"How? did you put any thing particular in it?"

41 Dupin comes to resemble his criminal adversary "D———" not just in his thoughts but in his actions as well. To truly defeat him, Dupin cannot stop at exposing the fraud—he must *duplicate* it. Dupin's duplicity extends to the Prefect as well, since Dupin isn't immediately forthcoming about the fact that he has recovered the letter, waiting tactically, it would seem, until a reward has been offered. In this case, he has taken some soft bread and formed it, claylike, into a shape he can use as a seal.

42 The Minister D———'s downfall is all the more menacing and disturbing for its indefiniteness and the fact that the Minister is completely unaware of his fate, as the victors, we imagine, keep him under close surveillance.

43 This quotation, which comes from Virgil's *Aeneid,* book VI, line 126, means, "Easy is the descent to Avernus." A volcanic crater near Cuma, Italy, Avernus expelled noxious sulphuric gases, which made it seem like a gateway to Hell.

44 Angelica Catalani (1780–1849), an Italian opera singer who established her reputation on the English stage, was well known for her vocal range, being able to jump over two octaves at once (Richard Edgecumbe, *Musical Reminiscences, Containing an Account of the Italian Opera in England, from 1773,* 4th ed. [London: John Andrews, 1834], 97).

45 From the *Aeneid,* book III, line 658, *monstrum horrendum* is the epithet that Virgil uses for the Cyclops Polyphemus.

46 Exchanging one letter for another to falsify its message is a traditional motif that frequently occurs in legends.

47   "A plot so deadly, if not worthy of Atreus, is worthy of Thyestes." These lines come from Prosper Jolyot de Crébillon's revenge tragedy *Atrée et Thyeste* (1707). Crébillon's play was influenced by the Greek myth of Thyestes, as was Shakespeare's bloody *Titus Andronicus*. Having seduced the wife of his brother Atreus, Thyestes plots to kill him, but Atreus escapes murder and takes revenge, killing Thyestes's three sons and serving them to him at a banquet. Gregory Hays argues that Dupin's classical allusions, like his name (C. Auguste Dupin) linking him to the Augustan Age of Latin Literature, "align him with the values of reason and order; he is the Aristotelian mean between the subhuman ape and the hypercivilized but amoral minister 'D.' Yet one of the Virgilian quotations in 'The Purloined Letter' describes the monstrous Cyclops, and the story closes with an allusion to the gory myth of Atreus and Thyestes—a hint that civilization may be no more than a veneer" (Gregory Hays, "Ancient Classics," *Edgar Allan Poe in Context*, ed. Kevin J. Hayes [New York: Cambridge University Press, 2013], 226–227).

"Why—it did not seem altogether right to leave the interior blank—that would have been insulting. D——, at Vienna once, did me an evil turn, which I told him, quite good- humoredly, that I should remember. So, as I knew he would feel some curiosity in regard to the identity of the person who had outwitted him, I thought it a pity not to give him a clue. He is well acquainted with my manuscript, and I just copied into the middle of the blank sheet the words—

> —Un dessein si funeste,
> S'il n'est digne d'Atrée, est digne de Thyeste.

They are to be found in Crébillon's *Atrée*."[47]

The Facts in the Case of M. Valdemar

Of course I shall not pretend to consider it any matter for wonder, that the extraordinary[1] case of M. Valdemar has excited discussion. It would have been a miracle had it not—especially under the circumstances. Through the desire of all parties concerned, to keep the affair from the public, at least for the present, or until we had farther opportunities for investigation—through our endeavors to effect this—a garbled or exaggerated account made its way into society, and became the source of many unpleasant misrepresentations, and, very naturally, of a great deal of disbelief.

It is now rendered necessary that I give the *facts*—as far as I comprehend them myself. They are, succinctly, these:

My attention, for the last three years, had been repeatedly drawn to the subject of Mesmerism;[2] and, about nine months ago, it occurred to me, quite suddenly, that in the series of experiments made hitherto, there had been a very remarkable and most unaccountable omission:—no person had as yet been mesmerized *in articulo mortis*.[3] It remained to be seen, first, whether, in such condition, there existed in the patient any susceptibility to the magnetic influence; secondly, whether, if any existed, it was impaired or increased by the condition; thirdly, to what extent, or for how long a period, the encroachments of Death might be arrested by the process. There were other points to be ascertained, but these most excited my curiosity—the last in especial, from the immensely important character of its consequences.

In looking around me for some subject by whose means I might test these particulars, I was brought to think of my friend, M. Ernest Valdemar, the well-known compiler of the *Bibliotheca Foren-

When Hugo Gernsback launched Amazing Stories—the world's first science fiction magazine—in 1926, he chose to reprint "The Facts in the Case of M. Valdemar" in the magazine's debut issue. That Gernsback and his readers could appreciate "The Facts in the Case of M. Valdemar" as a work of classic science fiction underscores the profound shift in scientific understanding that had taken place since the tale's appearance in 1845, when many readers believed it was not fiction but a truthful report about a man suspended in a hypnotic state at the moment of death.

The third and arguably the best of Poe's tales concerning mesmerism ("A Tale of the Ragged Mountains" and "Mesmeric Revelation" are the other two), "The Facts in the Case of M. Valdemar" appeared almost simultaneously in the American Review: A Whig Journal *and the* Broadway Journal. *Newspapers and magazines across the nation reprinted the story, and other reprints appeared in the British press, causing an international stir, as readers speculated on its accuracy. It was, as Poe later admitted, intended as a hoax. In a letter of April 1846, the poet Elizabeth Barrett (Browning) gave Poe some sense of the British response: the tale "is going the rounds of the newspapers . . . throwing us all into 'most admired disorder', or dreadful doubts as to 'whether it can be true'. . . . The certain thing in the tale in question is the power of the writer and the faculty he has of making horrible improbabilities seem near & familiar"* (Collected Letters of Edgar Allan Poe, *ed. John Ward Ostrom, Burton R. Pollin, and Jeffrey A. Savoye, 2 vols. [New York: Gordian Press, 2008], I, 581). Robert H. Collyer, an English mesmerist lecturing in Boston, wrote to Poe on December 16, 1845: "It requires from me no apology, in stating, that I have not the least doubt of the possibility of such a phenomenon; for I did actually restore to active animation a person who died from excessive drinking of ardent spirits. He was placed in his coffin ready for interment." In an installment of his* Marginalia *in 1848, Poe revisited the controversy, ridiculing "both the* London Morning Post *and the* Popular Record *for discussions written confidently without any investigation in New York"* (Thomas Ollive Mabbott, *ed.,* Collected Works of Edgar Allan Poe, *3 vols. [Cambridge, MA: The Belknap Press of Harvard University Press, 1969–1978], III, 1232).

1   In a close reading of the tale, Roland Barthes makes much of the fact that the word "extraordinary" is ambiguous, since it may or may not refer to something supernatural: "The word's ambiguity is significant here: a horrible story (outside the limits of nature) and yet covered by the alibi of science (here connoted by the 'discussion', which is a scientist's word). This blending is in fact cultural: the blend of the strange with the scientific reached its peak in that part of the nineteenth century to which Poe, broadly

Edward William Clay, *Animal Magnetism*, 1839. A contemporary cartoonist makes use of the same motifs of mesmerism that Poe employs in "The Facts in the Case of M. Valdemar." Edward William Clay (1799–1857) critiques President Martin Van Buren's monetary policies, seeing them as a continuation of those of Andrew Jackson. Seated in the chair, Jackson is the mesmerist, and Van Buren, seated on the sofa, is his patient.

speaking, belongs: it excited people to observe the supernatural (mesmerism, spiritualism, telepathy, etc.) scientifically; the supernatural takes the rationalist, scientific alibi; this, then is the *cri du coeur* of that positivist age: if only one could believe *scientifically* in immortality! This cultural code . . . [is] of great importance throughout the narrative" ("Textual Analysis of a Tale of Poe," *On Signs*, ed. Marshall Blonsky [Baltimore: Johns Hopkins University Press, 1985], 88–89).

sica,[4] and author (under the *nom de plume* of Issachar Marx) of the Polish versions of *Wallenstein* and *Gargantua*.[5] M. Valdemar, who has resided principally at Harlaem, N.Y.,[6] since the year 1839, is (or was) particularly noticeable for the extreme spareness of his person—his lower limbs much resembling those of John Randolph;[7] and, also, for the whiteness of his whiskers, in violent contrast to the blackness of his hair—the latter, in consequence, being very generally mistaken for a wig. His temperament was markedly nervous, and rendered him a good subject for mesmeric experiment. On two or three occasions I had put him to sleep with little difficulty, but was disappointed in other results which his peculiar constitution had naturally led me to anticipate. His will was at no period positively, or thoroughly, under my control, and in regard to *clairvoyance*,[8] I could accomplish with him nothing to be relied upon. I always attributed my failure at these points to the disordered state of his health. For some months previous to my becoming acquainted with him, his physicians had declared him in a confirmed phthisis.[9] It was his custom, indeed, to speak calmly of his approaching dissolution, as of a matter neither to be avoided nor regretted.

When the ideas to which I have alluded first occurred to me, it was of course very natural that I should think of M. Valdemar. I knew the steady philosophy of the man too well to apprehend any scruples from *him;* and he had no relatives in America who would be likely to interfere. I spoke to him frankly upon the subject; and, to my surprise, his interest seemed vividly excited. I say to my surprise; for, although he had always yielded his person freely to my experiments, he had never before given me any tokens of sympathy with what I did. His disease was of that character which would admit of exact calculation in respect to the epoch of its termination in death; and it was finally arranged between us that he would send for me about twenty-four hours before the period announced by his physicians as that of his decease.

It is now rather more than seven months since I received, from M. Valdemar himself, the subjoined note:

My Dear P——,

You may as well come *now.* D—— and F—— are agreed that I cannot hold out beyond to-morrow midnight; and I think they have hit the time very nearly.

Valdemar.

I received this note within half an hour after it was written, and in fifteen minutes more I was in the dying man's chamber. I had not seen him for ten days, and was appalled by the fearful alteration which the brief interval had wrought in him. His face wore a leaden hue; the eyes were utterly lustreless; and the emaciation was so extreme that the skin had been broken through by the cheekbones. His expectoration was excessive. The pulse was barely per-

2 Though Benjamin Franklin and others had debunked the theories of Viennese physician Franz Anton Mesmer (1734–1815) more than a half century earlier, mesmerism underwent a revival in Poe's day. According to Mesmer, animal magnetism permeated the universe, attuning itself to the human nervous system. Nervous illness thus resulted from an imbalance between a person's animal magnetism and the external world. Practicing mesmerists induced trancelike states in patients to restore harmony and allow the free circulation of magnetic fluid within the body.

Some people even believed that animal magnetism could put the living in contact with the dead.

3 This Latin phrase means "to be at the point of death." Barthes explains that Poe's Latin—the language of medicine—lends the sentence a scientific aura, yet it also serves as a euphemism because it expresses in a little-known language something people hesitate to say in everyday language.

4 There is no such book as *Bibliotheca Forensica*. Attributing this work—implicitly a collection of documents regarding criminal investigation—to Valdemar, Poe makes the character an expert in the nascent field of forensic science.

5 Genesis 49:14 provides an explanation of Valdemar's penname: "Issachar is a strong ass couching down between two burdens." The two burdens in this instance are literary ones, Friedrich Schiller's lengthy three-part tragedy *Wallenstein* (1798–1799) and François Rabelais's *Gargantua* (1534–1535), one of a series of five novels usually published together as *Gargantua and Pantagruel*. The sprawling nature of these works by Schiller and Rabelais is at odds with Poe's aesthetic concept of brevity. There is a further irony here. As a translator, Valdemar is someone who mediates between different languages and cultures: he will be called upon again as a mediator—between different worlds—in his mesmeric state.

6 When Poe moved to New York in 1844, he found lodgings at a farmhouse on 84th Street, which was just south of Harlem. A small farming village since the early days of Dutch settlement, Harlem was undergoing rapid economic and social changes during the 1840s. As the surrounding farmland became unproductive, the village found itself home to newly arrived Irish immigrants, who established themselves in shantytowns. This transition zone between rural and urban suggests an interesting parallel to Valdemar's transitional state.

Nathaniel Currier, *The High Bridge at Harlem, N.Y.*, 1849.

7 Poe's reference to the contentious Virginia congressman John Randolph of Roanoke (1773–1833) refers to his unusual physique. Randolph suffered from an undiagnosed disease that left his limbs in an almost skeletonlike state and turned his voice into a high-pitched whine. The comparison between Valdemar and Randolph raises intriguing interpretive possibilities. As a slaveholder and champion of the Southern aristocracy, Randolph represented a way of life that many Southerners were trying to sustain, though it was already dying. According to rumor, Randolph was buried facing west toward Kentucky, so that in death he could keep a watchful eye on his old adversary Henry Clay.

8 Through the practice of mesmerism, the word "clairvoyance" entered the English language to refer to the ability of mesmerized patients to perceive objects either at a distance or concealed from sight.

9 A wasting disease typically associated with the lungs, "phthisis" was often used as a synonym for consumption (tuberculosis). In contrast to incipient phthisis, confirmed phthisis is a fatal diagnosis. Poe was well acquainted with the symptoms of the disease: his wife, Virginia, had been diagnosed with consumption in 1842.

10 Martin Willis observes a profound schism in the story: the narrator, who has, until this point, behaved more like an amateur mesmerist than a medical professional, now speaks with newfound authority. His language becomes precise, exacting, and minutely descriptive, and the two attending physicians take their direction from him. Willis argues that this schism reflects the ambiguous status of mesmerism itself in the contemporary medical and scientific community (*Mesmerists, Monsters, and Machines: Science Fiction and the Cultures of Science in the Nineteenth Century* [Kent, OH: Kent State University Press, 2006], 118).

11 Tuberculosis causes the formation of hard fibrous nodules or tubercles that in Valdemar's advanced case have come to resemble cartilage.

12 The tubercles in the lower right lung are not yet cartilaginous—but are filled with pus.

13 A thinning of an arterial wall, resulting in a life-threatening dilation of the artery.

ceptible. He retained, nevertheless, in a very remarkable manner, both his mental power and a certain degree of physical strength. He spoke with distinctness—took some palliative medicines without aid—and, when I entered the room, was occupied in penciling memoranda in a pocket-book. He was propped up in the bed by pillows. Doctors D—— and F—— were in attendance.[10]

After pressing Valdemar's hand, I took these gentlemen aside, and obtained from them a minute account of the patient's condition. The left lung had been for eighteen months in a semi-osseous or cartilaginous state,[11] and was, of course, entirely useless for all purposes of vitality. The right, in its upper portion, was also partially, if not thoroughly, ossified, while the lower region was merely a mass of purulent tubercles,[12] running one into another. Several extensive perforations existed; and, at one point, permanent adhesion to the ribs had taken place. These appearances in the right lobe were of comparatively recent date. The ossification had proceeded with very unusual rapidity; no sign of it had been discovered a month before, and the adhesion had only been observed during the three previous days. Independently of the phthisis, the patient was suspected of aneurism of the aorta;[13] but on this point the osseous symptoms rendered an exact diagnosis impossible. It was the opinion of both physicians that M. Valdemar would die about midnight on the morrow (Sunday). It was then seven o'clock on Saturday evening.

On quitting the invalid's bed-side to hold conversation with myself, Doctors D—— and F—— had bidden him a final farewell. It had not been their intention to return; but, at my request, they agreed to look in upon the patient about ten the next night.

When they had gone, I spoke freely with M. Valdemar on the subject of his approaching dissolution, as well as, more particularly, of the experiment proposed. He still professed himself quite willing and even anxious to have it made, and urged me to commence it at once. A male and a female nurse were in attendance; but I did not feel myself altogether at liberty to engage in a task of this character with no more reliable witnesses than these people, in case of sudden accident, might prove. I therefore postponed operations until about eight the next night, when the arrival of a medical student with whom I had some acquaintance, (Mr. Theodore L——l,) relieved me from farther embarrassment. It had been my design, originally, to wait for the physicians; but I was induced to

John Marshal, *John Randolph of Roanoke on His Embarkation for Russia Onboard Ship "Concord,"* ca. 1830.

14 Eric Lewin Altschuler argues that Poe's tale offers one of the earliest descriptions of informed consent: "As his thoroughly modern description of informed consent shows, Poe was also decades ahead of his time in appreciating the process of research" ("Informed Consent in an Edgar Allan Poe Tale," *Lancet* 317 [November 1, 2003], 1504).

15 Noisy and labored breathing; he is snoring.

16 In *Human Physiology* (1835), John Elliotson coined the term "sleepwaking" for the mesmeric state. As a descriptive term, Elliotson says, "sleepwaking" is preferable to sleepwalking "because in this state patients may not walk, or may even be unable to walk." Poe's editors and translators have sometimes misread sleepwaking as sleepwalking. For her 1910 German translation of Poe's story, Gisela Etzel, for instance, mistranslated sleepwaking as *Somnambulen*. Her translation would have a major influence on one of the masterworks of German cinema, *The Cabinet of Dr. Caligari* (1920), which features a mad doctor and a hypnotized sleepwalker. In turn, American moviegoers were receptive to the German avant-garde film partly because it called to mind the tales of Poe.

proceed, first, by the urgent entreaties of M. Valdemar, and secondly, by my conviction that I had not a moment to lose, as he was evidently sinking fast.

Mr. L——l was so kind as to accede to my desire that he would take notes of all that occurred; and it is from his memoranda that what I now have to relate is, for the most part, either condensed or copied *verbatim*.

It wanted about five minutes of eight when, taking the patient's hand, I begged him to state, as distinctly as he could, to Mr. L——l, whether he (M. Valdemar) was entirely willing that I should make the experiment of mesmerizing him in his then condition.

He replied feebly, yet quite audibly, "Yes, I wish to be mesmerized"—adding immediately afterwards, "I fear you have deferred it too long."[14]

While he spoke thus, I commenced the passes which I had already found most effectual in subduing him. He was evidently influenced with the first lateral stroke of my hand across his forehead; but although I exerted all my powers, no farther perceptible effect was induced until some minutes after ten o'clock, when Doctors D—— and F—— called, according to appointment. I explained to them, in a few words, what I designed, and as they opposed no objection, saying that the patient was already in the death agony, I proceeded without hesitation—exchanging, however, the lateral passes for downward ones, and directing my gaze entirely into the right eye of the sufferer.

By this time his pulse was imperceptible and his breathing was stertorous,[15] and at intervals of half a minute.

This condition was nearly unaltered for a quarter of an hour. At the expiration of this period, however, a natural although a very deep sigh escaped the bosom of the dying man, and the stertorous breathing ceased—that is to say, its stertorousness was no longer apparent; the intervals were undiminished. The patient's extremities were of an icy coldness.

At five minutes before eleven I perceived unequivocal signs of the mesmeric influence. The glassy roll of the eye was changed for that expression of uneasy *inward* examination which is never seen except in cases of sleep-waking,[16] and which it is quite impossible to mistake. With a few rapid lateral passes I made the lids quiver, as in incipient sleep, and with a few more I closed them altogether. I was not satisfied, however, with this, but continued the manipu-

Hermann Wögel, engraving for "The Facts in the Case of M. Valdemar," from *The Tales and Poems of Edgar Allan Poe* (Philadelphia: George Barrie, 1895).

Conrad Veidt as the sleepwalker Cesare in the silent film *The Cabinet of Dr. Caligari* (1920). In what is widely considered the first true horror film, the mad hypnotist Caligari (Werner Krauss) uses Cesare to commit murder for him.

lations vigorously, and with the fullest exertion of the will, until I had completely stiffened the limbs of the slumberer, after placing them in a seemingly easy position. The legs were at full length; the arms were nearly so, and reposed on the bed at a moderate distance from the loins. The head was very slightly elevated.

When I had accomplished this, it was fully midnight, and I requested the gentlemen present to examine M. Valdemar's condition. After a few experiments, they admitted him to be in an unusually perfect state of mesmeric trance. The curiosity of both the physicians was greatly excited. Dr. D—— resolved at once to remain with the patient all night, while Dr. F—— took leave with a promise to return at day-break. Mr. L——l and the nurses remained.

We left M. Valdemar entirely undisturbed until about three o'clock in the morning, when I approached him and found him in precisely the same condition as when Dr. F—— went away—that is to say, he lay in the same position; the pulse was imperceptible; the breathing was gentle (scarcely noticeable, unless through the application of a mirror to the lips); the eyes were closed naturally; and the limbs were as rigid and as cold as marble. Still, the general appearance was certainly not that of death.

As I approached M. Valdemar I made a kind of half effort to influence his right arm into pursuit of my own, as I passed the latter gently to and fro above his person. In such experiments with this patient I had never perfectly succeeded before, and assuredly I had little thought of succeeding now; but to my astonishment, his arm very readily, although feebly, followed every direction I assigned it with mine. I determined to hazard a few words of conversation.

"M. Valdemar," I said, "are you asleep?" He made no answer, but I perceived a tremor about the lips, and was thus induced to repeat the question, again and again. At its third repetition, his whole frame was agitated by a very slight shivering; the eye-lids unclosed themselves so far as to display a white line of the ball; the lips moved sluggishly, and from between them, in a barely audible whisper, issued the words:

"Yes;—asleep now. Do not wake me!—let me die so!"

I here felt the limbs and found them as rigid as ever. The right arm, as before, obeyed the direction of my hand. I questioned the sleep-waker again:

"Do you still feel pain in the breast, M. Valdemar?"

The answer now was immediate, but even less audible than before:

"No pain—I am dying."

I did not think it advisable to disturb him farther just then, and nothing more was said or done until the arrival of Dr. F——, who came a little before sunrise, and expressed unbounded astonishment at finding the patient still alive. After feeling the pulse and applying a mirror to the lips, he requested me to speak to the sleep-waker again. I did so, saying:

"M. Valdemar, do you still sleep?"

As before, some minutes elapsed ere a reply was made; and during the interval the dying man seemed to be collecting his energies to speak. At my fourth repetition of the question, he said very faintly, almost inaudibly:

"Yes; still asleep—dying."[17]

It was now the opinion, or rather the wish, of the physicians, that M. Valdemar should be suffered to remain undisturbed in his present apparently tranquil condition, until death should supervene—and this, it was generally agreed, must now take place within a few minutes. I concluded, however, to speak to him once more, and merely repeated my previous question.

17   In a letter of July 2, 1844, to James Russell Lowell, Poe offers his thoughts on what the afterlife might look like: "Man exists as a 'person', by being clothed with matter (the particled matter) which individualizes him. Thus habited, his life is rudimental. What we call 'death' is the painful metamorphosis. The stars are the habitations of rudimental beings. But for the necessity of the rudimental life, there would be no worlds. At death, the worm is the butterfly—still material, but of a matter unrecognized by our organs—recognized, occasionally, perhaps, by the sleep-waker, directly—without organs—through the mesmeric medium. Thus a sleep-waker may see ghosts. Divested of the rudimental covering, the being inhabits *space*—what we suppose to be the immaterial universe—passing every where, and acting all things, by mere volition—cognizant of all secrets but that of the nature of God's volition—the motion, or activity, of the unparticled matter" (*Collected Letters*, I, 449–450).

18 The word "hectic" was often used to describe the recurrent fever produced by tuberculosis, marked by flushed cheeks and hot dry skin.

While I spoke, there came a marked change over the countenance of the sleep-waker. The eyes rolled themselves slowly open, the pupils disappearing upwardly; the skin generally assumed a cadaverous hue, resembling not so much parchment as white paper; and the circular hectic spots[18] which, hitherto, had been strongly defined in the centre of each cheek, *went out* at once. I use this expression, because the suddenness of their departure put me in mind of nothing so much as the extinguishment of a candle by a puff of the breath. The upper lip, at the same time, writhed itself away from the teeth, which it had previously covered completely; while the lower jaw fell with an audible jerk, leaving the mouth widely extended, and disclosing in full view the swollen and blackened tongue. I presume that no member of the party then present had been unaccustomed to death-bed horrors; but so hideous beyond conception was the appearance of M. Valdemar at this moment, that there was a general shrinking back from the region of the bed.

I now feel that I have reached a point of this narrative at which every reader will be startled into positive disbelief. It is my business, however, simply to proceed.

There was no longer the faintest sign of vitality in M. Valdemar; and concluding him to be dead, we were consigning him to the charge of the nurses, when a strong vibratory motion was observable in the tongue. This continued for perhaps a minute. At the expiration of this period, there issued from the distended and motionless jaws a voice—such as it would be madness in me to attempt describing. There are, indeed, two or three epithets which might be considered as applicable to it in part; I might say, for example, that the sound was harsh, and broken and hollow; but the hideous whole is indescribable, for the simple reason that no similar sounds have ever jarred upon the ear of humanity. There were two particulars, nevertheless, which I thought then, and still think, might fairly be stated as characteristic of the intonation—as well adapted to convey some idea of its unearthly peculiarity. In the first place, the voice seemed to reach our ears—at least mine—from a vast distance, or from some deep cavern within the earth. In the second place, it impressed me (I fear, indeed, that it will be impossible to make myself comprehended) as gelatinous or glutinous matters impress the sense of touch.

I have spoken both of "sound" and of "voice." I mean to say

that the sound was one of distinct—of even wonderfully, thrillingly distinct—syllabification. M. Valdemar *spoke*—obviously in reply to the question I had propounded to him a few minutes before. I had asked him, it will be remembered, if he still slept. He now said:

"Yes;—no;—I *have been* sleeping—and now—now—*I am dead.*"[19]

No person present even affected to deny, or attempted to repress, the unutterable, shuddering horror which these few words, thus uttered, were so well calculated to convey. Mr. L——l (the student) swooned. The nurses immediately left the chamber, and could not be induced to return. My own impressions I would not pretend to render intelligible to the reader. For nearly an hour, we busied ourselves, silently—without the utterance of a word—in endeavors to revive Mr. L——l. When he came to himself, we addressed ourselves again to an investigation of M. Valdemar's condition.

It remained in all respects as I have last described it, with the exception that the mirror no longer afforded evidence of respiration. An attempt to draw blood from the arm failed. I should mention, too, that this limb was no farther subject to my will. I endeavored in vain to make it follow the direction of my hand. The only real indication, indeed, of the mesmeric influence, was now found in the vibratory movement of the tongue, whenever I addressed M. Valdemar a question. He seemed to be making an effort to reply, but had no longer sufficient volition. To queries put to him by any other person than myself he seemed utterly insensible—although I endeavored to place each member of the company in mesmeric *rapport* with him. I believe that I have now related all that is necessary to an understanding of the sleep-waker's state at this epoch. Other nurses were procured; and at ten o'clock I left the house in company with the two physicians and Mr. L——l.

In the afternoon we all called again to see the patient. His condition remained precisely the same. We had now some discussion as to the propriety and feasibility of awakening him; but we had little difficulty in agreeing that no good purpose would be served by so doing. It was evident that, so far, death (or what is usually termed death) had been arrested by the mesmeric process. It seemed clear to us all that to awaken M. Valdemar would be merely to insure his instant, or at least his speedy dissolution.

19   With this tale and his earlier story "Mesmeric Revelation," Poe introduced to American literature a motif that would enjoy a long, ghastly cinematic afterlife beginning with George Romero's *Night of the Living Dead* (1968). Romero was profoundly influenced by Poe's portrayal of mesmerism, and he paid homage to Poe with his cinematic adaptation, "The Facts in the Case of Mr. Valdemar," the first segment of his two-part *Two Evil Eyes* (1990).

20   By "yellowish ichor," Poe means a watery, acrid dis-
charge that sometimes issues from wounds and sores. John
Lennon would borrow this image for "I Am the Walrus"
("Yellow matter custard dripping from a dead dog's eye").
Later in the song, Lennon acknowledges his debt with a di-
rect reference to Poe.

21   Poe's friend and fellow poet Philip Pendleton Cooke
was profoundly affected by this story. In a letter of August
4, 1846, to Poe, he wrote: "The 'Valdemar Case' I read in a
number of your *Broadway Journal* last winter—as I lay in
a Turkey blind, muffled to the eyes in overcoats, etc.,
and pronounce it without hesitation the most damnable,
vraisemblable, horrible, hair-lifting, shocking, ingenious
chapter of fiction that any brain ever conceived, or hands
traced. That gelatinous, viscous sound of man's voice!
there never was such an idea before. That story scared me
in broad day, armed with a double-barrel Tryon Turkey
gun. What would it have done at midnight in some old
ghostly countryhouse?" *Philip Pendleton Cooke: Poet, Critic,
Novelist*, ed. John Daniel Allen (Johnson City, TN: East
Tennessee State University, Research Advisory Council,
1969), 307.

From this period until the close of last week—*an interval of
nearly seven months*—we continued to make daily calls at M. Valdemar's house, accompanied, now and then, by medical and other
friends. All this time the sleeper-waker remained *exactly* as I have
last described him. The nurses' attentions were continual.

It was on Friday last that we finally resolved to make the experiment of awakening, or attempting to awaken him; and it is the
(perhaps) unfortunate result of this latter experiment which has
given rise to so much discussion in private circles—to so much of
what I cannot help thinking unwarranted popular feeling.

For the purpose of relieving M. Valdemar from the mesmeric
trance, I made use of the customary passes. These, for a time, were
unsuccessful. The first indication of revival was afforded by a partial descent of the iris. It was observed, as especially remarkable,
that this lowering of the pupil was accompanied by the profuse
out-flowing of a yellowish ichor (from beneath the lids) of a pungent and highly offensive odor.[20]

It now was suggested that I should attempt to influence the
patient's arm, as heretofore. I made the attempt and failed. Dr.
F—— then intimated a desire to have me put a question. I did so,
as follows:

"M. Valdemar, can you explain to us what are your feelings or
wishes now?"

There was an instant return of the hectic circles on the cheeks;
the tongue quivered, or rather rolled violently in the mouth (although the jaws and lips remained rigid as before;) and at length
the same hideous voice which I have already described, broke
forth:

"For God's sake!—quick!—quick!—put me to sleep—or,
quick!—waken me!—quick!—*I say to you that I am dead!*"[21]

I was thoroughly unnerved, and for an instant remained unde-
cided what to do. At first I made an endeavor to re-compose the
patient; but, failing in this through total abeyance of the will, I retraced my steps and as earnestly struggled to awaken him. In this
attempt I soon saw that I should be successful—or at least I soon
fancied that my success would be complete—and I am sure that all
in the room were prepared to see the patient awaken.

For what really occurred, however, it is quite impossible that
any human being could have been prepared.

As I rapidly made the mesmeric passes, amid ejaculations of

"dead! dead!" absolutely *bursting* from the tongue and not from the lips of the sufferer, his whole frame at once—within the space of a single minute, or even less, shrunk—crumbled—absolutely *rotted* away beneath my hands. Upon the bed, before that whole company, there lay a nearly liquid mass of loathsome—of detestable putridity.[22]

22   The image of Valdemar's sudden collapse into putrescence has disgusted or offended readers well into the twentieth century. William Dean Howells (1837–1920), the grand old man of American literary realism, for example, writes that Poe "cannot hold his hand from horror when he would move to awe, and such an otherwise well-managed inquiry into the unknowable as 'The Case of M. Valdemar' ends in mere loathsomeness, and you are left confronted with carrion, holding your nose" ("Edgar Allan Poe," *Harper's Weekly*, January 11, 1909, 12).

J. Gerald Kennedy observes about this "unforgettable final image": "Apart from effecting our revulsion, these details serve a figurative purpose, for 'Valdemar' dramatizes the scientific effort—undertaken in the eighteenth century and continuing in our era of medical technology—to understand, control, and perhaps finally conquer the major causes of death. . . . the final scene betrays the limitation of human efficacy and reaffirms the sovereignty of death. In effect, the illusion of a scientifically insured immortality disintegrates with Valdemar" ("Phantasms of Death in Poe's Fiction," *The Haunted Dusk: American Supernatural Fiction, 1820–1920*, ed. Howard Kerr, John W. Crowley, and Charles L. Crow [Athens: University of Georgia Press, 1983], 62).

Today one of Poe's most celebrated and frequently anthologized tales, "The Cask of Amontillado" took some time to catch on. Unlike many of the later tales, it was seldom reprinted in his lifetime. Not until the decadent movement of the late nineteenth century did it find readers so attuned to the narrator's excesses, obsession, and cruelly punitive impulses. Joris-Karl Huysmans, one of the foremost French decadents, paid tribute to its sublime power in his novel Against Nature *(1884). Huysmans has Des Esseintes, the novel's protagonist, enter a wine cellar within the arcades of the Rue de Rivoli, where he orders a glass of port, the taste of which calls to mind the "charming" novels of Charles Dickens, which lately he has taken to reading to soothe his nerves. Reinforcing the impression, the cellar is filled with English-speaking patrons, and soon he is sent into a reverie, imaginatively peopling the cellar with Dickens's characters. When Des Esseintes orders a glass of amontillado next, however, it has a much different effect: "He called for a glass of amontillado, and suddenly, beside this pale, dry wine, the lenitive, sweetish stories of the English author were routed, to be replaced by the pitiless revulsives and the grievous irritants of Edgar Allan Poe; the cold nightmares of 'The Cask of Amontillado,' of the man immured in a vault, assailed him; the ordinary placid faces of American and English drinkers who occupied the room, appeared to him to reflect involuntary frightful thoughts, to be harboring instinctive, odious plots."*

Since the fin-de-siècle, "The Cask of Amontillado" has become a classic tale of revenge, narrated—critics are divided on this point—either by a man consumed by guilt for a murderous deed committed in his youth or by an unrepentant psychopath entombed these long years within his own revenge. "The Cask of Amontillado" appeared in November 1846, in Godey's Lady's Book, *among the most widely circulated magazines of its day.*

The Cask of Amontillado

The thousand injuries of Fortunato I had borne as I best could; but when he ventured upon insult, I vowed revenge.[1] You, who so well know the nature of my soul, will not suppose, however, that I gave utterance to a threat. *At length* I would be avenged; this was a point definitively settled—but the very definitiveness with which it was resolved precluded the idea of risk. I must not only punish, but punish with impunity.[2] A wrong is unredressed when retribution overtakes its redresser. It is equally unredressed when the avenger fails to make himself felt as such to him who has done the wrong.[3]

It must be understood that neither by word nor deed had I given Fortunato cause to doubt my good will. I continued, as was my wont, to smile in his face, and he did not perceive that my smile *now* was at the thought of his immolation.

He had a weak point—this Fortunato—although in other regards he was a man to be respected and even feared. He prided himself on his connoisseurship in wine. Few Italians have the true virtuoso spirit. For the most part their enthusiasm is adopted to suit the time and opportunity—to practise imposture upon the British and Austrian *millionaires*. In painting and gemmary[4] Fortunato, like his countrymen, was a quack—but in the matter of old wines he was sincere. In this respect I did not differ from him materially: I was skilful in the Italian vintages myself, and bought largely whenever I could.[5]

It was about dusk, one evening during the supreme madness of the carnival season,[6] that I encountered my friend. He accosted me with excessive warmth, for he had been drinking much. The man

1 "How many good books suffer neglect through the inefficiency of their beginnings!" Poe complains in his *Marginalia.* "It is far better that we commence irregularly—immethodically—than that we fail to arrest attention; but the two points, method and pungency, may always be combined. At all risks, let there be a few vivid sentences *imprimis*, by way of the electric bell to the telegraph" (*Essays and Reviews*, ed. G. R. Thompson [New York: Library of America, 1984], 1322). In *Indolent Essays* (1889), Richard Dowling quotes a friend on Poe's electrifying opening: "Without reading a line further you are acquainted with the character of Fortunato, the doomed man, and of Montresor, the narrator and murderer. You know the narrator *is* a murderer, because so portentous a beginning must have an adequate ending, and the deliberateness of the opening, the solemn reference to the narrator's soul, and the asseveration that he uttered no threat, prepare you for vengeance of fatal horror."

Poe's second sentence perhaps suggests that Montresor, "probably on his deathbed," is narrating the story as a confession to a priest, that is, someone who would know the nature of his soul (Thomas Ollive Mabbott, ed., *Collected Works of Edgar Allan Poe*, 3 vols. [Cambridge, MA: The Belknap Press of Harvard University Press, 1969–1978], III, 1264).

Whether or not he is repentant is yet another matter. At the end of the tale, Montresor reveals that he is relating events that occurred a half century earlier.

2 As we soon learn, the Montresor family motto is *Nemo me impune lacessit* ("No one insults me without punishment"). Impunity means "without punishment." Montresor must punish without punishment, that is, take vengeance without being caught, something more easily accomplished during the evening revelries of carnival season, when many, including Fortunato, are inebriated and when Montresor can don his black silk mask. The second requirement of his successful vengeance, Monstresor says, is making sure Fortunato understands that he has been avenged.

The motive for Montresor's revenge has been the subject of considerable debate. "The thousand injuries of Fortunato" is hyperbole—but what are the most galling injuries? And what is the one unforgivable "insult"? Certainly the text offers intriguing hints, but Mabbott's summary of the matter in the late 1960s remains true, that "Poe's many subtleties have generated endless discussion, by serious readers, of the person or persons addressed, and of Montresor's fundamental motive." In a further note, Mabbott says, "These questions . . . will probably always remain moot" (Mabbott III, 1264, 1266). A novelist's perspective is interesting. John Gardner explains, "When Kafka writes in his 'Metamorphosis' that Gregor Samsa awakens to find himself transformed into a live vermin . . . what he's doing is reopening the 'Cask of Amontillado.' Poe was the first man in the world to discover that narrative fiction needn't be limited to the Aristotelian task of explaining how things happened. Poe said, 'I don't care how things *happened*, I'll tell you what happens now.' In 'Cask of Amontillado,' there

is no background for the story, not even an implied background." Poe's technique of starting near the end of the story Gardner calls "the name of the game in Post-Modern fiction" (*Conversations with John Gardner*, ed. Allan Chavkin [Jackson: University Press of Mississippi, 1990], 80).

3 Mabbott and others have pointed out that Poe's composition of "The Cask of Amontillado" was motivated, at least in part, by Poe's own desire for revenge against his former friend Thomas Dunn English. After Poe published a flippant notice of Thomas Dunn English in "The Literati of New York" (*Godey's Lady's Book*, June 20, 1846), English responded with a vicious personal attack in an ad taken out in the pages of the *New York Evening Mirror* (July 13, 1846). English accused Poe of forgery, securing unpaid debts under false premises, and drunken behavior (Poe successfully sued the *Mirror* for libel and was awarded $225.06 plus additional court costs). In a more coded way, English continued his attack on Poe in his serialized novel *1844: or, The Power of S. F.* (1846), in which he depicts Poe as "Marmaduke Hammerhead," a dishonest, abusive, and alcoholic critic who is the author of a popular poem called "The Black Crow." Putting Poe's story and English's novel side by side, Richard Dilworth Rust points out a number of specific details in "The Cask of Amontillado" that are direct responses to English's novel. Rust feels that Poe bests English. And "while Poe likely identified at least partially with Montresor," he observes, "yet just as Coverdale is not Nathaniel Hawthorne despite the numerous points of comparison and Ahab is not Herman Melville, so Montresor is not Poe" ("'Punish with Impunity': Poe, Thomas Dunn English, and 'The Cask of Amontillado,'" *The Edgar Allan Poe Review*, 2 [2001], 38). Biographer Silverman points out that, when the tale is read in the context of Poe's last years, there are a number of candidates for his revenge: "In Montresor, Poe figured the writer . . . [as] an avenger, and storytelling as a means of getting even with the world" (*Edgar A. Poe: Mournful and Never-Ending Remembrance* [New York: HarperCollins, 1991], 316).

4 An obsolete word, "gemmary," in its adjectival form, means "pertaining to gems." As a noun, it had always referred to an engraver of jewels or a jeweler. Here, Poe gives it a new meaning: the knowledge of gems.

5 Montresor ("my treasure") is a French name, and Mabbott argues that "Montresor's words prove he was not himself Italian" (Mabbott, III, 1264). Critics are divided over whether the tale is set in Italy or France.

6 In many Roman Catholic countries, carnival is a time of great feasts and merrymaking, occurring over the last three days before Lent: one last blowout preceding forty days of penance and privation. Masked balls, elaborate costumes, and outrageous behavior otherwise unacceptable outside of carnival typify the merrymaking.

7 Amontillado is a type of high-quality Spanish sherry. Pale, dry, delicate, amontillado has a distinctive taste, but it takes a discriminating palate to differentiate it from commonplace Spanish sherry. The production process may be the most unusual aspect of amontillado: In *Journal of a Clergyman* (1845), the Rev. William Robertson explains: "The most singular circumstance regarding the Amontillado is, that, in the finest sorts, its peculiar flavour and difference in quality from other wines are the result of accident, or at least of circumstances with which the grower himself is perfectly unacquainted, and over which he has no control." Since its production depends on pure chance, amontillado forms an analogue for art, the creation of which sometimes stems from chance occurrence.

A pipe of wine is equal to two hogsheads or 126 wine gallons (105 imperial gallons). Two pipes make a tun. Poe's phrase "a pipe of what passes" is a pun on the title of Robert Browning's closet drama *Pippa Passes* (1841) and thus turns "The Cask of Amontillado" into an ironic counterpoint to the most famous line from *Pippa Passes:* "God's in his heaven: All's right with the world!"

8 A private reference to the Baltimore musician and music teacher Frederick Lucchesi.

9 Montresor makes a bad joke (Fortunato is dressed as a court jester or fool), which Fortunato—drunk, vain, and eager to prove his superiority—misses. Generally, Fortunato is oblivious to Montresor's wit. If Fortunato were not so quick to demonstrate that Luchesi is a fool, he might suspect Montresor's motives—or perhaps not.

10 Nitre or saltpetre often crystallizes on the surface of damp caves and caverns.

11 Masks of black silk were common attire during the time of carnival. William Wilson wears a similar mask during carnival that "entirely covered his face." Poe's description may conjure up the idea of an executioner's headgear. Regardless, Montresor's all-black attire provides a somber contrast to Fortunato's colorful motley.

12 A roquelaire is a knee-length cloak, often furlined and luxuriously appointed. The old man in "The Man of the Crowd" wears an "evidently second-handed roquelaire."

wore motley. He had on a tight-fitting parti-striped dress, and his head was surmounted by the conical cap and bells. I was so pleased to see him, that I thought I should never have done wringing his hand.

I said to him—"My dear Fortunato, you are luckily met. How remarkably well you are looking to-day! But I have received a pipe of what passes for Amontillado,[7] and I have my doubts."

"How?" said he. "Amontillado? A pipe? Impossible! And in the middle of the carnival!"

"I have my doubts," I replied; "and I was silly enough to pay the full Amontillado price without consulting you in the matter. You were not to be found, and I was fearful of losing a bargain."

"Amontillado!"

"I have my doubts."

"Amontillado!"

"And I must satisfy them."

"Amontillado!"

"As you are engaged, I am on my way to Luchesi.[8] If any one has a critical turn, it is he. He will tell me—"

"Luchesi cannot tell Amontillado from Sherry."

"And yet some fools will have it that his taste is a match for your own."[9]

"Come, let us go."

"Whither?"

"To your vaults."

"My friend, no; I will not impose upon your good nature. I perceive you have an engagement. Luchesi—"

"I have no engagement;—come."

"My friend, no. It is not the engagement, but the severe cold with which I perceive you are afflicted. The vaults are insufferably damp. They are encrusted with nitre."[10]

"Let us go, nevertheless. The cold is merely nothing. Amontillado! You have been imposed upon. And as for Luchesi, he cannot distinguish Sherry from Amontillado."

Thus speaking, Fortunato possessed himself of my arm. Putting on a mask of black silk,[11] and drawing a *roquelaire*[12] closely about my person, I suffered him to hurry me to my palazzo.

There were no attendants at home; they had absconded to make merry in honor of the time. I had told them that I should not return until the morning, and had given them explicit orders not to

Corridor in the Cappuccino Cata-combs, Rome, Italy, 1897. This macabre tourist destination on the Via Veneto houses the bones and mummified corpses of thousands of Capuchin friars, arranged artfully in several tiny chapels. Visitors to the crypt, located along one of the swankiest streets in Rome, are greeted by a sign that reads, "What you are now, we once were; what we are now, you shall be."

stir from the house. These orders were sufficient, I well knew, to insure their immediate disappearance, one and all, as soon as my back was turned.

I took from their sconces two flambeaux,[13] and giving one to Fortunato, bowed him through several suites of rooms to the archway that led into the vaults. I passed down a long and winding staircase, requesting him to be cautious as he followed. We came at length to the foot of the descent, and stood together on the damp ground of the catacombs[14] of the Montresors.

The gait of my friend was unsteady, and the bells upon his cap jingled as he strode.

"The pipe," said he.

13   A sconce is a bracket, usually made of brass or iron, fastened to the wall and used to hold candlesticks or, in this case, lighted torches known as flambeaux.

14   Catacombs are subterranean galleries or passages for the burial of the dead, with recesses where the bodies are placed. In early Christian Rome, catacombs also served as the sites for funeral feasts celebrated on the day of entombment.

15   The Medoc region of France produces excellent wine, including Lafitte, Latour, and Margouz. According to tradition, Medoc has medicinal value, as well.

16   The Monstresor coat of arms depicts a large golden foot against a sky-blue background as it crushes a serpent whose fangs are embedded in the heel. These arms call to mind the prophecy of Genesis 3:14–15: "And the Lord God said unto the serpent, Because thou hast done this, thou art cursed above all cattle, and above every beast of the field; upon thy belly shalt thou go, and dust shalt thou eat all the days of thy life: And I will put enmity between thee and the woman, and between thy seed and her seed; it shall bruise thy head, and thou shalt bruise his heel."

William Stepp argues "that Montresor identifies himself with the golden foot, ponderously triumphing over the lashing serpent." Alternatively, Stepp argues, Poe may not so easily identify Montresor with the foot. The snake is the more obvious choice. Secrecy, cunning, serpentine subtlety—these are the themes Montresor demonstrated best of all. And the huge, golden boot fits very snugly the Fortunato that Montresor presents to us—large, powerful, and very clumsy. The larger story shows very well how to read the emblem: a giant has blindly stepped on a snake" ("The Ironic Double in Poe's 'The Cask of Amontillado,'" *Studies in Short Fiction* 13 [1976], 448).

17   "No one insults me with impunity." This Latin phrase is the motto of the Scottish people, but Poe may have encountered it in many places. In John Webster's revenge tragedy, *The White Devil* (1612), for example, Brachiano repeats the phrase. In a June 1, 1840, letter to William Burton, Poe wrote, "If by accident you have taken it into your head that I am to be insulted with impunity I can only assume that you are an ass" (*The Collected Letters of Edgar Allan Poe*, ed. John Ward Ostrom, Burton R. Pollin, and Jeffrey A. Savoye, 2 vols. [New York: Gordian Press, 2008], I, 217–218.

"It is farther on," said I; "but observe the white web-work which gleams from these cavern walls."

He turned towards me, and looked into my eyes with two filmy orbs that distilled the rheum of intoxication.

"Nitre?" he asked, at length.

"Nitre," I replied. "How long have you had that cough?"

"Ugh! ugh! ugh!—ugh! ugh! ugh!—ugh! ugh! ugh!—ugh! ugh! ugh!—ugh! ugh! ugh!"

My poor friend found it impossible to reply for many minutes.

"It is nothing," he said, at last.

"Come," I said, with decision, "we will go back; your health is precious. You are rich, respected, admired, beloved; you are happy, as once I was. You are a man to be missed. For me it is no matter. We will go back; you will be ill, and I cannot be responsible. Besides, there is Luchesi—"

"Enough," he said; "the cough is a mere nothing; it will not kill me. I shall not die of a cough."

"True—true," I replied; "and, indeed, I had no intention of alarming you unnecessarily—but you should use all proper caution. A draught of this Medoc[15] will defend us from the damps."

Here I knocked off the neck of a bottle which I drew from a long row of its fellows that lay upon the mould.

"Drink," I said, presenting him the wine.

He raised it to his lips with a leer. He paused and nodded to me familiarly, while his bells jingled.

"I drink," he said, "to the buried that repose around us."

"And I to your long life."

He again took my arm, and we proceeded.

"These vaults," he said, "are extensive."

"The Montresors," I replied, "were a great and numerous family."

"I forget your arms."

"A huge human foot d'or, in a field azure; the foot crushes a serpent rampant whose fangs are imbedded in the heel."[16]

"And the motto?"

"Nemo me impune lacessit."[17]

"Good!" he said.

The wine sparkled in his eyes and the bells jingled. My own fancy grew warm with the Medoc. We had passed through walls of piled bones, with casks and puncheons intermingling, into the inmost recesses of the catacombs. I paused again, and this time I made bold to seize Fortunato by an arm above the elbow.

"The nitre!" I said; "see, it increases. It hangs like moss upon the vaults. We are below the river's bed. The drops of moisture trickle among the bones. Come, we will go back ere it is too late. Your cough—"

"It is nothing," he said; "let us go on. But first, another draught of the Medoc."

I broke and reached him a flaçon of De Grâve.[18] He emptied it at a breath. His eyes flashed with a fierce light. He laughed and threw the bottle upwards with a gesticulation I did not understand.

I looked at him in surprise. He repeated the movement—a grotesque one.

"You do not comprehend?" he said.

"Not I," I replied.

"Then you are not of the brotherhood."

"How?"

"You are not of the masons."[19]

"Yes, yes," I said, "yes, yes."

"You? Impossible! A mason?"

"A mason," I replied.

"A sign," he said.

"It is this," I answered, producing a trowel from beneath the folds of my *roquelaire.*

"You jest," he exclaimed, recoiling a few paces. "But let us proceed to the Amontillado."

"Be it so," I said, replacing the tool beneath the cloak, and again offering him my arm. He leaned upon it heavily. We continued our route in search of the Amontillado. We passed through a range of low arches, descended, passed on, and descending again, arrived at a deep crypt, in which the foulness of the air caused our flambeaux rather to glow than flame.

At the most remote end of the crypt there appeared another less spacious. Its walls had been lined with human remains, piled to the vault overhead, in the fashion of the great catacombs of Paris. Three sides of this interior crypt were still ornamented in this manner. From the fourth the bones had been thrown down, and lay promiscuously upon the earth, forming at one point a mound of some size. Within the wall thus exposed by the displacing of the bones, we perceived a still interior recess, in depth about four

18 *Vin de grave* was so called because it comes from grapes grown in gravelly soil. The term originally referred to white wines, but in Poe's day it pertained to both red and white wines grown on the gravelly lands to the southeast and southwest of Bordeaux. Montresor makes a bad pun.

19 Originating with the guilds of medieval stonemasons in England and Scotland, Freemasonry became by the seventeenth century an international fraternal organization, appropriating the rites and trappings of religious orders and chivalric brotherhoods, whose goal was the improvement of society. Secrecy marks Masonic rituals and ceremonies of initiation. Fortunato uses a secret sign indicating he is a Masonic brother. Poe was not a Mason, nor is Montresor, since he fails to recognize Fortunato's gesture. In gothic literature, references to Freemasonry have their own purpose, evoking mystery, suspense, and a sense of the unknown.

20 Poe had several literary precedents for the motif of immuration, that is, being walled in alive. In *Marmion* (1808), Sir Walter Scott relates the story of a runaway nun immured for being unchaste. In "La Grand Bretêche," Honoré de Balzac presents the story of a cuckholded husband who walls up his wife's lover in her presence. An English translation of Balzac's tale appeared in the November 1843 issue of the *Democratic Review*. American literature also offers a precedent. Joel T. Headley's sketch "A Man Built in a Wall," which appeared in the August 1844 issue of the *Columbian Magazine*—the same issue as Poe's "Mesmeric Revelation"—describes a niche in a church wall containing a skeleton of a man, who, according to legend, had been walled in alive as an act of revenge (Mabbott, III, 1253–1254).

feet, in width three, in height six or seven. It seemed to have been constructed for no especial use within itself, but formed merely the interval between two of the colossal supports of the roof of the catacombs, and was backed by one of their circumscribing walls of solid granite.

It was in vain that Fortunato, uplifting his dull torch, endeavored to pry into the depths of the recess. Its termination the feeble light did not enable us to see.

"Proceed," I said; "herein is the Amontillado. As for Luchesi—"

"He is an ignoramus," interrupted my friend, as he stepped unsteadily forward, while I followed immediately at his heels. In an instant he had reached the extremity of the niche, and finding his progress arrested by the rock, stood stupidly bewildered. A moment more and I had fettered him to the granite. In its surface were two iron staples, distant from each other about two feet, horizontally. From one of these depended a short chain, from the other a padlock. Throwing the links about his waist, it was but the work of a few seconds to secure it. He was too much astounded to resist. Withdrawing the key I stepped back from the recess.

"Pass your hand," I said, "over the wall; you cannot help feeling the nitre. Indeed it is *very* damp. Once more let me *implore* you to return. No? Then I must positively leave you. But I must first render you all the little attentions in my power."

"The Amontillado!" ejaculated my friend, not yet recovered from his astonishment.

"True," I replied; "the Amontillado."

As I said these words I busied myself among the pile of bones of which I have before spoken. Throwing them aside, I soon uncovered a quantity of building stone and mortar. With these materials and with the aid of my trowel, I began vigorously to wall up the entrance of the niche.[20]

I had scarcely laid the first tier of my masonry when I discovered that the intoxication of Fortunato had in a great measure worn off. The earliest indication I had of this was a low moaning cry from the depth of the recess. It was *not* the cry of a drunken man. There was then a long and obstinate silence. I laid the second tier, and the third, and the fourth; and then I heard the furious vibrations of the chain. The noise lasted for several minutes, during which, that I might hearken to it with the more satisfaction, I ceased my labors and sat down upon the bones. When at last the clanking subsided, I resumed the trowel, and finished without interruption the fifth, the sixth, and the seventh tier. The wall was now nearly upon a level with my breast. I again paused, and holding the flambeaux over the mason-work, threw a few feeble rays upon the figure within.

A succession of loud and shrill screams, bursting suddenly from the throat of the chained form, seemed to thrust me violently back. For a brief moment I hesitated—I trembled. Unsheathing my rapier, I began to grope with it about the recess: but the thought of an instant reassured me. I placed my hand upon the solid fabric of the catacombs, and felt satisfied. I reapproached the wall. I replied to the yells of him who clamored. I re-echoed—I aided—I surpassed them in volume and in strength. I did this, and the clamorer grew still.

It was now midnight, and my task was drawing to a close. I had completed the eighth, the ninth, and the tenth tier. I had finished a portion of the last and the eleventh; there remained but a single stone to be fitted and plastered in. I struggled with its weight; I placed it partially in its destined position. But now there came from out the niche a low laugh that erected the hairs upon my head. It was succeeded by a sad voice, which I had difficulty in recognising as that of the noble Fortunato. The voice said—

"Ha! ha! ha!—he! he!—a very good joke indeed—an excellent jest. We will have many a rich laugh about it at the palazzo—he! he! he!—over our wine—he! he! he!"

"The Amontillado!" I said.

"He! he! he!—he! he! he!—yes, the Amontillado. But is it not getting late? Will not they be awaiting us at the palazzo, the Lady Fortunato and the rest? Let us be gone."

"Yes," I said, "let us be gone."

"For the love of God, Montressor!"

"Yes," I said, "for the love of God!"

But to these words I hearkened in vain for a reply. I grew impatient. I called aloud—

"Fortunato!"

No answer. I called again—

"Fortunato!"

No answer still. I thrust a torch through the remaining aperture and let it fall within. There came forth in return only a jingling of

21   In "The Merciful" (1971), an episode of Rod Serling's *Night Gallery* inspired by "The Cask of Amontillado," Imogene Coca plays a wife who erects a brick wall to seal her husband inside the basement but mistakenly walls in herself instead. Every adaptation of a literary work also constitutes a critical interpretation, and this television episode is no exception: In walling up Fortunato, Montresor has walled up himself, restricting his mind, his thought, his actions, rendering him unable to do anything else save think about what he had done. Daniel Hoffman offers a similar take: "But has not Montresor walled up himself in this revenge? Of what else can he think, can he have thought for the past half-century, but of that night's vengeance upon his enemy? His freedom to do otherwise stands chained in the dank vault with Fortunato" (*Poe Poe Poe Poe Poe Poe Poe* [Garden City, NY: Doubleday, 1972], 219).

22   Latin: "May he/she rest in peace." As part of the Catholic burial service, it is a prayerful request for the everlasting repose of the soul in the afterlife. Inscribed on Christian tombs and gravestones, it is a familiar epitaphic formulation. According to Joshua Scodel, "*Cuius anima requiescat in pace* was common at the end of Italian and French medieval epitaphs. . . . *Requiescat in pace* does not appear regularly on post-Reformation English tombstones until the eighteenth and nineteenth centuries, when its increasing appearance reflects the greater tolerance, de fact and eventually de jure, of Catholicism, with which the formula was associated" (*The English Poetic Epitaph: Commemoration and Conflict from Jonson to Wordsworth* [Ithaca: Cornell University Press, 1991], 94). The words here seem intended for Fortunato, but they may apply equally to Montresor, perhaps uttered by a priest during the administration of Last Rites.

the bells. My heart grew sick—on account of the dampness of the catacombs. I hastened to make an end of my labor. I forced the last stone into its position; I plastered it up. Against the new masonry I re-erected the old rampart of bones. For the half of a century no mortal has disturbed them.[21] *In páce requiescat!*[22]

Hop-Frog

Part fairy tale and part revenge tragedy, "Hop-Frog" appeared in print only months before Poe's death in 1849 in a Baltimore hospital. In the last years of his life he wrote relatively few stories. It was not the case that he had run out of ideas. "The true invention never exhausts itself," he once declared. "It is mere cant and ignorance to talk of the possibility of the really imaginative man's 'writing himself out'" (Essays and Reviews, ed. G. R. Thompson [New York: Library of America, 1984], 319). Rather, Poe now found himself in a similar situation to the one he faced in the mid-1830s after leaving the Southern Literary Messenger. Despite the successes of "The Gold-Bug" and "The Raven," Poe had trouble finding magazine editors and publishers willing to pay him a decent wage for his tales. Poe's "boast of having made 'permanent engagements with every magazine in America,'" biographer Kenneth Silverman writes, "came down to writing mostly for a single journal" (Edgar A. Poe: Mournful and Never-Ending Remembrance [New York: HarperCollins, 1991], 399). In January 1849, the Boston publisher Frederick Gleason invited Poe to become a regular contributor to the Flag of Our Union, a cheap newspaper-style weekly that promoted itself on its masthead as "A Literary and Miscellaneous Family Journal, containing News, Wit, Humor, and Romance—independent of Party or Sect." Poe was less than thrilled with the idea of publishing in its pages, but Gleason at least treated his authors respectfully. He offered Poe five dollars a page for contributions. In a letter of April 20, 1849, Poe writes to Nathaniel P. Willis: "[Flags of Our Union] pays well as times go— but unquestionably it ought to pay ten prices; for whatever I send it I feel I am consigning to the tomb of the Capulets" (Collected Letters of Edgar Allan Poe, ed. John Ward Ostrom, Burton R. Pollin, and Jeffrey A. Savoye, 2 vols. [New York: Gordian Press, 2008], II, 790–791). Poe had had the idea for "Hop-Frog" since at least 1845. Two weeks after receiving Gleason's offer, he completed the tale, which appeared as "Hop-Frog: or, the Eight Chained Ourang-Outangs" in the March 17, 1849, issue of Flag of Our Union.

I never knew any one so keenly alive to a joke as the king was. He seemed to live only for joking.[1] To tell a good story of the joke kind, and to tell it well, was the surest road to his favor. Thus it happened that his seven ministers were all noted for their accomplishments as jokers. They all took after the king, too, in being large, corpulent, oily men, as well as inimitable jokers.[2] Whether people grow fat by joking, or whether there is something in fat itself which predisposes to a joke, I have never been quite able to determine; but certain it is that a lean joker is a *rara avis in terris*.[3]

About the refinements, or, as he called them, the "ghosts" of wit, the king troubled himself very little. He had an especial admiration for *breadth* in a jest, and would often put up with *length*, for the sake of it. Over-niceties wearied him. He would have preferred Rabelais's *Gargantua*, to the *Zadig* of Voltaire:[4] and, upon the whole, practical jokes suited his taste far better than verbal ones.[5]

At the date of my narrative, professing jesters had not altogether gone out of fashion at court.[6] Several of the great continental "powers" still retained their "fools," who wore motley, with caps and bells, and who were expected to be always ready with sharp witticisms, at a moment's notice, in consideration of the crumbs that fell from the royal table.[7]

Our king, as a matter of course, retained his "fool." The fact is, he *required* something in the way of folly—if only to counterbalance the heavy wisdom of the seven wise men who were his ministers—not to mention himself.

1 The narrative has the quality of a fairy tale, a story set in some vague but distant past, but the narrator asserts himself as an authorial presence throughout. Nowhere does the narrator suggest these events actually occurred.

2 Julie Taymor brought "Hop-Frog" to the long-running PBS television program *American Playhouse* as *Fool's Fire* (1992). She cast little people in the roles of Hop-Frog (Michael J. Anderson) and Tripetta (Mireille Mossé) and used massive puppets for all the other roles. Taymor's aesthetic choices gave her an effective way to bring Poe's crippled dwarf to television, as she explained in a speech to the Na-

tional Press Club on November 15, 2000. Her casting decisions let her concentrate on Hop-Frog's humanity, allowing audiences to identify with him, to see the sweat on his
brow and the tears in his eyes. Her star, who had previously played dwarfs in many television shows, appreciated
Taymor's sensitivity, commenting that for the first time he
was the human being, not the special effect.

3   This well-known line from Juvenal's *Satires* may be
translated as "a rare bird upon the earth."

4   Here, we are given to understand that the king would
prefer Rabelais's *Gargantua* (1534) to Voltaire's *Zadig: ou,
La Destinée* (1747) for the coarseness of its humor. There
are Rabelaisian aspects to the humor in Poe's tale. Note the
use of subjunctive mood: the king *would* prefer *Gargantua*
to *Zadig*, perhaps because we are meant to understand the
events take place in a distant past, or perhaps because the
king is someone disinclined to actually read a book.

5   Though Poe placed verbal jokes, even the slightest
puns and conundrums, at a higher level than practical
jokes, he was himself sometimes a practical joker. When he
was at West Point, according to one story, Thomas Gibson, a fellow cadet, left their barracks one evening to visit a
nearby tavern for the purpose of replenishing their supply
of grog and goodies. Poe stood lookout as Gibson returned
with a bottle of brandy in one hand and a gunnysack dripping with blood in the other. The sack contained a recently
slaughtered goose, but, for a man of Poe's imagination, it
looked like it contained a severed head. He convinced Gibson to return to the barracks pretending he had decapitated
the instructor of infantry tactics (Mary E. Phillips, *Edgar
Allan Poe: The Man*, 2 vols. [Chicago: John C. Winston,
1926], I, 381–383).

6   The fool or jester died out as a court institution in Europe in the early eighteenth century. Beatrice K. Otto offers this description of the court jester's characteristics:
"He could be juggler, confidant, scapegoat, prophet, and
counselor all in one. If we follow his family tree along its
many branches we encounter musicians and actors, acro-
bats and poets, dwarfs, hunchbacks, tricksters, madmen,
and mountebanks" (*Fools Are Everywhere: The Court Jester
around the World* [Chicago: The University of Chicago
Press, 2001], 6).

7   Compare Luke 16:19–21: "There was a certain rich
man, which was clothed in purple and fine linen, and fared
sumptuously every day: And there was a certain beggar

His fool, or professional jester, was not *only* a fool, however.
His value was trebled in the eyes of the king, by the fact of his being also a dwarf[8] and a cripple.[9] Dwarfs were as common at court,
in those days, as fools; and many monarchs would have found it
difficult to get through their days (days are rather longer at court
than elsewhere) without both a jester to laugh *with*, and a dwarf to
laugh *at*. But, as I have already observed, your jesters, in ninety-
nine cases out of a hundred, are fat, round and unwieldy—so that
it was no small source of self-gratulation with our king that, in
Hop-Frog (this was the fool's name,) he possessed a triplicate treasure in one person.

I believe the name "Hop-Frog" was *not* that given to the dwarf
by his sponsors at baptism, but it was conferred upon him, by general consent of the several ministers, on account of his inability to
walk as other men do.[10] In fact, Hop-Frog could only get along
by a sort of interjectional gait—something between a leap and a
wriggle—a movement that afforded illimitable amusement, and of
course consolation, to the king, for (notwithstanding the protuberance of his stomach and a constitutional swelling of the head)
the king, by his whole court, was accounted a capital figure.

But although Hop-Frog, through the distortion of his legs,
could move only with great pain and difficulty along a road or
floor, the prodigious muscular power which nature seemed to have
bestowed upon his arms, by way of compensation for deficiency in
the lower limbs, enabled him to perform many feats of wonderful
dexterity, where trees or ropes were in question, or anything else
to climb. At such exercises he certainly much more resembled a
squirrel, or a small monkey, than a frog.[11]

I am not able to say, with precision, from what country Hop-
Frog originally came. It was from some barbarous region, however, that no person ever heard of—a vast distance from the court
of our king.[12] Hop-Frog, and a young girl very little less dwarfish
than himself (although of exquisite proportions, and a marvellous
dancer,) had been forcibly carried off from their respective homes
in adjoining provinces, and sent as presents to the king, by one of
his ever-victorious generals.

Under these circumstances, it is not to be wondered at that a
close intimacy arose between the two little captives. Indeed, they
soon became sworn friends. Hop-Frog, who, although he made
a great deal of sport, was by no means popular, had it not in his

power to render Trippetta many services; but *she*, on account of her grace and exquisite beauty (although a dwarf,) was universally admired and petted: so she possessed much influence; and never failed to use it, whenever she could, for the benefit of Hop-Frog.

On some grand state occasion—I forget what—the king determined to have a masquerade, and whenever a masquerade or anything of that kind, occurred at our court, then the talents both of Hop-Frog and Trippetta were sure to be called in play. Hop-Frog, in especial, was so inventive in the way of getting up pageants, suggesting novel characters, and arranging costume, for masked balls, that nothing could be done, it seems, without his assistance.[13]

The night appointed for the *fête* had arrived. A gorgeous hall had been fitted up, under Trippetta's eye, with every kind of device which could possibly give *éclat*[14] to a masquerade. The whole court was in a fever of expectation. As for costumes and charac-

---

named Lazarus, which was laid at his gate, full of sores, And desiring to be fed with the crumbs which fell from the rich man's table: moreover the dogs came and licked his sores."

8   In folk tradition, dwarfs often possess a mischievous nature, but they also serve as protectors. Think of the Seven Dwarfs in *Sleeping Beauty.*

9   Perhaps unsurprisingly, American photographer Diane Arbus (1923–1971) was fascinated with "Hop-Frog." Though she began her career as a commercial photographer, Arbus is best known for her portraits of "freaks" and marginalized people. "There's a quality of legend about freaks," she writes. "Like a person in a fairy tale who stops you and demands that you answer a riddle. Most people go through life dreading they'll have a traumatic experience. Freaks were born with their trauma. They've already passed their test in life. They're aristocrats" (*Diane Arbus: An Aperture Monograph* [Millerton, NY: Aperture, 1972], 3).

10   "Hop-frog" is the name of a children's game more commonly called "leap-frog," in which players vault or leap over each other's stooped backs. The name Hop-Frog was also inspired by the central character in John Poole's sketch "Frogére and the Emperor Paul," which anticipates several aspects of Poe's tale and features an emperor fond of cruel practical jokes. Poole's sketch was first published in the May 1830 issue of the *New Monthly Magazine* and later appeared in *Sketches and Recollections,* 2 vols. (Philadelphia: Carey, Lea, and Blanchard, 1835), II, 149–159.

11   Hop-Frog bears similarities to Quasimodo, Victor Hugo's memorable hunchback from *Notre-Dame de Paris* (1831), the first American edition of which appeared in two volumes as *The Hunchback of Notre-Dame* (Philadelphia: Carey, Lea, and Blanchard, 1834).

12   In part due to P. T. Barnum's promotion of Tom Thumb, there was a resurgence of public interest in little people in the midnineteenth century. Like Poe, Barnum fabricated exotic backgrounds for dwarfs, midgets, and other "curiosities" (Lindsey Hursh, "Curiosity," *Edgar Allan Poe in Context*, ed. Kevin J. Hayes [New York: Cambridge University Press, 2013], 91).

13   Hop-Frog's role as an entertainer, his quick invention, and his ability to create "novel characters" suggest obvious parallels to the literary performance of the writer. Leslie A. Fiedler calls Hop-Frog "a symbol for all alienated artists." Robert Shulman goes further, describing Poe's tale as "one of the most disturbing enactments of the American artist's feelings of hatred against his imprisoned servitude to the public." More recently, Leon Jackson has seen "Hop-Frog" as "a parable concerning the nature of celebrity culture" (Leslie A. Fiedler, *Freaks: Myths and Images of the Secret Self* [New York: Simon and Schuster, 1978], 73; Robert Shulman, *Social Criticism and Nineteenth-Century American Fictions* [Columbia: University of Missouri Press, 1987], 178; Leon Jackson, "'The Rage for Lions': Edgar Allan Poe and the Culture of Celebrity," *Poe and the Remapping of Antebellum Print Culture*, ed. J. Gerald Kennedy and Jerome McGann [Baton Rouge: Louisiana State University Press, 2012], 55).

14   "Brilliancy, radiance, dazzling effect" *(OED).*

15   Compare Luke 12:19: "And I will say to my soul, Soul, thou hast much goods laid up for many years; take thine ease, eat, drink, and be merry."

ters, it might well be supposed that everybody had come to a decision on such points. Many had made up their minds (as to what *rôles* they should assume) a week, or even a month, in advance; and, in fact, there was not a particle of indecision anywhere—except in the case of the king and his seven ministers. Why *they* hesitated I never could tell, unless they did it by way of a joke. More probably, they found it difficult, on account of being so fat, to make up their minds. At all events, time flew; and, as a last resource, they sent for Trippetta and Hop-Frog.

When the two little friends obeyed the summons of the king, they found him sitting at his wine with the seven members of his cabinet council; but the monarch appeared to be in a very ill humor. He knew that Hop-Frog was not fond of wine; for it excited the poor cripple almost to madness; and madness is no comfortable feeling. But the king loved his practical jokes, and took pleasure in forcing Hop-Frog to drink and (as the king called it) "to be merry."[15]

"Come here, Hop-Frog," said he, as the jester and his friend entered the room: "swallow this bumper to the health of your absent friends (here Hop-Frog sighed,) and then let us have the benefit of your invention. We want characters—*characters*, man—something novel—out of the way. We are wearied with this everlasting sameness. Come, drink! the wine will brighten your wits."

Hop-Frog endeavored, as usual, to get up a jest in reply to these advances from the king; but the effort was too much. It happened to be the poor dwarf's birthday, and the command to drink to his "absent friends" forced the tears to his eyes. Many large, bitter drops fell into the goblet as he took it, humbly, from the hand of the tyrant.

"Ah! ha! ha! ha!" roared the latter, as the dwarf reluctantly drained the beaker. "See what a glass of good wine can do! Why, your eyes are shining already!"

Poor fellow! his large eyes *gleamed*, rather than shone; for the effect of wine on his excitable brain was not more powerful than instantaneous. He placed the goblet nervously on the table, and looked round upon the company with a half-insane stare. They all seemed highly amused at the success of the king's "*joke.*"

"And now to business," said the prime minister, a *very* fat man.

"Yes," said the king; "Come, Hop-Frog, lend us your assistance. Characters, my fine fellow; we stand in need of characters—all of us—ha! ha! ha!" and as this was seriously meant for a joke, his laugh was chorused by the seven.

Hop-Frog also laughed, although feebly and somewhat vacantly.

"Come, come," said the king, impatiently, "have you nothing to suggest?"

"I am endeavoring to think of something *novel*," replied the dwarf, abstractedly, for he was quite bewildered by the wine.

"Endeavoring!" cried the tyrant, fiercely; "what do you mean by *that?* Ah, I perceive. You are sulky, and want more wine. Here, drink this!" and he poured out another goblet full and offered it to the cripple, who merely gazed at it, gasping for breath.

"Drink, I say!" shouted the monster, "or by the fiends—"

The dwarf hesitated. The king grew purple with rage. The courtiers smirked. Trippetta, pale as a corpse, advanced to the monarch's seat, and, falling on her knees before him, implored him to spare her friend.

The tyrant regarded her, for some moments, in evident wonder at her audacity. He seemed quite at a loss what to do or say—how most becomingly to express his indignation. At last, without uttering a syllable, he pushed her violently from him, and threw the contents of the brimming goblet in her face.

The poor girl got up as best she could, and, not daring even to sigh, resumed her position at the foot of the table.

There was a dead silence for about a half a minute, during which the falling of a leaf, or of a feather, might have been heard. It was interrupted by a low, but harsh and protracted *grating* sound which seemed to come at once from every corner of the room.

"What—what—*what* are you making that noise for?" demanded the king, turning furiously to the dwarf.

The latter seemed to have recovered, in great measure, from his intoxication, and looking fixedly but quietly into the tyrant's face, merely ejaculated:

"I—I? How could it have been me?"

"The sound appeared to come from without," observed one of the courtiers. "I fancy it was the parrot at the window, whetting his bill upon his cage-wires."

"True," replied the monarch, as if much relieved by the suggestion; "but, on the honor of a knight, I could have sworn that it was the gritting of this vagabond's teeth."

Hereupon the dwarf laughed (the king was too confirmed a joker to object to any one's laughing), and displayed a set of large, powerful, and very repulsive teeth. Moreover, he avowed his perfect willingness to swallow as much wine as desired. The monarch was pacified; and having drained another bumper with no very perceptible ill effect, Hop-Frog entered at once, and with spirit, into the plans for the masquerade.

"I cannot tell what was the association of idea," observed he, very tranquilly, and as if he had never tasted wine in his life, "but *just after* your majesty had struck the girl and thrown the wine in her face—*just after* your majesty had done this, and while the parrot was making that odd noise outside the window, there came into my mind a capital diversion—one of my own country frolics—often enacted among us, at our masquerades: but here it will be new altogether. Unfortunately, however, it requires a company of eight persons, and—"

"Here we *are!*" cried the king, laughing at his acute discovery of the coincidence; "eight to a fraction—I and my seven ministers. Come! what is the diversion?"

"We call it," replied the cripple, "the Eight Chained Ourang-Outangs, and it really is excellent sport if well enacted."

"*We* will enact it," remarked the king, drawing himself up, and lowering his eyelids.

"The beauty of the game," continued Hop-Frog, "lies in the fright it occasions among the women."

"Capital!" roared in chorus the monarch and his ministry.

"*I* will equip you as ourang-outangs," proceeded the dwarf; "leave all that to me. The resemblance shall be so striking, that the company of masqueraders will take you for real beasts—and of course, they will be as much terrified as astonished."

"O, this is exquisite!" exclaimed the king. "Hop-Frog! I will make a man of you."

"The chains are for the purpose of increasing the confusion by their jangling. You are supposed to have escaped, *en masse*, from your keepers. Your majesty cannot conceive the *effect* produced, at a masquerade, by eight chained ourang-outangs, imagined to be real ones by most of the company; and rushing in with savage cries, among the crowd of delicately and gorgeously habited men and women. The *contrast* is inimitable."

"It *must* be," said the king: and the council arose hurriedly (as it was growing late), to put in execution the scheme of Hop-Frog.

His mode of equipping the party as ourang-outangs was very simple, but effective enough for his purposes. The animals in question had, at the epoch of my story, very rarely been seen in any part of the civilized world; and as the imitations made by the dwarf were sufficiently beast-like and more than sufficiently hideous, their truthfulness to nature was thus thought to be secured.

The king and his ministers were first encased in tight-fitting stockinet[16] shirts and drawers. They were then saturated with tar. At this stage of the process, some one of the party suggested feathers; but the suggestion was at once overruled by the dwarf, who soon convinced the eight, by ocular demonstration, that the hair of such a brute as the ourang-outang was much more efficiently represented by *flax*. A thick coating of the latter was accordingly plastered upon the coating of tar. A long chain was now procured. First, it was passed about the waist of the king, *and tied;* then about another of the party, and also tied; then about all successively, in the same manner. When this chaining arrangement was complete, and the party stood as far apart from each other as possible, they formed a circle; and to make all things appear natural, Hop-Frog passed the residue of the chain, in two diameters, at right angles, across the circle, after the fashion adopted, at the present day, by those who capture Chimpanzees, or other large apes, in Borneo.[17]

The grand saloon in which the masquerade was to take place, was a circular room, very lofty, and receiving the light of the sun only through a single window at top. At night (the season for which the apartment was especially designed,) it was illuminated principally by a large chandelier, depending by a chain from the centre of the sky-light, and lowered, or elevated, by means of a counter-balance as usual; but (in order not to look unsightly) this latter passed outside the cupola and over the roof.

The arrangements of the room had been left to Trippetta's superintendence; but, in some particulars, it seems, she had been guided by the calmer judgment of her friend the dwarf. At his suggestion it was that, on this occasion, the chandelier was removed. Its waxen drippings (which, in weather so warm, it was quite impossible to prevent,) would have been seriously detrimental to the rich dresses of the guests, who, on account of the crowded state of

16 A knit fabric used to make underwear.

17 "Hop-Frog" may have been inspired in part by an episode described in the 138th chapter of Jean Froissart's *Chronicles of England, France, Spain, and the Adjoining Countries, from the Latter Part of the Reign of Edward II. to the Coronation of Henry IV.* In a footnote to his essay "Barbarities of the Theatre," published in the February 1, 1845, issue of the *Broadway Journal*, Evert Duyckinck relates the episode in detail. During a wedding party at the court of Charles VI of France in 1385, the king and a group of courtiers covered their bodies in long hair to assume the guise of wild men. Chained together, they entered a ballroom from which all torches had been removed as a precaution. Unaware of the danger, however, the Duke of Orleans, arriving late, entered with an entourage of torch-bearers, one of whom accidentally set the courtiers on fire. All the courtiers perished, but the king, who was not chained to them, escaped with his life, thanks to the Duchess of Berry, who smothered his burning body with the train of her dress.

18   Caryatides are supporting columns in the form of draped female figures. The Caryatid Porch of the Erechtheion is the most celebrated example.

19   Poe's use of slapstick humor—the stumbling entrance of the king and his seven ministers—enhances the shock and horror of what follows.

the saloon, could not *all* be expected to keep from out its centre—that is to say, from under the chandelier. Additional sconces were set in various parts of the hall, out of the way; and a flambeau, emitting sweet odor, was placed in the right hand of each of the Caryatides[18] that stood against the wall—some fifty or sixty altogether.

The eight ourang-outangs, taking Hop-Frog's advice, waited patiently until midnight (when the room was thoroughly filled with masqueraders) before making their appearance. No sooner had the clock ceased striking, however, than they rushed, or rather rolled in, all together—for the impediment of their chains caused most of the party to fall, and all to stumble as they entered.[19]

The excitement among the masqueraders was prodigious, and filled the heart of the king with glee. As had been anticipated, there were not a few of the guests who supposed the ferocious-looking creatures to be beasts of *some* kind in reality, if not precisely ourang-outangs. Many of the women swooned with affright; and had not the king taken the precaution to exclude all weapons from the saloon, his party might soon have expiated their frolic in their blood. As it was, a general rush was made for the doors; but the king had ordered them to be locked immediately upon his entrance; and, at the dwarf's suggestion, the keys had been deposited with *him*.

While the tumult was at its height, and each masquerader attentive only to his own safety—(for, in fact, there was much *real* danger from the pressure of the excited crowd,)—the chain by which the chandelier ordinarily hung, and which had been drawn up on its removal, might have been seen very gradually to descend, until its hooked extremity came within three feet of the floor.

Soon after this, the king and his seven friends, having reeled about the hall in all directions, found themselves, at length, in its centre, and, of course, in immediate contact with the chain. While they were thus situated, the dwarf, who had followed closely at their heels, inciting them to keep up the commotion, took hold of their own chain at the intersection of the two portions which crossed the circle diametrically and at right angles. Here, with the rapidity of thought, he inserted the hook from which the chandelier had been wont to depend; and, in an instant, by some unseen agency, the chandelier-chain was drawn so far upward as to take

James Ensor, *The Vengeance of Hop-Frog*, 1898.

the hook out of reach, and, as an inevitable consequence, to drag the ourang-outangs together in close connection, and face to face.

The masqueraders, by this time, had recovered, in some measure, from their alarm; and, beginning to regard the whole matter as a well-contrived pleasantry, set up a loud shout of laughter at the predicament of the apes.

"Leave them to *me!*" now screamed Hop-Frog, his shrill voice making itself easily heard through all the din. "Leave them to *me*. I fancy *I* know them. If I can only get a good look at them, *I* can soon tell who they are."

Here, scrambling over the heads of the crowd, he managed to get to the wall; when, seizing a flambeau from one of the Caryatides, he returned, as he went, to the centre of the room—leaped, with the agility of a monkey, upon the king's head—and thence clambered a few feet up the chain—holding down the torch to examine the group of ourang-outangs, and still screaming, "*I* shall soon find out who they are!"

And now, while the whole assembly (the apes included) were convulsed with laughter, the jester suddenly uttered a shrill whistle; when the chain flew violently up for about thirty feet—dragging with it the dismayed and struggling ourang-outangs, and leaving them suspended in mid-air between the sky-light and the floor. Hop-Frog, clinging to the chain as it rose, still maintained his relative position in respect to the eight maskers, and still (as if nothing were the matter) continued to thrust his torch down towards them, as though endeavoring to discover who they were.

So thoroughly astonished were the whole company at this ascent, that a dead silence, of about a minute's duration, ensued. It was broken by just such a low, harsh, *grating* sound, as had before attracted the attention of the king and his councillors, when the former threw the wine in the face of Trippetta. But, on the present occasion, there could be no question as to *whence* the sound issued. It came from the fang-like teeth of the dwarf, who ground them and gnashed them as he foamed at the mouth, and glared, with an expression of maniacal rage, into the upturned countenances of the king and his seven companions.

"Ah, ha!" said at length the infuriated jester. "Ah, ha! I begin to see who these people *are*, now!" Here, pretending to scrutinize the king more closely, he held the flambeau to the flaxen coat which enveloped him, and which instantly burst into a sheet of vivid flame. In less than half a minute the whole eight ourang-outangs were blazing fiercely, amid the shrieks of the multitude who gazed at them from below, horror-stricken, and without the power to render them the slightest assistance.

At length the flames, suddenly increasing in virulence, forced the jester to climb higher up the chain, to be out of their reach; and, as he made this movement, the crowd again sank, for a brief instant, into silence. The dwarf seized his opportunity, and once more spoke:

"I now see *distinctly*," he said, "what manner of people these maskers are. They are a great king and his seven privy-councillors—a king who does not scruple to strike a defenceless girl, and his seven councillors who abet him in the outrage. As for myself, I am simply Hop-Frog, the jester—and *this is my last jest*."

Owing to the high combustibility of both the flax and the tar to which it adhered, the dwarf had scarcely made an end of his brief speech before the work of vengeance was complete. The eight corpses swung in their chains, a fetid, blackened, hideous, and in-distinguishable mass. The cripple hurled his torch at them, clambered leisurely to the ceiling, and disappeared through the sky-light.[20]

It is supposed that Trippetta, stationed on the roof of the sa-loon, had been the accomplice of her friend in his fiery revenge, and that, together, they effected their escape to their own country: for neither was seen again.

20 Many readers feel that in his desire for revenge Hop-Frog has at last outdone the king and his ministers in their cruelty. There is no easy moral takeaway. Charles Baudelaire believed that Poe's tale's only repeatedly affirmed "the natural wickedness of man." In his letter of July 2, 1844, to James Russell Lowell, Poe writes: "I have no faith in human perfectibility. I think that human exertion will have no appreciable effect upon humanity. Man is now only more active—not more happy—nor more wise, than he was 6000 years ago. The result will never vary—and to suppose that it will, is to suppose that the foregone man has lived in vain—that the foregone time is but the rudiment of the future—that the myriads who have perished have not been upon equal footing with ourselves—nor are we with our posterity" (*Collected Letters*, I, 449).

First published in Poems *(1831), Poe's third collection of verse, "To Helen" is widely considered the finest of Poe's early poems. The poem underwent many revisions and reprintings before Poe was satisfied with it. It didn't achieve its final form until 1843. Its placement as the concluding work in* The Raven and Other Poems *(1845) indicates Poe's own sense of its importance in his oeuvre. The poem found many prominent readers among the leading Modernist poets in American literature. In an essay he contributed to the February 1915 issue of* Poetry, *Ezra Pound asks all poets to consider their literary palette, by which he means the set of authors who influenced them the most and whose works shaped their imagery and their prosody. Pound makes no mention of Poe, but in a note to his essay, the magazine's editor, Harriet Monroe, says that "To Helen" belongs on the palette of "most English-writing poets." H. D., also part of the Pound-Monroe circle, called "To Helen" her favorite of Poe's poems.*

In a letter of October 1, 1848, to Helen Whitman, Poe referred to the poem as "lines I had written in my passionate boyhood, to the first, purely ideal love of my soul—to Helen Stannard [Jane Stannard] of whom I told you." Thomas Mabbott says that "Poe's habit of giving names he liked to women for whose real names he did not care amply accounts for his substitution of 'Helen' for 'Jane'" (Thomas Ollive Mabbott, ed., Collected Works of Edgar Allan Poe, *3 vols. [Cambridge, MA: The Belknap Press of Harvard University Press, 1969–1978], I, 163).*

1   Poe selected the name "Helen" for its sound and allusion to Helen of Troy and her Hellenic world. He typically favored female names containing "el" and "en" sounds. Other female characters in his verse are named Annabel, Ellen, Elenore, and Lenore. Helen of Troy, a daughter of Zeus either by Leda or by Nemesis, was reputedly the most beautiful woman in the world and the indirect cause of the Trojan War. For many poets through the centuries she has been the personification of ideal beauty. In Marlowe's *Doctor Faustus* (1604) she is "the face that launch'd a thousand ships."

2   Poe echoes Coleridge's "Youth and Age," line 12: "Like those trim skiffs, unknown of yore," as Killis Campbell first suggested in his 1917 edition of Poe's verse. Pertaining to Nike, the Greek goddess of victory, "Nicéan" means victorious. It also refers to the ancient city of Nicaea in Asia Minor. The word "Nicaean" or, as it is sometimes spelled, "Nicene" was used to describe anything pertaining to the city, including, of course, the Nicene Creed, or profession of faith, which formed part of the liturgy Poe learned as a student in England. Poe chooses a term that

To Helen

Helen,[1] thy beauty is to me
    Like those Nicéan barks of yore,[2]
That gently, o'er a perfumed sea,
    The weary way-worn wanderer[3] bore
    To his own native shore.

On desperate seas long wont to roam,
    Thy hyacinth hair,[4] thy classic face,
Thy Naiad airs[5] have brought me home
    To the glory that was Greece,
And the grandeur that was Rome.[6]

Lo! in yon brilliant[7] window-niche
    How statue-like I see thee stand,
    The agate lamp[8] within thy hand!
Ah, Psyche,[9] from the regions which
    Are Holy-Land!

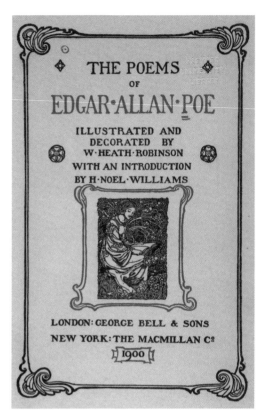

W. Heath Robinson, title page for *The Poems of Edgar Allan Poe* (1900). Robinson (1872–1944), a British cartoonist and illustrator, established his reputation with images of whimsical and unnecessarily complex machinery. During World War I, the name "Heath Robinson" would become a proverbial phrase meaning any unnecessarily complex contrivance, much as the term "Rube Goldberg machine" would enter the vernacular in the United States during the 1930s. Heath Robinson got his start with *The Poems of Edgar Allan Poe*, the first book he illustrated.

resonates in both pagan and Christian theology to articulate his own brand of worship, that is, the worship of ideal beauty.

3   Contemporary authors frequently described travelers as weary and way-worn. The Rev. William Sheperd, for one, translated a passage from Catullus depicting a traveler returning to his island home after a lengthy absence: "Hail! then, fair Isle!—with welcome sweet / Thy weary, way-worn master greet" (*Poems, Original and Translated* [London: Longman, Rees, Orme, Brown, and Green, 1829], 113).

4   Hyacinth hair is glossy, luxuriant black hair, having tight curls resembling a hyacinth flower. Mabbott notes: "In Pope's version of the *Odyssey*, VI, 231, which Poe almost surely did know, we read of the 'hyacinthine locks' of Ulysses . . . In his story 'Ligeia' Poe says his heroine had 'the raven-black, the glossy, the luxuriant and naturally-curling tresses, setting forth the full force of the Homeric epithet "hyacinthine"'" (Mabbott, *Collected Works*, I, 170).

5   In Greek mythology, Naiads are nymphs, that is, female spirits, associated with fountains, lakes, rivers, and other bodies of water.

6   Among Poe's most memorable and, indeed, most famous lines, lines 9–10 have become a commonplace expression for the many and varied achievements of Greco-Roman civilization. It took Poe several tries to perfect these two lines. In the first published version, they read:

> To the beauty of fair Greece,
> And the grandeur of old Rome.

Carol Rumens identifies the rhymes that "bookend" this stanza—"roam" and "Rome"—as "a subtle touch—a miniature history in a pair of homophones" ("Poem of the Week," *Guardian Unlimited*, April 26, 2010).

7   In the 1831 version, the phrase "that little" modifies the window-niche; it then became "that shadowy" before Poe settled on "yon brilliant" in 1843. His use of the antique word "yon" creates a sense of distance in time, which parallels the physical distance between the speaker of the poem and the window niche where Helen stands.

8   A substitution made in 1843, "agate lamp" was previously an "agate book" and before that a "folded scroll" in the earliest version of the poem. Often used in the making of lamp glass, agate is a semiprecious stone that occurs in bands of varying color and transparency. Perfumed oil sometimes enhanced the sensory qualities of agate lamps. British novelist Elizabeth Caroline Grey associates agate lamps with highly refined forms of art: "Resignation to the will of God yields a softer pillow to the dying one, than the utmost refinements of art; Christian faith beams more sweetly on the closing lid, than the attempered light shed by perfumed oil from an agate lamp" (*Hyacinthe; or, The Contrast* [London: James Cochrane, 1835], 231).

9   In Greek, psyche means soul and butterfly. The sight of Helen holding a lamp recalls to the speaker's mind the image of Psyche, beloved of Cupid, whose lamp marks a crucial moment in traditional stories about her. Not wishing to reveal his identity, Cupid visits his lover at night, always under the cloak of darkness. Curious to see what he looks like, Psyche one night lights a lamp to spy on him while he sleeps. When a drop of lamp oil accidentally falls on Cupid, he wakes and flees.

"To One in Paradise" originally appeared within "The Visionary" (1834), better known by its later title, "The Assignation." Thomas Mabbott calls the tale "the most romantic story" Poe ever wrote and the first of his imaginative works to treat one of his favorite themes, the death of a beautiful woman (Thomas Ollive Mabbott, ed., Collected Works of Edgar Allan Poe, *3 vols. [Cambridge, MA: The Belknap Press of Harvard University Press, 1969–1978], II, 148–149). It concerns an impossible love triangle—between an English poet, clearly modeled on Lord Byron, his beloved, and her much older aristocratic husband. The assignation in question is the anticipated union of the two star-crossed lovers in the afterlife (they enter a suicide pact). Within the context of the tale, the untitled poem is the composition of the male lover/Byronic protagonist. As a stand-alone poem, "To One in Paradise" appeared first as "To Ianthe in Heaven" and then "To One Beloved" before Poe settled on the final title. No less a poet and critic than William Carlos Williams considered it Poe's best poem.*

1   The poem is an echo-chamber of allusions. The phrase "green isle in the sea" appears in Shelley's "Lines Written among the Euganean Hills," but Poe may not be in debt to Shelley in this particular instance: it was a proverbial phrase. However, the words "dim gulf" late in the poem echo Shelley's *The Revolt of Islam*, canto III, stanza 1, and Henry Kirke White's "Written in the Prospect of Death," line 30. Poe took the phrase "thunder-blasted tree" in the third stanza from John G. C. Brainard's "Address to Connecticut River," line 105. As these examples indicate, poetry writing was for Poe a collective process. In his view, a poem was an approximation of the ideal beauty of the heavens. By drawing on the poetry of the past, new poets could bring their work ever closer to ideal beauty.

2   John 8:12: "Then spake Jesus again unto them, saying, I am the light of the world: he that followeth me shall not walk in darkness, but shall have the light of life."

3   The concluding stanza contains some of Poe's most famous and quoted lines of poetry. In *Batman* (Twentieth-Century Fox, 1966), a feature-length film based on the television series, Bruce Wayne (Adam West) recites lines 21–24. The Alan Parsons Project incorporates the stanza as part of its concept album, *Tales of Mystery and Imagination* (Twentieth-Century Fox, 1976). And a recent progressive rock band, Grey Eye Glances, takes its name from this

To One in Paradise

Thou wast that all to me, love,
     For which my soul did pine—
A green isle in the sea,[1] love,
     A fountain and a shrine,
All wreathed with fairy fruits and flowers,
     And all the flowers were mine.

Ah, dream too bright to last!
     Ah, starry Hope! that didst arise
But to be overcast!
     A voice from out the Future cries,
"On! on!"—but o'er the Past
     (Dim gulf!) my spirit hovering lies
Mute, motionless, aghast!

For, alas! alas! with me
     The light of Life[2] is o'er!
     No more—no more—no more—
(Such language holds the solemn sea
     To the sands upon the shore)
Shall bloom the thunder-blasted tree,
     Or the stricken eagle soar!

In this scene from *Batman* (1966), millionaire philanthropist Bruce Wayne (Adam West) flirts with Miss Kitka (Lee Meriwether), who, unbeknownst to him, is really Catwoman in disguise. Her beauty inspires Bruce Wayne to recite the first four lines of the final stanza of "To One in Paradise." It is appropriate that Batman can quote Poe. Bob Kane, who originally conceived the character for the comic books, came up with the idea for this superhero-detective while visiting the Poe Cottage in Fordham, New York.

And all my days are trances,
    And all my nightly dreams
Are where thy grey eye glances,
    And where thy footstep gleams[3]—
In what ethereal dances,
By what eternal streams.[4]

poem. Daniel Hoffman asks, "Who cannot but be charmed by the melodiousness of rhyme and alliteration, the lulling lilt, and the indefiniteness of meaning imposed by a syntax purposely inconclusive, of the last stanza in 'To One in Paradise'?" (*Poe Poe Poe Poe Poe Poe Poe* [Garden City, NY: Doubleday, 1972], 53).

4   When this poem first appeared as part of "The Visionary," it ended with an additional stanza, which alludes to the marriage of the beloved to her older, "titled" husband:

> Alas! for that accursed time
> They bore thee o'er the billow
> From me—to titled age and crime,
> And an unholy pillow—
> From Love, and from our misty clime
> Where weeps the silver willow!

Poe initially arranged to publish "The Raven" in the February 1845 issue of the American Review, *but his friend Nathaniel P. Willis obtained an advance copy of the* American Review *and published the poem under Poe's name in the New York* Evening Mirror, *January 29, 1845. In his headnote to the poem, Willis remarked, "It will stick to the memory of everybody who reads it." In the* American Review, *according to the magazine's policy, "The Raven" appeared pseudonymously—by "Quarles"—but since Willis had already identified the work as Poe's, news of his authorship spread quickly. Magazines and newspapers across the United States and Great Britain soon reprinted "The Raven," and, as Willis predicted, the poem did indeed stick. Everywhere, it seemed, people thrilled at its incantatory power. The word "Nevermore" was on everyone's lips. Poe's nickname became "Raven," and, for a time, he was the darling of New York literary society, invited to the most fashionable soirées and lionized by the leading literary women of the day. If ever a poem was designed for oral recitation, it is "The Raven." Its insistent meter and its rhyme and internal rhyme scheme of unusual complexity also lent it to parody, of which many examples were soon forthcoming: "The Owl," by Sarles; "The Veto," by Snarles; "A Vision," also by Snarles; "The Craven," by Poh!; "The Whippoorwill"; and "The Turkey." "'The Raven' has had a great 'run,' Thomas," Poe boasted in a letter of May 4, 1845, to his friend F. W. Thomas, "but I wrote it for the express purpose of running—just as I did the 'Gold-Bug,' you know. The bird beat the bug, though, all hollow" (*Collected Letters of Edgar Allan Poe, ed. John Ward Ostrom, Burton R. Pollin, and Jeffrey A. Savoye, 2 vols. [New York: Gordian Press, 2008], I, 505).*

1 "The Raven" has eighteen stanzas of six lines each. The meter, or pattern of emphasis, is trochaic, that is, each metrical foot is composed of an accented syllable followed by an unaccented syllable. The pounding meter, the rhyme and internal rhyme scheme of fiendish complexity, Poe's use of alliteration ("weak and weary"), and the catchy refrain invite oral recitation and memorization. The response of John M. Daniel, editor of the *Southern Literary Messenger*, gives some sense of the contemporary appreciation of the musical elements of the poem: the poem has "a versification indescribably sweet and wonderfully difficult—winding and convoluted about like the mazes of some complicated overture by Beethoven. To all who have a strong perception, of tune there is a music in it which haunts the ear long after reading" (I. N. Walker, ed., *Edgar Allan Poe: The Critical Heritage* [New York: Routledge and Kegan Paul, 1986], 147). More recently, Jerome McGann has ar-

The Raven

Once upon a midnight dreary, while I pondered, weak and weary,[1]
Over many a quaint and curious volume of forgotten lore[2]—
While I nodded, nearly napping, suddenly there came a tapping,
As of some one gently rapping, rapping at my chamber door.[3]
"'Tis some visiter," I muttered, "tapping at my chamber door—
    Only this and nothing more."

Ah, distinctly I remember it was in the bleak December;
And each separate dying ember wrought its ghost upon the floor.
Eagerly I wished the morrow;—vainly I had sought to borrow
From my books surcease of sorrow[4]—sorrow for the lost Lenore[5]—
For the rare and radiant maiden whom the angels name Lenore—
    Nameless *here* for evermore.

And the silken, sad, uncertain rustling of each purple curtain[6]
Thrilled me—filled me with fantastic terrors never felt before;
So that now, to still the beating of my heart, I stood repeating
"'Tis some visiter entreating entrance at my chamber door—
Some late visiter entreating entrance at my chamber door;—
    This it is and nothing more."

Presently my soul grew stronger; hesitating then no longer,
"Sir," said I, "or Madam, truly your forgiveness I implore;
But the fact is I was napping, and so gently you came rapping,
And so faintly you came tapping, tapping at my chamber door,

"The Room Where 'The Raven' Was Written," from William F. Gill, *The Life of Edgar Allan Poe* (New York: C. T. Dillingham, 1877). After Poe moved to New York in 1844, he rented rooms in a farmhouse near 84th St. from Mr. and Mrs. Patrick Henry Brennan. As Poe wrote "The Raven," so the story goes, he tossed the manuscript pages on the floor, and the Brennans' teenage daughter Martha gathered and arranged them for him.

gued that Poe's poetic intention is less the creation of meaning than the "rhythmical creation of beauty": "The method of Poe's poetry is less a function of what it means than of how it works" (*The Poet Edgar Allan Poe: Alien Angel* [Cambridge: Harvard University Press, 2014], 127).

2   The speaker of the poem is a scholar and antiquarian. In "The Philosophy of Composition," Poe's mock-serious essay about how he composed his widely popular poem, he refers more explicitly to the speaker as a "student."

3   In "The Philosophy of Composition," Poe says he deliberately chose the chamber of the bereaved lover as his setting for "The Raven" because "a close *circumscription of space* is absolutely necessary to the effect of insulated incident:—it has the force of a frame to a picture. It has an indisputable moral power in keeping concentrated the attention, and, of course, must not be confounded with mere unity of place" (*Essays and Reviews*, ed. G. R. Thompson [New York: Library of America, 1984], 21).

4   "The Philosophy of Composition" contains Poe's often-quoted declaration that the death of a beautiful woman is "the most poetical topic in the world." But Poe hastens to add, "and equally is it beyond doubt that the lips best suited for such topic are those of a bereaved lover" (*Essays*, 19).

5   Poe may have taken the name from "Lenore" (1773), a ballad by the popular German lyric poet Gottfried August Bürger, which Karl von Holtei had adapted for the stage as *Lenore* (1829). Bürger's poem exerted an enormous influence on Romantic literature and ballad writing of the late eighteenth and early nineteenth centuries. Of course, Poe had earlier used the name in "Lenore" (1843), yet another of his poems that concerns itself with the death of a beautiful woman.

6   Elizabeth Barrett Browning's "Lady Geraldine's Courtship" (1844) inspired some of the poem's imagery and more significantly gave Poe his metrical structure:

> With a murmurous stir, uncertain, in the air, the purple
>   curtain
> Swelleth in and swelleth out around her motionless pale
>   brows;
> While the gliding of the river sends a rippling noise for ever,
> Through the open casement whitened by the moonlight's
>   slant repose.

In his January 11, 1845, *Broadway Journal* review of Barrett Browning's *Drama of Exile and Other Poems*, Poe calls "Lady Geraldine's Courtship" a "palpable imitation of Tennyson's 'Locksley Hall.'" Poe's dedication of *The Raven and Other Poems* to Barrett Browning, Mabbott says, is "a tacit recognition of his own similar debt to her" (Thomas Ollive Mabbott, ed., *Collected Works of Edgar Allan Poe*, 3 vols. [Cambridge, MA: The Belknap Press of Harvard University Press, 1969–1978], I, 356–357). Dennis Eddings goes further: he sees "The Raven" as a parody of "Lady Geraldine's Courtship" ("Theme and Parody in 'The Raven,'" *Poe and His Times: The Artist and His Milieu*, ed. Benjamin Franklin Fisher [Baltimore: Edgar Allan Poe Society, 1990], 215).

7   "The idea of making the lover suppose, in the first instance, that the flapping of the wings of the bird against the shutter, is a 'tapping' at the door," Poe says in "The Philosophy of Composition," "originated in a wish to increase, by prolonging, the reader's curiosity, and in a desire to admit the incidental effect arising from the lover's throwing open the door, finding all dark, and thence adopting the half-fancy that it was the spirit of his mistress that knocked" (*Essays*, 21–22).

8   "I made the night tempestuous, first, to account for the Raven's seeking admission," Poe explains, "and secondly, for the effect of contrast with the (physical) serenity within the chamber" (*Essays*, 22).

John Tenniel, illustration from *The Poetical Works of Edgar Allan Poe*, 1858.

That I scarce was sure I heard you"—here I opened wide the
    door;—
    Darkness there and nothing more.[7]

Deep into that darkness peering, long I stood there wondering,
    fearing,
Doubting, dreaming dreams no mortal ever dared to dream be-
    fore;
But the silence was unbroken, and the stillness gave no token,
And the only word there spoken was the whispered word, "Le-
    nore?"
This I whispered, and an echo murmured back the word, "Le-
    nore!"—
    Merely this and nothing more.

Back into the chamber turning, all my soul within me burning,
Soon again I heard a tapping somewhat louder than before.
"Surely," said I, "surely that is something at my window lattice;
Let me see, then, what thereat is, and this mystery explore—
Let my heart be still a moment and this mystery explore;—
    'Tis the wind and nothing more!"[8]

Edward Hopper, "Quoth the Raven, 'Nevermore,'" *ca.* 1900–1906, pen and black ink on paper. Hopper (1882–1967), an American realist painter best known for his depictions of lonely cityscapes, was also an accomplished printmaker and etcher.

John Tenniel, illustration from *The Poetical Works of Edgar Allan Poe*, 1858. Sir John Tenniel (1820–1914) was an English artist best known for his illustrations for Lewis Carrol's *Alice's Adventures in Wonderland*. He was also the principal political cartoonist for *Punch* magazine for more than fifty years.

D. G. Rossetti, *The Raven, ca.* 1848. Dante Gabriel Rossetti (1828–1882), an English poet, illustrator, and painter, was an admirer of Poe's work. His enjoyment of Poe's verse is evident in both his art and his poetry. "The Blessed Damozel," one of Rossetti's most well-known poems, written when he was just eighteen years old, can be read as a response to "The Raven." Whereas Poe addressed the grief of the lover left behind when a partner has died, Rossetti reversed the perspective, expressing the yearnings of the deceased in heaven.

Joseph Ferdinand Keppler, *The Raven*, illustration from *Puck Magazine*, vol. 27, August 13, 1890. Keppler (1838–1894), the founder and illustrator of *Puck*, a weekly humor magazine, shows just how well known "The Raven" had become by the last decade of the nineteenth century. Keppler caricatures President Benjamin Harrison, emphasizing his diminutive stature and suggesting that he cannot fill the hat of his grandfather, President William Henry Harrison. On a bust of Pallas perches a raven with the face of Secretary of State James G. Blaine. Harrison and Blaine disagreed over the proposed McKinley Tariff, which raised duties on imports to protect domestic industries from foreign competition.

Udo J. Keppler, *Nevermore* (cover for *Puck Magazine*, November 7, 1900). Keppler, cartoonist and son of Joseph Ferdinand Keppler, the founder of *Puck Magazine*, depicts William Jennings Bryan, the 1900 Democratic presidential nominee, after he has just lost the election to William McKinley for the second time. As he had in 1896, Bryan campaigned on a Free-Silver platform, arguing that the United States should abandon the gold standard. The Raven's prediction, that Bryan would nevermore run for the presidency, did not come true. Bryan ran again in 1908, losing the election to William Howard Taft.

9   The raven has been a cultural icon for thousands of years, since at least the Paleolithic era, when people drew images of crows and ravens on cave walls. The French anthropologist Claude Lévi-Strauss accounts for the raven's mythic status by pointing to the fact that it is a carrion-eating animal and therefore functions as a "mediator" between life and death. In poetry and prose, the raven has a long and distinguished literary pedigree, dating back to Greek and Roman culture. In Book II of Ovid's *Metamorphoses*, for example, the raven, once a white bird, was turned black by Apollo for delivering an unwelcome message about his beloved's unfaithfulness. In John Gay's fable "The Farmer's Wife and the Raven" (1727), the sight and sound of a raven prompt the farmer's wife to scream:

> That raven on yon left hand oak
> (Curse on his ill-betiding croak)
> Bodes me no good.

In Poe's own words, the raven functions as a "bird of ill omen." In a more particular way, Poe's stately raven seems to have been inspired by the talking raven in Charles Dickens's *Barnaby Rudge* (1841), a novel that Poe reviewed in *Graham's Magazine*. In the Dickens novel, Barnaby and his pet raven, Grip, wander in and out of a story set amid the 1780 Gordon Riots in London. In Chapter 5, prompted by a sudden noise, Varden asks, "What was that—him tapping at the door?" Barnaby's mother replies, "It was in the street, I think. Hark! Yes. There again! 'Tis some one knocking softly at the shutter."

10   In ancient Greek religion, Pallas Athene is the goddess of wisdom, war strategy, handicraft, and all the arts. Poe tells us he "made the bird alight on the bust of Pallas . . . for the effect of contrast between the marble and the plumage . . . the bust of *Pallas* being chosen, first, as most in keeping with the scholarship of the lover, and, secondly, for the sonorousness of the word, Pallas, itself " (*Essays*, 22). Something Poe does not mention in "The Philosophy of Composition" is that the raven was traditionally associated with Athene. According to one fable, Athene hates the raven because of its powers of augury, so the raven makes sacrifices to Athene to appease her.

Mabbott notes in his edition that helmeted busts of the goddess of wisdom were popular mid-nineteenth century furnishings. In an April 1846 letter to Poe, Elizabeth Barrett Browning writes: "Your 'Raven' has produced a sensation, a 'fit horror,' here in England. Some of my friends are taken by the fear of it and some by the music. I hear of persons haunted by the 'Nevermore,' and one acquaintance of mine who has the misfortune of possessing a 'bust of Pal-

Open here I flung the shutter, when, with many a flirt and flutter,
In there stepped a stately Raven[9] of the saintly days of yore;
Not the least obeisance made he; not a minute stopped or stayed he;
But, with mien of lord or lady, perched above my chamber door—
Perched upon a bust of Pallas[10] just above my chamber door—
      Perched, and sat, and nothing more.

Then this ebony bird beguiling my sad fancy into smiling,
By the grave and stern decorum of the countenance it wore,
"Though thy crest be shorn and shaven, thou," I said, "art sure no craven,
Ghastly grim and ancient Raven wandering from the Nightly shore[11]—
Tell me what thy lordly name is on the Night's Plutonian[12] shore!"
      Quoth the Raven "Nevermore."[13]

Much I marvelled this ungainly fowl to hear discourse so plainly,
Though its answer little meaning—little relevancy bore;
For we cannot help agreeing that no living human being
Ever yet was blessed with seeing bird above his chamber door—
Bird or beast upon the sculptured bust above his chamber door,
      With such name as "Nevermore."

But the Raven, sitting lonely on the placid bust, spoke only
That one word, as if his soul in that one word he did outpour.
Nothing farther then he uttered—not a feather then he fluttered—
Till I scarcely more than muttered "Other friends have flown before—
On the morrow *he* will leave me, as my Hopes have flown before."
      Then the bird said "Nevermore."[14]

Startled at the stillness broken by reply so aptly spoken,
"Doubtless," said I, "what it utters is its only stock and store
Caught from some unhappy master whom unmerciful Disaster
Followed fast and followed faster[15] till his songs one burden bore—

Gustave Doré, illustration from Edgar Allan Poe's "The Raven," 1882. Harper and Brothers commissioned Doré (1832–1883) to prepare a set of images for an illustrated edition of "The Raven" edited by Edmund C. Stedman. Doré did not live to see the book, which was published in 1884, the year after his death. This image illustrates line 26 of "The Raven": "Doubting, dreaming dreams no mortal ever dared to dream before."

las' never can bear to look at it in the twilight" (Walker, ed., *Edgar Allan Poe*, 144).

11   Poe's diction echoes Luis de Camões, *The Lusiad:* "Deep in the days of yore / A holy pilgrim trod the nightly shore" (*The Lusiad; or, The Discovery of India: An Epic Poem*, trans. William Julius Mickle, 3 vols. [London: Lackington, Allen, 1809], II, 156).

12   Pertaining to the god Pluto, the ruler of the underworld, the adjective Plutonian means infernal and demonic, but it can also mean dark or gloomy.

13   In "The Philosophy of Composition," Poe explains how he searched for "a key-note in the construction of the poem—some pivot upon which the whole structure might turn." That pivot, he determined, would be the *refrain*. In poetry, the chief pleasure of the refrain has everything to do with "the sense of identity—of repetition." But he "resolved to diversify, and so vastly heighten, the effect, by adhering, in general, to the monotone of sound, while I continually varied that of thought: that is to say, I determined to produce continuously

novel effects, by the variation *of the application* of the *refrain*—the refrain itself remaining, for the most part, unvaried." Having resolved these important points, he determined that the refrain must be "brief" but "sonorous and susceptible of protracted emphasis" (*Essays*, 17–18).

Amplifying Poe's own criticial insights, Daniel Hoffman observes that with "The Raven" Poe succeeded in writing "a poem based upon the repetition of a single word, that word said o'er and o'er until its meaning becomes as nothing, or legion; the mesmeric spell of the same repeated syllables overpowering the mind of the narrator, the sonorous chiming and sorrowful repetitions of 'Nevermore' sweeping away all propensity for independent thought" (*Poe Poe Poe Poe Poe Poe Poe*, 74).

14   Poe says that this stanza marks an important dividing point in the poem's psychological drama. In a kind of delightful "self-torture," the speaker of the poem hereafter models the questions he puts to the bird in such a way "to bring him, the lover, the most luxury of sorrow, through the anticipated answer 'Nevermore'" (*Essays*, 24).

15   *Midsummer Night's Dream*, III.ii.416: "I followed fast, but faster did he fly."

16   Songs of mourning.

17   The highest order of angels.

18   According to Poe's friend Frederick W. Thomas, contemporary readers disliked this line, finding it absurd that angels' feet could make tinkling sounds on the carpet ("tufted floor"). Readers in later generations have disliked the line as well. Dennis Eddings suggests that its awkwardness is deliberate. As a poet, the bereaved lover cannot always control his mode of expression. Poe defended his imagery with reference to Isaiah 3:16: "Moreover the Lord saith, Because the daughters of Zion are haughty, and walk with stretched forth necks and wanton eyes, walking and mincing as they go, and making a tinkling with their feet" (J. H. Whitty, ed., *The Complete Poems of Edgar Allan Poe* [Boston: Houghton Mifflin, 1911], 195).

19   Nepenthe, a magic potion extending back to classical mythology, is said to make a person forget the past and so has the power to chase away sorrow.

20   The Common Raven (Corvus corax) is quite adept at imitating human speech. The clause "quoth the Raven" finds an antecedent in John Gay's "The Farmer's Wife and the Raven" (1727):

> Dame, quoth the Raven, spare your oaths,
> Unclench your fist, and wipe your cloaths.

21   Jeremiah 8:22: "Is there no balm in Gilead; is there no physician there? why then is not the health of the daughter of my people recovered?"

Till the dirges[16] of his Hope that melancholy burden bore
    Of 'Never—nevermore.'"

But the Raven still beguiling my sad fancy into smiling,
Straight I wheeled a cushioned seat in front of bird, and bust and
        door;
Then, upon the velvet sinking, I betook myself to linking
Fancy unto fancy, thinking what this ominous bird of yore—
What this grim, ungainly, ghastly, gaunt, and ominous bird of
        yore
    Meant in croaking "Nevermore."

This I sat engaged in guessing, but no syllable expressing
To the fowl whose fiery eyes now burned into my bosom's core;
This and more I sat divining, with my head at ease reclining
On the cushion's velvet lining that the lamp-light gloated o'er,
But whose velvet-violet lining with the lamp-light gloating o'er,
    She shall press, ah, nevermore!

Then, methought, the air grew denser, perfumed from an unseen
        censer
Swung by seraphim[17] whose foot-falls tinkled on the tufted floor.[18]
"Wretch," I cried, "thy God hath lent thee—by these angels he
        hath sent thee
Respite—respite and nepenthe,[19] from thy memories of Lenore;
Quaff, oh quaff this kind nepenthe and forget this lost Lenore!"
    Quoth the Raven "Nevermore."[20]

"Prophet!" said I, "thing of evil!—prophet still, if bird or
        devil!—
Whether Tempter sent, or whether tempest tossed thee here
        ashore,
Desolate yet all undaunted, on this desert land enchanted—
On this home by Horror haunted—tell me truly, I implore—
Is there—*is* there balm in Gilead?[21]—tell me—tell me, I im-
        plore!"
    Quoth the Raven "Nevermore."

Edouard Manet, illustration for "The Raven," 1875. This illustration forms part of *Le Corbeau*, a French edition of "The Raven" translated by Stephane Mallarmé and illustrated by Manet. In its review, the *Paris-Journal* said that Manet "transposed from one art into another the nightmare atmosphere and hallucinations that are so powerfully expressed in the works of Edgar Poe" (quoted in Kevin J. Hayes, "One-Man Modernist," in *The Cambridge Companion to Edgar Allan Poe* [New York: Cambridge University Press, 2002], 227).

"Prophet!" said I, "thing of evil!—prophet still, if bird or devil!
By that Heaven that bends above us—by that God we both
    adore—
Tell this soul with sorrow laden if, within the distant Aidenn,[22]
It shall clasp a sainted maiden whom the angels name Lenore—
Clasp a rare and radiant maiden whom the angels name Lenore."
    Quoth the Raven "Nevermore."

22 Poe had first used the word "Aidenn" in "The Conversation of Eiros and Charmion" (1839). Derived from the Arabic "And," it means Eden or Heaven.

23   "It will be observed that the words 'from out my heart,'" Poe says, "involve the first metaphorical expression in the poem. . . . The reader begins now to regard the Raven as emblematical—but it is not until the very last line of the very last stanza, that the intention of making him emblematical of *Mournful and Never-ending Remembrance* is permitted distinctly to be seen" (*Essays*, 25).

24   The success of "The Raven" made Poe a popular guest in New York's literary salons, where he gave readings of his poem. On January 7, 1846, one acquaintance wrote: "I meet Mr. Poe very often at the receptions. He is the observed of all observers. His stories are thought wonderful, and to hear him repeat the Raven, which he does very quietly, is an event in one's life. People seem to think there is something uncanny about him, and the strangest stories are told, and, what is more, *believed*, about his mesmeric experiences, at the mention of which he always smiles. His smile is captivating! . . . Everybody wants to know him; but only a very few people seem to get well acquainted with him" (quoted in Sarah Helen Whitman, "Introductory Letter," in Eugene L. Didier, *The Life and Poems of Edgar Allan Poe* [New York: W. J. Widdleton, 1879], 13).

"Be that word our sign of parting, bird or fiend!" I shrieked, up-
        starting—
"Get thee back into the tempest and the Night's Plutonian shore!
Leave no black plume as a token of that lie thy soul hath spoken!
Leave my loneliness unbroken!—quit the bust above my door!
Take thy beak from out my heart,[23] and take thy form from off my
        door!"
        Quoth the Raven "Nevermore."

And the Raven, never flitting, still is sitting, *still* is sitting
On the pallid bust of Pallas just above my chamber door;
And his eyes have all the seeming of a demon's that is dreaming,
And the lamp-light o'er him streaming throws his shadow on the
        floor;
And my soul from out that shadow that lies floating on the floor
        Shall be lifted—nevermore![24]

Ulalume: A Ballad

The skies they were ashen and sober;[1]
   The leaves they were crispéd and sere[2]—
   The leaves they were withering and sere:
It was night, in the lonesome October
   Of my most immemorial year:[3]
It was hard by the dim lake of Auber,
   In the misty mid region of Weir:[4]—
It was down by the dank tarn of Auber,
   In the ghoul-haunted woodland[5] of Weir.

Here once, through an alley Titanic,[6]
   Of cypress,[7] I roamed with my Soul—
   Of cypress, with Psyche, my Soul.[8]
These were days when my heart was volcanic
   As the scoriac[9] rivers that roll—
   As the lavas that restlessly roll
Their sulphurous currents down Yaanek,[10]
   In the ultimate climes of the Pole—
That groan as they roll down Mount Yaanek,
   In the realms of the Boreal Pole.[11]

Our talk had been serious and sober,
   But our thoughts they were palsied and sere—
   Our memories were treacherous and sere;
For we knew not the month was October,
   And we marked not the night of the year—
   (Ah, night of all nights in the year!)[12]

"Ulalume" has caused considerable difficulty for readers ever since its publication. In an article in the February 1863 issue of the Sixpenny Magazine, Poe's friend Mary Gove writes of her appreciation of the poem's musicality but says she remained as perplexed by it as the other members of her book club: "Heaven forgive us, we could not make head or tail to it. It might as well have been in any of the lost languages, for any meaning we could extract from its melodious numbers." More recently, Daniel Hoffman registers his own frustration with the poem: "For years 'Ulalume' made me sick. I refused to surrender my will, my rhythms, my hold on the reality of language, to go along on the trip [Poe's] melancholy ballad-singer describes" (Poe Poe Poe Poe Poe Poe Poe [Garden City, NY: Doubleday, 1972], 70).

Another of the poems concerning the death of a beautiful woman and a grief-stricken lover, "Ulalume" conveys through its monotonous repetitions and otherworldly geography (the "dank tarn of Auber," "Mount Yaanek," the "ghoul-haunted woodland of Weir") a mood of weariness, and hopefulness mixed with fear, as the speaker searches for the "Lethean peace of the skies." Its dramatic structure can be summarized as follows: on the anniversary of his beloved's death, the speaker of the poem, accompanied by the winged Psyche, a personification of his spirit or mind, sets out on a journey that ends with the shocking recognition that he has traveled the same path before. He has arrived at the tomb of his beloved Ulalume. Many readers have seen the poem's action as spiritual or psychological and its weird landscape as a mirror of the speaker's inner torment. Jerome McGann argues that the poem is less concerned with "a psychic condition than a poetical figure of deep estrangement that is available to the reader and not the speaker" (The Poet Edgar Allan Poe: Alien Angel [Cambridge: Harvard University Press, 2014], 143).

"Ulalume" began as an answer to a challenge. The Rev. Cotesworth P. Bronson, a well-known teacher of elocution, dared Poe to write something suitable for recitation, a poem filled with a wide variety of vocal expression. Poe first published the poem as "To———. Ulalume: A Ballad" in the December 1847 issue of the American Review. Though a ballad in name, it bears little resemblance to traditional narrative ballads beyond its musicality and its use of incremental repetition. "Ulalume" (pronounced Oo'la Loom, to rhyme with "tomb") is Poe's own creation, a portmanteau that, as Mabbott points out, combines "the elements of the Latin verb ululare, to wail (the English cognate), and lumen, a light—Light of Sorrow" (Thomas Ollive Mabbott, ed., Collected Works of Edgar Allan Poe, 3 vols. [Cambridge, MA: The Belknap Press of Harvard University Press, 1969–1978], I, 419).

1   Ashen is a pale shade of gray. The word "sober" in this instance has several possible connotations. When used to describe a person's demeanor, it means serious and solemn; when used to describe natural forces, it means gentle, quiet, not violent. When used to describe color or dress (literal or figurative), it means dull, not bright. Consider Milton's use of the word in *Paradise Lost*, book IV, lines 598–599:

> Now came still Evening on, and Twilight gray
> Had in her sober Liverie all things clad

2   Dry, brittle, withered. Poe borrowed the phrase "crispéd and sere" from Philip Pendleton Cooke's poem "A Song of the Seasons," which appeared in the January 1835 issue of the *Southern Literary Messenger:* "The roebuck wandered moodily, o'er leaves all crisped and sere." Cooke, in turn, paid homage to "Ulalume" in his serialized novel *The Crime of Andrew Blair:* "Miss Araminta approached with her lover. They came on, now swiftly, now cautiously—cantering and walking by turns—like the measure of Mr. Poe's 'Ulalume'" (*Southern Literary Messenger* 15 [1849], 108).

3   T. S. Eliot, whose relationship to Poe is extremely fraught and complex, objected to Poe's use of the word "immemorial," defined by the *Oxford English Dictionary* as something "beyond memory or out of mind; ancient beyond memory or record: extremely old." "None of these meanings," Eliot says, "seems applicable to this use of the word by Poe. The year was not beyond memory—the speaker remembers one incident in it very well" (Eric W. Carlson, ed., *The Recognition of Edgar Allan Poe: Selected Criticism since 1829* [Ann Arbor: University of Michigan Press, 1966], 210). Eliot here protests too much. Poe seldom hesitated to put a word to new uses whenever he saw fit. The speaker of "Ulalume" uses the word "immemorial" in a way that makes perfect sense within the context of the poem, that is, he indicates a part of his past that he has blocked from memory.

4   Auber alludes to the popular contemporary composer Daniel Francois-Esprit Auber (1782–1871), whose many operas include *Le Lac des fées* (*The Lake of Fairies*, 1839). Robert Walter Weir (1803–1889), a contemporary American artist and teacher who served as a professor of art at the U.S. Military Academy, was on his way to becoming one of America's most significant history painters. Poe and Weir most likely became acquaintances in the 1840s, when they traveled in the same literary circles. Setting his poem in the region of Weir by the lake of Auber, Poe situates "Ulalume" within the realm of imagination. Referring specifically to opera and painting, he places "Ulalume" at the conjunction of performance and image (Kevin J. Hayes, "Putting 'Ulalume' in Its Place," *The Cambridge Companion to Edgar Allan Poe* [New York: Cambridge University Press, 2002], 199).

5   Ghouls are evil spirits that rob graves and prey on human corpses.

6   Colossal.

7   Cypress (Cupressus sempervirens) is a long-lived coniferous tree native to the Near East. It has since the time of classical antiquity been a symbol of mourning and death, and often flanks the borders and avenues of cemeteries.

8   In classical mythology, Psyche's beauty causes much pain and grief. Patrick White argues that Psyche "functions in the poem not only as a personification of soul but also as a suggestion of the sorrow in earthly love." Psyche, however, as a personification of the speaker's soul, "has no superiority of vision and can attain no knowledge of which the narrator is unaware" ("The Thing Needed: Hope and Despair in 'Ulalume,'" *Masques, Mysteries, and Mastadons: A Poe Miscellany*, ed. Benjamin F. Fisher [Baltimore: Edgar Allan Poe Society, 2006], 3–4).

9   Poe derived this unusual adjective—the first recorded use of "scoriac" in the English language—from scoriae, volcanic rock formed as part of lava flow or ejecta.

10   In Poe's lifetime, the explorer and British naval officer Sir James Clark Ross (1800–1862) charted the coastline of the Antarctic and discovered the volcanoes Mount Erebus and Mount Terror. "The discovery of an active volcano in so high a southern latitude," Ross writes, "cannot but be esteemed a circumstance of high geological importance and interest, and contribute to throw some further light on the physical construction of our globe. I named it 'Mount Erebus,' and an extinct volcano to the eastward, little inferior in height, being by measurement ten thousand nine hundred feet high, was called 'Mount Terror.'" Poe's Mount Yaanek, Patrick White observes, presents a complex image, depicting creative and destructive fire within a frozen, lifeless region (James Clark Ross, *A Voyage of Discovery and Research in the Southern and Antarctic Regions, During the Years 1839–43*, 2 vols. [London: John Murray, 1847], 217; White, "Thing Needed," 9).

11   "Generally speaking *boreal* means *northern*, from Boreas, the north wind. But," William P. Trent notes, "Poe's imagination usually turned to the South Pole, so that it seems possible that he was following the French terminology, in which 'boreal pole' is that pole of the magnetic needle which points to the South. The whole expression would then be equivalent to 'Antarctic regions'" (*Poems and Tales from the Writings of Edgar Allan Poe*, ed. William P. Trent [Boston: Houghton, Mifflin, 1898], 13).

12   Mabbott and other critics suppose that the evening in question is Halloween, or All Hallow's Eve, when spirits of the dead are free to roam the earth. On the other hand, it may be a reference to the anniversary of Ulalume's death.

Robert Walter Weir, *Landscape*, n.d., ink wash and gouache.

We noted not the dim lake of Auber,
    (Though once we had journeyed down here)
We remembered not the dank tarn of Auber,
    Nor the ghoul-haunted woodland of Weir.

And now, as the night was senescent,[13]
    And star-dials[14] pointed to morn—
    As the star-dials hinted of morn—
At the end of our path a liquescent[15]
    And nebulous lustre was born,
Out of which a miraculous crescent
    Arose with a duplicate horn—
Astarte's bediamonded crescent,
    Distinct with its duplicate horn.[16]

13   Growing old.

14   It is of course possible to determine time of evening based on the relative position of stars in the night sky, and modern rotary star maps can tell the local time quite accurately. But a garden star-dial that functions like a sundial is fantastical.

15   In the process of becoming or, in this case, resembling liquid.

16   "Astarte's bediamonded crescent" is the planet Venus, contrasted with the moon in the stanza that follows. Like the moon, Venus goes through different phases. Those with keen eyes can see its extreme crescent phase without the aid of a telescope. Astarte, a powerful divinity of Syria, has been identified with both Venus of the Greeks and Ashtoreth of the Phoenicians; Astarte, Venus, and Ashtoreth

are connected with fertility and sexuality. Daniel Hoffman entertains the possibility that the presence of Astarte "signifies that [the speaker's] heart has been drawn away from the path of Psyche—the unending worship of his dead Ulalume—toward a new love, a more gross, less pure heartfelt passion for a living woman, from which Psyche only with difficulty—and with the aid of the ghouls, or shades of the dead—redeems him" (*Poe Poe Poe Poe Poe Poe Poe*, 72–73).

17   Poe contrasts Astarte with the goddess Diana, the pure and virginal huntress, often depicted with a bow and quiver. But Diana is also the goddess of light, closely associated with the moon.

18   Ether was formerly believed to be a material substance that occupied space between the stars and planets. In the nineteenth century, the word was often used figuratively, as it is here. The phrase "ether of sighs" is proverbial. As contemporary British novelist Louisa Sidney Stanhope observes, "Lovers, proverbially living upon the ether of sighs and recollections, can make small allowance for the vulgar cravings of corporeal appetite" (*Sydney Beresford: A Tale of the Day*, 3 vols. [London: Sherwood, Gilbert, and Piper, 1835], II, 206).

19   Isaiah 66:24: "And they shall go forth, and look upon the carcases of the men that have transgressed against me: for their worm shall not die, neither shall their fire be quenched; and they shall be an abhorring unto all flesh."

20   The constellation Leo.

21   In Greek mythology, the Lethe, one of the five rivers in Hades, had the power to make those who drank from it experience total forgetfulness.

22   Resembling or characteristic of the ancient sibyls; prophetic, oracular. Patrick White observes, "The Astarte star is another example of false light, false in an ironic sense because the narrator first entirely misinterprets it as a hopefully 'Sibyllic' sign prophetic of hope, but it is actually the narrator's own self-deluding projection. The false light leads him, finally, to the true light: Ulalume, the light of death, whose name is actually intoned by Psyche as they stand before the tomb" ("Thing Needed," 7).

23   Jerome McGann glosses this and the previous stanza: "Psyche's 'mistrust' (52) as well as his own confidence (61–71) together signal—did we miss this when we

And I said—"She is warmer than Dian;[17]
    She rolls through an ether of sighs—[18]
    She revels in a region of sighs.
She has seen that the tears are not dry on
    These cheeks where the worm never dies,[19]
And has come past the stars of the Lion,[20]
    To point us the path to the skies—
    To the Lethean[21] peace of the skies—
Come up, in despite of the Lion,
    To shine on us with her bright eyes—
Come up, through the lair of the Lion,
    With love in her luminous eyes."

But Psyche, uplifting her finger,
    Said—"Sadly this star I mistrust—
    Her pallor I strangely mistrust—
Ah, hasten!—ah, let us not linger!
    Ah, fly!—let us fly!—for we must."
In terror she spoke; letting sink her
    Wings till they trailed in the dust—
In agony sobbed; letting sink her
    Plumes till they trailed in the dust—
    Till they sorrowfully trailed in the dust.

I replied—"This is nothing but dreaming.
    Let us on, by this tremulous light!
    Let us bathe in this crystalline light!
Its Sybillic[22] splendor is beaming
    With Hope and in Beauty to-night—
    See!—it flickers up the sky through the night!
Ah, we safely may trust to its gleaming
    And be sure it will lead us aright—
We safely may trust to a gleaming
    That cannot but guide us aright
Since it flickers up to Heaven through the night."[23]

Thus I pacified Psyche and kissed her,
    And tempted her out of her gloom—
    And conquered her scruples and gloom;
And we passed to the end of the vista—

But were stopped by the door of a tomb—
   By the door of a legended[24] tomb;
And I said—"What is written, sweet sister,
   On the door of this legended tomb?"
She replied—"Ulalume—Ulalume—
'Tis the vault of thy lost Ulalume!"

Then my heart it grew ashen and sober
   As the leaves that were crispéd and sere—
   As the leaves that were withering and sere—
And I cried—"It was surely October,
   On *this* very night of last year,

   That I journeyed—I journeyed down here!—
   That I brought a dread burden down here—
   On this night, of all nights in the year,
   Ah, what demon hath tempted me here?[25]
Well I know, now, this dim lake of Auber—
   This misty mid region of Weir:—
Well I know, now, this dank tarn of Auber—
   This ghoul-haunted woodland of Weir."

Said we, then—the two, then—"Ah, can it
   Have been that the woodlandish ghouls—
   The pitiful, the merciful ghouls,
To bar up our way and to ban it
   From the secret that lies in these wolds[26]—
   From the thing that lies hidden in these wolds—
Have drawn up the spectre of a planet
   From the limbo of lunary souls—
This sinfully scintillant planet[27]
   From the Hell of the planetary souls?"

were reading?—that the speaker's amnesia measures the depth of his immemorial sorrow" (*The Poet Edgar Allan Poe*, 143).

24   Bearing a legend or inscription. The *OED* identifies the word as Poe's coinage.

25   Kenneth Silverman says the demon that has tempted the speaker here "is of course himself, his Imp of the Immemorial, whose voice is the strange new music Poe contrived in 'Ulalume,' the music of Hell" (*Edgar A. Poe: Mournful and Never-Ending Remembrance* [New York: HarperCollins, 1991], 337).

26   Forest, wooded upland.

27   "Scintillant" means sparkling, twinkling. The sinfully scintillant planet is Venus.

F. R. Pickersgill, illustration from *The Poetical Works of Edgar Allan Poe*, 1858.

Among Poe's last poems, "Eldorado" appeared in the Boston-based weekly newspaper the Flag of Our Union *on April 21, 1849. Though it does not concern romantic love or mourning, Mabbott calls it the "most universal in implication, and the most intensely personal" of his poems (Thomas Ollive Mabbott, ed.,* Collected Works of Edgar Allan Poe, *3 vols. [Cambridge, MA: The Belknap Press of Harvard University Press, 1969–1978], I, 461). As a singer of songs, Poe's knight is an obvious stand-in for the poet. More particularly, it is hard not to read this late-career poem in terms of Poe's own artistic questing in the face of poverty, disappointment, and personal adversity. In a letter to his friend Frederick W. Thomas, written February 14, 1849, Poe compares literary endeavor with the search for gold: "Literature is the most noble of professions. In fact, it is about the only one fit for a man. For my own part, there is no seducing me from the path. I shall be a* littérateur, *at least, all my life; nor would I abandon the hopes which still lead me on for all the gold in California" (*Collected Letters of Edgar Allan Poe, *ed. John Ward Ostrom, Burton R. Pollin, and Jeffrey A. Savoye, 2 vols. [New York: Gordian Press, 2008], II, 770).*

1   Bedight means furnished, equipped, bedecked.

2   The word "shadow" appears in the third line of each stanza, though its meaning shifts within the poem, as does the meaning of its rhyme-word—and the poem's keyword—"Eldorado." "Borrowing a device from 'The Raven,'" Kenneth Silverman observes, "[Poe] compressed the significance of the knight's career into the changing meanings of 'shadow.' Prominently set at the turning point of each stanza, the word first means simply the lack of sunshine, then gloom, then a ghost; its deepest sense is revealed to the knight in the final stanza by the 'pilgrim shadow' . . . The pilgrim imparts what Poe had always known about Eldorado, that the way to golden treasure lies through the valley of death" (*Edgar A. Poe: Mournful and Never-Ending Remembrance* [New York: HarperCollins, 1991], 403).

Eldorado

Gaily bedight,[1]
  A gallant knight,
In sunshine and in shadow,[2]
  Had journeyed long,
  Singing a song,
In search of Eldorado.[3]

  But he grew old—
  This knight so bold—
And o'er his heart a shadow
  Fell, as he found
  No spot of ground
That looked like Eldorado.

  And, as his strength
  Failed him at length[4]
He met a pilgrim shadow—
  "Shadow," said he,
  "Where can it be—
This land of Eldorado?"

  "Over the Mountains
  Of the Moon,[5]
Down the Valley of the Shadow,[6]
  Ride, boldly ride,"[7]
  The shade replied,—
"If you seek for Eldorado!"[8]

Currier and Ives, *Gold Mining in California*, 1871.

3 El Dorado is the legendary golden city sought by Spanish and English explorers in the Americas. As Mabbott notes, by Poe's day the word was used figuratively to mean any place, venture, or scheme that might bring wealth. More particularly, it became a buzzword and nickname for California after the first significant gold strike in Northern California, at Sutter's Mill in January 1848. Within a year, 80,000 "forty-niners" had picked up and headed to the far west in search of gold. Many more would follow. Written in the early frenzied days of the California Gold Rush, Poe's poem capitalizes on the new currency of the word—something Poe's contemporary readers would have immediately understood.

4 Poe's knight calls to mind the aging hero in Tennyson's great poem "Ulysses" (1842). In the Tennyson poem, Ulysses enjoins his faithful mariners to embark on one last adventure "beyond the sunset," at a point in their storied lives when they, like Poe's seeker, are old and somewhat the worse for wear but may yet achieve "something ere the end" (lines 65–70):

> Tho' much is taken, much abides; and tho'
> We are not now that strength which in old days
> Moved earth and heaven; that which we are, we are;
> One equal temper of heroic hearts,
> Made weak by time and fate, but strong in will
> To strive, to seek, to find, and not to yield.

5 A mountain range in central Africa, the Mountains of the Moon formed the mythical source of the Nile River, but the phrase was often used, as it is here, to mean a remote place, the ends of the earth, a place beyond human knowledge. Compare lines 30–33 of Tennyson's "Ulysses," where the discontented hero speaks of his yearning desire "To follow knowledge like a sinking star, / Beyond the utmost bound of human thought."

W. Heath Robinson, illustration for "El Dorado," published in *The Poems of Edgar Allan Poe* (1900). Portraying the gallant knight as a young and virile man, Robinson depicts him as he is at the beginning of the poem, that is, before he grows old and his strength starts to fail him.

In this early scene from the movie *El Dorado* (1966), Alan Bourdillion Traherne, a.k.a. "Mississippi" (James Caan), re-cites lines from Poe's "Eldorado" to characterize the situation of John Wayne's character, Cole Thornton. The poem becomes a touchstone through the rest of the film.

6   Psalm 23:4: "Yea, though I walk through the valley of the shadow of death, I will fear no evil: for thou art with me; thy rod and thy staff they comfort me."

7   Compare the opening lines of Christopher Wordsworth's award-winning poem "The Invasion of Russia": "Ride, boldly ride! for thee the vernal gale / Breathes life and fragrance o'er the teeming vale" (*Cambridge Prize Poems*, new ed. [London: Henry Washbourne, 1847], 207).

8   In Howard Hawks's Technicolor western *El Dorado* (Paramount, 1966), starring John Wayne and Robert Mitchum, Poe's "Eldorado" is quoted several times. The film tells the story of Cole Thornton, an aging gunfighter played by John Wayne, who returns to help an old sheriff-friend battle an unscrupulous rancher. Thornton's rallying cry is the line "Ride, boldly ride." Highlighting the moral of Poe's poem, film historian Peter Bogdanovich finds it applicable to Hawks himself as well as to numerous male characters throughout his oeuvre: "Hawks and his men know this instinctively: it is not whether the goal is achieved that matters, but rather how well it is sought" ("'Ride, Boldly Ride,'" *New York*, January 21, 1974, 49).

Annabel Lee

It was many and many a year ago,[1]
   In a kingdom by the sea,
That a maiden there lived[2] whom you may know
   By the name of Annabel Lee;—
And this maiden she lived with no other thought
   Than to love and be loved by me.

She was a child and *I* was a child,[3]
   In this kingdom by the sea,
But we loved with a love that was more than love—
   I and my Annabel Lee—
With a love that the wingéd seraphs of Heaven
   Coveted her and me.

And this was the reason that, long ago,
   In this kingdom by the sea,
A wind blew out of a cloud by night
   Chilling my Annabel Lee;
So that her highborn kinsmen[4] came
   And bore her away from me,
To shut her up, in a sepulchre[5]
   In this kingdom by the sea.

The angels, not half so happy in Heaven,
   Went envying her and me:—
Yes! that was the reason (as all men know,
   In this kingdom by the sea)

"Annabel Lee" was completed and circulated in manuscript shortly before Poe's mysterious death on October 7, 1849, several days after he was found delirious at Gunner's Hall, a Baltimore tavern. The poem first appeared in print in September 1849 in the Richmond Examiner *and was widely reprinted after news of his death spread. Many women whom Poe had known—some from his youth, others from the literary circles of New York that had lionized him—claimed to be the real-life inspiration for the poem. The* Brooklyn Eagle *carried this headnote along with the poem in its October 22, 1849, edition: "The following beautiful poem is said to have been the last thing written by Poe, whose death it was our painful duty to announce only a week since. Nothing that ever came from his pen better illustrates his surpassing mastery of the rhythm and melody of English verse." "Annabel Lee" has continued to thrill new generations of readers—readers as diverse as Vladimir Nabokov and Clint Eastwood. Nabokov makes several not-so-subtle allusions to it in the famous opening chapter of* Lolita *(1955)—a novel, by the way, that he had originally planned to call "A Kingdom by the Sea." In Eastwood's directorial debut,* Play Misty for Me *(1971), the psychotic stalker played by Jessica Walter identifies with Poe's title character and quotes snippets of "Annabel Lee" to Dave Garver, the poetry-loving DJ played by Eastwood.*

1 In a lengthy review of the poetry of William Cullen Bryant (1837), Poe highlights the way in which Bryant puts the "occasional excess" of meter to good use. To further illustrate the point about excess, Poe calls attention to Wordsworth's *"many and many* a song" in "Guilt and Sorrow" (*Essays*, 418):

> There was a youth whom I had loved so long,
> That when I loved him not I cannot say.
> Mid the green mountains many and many a song
> We two had sung like gladsome birds in May.

Poe had himself used this intentional redundancy in an earlier poem, "The City in the Sea" (1845), line 21: "Up many and many a marvellous shrine."

2 This phrase comes from a popular comic song: "A Maiden There Lived in a Large Market Town," *The Universal Songster; or, Museum of Mirth*, 3 vols. (London: Jones, 1834), I, 373.

3 Edward M. Alfriend, whose father knew Poe personally, observed that Poe "was extremely fond of children . . . My father said that he would romp with them by the hour, and in their childish sports would become himself a child again" ("Unpublished Recollections of Edgar Allan Poe," *Literary Era* 8 [1901], 491).

That the wind came out of the cloud, chilling
    And killing my Annabel Lee.

But our love it was stronger by far than the love
    Of those who were older than we—
    Of many far wiser than we—
And neither the angels in Heaven above
    Nor the demons down under the sea
Can ever dissever⁶ my soul from the soul
    Of the beautiful Annabel Lee:—

For the moon never beams without bringing me dreams
    Of the beautiful Annabel Lee;
And the stars never rise but I see the bright eyes
    Of the beautiful Annabel Lee;
And so, all the night-tide, I lie down by the side
Of my darling, my darling, my life and my bride
    In her sepulchre there by the sea—
    In her tomb by the side of the sea.⁷

4   These "highborn kinsmen" are, as Richard Wilbur observes, angels—a reference to the "wingéd seraphs of Heaven" mentioned in the previous stanza. The phrase reflects Poe's association between spirituality and aristocracy ("Edgar Allan Poe," *Major Writers of America*, ed. Perry Miller [New York: Harcourt, Brace and World, 1962], 398).

5   A tomb or burial place.

6   This phrase is indebted to lines 17–20 of a popular song entitled "The Complaint" (*Universal Songster*, III, 247):

> Think you that my love can possibly rove,
> Or from you, sweet, ever dissever?
> To banish your pain, I now swear again
> I love you more dearly than ever!

7   Scott Peeples calls attention to the fact that the speaker tells us almost nothing about his beloved. We know she was "a child" who lived in a "kingdom by the sea," but she is otherwise "present to him only as an absence, as if Annabel Lee is his name for love and grief. The inextricability of those emotions is heightened by the speaker's insistence that her death resulted not from random misfortune but from their love" (*Edgar Allan Poe Revisited* [New York: Twayne, 1998], 170–171).

James McNeill Whistler, *Annabel Lee*, 1885–1887, chalk and pastel on brown paper.

Appendix: First Printings, Reprints, and Translations Published during Poe's Lifetime

What follows is a list of authorized and unauthorized printings and translations of the tales and poems of Edgar Allan Poe included in this edition that were published in books and periodicals during his lifetime, with the exception of "Annabel Lee," which appeared posthumously. Many of the reprints represent new discoveries that have not been listed in any previous bibliography. Ambitious readers may use this list as a starting point to locate additional reprints. Many new discoveries await.

Metzengerstein

Philadelphia *Saturday Courier*, January 14, 1832.
Southern Literary Messenger 2 (January 1836), 97–100.
Tales of the Grotesque and Arabesque (1840), II, 151–165.

Manuscript Found in a Bottle

Baltimore *Saturday Visiter*, October 19, 1833.
Newburyport, Massachusetts *The People's Advocate*, October 26, 1833.
Cincinnati Mirror, and Western Gazette of Literature and Science 3 (November 9, 1833), 28–30.
The Gift: A Christmas and New Year's Present for 1836, ed. Eliza Leslie (Philadelphia: E. L. Carey and A. Hart, 1835), 67–87.
Southern Literary Messenger 2 (December 1835), 33–37.
Tales of the Grotesque and Arabesque (1840), I, 111–126.
Broadway Journal 2 (October 11, 1845), 203–206.

Berenice

Southern Literary Messenger 1 (March 1835), 333–336.
Tales of the Grotesque and Arabesque (1840), II, 167–181.
Broadway Journal 1 (April 5, 1845), 217–219.
Philadelphia *Spirit of the Times*, April 11, 1845.

Morella

Southern Literary Messenger 1 (April 1835), 448–450.
Burton's Gentleman's Magazine 5 (November 1839), 264–268.

Tales of the Grotesque and Arabesque (1840), I, 9–18.
Broadway Journal 1 (June 21, 1845), 388–389.

Ligeia

American Museum of Science, Literature, and the Arts 1 (September 1838), 25–37.
Tales of the Grotesque and Arabesque (1840), I, 171–192.
New York *New World* 10 (February 15, 1845), 100–101.
Broadway Journal 2 (September 27, 1845), 171–176.
Philadelphia *Illustrated Monthly Courier* 2 (August 1, 1848), 18–19.

The Man That Was Used Up

Burton's Gentleman's Magazine 5 (August 1839), 66–70.
Tales of the Grotesque and Arabesque (1840), I, 59–74.
Prose Romances of Edgar Allan Poe (Philadelphia: W. H. Graham, 1843), 40–48.
New Mirror 1 (September 9, 1843), 362–365.
Broadway Journal 2 (August 9, 1845), 68–71.
Philadelphia *Spirit of the Times*, September 12–13, 1845.

The Fall of the House of Usher

Burton's Gentleman's Magazine 5 (September 1839), 145–152.
Tales of the Grotesque and Arabesque (1840), I, 75–103.
Bentley's Miscellany 8 (August 1840), 158–170.
Boston Notion, September 5, 1840.
Tales (1845), 64–82.
The Prose Writers of America, ed. Rufus Wilmot Griswold (Philadelphia: Carey and Hart, 1847), 524–530.
Oquawka Spectator, August 23 and 30, 1848.

William Wilson

The Gift: A Christmas and New Year's Present for 1840, ed. Eliza Leslie (Philadelphia: Carey and Hart, 1839), 229–253.

Edgar Allan Poe House, 530 North Seventh Street, Philadelphia, PA. When Poe lived here with his wife, Virginia, and his mother-in-law, Maria Clemm, in the early 1840s, the landscaping was much more lush than this modern photograph indicates. Fruit trees grew in the yard; the garden was filled with flowers; and ivy crept partway up the walls of this tall but very narrow cottage.

Burton's Gentleman's Magazine 5 (October 1839), 205–212.
Tales of the Grotesque and Arabesque (1840), I, 27–57.
Broadway Journal 2 (30 August 1845), 113–119.

Why the Little Frenchman Wears His Hand in a Sling

Tales of the Grotesque and Arabesque (1840), II, 183–191.
Bentley's Miscellany 8 (July 1840), 45–48, "The Irish Gentleman and the Little Frenchman."
New York *Spirit of the Times* 10 [August 1, 1840], 254–255, "The Irish Gentleman and the Little Frenchman."
Broadway Journal 2 (September 6, 1845), 129–131.

The Business Man

Burton's Gentleman's Magazine 6 (February 1840), 87–89, "Peter Pendulum, The Business Man."
Providence Daily Journal, May 10, 1843.
Manufacturers and Farmers Providence and Pawtucket Advertiser, May 11, 1843.
Broadway Journal 2 (August 2, 1845), 49–52.

The Philosophy of Furniture

Burton's Gentleman's Magazine 6 (May 1840), 243–245.
Philadelphia *Spirit of the Times*, May 16, 1840.

Broadway Journal 1 (May 3, 1845), 273–275.
New York Mirror, May 17, 1845.

The Man of the Crowd

Burton's Gentleman's Magazine 7 (December 1840), 267–270.
Tales (1845), 219–228.

The Murders in the Rue Morgue

Graham's Magazine 18 (April 1841), 166–179.
Prose Romances of Edgar Allan Poe (Philadelphia: W. H. Graham, 1843), 9–40.
Tales (1845), 116–150.
La Quotidienne, June 11, 12, and 13, 1846, "Un Meurtre sans exemple dans les fastes de la justice," trans. Gustave Brunet.
Le Commerce, October 12, 1846, "Une Sanglante énigme," trans. E. D. Forgues.
La Démocratie pacifique, January 21, 1847, "L'Assassinat de la Rue Morgue," trans. Isabelle Meunier.

A Descent into the Maelström

Graham's Magazine 18 (May 1841), 235–241.
Baltimore *Sun*, May 11 and 12, 1841.
Baltimore *Weekly Sun*, May 15, 1841.

Portland Transcript, May 15, 1841.

Tales (1845), 83–99.

Revue britannique, 6th ser. 5 (September 1846), 182–203, trans. E. D. Forgues.

Frankfurter Konversationsblatt, October 14–18 and 20–21, 1846, "Auf dem Maelstrom: Reiseerinnerungen aus Norwegen."

La Démocratie pacifique, September 24 and 27, 1847, trans. Isabelle Meunier.

Boston Weekly Museum and Literary Portfolio, May 26, 1849.

The Oval Portrait

Graham's Magazine 20 (April 1842), 200–201, "Life in Death."

Broadway Journal 1 (April 26, 1845), 264–265.

The Masque of the Red Death

Graham's Magazine 20 (May 1842), 257–259, "The Mask of the Red Death."

Baltimore *Saturday Visiter*, April 30, 1842.

Literary Souvenir, June 4, 1842.

Iris and Literary Repository 1 (July 1842), 113–116.

Broadway Journal 2 (July 19, 1845), 17–19.

The Pit and the Pendulum

The Gift: A Christmas and New Year's Present. Mdcccxliii (Philadelphia: Carey and Hart, 1842), 133–151.

New-York Spectator, October 22, 1842.

Pennsylvania Inquirer and National Gazette, November 15, 1842.

New London, Connecticut *People's Advocate*, November 23, 1842.

Broadway Journal 1 (May 17, 1845), 307–311.

The Tell-Tale Heart

The Pioneer 1 (January 1843), 29–31.

Philadelphia *United States Gazette*, January 6, 1843.

New York Sun, January 11, 1843.

Philadelphia *Dollar Newspaper*, January 25, 1843.

London *Cleaves Penny Gazette*, June 17, 1843, "The Tell-Tale Heart, or, The Unconscious Madman."

Montreal *Literary Garland: A Canadian Magazine of Tales, Sketches, Poetry, Music, Engravings*, new ser. 2 (July 1844), 333–335, "Confession of a Maniac."

Broadway Journal 2 (August 23, 1845), 97–99.

Philadelphia *Spirit of the Times*, August 27, 1845.

Boston Daily Mail, August 30-September 1, 1845.

Boston Weekly Bee, December 20, 1845.

The Gold-Bug

Philadelphia *Dollar Newspaper*, June 21–28, 1843.

Philadelphia *Saturday Courier*, June 24, July 1 and 8, 1843.

Pennsylvania Inquirer and National Gazette, July 4, 6, and 7, 1843.

Baltimore *Sun*, July 24, 25, 26, and 27, 1843.

Baltimore *Weekly Sun*, July 29, 1843.

Montrose, Pennsylvania *Volunteer*, August 3, 10, and 17, 1843.

Revue britannique, 5th ser., 30 (November 1845), 168–212, "Le Scarabée d'or," trans. Amédée Pichot.

The Gold Bug (London: Arthur Dyson, 1846–1847?).

Novaja biblioteka dlja vospitanija [*New Library for Education*] 1 (1847), 154–220, "Zolotoj žuk."

Biblioteka dlja čtenija [*Library for Reading*] 89 (1848), 186–208, "Amerikanskij iskatel' kladov" [An American Searcher for Treasures].

La Démocratie pacifique, May 23, 25, 27, 1848, "Le Scarabée d'or," trans. Isabelle Meunier.

Le Journal du Loiret, June 17, 20, 22, and 24, 1848, "Le Scarabée d'or."

Boston Museum, July 22, 1848.

Maine Farmer, August 31 and September 7, 1848.

The Black Cat

United States Saturday Post, August 19, 1843.

Tales (1845), 37–46.

La Démocratie pacifique, January 27, 1847, "Le Chat Noir," trans. Isabelle Meunier.

Pictorial National Library 1 (November 1848), 255–259.

The Purloined Letter

The Gift: A Christmas, New Year, and Birthday Present. Mdcccxlv, ed. Eliza Leslie (Philadelphia: Carey and Hart, 1845), 41–61.

Chambers's Edinburgh Journal, new ser. 2 (November 30, 1844), 343–347. An abridged version.

Littell's Living Age 4 (January 18, 1845), 135–139. A reprint of the abridged version from *Chamber's*.

Philadelphia *Spirit of the Times*, January 20 and 22, 1845.

New York Weekly News, January 25, 1845.

Lowell Courier, January 28, 1845.

Tales (1845), 200–218.

Stockholm *Dagligt Allehanda*, June 30 and July 1, 1847.

The Facts in the Case of M. Valdemar

American Review: A Whig Journal 2 (December 1845), 561–565, "The Facts of M. Valdemar's Case."

Boston Courier, December 12, 1845.

Boston Semi-Weekly Courier, December 15, 1845.

Boston Weekly Courier, December 18, 1845.

Baltimore *Saturday Visiter*, December 20, 1845.

Broadway Journal 2 (December 20, 1845), 365–368.

Philadelphia *Spirit of the Times*, December 23 and 24, 1845.

Rochester *Daily Advertiser*, December 24, 1845.

Poe's bedroom in Edgar Allan Poe House, 530 North Seventh Street, Philadelphia, PA.

London *Sunday Times,* January 4, 1846, "Mesmerism in America: Astounding and Horrifying Narrative."

London *Morning Post,* January 5, 1846.

Popular Record of Modern Science, January 10, 1846.

Mesmerism "In Articulo Mortis": An Astounding and Horrifying Narrative, Shewing the Extraordinary Power of Mesmerism in Arresting the Progress of Death (London: Short, 1846).

Stockholm *Dagligt Allehanda,* February 12, 1846.

Boston Museum, August 18, 1849.

The Cask of Amontillado

Godey's Magazine and Lady's Book 33 (November 1846), 216–218.

New England Weekly Review, November 14, 1846.

Hop-Frog

Flag of Our Union, March 17, 1849, "Hop-Frog: or, the Eight Chained Ourang-Outangs."

Maine Farmer 17 (March 29, 1849), 4.

To Helen

Poems: Second Edition (New York: Elam Bliss, 1831), 39.

Atkinson's Casket 5 (May 1831), 239.

Southern Literary Messenger 2 (March 1836), 238.

Graham's Magazine 19 (September 1841), 123.

Philadelphia *Saturday Museum,* March 4, 1843.

Graham's Magazine 27 (February 1845), 51.

The Raven and Other Poems (New York: Wiley and Putnam, 1845), 91.

The Lover's Gift; or, Tributes to the Beautiful, ed. E. Oakes Smith (Hartford: Henry S. Parsons, 1848), 108.

To One in Paradise

Lady's Book 8 (January 1834), 42–43, within "The Visionary."

Burton's Gentleman's Magazine 5 (July 1839), 49, "To Ianthe in Heaven."

American Melodies, ed. George P. Morris (New York: Linen and Fennell, 1841), 186–187, "To Ianthe in Heaven."

Saturday Evening Post, January 9, 1841, "To One Beloved."

Philadelphia *Saturday Museum,* March 4, 1843.

Broadway Journal 1 (May 10, 1845), 295.

The Raven and Other Poems (1845), 23.

The Raven

New York *Evening Mirror,* January 29, 1845.

American Review 1 (February 1845), 143–145.

New York *Morning News,* February 3, 1845.

New-York Tribune, February 4, 1845.

Alexandria Gazette, February 8, 1845.

Broadway Journal 1 (February 8, 1845), 90.

New-York Mirror, February 8, 1845.

New-York Weekly Tribune, February 8, 1845.

Ellicott City, Maryland *Howard District Press*, February 15, 1845.

Pennsylvania Inquirer and National Gazette, February 15, 1845.

Boston Post, February 17, 1845.

Liberator 15 (February 21, 1845), 32.

New World 10 (February 22, 1845), 120.

Western Literary Messenger 4 (February 22, 1845), 237–238.

Southern Literary Messenger 11 (March 1845), 186–188.

Exeter News-Letter and Rockingham Advertiser, March 3, 1845.

Ogdensburgh, New York *St. Lawrence Republican*, March 4, 1845.

Massachusetts Temperance Standard, June 6, 1845.

London *Critic* 2 (June 14, 1845), 148.

Littell's Living Age 6 (July 26, 1845), 185–186.

New York *Literary Emporium* 2 (December 1845), 376–378.

A Plain System of Elocution: or, Logical and Musical Reading and Declamation, ed. George Vandenhoff, 2nd ed. (New York: C. Shepard, 1845), 264–267.

The Raven and Other Poems (1845), 1–5.

London *World of Fashion* 266 (May 1, 1846), 102–104.

Birmingham Journal, June 28, 1845.

Philadelphia *Saturday Courier*, July 25, 1846.

Ladies Wreath and Literary Gatherer, December 1846.

Poets and Poetry of America, ed. Rufus W. Griswold, 8th ed. (Philadelphia: Carey and Hart, 1847), 432–433.

Oquawka Spectator, September 12, 1849.

Richmond *Semi-Weekly Examiner*, September 25, 1849.

Ulalume: A Ballad

American Review 6 (December 1847), 599, "To ———. Ulalume: A Ballad."

Home Journal, January 1, 1848.

Philadelphia *Saturday Courier*, January 22, 1848.

Providence Journal, November 22, 1848.

Literary World 4 (March 3, 1849), 202.

Portland Transcript, September 8, 1849.

Eldorado

Boston *Flag of Our Union*, April 21, 1849.

Annabel Lee

New-York Daily Tribune, October 9, 1849.

Further Reading

The following bibliography of biographical and critical works about Edgar Allan Poe lists books only. There are numerous excellent periodical essays that illuminate Poe's life and writings, many of which are cited in the annotations to the present edition.

Allen, Michael L. *Poe and the British Magazine Tradition*. New York: Oxford University Press, 1969.

Anderson, Douglas. *Pictures of Ascent in the Fiction of Edgar Allan Poe*. New York: Palgrave Macmillan, 2009.

Asselineau, Roger. *Edgar Allan Poe*. Minneapolis: University of Minnesota Press, 1970.

Baudelaire, Charles. *Baudelaire on Poe: Critical Papers*. Trans. and ed. Lois Hyslop and Francis E. Hyslop, Jr. State College, PA: Bald Eagle Press, 1952.

Bonaparte, Marie. *The Life and Works of Edgar Allan Poe: A Psycho-Analytic Interpretation*. Trans. John Rodker. London: Imago, 1949.

Bondurant, Agnes Meredith. *Poe's Richmond*. Richmond: Garrett and Massie, 1942.

Budd, Louis J., and Edwin Harrison Cady, eds. *On Poe*. Durham: Duke University Press, 1993.

Campbell, Killis. *The Mind of Poe, and Other Studies*. Cambridge, MA: Harvard University Press, 1933.

Cantalupo, Barbara. *Poe and the Visual Arts*. University Park: Pennsylvania State University Press, 2014.

Carlson, Eric W., ed. *A Companion to Poe Studies*. Westport, CT: Greenwood Press, 1996.

———, ed. *Critical Essays on Edgar Allan Poe*. Boston: G. K. Hall, 1987.

———, ed. *The Recognition of Edgar Allan Poe: Selected Criticism since 1829*. Ann Arbor: University of Michigan Press, 1966.

Chivers, T. H. *Life of Poe*. Ed. Richard Beale Davis. New York: Dutton, 1952.

Davidson, Edward H. *Poe: A Critical Study*. Cambridge, MA: Belknap Press of Harvard University Press, 1957.

Deas, Michael. *The Portraits and Daguerreotypes of Edgar Allan Poe*. Charlottesville: University Press of Virginia, 1989.

Eddings, Dennis W. *The Naiad Voice: Essays on Poe's Satiric Hoaxing*. Port Washington, NY: Associated Faculty Press, 1983.

Fagin, Nathan Bryllion. *The Histrionic Mr. Poe*. Baltimore: Johns Hopkins Press, 1949.

Fisher, Benjamin Franklin. *The Cambridge Introduction to Edgar Allan Poe*. New York: Cambridge University Press, 2008.

———, ed. *Masques, Mysteries, and Mastodons: A Poe Miscellany*. Baltimore: Edgar Allan Poe Society, 2006.

———, ed. *Poe and His Times: The Artist and His Milieu*. Baltimore: Edgar Allan Poe Society, 1990.

———, ed. *Poe and Our Times: Influences and Affinities*. Baltimore: Edgar Allan Poe Society, 1986.

———, ed. *Poe at Work: Seven Textual Studies*. Baltimore: Edgar Allan Poe Society, 1978.

———, ed. *Poe in His Own Time: A Biographical Chronicle of His Life, Drawn from Recollections, Interviews, and Memoirs by Family, Friends, and Associates*. Iowa City: University of Iowa Press, 2010.

Forrest, William Mentzel. *Biblical Allusions in Poe*. New York: Macmillan, 1928.

Frank, Frederick S., and Tony Magistrale. *The Poe Encyclopedia*. Westport, CT: Greenwood Press, 1997.

Hartmann, Jonathan H. *The Marketing of Edgar Allan Poe*. New York: Routledge, 2008.

Hayes, Kevin J., ed. *The Cambridge Companion to Edgar Allan Poe*. New York: Cambridge University Press, 2002.

———, ed. *Edgar Allan Poe in Context*. New York: Cambridge University Press, 2013.

———. *Poe and the Printed Word*. New York: Cambridge University Press, 2000.

———. *Edgar Allan Poe*. London: Reaktion, 2009.

Hoffman, Daniel. *Poe Poe Poe Poe Poe Poe Poe*. Garden City, NY: Doubleday, 1972.

Hutchisson, James M., ed. *Edgar Allan Poe: Beyond Gothicism*. Newark: University of Delaware Press, 2011.

———. *Poe*. Jackson: University Press of Mississippi, 2005.

Jackson, David Kelly. *Poe and the Southern Literary Messenger*. Richmond, VA: Dietz, 1934.

Levin, Harry. *The Power of Blackness: Hawthorne, Poe, Melville*. New York: Knopf, 1958.

McGann, Jerome J. *The Poet Edgar Allan Poe: Alien Angel*. Cambridge, MA: Harvard University Press, 2014.

Miller, Perry. *The Raven and the Whale: The War of Words and Wits in the Era of Poe and Melville*. New York: Harcourt, Brace, 1956.

Mills, Bruce. *Poe, Fuller, and the Mesmeric Arts: Transition States in the American Renaissance*. Columbia: University of Missouri Press, 2006.

Moss, Sidney P. *Poe's Literary Battles: The Critic in the Context of His Literary Milieu*. Durham: Duke University Press, 1963.

———. *Poe's Major Crisis: His Libel Suit and New York's Literary World*. Durham: Duke University Press, 1970.

Parks, Edd Winfield. *Edgar Allan Poe as Literary Critic*. Athens: University of Georgia Press, 1964.

Phillips, Mary Elizabeth. *Edgar Allan Poe: The Man*. 2 vols. Chicago: John C. Winston, 1926.

Quinn, Patrick F. *The French Face of Edgar Poe*. Carbondale: Southern Illinois University Press, 1957.

Rans, Geoffrey. *Edgar Allan Poe*. Edinburgh: Oliver and Boyd, 1965.

Silverman, Kenneth. *Edgar A. Poe: Mournful and Never-Ending Remembrance*. New York: HarperCollins, 1991.

Taylor, Jonathan. *Science and Omniscience in Nineteenth Century Literature*. Brighton: Sussex Academic Press, 2007.

Thomas, Dwight, and David K. Jackson. *The Poe Log: A Documentary Life of Edgar Allan Poe, 1809–1849*. Boston: G. K. Hall, 1987.

Thoms, Peter. *Detection and Its Designs: Narrative and Power in 19th-Century Detective Fiction*. Athens: Ohio University Press, 1998.

Urakova, A. P., ed. *Deciphering Poe: Subtexts, Contexts, Subversive Meanings*. Bethlehem: Lehigh University Press, 2013.

Vines, Lois. *Poe Abroad: Influence, Reputation, Affinities*. Iowa City: University of Iowa Press, 1999.

Walker, I. M., ed. *Edgar Allan Poe: The Critical Heritage*. New York: Routledge & K. Paul, 1986.

Walsh, John Evangelist. *Midnight Dreary: The Mysterious Death of Edgar Allan Poe*. New Brunswick: Rutgers University Press, 1998.

———. *Poe the Detective: The Curious Circumstances behind The Mystery of Marie Rogêt*. New Brunswick: Rutgers University Press Year, 1967.

Weinstock, Jeffrey A., and Tony Magistrale, eds. *Approaches to Teaching Poe's Prose and Poetry*. New York: Modern Language Association of America, 2008.

Werner, James V. *American Flaneur: The Cosmic Physiognomy of Edgar Allan Poe*. New York: Routledge, 2004.

Whalen, Terence. *Edgar Allan Poe and the Masses: The Political Economy of Literature in Antebellum America*. Princeton: Princeton University Press, 1999.

Zimmerman, Brett. *Edgar Allan Poe: Rhetoric and Style*. Montreal: McGill-Queen's University Press, 2005.

Samuel Masury and S. W. Hartshorn, *Edgar Allan Poe* (1848). This photographic copy of the "Ultima Thule" daguerreotype, the favorite of many Poe enthusiasts, was taken in Providence, Rhode Island, in November 1848, four days after Poe attempted to kill himself with an overdose of laudanum. "Ultima Thule" is a Latin phrase referring to the extreme limits of travel and discovery.

Illustration Credits

"She Now Stands Without the Door!" from Poe, *Tales of Mystery and Imagination*, illustrated by Harry Clarke (London: George G. Harrap, 1919). frontispiece and 116

Rotunda of the University of Virginia, photograph, by John Collier, 1943. Reproduction no. LC-DIG-fsac-1a34518, Library of Congress Prints and Photographs Division. 2

Baltimore from Federal Hill, aquatint with watercolor, by W. J. Bennett, c. 1831 (New York: H. I. Megarey). Reproduction no. LC-USZ62-3691, Library of Congress Prints and Photographs Division. 3

Poe Returning to Boston, bronze, by Steff Rocknak, Boston, 2014. Photo courtesy of the artist and Russ Rocknak. 5

Richmond, from the Hill above the Waterworks, colored aquatint, by W. J. Bennett, c. 1834, after a painting by G. Cooke (New York: Lewis P. Clover). Reproduction no. LC-USZC4-4539, Library of Congress Prints and Photographs Division. 6

John Pendleton Kennedy, frontispiece from Henry T. Tuckerman, *The Life of John Pendleton Kennedy* (New York: G. P. Putnam and Son, 1871). 9

Title page, *Burton's Gentlemans' Magazine and American Monthly Review*, vol. 5 (July–December 1839). Courtesy of Widener Library, Harvard University. 10

A Market Square, Philadelphia, Pennsylvania, color lithograph, by Paolo Fumagalli, from Jules Ferrario, *Le Costume Ancien et Moderne, Amerique*, vol. 1 (1820), plate 43. Private collection/The Stapleton Collection/Bridgeman Images. 11

Evert A. Duyckinck, engraving, c. 1860–1890. Reproduction no. LC-USZ62-123838, Library of Congress Prints and Photographs Division. 13

Rufus W. Griswold, engraving, n.d. Item no. 510d47df-d794-a3d9-e040-e00a18064a99, Print Collection, Miriam and Ira D. Wallach Division of Art, Prints and Photographs, The New York Public Library, Astor, Lenox and Tilden Foundations. 15

Edgar A. Poe trading card, W. Duke Sons & Co., Tobacco Collections, item #D0195. Emergence of Advertising in America Collection, John W. Hartman Center for Stales, Advertising and Marketing History, Duke University Rare Book, Manuscript, and Special Collections Library. 17

Portrait of Edgar Allen Poe, from Poe, *Tales of Mystery and Imagination*, illustrated by Harry Clarke (London: George G. Harrap, 1919). 23

The Stables of Caligula's Horse, Incitata, colored engraving, by Angelo Biasioli, c. 1800–1818. Private collection/The Stapleton Collection/The Bridgeman Art Library. 29

Baron on horse, illustration by Hermann Wögel, from Poe, *The Tales and Poems of Edgar Allen Poe* (Philadelphia: George Barrie, 1895). 33

"A cloud of smoke settled heavily over the battlements in the distinct collosal figure of—a horse," illustration for "Metzengerstein," from Poe, *Selected Tales of Mystery*, illustrated by Byam Shaw (London: Sidgwick and Jackson, 1909), facing p. 174. 35

Approach of the Simoom—Desert of Gizeh, color lithograph, by Louis Haghe, after a drawing by David Roberts, from *Egypt and Nubia* (London: F. G. Moon, 1846–1849), vol. 3, p. 28. Reproduction no.

LC-USZC4-4038, Library of Congress Prints and Photographs Division. 39

Portrait of Samuel Taylor Coleridge, oil on canvas, by Thomas Phillips, c. 1818–1821. Private collection/The Bridgeman Art Library. 41

Balbec, undated print. Reproduction no. LC-DIG-pga-00134, Library of Congress Prints and Photographs Division. 47

Bootes Canes Venatici, Coma Berenices, and Quadrans Muralis, hand-colored etching, by Sidney Hall, from Jehoshaphat Aspin, *A Familiar Treatise on Astronomy: Explaining the General Phenomena of the Celestial Bodies* (London: Samuel Leigh, 1825), plate 10. Reproduction no. LC-USZC4-10059, Library of Congress Prints and Photographs Division. 51

Title page, Poe, *Al Aaraaf, Tamerlane, and Minor Poems* (Baltimore: Hatch and Dunning, 1829). Courtesy of Houghton Library, Harvard University. 54

View on the Rhine, hand-colored lithograph, by Currier and Ives, c. 1856–1901. Reproduction no. LC-USZC2-3142, Library of Congress Prints and Photographs Division. 66

Vahine No Te Tiare [Woman with a Flower], oil on canvas, by Paul Gaugin, 1891. Ny Carlsberg Glyptotek, Copenhagen, Denmark/Bridgeman Images. 69

"Ligeia," by Harry Clarke, from Poe, *Tales of Mystery and Imagination,* illustrated by Harry Clarke (London: George G. Harrap, 1919). 71

Attack of the Seminoles on the Block House, hand-colored lithograph, by Gray and James (Charleston SC: T. F. Gray and James, 1837). Reproduction no. LC-DIG-ppmsca-19924, Library of Congress Prints and Photographs Division. 85

Royal Gardens, Vauxhall. Grand Day and Evening Fete, Next Tuesday, August 7, 1838. Ascent of the Nassau Balloon, Combined with the Evening Entertainments, broadside print (London: Balne, 1838). Reproduction no. LC-DIG-ppmsca-07185, Library of Congress Prints and Photographs Division. 87

L'homme au masque de fer [The Man in the Iron Mask], hand-colored etching and mezzotint, 1789. Reproduction no. LC-DIG-

ppmsca-07185, French Political Cartoons Collection, Library of Congress Prints and Photographs Division. 91

Peter Weller as RoboCop in *RoboCop,* directed by Paul Verhoeven, Orion, 1987. 94

Dr. Spurzheim: Divisions of the Organs of Phrenology Marked Externally, lithograph, by Wm. S. Pendleton (Boston: Pendleton's Lith., c. 1834). Reproduction no. LC-USZC4-4556, Library of Congress Prints and Photographs Division. 101

Titania, Queen of the Fairies, with Bottom and attending fairies, illustration for Shakespeare, *Midsummer Night's Dream,* Act IV, Scene 1—A wood, engraving, by John Peter Simon after a painting by Henry Fuseli (London: J. and J. Boydell, 1796). Reproduction no. LC-DIG-pga-02780, Library of Congress Prints and Photographs Division. 104

The Nightmare, oil on canvas, by Henry Fuseli, 1781. Founders Society purchase with Mr. and Mrs. Bert L. Smokler and Mr. and Mrs. Lawrence A. Fleischman Funds, Detroit Institute of Arts/Bridgeman Images. 111

Thomas Dunn English. Photography © New-York Historical Society. 115

Alain Delon as William Wilson in "William Wilson," directed by Louis Malle, segment of omnibus film *Histoires extraordinaires,* Cocinor (France), 1968. 118

"Rev. Dr. Bransby's Establishment at Stoke-Newington," from William F. Gill, *The Life of Edgar Allan Poe* (New York: C. T. Dillingham, 1877), opposite p. 29. 119

"The Rev. Dr. Bransby (Poe's English schoolmaster)," from William F. Gill, *The Life of Edgar Allan Poe* (New York: C. T. Dillingham, 1877), opposite p. 30. 121

"A Masquerade in the Palazzo of the Neapolitan Duke Di Broglio," frontispiece, from Poe, *Selected Tales of Mystery,* illustrated by Byam Shaw (London: Sidgwick and Jackson, 1909). 136

Benjamin Franklin: The Statesman and Philosopher, hand-colored lithograph, by Nathaniel Currier, 1847. Reproduction no. LC-USZC2-2004, Library of Congress Prints and Photographs Division. 147

Wall Street, N.Y., 1847, colored lithograph, by Laurent Deroy after a drawing by August Köllner, 1847. Reproduction no. LC-USZC4-2461, Library of Congress Prints and Photographs Division. 151

George III commode, mahogany and ormolu, English School, 18th century. Private collection/Bridgeman Images. 159

Lake of the Dismal Swamp, painted firescreen, by John Gadsby Chapman, 1825. Lora Robins Collection of Virginia Art, Virginia Historical Society (1995.120). 161

Portrait of Charles Baudelaire, oil on canvas, by Gustave Courbet, 1847. Musée Fabre, Montpellier, France/Bridgeman Images. 164

Harrison Ford as Rick Deckard in *Blade Runner,* directed by Ridley Scott, Warner Brothers, 1982. 165

"Faust and Mephistopheles in the Witches' Cave," by Moritz Retzsch, from *Illustrations to Goethe's* Faust, engraved by Henry Moses (London: Tilt and Bogue, 1843). 169

Running Legs, New York, gelatin silver print, by Lisette Model, c. 1940–1941. © Lisette Model Foundation, accession no. 29359, National Gallery of Canada, Ottawa. Photo © National Gallery of Canada, Ottawa. Courtesy of the Lisette Model Foundation, Inc. (1983). Used by permission. 172

Stele of Zezen-nakht, limestone with stucco and paint, from the chapel near the tomb of Zezen-nakht at Naga ed-Deir, Egypt, First Intermediate Period, early Dynasty 11, c. 2000 BCE. 29½ X 36 inches (74.9 X 91.4 cm.). Purchased with funds from the Libbey Endowment, Gift of Edward Drummond Libbey. Object no. 1947.61, Toledo Museum of Art, Toledo, OH. Photo: Tim Thayer, Oak Park, MI. 177

Mr. Dupin, engraving, English School. Private collection/Bridgeman Images. 179

Bishop Odenheimer, wet collodion glass negative, c. 1855–1865. Reproduction no. LC-DIG-cwbph-01918, Brady-Handy Photograph Collection, Library of Congress Prints and Photographs Division. 186

Barry O' Moore as Herbert Yost (Edgar Allen Poe), in *Edgar Allen Poe,* directed by D. W. Griffith (American Mutoscope and Biograph, 1909). 189

Illustration for "The Murders in the Rue Morgue," from Poe, *Tales of Mystery and Imagination,* illustrated by Harry Clarke (London: George G. Harrap, 1919). 208

Woodcut illustration from Poe, *Une descente dans le maelstrom,* illustrated by Marc Roux, translated by Charles Baudelaire (Paris: Devambez, 1920), p. 17. Courtesy of Éditions d'Art Devambez. 217

Dramas of the Sea: A Descent into the Maelstrom, zincograph, by Paul Gaugin, 1889. Sterling and Francine Clark Art Institute, Williamstown, MA/Bridgeman Images. 221

Woodcut illustration from Poe, *Une descente dans le maelstrom,* illustrated by Marc Roux, translated by Charles Baudelaire (Paris: Devambez, 1920), p. 33. Courtesy of Éditions d'Art Devambez. 223

Woodcut illustration from Poe, *Une descente dans le maelstrom,* illustrated by Marc Roux, translated by Charles Baudelaire (Paris: Devambez, 1920), p. 41. Courtesy of Éditions d'Art Devambez. 228

Eric Schlumberger as Luigi in *Vivre sa vie,* directed by Jean-Luc Godard (Les Films de la Pléiade, 1962). 230

Anna Karina as Nana Kleinfrankenheim in *Vivre sa vie,* directed by Jean-Luc Godard (Les Films de la Pléiade, 1962). 231

Storm and shipwreck, illustration for Shakespeare's *Tempest,* Act I, Scene 1, engraving by B. Smith after a painting by G. Romney (London: J. and J. Boydell, c. 1797). Reproduction no. LC-DIG-pga-03317, Library of Congress Prints and Photographs Division. 234

Illustration for Poe's Masque of Red Death, watercolor on paper, by Charles Demuth, 1918. The Barnes Foundation, Philadelphia/Bridgeman Images. 237

Lon Chaney as the Phantom in *The Phantom of the Opera,* directed by Rupert Julian (Universal Pictures, 1925). 239

Illustration for "The Pit and the Pendulum," from Poe, *Tales of Mystery and Imagination,* illustrated by Arthur Rackham (London: G. G. Harrap, 1935). Courtesy of Houghton Library, Harvard University. 241

The Pit and the Pendulum, color offset photomechanical print, in *Puck,* vol. 65, no. 1682 (May 26, 1909), centerfold. Reproduction no.

LC-DIG-ppmsca-26378, Library of Congress Prints and Photographs Division. 249

"They swarmed upon me in ever-accumulating heaps," illustration for "The Pit and the Pendulum," from Poe, *Selected Tales of Mystery*, illustrated by Byam Shaw (London: Sidgwick and Jackson, 1909), facing p. 190. 255

Le Général Lasalle, engraving, 1825. Reproduction no. LC-USZ62-51970, Library of Congress Prints and Photographs Division. 257

Illustration for "The Tell-Tale Heart," by Virgil Finlay from *Fantastic*, vol. 1, no. 2 (September 1952). Collection of Kevin J. Hayes. Courtesy of Lail M. Finlay. 261

Lady MacBeth, illustration for Shakespeare, *MacBeth*, Act V, "One, two; why then 'tis time to do't," mezzotint, engraved by J. R. Smith after a painting by H. Fuseli (London: I. R. Smith, 1784). Reproduction no. LC-USZC4-5857, Library of Congress Prints and Photographs Division. 262

Ralph Lewis as the Detective in *The Avenging Conscience*, directed by D. W. Griffith (Majestic, 1914). 263

Hand in *The Avenging Conscience*, directed by D. W. Griffith (Majestic, 1914). 263

Henry B. Walthall as the Nephew in *The Avenging Conscience*, directed by D. W. Griffith (Majestic, 1914). 263

Fort Moultrie, Charleston Harbor, black ink and watercolor on tan paper, by A. Vizitelly, 1861. Reproduction no. LC-DIG-ppmsca-22981, Library of Congress Prints and Photographs Division. 267

Illustration for Poe, *The Gold-Bug*, illustrated by G. C. Widney (Chicago: Rand McNally, 1901). 269

Illustration by J. W. Kennedy for Poe, *The Gold Bug* (Boston: Dana Estes, 1899). 271

Geoffrey Holder as Jupiter and Anthony Michael Hall as Boy, publicity still for *ABC Weekend Special*, season 3, episode 8, "The Gold Bug," February 2, 1980. Collection of Kevin J. Hayes. 275

"A Map Showing the Lay of the Land and the Places Mentioned in 'The Gold Bug' by Edgar Allen Poe," illustration for Poe, *The Gold Bug*, illustrated by G. C. Widney (Chicago: Rand McNally, 1901). 281

"I Proceeded to Use the Glass," illustration for Poe, *The Gold Bug*, illustrated by G. C. Widney (Chicago: Rand McNally, 1901). 302

The Black Cat, engraving, from *Four Illustrations for the Tales of Edgar Allan Poe*, drawn by Aubrey Beardsley (Chicago: Herbert S. Stone, 1901). Reproduction number LC-USZ62-108227, General Collections, Library of Congress. 308

Harvey Keitel as Roderick Usher, from *Two Evil Eyes*, "The Black Cat" segment, directed by Dario Argento (ADC Films, 1990). 309

Rod Usher's book *Metropolitan Horrors*, from *Two Evil Eyes*, "The Black Cat" segment, directed by Dario Argento (ADC Films, 1990). 310

Moyamensing Prison, Philadelphia, lithograph, by John Caspar Wild, 1840. © Philadelphia History Museum at the Atwater Kent/Bridgeman Images. 313

Illustration for "The Black Cat," by H. Meyer, from Poe, *The Tales and Poems of Edgar Allen Poe* (Philadelphia: George Barrie, 1895). 317

Edgar Allan Poe, oil on canvas, by Samuel Osgood, 1845. Collection of the New-York Historical Society/Bridgeman Images. 321

Animal Magnetism, lithograph on wove paper, by Edward William Clay (New York: J. Childs, 1839). Reproduction no. LC-USZ62-37917, American Cartoon Print Filing Series, Library of Congress Prints and Photographs Division. 338

The High Bridge at Harlem, N.Y., hand-colored lithograph (New York: N. Currier, c. 1849). Reproduction no. LC-USZC2-2574, Library of Congress Prints and Photographs Division. 340

John Randolph of Roanoke on His Embarkation for Russia Onboard Ship "Concord," ink over graphite underdrawing, by John Marshal, c. 1830. Reproduction no. LC-DIG-ppmsca-22818, Library of Congress Prints and Photographs Division. 341

Illustration for "The Facts in the Case of M. Valdemar," by Hermann Wögel, from Poe, *The Tales and Poems of Edgar Allen Poe* (Philadelphia: George Barrie, 1895). 343

Conrad Veidt as Cesare, in *The Cabinet of Dr. Caligari*, directed by Robert Weine (Decla-Bioscop AG, 1920). 344

Corridor in the Cappuccino Catacombs, Rome, Italy, stereograph (photographic print on stereo card), c. 1897. Reproduction no. LC-USZ62-54103, Library of Congress Prints and Photographs Division. 353

The Vengeance of Hop-Frog, hand-colored etching, by James Ensor, 1898. William Rockhill Nelson Trust, 73-17. Nelson-Atkins Museum of Art, Kansas City, MO. Photo: Robert Newcombe. 367

Title page, Poe, *The Poems of Edgar Allen Poe*, illustrated by W. Heath Robinson (London: George Bell and Sons; New York: Macmillan, 1900), p. 65. Courtesy of Widener Library, Harvard University. 371

Adam West as Bruce Wayne and Lee Meriwether as Miss Kitka, in *Batman*, directed by Leslie H. Martinson (Twentieth Century Fox, 1966). 373

"The Room Where 'The Raven' Was Written," from William F. Gill, *The Life of Edgar Allan Poe* (New York: C. T. Dillingham, 1877), opposite p. 148. 375

"And the Raven, never flitting, still is sitting, still is sitting/On the pallid bust of Pallus just above my chamber door," illustration for "The Raven" by John Tenniel, engraved by J. Cooper, for Poe, *The Poetical Works of Edgar Allan Poe* (New York: J. S. Redfield, 1858), p. 8. 376

"Quoth the Raven, 'Nevermore,'" pen and black ink on paper, sheet (irregular), by Edward Hopper, n.d. Josephine N. Hopper Bequest 70.1561.13, Whitney Museum of American Art, New York. Photograph: Robert Gerhardt. 377

"And the silken and uncertain rustling of each purple curtain/Thrilled me—filled me with fantastic terrors never felt before," illustration for "The Raven" by John Tenniel, engraved by J. Cooper, for Poe, *The Poetical Works of Edgar Allan Poe* (New York: J. S. Redfield, 1858), p. 1. 377

The Raven, pen and ink on paper, Dante Gabriel Rossetti, c. 1848. Given by Mrs. Felix Moeller, E.3415-1922, © Victoria and Albert Museum, London. 378

The Raven, lithograph, by Joseph Ferdinand Keppler, from *Puck*, vol. 27 (August 13, 1890): 400–401. Reproduction no. LC-USZC4-5412, Library of Congress Prints and Photographs Division. 379

Nevermore, chromolithograph, by Udo J. Keppler, cover of *Puck*, vol. 48, no. 1235 (November 7, 1900). Reproduction no. LC-DIG-ppmsca-25470, Library of Congress Prints and Photographs Division. 379

"Doubting, dreaming dreams no mortal ever dared to dream before," engraving, by Gustave Doré, illustration from Edgar Allan Poe's "The Raven," 1882. Private collection/Bridgeman Images. 381

Illustration for "The Raven" by Edgar Allan Poe, lithograph, by Edouard Manet, 1875. On loan to the Hamburg Kunsthalle, Hamburg, Germany/Bridgeman Images. 383

Landscape, ink wash and gouache, by Robert Walter Weir, c. 1830–1880. Reproduction no. LC-DIG-ppmsca-23023, Library of Congress Prints and Photographs Division. 387

"That I brought a dread burden down here—/On this night of all nights of the year," illustration for "Ulalume" by F. R. Pickersgill, engraved by W. J. Linton, for Poe, *The Poetical Works of Edgar Allan Poe* (New York: J. S. Redfield, 1858), p. 27. 389

Gold Mining in California, hand-colored lithograph (New York: Currier and Ives, 1871). Reproduction no. LC-USZC2-1755, Library of Congress Prints and Photographs Division. 391

In Search of El Dorado, from Poe, *The Poems of Edgar Allen Poe*, illustrated by W. Heath Robinson (London: George Bell and Sons; New York: Macmillan, 1900), p. 65. Courtesy of Widener Library, Harvard University. 391

John Wayne as Cole Thornton and James Caan as Mississippi, in *El Dorado*, directed by Howard Hawks (Paramount, 1966). 392

Annabel Lee, chalk and pastel on brown paper, by James McNeill Whistler, c. 1885–1887. Gift of Charles Lang Freer F1905.129a–b, Freer Gallery of Art, Smithsonian Institution, Washington, D.C. 395

Edgar Allan Poe House, 530 North Seventh Street, Philadelphia (rear), Historic American Buildings Survey. In HABS PA, 51-PHILA,663A-1, photos from Survey HABS PA-1735, photo no. 1, Library of Congress Prints and Photographs Division. 398

Poe's bedroom, 2nd floor, in Edgar Allan Poe House, 530 North Seventh Street, Philadelphia, Historic American Buildings Survey. In HABS PA, 51-PHILA,663A-1, photos from Survey HABS PA-1735, photo no. 4, Library of Congress Prints and Photographs Division. 400

Edgar Allan Poe, photograph by C. T. Tatman, 1904, of daguerreotype, by S. W. Hartshorn and Samuel Masury, 1848. Reproduction no. LC-USZ62-10610, Library of Congress Prints and Photographs Division. 403

Acknowledgments

While preparing this volume, I had the opportunity to teach my biannual Poe seminar twice. I am grateful to the students of the seminar both times I taught it for their lively classroom discussions. Students from other classes contributed to this work as well. My second-semester freshmen students must write a cultural history as their major assignment. Caleb Glennie's "Cultural History of Batman" let me know how influential Poe's works were on Bob Kane, the creator of Batman. Researching the cultural history of black cats, Daniel Wyatt brought Hartley Coleridge's essay on the subject to my attention.

Heartfelt thanks go to Jeffrey A. Savoye of the Edgar Allan Poe Society of Baltimore for maintaining the society's website and making so many important Poe-related documents available.

I would also like to thank many people at libraries and museums across North America. Charles Melson and his interlibrary loan staff at Max Chambers Library worked hard to obtain my numerous and difficult requests. Others who deserve my heartfelt thanks include Stan Ackert, Lisette Model Foundation; Belma Buljubasic, National Gallery of Canada; Jamison Davis, Virginia Historical Society; Lail M. Finlay; Katharine French-Fuller, Rare Book, Manuscript, and Special Collection Library, Duke University; Kiowa Hammons, Whitney Museum of American Art; Rosana Hart; Betsy Kohut, Freer Gallery of Art and Arthur M. Sackler Gallery; Timothy Motz, Toledo Museum of Art; Maria Murguia-Harding, Bridgeman Art Library; Stacey Sherman, Nelson-Atkins Museum of Art; and Pierre Tzenkoff, Éditions d'Art Devambez.

I would also like to thank my editor at Harvard University Press, John Kulka, for asking me to undertake this project and helping me throughout its composition. John puts a tremendous amount of effort into his editing, and I am extremely grateful for the meticulous care he took with my manuscript. His numerous suggestions helped me shape my scholarship into prose everyone can appreciate. John is more than an editor: he is a teacher. Matthew Hills, Heather Hughes, Hope Stockton, Christine Thorsteinsson, and Annamarie Why of Harvard University Press also worked hard to bring this work to completion. As always, I thank my wife, Myung-Sook, for her encouragement and support, her patience and her love.